Dead or Alive

Twenty years ago Tom Clancy was a Maryland insurance broker with a passion for naval history. Years before, he had been an English major at Baltimore's Loyola College and had always dreamed of writing a novel. His first effort, *The Hunt for Red October*, sold briskly as a result of rave reviews, then catapulted on to *The New York Times* bestseller list after President Reagan pronounced it 'the perfect yarn'. Since then Clancy has established himself as an undisputed master at blending exceptional realism and authenticity, intricate plotting and razor-sharp suspense.

Grant Blackwood, a US Navy veteran, spent three years aboard a guided missile frigate as operations specialist and pilot rescue swimmer. He is co-author, with Clive Cussler, of *The New York Times* bestsellers *Spartan Gold* and *Lost Empire*. He is also the author of the Briggs Tanner series: *The End of Enemies, The Wall of Night* and *An Echo of War*. He lives in Colorado.

Dead or Alive

TOM CLANCY
with GRANT BLACKWOOD

MICHAEL JOSEPH
an imprint of
PENGUIN BOOKS

MICHAEL JOSEPH

Published by the Penguin Group
Penguin Books Ltd, 80 Strand, London WC2R ORL, England
Penguin Group (USA) Inc., 375 Hudson Street, New York, New York 10014, USA
Penguin Group (Canada), 90 Eglinton Avenue East, Suite 700, Toronto, Ontario, Canada M4P 2Y3
(a division of Pearson Penguin Canada Inc.)
Penguin Ireland, 25 St Stephen's Green, Dublin 2, Ireland (a division of Penguin Books Ltd)
Penguin Group (Australia), 250 Camberwell Road, Camberwell, Victoria 3124, Australia
(a division of Pearson Australia Group Pty Ltd)
Penguin Books India Pvt Ltd, 11 Community Centre, Panchsheel Park, New Delhi – 110 017, India
Penguin Group (NZ), 67 Apollo Drive, Rosedale, North Shore 0632, New Zealand
(a division of Pearson New Zealand Ltd)
Penguin Books (South Africa) (Pty) Ltd, 24 Sturdee Avenue, Rosebank, Johannesburg 2196, South Africa

Penguin Books Ltd, Registered Offices: 80 Strand, London WC2R ORL, England

www.penguin.com

First published in the United States of America by G. P. Putnam's Sons 2010
First published in Great Britain by Michael Joseph 2010

1

Copyright © Rubicon, Inc., 2010

Maps by Jeffrey L. Ward

The moral right of the authors has been asserted

This is a work of fiction. Names, characters, places and incidents either
are the product of the author's imagination or are used fictitiously, and any resemblance
to actual persons, living or dead, businesses, companies, events or locales is entirely coincidental

Set in 13.5/16 pt Garamond MT
Typeset by Palimpsest Book Production Limited, Falkirk, Stirlingshire

Printed in Great Britain by Clays Ltd, St Ives plc

A CIP catalogue record for this book is available from the British Library

HARDBACK ISBN: 978-0-718-15741-8

TRADE PAPERBACK ISBN: 978-0-718-15768-5

www.greenpenguin.co.uk

Mixed Sources
Product group from well-managed
forests and other controlled sources
www.fsc.org Cert no. SA-COC-1592
© 1996 Forest Stewardship Council

FSC

Penguin Books is committed to a sustainable future
for our business, our readers and our planet.
The book in your hands is made from paper
certified by the Forest Stewardship Council.

Dead or Alive

I

Light troops—an Eleven-Bravo light infantryman, according the United States Army's MOS (military occupational specialty) system—are supposed to be "pretty" spit-and-polish troops with spotless uniforms and clean-shaven faces, but First Sergeant Sam Driscoll wasn't one of those anymore, and hadn't been for some time. The concept of camouflage often involved more than patterned BDUs. No, wait, they weren't called that anymore, were they? Now they were called "Army combat uniforms," ACUs. *Same, same.*

Driscoll's beard was fully four inches long, with enough flecks of white in it that his men had taken to calling him Santa—rather annoying to a man hardly thirty-six years old, but when most of your compatriots were an average of ten years younger than you . . . Oh, well. Could be worse. Could be "Pops" or "Gramps."

He was even more annoyed to have long hair. It was dark and shaggy and greasy, and his beard coarse, which was useful here, where the facial hair was important to his cover and the local people rarely bothered with haircuts. His dress was entirely local in character, and this was true of his team as well. There were fifteen of them. Their company commander, a captain, was down with a broken leg from a misstep—which was all it took to sideline you in this terrain—sitting on a hilltop and waiting for the Chinook to evac him, along with one of the team's two medics who'd stayed behind to make sure he didn't go into shock. That left Driscoll in command for the mission. He didn't mind. He had more time in the field than Captain Wilson had, though the captain had a college degree, and Driscoll didn't have his yet. One thing at a time. He had to survive this deployment still, and after that he could go back to his classes at the University of Georgia. Funny, he thought, that it had taken him nearly three decades to start enjoying school. Well, hell, better late than never, he supposed.

He was tired, the kind of mind-numbing, bone-grinding fatigue Rangers knew only too well. He knew how to sleep like a dog on a granite block with only a rifle stock for a pillow, knew how to stay alert when his brain and body were screaming at him to lie down. Problem was, now that he was closer to forty than thirty, he felt the aches and pains a little more than he had when he was twenty, and it took twice as long to work out the kinks in the morning. Then again, those aches were offset by wisdom and experience. He'd learned over the years that despite it being a cliché, it was in fact mind over matter. He'd learned to largely block out pain, which was a handy skill when you were leading much younger men whose packs undoubtedly felt much lighter on their shoulders than Driscoll's did on his own. Life, he decided, was all about trade-offs.

They'd been in the hills for two days, all of it on the move, sleeping two to three hours a night. He was part of the special operations team of the 75th Ranger Regiment, based permanently at Fort Benning, Georgia, where there was a nice NCO club with good beer on tap. By closing his eyes and concentrating, he imagined he could still taste the cold beer, but that moment passed quickly. He had to focus here, every second. They were fifteen thousand feet above sea level, in the Hindu Kush mountains, in that gray zone that was both Afghanistan and Pakistan, and neither—at least to the locals. Lines on maps didn't make borders, Driscoll knew, especially in Indian country like this. He'd check his GPS equipment to be sure of his position, but latitude and longitude really didn't matter to his mission. What mattered was where they were headed, regardless of where it fell on the map.

The local population knew little about borders, and didn't especially care. For them reality was which tribe you were in, which family you were a part of, and which flavor of Muslim you were. Here memories lasted a hundred years, and the stories even longer. And grudges even longer than that. The locals still boasted that their ancestors had driven Alexander the Great out of the country, and some of them still remembered the names of the warriors who had bested the Macedonian spearmen who had up until then conquered every other place they'd wandered into. Most of all, though, the locals spoke of the Russians, and how many of those they'd killed, mostly by ambush, some with knives, face-to-face. They smiled and laughed with those stories, legends passed on from father to son. Driscoll doubted the Russian soldiers who made it out of Afghanistan did much laughing about the experience. No, sir, these were not nice folks, he knew. They were scary-tough, hardened by weather, war, famine, and just generally trying to stay alive in a country that seemed to be doing its best to kill you most of the time. Driscoll knew he ought to feel some sympathy for them. God had just dealt them a bad hand, and maybe that wasn't their fault, but it wasn't Driscoll's fault, either, nor his concern. They were enemies of Driscoll's country, and the powers-that-be had pointed the stick at them and ordered "Go," and so here they were. That was the central truth of the moment, the reason he was in these goddamned mountains.

One more ridge was the other central truth, especially here, it seemed. They'd legged it fifteen klicks, almost all of it uphill and over sharp rock and scree, since they'd hopped off the CH-47 Chinook helicopter, a Delta variant, the only one at their disposal that could handle the altitude here.

There . . . the ridgeline. Fifty meters.

Driscoll slowed his pace. He was walking point, leading the patrol as the senior NCO present, with his men stretched out a hundred meters to his rear, alert, eyes sweeping left and right, up and down, M4 carbines at ready-low and trained at their sectors. They expected there to be a few sentries on the ridge-line. The locals might be uneducated in the traditional sense, but they weren't stupid by any measure, which was why the Rangers were running this op at night—zero-one-forty-four, or a quarter to two in the morning—according to his digital watch. No moon tonight, and high clouds thick enough to block whatever light came from the stars. Good hunting weather, he thought.

His eyes traced more down than up. He didn't want to make any noise, and noise came from the feet. One damned rock, kicked loose and rolling down the hillside, could betray them all. Couldn't have that, could he? Couldn't waste the three days and fifteen miles it had taken them to get this close.

Twenty meters to the ridgeline. Sixty feet.

His eyes searched the line for movement. Nothing close. A few more steps, looking left and right, his noise-suppressed carbine cradled to his chest at ready-low, finger resting lightly on the trigger, just enough to know it was there.

It was hard to explain to people how hard this was, how tiring and debilitating—far more so than a fifteen-mile hike in the woods—knowing there might be someone with an AK-47 in his hands and his finger on a trigger, the selector switch set to full auto, ready to cut your ass in half. His men would take care of such a person, but that wouldn't do him any good, Driscoll knew. Still, he consoled himself, if it happened, the odds were that he wouldn't even know it. He'd dispatched enough enemies to know how it worked: One moment you're stepping forward, eyes scanning ahead, ears tuned, listening for danger . . . the next nothing. Death.

Driscoll knew the rule out here, in the badlands, in the dead of night: Slow is fast. Move slow, walk slow, step carefully. It had served him well lo these many years.

Just six months earlier he'd finished third in the Best Ranger Competition, the Super Bowl of special operations troops. Driscoll and Captain Wilson, in fact, entered as Team 21. The captain had to be pissed at the broken leg. He was a pretty good Ranger, Driscoll thought, but a broken tibia was a broken tibia. When a bone broke, there wasn't a whole hell of a lot to be done about it. A torn muscle hurt like hell but got better rapidly. On the other hand, a broken bone had to knit and mend, and that meant lying on your back for a few weeks at an Army hospital before the docs let you put weight on it again. Then you had to learn to run again, after you relearned how to walk. What a pain in the ass that would be. . . . He'd been lucky in his career, having suffered nothing worse than a twisted ankle, a broken pinkie, and a bone-bruised hip, none of which had sidelined him for much longer than a week. Not so much as a bullet or shrapnel graze. The Ranger gods had smiled on him for sure.

Five more steps . . .

Okay, there you are . . . Yep. As he'd expected, there was the sentry, right where he should be. Twenty-five meters to his right. It was just too obvious a spot for a sentry, though this particular one was doing a piss-poor job of it, sitting there, looking backward mostly, probably bored and half asleep and counting the minutes until his relief arrived. Well, boredom could kill you, and it was about to kill this guy in less than a minute, though he'd never even realize it. *Unless I miss the shot,* Driscoll reminded himself, knowing he wouldn't.

He turned one last time, scanning the area through his PVS-17 night-vision goggles. *Nobody else close. Okay.* He settled down, tucked the carbine to his right shoulder and centered the sights on the guy's right ear, controlled his breathing—

To his right, down a narrow trail, came the rasp of leather on rock.

Driscoll froze.

He did a quick mental recheck, placing the rest of the team in his mind's eye. Anyone down that way? No. Most of the team was spread out behind him and to his right. Moving with exaggerated slowness, Driscoll rotated his head in the direction of the sound. Nothing in the night vision. He lowered his carbine, laying it diagonally across his chest. He looked left. Ten feet away, Collins crouched behind a rock. Driscoll gestured: *Sound to the left; take two men.* Collins nodded and crab-walked backward out of sight. Driscoll did the same, then laid himself flat between a pair of scrub bushes.

Down the trail, another sound now: liquid splattering against stone. This brought a smile to Driscoll's lips. *The call of nature.* The urinating tapered off, then stopped. Footsteps began padding down the trail. Twenty feet away, Driscoll estimated, around the bend.

Moments later a figure appeared on the trail. His gait was unhurried, almost lazy. In the night vision Driscoll could see an AK-47 slung over his shoulder, barrel down. The guard kept coming. Driscoll didn't move. Fifteen feet . . . ten.

A figure rose up from the shadows along the trail and slipped in behind the guard. A hand appeared over the guard's shoulder, then the flash of a blade came over the other shoulder. Collins twisted the man to the right and down to the ground, and their shadows melted together. Ten seconds passed. Collins rose, ducked off the trail, and dragged the guard out of sight.

Textbook sentry takedown, Driscoll thought. Movie portrayals aside, knifework was something of a rarity in their business. Even so, Collins clearly hadn't lost the skill.

Moments later Collins reappeared on Driscoll's right.

Driscoll returned his attention to the sentry on the ridge.

Still there. Hadn't moved at all. Driscoll brought his M4 up, settled the sights on the nape of the man's neck, and then tightened his finger on the trigger.

Easy, easy . . . squeeze . . .

Pop. Not much of a sound. Hard to hear at all at a range of more than fifty meters, but the bullet flew true and transited the target's head, leaving a puff of green vapor behind, and he went off to see Allah, or whatever god he acknowledged; at twenty-odd years old, growing and eating and learning, and probably fighting, came to an abrupt and unwarned end.

The target crumpled, folding sideways out of sight.

Tough luck, Gomer, Driscoll thought. *But we're after bigger game than you tonight.*

"Sentry down," Driscoll said quietly into his radio. "The ridgeline is clear. Move on up. Keep it nice and tight." That last bit wasn't really necessary—not with these guys.

He looked back to see his men moving a little faster now. They were excited but under control, ready to get down to business. He could see it in their postures, the economy of movement that separated real shooters from wannabees and in-and-outers who were just waiting to return to civilian life.

Their real target might be less than a hundred meters away now, and they'd worked hard over the previous three months to bag this bastard. Mountain climbing was not anyone's idea of fun, except maybe for those nutjobs who pined after Everest and K2. Be that as it may, this was part of the job, and part of their current mission, so everybody sucked it up and kept moving.

The fifteen men formed up in three fire-teams of five Rangers each. One would stay here with their heavy weapons—they'd brought two M249 SAW (Squad Automatic Weapon) machine guns for fire cover on overwatch. No telling how many bad guys there might be about, and the SAW was a great equalizer. Satellites could give you only so much intel; some variables you just had to deal with as they came to you. All his men were scanning the rocks, looking for movement. Any movement. Maybe just a bad guy who came out to take a dump. In this neck of the woods, there was a ninety percent chance that anybody you encountered was a bad guy. Made their job that much easier, Driscoll thought.

Moving even more slowly now, he stalked forward, eyes flicking from his feet, watching each placement for loose rocks and twigs, then ahead, scanning, scanning. . . . This was another benefit of wisdom, he thought, knowing how to quash the excitement of being so close to the goal line. This is often where rookies and dead men made their mistakes, thinking the hard part was behind them and their target was so close. And that, Driscoll knew, is when Old Man Murphy, of Murphy's Law fame, usually snuck up behind you, tapped you on the shoulder, and handed you an ugly surprise. Anticipation and expectation were lethal sides of the same coin. Either one in the right dose at the wrong moment would get you killed.

Not this time, though. Not on my damned watch. And not with a team as good as his.

Driscoll saw the ridgeline looming ahead not more than ten feet away, and he hunched over, careful to keep his head below the lip, lest he present a tantalizing silhouette target for some alert gomer. He covered the last few feet on flat feet, then leaned forward, left hand flat against the rock, and peeked his head up.

And there you are . . . The cave.

2

"Low fuel," whoop, whoop, "low fuel," the computer-generated voice announced. "I know, I know," the pilot growled in reply.

He could see the necessary information on his instrument/ CRT display panel. The onboard computer master-trouble light had been blinking for fifteen minutes. They'd crossed the Canadian coast ten minutes earlier, and they could look down at what in daylight would have been green terrain covered with stunted trees. Unless he'd really screwed the navigational pooch, they'd see some lights soon. Anyway, they were feet-dry, which was a relief.

The North Atlantic winds had been far stiffer than predicted. Most of the night traffic was eastbound this time of day, and those aircraft carried a lot more fuel than a Dassault Falcon 9000. Twenty minutes' more fuel. Ten minutes more than they needed. Their indicated air speed was just over five hundred knots, altitude twenty-five thousand feet and falling.

"Gander Approach," he said into his radio microphone, "this is Hotel zero-niner-seven Mike Foxtrot, inbound for gas, over."

"Mike Foxtrot," came the reply, "this is Gander. Winds are calm. Recommend runway two-niner for a normal approach."

"Calm winds?" the copilot observed. "Damn." They'd just come through more than a hundred knots of jet stream right on the nose for three hours of minor buffeting, not too bad at forty-one thousand feet, but still noticeable. "This is about as long a hop over water as I like."

"Especially with winds like this," the pilot replied. "I hope the engines work on fumes."

"We set with customs?"

"Should be. We've done the CANPASS, and we're cleared into Moose Jaw. Do immigration there?"

"Yeah, right." Both knew better. This flight would be a little on the unusual side from Gander on in to their final destination. But they were being paid for it. And the euro–dollar exchange rate would be working in their favor. Especially Canadian dollars.

"Got the lights. Five minutes out," the copilot said.

"Roger, runway in view," the pilot said. "Flaps."

"Flaps coming down to ten." The copilot worked the controls, and they could hear the whine of the electric motors extending the flaps. "Wake up the passengers?"

"No. Why bother?" the pilot decided. If he did this right, they wouldn't notice a thing until the acceleration for the next takeoff. Having earned his spurs and twenty thousand hours with Swissair, he'd retired and bought his own used Dassault Falcon to charter millionaires and billionaires across Europe and around the globe. Half the people who could afford his services ended up going to the same places—Monaco, Harbor Island in the Bahamas, Saint-Tropez, Aspen. The fact that his current passenger was going none of those places was a curiosity, but as long as he paid, the destination was none of his business.

They passed downward through ten thousand feet. The runway lights were easy to see, a straight lane in the darkness that had once accommodated a wing of United States Air Force F-84 interceptors.

Five thousand feet and descending. "Flaps to twenty."

"Roger flaps twenty," the pilot acknowledged.

"Gear," he commanded next, and the copilot reached for the levers. The sound of rushing air entered the cabin as the landing-gear doors opened and the struts came down. Three hundred feet.

"Down and locked," the copilot replied.

"One hundred feet," the computer voice said.

The pilot tensed his arms, then relaxed them, easing the aircraft down, gently, gently, picking the proper spot to touch down. Only his skilled senses could tell when the Falcon touched down on the ten-meter concrete squares. He activated the thrust-reversers, and the Dassault slowed. A truck with blinking lights showed him where to go and whom to follow as he headed off to where the fuel truck would be waiting.

They were on the ground for a total of twenty minutes. An immigration officer queried them over the radio and determined that there were no changes from the CANPASS data. Outside, the fuel truck's driver disconnected his hose and secured the fuel valve.

Okay. That's done, the pilot thought. Now for the second segment of the three-part flight.

The Falcon taxied back out to the north end of the runway, going through the pre-liftoff checklist, as he always did, after waiting at the end of the runway. The acceleration went smoothly; then the wheels came up, then the flaps, followed by the climb-out. Ten more minutes and they were at thirty-seven thousand, their initial assigned altitude from Toronto Center.

They cruised west at Mach 0.81—about 520 knots, or 600 miles per hour true air speed—with their passengers asleep aft while the engines gobbled fuel at a fixed rate of 3,400 pounds per hour. The aircraft transponder broadcast their speed and altitude to the air-traffic-control radars, and aside from that there was no need for radio traffic of any sort. In rough weather they might have requested a different, probably higher, altitude for more comfortable cruising, but Gander tower had been correct. Having passed through the cold front that had opposed their flight into Newfoundland, they might not have been moving at all, except for the muted roar of the jet engines hanging on the tail. Pilot and copilot didn't even speak very much. They'd flown together enough that they knew all the same jokes, and on such an uneventful flight there was no need to swap information. Everything had been planned, down to the proverbial gnat's ass. Both wondered what Hawaii might be like. They could look forward to a pair of suites at the Royal Hawaiian, and a long sleep to ward off the inevitable jet lag, sure to accompany the ten hours of additional day they were going to experience. Well, both liked a nap on a sunny beach, and the weather in Hawaii was forecast to be as monotonously perfect as it usually was. They planned a two-day layover before proceeding back east to their home field outside of Geneva, with no scheduled passengers on that leg.

"Moose Jaw in forty minutes," the copilot observed.

"Time to get back to work, I guess."

The plan was simple. The pilot got on the HF radio—a holdover from World War Two—and called Moose Jaw, announcing his approach and his early descent, plus estimated time of arrival. Moose Jaw's approach control took the information from the area control systems and spotted the transponder alphanumerics on its scopes.

The Dassault began bleeding altitude on a completely normal approach, which was duly noted by Toronto Center. The local time was 0304, or Zulu -4:00, keeping homage to Greenwich Mean/Universal time, four hours to the east.

"There it is," the copilot announced. The approach lights for Moose Jaw showed up on the black countryside. "Altitude twelve thousand, descending one thousand per minute."

"Stand by the transponder," the pilot ordered.

"Roger," the copilot replied. The transponder was a custom installation, done by the flight crew themselves.

"Six thousand feet. Flaps?"

"Leave 'em," the pilot commanded.

"Roger. Runway in view." The sky was clear, and the Moose Jaw approach lights strobed in the cloudless air.

"Moose Jaw, this is Mike Foxtrot, over."

"Mike Foxtrot, Moose Jaw, over."

"Moose Jaw, our gear doesn't want to come down. Please stand by. Over." That notification woke people up.

"Roger. Are you declaring an emergency, over?" the approach radio inquired at once.

"Negative, Moose Jaw. We're checking the electrics. Stand by."

"Roger, standing by." Just a hint of concern in the voice.

"Okay," the pilot said to his copilot, "we'll drop off their scope at one thousand feet." They'd been through all this, of course. "Altitude three thousand and descending."

The pilot eased right. This was to show a course change on the Moose Jaw approach radar, nothing serious but a change nonetheless. With altitude dropping it might look interesting on the radar tapes if anyone cared to look, which was doubtful. Another blip lost in the airspace.

"Two thousand," the copilot said. The air was a little bumpier at the lower altitude but not as bumpy as it was going to get. "Fifteen hundred. Might want to adjust the descent rate."

"Fair enough." The pilot inched back on the yoke to flatten out the down-angle so that he could level out at nine hundred feet AGL. That was low enough to enter Moose Jaw's ground clutter. Though the Dassault was anything but stealthy, most civilian traffic-control radars primarily saw transponder signals, not "skin-paints." In commercial aviation, a plane on radar was nothing more than a notional signal in the sky.

"Mike Foxtrot, Moose Jaw, say altitude, over."

They'd be doing this for a while. The local tower team was unusually awake. Maybe they'd flown into a training exercise, the pilot thought. Too bad, but not a major problem.

"Autopilot off. Hand-flying the airplane."

"Pilot's airplane," the copilot replied.

"Okay, looping right. Transponder off," the pilot commanded.

The copilot killed power to transponder one. "Powered off. We're invisible." That got Moose Jaw's attention.

"Mike Foxtrot, Moose Jaw. Say altitude, over," the voice commanded more crisply. Then a second call.

The Falcon completed its northern loop and settled down on a course of two-two-five. The ground below was flat, and the pilot was tempted to reduce altitude to five hundred feet but decided against it. No need. As planned, the aircraft had just evaporated off the Moose Jaw radar.

"Mike Foxtrot, Moose Jaw. Say altitude, over!"

"Sounds excited," the copilot observed.

"I don't blame him."

The transponder they'd just shut down was for another plane entirely, probably parked in its hangar outside Söderhamn, Sweden. This flight was costing their charter party seventy thousand extra euros, but the Swiss flight crew understood about making money, and they weren't flying drugs or anything like that. Money or not, that sort of cargo was not worth the trouble.

Moose Jaw was forty miles behind them now, and dwindling at seven miles per minute, according to the plane's Doppler radar. The pilot adjusted his yoke to compensate for the crosswind. The computer by his right knee would compute for drift, and the computer knew exactly where they were going.

Part of the way, anyway.

3

It looked different than it had in the imagery—they always did—but they were in the right place, that was for sure. He felt his exhaustion drain away, replaced by focused anticipation.

Ten weeks earlier a CIA satellite had tapped into a radio

transmission here, and another had taken a photo, which Driscoll now had in his pocket. This was it, no question. A triangular formation of rocks over the top identified the spot. It wasn't decoration, despite its man-made appearance, but rather something left behind by the last set of glaciers that had ground their way through this valley God knew how many thousands of years ago. Probably the same meltwater that had carved the triangle had helped bore out the cave. Or however caves were formed. Driscoll didn't know, and didn't especially care. Some of them were pretty deep, some hundreds of meters deep, perfect safe holes to hide in. But this one had originated a radio signal. And that made it special. Special as hell. It had taken Washington and Langley more than a week to localize this place, but they'd been oh-so-careful following it up. Almost nobody knew about this mission. Fewer than thirty people in total, and most of those were at Fort Benning. Where the NCO club was. Where he and his team would return in less than forty-eight hours. God willing—*inshallah,* as they said locally. Not his religion, but the sentiment made sense. Driscoll was a Methodist, though that didn't keep him from having the occasional beer. Mostly he was a soldier.

Okay, how do we do this? he asked himself. Hard and fast, of course, but how to do it hard and fast? He was carrying half a dozen grenades. Three real ones and three M84 flashbangs. The latter were sheathed in plastic instead of steel, heavy on noisemaking explosives, made from some kind of mix of magnesium and ammonium to make it seem as though the surface of the sun had paid an unexpected visit, to dazzle and blind anyone nearby. Again, the chemistry and physics of the things didn't really concern him. They worked damned well, and that was what counted.

The Rangers were not in the business of fair fights. This was combat operations, not the Olympic Games. They might

15

apply first aid to whatever bad guys survived, but that was as far as it went, and only then because survivors tended to be somewhat more talkative than the dead. Driscoll peered again at the cave's entrance. Somebody had stood right in that spot to make his satellite phone call, and a RHYTHM e-lint satellite had copied it, and a KEYHOLE satellite had marked the location, and their mission had been authorized by SOCOM himself. He stood still, next to a large rock, close enough that his silhouette would blend with it. No evident movement inside. He wasn't surprised. Even terrorists had to sleep. And that worked for him. Just fine, in fact. Ten meters. He approached with movements that would have appeared comical to the uninitiated, exaggerated straight-up-and-down movements of his feet and lower legs, carefully avoiding loose stones. Then he got there. Dropped to one knee and looked inside. He glanced over his shoulder to ensure that the rest of the team wasn't bunching up. No worries there. Still, Driscoll felt the flutter of apprehension in his belly. Or was it fear? Fear of screwing the pooch, fear of repeating history. Fear of getting men killed.

A year earlier in Iraq, Captain Wilson's predecessor, a green second lieutenant, had planned a mission—a straightforward insurgent hunt along the southern shores of Buhayrat (Lake) Saddam, north of Mosel—and Driscoll had concurred. Problem was, the young lieutenant was more interested in filing a glowing report than he was in the safety of his Rangers. Against Driscoll's advice and with night falling, he'd split the team to flank a bunker complex, but as was their tendency, the hastily redrawn plan didn't survive its first contact with the enemy—in this case, a company-sized gathering of Saddam ex-army loyalists who encircled and butchered the young lieutenant's fire team before turning their attention on Driscoll and his men. The fighting withdrawal had taken most of the night, until finally Driscoll and three others made their way back across the Tigris and within range of a firebase.

Driscoll had known the lieutenant's plan was a disaster in the making. But had he argued strongly enough against it? If he'd pushed it . . . Well. This was the question that had haunted him for the past year. And now here again in Indian country, but this time all the decisions—good, bad, disastrous—were all his own.

Eye on the ball, Driscoll commanded himself. *Head back in the game.*

He took another step forward. Still nothing ahead. The Pashto people might be tough—they damned well were tough, Driscoll had learned—but they hadn't been trained beyond how to point a rifle and pull the trigger. There should have been somebody in the cave entrance doing overwatch. He saw some cigarette butts nearby. Maybe a sentry had been here and run out of smokes. *Bad habit, Gomer,* Driscoll thought. *Bad fieldcraft.* Slowly, carefully, he eased inside. His night-vision goggles were a godsend. The cave was straight for about fifteen meters, rough sides, mostly oval-shaped in cross-section. No lights. Not even a candle, but he could see a right turn coming, so Driscoll kept his eyes tuned for light. The cave floor was devoid of clutter. That told the sergeant much: Somebody lived here. They'd been given solid information. *Will miracles never cease?* Driscoll thought. As often as not, these hunting expeditions turned up nothing but an empty hidey-hole and a bunch of pissed-off Rangers holding their own dicks.

Maybe the right cave? He didn't often allow himself to think such thoughts. *Wouldn't that be something?* Driscoll thought for a bare instant. *Big prize, this one.* He set the thought aside. The size of the prize didn't change how they did their jobs.

The soles of his boots were flexible. Easier on his feet, but more important, quiet. He tucked his M4 carbine in close to his shoulder. He'd left his backpack outside. No need for additional weight or bulk inside the cave. Driscoll was not overly big. A hair under six feet, he weighed a hundred and eighty pounds, lean and tough, his blue eyes tracing forward. He had two soldiers a few meters behind him, and while they heard his breathing over the radio links they all carried, he didn't speak a word. Just hand signals, which were in any case data-dense in their content.

Movement. Somebody was coming their way.

Driscoll dropped to one knee.

The footsteps approached. Driscoll held up his left fist, telling those behind him to drop, as his carbine came up. The footsteps were casual. Alert ones sounded different to his trained ear. This guy was home, and was comfortable there. Well, too bad for him. Behind him, pebbles skittered and Driscoll knew the source; he'd done it before himself: a boot slip. He froze. Around the corner, the footsteps stopped. Ten seconds passed, then twenty. For a full thirty seconds, nothing moved. Then the footsteps began moving again. Still casual.

Driscoll tucked the M4 to his shoulder and turned the corner and there was the gomer. A moment later he had two rounds in the chest and a third one in the forehead, and he went down without a sound. He was older than the one outside, maybe twenty-five, with a mature beard, Driscoll saw. *Too bad for you.* Driscoll pressed on, stepping around the body and taking the right turn, then pausing to wait for his companions to catch up. Ahead he could see another six meters or so. Nothing directly ahead. *Press on.* How deep did this cave go? No telling that at the moment. He cradled the carbine tight in his hands.

There was more light ahead, flickering. Candles, probably. Maybe the gomers needed a night-light, like Driscoll's young kids. Still the cave floor was devoid of clutter. Somebody had cleaned this place up. Why? Driscoll wondered. How long ago?

He kept moving forward.

The next turn was to the left, a shallow, sweeping turn in the limestone rock, and at the next turn, a lot of light—relatively speaking. Without the PVS-17s it would have been a dull glow at most.

That's when he heard noise. Snoring. Not too far forward. Driscoll wasn't moving fast, but now he slowed a bit. Time to be careful. He approached the turn, weapon foremost, turning, turning, turning slowly.

There. That's what he was looking for. Semifinished lumber. Plain old untreated two-by-fours, and those didn't grow out of the ground. Somebody had carried them in here from civilization, and that somebody had used a saw to cut them and shape them to size.

Sure as hell, somebody lived here, and it wasn't just a temporary bolt-hole. That was a damned good sign for this cave.

He started to get excited, could feel the tingle of it in his belly. That didn't often happen to First Sergeant (E-8) Sam Driscoll. His left hand motioned for his companions to close up. They closed to an interval of maybe three meters and followed his lead.

Double-decker bunks. That's what the lumber was for. Eight of them he could see. All were occupied. Six bunks, six gomers. One even appeared to have a mattress, the blow-up plastic kind you could buy at Gander Mountain. On the floor was a foot-powered air pump. Whoever that one was, he liked sleeping in comfort.

Okay. Now what? he asked himself. It wasn't often that he didn't know what to do, and more often than not he advised his company commander at times like this, but Captain Wilson was stuck on a hilltop ten miles behind them, and that put Driscoll in command, and command was suddenly pretty damned lonely. Worst of all, this wasn't the last room. The cave went on forward. No telling how far. *Oh, shit.*

Back to work.

He eased forward. His orders were fairly simple, and for that purpose he had a noise suppressor for his pistol. This he now drew out of his web holster. Moving forward, he reached the first sleeping man. He put his Beretta next to the man's head and squeezed off the first round. The suppressor worked as advertised. The sound of the cycling pistol action was far louder than the report of the shot itself. He even heard the brass cartridge case rattling on the stone floor with its small, toylike tinkling clatter. Whatever the guy had been dreaming about was now as real as hell. The guys sleeping on the lower bunk went the same way.

It occurred briefly to Driscoll that in the civilian world this would be considered pure murder, but that wasn't his worry. These guys had thrown their lot in with people who were making war on his country, and it was their fault that they hadn't mounted a sufficient guard on their quarters. Laziness had consequences, and war had rules, and those rules were hard on those who violated them. Inside of three seconds, the remaining men were dispatched. Maybe they'd get their virgins. Driscoll didn't know. Nor did he especially care. Nine bad guys down and dead. He moved forward. Behind him, two more Rangers were following, not too close but close enough, pistol up in one case, M4 carbine in the other for overwatch, just like it said in The Book. The cave turned to the right a few feet ahead. Driscoll pressed on, taking time only to breathe. More bunks, he saw. Two of them.

But neither of these was occupied. The cave kept going. He'd been in a bunch of similar caves. A few had stretched on for as much as three, four hundred meters. Most didn't. Some were mere walk-in closets, but this wasn't one of those, either. He'd heard that some, in Afghanistan, went on for half of forever, too long for the Russians to defeat them, despite significant measures up to and including filling them with diesel fuel and tossing a match. Maybe gasoline would have been better here, Driscoll thought. Or explosives, maybe. The Afghans were tough enough, and most of them were not afraid to die. Driscoll had never encountered people like that before coming to this part of the world. But they died, just like everybody else, and then the problems they made ended with them.

One step at a time. Nine bodies behind him, all men, all in their twenties, too young to have any useful information, probably, and Gitmo had enough useless people sitting inside the wire. Thirty years or older—then maybe he would have been better advised to spare their lives and have an intel guy talk to them. But they'd all been too young, and they were all now dead.

Back to work.

Nothing more to be seen here. But there was still a faint glow ahead. Maybe another candle. His eyes looked down every few feet, looking for some stones that might have generated some noise, and noise was his most dangerous enemy at the moment. Noise woke people up, especially in a place like this. Echoes. That was why he had soft soles on his boots. The next turn went to the left, and it looked sharper. Time to slow down again. A sharp turn meant a sentry spot. Slowly, slowly. Four meters. Twelve feet or so. Slowly, gently. Like creeping into his baby's bedroom to look at her lying in her crib. But he worried about a grown man around the corner, holding a rifle, and fitfully asleep. He still had his pistol out, held in both hands, the soda can–like suppressor screwed on the front end. Eleven rounds left in the magazine. He stopped and turned. Both of the other Rangers were still there, eyes locked on him. Not scared but tense and focused as hell. Tait and Young, two sergeants from Delta Company, Second Battalion, 75th Ranger Regiment. Real serious pros, as he was, both looking to make the Army a career.

Eyes on the job. It was hard, sometimes, to keep focus. Another couple of feet to the corner. It was a sharp corner. Driscoll eased up to it . . . and stuck his head around the corner. There was somebody nearby. An Afghan, or some sort of gomer, sitting on a . . . chair? No, a rock, it appeared. This one was older than he'd expected. Maybe thirty. The guy was just sitting, not quite asleep, but not awake, either. Sort of in between, and definitely not paying attention. The man had a weapon, an AK-74, maybe four feet away from his hands, leaning against a rock. Close, but not close enough to reach in a real emergency, which the guy was about to have on his hands.

Driscoll approached quietly, moving his legs in an exaggerated way, getting close, and—

He clubbed the guy's head on the right side. Maybe enough to kill, but probably not. Driscoll reached into his field-jacket pockets and pulled out a set of plastic flex-cuffs. This one was probably old enough for the spooks to talk to, would probably end up at Gitmo. He'd let Tait and Young wrap him up for transport. He caught Tait's attention, pointed to the unconscious form, and made a twirling motion with his index finger: *Wrap him up.* Tait nodded in return.

Another turn ahead, five more meters away, to the right, and the glow was flickering.

Six more feet, then right.

Driscoll didn't lose focus now. Slow, careful steps, weapon held in tight.

The next chamber, which measured roughly ten meters by ten meters, turned out to be the end. He was, what, maybe seventy meters inside the cave. Deep enough. This cave probably had been set up for one of the important ones. Maybe the important one? He'd know in three more minutes. He didn't often allow himself that sort of thought. But that was the underlying reason for this mission. Maybe, maybe, maybe.

That was why Driscoll was a special ops Ranger. Forward, slowly. His hand went up behind him.

It was so dark now that his PVS-17 night-vision goggles were displaying as much receiver noise as proper image now, like little bits of popcorn in his field of view, popping and flitting around. He eased to the edge of the turn and very carefully looked around the corner. Somebody there, lying down. There was an AK-47 close by, complete with a preloaded plastic magazine, within easy reach. The guy appeared to be asleep, but in that respect they were good soldiers. They didn't sleep all the way, like civilians did, but hovered just below full wakefulness. And he wanted this one alive. Okay, fine, he'd killed a handful of people so far this night, just in the last ten minutes, but this one they wanted alive . . . if possible . . .

All right. Driscoll switched his pistol to his right hand, and with his left pulled a flashbang off his chest web gear. Tait and Young saw this and froze in place. The cave was about to change. Driscoll held up one finger. Tait gave his senior sergeant a thumbs-up. Time to rock and roll. Gomer was about to get his wake-up call. Tait looked around. One small candle that lit up the chamber nicely. Driscoll took a step or two back, flipped off his NV, and pulled the pin on the grenade. He let the safety spoon fly free, let it cook for a beat, then he tossed it, counting, a thousand one, a thousand two, a thousand three . . .

It sounded like the end of the world. The ten grams of magnesium powder bloomed like the noonday sun, but even brighter than that. And the noise. The noise did sound and feel like the end of the world, a crashing BANG that ended whatever sleep the gomer was enjoying. Then Driscoll went in. He was not stunned by the explosion. He'd expected it, and so his ears had adjusted to the noise and he'd closed his eyes to attenuate the magnitude of the flash. The gomer had enjoyed no such protection. His ears had been assaulted, and that adversely affected his balance. He didn't even reach for his nearby weapon—but Driscoll had leaped inward to bat it away, and a moment later he had his pistol right in the gomer's face. He had no chance to resist at all, but that was Driscoll's intention.

That's when Driscoll saw it was the wrong target. He had a beard, but he was in his early thirties, not anywhere near his forties. *Wrong gomer* was his immediate thought, followed by *Shit.* The face was the embodiment of confusion and shock. He was shaking his head, trying to get his brain initialized, but young and tough as he was, he wasn't fast enough for the necessities of the moment.

Near the back wall of the chamber Driscoll saw movement, a shadow hunched over, sliding along the rock wall. Not moving toward them but somewhere else. Driscoll holstered his pistol, turned to Tait, then pointed at the gomer on the ground—*Cuff 'em*—then flipped on his NV and dropped the M4's sights over the moving shadow. Another bearded gomer. His finger tightened on the trigger, but he held off, now curious. Ten feet behind the man, still leaning against the wall where he'd left it, was an AK-47. Clearly he'd heard the flashbang and knew the shit was coming down, so was he making a break for it? Driscoll wondered. Still tracking him with the M4's sights, Driscoll held him, looking for an exit . . . There: a five-foot-wide alcove in the rock wall. He scanned back and now saw the gomer had a grenade in his right hand. It was a 40-millimeter version of an RPG-7; locals were fond of converting the round into hand-thrown versions.

Not so fast, bud, Driscoll thought, and laid the M4's sights across the man's ear. Even as he was doing this the man cocked his arm back, underhand, to toss the grenade. Driscoll's 5.56-millimeter slug entered just above the man's ear and just behind his eye. His head snapped sideways, and he crumpled, but not before the grenade was flying, bouncing toward the alcove.

"Grenade!" Driscoll shouted and dropped flat.

Crump!

Driscoll looked up and around. "Head count!"

"Okay," Tait replied, followed in quick succession by Young and the others.

The grenade had bounced off the wall and rolled to a stop before the alcove, leaving behind a beach ball–sized crater in the dirt.

Driscoll took off his PVS-17s and took out his flashlight. This he turned on and played it about. This was the command segment of the cave. Lots of bookshelves, even a rug on the floor of the cave. Most Afghans they'd met were only semi-literate, but there were books and magazines in evidence, some of the latter in English, in fact. One sparsely filled shelf with nicely bound leather-sided books. One in partic-ular . . . green leather, gold-inlaid. Driscoll flipped it open. An illuminated manuscript, printed—not printed by a machine but by the hand of some long-dead scribe in multi-colored ink. This book was old, really old. In Arabic, so it appeared, written by hand and illuminated with gold leaf. This had to be a copy of the Holy Koran, and there was no telling its age or relative value. But it had value. Driscoll took it. Some spook would want to look at it. Back at Kabul they had a couple of Saudis, senior military officers who were backing up the Special Operations people and the Army spooks.

"Okay, Peterson, we're clear. Code it up and call it in," Driscoll radioed to his communications specialist. "Target secure. Nine tangos down for the count, two prisoners taken alive. Zero friendly casualties."

"But nothing under the Christmas tree, Santa," Sergeant Young said quietly. "Damn, this one felt pretty good coming in. Had the right vibe, I thought." One more dry hole for the Special Operations troops. They'd drilled too many of those already, but that was the nature of Special Operations.

"Me, too. What's your name, Gomer?" Driscoll asked Tait's prisoner. There was no response. The flashbang had really tumbled this bastard's gyros. He didn't yet understand that it could have been worse. A whole shitload worse. Then again, once the interrogators got ahold of him . . .

"All right, guys, let's clean this hole out. Look for a computer and any electronic stuff. Turn it upside down and inside out. If it looks interesting, bag it. Get somebody in here to take our friend."

There was a Chinook on short-fuse alert for this mission, and maybe he'd be aboard it in under an hour. Damn, he wanted to hit the Fort Benning NCO club for a glass of Sam Adams, but that wouldn't be for a couple of days at best.

While the remainder of his team was setting up an over-watch perimeter outside the cave entrance, Young and Tait searched the entrance tunnel, found a few goodies, maps and such, but no obvious jackpot. That was the way with these things, though. Weenies or not, the intel guys could make a meal out of a walnut. A little scrap of paper, a handwritten Koran, a stick figure drawn in purple crayon—the intel guys could sometimes work miracles with that stuff, which was why Driscoll wasn't taking any chances. Their target hadn't been here, and that was a goddamned shame, but maybe the shit the gomers had left behind might lead to something else, which in turn could lead to something good. That's the way it worked, though Driscoll didn't dwell on that stuff much. Above his pay grade and out of his MOS—military occupational specialty. Give him and the Rangers the mission, let somebody else worry about the hows and whats and whys.

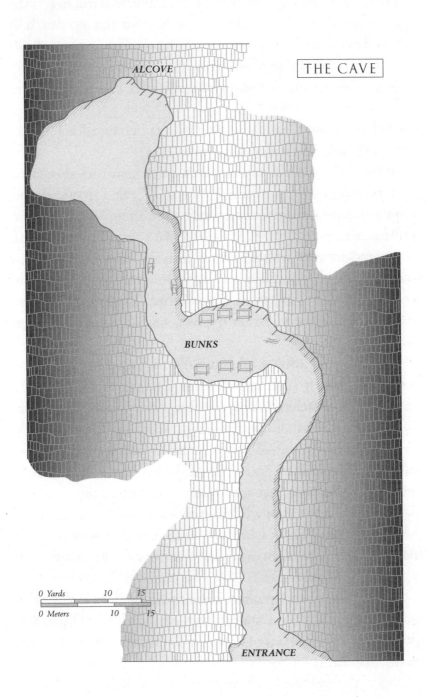

ALCOVE

THE CAVE

BUNKS

0 Yards   10   15

0 Meters   10   15

ENTRANCE

Driscoll walked to the rear of the cave, playing his flashlight around until he reached the alcove the gomer had seemed so keen to frag. It was about the size of a walk-in closet, he now saw, maybe a little bigger, with a low-hanging ceiling. He crouched down and waddled a few feet into the alcove.

"Whatcha got?" Tait said, coming up behind him.

"Sand table and a wooden ammo crate."

A flat piece of three-fourths-inch-thick plywood, about two meters square to each side, covered in glued-on sand and papier-mâché mountains and ridges, scatterings of boxlike buildings here and there. It looked like something in one of those old-time World War Two movies, or a grade-school diorama. Pretty good job, too, not something half-assed you sometimes see with these guys. More often than not the gomers here drew a plan in the dirt, said some prayers, then went at it.

The terrain didn't look familiar to Driscoll. Could be anywhere, but it sure as hell looked rugged enough to be around here, which didn't narrow down the possibilities much. No landmarks, either. No buildings, no roads. Driscoll lifted the corner of the table. It was damned heavy, maybe eighty pounds, which solved one of Driscoll's problems: no way they were going to haul that thing down the mountain. It was a goddamned brick hang glider; at this altitude the wind was a bitch, and they'd either lose the thing in a gust or it would start flapping and give them away. And breaking it up might ruin something of value.

"Okay, take some measurements and some samples, then go see if Smith is done taking shots of the gomers' faces and photograph the hell out of this thing," Driscoll ordered. "How many SD cards we got?"

"Six. Four gigs each. Plenty."

"Good. Multiple shots of everything, highest resolution.

Get some extra lights on it, too, and drop something beside for scale."

"Reno's got a tape measure."

"Good. Use it. Plenty of angles and close-ups—the more, the better." That was the beauty of digital cameras—take as many as you want and delete the bad ones. In this case they'd leave the deleting to the intel folks. "And check every inch for markings."

Never could tell what was important. A lot would depend on the model's scale, he suspected. If it was to scale they might be able to plug the measurements into a computer, do a little funky algebra or algorithms or whatever they used, and come up with a match somewhere. Who knew, maybe the papier-mâché stuff would turn out to be special or something, made only in some back-alley shop in Kandahar. Stranger shit had happened, and he wasn't about to give the higher-ups anything to bitch about. They'd be angry enough that their quarry hadn't been here, but that wasn't Driscoll's fault. Pre-mission intelligence, bad or good or otherwise, was beyond a soldier's control. Still, the old saying in the military, "Shit runs downhill," was as true as ever, and in this business there was always someone uphill from you, ready to give the shit ball a shove.

"You got it, boss," Tait said.

"Frag it when you're done. Might as well finish the job they should have done."

Tait trotted off.

Driscoll turned his attention to the ammo box, picking it up and carrying it into the entrance tunnel. Inside was a stack of paper about three inches thick—some lined notebook paper covered in Arabic script, some random numbers and doodles—and a large two-sided foldout map. One side was labeled "Sheet Operational Navigation Chart, G-6, Defense Mapping Agency, 1982" and displayed the Afghanistan-

Pakistan border region, while the other, held in place with masking tape, was a map of Peshawar torn from a Baedeker's travel guide.

4

"Welcome to American airspace, gentlemen," the copilot announced.

They were about to overfly Montana, home of elk, big skies, and a whole lot of decommissioned ICBM bases with empty silos.

They'd be burning fuel a lot faster down here, but the computer took notice of all that, and they had a much better reserve than what they'd had westbound over the Atlantic a few hours before—with a lot of usable fields down below to land on. The pilot turned on the heads-up display, which used low-light cameras to turn the darkness into green-and-white mono-color TV. Now it showed mountains to the west of their course track. The aircraft would automatically gain altitude to compensate, programmed as it was to maintain one thousand feet AGL—above ground level—and to do so with gentle angles, to keep his wealthy passengers happy and, he hoped, turn them into repeat customers.

The aircraft eased up to a true altitude of 6,100 feet as they passed over the lizard-back spine of the Grand Teton Range. Somewhere down there was Yellowstone National Park. In daylight he could have seen it, but it was a cloudless and moonless night.

The radar-sending systems showed they were "clear of conflict." No other aircraft was close to their position or altitude. Mountain Home Air Force Base was a few hundred miles behind them, along with its complement of young piss-and-vinegar fighter pilots.

"Pity we can't steer the HUD off the nose. Might even see the buffalo on the infrared sensors," he observed. "They are making a real comeback in the West, I've read."

"Along with the wolves," the copilot responded. Nature was about balance, or so the Discovery Channel said. Not enough bison, the wolves die. Not enough wolves, the bison overproduce.

Utah's countryside started off mountainous but gradually settled down to rolling flatness. They again maneuvered east to avoid Salt Lake City, which had an international airport and, probably, a sufficiently powerful radar to get a skin-paint.

This entire exercise would have been impossible thirty years earlier. They would have had to cross the Pinetree Line, one of the predecessors to America's DEW—Distant Early Warning—Lines, and alert the North American Air Defense Command at Cheyenne Mountain. Well, given the current tensions between the United States and Russia, maybe the DEW and Pinetree would be recommissioned.

The ride was smoother than he'd expected. Riding in daylight, in summer, over the desert, could be bumpy indeed, what with the irregular rising thermal currents. Except for a few automobile headlights, the land below might as well have been the sea, so empty and black it was.

Thirty minutes to go. They were down to 9,000 pounds of fuel. The engines burned it a lot faster down here, just over 5,000 pounds per hour instead of the usual 3,400 or so.

"Wake the passengers up?" the copilot asked.

"Good idea." The pilot lifted the microphone. "Attention. We expect to land in thirty minutes. Let us know if you have any special needs. Thank you," he added. *Thank you indeed for the money, and the interesting flight profile,* he did not add.

The pilot and copilot both wondered who the passengers were but asked no questions. Upholding customer anonymity was part of the job, and though what they were doing was technically illegal, probably, by American law, they weren't American citizens. They were not carrying guns, drugs, or anything else illegal. In any case, they didn't know their passenger from Adam, and his face was wrapped in bandages anyway.

"Hundred miles, according to the computer. I hope the runway really is that long."

"Chart says it is. Two thousand six hundred meters. We'll know soon enough."

In fact, the airstrip had been built in 1943, and was scarcely used since, built by an engineer battalion that had been trucked to Nevada and told to build an air base—as practice, really. All the fields looked the same, built from the same manual, like a triangle with one line segment longer than the other two. They were angling for runway two-seven, indicating a due-west approach run into the prevailing winds. It even had runway lights installed, but the cabling had long since degraded, as had the airport's diesel generator. But as there was little in the way of snow and ice here to damage the concrete runways, they were as good as the day they'd cured out, twelve inches thick of rebarred concrete.

"There."

"I see 'em."

They were, in fact, neon-green chemical lights being broken, shaken, and tossed onto the runway perimeter, and they blazed brightly on the low-light HUD display. Then even more as a truck's headlights turned on. One such pair even drove down the northern border of the runway, as though to outline it for the approaching aircraft. Neither pilot nor copilot knew, but they assumed that one of the passengers had called ahead on a cell phone to wake someone up.

"Okay, let's shoot the approach," the pilot-in-command

ordered. He eased the throttles back and lowered flaps to chop air speed. Again the altitude sensor announced their height above the ground, lower … lower … lower … then the wheels kissed the ground. At the west end of the runway, a truck flipped its headlights from high beams to low, back and forth a few times, and the pilot let the aircraft coast all the way.

"We have arrived at our destination," the pilot said over the intercom as the aircraft came to a slow and gentle halt. He took off his headset and stood to move aft. He opened the left-side door and lowered the stairs, then turned to look at his charter party, most of whom were up and moving forward.

"Welcome to American soil," he said.

"It was a long flight, but a good one even so," the chief of the group said. "Thank you. Your fee is already on deposit."

The pilot nodded his thanks. "If you need us again, please let me know."

"Yes, we will do that. In two or three weeks, perhaps."

Neither his voice nor his face gave much away, though now his face was somewhat obscured by bandages. Maybe he was just here to sit through the recovery period for whatever surgery he'd just had. Car accident was the pilot's best guess. At least it was a healthy climate.

"I trust you noticed the fuel truck. They will make sure you are topped off. You leave for Hawaii when?"

"As soon as we're fueled," the pilot answered. Four, five hours. He'd do autopilot for most of it, after clearing the California coast.

Another passenger came forward, then turned to go aft. "One moment," he said, entering the lavatory and closing the door behind him. There was another door aft of the lavatory. It led into the luggage compartment. There he'd left a duffel bag. He pulled down the zipper and flipped the cover open. Here he activated an electronic timer. He figured two and a half hours would be more than sufficient, then rezipped the closure and came forward. "Forgive me," he said, heading forward and left for the ten-step stairs. "And thank you."

"My pleasure, sir," the pilot said. "Enjoy your stay."

The copilot was already out, supervising the fueling operation. The last passenger followed his boss to the stretch limo that waited on the concrete, got in, and the car drove off. Fueling took five minutes. The pilot wondered how they'd managed to get what looked like an official fuel truck, but it drove off soon thereafter, and the flight crew made their way back to the cockpit and went through their start-up procedures.

After a total of thirty-three minutes on the ground, the Falcon taxied back east to the far end of the runway, and the flight crew advanced the throttles to takeoff power and raced back west to rotate and climb back into the sky for the third flight of what was already a long day. Fifty minutes later, and four thousand pounds lighter in fuel, they transited the California coast just over Ventura and were "feet wet" over the Pacific Ocean, cruising at Mach 0.83 at an altitude of forty-one thousand feet. Their primary transponder was switched on, this one with the aircraft's "official" registration information. The fact that it had just appeared on San Francisco Center's master scopes was not a matter of concern for anyone, since flight plans were neither computerized nor really organized in any systematic way. So long as the aircraft did nothing contrary to the rules, it attracted no attention. It was inbound to Honolulu, two thousand miles away, for an estimated flight time of four hours and fifty-four minutes. The home stretch.

Pilot and copilot relaxed, the aircraft on autopilot and all the gauges within norms. The pilot lit another cigarette as he departed the U.S. coast at 510 miles per hour true ground speed.

He didn't know that in the aft luggage compartment was a bomb made of almost nine pounds—four kilograms—of PETN and RDX plastic explosive—commonly referred to as Semtex—working off an electronic timer. They'd let the passengers and the welcoming party handle such luggage as there had been. Just as the aircraft passed six hundred miles off the California coast, the timer went to zero.

The explosion was immediate and catastrophic. It blew the tail and both engines off the airframe. The main fuel lines, which ran just under the deck, were vented to the sky, and the fuel that was being pumped created a meteor-like trail in the sky. It might have been seen by any aircraft trailing the Falcon, but there were none at this time of night, and the twin gouts of yellow flame flickered out and died in a few seconds.

Forward, pilot and copilot could not have known what had happened, just a sudden noise, a firewall full of flashing emergency lights and alarms, and an aircraft that did not answer to the controls. Aviators are trained to deal with emergencies. And it took five or ten seconds before they realized they were doomed. Without a tail plane, the Dassault could not be controlled; the physics were undeniable. The craft started spiraling downward to an ink-black sea. Both aviators tried to work the controls, hoping against hope. A lifetime of training and endless hours on computerized flight simulators had ingrained in them what to do when their airplane didn't respond to commands. They tried everything they knew, but the nose didn't come up. They didn't really have time to notice that the attempts at adjusting engine power did nothing at all. Locked in their seats by four-point safety belts, they couldn't look back into the passenger cabin, and both were soon anoxic with the loss of cabin pressure that had ruptured the door aft. Their minds never had a chance to catch up.

In all, it took just over a minute. The nose went up and down, left and right, of its own accord and at the mercy of the air currents until they smashed into the sea at a speed of 240 knots, which was instantly fatal. By that time their charter party was at its final destination, and hardly thinking about them at all.

5

As if a sign from Allah that his course was true and right, Dirar al-Kariim heard the Adhan, the call to prayer, echo over Tripoli's rooftops and down to where he sat in the café, drinking tea. The timing was no coincidence, he knew. So focused had he been on playing and replaying the operation in his mind, he'd failed to see the sun dipping toward the horizon. No matter. Certainly Allah would forgive him the oversight— especially if he succeeded in his task—and it was his, wasn't it, for better or worse? That his superiors had failed to see the value of the mission was an unfortunate waste, but Dirar was unconcerned. Initiative, as long as it was in keeping with Allah's will and Islam's laws, was a blessing, and surely his superiors would see that once the mission was complete. Whether he would still be alive to accept their praise was a matter for Allah to decide, but his reward was assured, in this life or the next. Dirar took comfort in the thought and used it to calm the churning in his belly.

Up until recently his role in the jihad had been largely supportive, providing transportation and information, offering his home to fellow soldiers, and occasionally aiding in reconnaissance and intelligence collection. He had handled weapons, of course, but to his great shame, he had never wielded one against an enemy. That would soon change— before the next dawn, in fact. Still, just as he'd been taught at the training camp outside Fuqha, proficiency in weapons and their use was only a small part of an operation. In that at least the American military was correct. Most fights are won and lost before the soldiers even take to the battlefield. Plan, replan, then triple-check your plans. Mistakes are born of poor preparation.

His target of choice had proven unfeasible, not only given the limited number of soldiers under his command but also because of the target's location. The hotel was one of the newest in Tripoli, with enough exits and floors and unknown entry points that it would take two dozen or more men to secure it, and that didn't even take into account the on-site security force, all former soldiers and police officers armed with advanced weapons and backed up by a surveillance system second-to-none. Given time and enough resources, Dirar was confident he could make such a mission work, but he had neither at his disposal. Not yet, at least. Next time, perhaps.

Instead he had chosen a secondary target, one that had already been proposed by another cell—the Benghazi group, Dirar suspected—but was subsequently rejected by the leadership. No reason had been given, nor an alternative suggested, and like many of his compatriots, Dirar was tired of waiting while the West continued its crusade unchecked. Unsurprisingly, he'd had little trouble finding other cell members who felt the same, though the recruitment had been a hazardous affair, Dirar never knowing whether word of his plan had found its way to unwelcome ears, both from within and without the organization. Over the past year Qaddafi's Haiat amn al Jamahiriyya had successfully infiltrated a number of cells, one of which had been led by a childhood friend of Dirar's. Those nine men, good soldiers and true believers each, had disappeared into the Bab al-Azizia barracks and never come out—not alive, at least.

The secondary target was softer to be sure, and only peripherally responsible for the act it would soon be punished for, but if he succeeded, Dirar was confident the message would be clear: Allah's soldiers had long memories and even longer knives. Kill one of ours and we kill a hundred of yours. He doubted he would reach a hundred here, but no matter.

Along with several of the café's other patrons, Dirar stood up and walked to a shelf built into the café's wall and took down a rolled sajada. As was required, the prayer rug was clean and free of debris. He returned to his table and unrolled the rug on the brick patio, taking care to ensure that the top was pointed in the direction of the Qibla, Mecca, then stood erect, hands at his sides, and began the *salaat*, starting with a whispered Iqama, the private call to prayer. He immediately felt a wave of peace wash through his mind as he proceeded through the remaining seven steps of the *salaat*, ending with the *salawat*.

O Allah, bless our Muhammad and his people;
Surely you are the Glorious.
O Allah, be gracious unto Muhammadand the people of Muhammad;
As you were merciful unto Abraham and the people of Abraham.
Surely you are the Eternal, the Glorious. . . .

Dirar finished with a lingering glance over each shoulder—acknowledging the angels that recorded each believer's good deeds as well as his wrongful deeds—then cupped his hands at his chest and wiped his face with his palms.

He opened his eyes and drew in a deep breath. In His wisdom, Allah had seen fit to require believers to perform the *salaat* at least five times per day, before dawn, at noon, at midafternoon, at sunset, and in the evening. As did most Muslims, Dirar found the frequent rituals were as much a personal recentering as they were a tribute to Allah's power and grace. He'd never spoken of this feeling to others, afraid it was blasphemous, but in his heart he doubted Allah condemned him for it.

He checked his watch. Time to go.

The only question that remained now was whether he would be alive to perform the day's final *salaat*. That was in Allah's hands now.

Though Driscoll didn't consider their stroll through the Hindu Kush mountaineering per se, it was close enough to remind him of an old Everest saying: Reach the summit and you've only climbed half the mountain. Translation: Oftentimes getting back down safely was the real bitch. And for him and his team this was especially true: Mountaineers usually follow the same route up and down. He and his Rangers couldn't do that, lest they risk ambush. To complicate matters, they were hauling along two prisoners, both of whom had so far been cooperating, but that could change quickly enough.

Driscoll reached a flat spot in the trail between a pair of boulders and stopped, raising his fist as he did so. Behind him, the rest of the team halted in near unison and crouched down. They were five hundred feet from the valley floor. Another forty minutes, Driscoll estimated, then another two klicks along the valley floor, then head to the LZ, or landing zone. He checked his watch: making good time.

Tait sidled up alongside and offered Driscoll a hunk of jerky. "Prisoners are starting to drag ass a bit."

"Life's a bitch."

"Then you die," Tait replied.

Handling prisoners was always dicey, and even more so in terrain like this. If one of them snapped an ankle or decided to simply sit down and refuse to get up, you had three choices: leave him behind, haul him, or shoot him. The trick was convincing the prisoners that only one fate—the last one—

awaited them. Probably true in any case, Driscoll thought. No way he'd put two gomers back into circulation.

Driscoll said, "Five minutes and we're moving again. Pass the word."

The boulder-strewn terrain slowly leveled out and gave way to barrel-sized rocks and gravel. A hundred meters from the valley floor, Driscoll called another halt and checked the way ahead through the night vision. He followed the trail's zigzagging course to where it bottomed out, pausing at every potential area of concealment until he was certain nothing was moving. The valley was two hundred meters wide and bordered by sheer rock walls. *Perfect place for an ambush,* Driscoll thought, but then again, the geography of the Hindu Kush made that more the rule than the exception, a lesson that had been passed down through the millennia, starting with Alexander the Great, then the Soviets, and now the U.S. military. Driscoll and their now–leg-broke captain had planned this mission backward and forward, each time looking for a better exfiltration route, but had found no alternatives, at least not within ten klicks, a detour that would have put their extraction into the daylight hours.

Driscoll turned around and did a quick head count: fifteen and two. Coming out with the same he'd taken in, a victory in itself. He signaled to Tait—*moving*—who passed it down the line. Driscoll stood up and started down the trail. Ten minutes later they were within a stone's throw of the valley floor. He paused to check that nobody was bunching up, then started out again, then stopped.

Something not right . . .

It took a moment for Driscoll to nail down the source: One of their prisoners, the one in the number-four position with Peterson, no longer seemed as tired. His posture was stiff, his head swiveling left and right. *A worried man. Why?* Driscoll called another halt, brought the column into a crouch. Tait was there a few moments later.

"What's up?"

"Peterson's gomer is nervous about something."

Driscoll did a scan ahead with the night vision but saw nothing. The valley floor, level and clear of debris save the occasional boulder, appeared empty. Nothing moving, and no sound except the faint whistling of wind. Still, Driscoll's gut was talking to him.

Tait asked, "See something?"

"Not a thing, but something's got what's-his-face jumpy."

"Grab Collins, Smith, and Gomez, then backtrack fifty yards and pick your way along the hillside. Tell Peterson and Flaherty to put their prisoners in the dirt and keep them quiet."

"Roger."

Tait disappeared back down the trail, pausing to whisper instructions to each man. Through the night vision, Driscoll watched Tait's progress as he and the other three snaked their way back up the slope, then off the trail, moving from boulder to boulder, paralleling the valley.

Zimmer had moved up the line to Driscoll's position. "Little voice talking to you, Santa?" he asked.

"Yeah."

Fifteen minutes passed. In the green, washed-out glow of the NV, Driscoll saw Tait suddenly stop. Over the radio: "Boss, we got an open space ahead of us—a notch in the rock. I can see the peak of a tent."

Which explains the nervous gomer, Driscoll thought. *He knows the camp is there.* "Life signs?"

"Muffled voices—five, maybe six."

"Roger, hold pos—"

To the right, fifty meters up the valley, came a pair of headlights. Driscoll turned to see a UAZ-469 jeep skid around the corner and head in their direction. Throwbacks to the Soviet

41

invasion of Afghanistan, UAZs were favored among the country's sundry bad guys. This one was open-topped and equipped with another piece of Soviet Army equipment, a mounted NSV 12.7-millimeter heavy machine gun. *Thirteen shots a second, 1,500-meter range,* Driscoll thought. Even as he recognized it for what it was, the muzzle began flashing. Bullets thudded into rock and soil, throwing up shards and plumes of dust. Farther down the valley, atop the cliff opposite Tait and the others, muzzles began flashing. Peterson's prisoner began shouting in Arabic, none of which Driscoll understood, but the tone was unmistakable: encouragement for his compatriots. Peterson popped him behind the ear with the butt of his M4, and the man went limp.

Tait's team opened up, their M4s cracking and echoing through the valley. Driscoll's remaining men had found cover and were lighting up the UAZ, which had skidded to a stop twenty meters away, its headlights aimed at the Rangers.

"Tait, put some grenades into those tents!" Driscoll ordered, then ducked left and snapped off two quick bursts at the UAZ.

"On it!" Tait replied.

Up the trail, Barnes had found a niche between some rocks and had his M249 SAW—Squad Automatic Weapon—up on its tripod. The muzzle started flashing. Its windshield spider-webbed, the UAZ started backing up now, the 12.7-millimeter still pumping rounds into the hillside. From Tait's direction Driscoll heard the crump of a grenade, then another, then two more in quick succession. Now more shouting in Arabic. Screams. It took a half-second for Driscoll to realize the screams were coming from behind. He spun, M4 to his shoulder. Fifteen meters up the trail, Gomez's prisoner was on his feet, facing the UAZ and shouting. Driscoll caught a snippet—*Shoot me. . . . Shoot me. . . .*—and then the top of the man's head exploded and he toppled backward.

"Barnes, get that thing stopped!" Driscoll shouted.

In answer, the SAW's tracers dropped from the UAZ's cab and roof to its front grille, which began sparking. Bullets thudded into the engine block, followed seconds later by a geyser of steam. The driver's-side door opened and a figure staggered out. The SAW cut him down. In the truck's bed, the NSV went silent, and Driscoll could see a figure scrambling. Reloading. Driscoll turned around and signaled to Peterson and Deacons—*grenades*—but they were already on their feet, arms cocked. The first grenade went long and right, exploding harmlessly behind the UAZ, but the second landed beside the truck's rear tire. The explosion lifted the truck's rear end a few inches off the ground. The gunner in the bed tumbled over the side and lay still.

Driscoll turned back, scanned the far cliff wall through the NV. He counted six gomers, all prone and pouring fire into Tait's position. "Light those fuckers up!" Driscoll ordered, and eleven guns began hosing down the cliff face. Thirty seconds was all it took. "Cease fire, cease fire!" Driscoll ordered. The gunfire ceased. He got on the radio: "Tait, head count."

"Still got four. Caught a few rock splinters, but we're good."

"Check the tents, mop it up."

"Roger."

Driscoll picked his way up the trail, checking each man in turn and finding only minor scrapes and cuts from flying rock. "Barnes, you and Deacons check the—"

"Santa, you're—"

"What?"

"Your shoulder. Sit down, Sam, sit down! Medic up!"

Now Driscoll could feel the numbness, as though his right arm had fallen asleep from the shoulder down. He let Barnes sit him down on the trail. Collins, the team's second medic, came running up. He knelt down, and he and Barnes eased Driscoll's pack off his right shoulder, then the left. Collins clicked on his hooded flashlight and examined Driscoll's shoulder.

"You got a rock splinter in there, Santa. About the size of my thumb."

"Ah, shit. Barnes, you and Deacons go check that truck."

"Got it, boss."

They trotted down the trail, then across to the truck. "Two dead," Deacons called.

"Frisk 'em, check for intel," Driscoll said through gritted teeth. The numbness was giving way to white-hot pain.

"You're bleeding pretty bad," Collins said. He pulled a field dressing from his pack and pressed it against the wound.

"Pack it up as best you can."

Tait, on the radio: "Santa, we got four KIA and two wounded, both are on their way out."

"Roger. Intel check, then get back here."

Collins said, "I'm gonna call for an evac—"

"Bullshit. In about fifteen minutes we're gonna be drowning in gomers. We're humping out of here. Get me up."

6

It was going to be a sad day, Clark knew. His gear was already packed—Sandy always handled that, as efficiently as ever. It would be the same at Ding's place—Patsy had learned packing from her mother. Rainbow Six was moving into its second generation, much of the original crew gone by now, rotated back stateside in the case of the Americans, mainly back for Fort Bragg and Delta School, or Coronado, California, where the Navy trained its SEAL candidates, there to tell such stories as the rules allowed over beers to a very few trusted fellow instructors. Every so often they'd come through Hereford in Wales, to drink pints of John Courage at the Green Dragon's comfortable bar and trade war stories rather more freely with fellow graduates of the Men of Black. The locals knew who they were, but they were as security-conscious as the Security Service agents—called "Five" men in a nod to the former British MI-5—who hung out there, too.

Nothing was permanent in the service, regardless of the country. This was healthy for the organizations, always bringing in fresh people, some of them with fresh ideas, and it made for warm reunions in the most unlikely of places—a lot of them airport terminals, all over the freaking world—and a lot of beers to be drunk and handshakes to be exchanged before the departing flights were called. But the impermanence and uncertainty wore at you over time. You started wondering when a close friend and colleague would be called away, to disappear into some other compartment of the "black" world, often remembered but rarely seen again. Clark had seen a lot of friends die on "training missions"—which usually meant catching a bullet in a denied area. But such things were the cost of belonging to this exclusive fraternity, and there was no changing it. As the SEALs were fond of saying, "You don't have to like it; you just have to do it."

Eddie Price, for example, had taken retirement as Regimental Sergeant Major of the 22nd Special Air Service Regiment, and was now the Yeoman Gaoler at Her Majesty's Royal Palace and Fortress, the Tower of London. John and Ding had both wondered if the UK's Chief of State understood how much more secure her Palace and Fortress was today, and if Price's ceremonial ax (the Yeoman Gaoler is the official executioner there) had a proper edge to it. For damned sure he still did his morning run and PT, and woe betide any member of the regular-Army security force quartered there who didn't have his boots spit-shined, his gig-lines in order, and his rifle cleaner than when it had left the factory.

It was a damned shame that you had to get old, John Clark told himself, close enough to sixty to see the shadow of it, and the worst part of getting old was that you could remember being young, even the things best forgotten, in his case. Memories were a double-edged sword.

"Hey, Mr. C.," said a familiar voice at the front door. "Hell of a day out, isn't it?"

"Ding, we talked about this," John said without turning.

"Sorry . . . John."

It had taken John Clark years to get Chavez, colleague and son-in-law, to call him by his first name, and even now Ding was having trouble with it.

"Ready if somebody tries to hijack the flight?"

"Mr. Beretta is in his usual place," Ding responded. They were among the handful of people in Britain who got to carry firearms, and such privileges were not lightly set aside.

"How are Johnny and Patsy?"

"The little guy is pretty excited about going home. We have a plan after we get there?"

"Not really. Tomorrow morning we make a courtesy call at Langley. I might want to drive over and see Jack in a day or two."

"See if he's leaving footprints on the ceiling?" Ding asked with a chuckle.

"More likely claw marks, if I know Jack."

"Retirement ain't fun, I suppose." Chavez didn't push it further. That was a touchy subject for his father-in law. Time passed, no matter how much you wished it wouldn't.

"How's Price handling it?"

"Eddie? He takes an even strain with life—that's how you sailors say it, right?"

"Close enough for a doggie."

"Hey, man, I said 'sailor,' not 'squid.'"

"Duly noted, Domingo. I beg your pardon, Colonel."

Chavez enjoyed the next laugh. "Yeah, I'm gonna miss that."

"How's Patsy?"

"Better than the last pregnancy. Looks great. Feels great—least she says she does. Not a big complainer, Patsy. She's a good girl, John—but then again, I ain't telling you anything you didn't already know, am I?"

"Nope, but it's always nice to hear it."

"Well, I have no complaints." And if he did, he'd have to approach the subject with great diplomacy. But he didn't. "The chopper is waiting, boss," he added.

"Damn." A sad whisper.

Sergeant Ivor Rogers had the luggage well in hand, loaded in a green British Army truck for the drive to the helipad, and he was waiting outside for his personal Brigadier, which was John's virtual rank. The Brits were unusually conscious of rank and ceremony, and he saw more of that when he got outside. He'd hoped to have a low-profile departure, but the locals weren't thinking that way. As they rolled onto the helipad, there was the entire Rainbow force, the shooters, the Intel support, even the team armorers—Rainbow had the best three gunsmiths in all of Britain—formed up—the local term was "paraded"—in whatever uniforms they were authorized to wear. There was even a squad from the SAS. Stone-faced, they collectively snapped to Present Arms, in the elegant three-count movement the British Army had adopted several centuries earlier. Tradition could be a beautiful thing.

"Damn," Clark muttered, getting out of the truck. He'd come pretty far for an old Navy chief bosun's mate, but he'd taken a lot of strange steps along the way. Not knowing quite what to do, he figured he had to review the troops, as it were, and shake hands with all of them on the way to the MH-60K helicopter.

It took more time than he'd expected. Nearly every person there got a word or two with the handshake. They all deserved it. His mind went back to 3rd SOG, a lifetime before. These were as good as those, hard to believe though that might be. He'd been young, proud, and immortal back then. And remarkably, he hadn't died of being immortal, as so many good men had. Why? Luck, maybe. No other likely explanation. He'd learned caution, mostly in Vietnam. Learned from seeing men who'd not been lucky go down hard from making some dumb mistake, often as simple as not paying attention. Some chances you had to take, but you tried to run them through your mind first and take only the necessary chances. Those were plenty bad enough.

Alice Foorgate and Helen Montgomery both gave him hugs. They'd been superb secretaries, and those were hard to find. Clark had been half tempted to try to find them jobs in the United States, but the Brits probably valued them as much as he had and would've put up a fight.

And finally Alistair Stanley, the incoming boss, was standing at the end.

"I'll take good care of them, John," he promised. They shook hands. There was not much else to be said. "Still no word on the next posting?"

"I expect they'll tell me before the next check comes." The government was usually good about getting the paperwork done. Not much else, of course, but paperwork, surely.

With nothing left to be said, Clark walked to the helicopter. Ding, Patsy, and J.C. were already strapped in, along with Sandy. J.C. especially loved flying, and he'd get a gut full in the next ten hours. On lifting off they turned southeast for Heathrow Terminal Four. Landing on their own pad, a van took them to the aircraft, and so they were absolved of passing through the magnetometers. It was a British Airways 777. The same type they'd flown over on four years earlier, then with the Basque terrorists aboard. They were in Spain, though in which prison and how the conditions were they'd never asked. Probably not the Waldorf Astoria.

"Are we fired, John?" Ding asked as the aircraft rotated off the Heathrow tarmac.

"Probably not. Even if we are, they're not going to call it that. They might make you a training officer down at The Farm. Me . . . ? Well, they can keep me on the payroll a year or two, maybe I can hold down a desk in the operations center until they take my parking sticker away. We're too senior to fire. Not worth the paperwork. They're afraid we might talk to the wrong reporter."

"Yeah, you still owe Bob Holtzman a lunch, don't you?"

John almost spilled his preflight champagne at that reminder. "Well, I did give my word, didn't I?"

They sat in silence for a few minutes, then Ding said, "So we make a courtesy call on Jack?"

"We kinda sorta gotta, Domingo."

"I hear you. Hell, Jack Junior's out of school now, isn't he?"

"Yeah. Not sure what he's doing, though."

"Some rich-kid job, I bet. Stocks and bonds, money shit, I bet."

"Well, what were you doing at that age?"

"Learning how to handle a dead drop from you, down at The Farm, and studying nights at George Mason University. Sleepwalking, mostly."

"But you got your master's, as I recall. Lot more than I ever got."

"Yeah. I got a piece of paper that says I'm smart. You left dead bodies all over the world." Fortunately, it was virtually impossible to bug an airliner's cabin.

"Call it foreign-policy laboratory work," Clark suggested, checking the first-class menu. At least British Airways pretended to serve decent food, though why airlines didn't just stock up on Big Macs and fries still mystified him. Or maybe a Domino's pizza. All the money they'd save—but the McDonald's in the UK just didn't seem to have the right beef. In Italy it was even worse. But their national dish was veal Milanese, and that had a Big Mac beat. "You worried?"

"About having a job? Not really. I can always make real money consulting. You know, the two of us could start up a company, executive security or like that, and really clean up. I'd do the planning, and you'd do the actual protection. You know, just stand there and stare at people in that special 'don't fuck with me' way you do."

"Too old for that, Domingo."

"Ain't nobody dumb enough to kick an old lion in the ass, John. I'm too short to scare bad guys away."

"Bullshit. I wouldn't mess with you for the fun of it."

Chavez had rarely received that magnitude of compliment. He was overly sensitive about his diminutive height—his wife was an inch taller—but it had its tactical value. Over the years, several people had underestimated him and then come within his reach. Not professionals. Those could read his eyes and see the danger that lay behind them. When he bothered to turn the lights on. It rarely came to that, though one street tough in east London had gotten impolite outside a pub. He'd been awakened later with a pint of beer and a playing card tucked in his pocket. It was the queen of clubs, but the back of the card had been a glossy black. Such instances were rare. England remained a civilized country for the most part, and Chavez never went looking for trouble. He'd learned that lesson over the years. The black deck of cards was an unauthorized souvenir for the Men of Black. The newspapers had picked up on it, and

Clark had come down hard on the men who carried the cards. But not that hard. There was security, and there was panache. The boys he'd left behind in Wales had both, and that, really, was okay, as long as the troops knew where the line was.

"What do you think our best job was?"

"Gotta be the amusement park. Malloy did a great job of setting your team down on the castle, and the takedown you did was damned near perfect, especially since we couldn't rehearse it."

"Damn, those were good troops," Domingo agreed with a smile. "My old Ninjas didn't even come close, and I thought they were as good as soldiers got."

"They were, but experience counts for a lot." Every one of the Rainbow team was at least an E-6 or equivalent, which took some years in uniform to achieve. "A lot of smarts comes along with time, and it's not the sort of thing you get out of a book. Then we trained the hell out of them."

"Tell me about it. If I run any more, I'll need two new legs."

Clark snorted. "You're still a pup. But I'll tell ya this: I've never seen a better bunch of triggers, and I've seen a fair share. Christ, it's like they were born with H-and-P's in their hands. How about it, Ding, got a personal champ?"

"Have to measure it with an O-scope and calipers. I'd take Eddie Price for brains. Weber or Johnston on a rifle, hell, there ain't nothing to choose from. For short guns, that little Frenchie, Loiselle . . . He could have scared Doc Holliday out of Tombstone. But you know, all you can really do is put a bullet in the X-ring. Dead is dead. We could all do it, close or far, day or night, awake or asleep, drunk or sober."

"Which is why we're paid the big money."

"Shame they're pulling back on the reins."

"A damned shame."

"Why, goddamn it? I just don't get it."

"Because the European terrorists have gone to ground. We shut them down, Ding, and in the process worked ourselves out of a full-time job. At least they didn't pull the plug altogether. Given the nature of politics, we'll call that a success and ride into the sunset."

"With a pat on the back and an attaboy."

"You expect gratitude from democratic governments?" John asked with a slight grimace. "You poor, naive boy."

The European Union bureaucrats had been the main reason. No European countries tolerated capital punishment anymore—what the common folk might have wanted was not considered, of course—and one such representative of the people had said aloud and repeatedly that the Rainbow team had been too ruthless. Whether or not he insisted on humane capture and medical treatment for rabid dogs had never quite been asked. The people had never disapproved of team actions in any country, but their kind and gentle bureaucrats had gotten their panties in a wad, and those faceless people had the real political power. Like every place else in the civilized world.

"You know, in Sweden it's illegal to raise calves the efficient way. You have to give them social contact with other critters. Next you won't be able to cut their balls off until they get laid at least once," Chavez grumped.

"Seems reasonable to me. That way they'll know what they're missing." Clark chuckled. "One less thing for the cowboys to have to do. Probably not a fun job for a man to do that to somebody else."

"Jesus said the meek shall inherit the earth, and that's fine with me, but it's still nice to have cops around."

"You hear me arguing with you? Rock your seat back and have a glass of wine and get some sleep, Domingo."

And if some asshole tries to hijack this airplane, we'll deal with him,
Clark didn't add.

One could always hope. One last jolt of action before going
out to pasture.

7

"So what's cooking?" Brian Caruso asked his cousin.

"Same stew, different day, I expect," Jack Ryan Jr. replied.

"'Stew'?" Dominic, the other Caruso, replied. "Don't you
mean shit?"

"Trying to be optimistic."

All three armed with their first cups of coffee of the day,
they walked down the corridor to Jack's office. It was 8:10
a.m., about time for another day to start at The Campus.

"Any word on our friend the Emir?" Brian asked, taking a
gulp of coffee.

"Nothing firsthand. He's not stupid. He even has his e-mails
relayed through a series of cutouts now, some of them through
ISP accounts that open and close within hours, and even then
the account financials turn out to be dead ends. The Pakistan
badlands is the best current guess. Maybe next door. Maybe
wherever he can buy a safe spot. Hell, at this point I'm tempted
to look in our own broom closet."

It was frustrating, Jack thought. His first adventure into
field operations had been a slam dunk. Or beginner's luck,
maybe? Or fate. He'd gone to Rome as Brian and Dominic's
intel support, nothing more, and had by sheer chance spotted
MoHa in the hotel. From there things had moved fast, too
damned fast, and then it'd been him and MoHa in the bathroom . . .

He wouldn't be as frightened the next time, Jack told himself with enormous—and false—confidence. He remembered the killing of MoHa as clearly as the first time he'd gotten laid. Most vivid of all was the look on the man's face when the succinylcholine had taken hold. Jack might have felt regret for the killing except for the adrenaline rush of the moment, and for what Mohammed had been guilty of. He'd found no regret in his soul for that action. MoHa had been a murderer himself, someone who had taken it upon himself to deliver death to innocent civilians, and Jack hadn't missed a wink of sleep over it.

It had helped that he'd been among family. He and Dominic and Brian shared a grandfather, Jack Muller, his mom's father. Their fraternal grandfather, now eighty-three, was first-generation Italian, having emigrated from Italy to Seattle, where for the past sixty years he'd lived and worked at the family-owned and -run restaurant.

Grandpa Muller, former Army veteran and Merrill Lynch VP, had a strained relationship with Jack Ryan Sr., having decided that his son-in-law's abandonment of Wall Street for government service was sheer idiocy—idiocy that had eventually led to his daughter and granddaughter, Little Sally, nearly losing their lives in a car crash. But for his son-in-law's ill-advised return to the CIA, the incident would have never happened. Of course, no one except Grandpa Muller believed that, including Mom and Sally.

It also helped, Jack Junior had decided, that Brian and Dominic were relatively new to this as well. Not new to the danger—Brian a Marine and Dominic an FBI agent—but to the "Wilderness of Mirrors," as James Jesus Angleton had called it. They'd adapted well and quickly, having taken out three URC soldiers in short order—four at the Charlottesville Mall shooting and three in Europe with the Magic Pen. Still, Hendley hadn't hired them because they were good triggers.

"Smart shooters" was the phrase Mike Brennan, his USSS principal, had often used, and it sure as hell fit his cousins.

"Gimme *your* best guess," Brian said now.

"Pakistan, but close enough that his people can hop across the border. Somewhere with plenty of evacuation routes. He's in a place with electricity, but portable generators are easy to come by, so that doesn't mean much. Maybe a phone line, too. They've gotten away from satellite phones. Learned that one the hard way—"

"Yeah, when they read about it in the *Times*," Brian growled.

Journalists think they can print anything they want to; it was hard to see those kinds of consequences while sitting in front of a keyboard.

"Bottom line is we don't know where His Highness is right now. Even my best guess is just a guess, but the truth be told, that's usually all intelligence amounts to—a guess based on the available info. Sometimes it's rock-solid, sometimes as thin as air. The good news is we're reading a lot of mail."

"How much?" Dominic asked.

"Maybe fifteen or twenty percent." Still, the sheer volume was overwhelming, but with volume came opportunities. *Kind of like Ryan Howard,* Jack thought. *Swing at a lot of pitches, strike out a lot, but hit a ton of home runs. Hopefully.*

"So let's go shake the trees and see what falls out." Ever the Marine, Brian was always ready to charge a beachhead. "Snatch somebody up and sweat him."

"Don't want to tip our hand," Jack said. "You save something like that for an op that's worth blowing it all for."

The one thing they both knew not to talk about was how cagily the intelligence community was playing with what data it had. A lot of it stayed in-house, not even forwarded to its own directors, who tended to be political appointees, loyal to the people who appointed them, if not always to the oath they'd taken on occupying their offices. The President—

known in the community as NCA, for National Command Authority—had a staff that he trusted, though the trust must have been to leak things he wished to leak, and only those things, and only to reporters who could be trusted to accept the spin placed on a leak. The spook community was holding out on the President, a firing offense if anyone got caught. They withheld data from end-user field people, too, which was also something with a history behind it, and which also explained why special ops people rarely trusted the intelligence community. It was all about need-to-know. You could have the highest clearance level available, but if you didn't need to know, you were still out of the loop. Same went for The Campus, which was officially out of all the loops, which was sort of the point. Still, they'd had a lot of success slipping themselves into the loop. Their hacker-in-chief, an über-geek named Gavin Biery who ran their IT section, had yet to meet an encryption system into which he couldn't poke a hole.

A former IBM employee, he'd lost two brothers in Vietnam, and thereafter had come to work for the federal government, then to be talent-scouted and cherry-picked to the Fort Meade headquarters of the National Security Agency, the government's premier center for communications and electronic security. His government salary had long since topped him out as a Senior Executive Service genius, and indeed he still collected his reasonably generous government pension. But he loved the action and had snapped up the offer to join The Campus within seconds of its being made. He was, professionally, a mathematician, with a doctorate from Harvard, where he'd studied under Benoit Mandelbrot himself, and he occasionally lectured at MIT and Caltech as well in his area of expertise.

Biery was a geek through and through, right down to the heavy black-rimmed glasses and doughy complexion, but he kept The Campus's electronic gears oiled and the machines purring.

"Compartmentalization?" Brian said. "Don't gimme that cloak-and-dagger shit."

Jack held up his hands and shrugged. "Sorry." Like his dad, Jack Ryan Jr. wasn't one to break the rules. Cousin or not, Brian didn't have the need to know. Period.

"You ever wonder about the name?" Dominic asked. "The URC? You know how much these guys love double meanings."

Interesting idea, Jack thought.

The Umayyad Revolutionary Council had been the Emir's own invention, they'd always guessed. Was it what it seemed— just another oblique reference to the tried-and-true Islamic symbol of jihad; namely, Saladin—or something more?

Born Salah Ad-din Yusuf Ibn Ayyub in about 1138 in Tikrit—current-day Iraq—Saladin had quickly risen to figure-head status during the Crusades, first as the defender of Baalbek, then as the sultan of Egypt and Syria. The fact that Saladin's battlefield record was by some accounts spotty at best was of little consequence in Muslim history, but as was the case with many historical figures, East and West alike, it was what Saladin came to represent that mattered. To Muslims he was the avenging sword of Allah standing against the flood of infidel crusaders.

If there was any insight to be gained from the URC's name, it probably lay in the first word, *Umayyad,* after the Damascus mosque that housed Saladin's final resting place, a mausoleum containing both a marble sarcophagus donated by Emperor Wilhelm II of Germany and a plain wooden coffin, in which Saladin's body still remained. The fact that the Emir had chosen *Umayyad* as his organization's operational word suggested to Jack that the Emir saw his jihad as a turning point, just as Saladin's death had been a transition from this life of struggle and suffering to everlasting paradise.

"I'll give it some thought," Jack said. "Not a bad hunch, though."

"It ain't all sand up here, cuz," Brian said, smiling, as he tapped his temple with his index finger. "So what's your dad doing with all his spare time now?"

"Don't know." Jack didn't spend much time at home. That would mean talking to his parents, and the more he talked about his "job," the more likely his dad would be to get curious, and if his father found out what he was doing here, he might blow a gasket somewhere in his head. And how Mom would react didn't bear contemplation. The thought grated on Jack. He wasn't a mama's boy, that was for sure, but did anyone ever really get past trying to impress their parents or seek their approval? What was that saying? A man isn't truly a man until he kills his father—metaphorically, of course. He was an adult, on his own, doing some serious shit at The Campus. *Time to step out from under Dad's shadow,* Jack reminded himself for the umpteenth time. And a damned big shadow it was.

Brian said, "Bet you he gets fed up and—"

"Runs?"

"Wouldn't you?"

"I've lived in the White House, remember? I had my fill. I'll gladly take my cubicle here, hunting bad guys."

Mostly on the computer so far, Jack thought, but maybe, if he played his cards right, more in the field. He was already rehearsing his pitch to The Campus's head, Gerry Hendley. The MoHa thing had to count for something, didn't it? His cousins were smart shooters. Did the term fit him? Jack wondered. *Could* it fit him? In comparison, his life had been a sheltered one, the well-protected son of President John Patrick Ryan, but that had come with benefits, hadn't it? He'd learned to shoot from Secret Service agents, had played chess against the Secretary of State, had lived and breathed, albeit obliquely, the inner worlds of the intelligence and military communities. Had he, by osmosis, picked up some of the traits for which Brian and Dominic had trained so hard? Maybe. Or maybe it was just wishful thinking. Either way, he had to get past Hendley first.

"But you ain't your dad," Dominic reminded him.

"True enough." Jack turned in his chair and powered up his PC for the morning news dose, public and classified. Too often, the latter was only three days in advance of the former. The first thing Jack logged in to was the Executive Intercept Transcript Summary from the NSA. Called EITS or XITS—and bearing the unfortunate moniker "zits"—it went only to high-level officers at the NSA and the CIA, and the National Security Council at the White House.

Speaking of the devil . . . There he was, the Emir himself, in the XITS again. An intercept. The message had been strictly administrative. The Emir wanted to know what someone—just an anonymous code name—was doing, whether he had made contact with some unknown foreign national, for some unknown purpose. That was the standard with most of these intercepts—a lot of unknowns, sort of like fill-in-the-blank, which was, in truth, what intelligence analysis was all about. The biggest and most complex jigsaw puzzle in the world. This particular piece had prompted a brainstorming meeting at the CIA.

The proposed agenda was the topic of a full single-spaced report (almost all of it speculation) by some middle-level analyst who probably wanted a better office and liked to spitball his speculation in the hopes that someday something would stick to the wall and so hike him to a supergrade's salary. And maybe someday he would, but that wouldn't make him any smarter, except maybe in the eyes of a superior who'd clawed his way up in similar fashion and liked having his back scratched.

Something was nagging at Jack's brain, something about this particular query. . . . He rolled his mouse's pointer over the XITS folder on his hard drive, double-clicked it, and brought up the summary document he'd been keeping of XITS. And there it was, the same intercept reference number, this one attached to a trio of week-old e-mails, the first from an NSC staffer to the NSA. Seems somebody at the White House wanted to know how exactly the information had been obtained. The query was then forwarded to the DNSA—a billet for a three-star professional military intelligence officer, at the moment an Army officer named Lieutenant General Sam Ferren—who responded curtly: BACKPACK. DO NOT REPLY. WILL HANDLE ADMINISTRATIVELY.

Jack had to smile at this. Currently "Backpack" was the NSA's rotating, in-house code name for Echelon, the agency's all-knowing, all-seeing electronic monitoring program. Ferren's response was understandable. The NSC staffer was asking for "sources and methods," the nuts and bolts of how the NSA worked its magic. Such secrets were simply not shared by intel consumers such as the White House, and for an NSC staffer to request them was idiotic.

Predictably, Ferren's subsequent XITS summary for the NSC simply listed the intercept source as "overseas coop-erative ELINT," or electronic intelligence, essentially telling the White House that the NSA got the info from a friendly intelligence agency. In short, he lied.

There could be only one reason for this: Ferren suspected the White House was showing the XITS around. *Jesus,* Jack thought, *must be quite a strain for a three-star to have to watch what he says to the sitting President.* But if the spook world didn't trust the President, who, then, was looking after the country? And if the system broke down, Jack further thought, whom the hell did you go to? That was a question for a philosopher, or a priest.

Deep thoughts for an early morning, Jack told himself, but if he was reading the XITS—supposedly the sanctum sanctorum of government documents—what was he not reading? What wasn't being disseminated? And who the hell got that info? Was there an insulated communications link at the director level only?

Okay, so the Emir was talking again. NSA didn't have the key to his personal encryption system, but The Campus had it—something Jack had bagged himself, by borrowing the data off MoHa's personal computer and handing it over to Biery and his geeks, who'd transferred the data to a FireWire hard drive. Inside of a day they'd picked it apart for all its secrets—including passwords, which had cracked open all manner of encrypted communications, some of which had been read at The Campus for five months before being changed routinely. The opposition had been fairly careful about that, and/or had been properly trained by somebody who'd worked for a real spook shop. But not that carefully. The passwords were not changed daily or even weekly. The Emir and his people were very confident in their security measures, and that failing had destroyed whole nation-states. Crypto spooks were always for hire on the open market, and most of them spoke Russian and were poor enough that any offer looked good. The CIA had even dangled a few at the bad guys as consultants to the Emir. At least one of them had been found under a trash heap in Islamabad with his throat slit from earlobe to earlobe. It was a rough game being played out there, even for professionals. Jack hoped that Langley took proper care of whatever family the man had left behind. That didn't always happen with agents. CIA case officers got plenty of death benefits, and their families were never forgotten by Langley, but agents were a different thing altogether. Usually unappreciated, and often quickly forgotten when a better asset came along.

It appeared the Emir was still wondering about the people he'd lost on the streets of Europe—all at the hands of Brian and Dominic Caruso and Jack, though the Emir didn't know that. Three heart attacks, the Emir speculated, seemed an inordinately large number for fit, young people. He'd had his agents delve carefully into the medical records, but those had been picked clean, overtly and covertly—the former by lawyers representing the estates of the deceased, and the latter by bribing petty bureaucrats for the original documents and further checking for evidence of a hidden addendum that might be filed separately, all to no avail. The Emir was writing to an operative evidently living in Vienna who'd been sent to look into an odd case, the man who'd apparently stumbled under a streetcar, because, the Emir said, he'd been such a spry boy as a youngster with horses—not the type to fall under a moving vehicle. But sure enough, the Emir's man replied, fully nine people had seen the incident, and by all accounts he'd just slipped right in front of a tram, something that could have happened to anyone, however sure-footed he might have been at the age of eleven. The Austrian physicians had been thorough, and the official autopsy had been clear: Fa'ad Rahmin Yasin had been carved rather messily into half a dozen chunks by a streetcar. His blood had been checked for alcohol, but nothing was found but some residual traces from the previous night—so the pathologist assumed—certainly not enough to affect cognitive judgment. Nor were there any traces of narcotics of any sort in such blood as they'd managed to recover from the mangled body. Conclusion: He'd slipped and fallen and died of blunt-force trauma and exsanguination—a fancy way of saying he'd bled to death.

Couldn't have happened to a nicer guy, Jack decided.

8

One thing Driscoll and his Rangers had long ago learned was that distances on a map of the Hindu Kush bore little semblance to the reality on the ground. In fairness, even digital-age cartographers had no way of calculating the spatial impact of every rise, fall, and switchback in the terrain. In planning the mission, he and Captain Wilson had multiplied all their estimates by two, a variable that seemed to generally work, and though this mathematical adjustment was never far from Driscoll's mind, realizing that their hump to the LZ was not in fact three klicks but closer to six—almost four miles—was almost enough to bring a string of curses to his lips. He quashed the impulse. It wouldn't do them any good. Might even do a little harm, showing a crack in front of the team. Even if their eyes weren't on him every minute, each of his Rangers was taking his cues from him. Both shit and attitude did indeed roll downhill.

Walking point, Tait stopped and held up a closed fist, bringing the staggered column to a halt. Driscoll dropped into a crouch, as did the rest of the team in near unison. Down the line, M4s came around, each man taking a sector, eyes watching and ears listening. They were in a narrow canyon—so narrow, Driscoll doubted the ten-foot-wide ravine actually qualified as a canyon—but they had little choice. It was either take this three-hundred-meter shortcut or tack another two klicks onto their route and risk a daylight pickup. They'd heard and seen nothing since the ambush, but that didn't mean much. The URC knew this ground better than anyone, and knew from experience how long it took pack-laden soldiers to cover it. Worse still, they knew there were a limited number of LZs from which the enemy could be retrieved. From there, setting up another ambush was simply a matter of doing the math of moving faster than your quarry.

Without turning, Tait gave Driscoll the underhand *move up* signal. Driscoll did so. "What's up?" he whispered.

"Coming to the end. Another thirty meters or so."

Driscoll turned around, pointed at Barnes, held up two fingers, then gave the *move up* signal. Barnes, Young, and Gomez were there in ten seconds. "End of the ravine," Driscoll explained. "See what there is to see."

"Right, boss."

They moved off. Behind Driscoll came Collins's voice: "How's the shoulder?"

"Fine." The six ibuprofen Collins had given him had taken the edge off, but every jostle sent ripples of pain through his shoulder, back, and neck.

"Get your pack off." Collins didn't wait for Driscoll to protest, slipping off the shoulder strap. "Bleeding's slowed. You feel your fingers?"

"Yeah."

"Move 'em."

Driscoll flipped him the bird and grinned. "How's that?"

"Touch each finger to your thumb."

"Jesus, Collins—"

"Do it." Driscoll complied, but each of his fingers moved sluggishly, as though rusted at the joint. "Get your pack off. I'm distributing your load." Driscoll opened his mouth to protest, but the medic cut him off. "Look, you keep that pack on, you can just about count on losing that arm later. Good chance you already got some nerve damage, and that sixty pounds ain't helping."

"Okay, okay . . ."

Barnes, Young, and Gomez returned. Collins handed the pack to Barnes, who went back down the line to divide up the contents. Young reported to Driscoll, "Didn't see nothing, but something's moving out there. Heard a truck engine about half a klick to the west."

"Okay, back in line. Collins, you, too."

Driscoll pulled out the map and clicked on his red-hooded penlight. Not exactly standard-issue, but as good as their NV was for most things, it was shit for reading maps. Some old-school habits were hard to break; some shouldn't be broken at all.

Tait scooted closer. Driscoll traced his finger along the ravine in which they sat; at its terminus was yet another canyon bordered on both sides by plateaus. The terrain was, Driscoll thought, not unlike an urban neighborhood: canyons were the main roads; plateaus the houses; and ravines the back alleys. They were essentially dashing across the roads, using the alleys between the houses to reach the airport. Or in this case, the heliport. *Two more canyons, one more ravine,* he thought, *then up the side of a plateau to the LZ.*

"Home stretch," Tait observed.

Which is where most racehorses go down, Driscoll thought but didn't say.

They sat at the mouth of the ravine for fifteen minutes, Tait and Driscoll scanning the length of the canyon through the NV until certain there were no eyes about. In pairs the team crossed the canyon floor to the opposite ravine while the rest provided cover and Driscoll and Tait played traffic cops. Young and his prisoner went last, and they had just slipped into the far ravine when a pair of headlights appeared to the east. Another UAZ, Driscoll saw immediately, but this one was moving at a leisurely pace.

"Hold," Driscoll ordered. "Truck coming from the east."

Like the one they'd encountered earlier, this UAZ bore an NSV 12.7-millimeter gun in the bed, but Driscoll counted only one man manning it. Same for the cab: a driver and no one else. They'd split their forces in hopes of cutting off their quarry. Small-unit tactics were often as much about instinct as they were rules, but whoever had dispatched this truck had made a mistake. The UAZ kept coming, tires crunching over the rubble, its headlights bouncing off the canyon.

Driscoll caught Tait's attention and mouthed *driver* and got a nod in return. On the radio, Driscoll whispered, "Hold fire," and got a double-click in reply.

The UAZ was twenty meters away now, close enough that Driscoll could see the NSV gunner's face clearly in the green-white glow of the night vision. Just a kid, maybe eighteen or nineteen, with a patchy beard. The NSV's barrel was pointed straight down the canyon, not traversing, as it should be. *Lazy's as good as dead,* he thought.

The UAZ drew even with the ravine and ground to a halt. In the cab, the driver leaned sideways, reaching for something, then came up with a handheld spotlight. He pointed it out the passenger window. Driscoll laid his M4's crosshairs just above the gunner's left ear. He squeezed the trigger, softly, softly, and the M4 bucked. In the NV, a halo of mist appeared around the gunner's head. He fell straight down below the truck bed's side. The driver went down a split second later, his spotlight dancing crazily before coming to rest on the seat.

Driscoll and Tait moved out, crossing to the truck and taking twenty seconds to kill the spotlight and make sure no one was still alive before continuing on to the ravine. To the west, an engine revved. Headlights pinned them. Driscoll didn't bother looking but barked, "Move, move!" and kept going with Tait a step ahead. The rapid, overlapping cough of another NSV started up, peppering the ground and rocks around them, but Driscoll and Tait were already in the ravine. On point, Gomez was moving deeper into the ravine. Driscoll signaled for Tait to continue and waved Barnes over. "SAW," he said, and Barnes dropped prone beside a boulder, extended the SAW's legs, and tucked the butt into his shoulders. At the mouth of the ravine they could see headlights coming closer. Driscoll slipped a grenade off his harness and pulled the pin. Out in the canyon came the skidding of tires; dust washed past the mouth of the ravine. Driscoll let the spoon go, counted one-one-thousand, two-one-thousand, letting the grenade cook, then arced it high toward the canyon. The UAZ slewed to a stop. The grenade exploded ten feet over the cab. Barnes opened up with the SAW, hosing down the doors and sides. In the bed, the NSV's muzzle spouted fire but went silent a moment later as the SAW's fusillade cut the gunner down. The UAZ's gears crunched, and then it was moving again and out of sight.

"Go," Driscoll ordered, waited for Barnes to get a head start, then turned to follow.

By the time they caught up with the column, Gomez had split the team, one half across the canyon, behind cover and on overwatch, the other waiting at the mouth of the ravine. Driscoll made his way up the line to Gomez. "Activity?"

"Engines, no movement."

Across the canyon, thirty meters west of the overwatch, was a natural ramp winding its way up the side of the plateau. Sure as hell looked man-made, Driscoll thought, but time and erosion did strange things to terrain. And they weren't going to bitch about this oddity; it would make their final push for the LZ relatively easy.

"Peterson, get Blade on the line and tell 'em we're ready. Call it hot."

Their Chinook would be orbiting, awaiting their signal. Like most things in combat and certainly most things in Afghanistan, their LZ was suboptimal, partly due to the landscape and partly due to the Chinook's design trade-off: a high operational ceiling but a big landing footprint. The 47 could get to troops at altitude but needed a fair amount of square footage to embark them. In this case, their LZ was hemmed in to the west and south by ravines and ridgelines so close that small-arms fire could reach it.

"Blade, this is Sickle, over."

"Go ahead, Sickle."

"Ready for pickup. Winds three to six from north to south. Lima zulu hot; composition and direction unknown."

"Roger, copy lima zulu hot. Three minutes out." Two minutes later: "Sickle, Blade is inbound, mark your location."

"Roger, stand by," Driscoll said, then radioed Barnes. "Chemlights, Barnes."

"Roger, boss. I've got blue, yellow, red."

Across the canyon the chemlights glowed to life, then sailed through the air and landed atop the plateau. Driscoll would've preferred an IR strobe, but S4 had been out when they'd left.

Driscoll called, "Blade, Sickle, I pop blue, yellow, red."

"Roger, I see it."

Now they heard it, the chopping of the Chinook's rotors. Then: "Sickle, this is Blade, I have inbound vehicles three hundred meters to your west and closing. I count two UAZs, over."

Shit. "Wave off, wave off. Mark the LZ and hold in orbit." The only other option was to have the Chinook's gunners light up the UAZs, but doing so from altitude would serve as a "here we are" flare for other enemy units in the area. The Chinook pilot would have his own ROE, or Rules of Engagement, but as he and his Rangers were on scene and in the shit, it was Driscoll's order to give. That the UAZs weren't racing toward them told him his unit hadn't yet been seen. They'd been lucky so far with these things; there was no use pushing it.

"Roger, waving off," replied the Chinook pilot.

68

To Barnes: "We got company to the west. Douse those chemlights. Everybody hunker down." Behind him, the column dropped flat.

He got a double-click in reply, then a few moments later saw a pair of hunched-over figures scrambling up to the plateau. The chemlights went dark.

Down the canyon, the UAZ headlights were now stationary. Faintly, Driscoll heard the rumble of their unmuffled engines. A long thirty seconds passed, then the engines revved up and the trucks began moving, separating into a staggered line as they headed down the canyon. *Bad sign,* Driscoll thought. On the move, the UAZs tended to prefer single-file formation. It was only when they were expecting trouble did they stagger.

"Cover," Driscoll radioed the team. "Gomers are hunting." Then to the Chinook: "Blade, Sickle, stay close. We may need you."

"Roger."

Preceded by headlights bouncing over the uneven ground, the crunch of the UAZ tires continued down the canyon until the first truck drew even with the ravine in which Driscoll and his column were hidden. The brakes squealed. The UAZ came to a stop; the second one, trailing thirty feet behind, also halted. A spotlight appeared in the passenger window and played over the walls, pausing as it reached the ravine. *Move on, Gomer,* Driscoll thought. *Nothing to see here.* Now the spotlight swung around, pointing out the driver's window and scanning the opposite ravine. After sixty seconds of this the spotlight went dark. The lead UAZ's transmission crunched and growled, then it began moving forward and beyond Driscoll's line of sight.

"Who's got eyes?" he radioed.

"Got him," Barnes called. "Fifty meters away, continuing east." Then: "Hundred meters . . . They're stopping."

Driscoll eased himself up and hunch-walked out of the ravine, taking care to keep close to the canyon's rock wall until he could see the halted UAZs. He dropped to his belly and peered through the NV. Each truck had taken up position at the northern and southern sides of the canyon. Their headlights and engines were off. Ambush position.

"Everybody stay put and stay quiet," Driscoll ordered, then got the Chinook on the line. "Blade, Sickle."

"Go ahead."

"Our UAZs have taken up position at the eastern end of the canyon."

"Roger, we see 'em. Be advised, Sickle, we are eight minutes to bingo."

Eight minutes until the Chinook was at the do-or-die turnaround point. A delay beyond that and they wouldn't have enough fuel to RTB, or return to base. For Rangers, working with thin margins was par for the course, but there were some things you fucked with at your peril, and your ride home was chief among them.

"Understood. Engage UAZs. Anything on wheels is yours."

"Roger, engaging."

The Chinook appeared over the top of the plateau, its nav lights flashing as it wheeled and started easing west down the canyon. Driscoll could see the door gunner swiveling the minigun about. Driscoll radioed, "Gomez, get your team moving up the ramp."

"Roger, boss."

"Eyes on the target," the Chinook pilot called. "Engaging . . ."

The Dillon M134 minigun opened up, casting the side of the Chinook in orange. The barrage lasted less than two seconds, then came another, and one more, then the pilot was back: "Targets destroyed." With a firing rate of three thousand rounds per minute, in those five or so seconds it had poured two hundred fifty 7.62-millimeter bullets into the approaching

70

UAZs. The Chinook reappeared, sideslipped over the LZ, and touched down. The ramp came down.

Gomez called, "Up on overwatch, Santa."

"Roger, moving to you."

Driscoll gave the order, and again in pairs the remainder of the team crossed the canyon floor, leapfrogging from cover to cover until Driscoll and Tait were across and headed up the ramp.

"Target!" Driscoll heard over his headset. Not one of his, he decided, but somebody aboard the Chinook. "On the tail, seven o'clock!" West across the plateau came the chatter of automatic weapons—AK-47s, quickly followed by the crack of returning M4 fire.

Driscoll and Tait reached the top of the ramp, dropped to their bellies, and crawled the last few feet. Fifty meters ahead, from inside a ravine and atop the ridgeline, muzzles were flashing. Driscoll counted at least three dozen. Down the canyon four pairs of headlights appeared in the dark. More UAZs.

Peterson's voice: "RPG, RPG . . ."

To their right, something bright streaked past. The ground beside the Chinook erupted.

"Move away, move away," the pilot called, then did something Driscoll had never seen: Neat as you please, the pilot lifted off, stopped in a hover at six feet, then wheeled, bringing the door gunner to bear. "Heads down, heads down!" The Dillon opened up, arcing fire into the ravine and ridgeline.

"Runner!" Driscoll heard faintly in his ear. "Heading west!"

Sidelit by the Dillon's tracers, their prisoner, still handcuffed, was staggering away from the Chinook and toward the draw. Tait muttered, "I got him, Santa."

"Drop him."

Tait's M4 popped and their prisoner went down. The AK fire tapered off, then died. Driscoll called, "Blade, we got

71

UAZs in the canyon. Two hundred meters and closing. Your three o'clock."

"Roger," the pilot replied, and brought the Chinook around. Again the minigun opened up. Ten seconds was all it took. The dust drifted away, revealing the four demolished UAZs.

"Head count," Driscoll ordered. No response. "Head count!" he repeated. Collins replied. "Two KIA, Santa, and two wounded."

"Motherfucker."

The pilot called—calmly, Driscoll thought, *Sickle, what say you fellas get aboard and we go home before our luck runs out?*

9

In all his years living in Saint Petersburg, Yuriy Beketov had walked its darkened streets hundreds of times, but this time was different, and it didn't take much contemplation to understand why. Wealth—or at least potential wealth—had a way of changing one's perspective. And this kind of wealth was of a different sort. He wasn't proud of the money in and of itself but rather the way in which he planned to apply it. What he was less certain about was whether that was truly a distinction or just a rationalization. If you danced with the devil for a very good reason, have you not still danced with the devil?

Of all the cities in his homeland, Saint Petersburg was Yuriy's favorite. The city's own history was a near-perfect reflection of Russia's history. In 1703 Peter the Great had founded the city during the Great Northern War with the Swedes; during World War One, Saint Petersburg's name, deemed excessively Teutonic by the powers-that-be, was changed to Petrograd; in 1924, seven years after the Bolshevik

Revolution and a few days after the death of Vladimir Lenin, it was dubbed Leningrad; and finally, in 1991, with the collapse of the Soviet Union, it was renamed once again—reverted to—Saint Petersburg.

Saint Petersburg, a Time Capsule of Russian History. Not a bad title for a book, he thought. Too bad he had no literary aspirations. The tsars, the Bolsheviks, the fall of the empire, then finally democracy—though perhaps democracy tainted with a bit of totalitarianism.

Tonight was especially chilly, with a brisk wind blowing off the Neva River and whistling through the branches of the trees. Unseen in the darkness, bits of litter skittered across concrete and cobblestones. Down a nearby alley came the clink of a bottle on brick, then a slurred curse. Another *bic* had either run out of vodka or spilled his last bit of it. For all his love for Saint Petersburg, Yuriy knew she'd fallen far from her zenith. This was true of the whole country.

The collapse of the Union had been tough on everyone but had been especially tumultuous for his former employer, the KGB, now known dually as the Federalnaya Sluzhba Bezopasnosti, or Federal Security Service (FSB), and the Sluzhba Vneshney Razvedki, or Foreign Intelligence Service (SVR). These were only the latest in a long string of acronyms under which the Russian intelligence services had operated, starting with the dreaded Cheka. Arguably, though, the KGB—the Committee for State Security—had been the most effective and the most feared of all its alphabet-soup predecessors and descendants alike.

Before taking retirement at a fractional pension in 1993, Yuriy had worked for the cream of the KGB crop, Directorate S—Illegals—of the First Chief Directorate. The real spies. No diplomatic cover, no embassy to which you can run, no deportation if caught but rather imprisonment or death. He'd had some successes, but nothing that had cast him into the stratosphere of the KGB's upper echelons, and so at forty-five years of age he'd found himself unemployed on the streets of Moscow with a set of skills that left him few career paths: contract intelligence and security or crime. He'd chosen the former, opening up a consultation firm that catered to the hordes of Western investors that had in the early days of post-Soviet rule flooded Russia. Yuriy owed, at least obliquely, many of his early successes to the Krasnaya Mafiya, the Red Mafia, and its biggest gangs, the Solntsevskaya Bratva, the Dolgoprudnenskaya, and the Izmailovskaya, all of which had wasted even less time than had foreign investors in pillaging Russia's chaotic economy. Of course, the Krasnaya Mafiya was unconcerned with the subtle niceties of business conduct, and investors from Europe and America were only too aware of this, a circumstance Yuriy was only too happy to exploit himself. That was the operative word back then—*exploit*—and the only difference among himself, the Mafia, and the common street hood was the methods each employed to obtain the desired ends. For Yuriy, the method was simple: protection. Keep visiting businessmen alive and out of the hands of kidnappers. Some of the lesser gangs, too small to run their own sophisticated protection and extortion games, had taken to kidnapping well-dressed Europeans or Americans staying in Moscow's finest hotels, then sending a ransom note along with a severed ear or a finger or toe—or worse. The local militia, underpaid and overwhelmed, was of little help, and more often than not the victim was killed, ransom paid or unpaid. There was no honor among kidnappers. Only brutal pragmatism.

Yuriy had hired former KGB colleagues and paramilitary types—mostly former Spetsnaz commandos who'd been similarly disenfranchised—to escort clients to and from their meetings and make sure they left the country alive and still in possession of all their parts. The money had been good, but as Moscow's economy (both official and underground) had burgeoned, so too had the cost of living soared, and while many entrepreneurs like Yuriy were seeing more money than they ever thought existed, they were also seeing it bleed away into the volatile market and an insanely high cost of living. It was sad irony to make so much money while having the cost of bread rise right along with your income.

By the late nineties Yuriy had saved enough money to see his three grandchildren through university and into self-sustaining adulthood but not enough money to retire to that idyllic remote cottage on the Black Sea he'd been dreaming about for twenty years.

The opportunities came, slowly at first and then with more regularity, just before, and then after, the events of September 11. On that morning America awoke to a fact the KGB and many non-Western intelligence services had long known: Islamic fundamentalists had declared war on America and her allies. Unfortunately for the United States, these fundamentalists had in the last half-decade evolved from the disorganized and irrational madmen they were so often depicted as in Western newspapers to organized, trained soldiers with a clear goal. Worse still, they had learned the value of intelligence networks, agent recruitment, and communication protocols, all things that had traditionally been advantages at the sole disposal of national intelligence agencies.

For all her achievements and boons, America was the archetypical giant, blithely ignoring arrows and stones in favor of the notional cannon on the horizon, the mini-9/11s that were few and far between, and impossible to quickly consign to the back pages of *The New York Times* or off the fifteen-minute rotation at MSNBC or CNN. Historians would forever be arguing whether American intelligence could have or should have heard the galloping hoofbeats of 9/11, but the escalation certainly could have been tracked, going as far back as the first World Trade Center bombing in 1993, up through the 1998 bombing of the U.S. embassy in Kenya and the attack on the USS *Cole* in 2000. Only to the CIA had these been isolated incidents; to the affiliated terrorist cells that had carried them out, they'd been battles within a war. It was only when war had been loudly declared on the United States—in both word and deed—that the U.S. intelligence community started to realize these arrows and stones could not be ignored.

Worse still, the U.S. government and CIA had only in recent years steered themselves away from what Yuriy had dubbed the "golem mind-set"—the obsessive focus on the enemy giant's head while ignoring its fingers and toes. Of course, that would never fully change, especially when it came to Public Enemy Number One, the Emir, who had become by design as much as by default, Yuriy believed, American's golem. Nations needed definable enemies, someone they could point to and cry "danger!"

Of course, Yuriy had little to complain about. Like so many of his countrymen, he'd benefited from this new war—though only recently, and with much reluctance and not a little regret. Starting in the mid-1990s, cash-bloated Islamic fundamentalist groups had begun knocking on Russia's door, seeking to hire errant intelligence officers, nuclear scientists, and Special Forces soldiers. Like so many of his countrymen, Yuriy had answered the door, but he was old and tired, and needed only a bit more money for that Black Sea cottage. With luck, tonight's meeting would solve that issue.

Yuriy shook himself from his reverie, stepped back from the railing, and continued across the bridge, then down two more blocks to a neon-lit restaurant bearing the name Chiaka in both Arabic and Cyrillic. He crossed the street and found a park bench in the blind spot between a pair of streetlights, then sat down and watched. He lifted his collar against the wind and shoved his hands deeper into the pockets of his greatcoat.

Chiaka was a Chechnyan restaurant, locally owned and operated by a Muslim family who'd thrived under the aegis of the Obshina, or Chechen Mafia. Similarly, the man he was meeting—known to him only as Nima—had likely slipped into Russia by the graces of the Obshina. *No matter*, Yuriy reminded himself. He'd dealt with the man twice before, once to consult on a relocation of what they had called an "associate," and more recently as an intermediary for a recruitment. That one had been an interesting affair. What these men wanted with a woman of that particular caliber he had no idea, and he didn't care. He'd learned long ago to stifle such curiosity.

He watched for another twenty minutes before satisfying himself that nothing seemed out of place. No watchers about, police or otherwise. He stood up and crossed the street and entered the restaurant, which was brightly lit and spartanly furnished, with black and white vinyl tiles, round Formica tables, and hard-backed wooden chairs. It was the late dinner rush, and almost every table was occupied. Overhead, speakers emitted the tinny sound of Chechnyan pondur music, similar in sound to that of the Russian balalaika.

Yuriy scanned the restaurant. A few customers had looked up upon his entry but had almost immediately returned to their meals or conversation. While Russians weren't a common sight in Chechnyan restaurants, neither were they rare. Despite their reputation, Yuriy had never had much trouble with Chechnyans. For the most part they were live-and-let-live, but woe betide the person they decided to kill. Few organizations were as brutal as the Obshina. They liked their knives, the Chechnyans, and they were handy with them.

In the rear, down a short hall, he saw Nima sitting at the last booth against the wall, beside the kitchen door and the bathroom. Yuriy walked back, held up a "wait a moment" finger to Nima as he passed, then slipped into the bathroom to wash his hands. His hands were perfectly clean, of course; his interest lay primarily in confirming that the bathroom was unoccupied and offered no alternative entrances. Care and caution that the normal person would think excessive had kept him alive as an Illegal for many years, and he saw no reason to change his habits now. He dried his hands, then took a moment to ensure that the Makarov 9-millimeter pistol was seated safely in its holster in the rear waistband of his trousers, then walked out and sat down in the booth, facing the front of the restaurant. The swinging kitchen door was to his left. While Yuriy had been in the bathroom, Nima had removed his sport jacket. It lay draped across the back of the booth. The message was clear: *I'm unarmed.*

Now the Arab spread his hands and smiled at Yuriy. "I know you're a careful man, my friend."

In return, Yuriy opened his sport coat. "As are you."

A waiter appeared, took their drink orders, then disappeared again.

"Thank you for coming," Nima said.

His Russian was good, with only a slight Arabic accent, his skin light enough that he could pass for a local with some Tartar in his blood. Yuriy absently wondered if the man had been schooled somewhere in the West.

"Of course. It's my pleasure."

"I was unsure if you were available."

"For you, my friend, always. Tell me: Your colleague arrived safely at his destination?"

"He did indeed. The woman as well. As I understand it, she is everything you told us she would be. My superiors are very pleased with the help you've already offered. I trust the compensation was satisfactory? No problems?"

"No problems." In fact, the money sat securely in a Liechtenstein account, admittedly earning very little interest but safe from the prying digital eyes of curious intelligence and police agencies. How he would move the funds once he needed them he hadn't decided, but there were always ways, especially if you were careful and willing to pay for such services. "Please pass along my thanks to your superiors."

Nima tipped his chin. "Of course." The drinks came—vodka for Yuriy and sparkling water for Nima, who took a sip, then said, "We have another proposal, Yuriy, something we believe you are uniquely qualified for."

"I am at your disposal."

"As with our other two arrangements, it is a delicate matter, and not without some risk to yourself."

Yuriy spread his hands and smiled. "Anything worthwhile in life usually is, yes?"

"Very true. Of course, as you know . . ."

From the front of the restaurant came a shout, then the shattering of glass. Yuriy looked up in time to see a man, clearly drunk, pushing back from his chair, a plate of unidentified food resting on his upraised palm. The other customers stared at him. The man uttered a string of what Yuriy assumed were Chechen curse words he felt best described the subpar quality of his meal, then stumbled toward a waiter in a white apron.

Yuriy chuckled. "An unhappy customer, it seems . . ." His words trailed off as he realized Nima had never turned in his seat to watch the commotion but was instead looking squarely into Yuriy's eyes with something akin to regret. Alarm bells began ringing in the former KGB officer's head. *Distraction, Yuriy, an arranged distraction.*

Time seemed to slow.

Yuriy leaned forward, his hand reaching behind him toward the Makarov in his waistband at the small of his back. His fingers had just reached the gun's checkered grip when he realized the swinging kitchen door to his left was standing open, a man-shaped figure standing at the threshold.

"I'm sorry, my friend," he heard Nima say in some distant part of his mind. "It is for the best. . . ."

Over the Arab's shoulder, Yuriy saw another waiter walking toward them, holding up a tablecloth, ostensibly going through the motions of folding it. A curtain to shield the deed . . . Yuriy saw movement in the corner of his eye. He rotated his head to the left in time to see the figure in the doorway— another waiter in a white apron—raising something dark and tubular in his hand.

Somewhere in a still-calm, analytical part of his brain, Yuriy thought, *Makeshift noise suppressor.* . . . He knew he would hear no noise, see no flash. Nor would there be any pain.

He was right. The 9-millimeter Parabellum hollow-point bullet struck him just above the left eyebrow before mush-rooming into a tangled lump of lead that turned a softball-sized chunk of his brain into so much jelly.

10

"Goddamn it," former President of the United States John Patrick Ryan muttered into his morning coffee.

"What is it now, Jack?" Cathy asked, though fully aware of what "it" was. She dearly loved her husband, but when a topic attracted his attention, he was like the proverbial dog with a bone, a trait that had made him a good spook and an even better President but not always the easiest of souls to get along with.

"This idiot Kealty doesn't know what the hell he's doing. What's worse, he doesn't care. He killed twelve Marines yesterday in Baghdad. You know why?" Cathy Ryan didn't answer; she knew the question was rhetorical. "Because somebody on his staff decided that Marines having loaded rifles might send the wrong message. Goddamn it, you don't send messages to people pointing weapons at you. Then get this: Their company commander went after the bad guys and whacked about six of them before he was ordered to pull back."

"By whom?"

"By his battalion commander, who probably got instructions from brigade, who got his from some lawyer Kealty's goons slipped into the chain of command. The worst part is he doesn't care. After all, the budget process is under way, and there's that flap over those friggin' trees in Oregon that has his undivided attention."

"Well, for better or worse, a lot of people get their panties in a twist over the environment, Jack," Professor Ryan told her husband.

Kealty, Jack seethed. He'd had it all figured out. Robby would have been a great President, but he hadn't considered the twisted mind of that old Ku Klux Klan bastard who was still waiting to die on Mississippi's Death Row. Jack had been in the Oval Office on that day—what had it been? Six days before the election, with Robby comfortably ahead in the polls. Not enough time to set things back in place, the election in chaos, Kealty the only major candidate left standing, and all the votes cast for Robby voided by circumstance. So many voters had simply stayed home in confusion. Kealty, President by default; election by forfeit.

The transition period had been even worse, if that was possible. The funeral, held at Jackson's father's Baptist church in Mississippi, was one of Jack's worst-ever memories. The media had sneered at his display of emotion. Presidents were supposed to be robots, after all, but Ryan had never been one of those.

And with good damned reason, Ryan thought.

Right here, right here in this very room, Robby had saved

his life, and his wife's, and his daughter's, and his as yet unborn son's. Jack had rarely known rage in his life, but this was one subject that caused it to erupt like Mount Vesuvius on a particularly bad day. Even Robby's father had preached forgiveness on the subject, proof positive that the Reverend Hosiah Jackson was a better man than he would ever be. So what fate suited Robby's killer? A pistol round in the liver, perhaps . . . might take five or ten minutes for the bastard to bleed out, screaming all the way to hell . . .

Worse still, rumor had it the current President was contemplating a blanket commutation of every death sentence in America. His political allies were already lobbying for him in the media, planning a public mercy demonstration on the Washington Mall. Mercy for the victims of the killers and kidnappers was something they never quite addressed, of course, but for all that it was for them a deeply held principle, and Ryan actually respected it.

The former President took a calming breath. He had his work to do. He was two years into his memoirs and in the home stretch. The work had gone quicker than he'd expected, so much so that he'd also written a confidential annex to his autobiography that would not see the light of day until twenty years after his death.

"Where are you?" Cathy asked, thinking of her schedule for the day. She had four laser procedures scheduled. Her Secret Service detail had already checked out the patients, lest one come into the OR with a pistol or knife, an event so unlikely to happen that Cathy had long ago stopped thinking about it. Or maybe she had stopped thinking about it because she knew her detail *was* worrying about it.

"Huh?"

"In the book," his wife clarified.

"The last few months." His tax and fiscal policy, which had actually worked until Kealty had applied a flamethrower to it.

And now the United States of America was muddling along under the presidency—or reign—of Edward Jonathan Kealty, a silver-spooned member of the aristocracy. In time it would be fixed one way or another, the people would see to that. But the difference between a mob and a herd was that a mob had a leader. The people didn't really need that. The people could do without it—because a leader usually came along somehow or other. But who chose the leader? The people did. But the people chose a leader from a list of candidates, and they had to be self-selected.

The phone rang. Jack got it.

"Hello?"

"Hey, Jack." The voice was familiar enough. Ryan's eyes lit up.

"Hi, Arnie. How's life in academia?"

"As you might expect. See the news this morning?"

"The Marines?"

"What do you think?" Arnie van Damm asked.

"Doesn't look very good."

"I think it's worse than it looks. The reporters aren't telling the whole story."

"Do they ever?" Jack wondered sourly.

"No, not when they don't like it, but some of them have integrity. Bob Holtzman at the *Post* is having a conscience attack. He called me. Wants to talk to you about your views— off the record, of course."

Robert Holtzman of *The Washington Post* was one of the few reporters Ryan almost trusted, partially because he'd always been straight with Ryan and partially because he was a former naval officer—a 1630, the code the Navy used to designate an intelligence officer. While he was at odds with Ryan on most political issues, he was also a man of integrity. Holtzman knew things about Ryan's background that he'd never published, despite the fact that they would have made juicy stories, perhaps even career-making stories. But then again, maybe he was just saving them for a book. Holtzman had written a few of those, one a bestseller, and had made decent money from the effort.

"What did you tell him?" Jack asked Arnie.

"I told him I'd ask, but you'd probably say not just no but hell, no."

"Arnie, I do like the guy, but a former President can't trash his successor. . . ."

"Even if he's a worthless piece of shit?"

"Even then," Jack confirmed sourly. "Maybe especially then. Hold on. I thought you liked him. What happened?"

"Maybe I hung around you too much. Now I have this crazy notion that character counts for something. It's not all political maneuvering."

"He's damned good at that, Arnie. Even I have to grant him that. Arnie, you want to come down for a talk?" Ryan asked. Why else would he call on a Friday morning?

"Yeah, okay, so I'm not exactly subtle."

"Fly on down. You're always welcome in my house, you know that."

Cathy asked sotto voce, "What about Tuesday? Dinner."

"How about Tuesday for dinner?" Jack asked Arnie. "You can stay the night. I'll tell Andrea to expect you."

"Do that. I'm always half worried that woman's going to shoot me, and as good as she is, I doubt it'd be a flesh wound. See you around ten."

"Great, Arnie, see ya." Jack set the phone back down and stood up to walk Cathy to the garage. Cathy had moved up in class. Now she drove a two-seat Mercedes, though she'd recently admitted she missed the helicopter into Hopkins. On the upside, now she got to play race-car driver, with her Secret Service agent, Roy Altman, former captain in the 82nd Airborne, holding on for dear life in the passenger seat. A serious guy. He was standing by the car, jacket unbuttoned, paddle holster visible.

"Morning, Dr. Ryan," he greeted.

"Hi, Roy. How are the kids?"

"Just fine, thank you, ma'am." He opened the car door.

"Have a productive day, Jack." And the usual morning kiss.

Cathy settled in, buckled her seat belt, and started up the twelve-cylinder beast that lived under the hood. She waved and backed out. Jack watched her disappear down the driveway, out to where the lead and chase cars were waiting, then turned back to the kitchen door.

"Good morning, Mrs. O'Day," he said in greeting.

"And to you, Mr. President," said Special Agent Andrea Price-O'Day, Jack's principal agent. She had a two-plus-year-old boy of her own, named Conor, and a handful he was, Jack knew. Conor's dad was Patrick O'Day, Major Case Inspector for FBI Director Dan Murray, another of Jack's government appointments that Kealty couldn't mess with, because the FBI wasn't allowed to be a political football—or least it wasn't supposed to be.

"How's the little one?"

"Just fine. Not quite sure about the potty yet, though. He cries when he sees it."

Jack laughed. "Jack was the same way. Arnie is coming down Tuesday, about ten in the morning," he told her. "Dinner, then overnight."

"Well, we don't have to check him out very thoroughly," Andrea replied. But they'd still run his Social Security number through the National Crime Information Computer, just to be sure. The Secret Service trusted few—even in its own ranks, since Aref Raman had gone bad. That had caused a major bellyache for the Service. But her own husband had helped to settle that one down, and Raman would be in the Florence, Colorado, federal prison for a long, long time. The grimmest of all federal penitentiaries, Florence was as max as a maximum-security prison got, dug as it was into hard bedrock and entirely belowground. The guests of Florence mostly saw sunlight on black-and-white TV.

Ryan walked back into the kitchen. He could have asked more. The Service kept lots of secrets. He could have gotten an answer, however, because he, too, had been a sitting President, but that was something he just didn't want to do.

And he still had work to do. So he poured another cup of coffee and headed off to his library to work on Chapter 48, mod 2. George Winston and the Tax System. It had worked well, until Kealty decided that some people weren't paying "their fair share." Kealty, of course, was the sole and final arbiter on what was "fair."

I I

The XITS this morning contained an encrypted intercept for which The Campus had the key. The content could hardly have been more bland, so much so that encryption was superfluous. Somebody's cousin had delivered a baby girl. Had to be plain text code. "The chair is against the wall" had been such a phrase used in World War Two to alert the French resistance to do something to the occupying German Army. "Jean has a long mustache" had told them that the D-day invasion was about to take place, as did "Wounds my heart with a monotonous languor."

So what does this mean? Jack asked himself. Maybe somebody had just had a baby, and a girl, which was not an event of great moment to the Arab culture. Or maybe there had been a big (or small) money transfer, which was how they tried to keep track of the opposition's activities. The Campus had eliminated those who made such money moves. One had been named Uda Bin Sali, and he'd died in London from the same pen that Jack had used in Rome to take down MoHa, who, he'd learned, had been a very bad boy.

Something caught Jack's eye. *Huh.* The e-mail's distribution contained an inordinate number of French addresses. *Something brewing there?* he wondered.

"You grasping at straws again?" Rick Bell asked Jack ten minutes later. Like Jack, The Campus's chief of analysis felt on its face the birth announcement too amorphous to get excited about.

"What else do you do in a hay field?" Jack replied. "Aside from the baby, there're some bank transfers, but the guys downstairs are into those."

"Big ones?"

Ryan shook his head. "No, the whole bunch doesn't total up to half a million euros. Housekeeping money. They've set up a new collection of credit cards. So no airline tickets to track. The Bureau is into that anyway, insofar as they can without our cipher-key collection."

"And that won't last," Bell opined. "Can't be much longer before they change their encryption systems, and we'll have to start over. The best we can hope for is they won't do that before we break something worthwhile. Nothing else?"

"Only questions, like where is Big Bird hiding? Not a whiff on that one."

"NSA has been watching every phone system in the world. To the point that it's taxing their computers. They want to buy two new mainframes from Sun Microsystems. The appropriation is going through this week. The weenies out in California are already assembling the boxes."

"Does NSA ever get shot down or underfunded?" Ryan wondered.

"Not in my lifetime," Bell reported. "Just so they fill out the forms right and grovel properly in front of the congressional committees."

The NSA always got what it wanted, Jack knew. But not so the CIA. But the NSA was more trusted and kept a lower profile. Except for Trailblazer, that was. Not long after 9/11, the NSA realized its SIGINT intercept technology was woefully inadequate to handle the volume of traffic it was trying to not only digest but disseminate, so a company out in San Diego, SAIC (Science Applications International Corporation), was hired to upgrade Fort Meade's systems. The twenty-six-month, $280 million project called Trailblazer went nowhere. SAIC was then awarded a $360 million contract for Trailblazer's successor. The waste of money and time had sent heads rolling at the NSA and damaged its otherwise untarnished image on Capitol Hill. Execute Locus, though still on track, was not yet out of the beta stage, so the NSA was supplementing its intercept computers with Sun mainframes, which, though powerful in their own right, were tantamount to sandbags holding back a tsunami. Worse still, by the time Execute Locus comes online it will have already started down the hill toward obsolescence, thanks mainly to IBM's übercomputer, Sequoia.

As tech-saavy as Jack liked to think himself, Sequoia's capacity was mind-boggling. Faster than the world's top five hundred supercomputers combined, Sequoia could perform twenty quadrillion mathematical processes per second, a statistic that could be grasped only by reductive comparison: If each of the 6.7 billion people on earth was armed with a calculator and worked together on a calculation twenty-four hours a day, every day of the year, it would take more than *three centuries* to do what Sequoia will do in one hour. On the downside, Sequoia wasn't quite ready for prime time; at last report it was being housed in ninety-six refrigerators covering more than three thousand square feet.

As big as a good-sized two-story house, Jack thought. Then: *Wonder if they're giving tours?*

Bell now asked, "So what tells you this is important?"

"Why encrypt a birth announcement?" Ryan replied. "And we cracked it on their in-house key. Okay, maybe bad guys have kids in their families, but no name on the mother, the father, or the kid. It's too clinical."

"True," Bell replied.

"One more thing: There's a new addressee on the distribution list, and he's using a different ISP. Might be worth a look. Maybe he's not as careful with his backstops and financials as the others."

So far all of their "French Connection" e-mails had come from cloaked Internet service providers or fire-and-forget e-mail accounts with nothing but a ghost at the other end, and since all originated from overseas providers, The Campus had little way of prying back the floorboard. If the French were in the loop, they'd simply walk into the Internet service provider and pull up his account information. They'd at least get his credit card number, and from that they'd get the address the credit card bill goes to every month, unless it was a falsely backstopped card, but even then they'd be able to launch a tracking operation and try to start gathering pieces. Back to the jigsaw theory: A lot of little pieces end up painting a big picture. With luck.

"Might take some hacking, but we might be able to grab enough to start a line on this guy."

"Worth a try," Bell agreed. "Run with it."

For his part, the birth announcement had come as a happy surprise to Ibrahim. Hidden within the seemingly innocuous language were three messages: His part of Lotus was moving to the next phase, communication protocols were changing, and a courier was en route.

It was late afternoon in Paris, and the city bustled with rush-hour traffic. The weather was pleasant. Tourists were coming back—from America, to the commercial pleasure and philosophical discontent of Parisians, to taste the food and wine, and see what sights there were. So many came by train from London now, but you couldn't tell from their clothing. The taxi drivers hustled their fares around, giving informal lessons on pronunciation along the way and grumbling at the size of their tips—at least Americans understood about tipping, while most Europeans did not.

Ibrahim Salih al-Adel was fully acclimated. His French was sufficiently perfect that Parisians had trouble fixing his accent, and he walked about like any other local, not gawping about like a monkey in the zoo. It was, oddly, the women who most offended him. So proudly they pranced about in their fashionable clothes, often with lovely and expensive leather bags dangling from their hands but usually with comfortable walking shoes, because people walked here more often than they rode. The better to parade their pride, he thought.

He'd had a routine day at work, mostly selling movie videos and DVDs, mainly of American films dubbed in French or with subtitles—which allowed his business clients to try out the English skills they'd learned in school. (Much as the French disdained America, a movie was a movie, and the French loved the cinema more than most nationalities.)

So tomorrow he would begin assembling the team and begin actual mission planning, something more easily discussed over a dinner table than actually accomplished. But he'd considered that, albeit in the private confines of his flat and not actually in the field. Some of that could be done here, over the Internet, but only in broad terms. The particulars of their target could be assessed only once they were on the ground, but homework here would save them precious time in the future. Some of the logistical pieces were already in place, and so far their informant at the facility had proven steady and reliable.

What did he need for the mission? A few people. Believers, all. Four. No more than that. One needed expertise with explosives. Untraceable automobiles—no problem there, of course. Good language skills. They had to look the part, which wouldn't be hard, given the target's location; few people could discern the subtleties of skin color, and he spoke English without much accent, so that wouldn't present a problem, either.

Most of all, though, each member of his team had to be a true believer. Willing to die. Willing to kill. It was easy for outsiders to think that the former was more important than the latter, but while there were many willing to throw their lives away, it was far more useful to discard your life only for something to advance the cause. They thought of themselves as Holy Warriors and sought after their seventy-two virgins but were in fact young people with few prospects, to whom religion was the path to greatness they would otherwise never achieve. It was remarkable that they were too stupid even to see that. But that was why he was the leader and they the followers.

I 2

Even if she had not been to the motel before, she would have had little trouble finding it, sitting beside what the town of Beatty optimistically called Main Street, which was in truth nothing more than a half-mile gap of thirty-mile-per-hour road between highways 95 and 374.

The hotel itself—the Motel 6 of Death Valley—had, despite

its outward appearance, relatively clean rooms that smelled of disinfectant soap. Not only had she seen worse, but she had applied her . . . special skills in worse places. And with worse men, for much less money. If anything, the name of the motel bothered her most of all.

A Keräˌsen Tatar by birth, Allison—her real name was Aysılu, which in Turkik meant Beauty as Moon—had inherited from her mother and father and ancestors a healthy respect for omens, both subtle and overt, and the name Motel 6 of Death Valley certainly qualified as the latter, she believed.

No matter. Omens were mercurial, and meaning was always open to interpretation. In this case the motel's name was unlikely to apply to her; her subject was too entranced by her to be of any threat, either directly or indirectly. And what she'd come here to do required little thinking on her part, so well had she been trained. And it helped that men were simple, predictable creatures, driven by the basest of needs. "Men are clay," her first instructor, a woman named Olga, had once told her, and even at the tender age of eleven she'd known the truth of it, having seen it in the lingering gazes of the boys in her village, and even in the always watching eyes of some of the men.

Even before she'd started going through her changes and her body had begun to blossom, she'd instinctively known which was not only the fairer sex but the stronger one as well. Men were physically strong, and that had its benefits and pleasures, but Allison plied a different kind of strength, one that had served her well, keeping her alive in dangerous situations and keeping her comfortable in hard times. And now, at twenty-two, with her village far behind her, her strength was making her wealthy. Better still, unlike many of her previous employers, her current one hadn't required an audition from her. Whether that was a function of their strict religious ideals or simply one of professionalism, she didn't know, but they had taken her bona fides at face value, along with a recom-mendation—though from whom was unclear. Certainly someone with influence. The now-discontinued program that had trained her had existed under closely guarded secrecy.

She drove past the motel's parking lot, then circled the block once and came back in the other direction, looking for anything out of place, anything that tickled her intuition. She saw his vehicle, a blue 1990 Dodge pickup, along with half a dozen others, all with in-state plates, save one from California and one from Arizona. Satisfied all was in order, she pulled into a gas station, did a quick Y-turn, then returned to the motel and pulled into the lot, parking two stalls down from the Dodge truck. She took a moment to check her makeup in the rearview mirror and retrieve a pair of condoms from the glove compart-ment. She dropped them in her purse and snapped it closed with a smile. He had begun to complain about the condoms, saying he wanted nothing between them, but she had demurred, saying she wanted to wait until they knew each other better, perhaps get tested for sexually transmitted diseases, before they took their relationship to the next level. The truth was, familiarity and caution had nothing to do with her hesitation. Her employer had been thorough, giving her a detailed dossier of the man, from his daily routine to his eating habits to his relationship history. He'd had two lovers before her, a high school girlfriend who had dumped him between his junior and senior years, and another shortly after he graduated from college. That, too, had been a brief affair. The likelihood he had a disease was almost nonexistent. No, the use of a condom was but another tool in her arsenal. The closeness he so craved was a need, and needs were merely leverage points. When she finally "gave in" and let him have her without the protection, it would serve only to strengthen her grasp on him.

Clay, she thought.

She couldn't delay much longer, though, as her employer

93

was already asking for information she'd yet to extract. Why they were impatient or what exactly they planned to do with the information she was funneling to them was their business, but clearly this man's secrets were of critical importance. This sort of thing could not be hurried, though. Not if you wanted good results.

She got out, locked the car door, and walked toward the room. As was his custom, he had left a red rose dangling in the gap between the doorknob and the jamb—"their" code to let her know where to find him. He was a sweet man, truth be told, but so weak and so needy that she found it nearly impossible to feel anything but disdain for him.

She knocked on the door. She heard footsteps rapidly padding toward the door, then the chain lock rattling as it was unhooked. The door swung open, and he stood there in his corduroy pants and one of the half-dozen tattered T-shirts he owned, all of which referenced some science-fiction movie or television show.

"Hey, there," she cooed, shooting a hip like a runway model. Years of training had left her without a trace of an accent. "Happy to see me?"

Her sundress—in the light peach color he liked so much— was clingy in all the right places and billowy in the others, the perfect balance of chasteness and spice. Most men, even if they didn't realize it, wanted their women to be ladies in daily life and whores in the bedroom.

His hungry eyes finished their scan of her legs and breasts, and then came to rest on her face. "Uh, yeah . . . God, yeah," he mumbled. "Come on, get in here."

They made love twice over the next two hours, the first time lasting only a few minutes, the second time ten minutes, and only that long because she'd held him off. *Muscles of a different sort,* she thought. But no less powerful. When they were done

94

he lay on his back, panting, his chest and face slick with sweat. She rolled off and snuggled into his shoulder, exhaling heavily.

"Wow," she murmured. "That was . . . Wow . . ."

"Yeah, it was," he replied.

Steve wasn't a bad-looking man, with curly reddish-blond hair and light blue eyes, but he was too skinny for her tastes, and his beard made her face and thighs itchy. He was clean, though, and he didn't smoke, and his teeth were straight, so all in all she knew it could be worse.

As for his lovemaking skills . . . They were almost non-existent. He was an overly considerate lover and too gentle by far, always worried he was doing something wrong or should be doing something different. She did her best to reassure him, saying all the right things and making all the right noises at all the right moments, but she suspected in the back of his head he was worried about losing her—not that he "had" her, really.

It was the quintessential beauty-and-the-beast syndrome. He wasn't going to lose her, of course, at least not until she'd gotten the answer her employers needed. Allison felt a momentary pang of guilt, imagining how he would react when she disappeared. She was fairly certain he'd fallen in love with her, which was the point, after all, but he was so . . . harmless it was hard not to occasionally feel sorry for him. Hard but not impossible. She pushed the thought from her mind.

"So how's work?" he asked.

"It's fine, the same old thing: making the rounds, giving my pitch, handing out my phone numbers, and showing the doctors a little cleavage. . . ."

"Hey!"

"Relax, I'm kidding. A lot of the doctors are worried about the recalls."

"On TV, the pain meds?"

"Those are the ones. We're getting a lot of pressure from the manufacturer to keep pushing them."

As far as he knew, she was a pharmaceutical saleswoman based in Reno. They "met" at a Barnes & Noble, where, at the in-house Starbucks, she'd found herself a nickel short in paying for her Caffè Mocha. Behind her in line, Steve had nervously offered to cover the difference. Armed with his dossier—or what little of his dossier they felt she needed to have—and well aware of his habits, the meeting had been easy to arrange and easier still to exploit when she'd expressed an interest in a book he was reading, something about mechanical engineering that she actually cared nothing about. He hadn't noticed, so thrilled to have a pretty girl paying attention to him.

"So all that engineering stuff," she said. "I don't know how you do it. I tried to read one of those books you gave me, but it went right over my head."

"Well, you're plenty smart, that's for sure, but it's pretty dry stuff. Don't forget, I went to four years of college for it, and even then I didn't really learn anything practical until I got on the job. MIT taught me a lot, but nothing compared to what I've learned since then."

"Like what?"

"Ah, you know, just stuff."

"Such as?"

He didn't reply.

"Okay, okay, I get the point, Mr. Important Top-Secret Guy."

"It's not that, Ali," he replied in a slightly whiny tone. "It's just that they make you sign all this paperwork—confidentiality agreements and all that."

"Wow, you must be important."

He shook his head. "Nah. You know how the government

is . . . paranoid to the end. Hell, I'm a little surprised they haven't polygraphed us, but who knows?"

"So what is it, then? Weapons and bombs and stuff like that? Wait a second. . . . Are you a rocket scientist?"

He chuckled. "No, not a rocket scientist. Mechanical engineer—average, run-of-the mill engineer."

"A spy?" She propped herself up on an elbow, letting the sheet fall away to reveal a pale breast. "That's it, isn't it? You're a spy."

"No, not a spy, either. I mean, come on, look at me. I'm a nerd."

"The perfect cover."

"Boy, you've got some imagination there, I'll give you that."

"You're dodging the question. That's a giveaway—a telltale spy move."

"Nope. Sorry to disappoint you."

"Then what? Tell me. . . ."

"I work for the DOE—Department of Energy."

"Like nuclear energy and all that."

"Right."

The truth was she knew exactly what he did for a living, where he worked, and what went on there. What she was looking for—what they were looking for—was much more specific. They were confident he had the information, perhaps already in his head, and if not, he certainly had access to it. She absently wondered why they had chosen to use her rather than to simply snatch him off the street and extract the information through blunt force. She suspected the answer had as much to do with where he worked as it did the unreliability of torture. If Steve disappeared or turned up dead under even remotely suspicious circumstances, there would be an investigation by not only the local police but the FBI as well, and that kind of scrutiny was something her employer was probably quite anxious to avoid. Still, the fact that they hadn't chosen the more direct method told her something: The information they needed was both critical and extraordinary. Steve was perhaps their only viable source of the information, which meant it was either highly protected elsewhere or his grasp of it was singular.

Not that it mattered. She would do the job, take the money, and then . . . well, who knew?

Her fee was considerable, enough perhaps to give her a head start on a new life somewhere else, doing something else for a living. Something ordinary, like being a librarian or a bookkeeper. She smiled at the thought. Ordinary might be nice. She would have to be very careful, though, with these people. However they were planning to use this information, it was clearly of deadly importance. Important enough to kill over, she suspected.

Back to work . . .

She lazily traced her fingernails over his chest. "You're not, like, in danger or anything, are you? I mean, from cancer or anything?"

"Well, no," he said, "not really. I guess there's some risk, but they've got protocols and rules and regulations—enough that you'd have to really screw up to get hurt."

"So it's never happened—to anyone?"

"Sure, but usually it's dumb stuff, like some guy getting his foot run over by a forklift or choking on nachos in the cafeteria. We've had a couple close calls in . . . in other places, but that was usually because somebody tried to cut a corner, and even when that happens, there're backup systems and procedures. Believe me, babe, I'm pretty safe."

"Good; I'm glad. I hate to think of you hurt or sick."

"That's not going to happen, Ali. I'm very careful."

We'll see, she thought.

13

Jack Junior pressed himself flat against the wall and slid forward along it, feeling the splinters in the rough plank boards catch on his shirt. He reached the corner and stopped, weapon held in the Weaver stance doublehanded grip, barrel pointed downward. Not like Hollywood or cop TV shows, he thought, where they carried the gun pointed barrel-up beside their faces. Sure, it looked cool—nothing framed a hero's lantern jaw and steely blue eyes like a chunky Glock— but this wasn't about cool, this was about staying alive and putting down the bad guys. Growing up in the White House surrounded by Secret Service pros who knew guns better than they knew their own kids certainly had its advantages, didn't it?

The problem with the Hollywood model of gun handling was twofold: site picture and ambush. Real-world combat handgunning was about shooting straight and true under pressure, and that, in turn, was all about mind-set and site picture. The former was about conditioning; the latter, mechanics. It was a lot easier and a lot more effective to bring a weapon up, get a good site picture of the target, and snap off a shot than it was doing it in the reverse. The other factor— the ambush—was all about what happens when you turn a corner to find yourself face-to-face with a bad guy. Do you want your gun up, by your face, or do you want it down where you might, just might, have a chance to snap off a shot into the guy's legs before he tackles you and the situation devolves into a no-holds-barred wrestling match? That didn't happen very often, of course, but as far as Jack was concerned, and as far as real shooters were concerned, it was much better to be wrestling a bad guy who had a 9-millimeter slug or two in his leg than not.

Theory, Jack, he reminded himself, returning to the here and now. Theories are for the classroom, not the real world.

Where the hell was Dominic? They'd separated at the front door, Dominic moving right to take the house's back rooms—the potentially more "heavy" rooms—Jack to the left, heading for the more open kitchen and living room. *Don't worry about Dominic, worry about you.* His cousin was FBI—at least officially—so he needed no lessons on this stuff.

Jack changed the gun to his left hand, dried his palm on his pants leg, then changed it back again. He took a breath, took a short step back, then peeked his head around the corner. Kitchen. Refrigerator to the right; avocado-green counter, stainless-steel sink, and desktop microwave to the left; dining table and chairs down a ways, past the end of the counter, beside the back door.

Jack scanned for movement but saw nothing, so he stepped out, gun raised to near shoulder height, eyes scanning, gun barrel following, then crept into the kitchen. Ahead and to the right was an archway, this one leading to the living room, he assumed, picturing the layout in his head. Dominic should be coming through the other room on the right to link up with him—

"Jack, rear bedroom window!" Dominic shouted from somewhere deeper inside the house. "Got a runner! Out the side window! White male, red jacket, armed . . . I'm on him!"

Jack resisted the impulse to charge ahead, instead moving slow and steady, clearing the remainder of the kitchen, then peeking around the corner into the living room. Clear. He stepped to the patio door, body aligned to the left of the door-jamb and hopefully behind the wooden 2 × 4 studs under the drywall that would, in theory, stop or slow down any bullets meant for him, then ducked down to peer out the porthole-style window into the alley beyond. To his right he saw a figure moving down the alley: blue windbreaker, yellow letters. Dominic's FBI windbreaker. Jack opened the door, looked again, then pushed open the screen door. Directly across from him was a darkened doorway in the brick wall; to his left a green Dumpster. He moved that way, gun up, tracking for targets. He saw a shadow moving in the doorway and pivoted in time to see a man-shaped silhouette appear on the threshold.

"Freeze! Don't move, don't move!" he shouted, but the figure kept moving, left arm coming into the light, hand holding a revolver. "Drop it!" Jack shouted again, gave him another beat, then fired twice, both shots striking center mass. The figure fell back into the doorway. Jack turned again, back toward the Dumpster, moving until he could see around its corner, looking for—

And then something slammed into his back, between the shoulder blades, and he staggered forward. He felt the blood rush to his head and thought, *Ah, shit, goddamn it . . .* He bounced against the Dumpster, left shoulder taking the brunt of the impact, and tried to pivot on his heel toward the source of the gunfire. . . . He felt another round slam into his side, just below his armpit, and knew it was too late.

"Hold!" a voice shouted over a bullhorn, followed by three rapid whistle blasts that echoed down the alley. "Cease exercise, cease exercise!"

"Ah, man . . ." Jack muttered, then leaned back against the Dumpster and exhaled heavily.

The man who'd just shot him—Special Agent Walt Brandeis—stepped out of the doorway and shook his head sadly. "My God. To die like that, son, with a green paint splatter in the middle of your back . . ." Jack could see the half-smile playing across Brandeis's lips as he looked Jack up and down, then clicked his tongue. "It's just a plain shame, that's what it is."

Down the alley, Dominic came jogging around the corner and stopped in his tracks, then said, "Again?"

"Here's the problem, Jack: You were—"

"Hurrying, I know."

"No, not this time. It's more than that. Hurrying wasn't your real problem—it was part of it but not really what got you killed. Care to take a guess?"

Jack Junior thought it over a moment. "I assumed."

"Damn right you assumed. You assumed the target you saw in that door was the only one in there. You assumed you'd put him down, then stopped worrying about it. It's what I call Ambush Relief Syndrome. You won't find it in the textbooks, but it goes like this: You survived an ambush, a real near thing, and you feel like you're golden. In your head you subconsciously relabeled that door and the room inside from 'uncleared' to 'cleared.' Now, if this was real life and there had been two of them in there, your average dumb criminal probably would've opened up on you the moment his partner did, but there are always exceptions out there—like that rare creature, a smart bad guy—and exceptions get you killed."

"You're right," Jack muttered, taking a sip of Diet Coke. "Damn."

Along with Brian, who'd sat out the last exercise, he and Dominic had regrouped in the break room after being debriefed by Brandeis, who hadn't pulled any punches, former President's son or not. He'd told Jack basically the same thing Dominic was saying, only in a more entertaining fashion. Brandeis, a native Mississippian, had an aw-shucks, Will Rogers way about him that took some sting out of the criticism. Some, but not all of it. *What'd you think, Jack, that you'd come here and walk out an expert?*

Like much of the FBI's Quantico urban tactical training facility known affectionately as Hogan's Alley, the break room was a Spartan affair, with plywood walls and floors, and Formica tables that looked like they'd been beaten with hammers. The course itself was anything but slapdash, though, right down to its bank, post office, barbershop, and pool hall. *And dark doorways,* Jack thought. That sure as hell felt real, as had the paintball pellet he'd caught between the shoulder blades. It still itched, and he suspected he'd see a good-sized welt later in the shower. But pellet or not, dead was dead. He suspected they'd used paintballs for his benefit. Depending on the scenario being run and the agents running it, Hogan's Alley could be a lot louder and a lot hairier. Jack had even heard rumors that the HRT—the Hostage Rescue Team— sometimes went live fire. But then again, those guys were the best of the best.

"What about you? You don't pile on?" Jack asked Brian, who sat slumped in his chair, rocking on two legs. "Might as well get the full lecture."

Brian shook his head and smiled, nodding at his brother. "His turf, cuz, not mine. You come out to Twenty-nine Palms and we'll talk." The Marines had their own frighteningly realistic urban combat training center called MOUT—Military Operations on Urbanized Terrain. "Till then, I'll keep my mouth shut, thank you very much."

Dominic rapped a knuckle on the table before Jack. "Cuz, goddamn it, you asked us to bring you here, right?"

The steel in Dominic's voice was unmistakable, and Jack was momentarily taken aback. *What is going on?* he wondered. "Right."

"You wanted to feel what it's really like, right?"

"Yeah."

"Well, then stop acting like a little boy who got caught cheating on the spelling bee. This ain't about lectures. Nobody gives a shit who you are, or whether you made some rookie mistake your third time out. Hell, the first ten times I ran this course I caught a bullet. That doorway you missed? They almost named that damned thing after me, the number of shots I took there."

Jack believed him. Hogan's had been training FBI agents for twenty-plus years, and the only ones who shot it perfectly were the ones who'd run it so much they saw it in their dreams. That was the way of everything, Jack knew. Practice makes perfect was not a cliché but in fact an axiom, especially in the military and in law enforcement. Practice cut new grooves into your mental wiring while your body developed muscle memory— performing the same action over and over until muscle and synapse worked in unison and thinking was erased from the equation. *How long does that kind of thing take?* he wondered.

"Come on. . . ." Jack said.

"Nope. Ask Brandeis. He'll be happy to tell you. I took plenty of his bullets. Shit, the first two times I walked right by that door and got killed for it. Look, I'm not all that keen on telling you this, but the truth is you did damned good your first time out. Scary good. Hell, who would've figured it . . . My braniac cousin a gen-u-ine gunslinger."

"Now you're humoring me."

"No, I'm not. Really, man. Jump in, Brian. Tell him."

"He's right, Jack. You're really rough around the edges— hell, you crossed Dom twice in the Laundromat—"

"Crossed?"

"When you're stacked up outside a room, you know, just before you go in, and then you split up inside, one group moving to the heavy side, the other to the light side—"

"Yeah, I remember."

"In the Laundromat you sidestepped and tracked your gun outside your zone. Your barrel crossed me—right across the back of the head, in fact. A real no-no."

"Okay, so lesson number one: Don't point your gun at your friends."

Brian laughed. "That's a way of putting it, yeah. Like I was saying . . . you're rough around the edges, but you've got great instincts. What, you been holding out on us? Do some training with the Secret Service when you were a kid? Maybe a few vacations with Clark and Chavez?"

Jack shook his head. "No, none of that. I mean, yeah, I shot some guns but nothing like this. I don't know. . . . It just seemed to play out in my head before it was happening. . . ." Jack shrugged, then smiled. "Maybe got a little of Dad's Marine DNA. Hell, who knows, maybe I've just watched *Die Hard* too many times."

"Somehow I don't think so," Brian replied. "Well, whatever it is, I wouldn't mind having you on my six."

"I'll second that."

They raised their cans of Diet Coke and clunked them together.

"About that, guys . . ." Jack said tentatively. "You remember that thing last year . . . in Italy?"

Brian and Dominic exchanged glances. "We remember," Dom said. "Hell of a deal, that."

"Yeah, well, I was thinking I wouldn't mind doing some more of it—not that exactly, maybe, but something like it."

Brian said, "Jesus, cuz, are you talking about unplugging from your keyboard and living in the real world? I can see the devil lacing up his ice skates as we speak."

"Very funny. No, I like what I do, I know it makes a difference, but that stuff is so intangible. What you guys do—what we did in Italy—that's the real deal. Hands on, you know? You can see the results with your own eyes."

"Now that you've brought it up," Dominic said, "I've always meant to ask you: Did any of that bother you afterward—not that it should have, necessarily, but let's face it: You were kind of dumped ass-backward into a shitty situation—if you'll pardon the pun."

Jack considered this. "What do you want me to say? That it bothered me? Well, it didn't. Not really. Sure, I was nervous, and there was a quarter-second just before it happened where I thought, *What the hell am I doing?* But then it was gone, and it was just me and him, and I just did it. To answer the question I think you're trying to ask—no, I haven't lost a wink of sleep over it. You think I should have?"

"Shit, no." Brian looked around to make sure they were alone, then leaned in close, forearms on the table. "There's no should about it, Jack. You either do or you don't. You don't, and that's okay. The asshole deserved it. First time I popped a guy, Jack, he had me dead to rights. It was kill or be killed. I put him down, and I knew it was the right thing. Still had a few nightmares, though. Right or wrong, whether he deserves it or not, killing a man ain't a pleasant thing. Anybody who thinks it is a little touched in the head. All that gung-ho stuff ain't really about killing; it's about doing the job you've trained your ass off to be good at, taking care of the guys to your left and right, and coming out the other side with all your fingers and toes."

"Besides, Jack," Dominic added, "that guy in Italy, he wouldn't have just up and quit one day. He would've cost a lot of people their lives before somebody sent him on his way. For me, that's the deal-breaker. A bad guy deserving what he gets is all well and good, but what we're doing— what this whole thing is about—isn't revenge, at least not for its own sake. Playing it that way is sort of like shutting the barn door after horses get out. Me, I'd much rather stop the guy who's planning on opening the barn door in the first place."

Brian stared hard at his twin brother for a couple of beats and then shook his head and grinned. "I'll be damned. Mom always said you were the philosopher of the family. I just never believed her till now."

"Yeah, yeah . . ." Dominic muttered. "Not so much philosophy as math. Kill one, save hundreds or thousands. If we were talking about decent, law-abiding folks, that'd be a harder equation, but they're not."

"I agree with him, Jack," said Brian. "We've got a chance to do some real good here. But if you're thinking about doing this kind of stuff because you think revenge is the answer, or that it's all James Bond shit—"

"That's not what—"

"Good, because it ain't, not even close. It's ugly shit, period. And revenge is a piss-poor motivator. It makes you sloppy, and sloppy is dead."

"I know."

"So what're you going to do about it?"

"Talk to Gerry, I guess, and see what he says."

"You better have one hell of a pitch," Dominic said. "Hell, as it stands Gerry took a risk hiring you in the first place. Your dad would have a fit—"

"Let me worry about my dad, Dom."

"Fine, but if you think Gerry's just going to hand you a gun and say, 'Go forth and make the world safe for democracy,' you got another think coming. If you were to buy the farm, he'd be the one making the call."

"I know."

"Good."

"So," Jack said, "if I talk to him, you guys'll back me up?"

"For what it's worth, sure," Brian replied. "But this isn't a democracy, Jack. Assuming he doesn't shoot down the idea on the spot, he'll probably run it by Sam." Sam Granger was The Campus's Chief of Operations. "I doubt he's going to ask us."

Jack nodded. "Probably right. Well, like you said, I'd better make my pitch a damn good one, then."

14

Autumn was here. You could tell from the wind and the ice pack, which had begun pulling away from the coast to reveal the black water of the Arctic Ocean. It could not be colder without turning to ice, and there was plenty of that still in sight, just to remind one that summer up here was fleeting at best. Mother Nature remained as grim and heartless as ever, even under a sky of crystal blue and a few cotton-ball white clouds.

This place was not unlike his first Navy posting to Polyyarniy twelve years before, just as the Soviet Navy was starting to shut down. Oh, sure, they had a few ships left, most of them tied at the working ports of the Kola Fjord, manned by men who stayed in the Navy because they either had to or had nothing to go home to. There were a few ships with crews composed almost entirely of officers who actually got paid a few times a year. Vitaliy had been among the last men drafted into the former Soviet Navy and, to his astonishment, found himself liking the work.

After the mindless basic training he'd been made a junior *starshina,* or petty officer, and a bosun's mate. It had been hard, backbreaking work but satisfying, and it had ended up giving him a useful trade. He'd profited personally from the demise of the Soviet Navy by buying at a discount an old but well-maintained T-4 amphibious landing craft that he'd nominally converted into a passenger craft. Mostly he took scientific parties, exploring the region for obscure reasons beyond his interest, while some were hunters looking to convert a polar bear into an expensive rug.

His charter for the week was waiting for him down the coast

at a small fishing village. Two days ago he'd preloaded their equipment—a GAZ truck with all-wheel drive, new tires, and a fresh paint job, equipped with a heavy-duty A-frame, taking delivery from an anonymous driver who, like him, had probably been paid in euros. As any good captain did, Vitaliy had inspected the cargo and had been surprised to find the truck stripped of all identification codes, right down to the one on the engine block. While such a task wasn't particularly complicated, and neither did it require a mechanic, something told Vitaliy that his charters hadn't done the work themselves. So they'd come here, bought a GAZ in good condition, paid someone handsomely to strip it, then hired a private charter. Plenty of money to spread around and overly concerned with anonymity. What did that mean?

But there was no point in being too curious. Smart cats knew the danger of curiosity, and he liked to think he was smart enough. The euros would also take care of his memory, something in which his party seemed supremely confident; the leader of the group, clearly of Mediterranean descent, had told Vitaliy to call him Fred. It wasn't so much an artifice as it was a moniker of convenience, almost a private joke between them, and Fred's smirk during their initial meeting had confirmed it.

He watched his charter party come aboard and wave at him, and with that done, he signaled to Vanya, his engineer/deckhand, who cast off the lines. Vitaliy started the diesel engines and pulled away from the dock.

Soon enough he was in the fairway and headed out to sea. The black water didn't exactly beckon, but it was where he and the boat belonged, and it felt good to be heading back out. All he needed to make the morning perfect was a tranquilizer, and that Vitaliy handled with an American Marlboro Lights 100 cigarette. And then the morning was perfect. The local fishing fleet had already cleared the harbor—such dreadful hours they worked—and the water was clear for easy navigation, with only a slight chopping breaking on the marker buoys.

As he passed the breakwater, he turned to starboard and headed east.

Per his instructions, Adnan had kept his team small, himself and three others that he trusted implicitly, just enough bodies to do the heavy lifting but not enough to present a problem when the inevitable conclusion to their mission arrived. He didn't mind that part of it, actually. He would, after all, suffer the same general fate as his compatriots. A sad necessity, he thought. No, his biggest worry was that they might fail. Failure here would undoubtedly have a resonant effect on the larger operation, whatever that might be, and Adnan would do everything in his power to make sure that didn't happen.

His life. Adnan smiled at the notion. Nonbelievers saw all this—trees and water and material possessions—as life. Nor was life defined by what you ate and drank and defiled with your bodily lusts. The time you spend on this earth is but preparation for what comes after, and if you are devout and obedient to the one true God, your reward will be glorious beyond imagining. What was less certain, Adnan realized, was his fate should he succeed here. Would he be given greater missions, or would his silence be more valuable to the jihad? He would prefer the former, if only to continue serving Allah, but if the latter was to be his destiny, then so be it. He would meet either outcome with the same equanimity, confident he'd lived his earthly life as best he could.

Whatever was to come, he thought, was in the future, and he would let that worry about itself. In the here and now he had a job to do. An important one, though he wasn't sure how exactly it fit into the larger picture. That was for wiser minds.

They'd arrived at the fishing village the day before, after

parting company with the driver who was to deliver their truck to the docks and into the hands of the charter captain they had hired. The village was largely abandoned, most of its occupants having moved on after the waters had gone barren from years of overfishing. What few villagers remained kept to themselves, scraping by as best they could as autumn moved toward winter. Adnan and his men, bundled in parkas and their faces covered in scarves against the cold, had drawn little attention, and the hostel manager, who was only too surprised and happy to have paying customers, asked them no questions—neither about where they had come from nor about their future travel plans. Even had the manager asked, Adnan couldn't have answered if he'd wanted to. The future belonged to Allah, whether the rest of the world knew it or not.

It was dark in Paris, and there was a chill in the air that affected the two Arabs more than the Parisians. But that was an excuse for more wine, which was welcome. And the sidewalk tables had thinned out enough that they could talk more openly. If anyone was observing them, then he was being very careful about it. And you couldn't be afraid of everything all the time, even in this business.

"You're waiting for another communication?" Fa'ad asked.

Ibrahim nodded. "It's supposed to be en route. A good courier. Very reliable."

"What do you expect?"

"I've learned not to speculate," Ibrahim said. "I take my directions as they come. The Emir knows what to do, doesn't he?"

"So far he has been effective, but sometimes I think he's an old woman," Fa'ad groused. "If you plan your operation intelligently, then it will work. We are the Emir's hands and eyes in the field. He picked us. He should trust us more."

"Yes, but he sees things which we do not see. Never forget

that," Ibrahim reminded his guest. "That is why he decides on all the operations."

"Yes, he is very wise," Fa'ad conceded, not entirely meaning it but having to talk that way even so. He had sworn his allegiance to the Emir, and that, really, was that, even though he'd done it five years before, still in his enthusiastic teens. People believed much at that age, and swore loyalty easily. And it took years for that sort of oath to wear off. If ever.

But that didn't entirely stop doubts. He'd met the Emir only once, while Ibrahim could claim to know the man. Such was the nature of their work. Neither Ibrahim nor Fa'ad knew where their leader was living. They were familiar with just one end of a lengthy electronic trail. That was a sensible security precaution: American police were probably as efficient as the European sort, and European police were men to be feared. Even so, there was much old woman in the Emir. He didn't even trust those who had sworn to die in his place. Whom, then, did he trust? Why them and not . . . him? Fa'ad asked himself. Fundamentally, Fa'ad was too bright to accept things "because I said so," as every mother in the world said to every five-year-old son. Even more frustratingly, he could not even ask certain questions, because they would imply disloyalty to certain others. And disloyalty in the organization was tantamount to a request for self-immolation. But Fa'ad knew that this actually made sense, both from the Emir's point of view and for the organization as a whole.

It wasn't easy doing Allah's work, but Fa'ad had known that going in. Or so he told himself. Well, at least in Paris you could look at the passing women, dressed as whores, most of them, showing their bodies off as though advertising their business. It was good, Fa'ad thought, that Ibrahim had chosen to live in this area. At least the scenery was pretty.

"That's a pretty one," Ibrahim said in agreement to the

unspoken observation. "She's a doctor's wife, and sadly she does not commit adultery, in my experience."

"Mind reading." Fa'ad laughed. "French women are open to advances?"

"Some are. The hard part is reading their minds. Few men have that ability, even here." And he had a good laugh. "In that sense, French women are no different from our own. Some things are universal."

Fa'ad took a sip of coffee and leaned closer. "Will it work?" he asked, meaning their planned operation.

"I see no reason why it would not, and the effects will be noteworthy. The one drawback is that it will give us new enemies, but how will we notice the difference? We have no friends among the infidels. For us, now, it's just a matter of getting the tools in place for our strike."

"*Inshallah,*" Fa'ad replied.

And both clicked their glasses, just like Frenchmen after an agreement is reached.

There was nothing like home court advantage, former President Ryan thought. He'd gotten his doctorate in history at Georgetown University, so he knew the campus almost as well as he did his own home. All in all, he'd found the lecture circuit surprisingly agreeable. It was easy duty, being paid an embarrassing amount of money to talk about a subject he knew well: his time in the White House. So far there'd been only a smattering of audience loonies, eighty percent of them conspiracy nuts who'd been quickly shouted down by the other attendees. The other twenty percent were lefties who held the opinion that Edward Kealty had pulled the country back from an abyss Ryan had created. It was nonsense, of course, but there was no doubting their sincerity, a reminder Ryan took to heart: There was reality, and then there was perception, and rarely the two shall meet. It was a lesson Arnie van Damm had tried—mostly in vain—to pound into Ryan's head during his presidency, and a lesson Ryan's stubborn pride did not allow him to swallow easily. Some things were just *true*. Perception be damned. The fact that a majority of the American electorate seemed to have forgotten this fact by electing Kealty still boggled Ryan's mind, but then again, he was no objective observer. Should have been Robby in the Oval Office. The trick was to not let this disappointment taint his speech. As much as he might like to, criticizing a sitting President—even a jackass—was bad form.

The door to the greenroom—in this case a small lounge adjoining McNeir Auditorium—opened, and Andrea Price-O'Day, his principal Secret Service agent, stepped past the agents at the door.

"Five minutes, sir."

"How's the crowd?" Ryan said.

"Full house. No torches and pitchforks."

Ryan laughed at this. "Always a good sign. How's my tie?"

He'd learned early on that Andrea was far handier with a Windsor knot than he was—almost as good as Cathy, but the good doctor had left early for the hospital that morning, so he'd tied the knot himself. A mistake.

Andrea cocked her head and appraised it. "Not bad, sir." She made a slight adjustment and gave a curt nod of approval. "I feel my job security slipping away."

"Not gonna happen, Andrea." Price-O'Day had been with the Ryan family a long time, so long, in fact, that most of them rarely remembered she was armed and ready to kill and die for their safety.

There came a knock on the door, and one of the agents poked his head through the gap. "SHORTSTOP," he announced, then opened the door to admit Jack Junior.

"Jack!" the elder Ryan said, walking over.

"Hey, Andrea," Jack Junior said.

"Mr. Ryan."

"Nice surprise," said the former President.

"Yeah, well, my date canceled on me, so . . ."

Ryan laughed. "Man's gotta have his priorities."

"Hell, I didn't mean it like that—"

"Forget it. Glad you came. You got a seat?"

Jack Junior nodded. "Front row."

"Good. If I get into trouble you can throw me a softball."

Jack left his father, walked down the hall, took the stairs down one level, then headed toward the auditorium. Ahead, the hall was mostly dark, every other fluorescent ceiling fixture turned off. Like most educational institutions, Georgetown was trying to be more "green." As he passed a conference room he heard a metallic scraping sound from within, like a chair being dragged across a floor. He stepped back and peeked through the slit window. Inside, a janitor in blue coveralls was kneeling down beside an upturned floor buffer, poking at the polishing pad with a screwdriver. On impulse, Jack pushed open the door and poked his head inside. The janitor looked up.

"Hi," Jack said.

"Hello." The man appeared to be Hispanic and spoke with a heavy accent. "Change pad," he said.

"Sorry to bother you," Jack said, then shut the door behind him. He pulled out his cell phone and dialed Andrea's number. She picked up on the first ring. Jack said, "Hey, I was on my way to the auditorium. . . . There's a janitor down here—"

"Conference room two-b?"

"Yeah."

"We cleared him, and we'll sweep again. We're taking the basement route anyway."

"Okay, just checking."

"You looking for a second job?" Price-O'Day asked.

Jack chuckled. "How's the pay?"

"Lot less than you make. And the hours are hell. See you later."

Andrea disconnected. Jack headed toward the auditorium.

"Showtime, sir," she told former President Ryan, who stood up and shot his cuffs; the gesture was uniquely Jack Ryan Sr., but Price-O'Day saw a bit of the son in the father, and SHORTSTOP's call about the janitor had told her something more: The son hadn't fallen far from the intellectual tree, either. Was there such a thing as a spook gene? she wondered. If so, Jack Junior probably had it. Like his father, he was intensely curious and took few things on face. Of course they'd swept the building, and of course Jack knew this. Even so, he'd spotted the janitor and immediately thought, *Anomaly.* It had been a false alarm, but the question had been valid— something Secret Service agents learned to ask through training and experience.

Andrea now checked her watch and replayed their route in her mind, seeing the map in her head, timing the turns and distances. Satisfied, she knocked twice on the door, signaling to the agents there that SWORDSMAN was ready to move. She waited a moment for the cordon to form up, then opened the door, checked the hall, and stepped out, signaling for Ryan to follow.

In his auditorium seat, Jack Junior absently flipped through the night's program, his eyes taking in the words but his brain failing to register them. Something was itching at his subconscious, that nebulous feeling of something left undone. . . . Something he'd meant to do before leaving The Campus, perhaps?

The president of Georgetown appeared on the stage and walked to the podium, accompanied by polite applause. "Good evening, ladies and gentlemen. As we have only one item on tonight's program, I'll be brief with my introductions. Former President John Patrick Ryan has a long history of government service—"

Janitor. The word popped, unbidden, into Jack's mind. He'd been cleared, Andrea had said. Even so . . . He reached for his cell phone, then stopped. What would he say? That he had a feeling? From his seat, he could see the left side of the stage. Two black-suited Secret Service agents appeared; behind them, Andrea and his dad.

Before he realized what he was doing, Jack was on his feet and headed for the side exit. He trotted up the stairs, turned left, headed down the hall, counting conference room doors as he went.

Screwdriver, he thought, and suddenly the subconsious itch he'd felt two minutes earlier snapped into focus. The janitor had been using a screwdriver to remove a pad that had been secured to the buffer by a center locknut.

Chest now pounding, Jack reached the correct conference room and stopped a few feet short. He saw light coming through the slit window but could hear no sounds from within. He took a break, walked to the door, and tried the knob. Locked. He peeked through the window. The buffer was still there. The janitor was gone. The flathead screwdriver lay on the floor.

Jack turned and started jogging back to the auditorium. He stopped at the door, collected himself, then gently pushed open the door and eased it shut. A few people looked up as he entered, as did one of Andrea's agents standing in the center aisle. He gave Jack a nod of recognition, then returned to his scan of the auditorium.

Jack started his own scan, looking first for any sign of blue coveralls but quickly abandoning this; the janitor wouldn't have gotten into the auditorium. Backstage would be clear as well, locked down by Andrea's team. *Who else?* he thought, picking through the sea of faces. Audience members, agents, campus security . . .

Standing beside the east wall, his face partially in shadow and his hands clasped before him, was a rent-a-cop. Like the agents, he, too, was scanning the crowd. Like the agents . . . Jack kept scanning, counting campus security officers. Five in total. And none of them scanning the crowd. Untrained in personal protection, their attention was not focused on the audience—the most likely area of threat—but rather on the stage. Except for the guard on the east wall. The man turned his head, and his face passed briefly into the light.

Jack pulled out his cell phone and texted Andrea: GUARD, EAST WALL = JANITOR.

Onstage, Andrea was standing ten feet behind and to the left of the podium. Jack saw her pull out her cell phone, check the screen, then return it to her pocket. Her reaction was immediate. Her cuff mike came up to her mouth, then down again. The agent in the center aisle casually headed back up the aisle steps, then turned right at the carpeted intersection, heading toward the east wall. Now Jack saw Andrea sidestep behind his dad, moving into what he assumed was an intercept angle between his dad and the guard.

The center-aisle agent had reached the east wall's aisle. Thirty feet away, the guard rotated his head in that direction, paused ever so briefly on the agent, then rotated back to the stage, where Andrea had moved into blocking position. His dad, noticing this, cast a brief glance in her direction but kept talking. He would know, of course, what Andrea was doing, Jack reasoned, but not whether there was a specific threat.

On the east wall, the guard also noticed Andrea's movement. Casually, he took two steps down the aisle and bent over to whisper in an audience member's ear. The woman looked up at the guard, surprise on her face, then stood up. Now smiling, the guard took her by the elbow and, stepping around to her right side, guided her down the aisle toward the exit by the stage. As they passed the fourth row, Andrea took another step forward, maintaining her blocking position.

She unbuttoned her suit coat.

The guard suddenly switched his left hand from the woman's elbow to her collar, then sidestepped, moving sideways past the front row. The woman let out a yelp. Heads turned. The guard's right hand slipped into the front waistband of his pants. He jerked the woman around, using her as a shield. Andrea's gun came out and up.

"Freeze, Secret Service!"

Behind her, the other agents were already moving, swarming the former President, pushing him down and hurrying him toward the opposite side of the stage.

The guard's hand emerged from his waistband with a semi-automatic 9-millimeter. Seeing his target moving out of range, the guard made the mistake for which Andrea was waiting. Gun coming level with the stage, he took a step forward. And a half-foot beyond the protection of his human shield.

Andrea fired once. At fifteen feet, the low-velocity hollow-point bullet struck home, punching into the guard's head between his left eye and his ear. Designed for close-quarters, crowd-dense firing, the round worked as advertised, mushrooming inside the guard's brain, expending all its energy in a thousandth of a second and stopping, as the autopsy would later show, three inches from the opposite side of the skull.

The guard dropped straight down, dead before he reached the carpet.

"Andrea tells me you saved the day," former President Ryan said twenty minutes later in the limousine.

"Just sent up the flare," Jack replied.

The whole thing had been a surreal experience, Jack thought, but somehow less surreal than its aftermath. Though the series of events had been brief—five seconds from the time the guard had gotten the woman from her seat to when Andrea's head shot had dropped him—the mental replay in Jack's mind moved, predictably, he supposed, in slow motion. So shocked by the shooting was the audience that it had emitted only a few screams, all of those from the attendees before whom the assassin had fallen dead.

For his part, Jack had known better than to move, so he remained standing against the west wall as campus security and Andrea's agents cleared the auditorium. His dad, at the center of the Secret Service scrum, had been offstage before Andrea had fired the killing shot.

"Even so," Ryan said. "Thanks."

It was an awkward moment that drifted into an even more uncomfortable silence. Jack Junior broke it. "Scary shit, huh?"

Former President Ryan nodded at this. "What made you go back there—to check on the janitor, I mean?"

"When I saw him, he was trying to take off the buffer pad with a screwdriver. He needed a crescent wrench."

"Impressive, Jack."

"Because of the screwdriver—"

"Partially that. Partially because you didn't panic. And you let the professionals do their job. Eight outta ten people wouldn't have noticed the buffer thing. Most of those would have panicked, frozen up. The others would've tried to move on the guy themselves. You did it right, from soup to nuts."

"Thanks."

Ryan Senior smiled. "Now let's talk about how to break this to your mother. . . ."

They didn't get far before the plane returned to the gate, the front wheels having never even begun their rotation onto the tarmac proper. There was no explanation offered, only a fixed smile and a curt "Will you come with me, please?" to himself and Chavez, followed by the fixed and firm smile that only a professional flight attendant can mount—and one that told Clark the request wasn't open to discussion.

"You forget to pay a parking ticket, Ding?" Clark asked his son-in-law.

"Not me, *mano*. I'm a straight arrow."

Each of them gave his wife a quick kiss and a "Don't worry," then followed the flight attendant up the aisle to the already open door. Waiting for them in the jet bridge was a London Metropolitan Police Service officer. The black-and-white checkerboard pattern on the man's cap told Clark he wasn't your run-of-the-mill bobby, and the patch on his sweater told him he belonged to SCD11—intelligence—part of the Specialist Crime Directorate.

"Sorry to interrupt your jaunt home, gentlemen," the cop said, "but your presence has been requested. If you'll follow me, please."

British manners—along with driving on the wrong side of the road and french fries being called "chips"—was one of the things Clark had never quite gotten used to—especially among the upper echelons of the Army. Polite was always better than rude, mind you, but there was something unnerving about being talked to oh, so civilly by a guy who had probably killed more bad guys than most people would ever see in their lifetime. Clark had met some folks here who could explain in detail how they planned to kill you with a fork, drink your blood, then skin you, all the while making it sound like an invitation to afternoon tea.

Clark and Chavez followed the cop down the jetway, through several checkpoints, then through a card reader–controlled door into Heathrow's security center. They were led to a small conference room where they found Alistair Stanley, still officially second-in-command of Rainbow Six, standing at the diamond-shaped table under the cold glare of fluorescent lights. Stanley was SAS, or Special Air Service, Britain's premier special warfare unit.

Though Clark was reluctant to admit it in mixed company, as far as he was concerned, when it came to efficacy and longevity, the SAS was without peer. Certainly there were outfits out there that were as good as the SAS—his alma mater, the Navy SEALs, came to mind—but the Brits had long ago set the gold standard for modern-era special ops troops, going back as far as 1941 when a Scots Guards officer named Stirling—later of Stirling submachine-gun fame—and his L Detachment of sixty-five men harried the German *Wehrmacht* across North Africa. From their early behind-the-lines sabotage missions in North Africa to Scud hunting in the Iraqi desert, the SAS had done it all, seen it all, and written the book on special ops along the way. And like all his brethren before him, Alistair Stanley was a top-notch troop. In fact, Clark had rarely thought of Stanley as his second but rather his co-commander, so great was his respect for the man.

Along with driving lanes and french fries, SAS organization had been another adjustment for Clark. In characteristically British fashion, the SAS's organization was unique, divided into regiments—the 21st, the 22nd, and the 23rd—and squadrons—ranging from A through G, with a few alphabetical gaps thrown in for good measure. Still, Clark had to further admit, the Brits did everything with flair.

"Alistair," Clark said with a solemn nod. The look on Stanley's face told him something serious had already happened or was in the process of happening.

"Miss us already, Stan?" Ding said, shaking his hand.

"I wish that were it, mate. Feel bloody awful interrupting your trip and all. Thought you boys might like to have one more go before you go soft. Got something interesting in the works."

"From?" Clark asked.

"The Swedes, in a roundabout fashion. Seems they've gone and lost their consulate in Tripoli. Bloody embarrassing for them."

Chavez said, "By 'lost,' I assume you don't mean misplaced?"

"Right, sorry. Typical British understatement. Charming but not always practical. The intelligence is still filtering in, but given the location, it doesn't take much of a leap to venture a guess as to the culprit's general identity."

Clark and Chavez pulled out chairs and sat down at the table. Stanley did the same. He opened a leather portfolio containing a legal pad covered in handwritten notes.

"Let's hear it," Clark said, switching mental gears.

Ten minutes earlier he'd been in civilian mode—or at least as much of a civilian mode as he allowed himself—sitting with his family and getting ready to head home, but that was then and this was now. Now he was the commander of Rainbow Six again. It felt good, he had to admit.

"Best as we can tell, there are eight men in all," Stanley said. "Bypassed the local cops quick as you please with nary a casualty. Satellite images show four Swedes—probably Fallskarmsjagares—down and out within the compound's grounds."

The Fallskarmsjagares were essentially Sweden's version of airborne rangers, culled from the best of the Army. Probably members of the Särskilda Skyddsgruppen—Special Protection

Group—that had been seconded to SÄPO, the Swedish Security Service, for embassy duty.

"Those are some tough boys," Chavez said. "Somebody did their homework—and some good shooting. Anything from inside the consulate?"

Stanley shook his head. "Radio-silent."

Which made sense, Clark decided. Anyone good enough to get into the grounds that quickly and take down four Fallskarmsjagares would also be smart enough to go straight for the communications room.

"Nobody taking credit?" Chavez asked.

"None so far, but that won't last long, I suspect. So far the Libyans have a lid on the press, but it's only a matter of time, I'm afraid."

The hodgepodge of terrorist groups in the Middle East tended to take overlapping credit for any act of significant violence, and it wasn't always about prestige, either, but rather a deliberate attempt to muddy the intelligence waters. It was a lot like what a police homicide unit went through during big murder cases. Quick confessions and nutjob suspects were a dime a dozen, and each one had to be taken seriously, lest you miss a real tango. The same applied to terrorism.

"And no demands, I assume?" Clark added.

"Right."

As often as not there were no demands. In the Middle East most hostage takers just wanted to grow an international audience before they started executing people, only belatedly explaining the whys and wherefores. Not that that made any difference to Clark and his team, but until some government functionary somewhere said "Go," Rainbow was, like every other special ops outfit, at the mercy of politics. Only once the pols had satisfied themselves that unleashing the dogs of war was appropriate did Rainbow get to do what it did best.

"Now here's the tricky part," Stanley said.

"Politics," Clark guessed.

"Right again. As you might imagine, our friend the Colonel wants to send in his Jamahiriyyah—he already has them staged, in fact—but the Swedish Consul General isn't so keen on the idea, what with the Jamahiriyyah's rules of engagement being what they are."

The Jamahiriyyah Guard were essentially Colonel Muammar Qaddafi's own personal Special Forces unit, composed of two thousand or so men drawn from his own backyard, the Surt region of Libya. The Jamahiriyyah were good, Clark knew, and well supported with their own in-house logistics and intelligence units, but the Jamahiriyyah were not known for their discretion, nor for any deep concern for collateral damage, inanimate and animate alike. With the Jamahiriyyah making the assault, the Swedes were likely to lose a fair number of staff.

An interesting bastard, Qaddafi, Clark thought. Like much of the U.S. intelligence community, Clark had his doubts about Qaddafi's recent character transformation from bad boy of North Africa to humanitarian and denouncer of terrorism. The old phrase "a leopard can't change its spots" might be a cliché that rang false for some, but as far as Clark was concerned, Colonel Muammar Abu Minyar al-Qaddafi, "Brotherly Leader and Guide of the Revolution," was a leopard through and through, and would be until the day he died of natural causes or not-so-natural causes.

In 2003, at Qaddafi's command, the Libyan government officially informed the United Nations it was prepared to accept responsibility for the downing of Pan Am 103 over Lockerbie some fifteen years earlier and was further prepared to compensate the victims' families to the tune of nearly $3 billion. The gesture was immediately rewarded with not only praise from the West but also the lifting of economic sanctions and diplomatically couched "attaboys" from many

European countries. And the leopard didn't stop there, first opening up his weapons programs to international inspectors, then denouncing the 9/11 attacks.

Clark had a guess about Qaddafi's change of heart, and it had nothing to do with the mellowing of old age but rather with plain old economics. In other words, oil prices—which had plummeted throughout the '90s, leaving Libya poorer than it had been since camels and not black gold had been king in the desert nation, and less able to fund the Colonel's pet terrorist projects. Of course, Clark reminded himself, Qaddafi's nice-guy routine was probably helped along by the U.S. invasion of Iraq, which he probably saw as just a preview of what could happen to his little fiefdom. In fairness, Clark conceded that it was always better to have a leopard only pretending to change its spots as long as its fangs were in fact blunted. The question was, now that oil prices were back up, would the Colonel be feeling frisky again? Would he use this incident to roar?

"Of course, the Supreme Command in Stockholm wants to call in their own blokes, but Qaddafi is having none of it," Stanley continued. "Last I heard, Rosenbad Street was talking to Downing Street. At any rate, we've been put on standby. Herefordshire is putting out the call for the rest of the team. We've got two on leave—one medical, one on holiday—but the bulk of them should be assembled and equipped within the hour and en route to us shortly after that." Stanley checked his watch. "Say, seventy minutes to wheels up."

"You said 'staged,'" Chavez said. "Staged where?" Time was critical, and even in the fastest of transports, London to Tripoli was a long hop—perhaps longer than the hostages inside that consulate had to live.

"Taranto. The Marina Militare has kindly offered to put us up until the pols sort things out. If we get the call, we're just a skip across the water to Tripoli."

16

Lieutenant Operativnik (Detective) Pavel Rosikhina pulled back the sheet—a tablecloth, really—that some kind soul had draped over the body and stared into the wide-eyed face of what he'd assumed was yet another Mafia execution. Maybe not. Despite the man's pallor, it was clear he wasn't Chechnyan or an ethnic Russian, which surprised him, given their location. A Caucasian Russian. *Interesting.*

The single bullet had entered the man's skull just above and an inch forward of his left ear and exited. . . . Rosikhina leaned over the table, careful to touch nothing but the tablecloth, and peered at the right side of the man's head, which lay resting on the booth's cushioned upper edge. *There.* An egg-sized exit hole behind the man's right ear. The blood and brain matter splattered on the wall behind the booth fit with the bullet's trajectory, which meant the killer would have been standing . . . here. Right in front of the kitchen door. How close would be a matter for the coroner to decide, but looking at the entry wound, Rosikhina knew it wasn't done at close-contact range. There were no powder-burn marks on the skin around the wound, nor any stippling. The wound itself was perfectly round, which further ruled out a contact shot, which usually left behind a distinctive star-shaped rip in the skin. Rosikhina covered his nose against the fecal stink. As did many victims of sudden death, the man's bowels and bladder had relaxed. He carefully pulled back the man's sport coat, first the left side, then the right, patting the pockets for a wallet. There was nothing but a silver ballpoint pen, a white handkerchief, and an extra button for the man's suit coat.

"How close, you think?" he heard, and turned around.

His sometimes partner, Gennady Oleksei, stood a few feet away, cigarette dangling from his half-smiling lips and hands shoved into the pockets of his leather coat.

Over Oleksei's shoulder Rosikhina could see that the uniformed militia officers had finished herding the restaurant's customers out the front door, where they stood milling around, waiting to be questioned. The restaurant's staff—four waiters, a cashier, and three cooks—were seated at the now-empty tables, giving their names to another officer.

Oleksei and Rosikhina worked in the Saint Petersburg militia's Main Office for Combating Financial Crimes, a subdivision of the Criminal Investigations Department. Unlike most Western police agencies, Russian operativniks were not assigned permanent partners. Why this was no one had ever explained to Rosikhina, but he assumed it had something to do with funding. Everything had to do with funding, from whether they got their own cars from week to week to whether they worked alone or with partners.

"You're assigned?" Rosikhina asked.

"Called me at home. How close?" Oleksei repeated.

"Two to six feet. Easy shot." He noticed something lying on the seat behind the victim's buttocks. He leaned over for a closer look. "Got a gun," he told Oleksei. "Semiautomatic. Looks like a Makarov. He was trying, at least. A second faster on the draw and maybe . . ."

"Now, there's a question for you," Oleksei said. "Would you rather go like our friend here, knowing it was coming, or would you rather just . . . poof. Be gone. Nothing."

"Good Christ, Gennady . . ."

"Come on, play along."

Rosikhina sighed. "I guess I'd rather go in my sleep—a hundred years old and lying next to Natalia."

"Pavel, Pavel . . . You never humor me."

"Sorry. I don't like this. Something's off. It feels like and looks like your standard Mafia hit, but this sure isn't your standard victim—not sitting in a place like this, at least."

"He was either very brave or very stupid," Oleksei said.

"Or desperate." To come into a place like this, their Caucasian Russian victim had to be in search of something more than a good bowl of *djepelgesh* and some of that god-awful pondur music—music that sounded to Pavel like cats in heat.

"Or really hungry," Oleksei added. "Another boss, maybe? He doesn't look familiar, but he could be on the books."

"I doubt it. They never travel without their own little army. Even if somebody had managed to get to him here and put a bullet into his head at this range, his bodyguards would have started a god-awful firefight. There'd be holes everywhere, and a lot more bodies. No, we've got one bullet and one dead man. Very deliberate. An ambush, professionally done. The question is, who is he and why was he important enough to kill?"

"Well, we're not going to get any answers out of this bunch."

Rosikhina knew his partner was right. Fear of, or loyalty to, the Obshina tended to silence even the most helpful of souls. The witness reports would invariably fall into one of three general categories: I saw nothing; someone in a mask ran in, shot the man, and ran out, it all happened so fast; and Rosikhina's favorite, *Ya ne govo'ryu po russki*. I don't speak Russian.

And of those accounts, the only true statement they'd get was likely the last one: It all happened so fast. Not that he blamed any of them. The Krasnaya Mafiya, or Bratva (brotherhood), or Obshina—whatever the name or denomination—was ruthless beyond compare. Witnesses and their entire families were often targeted for death simply because some boss in some dark basement somewhere had decided the person might have information they might disclose to authorities. And it wasn't merely a matter of dying, Rosikhina reminded himself. The Mafia was often ingenious and unhurried in its execution methods. What, he wondered, would he do in similar circumstances?

Though the Mafia generally refrained from killing militia officers—it was bad for business—it had happened in the past.
Armed and trained as they were, cops could protect themselves,
but the average citizen, the teacher or factory worker or accoun-
tant, what chance did they have? None, really. The militia had
neither the money nor the manpower to protect every witness,
and the average citizen knew it, so they kept their mouths shut
and kept their heads down. Even now, some of the restaurant's
patrons were terrified for their lives, having simply been in the
wrong place at the wrong time. It was a wonder places like this
managed to stay open at all.

It was that kind of fear, Rosikhina thought, that made
people wish for the old days, the return of Stalinesque control
of the country, and in many ways Putin was doing just that
with his "reform programs." There was no middle ground
with that, though. As long as there were political freedoms,
personal rights, and an open market in Russia, there would be
crime, both large and small—and there was in Stalin's time,
too, but not nearly as much. But that argument was something
of a straw man, wasn't it? Something that old communist
hard-liners and ultranationalists used to decry democracy and
capitalism, all the while forgetting or ignoring that the iron-
fisted control of Soviet Russia had come at a high price indeed.
What was that old saying? Hardship truncates memory?
Rosikhina's father, a Yakut fisherman by birth, had his own
take on the concept: "When you've got a shrew for a wife,
even the ugliest ex-girlfriend looks enticing." And that, he
knew, was what Soviet Russia really was, an ugly ex-girlfriend.
Certainly she had her positive traits, but nothing you'd like to
be reunited with. Unfortunately, that wasn't an opinion many
of his fellow citizens—some forty percent of them, according to the latest polls, suspect as they may be—shared. Or
maybe it was what Oleksei had once accused him of being, a
cockeyed optimist. Or was it "blind optimist"?

Now he gazed out the front windows of the restaurant, watching the grim-faced customers standing in tight clusters, their breath steaming in the cold night air, and wondered if his optimism was in fact unwarranted. A restaurant of thirty or so people who'd just twenty minutes earlier watched a man's brains get blown out the side of his skull, and not a one would probably lift a finger to help them catch the killer.

"True, but you never know," Rosikhina replied. "Better to ask and be surprised than the converse, don't you think?"

Oleksei shrugged and smiled as only a Russian fatalist can. What can you do? Not much excited Oleksei; his composure was as permanent as the cigarette he seemed to always be smoking.

Then again, on rare occasions a few useful witness details would inadvertently slip through and give them something to pick at. More often, though, the statements were vague or contradictory, or both, leaving investigators with nothing but what they could glean from the body or bodies left behind.

"Besides," Rosikhina said, "without all those useless witness statements to process, we won't have four glorious hours of paperwork and bad coffee ahead of us."

"Four hours? If we're lucky."

"Damn it, where's the coroner?"

Until the victim was officially pronounced dead, the body would remain where it was, dead and glazed eyes staring at the ceiling.

"He's on his way," Oleksei said. "I checked before I came. Busy night, I guess."

Rosikhina leaned over and snagged the gun's trigger guard with his index finger and lifted it from the seat. "Nine millimeter." He ejected the magazine and cycled back the slide. A bullet tumbled out of the chamber and clinked onto the floor.

"Well, he was ready for something. Any missing?"

Rosikhina shook his head and sniffed the barrel. "Happened

too fast, I suspect. Recently cleaned. Well, I'll be damned. . . . Look, of all things, Gennady, the serial number's been erased."

"Will miracles never cease?"

Bad guys often acid-erased the serial numbers on murder weapons but rarely re-inscribed them. If that was the case here, the Makarov's number might actually lead somewhere. Cockeyed optimism.

And probably misplaced, Rosikhina reminded himself.

As often happened in homicide cases, whether in the West or in Moscow, Lieutenant Rosikhina and Oleksei would learn little either from those present in the restaurant at the time of the murder or from the canvass of the surrounding neighborhood. The Chechnyan community was tight-knit, distrusting of the police, and deeply afraid of the Obshina. And with good reason. Its brutality knew few bounds. A witness would pay not only with his own life but with those of his family as well, a spectacle which he'd likely be forced to watch before he, too, was killed. The prospect of seeing one's children carved up with a hacksaw tended to close loose lips. Even so, Rosikhina had little choice but to go through the motions of taking statements, however unproductive, and tracking down leads, however insubstantial.

They would diligently work the murder, but in the end what few small leads they had would evaporate and they'd be forced to set the case aside. With this thought, Rosikhina looked sadly at the victim. "Sorry, my friend."

17

It was a funny thing, Jack Ryan Jr. thought, that there'd been no congratulatory replies to the birth announcement. Not one. He had everything cross-filed on his computer, all of it in the terabytes of RAM on The Campus's monstrous server, and he called up the most recent documents, making a written note of initiator and recipient, but those were always nothing more than an alphanumeric handle that might or might not have a relationship to their real names. Jack extended his search of past e-mails to six months prior and ran a quick spreadsheet. Sure enough, the traffic had been steady, rarely varying more than five percent from month to month. And now, within days of the birth announcement, a precipitous drop. In fact, aside from a few routine messages that had probably been sent before the announcement and had been stuck in cyberspace, there were *no* e-mails. The Emir and his URC—the Umayyad Revolutionary Council—had in essence gone radio-silent, and that thought gave Jack a chill. There were three options: Either they'd switched communication protocols as a general security measure, or they'd somehow figured out someone was reading their mail, or this was an OpSec change, a zipping of the electronic lips prior to a high-level operation. The first two options were possible but unlikely. The URC had changed its procedures little in the last nine months, and The Campus had been careful not to tip its hand. So option three. There was precedent, of course. Just before 9/11, Al-Qaeda standard electronic chatter level dropped like a stone; so, too, with the Japanese before Pearl Harbor. Part of Jack wanted his hypothesis to be proven out; another part hoped to hell he was wrong.

How, then, would the Emir get his messages out? Couriers were the most secure method, if not the quickest: Write up the messages, burn the disk, and have someone take it for a handoff rendezvous. With modern air travel, a man could get from Chicago to Calcutta in less than a day, so long as he didn't mind airline food. Hell, international air travel was designed with that idea in mind, wasn't it? It might have been designed with the "black" community in mind, not just the sales force of Frederick's of Hollywood or Dow Chemical.

Chicago to Calcutta. What if the Emir was in Chicago, or New York, or Miami? What was to stop him from living there? Not a goddamned thing. The CIA and everyone else assumed he was somewhere in the Stans—why? Because that was the last place they'd known him to be. Not because of any evidence that would place him anywhere. And there was a good half of the United States government's Special Forces in Pakistan and Afghanistan beating the bushes and looking into every hole in the rocks, asking endless questions, tossing money around, looking for the one man—or woman—who might know his face and might know where he might be. And still nothing. What were the odds of that? Jack wondered.

A man like the Emir could never feel secure enough, not with every intelligence agency in the world looking for him—even dedicated, patriotic intelligence officers could look at the public reward America had placed on his head and think of a nice house on the Riviera and a comfortable retirement, just for one phone call and a little bit of information. . . .

The Emir would know all of that. He'd limit the number of people who knew his location. He'd limit that number to people whom he could absolutely trust, and he'd take good care of them. The best of care. Money, comfort, such luxuries as circumstances permitted. He'd reinforce their desire to earn his trust. He'd reinforce their faith in Allah and in himself, be solicitous as hell to them. But he would also maintain his aura of command, because the source of that authority was always on a man-to-man basis, as with all the really important things in life, a thing of the mind.

So what would it take for the Emir to relocate beyond Pakistan and Afghanistan? How does one go about moving the most wanted man on the face of the earth?

The CIA's master file on the Emir had mediocre photos, some of them raw and some digitally enhanced, all of which had been distributed to virtually every intelligence and police agency in the world. Same with the general public. If Brad Pitt and Angelina Jolie can't go out to Sunday brunch without being mobbed, the Emir would certainly find it difficult to travel beyond his regular stomping grounds.

The Emir couldn't change his height, though it *was* technically possible, but it involved major and somewhat painful surgery, followed by a lengthy recovery period, which would necessitate being immobile for several weeks—bad joss for a guy on the run. He could change his face, his skin color, his hair. He could wear colored contact lenses to change his eye color and maybe improve his eyesight, which, the file said, was about average. He walked erectly, not slumped over, and the talk about how he suffered from Marfan syndrome had been shot down by a doc at Johns Hopkins who was an expert in the disorder, rather to Langley's surprise, as that had become gospel to the intelligence community. So he did *not* need a dialysis machine in constant proximity.

Wait a second, Jack. The intel community had been assuming a lot about the Emir. They'd gotten, what, one opinion on the Marfan angle? Was that enough to discount the theory? As far as Jack could tell, no one had ever laid hands on someone close enough to the Emir to know one way or another. Something to think about.

"Hey, Jack," said a familiar voice. He turned to see Dominic and Brian standing in the doorway.

"Hey, guys, come on in. What's happening?"

Each brother took a chair. Dominic said, "Reading a computer all morning gives me a headache, so I came up to harass you. Whatcha reading? Application to the Treasury Department?"

It took a moment for Jack to get it. Treasury oversaw the Secret Service. These kind of jokes had been coming since the Georgetown thing. While the press was giving the incident heavy coverage, his name had so far remained out of it, which suited him just fine. Hendley knew the whole story, of course, which didn't bother Jack at all. More ammunition when it came to pitch his boss.

"Smart-ass," Jack shot back.

"They know anything about the mutt?" Brian asked.

"Not that I've heard. The press is saying no accomplices, but in something like this they only get what the Secret Service wants them to get." In a town where leaks were more the rule than the exception, the Secret Service knew how to run a tight ship. Jack changed the subject. "You heard about the Marfan theory, right? About the Emir?"

"Yeah, I think so," Dominic replied. "Didn't pan out, right?"

Jack shrugged. "Trying to think outside the box. His location, for example: My gut tells me he's not in Afghanistan, but we've never thought beyond there or Pakistan. What if we should be? He's got all kinds of money, and money buys you a lot of flexibility."

Brian shrugged. "Still, kinda hard to imagine a guy like that getting even fifty miles away from his bolt-hole without being spotted."

"Assumptions and intel analysis are dangerous bedfellows," Jack observed.

"True. If he's moved on, I bet that fucker's laughing his ass off watching everybody hump those mountains looking for him. How would he do it, though? Sure as hell couldn't just walk into the Islamabad airport and ask for a ticket."

Dominic said, "Money can buy you a lot of knowledge, too."

"What do you mean?" Jack asked.

"There's an expert for every problem, Jack. The trick is knowing where to look."

The day passed quickly. At five, Jack poked his head into Dominic's office. Brian was sitting in the chair across from his brother's desk. "Hey, guys," Jack called.

"Yo," Brian responded. "How's the computer maven?"

"Chipping away."

"What's for dinner?" Dominic wondered.

"Open for ideas."

"His love life must be like mine," Brian muttered.

"Found a new place in Baltimore. Wanna give it a try?"

"Sure." *What the hell,* Jack thought. Eating alone was never fun.

The three-car convoy headed north on U.S. 29, then turned east on U.S. 40 for the trip into Baltimore's Little Italy—nearly every American city has one—off Eastern Avenue. The trip was almost identical to Jack's normal drive home, a few blocks from the baseball stadium at Camden Yards. But that season had ended, again without a trip into the playoffs.

Baltimore's Little Italy is a rabbit warren of narrow streets and few parking lots, and for Jack, parking his Hummer was not unlike bringing an ocean liner alongside. But in due course he found a spot in a small parking lot and then walked the two blocks to the restaurant on High Street, which specialized in Northern Italian food. On walking in, he saw that his cousins were camped out in a corner booth, with nobody else close by.

"How's the food here?" he asked, taking a seat.

"The head chef is as good as our grandfather, and that's high praise, Jack. The veal is really first-class. They say he buys it himself every day at Lexington Market."

"Must be tough, being a cow," Jack observed, scanning the menu.

"Never asked," Brian noted. "Never heard any complaints, though."

"Talk to my sister. She's turning into a vegan, except for the shoes." Jack chuckled. "How's the wine list?"

"Ordered," the Marine responded. "Lacrima Christi del

Vesuvio. I discovered it in Naples on a Med cruise. The Tears of Christ from Vesuvius. Took a trip to Pompeii, and the guide said they've been growing wine grapes there for about two thousand years, and I assumed they have it pretty well figured out. If you don't like it, I'll drink it all," Brian promised.

"Brian knows his wine, Jack," Dominic said.

"You say it like you're surprised," Brian shot back. "I'm not your typical jarhead, you know."

"I stand corrected."

The bottle came a minute later. The waiter opened it with a flourish.

"Where do you eat in Naples?"

"My boy, you have to work real hard to find a bad restaurant in Italy," Dominic told him. "The stuff you buy on the street is as good as most sit-down restaurants over here. But this place is seriously okay. He's a *paisano*."

Brian tuned in: "In Naples, there's a place on the waterfront called La Bersagliera, about a mile from the big fortress. Now, I'll risk a fistfight and say that's the best restaurant in the entire world."

"No. Rome, Alfonso Ricci's, 'bout half a mile east of Vatican City," Dominic pronounced.

"Guess I'll take your word for it."

The food came, along with more wine, and the conversation turned to women. All three dated, but casually. The Carusos joked that they were looking for the perfect Italian girl; for Jack's part, he was looking for a girl he could "bring home to Mom."

"So what're you saying, cuz?" Brian asked. "You don't like 'em a little slutty?"

"In the bedroom, hell, yes," Jack replied. "But out in public . . . Not a big fan of halter tops and giant tramp stamps."

Dominic chuckled at this. "Brian, what was the name of that girl, you know the one, the stripper with the tattoo?"

"Ah, shit . . ."

Dominic was still laughing. He turned to Jack and said, half conspiratorially, "She had this tattoo just below her belly button: a downward arrow with the words *Slippery When Wet*. Problem was, she spelled *slippery* with one *p*."

Jack burst out laughing. "What was her name?"

Brian shook his head. "No way."

"Tell him," Dominic said.

"Come on," Jack prodded.

"Candy."

More laughter. "Spelled with a *y* or an *ie*?" Jack asked.

"Neither. Two *e*'s. Okay, okay, so she wasn't the brightest bulb. We weren't exactly on the marriage track. What about you, Jack? What's your taste? Jessica Alba, maybe? Scarlett Johansson?"

"Charlize Theron."

"Good choice," Dominic observed.

From a nearby stool at the bar they heard, "I'd go for Holly Madison. Great boobs."

The three of them turned to see a woman smiling at them. She was a redhead, tall, with green eyes and a wide smile. "Just my two cents," she added.

"The woman has a point," Dominic observed. "Then again, if we're talking about intellect . . ."

"Intellect?" the woman replied. "I thought we were talking about sex. If you're going to bring brainpower into it, then I'd have to go with . . . Paris Hilton."

There were a few moments of silence before the woman's deadpan expression showed a hint of a smile. Jack, Dominic, and Brian burst out lauging. The Marine said, "I suppose now would be the time to ask if you want to join us."

"Love to."

She picked up her freshly refilled glass of wine and moved to their table, taking a seat beside Dominic. "I'm Wendy," she said. "Spelled with a *y* on the end," she added. "Sorry, I couldn't help eavesdropping." She said to Dominic, "So we know Jack likes Charlize and Brian goes for dyslexic strippers—"

"That hurts," Brian said.

"—but what about you?"

"You want my real answer?"

"Of course."

"It's going to sound like a line."

"Try me."

"I prefer redheads."

Jack groaned. "So smooth."

Wendy studied Dominic's face for moment. "He's telling the truth, I think."

"He is," Brian confirmed. "He's still got a poster of Lucille Ball in his room."

General laughter.

"Bullshit, bro." To Wendy: "You meeting someone?"

"I was. A girlfriend. She texted me, said she couldn't make it."

The four of them ate dinner, shared more wine, and talked until nearly eleven, when Jack announced he was going home. Brian, having seen the same signs his cousin had, bowed out as well, and soon Dominic and Wendy were alone. They chatted for a few more minutes before she said, "So . . ."

The opening was there, and Dominic took it. "You wanna get out of here?"

Wendy smiled at him. "My place is a couple blocks from here."

They were kissing before the elevator doors closed, parted briefly when the car reached her floor, then moved together to her door, then inside, where the clothes started coming off. Once in the bedroom, Wendy wriggled the rest of the way out of her dress, revealing a lacy black bra and matching panties. She sat down on the bed before Dominic, grabbed the end of his belt, whipped it free, then lay back on the bed. "Your turn." A lock of red hair had fallen over one of Wendy's eyes.

"Wow," Dominic breathed.

"I'll take that as a compliment," she replied with a giggle.

Dominic took off his pants and got onto the bed. They kissed for thirty seconds before Wendy pulled away. She rolled over and opened her nightstand drawer. "A little something to set the mood," she said, looking back at him, then rolled over with a tiny rectangular mirror and a thumb-sized glass vial.

"What's that?" Dominic asked.

"It'll make it better," Wendy said.

Ah, shit, Dominic thought. She saw his expression change and said, "What?"

"This isn't going to work."

"Why, what's the matter? It's just a little coke."

Dominic got up, retrieved his pants, and slipped them on.

"You're going?" Wendy said, sitting up.

"Yep."

"You're kidding me? Just because of—"

"Yep."

"God, what's your problem?"

Dominic didn't answer. He grabbed his shirt from the floor and slipped it on. He headed for the door.

"You're an asshole," Wendy said.

Dominic stopped and turned around. He fished his wallet from his pants and flipped it open to reveal his FBI badge.

"Oh, shit," Wendy whispered. "I didn't . . . Are you going to—"

"No. This is your lucky day."

He walked out.

*

Tariq Himsi was contemplating the power of money. And the vagaries of choice. Finding the Emir a companion, even for a fleeting assignation, was a delicate proposition. His tastes were specific; his security paramount. Fortunately, the whores here were plentiful, easy to find on the street, and, as it turned out, quite accustomed to unusual requests, such as being driven to an undisclosed location in a vehicle with blacked-out windows. His earlier surveillance had shown that while morally corrupt, these women were far from stupid: They patrolled their corners in twos and threes, and whenever one of their cohorts got into a car, one of the others would take down the license plate number. A quick trip to one of the local airport's off-property park-and-ride lots had solved this problem. License plates were easy to install and even easier to dispose of. Almost as easy as disguising his appearance with thick black glasses and a baseball cap.

Tariq had initially considered engaging an escort service, but that brought its own complications—not insurmountable, certainly, but complicated nonetheless. Through their network here he had obtained the name of a service known for zealously protecting its clients' privacy, so much so that it was used by many celebrities and politicians, including several U.S. senators. The irony of using such a service was tempting, Tariq had to admit.

For now he would satisfy himself with engaging one of the street whores he'd been observing for the last week. Though she generally dressed as did all the others—in obnoxiously revealing outfits—her taste seemed slightly less appalling, her manner slightly less shameless. In the short term, she would do as a receptacle.

He waited until well after the sun had set, then waited down the block, watching for a lull in traffic before pulling out and driving down to where the woman and her two companions stood. He pulled to a halt beside the curb and rolled down the passenger window. One of the women, a redhead with impossibly large breasts, strode toward the window.

"Not you," Tariq said. "The other one. The tall blonde."

"Suit yourself, mister. Hey, Trixie, he wants you."

Trixie sashayed over. "Hey," she said. "Looking for a date?"

"For a friend."

"Where is this friend?"

"At his condominium."

"Don't do in-home dates."

"Two thousand dollars," Tariq replied, and immediately saw Trixie's eyes change. "Your friends may take down my license plate, if they wish. My friend is . . . well known. He simply wants some anonymous companionship."

"Straight sex?"

"Pardon me?"

"I don't do rough trade. No water sports, nothing like that."

"Of course."

"Okay, hang on a sec, hon." Trixie walked back to her friends, exchanged a few words, then returned to Tariq, who said, "You may ride in the back," and clicked open the lock.

"Oh, hey, fancy," Trixie said, and got in.

"Please sit down," the Emir said to her thirty minutes later, as Tariq brought her into the living room and made the introductions. "Would you like some wine?"

"Uh, sure, I guess," Trixie said. "I like that zinfandel stuff. That's how you say it, right?"

"Yes." The Emir signaled to Tariq, who disappeared and returned a minute later with two glasses of wine. Trixie took hers, looked around anxiously, then dug in her purse and came up with a tissue, into which she spit the piece of gum she'd been chewing. She took a gulp of wine. "Pretty good stuff."

"Yes, it is. Is Trixie your real name?"

"Yeah, actually. What's yours?"

"Believe it or not, my name is John."

Trixie barked out a laugh. "If you say so. So, what, you're Arab or something?"

Standing in the doorway behind Trixie, Tariq's brows furrowed. The Emir lifted his index finger from the arm of his chair. Tariq nodded and stepped back a few feet.

"I'm from Italy," the Emir said. "Sicily."

"Hey, like *The Godfather,* right?"

"Pardon me?"

"You know, the movie. That's where the Corleones were from: Sicily."

"I suppose so, yes."

"Your accent sounds kind of funny. You live here, or just on vacation?"

"Vacation."

"It's a really nice house. You must be loaded, huh?"

"The house belongs to a friend."

Trixie smiled. "A friend, huh? Maybe your friend would like some company."

"I'll be sure to ask him," the Emir said drily.

"Just so you know: I only do straight, okay? Nothing kinky."

"Of course, Trixie."

"And no kissing on the mouth. Your guy said two thousand?"

"Would you like your reimbursement now?"

Trixie took another gulp of wine. "My what?"

"Your money."

"Sure, then we can get started." At the Emir's signal, Tariq came forward and handed Trixie a wad of $100 bills. "No offense," she said, then counted the bills. "You wanna do it here, or what?"

An hour later the Emir emerged from the bedroom. Behind him, Trixie was slipping on her panties and humming to herself. At the dining room table, Tariq stood up to meet his boss. The Emir merely said, "Too many questions."

A few minutes later in the garage, Tariq walked around the car to the rear door and opened it for her. "That was fun," she said. "If your guy wants to do it again, you know where to find me."

"I'll inform him."

As Trixie ducked down to enter the car, Tariq toe-kicked her behind the knee and she dropped down. "Hey, what—" were the only words she managed to get out before Tariq's garrote, a two-foot piece of half-inch smooth nylon rope, looped around her neck and cinched down on her windpipe.

As he'd planned, the rope's twin knots, spaced five inches apart in the middle of the rope, immediately compressed the carotid arteries on either side of her trachea. Trixie began bucking, clawing at the rope, her back arching until Tariq could see her eyes—at first wide and bulging, and then slowly, as the blood flow to her brain dwindled, fluttering and rolling back into her head. After another ten seconds Trixie went limp. Tariq kept the pressure on the rope for another three minutes, standing perfectly still as the life slowly drained from her body. Strangulation was never the quick task one saw in Hollywood movies.

He took two steps backward, dragging her along and slowly laying her body flat on the garage's concrete floor. Carefully he unwrapped the rope from around her neck, then examined the skin beneath. There was some slight bruising but no blood. Even so, the rope would later be burned in a steel pail. He felt for a pulse at her neck and found none. She was dead, of that he was certain, but given their circumstances, an extra measure of caution was required.

Placing one hand beneath her shoulders and the other beneath her buttocks, Tariq rolled Trixie onto her stomach, then straddled her at the waist. He placed his left hand beneath her chin, drew her head up toward him, then placed the flat of his right palm on the side of her head and levered his hands in opposite directions. The neck snapped. He reversed his hands and twisted the head back in the other direction, getting one more muffled pop. The body's residual nerve impulses caused her legs to jerk once. He gently lowered the head back to the ground and stood up.

Now all that remained was to decide how far into the desert to drive her.

18

The reception they received upon touching down in Tripoli should have told Clark and Chavez all they needed to know about the mood of Colonel Muammar Qaddafi and his generals, as well as what level of support they could expect. The People's Militia lieutenant they found waiting at the bottom of the plane's stairs was polite enough but green as the Libyan sun was hot, and the twitch under his left eye told Clark the man knew enough about his charges to be nervous. *Good for you, boy.* Clearly Qaddafi was less than pleased to have Western soldiers on his soil, let alone Western Special Forces soldiers. Whether his displeasure was born of pride or some deeper political motive Clark neither knew nor cared. As long as they stayed out of Rainbow's way and didn't get anyone inside the embassy killed, Muammar could be as pissy as he liked.

The lieutenant snapped off a sharp salute to Clark, said "Masudi," which Clark assumed was his name, then stepped aside and gestured toward a circa-1950 canvas canopied Army truck that sat idling fifty feet away. Clark gave the nod to

Stanley, who ordered the team to gather the gear and head toward the truck.

The sun was so hot it almost stung Clark's skin, and sucking the superheated air into his lungs caused them to burn a bit. There was a slight breeze fluttering the flags on the hangar roof but not nearly enough to provide any cooling.

"Hell, at least they sent somebody, huh?" Chavez muttered to Clark as they walked.

"Always look on the bright side, eh, Ding?"

"You got it, *mano*."

Within an hour of being pulled off the plane at Heathrow and getting the dump from Alistair Stanley, Clark, Chavez, and the remainder of the on-call R6 shooters were aboard a British Airways jet bound for Italy.

As did all military teams, Rainbow had its fair share of personnel turnover as men returned to their home country's unit, most of them for well-earned promotions after their work on Rainbow. Of the eight Stanley had picked for the op, four were originals: Master Chief Miguel Chin, Navy SEAL; Homer Johnston; Louis Loiselle; and Dieter Weber. Two Americans, a Frenchman, a German. Johnston and Loiselle were their snipers, and each was scary-good, their rounds rarely finding anything but X-ring.

In fact, all of them were good shooters. He wasn't in the least worried about them; you didn't get to Rainbow without, one, having a lot of time in service, and two, being the best of the best. And you certainly didn't stay in Rainbow without passing muster with Alistair Stanley, who was, though polite to the core, a real ass-kicker. *Better to sweat in training than to bleed on an op,* Clark reminded himself. It was an old SEAL adage, one that any Special Forces service worth a damn adhered to as if it were the word of God.

After a brief stop in Rome they were shuttled to a waiting Piaggio P180 Avanti twin-engine turboprop kindly supplied by the 28th Army Aviation "Tucano" Squadron for the final hop to Taranto, where they sat and drank Chinotto, Italy's herbal answer to American Sprite, while getting a history lesson from the base's public-affairs officer on the history of Taranto, the Marina Militare, and its predecessor, the Regia Marina. After four hours of this, Stanley's satellite phone went off. The politics had been settled. How they'd talked Qaddafi out of sending in his shock troops Clark didn't know, and he didn't care. Rainbow was green-lit.

An hour later they reboarded the Avanti for the five-hundred-mile hop across the Med to Tripoli.

Clark followed Chavez to the truck and climbed aboard. Sitting across the wooden bench seat from him was a man in civilian clothes.

"Tad Richards," the man said, shaking Clark's hand, "U.S. embassy."

Clark didn't bother asking the man's position. The answer would likely involve a combination of words like *attaché, cultural, junior,* and *state department,* but he was in fact a member of CIA station Libya, which worked out of the embassy in the Corinthia Bab Africa Hotel. Like the People's Militia lieutenant who'd greeted them, Richards looked too fresh by half. Probably his first overseas posting, Clark decided. Didn't matter, really. As long as the man had the intel dump for them.

With the crunching of gears and a plume of diesel exhaust, the truck lurched forward and started moving.

"Sorry for the delay," Richards said.

Clark shrugged, noting that the man hadn't asked for names. *Maybe a little sharper than I thought.* He said, "I gather the colonel is less than enthusiastic about hosting us."

"You gather correctly. Not sure of the hows, but the phones have been nuts for the past eight hours. Army's got extra security posted around the hotel."

This made sense. Whether a real threat or not, the Libyan

148

government's enhanced "protection" of the U.S. embassy was certainly a signal: The people of Libya were so unhappy about having Western soldiers on their soil that attacks on American assets were possible. It was crap, of course, but Muammar had to walk the fine line between being America's newest ally in North Africa and presiding over a population that was still largely sympathetic to the Palestinian cause and therefore unsympathetic to their oppressors, the United States and Israel.

"The joy of international politics," Clark observed.

"Amen."

"You got Arabic?"

"Yeah, passable. Getting better. Working on a level-three Rosetta Stone course."

"Good. I'll need you to stick around, translate for us."

"You got it."

"You have intel for us?"

Richards nodded, wiping his sweating forehead with a handkerchief. "They've got a command post set up on the top floor of an apartment building a block from the embassy. I'll show you what we've got when we get there."

"Fair enough," Clark replied. "Any contact from inside the compound?"

"None."

"How many hostages?"

"According to the Swedish foreign ministry, sixteen."

"What've they done so far? The locals, I mean."

"Nothing, as far as we can tell, beyond setting up a perimeter and keeping the civilians and reporters back."

"The news broke?" Chavez asked.

Richards nodded. "Couple hours ago, while you were in the air. Sorry, forgot to tell you."

Clark asked, "Utilities?"

"Water and electricity are still running to the compound."

Cutting off these essentials was near the top of the to-do list for any hostage situation. This was important for two reasons: One, no matter how tough they were, a lack of amenities would begin to wear on the bad guys. And two, the resumption of water and electricity could be used during negotiations: Give us five hostages and we'll turn your air-conditioning back on.

Here again, the Libyan government, having gotten the political "butt the fuck out," was washing its hands of the situation. This could work in their favor, however. Unless the bad guys inside the embassy were complete idiots, they would have taken note of the utilities and perhaps made some guesses about what was happening outside, assuming that the security forces were either unprepared or waiting to cut the power in advance of an assault.

Maybe . . . if, Clark thought. Hard to get into anyone's head, let alone some dirtball who thinks it's okay to take hostage a bunch of innocent civilians. It was just as likely the bad guys weren't strategic thinkers at all and hadn't given a second thought to the power-and-water question. Still, they'd been good enough to dispatch those Särskilda Skyddsgruppens, which at the very least suggested Rainbow was dealing with people with some training. Didn't matter, really. There was none better than Rainbow, of that Clark was certain. Whatever the situation inside, it'd get sorted out—and most likely to the detriment of the bad guys.

The trip took twenty minutes. Clark spent most of it running scenarios in his head and watching the dusty, ochre-colored roads of Tripoli skim past the end of the tailgate. Finally the truck grumbled to a stop in an alley whose front and rear entrances were shaded by a pair of date palms. Lieutenant Masudi appeared at the rear and dropped the tailgate. Richards climbed out and led Clark and Stanley down the alley, while Chavez and the others gathered the gear and followed. Richards took them up two flights of stone stairs mounted on the stone wall's exterior, then through a door into a half-finished apartment. Stacks of drywall lay against the wall along with five-gallon tubs of Sheetrock mud. Of the four walls, only two were finished, these painted a shade of sea-foam green that belonged in an episode of *Miami Vice*. The room smelled of fresh paint. A large picture window framed by date palms overlooked at a distance of two hundred meters what Clark assumed was the Swedish embassy, a Spanish-style two-story villa surrounded by eight-foot-high white stucco walls topped with black wrought-iron spikes. The building's ground floor sported plenty of windows, but all of them were barred and shuttered.

Six thousand square feet at least, Clark thought sourly. *A lot of territory. Plus maybe a basement.*

He had half expected to find a colonel or general or two from the People's Militia waiting for them, but there was no one. Evidently, Masudi was to be their only contact with the Libyan government, which suited Clark fine, as long as the man had the requisite horsepower to provide what they requested.

The street below looked like a damned military parade. Of the two visible streets adjacent to the embassy, Clark counted no fewer than six Army vehicles, two jeeps and four trucks, each surrounded by a group of soldiers, smoking and milling about, bolt-action rifles casually dangling from their shoulders. If he hadn't already known it, the soldiers' weapons would have told Clark everything he needed to know about Qaddafi's attitude toward the crisis. Having been pushed out of the loop in his own country, the colonel had taken his elite troops off the perimeter and replaced them with the shabbiest grunts he could field.

Like a spoiled little boy taking his marbles and going home.

While Chavez and the others started unpacking the gear and sorting it in the unfinished breakfast nook, Clark and

Stanley surveyed the embassy compound through binoculars. Richards and Lieutenant Masudi stood off to one side. After two minutes of silence, Stanley said without lowering his binoculars, "Tough one."

"Yep," Clark answered. "You see any movement?"

"No. Those are plantation shutters. Good and solid."

"Fixed surveillance camera on each corner, just below the eaves, and two along the front façade."

"Best assume the same for the rear façade," Stanley replied. "The question is, did the security folks have time to mash the button?"

Most embassies had an emergency checklist that any security detail worth a damn would know by heart. At the top of the list, titled "In Case of Armed Intrusion and Embassy Takeover" or something similar, would be an instruction to fatally disable the facility's external surveillance system. Blind bad guys are easier to take down. Whether or not the Swedes had done this there was no way of telling, so Rainbow would assume the cameras were not only functional but also being monitored. The good news was the cameras were fixed, which made it much easier to pick out blind spots and coverage gaps.

Clark said, "Richards, when's sunset?"

"Three hours, give or take. Weather report is for clear skies."

Shit, Clark thought. Operating in a desert climate could be a pain in the ass. Tripoli had a bit of pollution, but nothing like a Western metropolis, so the ambient light from the moon and stars would make movement tricky. A lot would depend on how many bad guys were inside and where they were positioned. If they had enough bodies, they'd almost certainly have surveillance posted, but that wasn't anything Johnston and Loiselle couldn't handle. Still, any approach on the compound would have to be planned carefully.

"Johnston . . ." Clark called.

"Yeah, boss."

"Go for a stroll. Pick your perches, then come back and sketch it out for coverage and fields of fire. Richards, tell our escort to pass the word: Let our men work and don't get in their way."

"Okay." Richards took Masudi by the elbow, moved him a few feet away, then started talking. After half a minute, Masudi nodded and left.

"We have blueprints?" Stanley asked Richards.

The embassy man checked his watch. "Should be here within the hour."

"From Stockholm?"

Richards gave a negative shake of his head. "Here. Interior ministry."

"Christ."

There was no use having them transmitted in piecemeal JPEGs, either. No guarantee they'd be any better than what they already had—unless the Libyans were willing to take the shots to a professional printer and have the pieces stitched together. Clark wasn't going to hold his breath for that.

"Hey, Ding?"

"Here, boss."

Clark handed him the binoculars. "Take a look." Along with Dieter Weber, Chavez would be leading one of the two assault teams.

Chavez scanned the building for sixty seconds, then handed back the binoculars. "Basement?"

"Don't know yet."

"Bad guys usually like to hunker down, so I'd say they're concentrated on the first floor, or in the basement if there is one, though that's iffy—unless they're really dumb."

No exits belowground, Clark thought.

"If we can halfway nail down where the hostages are and whether they're lumped together or split up . . . But if I had to make a snap call, I'd say enter on the second floor, south and east walls, clear that level, and then head down. Standard small-unit tactics, really. Take the high points on the map and the bad guys are at an automatic disadvantage."

"Go on," Clark said.

"The first-floor windows are out. We could handle the bars, but not quickly, and it would make a lot of noise. But those balconies . . . the railing looks pretty solid. Should be easy to get up there. A lot's going to depend on the layout. If it's more open, not too broken up, I say start high. Otherwise, we rattle their cages with some flashbangs, breach the walls in a couple places with Gatecrashers, then swarm 'em."

Clark looked to Stanley, who nodded his approval. "The boy is learning," he said with a grin.

"Fuck you very much," Chavez replied with his own smile.

Clark checked his watch again. Time.

The bad guys hadn't made contact, and that worried him. There were only a couple reasons to explain the silence: Either they were waiting to make sure they had the world's attention before announcing their demands, or they were waiting to make sure they had the world's attention before they started tossing bodies out the front door.

19

Surprising no one, the blueprints did not arrive within the hour but closer to two, and so it was not quite ninety minutes before sunset when Clark, Stanley, and Chavez unrolled the plans of the compound and got their first look at what lay ahead of them.

"Bloody hell," Stanley growled.

The blueprints weren't the original architect's set but rather a taped-together photocopy of a photocopy. Many of the notations were blurred beyond recognition.

"Ah, Jesus . . ." Richards said, looking over their shoulders. "I'm sorry, they said—"

"Not your fault," Clark replied evenly. "More games. We'll make it work." This was another thing Rainbow did very well: adapt and improvise. Bad blueprints were just another form of insufficient intel, and Rainbow had dealt with its fair share of that. Worse still, the good colonel's intelligence service had refused to give the Swedes blueprints to their own damned building, so they were out of luck there, too.

The good news was the embassy building did not have a basement, and the floor plan looked relatively open. No chopped-up hallways and cookie-cutter spaces, which made room clearing tedious and time-consuming. And there was a wraparound balcony on the second floor overlooking a large open space that abutted a wall of smaller rooms along the west wall.

"Forty by fifty feet," Chavez observed. "Whaddya think? Main work area?"

Clark nodded. "And those along the west wall have gotta be executive offices."

Opposite them, down a short hall that turned right at the base of the stairs, was what looked like a kitchen/dining area, a bathroom, and four more rooms, unlabeled on the plans. Maybe storage, Clark thought, judging by their size. One's probably the security office. At the end of the hall was a door leading to the outside.

"There's no electrical or water on these plans," Chavez said.

"If you're thinking sewer to get in," Richards replied, "forget it. This is one of the oldest neighborhoods in Tripoli. The sewer system is for shit—"

"Very funny."

"The pipes are no bigger around than a volleyball, and they

collapse if you look sideways at them. Just this week I've had to detour twice on the way to work to avoid sinkholes."

"Okay," Clark said, bringing things back on track. "Richards, you talk to Masudi and make sure we can get the power cut when we give the go." They'd decided to leave the utilities on, lest they agitate the bad guys this close to Chavez and his teams going in.

"Right."

"Ding, weapons check?"

"Done and done."

As always, the assault teams would be armed with Heckler & Koch MP5SD3s. Noise-suppressed and chambered in 9 millimeters with a 700-round-per-minute rate of fire.

Along with the standard load-out of fragmentation grenades and flashbangs each man would also be armed with an MK23 .45-caliber ACP with a modified KAC noise suppressor and a tritium laser aiming module—LAM—with four selector modes: visible laser only, visible laser/flashlight, infrared laser only, and infrared laser/illuminator. Favored by Navy Special Warfare teams and the British Special Boat Service, the MK23 was a marvel of durability, having been torture-tested by both the SEALs and the SBS for extreme temperature, saltwater submersion, dry-firing, impact, and a weapon's worst enemy, dirt. Like a good Timex watch, the MK23 had taken a licking and kept on ticking—or in this case, kept on firing.

Johnston and Loiselle had bright and shiny new toys to play with, Rainbow having recently switched from the M24 sniper rifle to the Knights Armament M110 Sniper System, equipped with Leupold scope for daylight conditions and the tried-and-true AN/PVS-14 night sight. Unlike the bolt-action M24, the M110 was semiautomatic. For the assault teams, it meant Johnston and Loiselle, shooting cover fire, could put more rounds on target in a whole lot less time.

At Clark's direction, each sniper had earlier done a walkabout of the area, circumnavigating the blocks surrounding the embassy compound, picking out perches and sketching out his fields of fire. Of the spots Chavez and Weber had chosen as their entry points, Johnston and Loiselle would be able to provide absolute cover—until the teams entered the building proper, that was. Once inside, the assault teams would be on their own.

Fifty minutes after sunset the team sat hunkered down in their makeshift command post, lights out, waiting. Through the binoculars Clark could see the faint glow of light seeping through the embassy's plantation shutters. The exterior lights had popped on, too, four twenty-foot-high poles, one at each corner of the compound and each topped with a sodium-vapor lamp pointed in toward the building.

An hour earlier the muezzin's call to *salaat* had echoed over Tripoli, but now the streets were deserted and quiet, save the distant barking of dogs, the occasional car horn, and the faint voices of the People's Militia guards still on perimeter duty around the embassy. The temperature had dropped only a few degrees, hovering somewhere in the upper eighties. Between now and sunrise, as the heat dissipated into the cloudless desert air, the temperature would plummet another thirty degrees or more, but Clark was confident that by sunrise the embassy would be secure and Rainbow would be packing up. He hoped with no friendly casualties and a few live bad guys to hand over to . . . whomever. Who would oversee the post-mission mop-up and subsequent investigation was probably still being debated.

Somewhere in the dark a cell phone trilled softly, and a few moments later Richards appeared at Clark's shoulder and whispered, "Swedes on the ground at the airport."

The Swedish Security Service, the Säkerhetspolisen, fielded the county's antiterrorist division, while the Rikskriminalpolisen, or Criminal Investigation Department, was its version of the FBI. Once Rainbow had secured the embassy, it would be turned over to them.

"Good, thanks. Guess that answers the question. Tell them to stand by. As soon as we're finished they can come in. Nothing about our timeline, though. Don't want that getting out."

"You think the Swedes would—"

"No, not intentionally, but who knows who they're talking to." Though Clark thought it unlikely, he couldn't discount the possibility of the Libyans throwing a wrench into the works: The Americans came here, failed in their mission, and now people are dead. A publicity coup for the colonel.

It had been nearly twenty-four hours since the embassy had been stormed, and still no sign of life from inside. Clark had chosen 0215 as their go-time, reasoning that the terrorists were likely assuming any assault would come with nightfall. Clark was hoping the delay would cause them to relax, even if only a bit. Plus, statistically, the hours between two and four in the morning were when the human mind starts to lose its edge—especially human minds that have been saddled with the twin demons of stress and uncertainty for the past twenty-eight hours.

At 0130 hours Clark told Johnston and Loiselle to get ready, then gave the nod to Richards, who in turn gave it to Lieutenant Masudi. Five minutes and an extended walkie-talkie discussion later, the Libyan reported back: the perimeter guards were ready. Clark didn't want some nervous grunt taking a potshot at his snipers as they moved into position. Similarly, he had Stanley and Chavez on the binoculars, keeping a close watch. However unlikely, there was always the possibility that someone—a sympathizer or just some asshole private who hated Americans—might try to signal the terrorists that the game was about to start. If this happened, there wouldn't be much Clark could do except recall Johnston and Loiselle and try again later.

With Johnston and Loiselle geared up, M110s draped across their shoulders, Clark waited five minutes, then whispered to Stanley and Chavez, "How're we doing?"

"No change," Ding reported. "Some walkie-talkie action, but that's probably the word getting passed."

At 0140 Clark turned to Johnston and Loiselle and nodded. The two snipers slipped out the door and disappeared into the darkness. Clark donned his headset.

Five minutes passed. Ten minutes.

Over the radio came Loiselle's voice: "Omega One, in position." Followed ten seconds later by Johnston: "Omega Two, in position."

"Roger," Clark replied, checking his watch. "Stand by. Assault teams moving in ten."

He could hear a pair of "Roger" double-clicks in reply.

"Alistair . . . Ding?"

"No movement. All quiet."

"Same here, boss."

"Okay, get ready."

At this, Chavez handed his binoculars to Clark and joined his team at the door. Weber and his team, who were tasked with the ground-floor breach on the front/west corner wall, had farther to go to get into position, so they would go first, followed four minutes later by Chavez and his shooters.

Clark scanned the embassy compound one more time, looking for movement, changes—anything that didn't pass his k-check, or kinesthetic check. Do this kind of thing long enough, he'd learned, and you develop something akin to a sixth sense. Does it feel right? Any nagging voices in the back of your head? Any unchecked boxes or overlooked details? Clark had seen too many otherwise good operators ignore the k-check—more often than not to their detriment.

Clark lowered his binoculars and turned to his teams, poised in the doorway. "Go," he whispered.

20

Chavez waited the requisite four minutes, then led his team down the steps and to the head of the alley. As Clark had requested, the Libyans had turned off the streetlights for a block around the embassy, something they all hoped the bad guys wouldn't notice, since the compound's pole lights were still on and pointing inward. Also by request, a trio of Army trucks had been parked single file down the middle of the street between the command-post apartment and the east side of the compound.

Using hand signals, he sent each man down the sidewalk, using the shadows and the trucks as cover until they reached the next alley, where a line of hedges ran in front of the next building, a private medical practice, Ding had been told, cleared of civilians earlier that day.

Once the team was safely behind the hedges, he followed at a walking pace, half hunched over, MP5 at ready-low, his eyes scanning ahead and to the right and over the top of the embassy compound's wall. No movement. *Good. Nothing to see here, tango.*

Chavez reached the hedges and stopped in a crouch. Over his headset he heard Weber's voice: "Command, Red Actual, over."

"Go, Red Actual."

"In position. Setting up Gatecrasher."

Chavez half wished he had Weber's job. Though he'd used Rainbow's newest toy in training, he'd yet to see it in live action.

Developed by Alford Technologies in Great Britain, the Gatecrasher—which Loiselle had dubbed the "magic door maker"—reminded Ding of one of those tall, rounded rectangular shields the Spartans carried in *300,* but a more accurate analogy would be that of a quarter-scale rubber raft. Instead of air in the outside ring of tubes, there was water, and opposite them, on the hollow side of the Gatecrasher, a sunken strip into which strands of PETN detonator cord were packed. The det cord, backed by the water jacket, created what was known as a tamping effect, essentially turning the det cord into a shaped charge—a focused explosive cutting ring that could cut through a foot and a half of solid brick.

The Gatecrasher addressed a number of issues that had long plagued special operators and hostage rescue teams: one, booby-trapped entry points, and two, the "fatal funnel." Terrorists, knowing the good guys had to come through either doors or windows, often rigged them with explosives—as they did during the Breslan school massacre in Russia—and/or concentrated their firepower and attention on likely entry points.

With the Gatecrasher, Weber and his team would be through the front west wall of the building about three seconds after detonation.

"Roger," Clark replied to Weber. "Blue Actual?"

"Three minutes to wall," Chavez reported.

He scanned the compound one last time through his night vision, saw nothing, then moved out.

For getting over the wall, they'd chosen a decidedly low-tech method: a four-foot stepladder and a Kevlar flak jacket. Among the many axioms special operators lived by, KISS was one of the most important: Keep it simple, stupid. Don't overthink a simple problem, or as Clark often put it, "You don't use a shotgun on a cockroach." In this case, the stepladder would get them level with the top of the wall; the flak jacket, draped over the glass shards jutting from the top of the wall, would keep Chavez and his team from losing some fluid while going over.

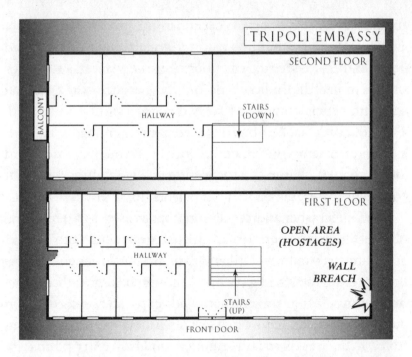

Chavez slipped out from behind the hedges, dashed to the wall, crouched down. He keyed his headset: "Command, Blue Actual. At the wall."

"Roger." Stanley's voice.

A few seconds later a red laser dot appeared on the wall three feet to Chavez's right. Having already mapped out the surveillance camera's blind spots, Alistair was using his MK23's LAM to show Ding the way.

Chavez sidestepped until the laser dot was resting on his chest. The dot disappeared. He quickly and quietly set up the ladder, then gave the *move up* signal to the rest of his team.

Showalter went first. Chavez handed him the flak jacket, and he mounted the ladder. Ten seconds later he was up, over, and out of sight. One by one, the rest of the team followed suit until it was Ding's turn.

Once on the other side, he found himself standing on a plush green lawn bordered by hibiscus bushes. *The Swedes' monthly sprinkler bills must be a bitch,* he thought absently. To his right lay the front of the building, and directly ahead, twenty feet away, the east wall. Showalter and Bianco had taken up overwatch at each corner of the building. Ybarra sat crouched beneath the balcony. Ding started toward him.

"Hold." Loiselle's voice. "Movement, south side."

Ding froze.

Ten seconds later. "Clear. Just a cat."

Chavez crossed over to Ybarra, slung his MP5, then climbed on the stout Spaniard's back. The balcony's lowermost rail was just beyond finger reach. Chavez stretched. Ybarra steadied himself and stood a little straighter. Chavez caught the railing, first with his right hand, then with his left, then chinned himself up. Five seconds later he was crouched on the balcony. He unclipped a section of knotted rope from his harness, clipped the D ring to the rope railing, and dropped the end over the side.

He turned to face the door. Like the windows, it was shuttered and, of course, locked. Behind him he heard a faint creaking as Ybarra came over the railing, then felt an "I'm here" pat on his shoulder.

Chavez keyed his headset. "Command, Blue Actual, at the door."

"Roger."

Ding pulled the flexi-cam from his right-thigh cargo pocket, linked it to his goggles, then slipped the lens beneath the door, slowly, gently, going almost as much by touch as he was by sight. Like everything they did, each Rainbow member had trained and retrained, then trained some more, with every tool in their arsenal, the flexi-cam included. If the door was wired, Chavez was just as likely to feel it as he was to see it.

He scanned first the bottom threshold, then, finding nothing, he moved on to the hinges before finishing with the doorknob and striker plate. Clear. There was nothing. He withdrew the cam. Behind him, Showalter and Bianco had made it over the railing. Ding pointed at Bianco, then at the doorknob. The Italian nodded and went to work with his pick set. Thirty seconds later the lock snicked open.

Using hand signals, Ding gave them final instructions: He and Bianco would take point and clear the rooms on the right; Showalter and Ybarra the left.

Ding gently turned the knob, opened the door a crack. He waited for ten beats, then swung the door open another foot and peeked his head through. The hall was clear. Three doors, two on the right, one on the left. In the distance he heard murmured voices, then silence. A sneeze. He withdrew his head and swung the door open all the way, letting Showalter catch it and hold it.

MP5 at ready-low, Ding stepped into the hall. Bianco followed two paces behind and to his left, taking the hall's centerline. On the south wall, Showalter reached the left-hand doorway and stopped. The door was partially closed. "At south-hall door," Showalter radioed.

"Looking," Loiselle replied. "No movement."

Showalter squared himself with the door, swung it open, and went in. He emerged twenty seconds later and gave a thumbs-up. Chavez crept down the north wall.

Johnston's voice: "Hold."

Ding held up a closed fist, and the other three stopped, dropped into a crouch.

"Movement," Johnston said. "North wall, second window from east corner."

The next room, Ding thought. Twenty seconds passed. Tempted as he was to press Johnston for an update, he resisted. The sniper would respond when he had something.

"Window's covered in mini-blinds," Johnston radioed. "Half open. I see one body moving."

"Weapon?"

"Can't tell. Stand by. Moving to the door. Three seconds."

Chavez slung his MP5, drew his suppressed MK23, stood up, and slid down the wall until he was within arm's reach of the door.

"At door," Johnston called.

It swung open, and a figure stepped out. Chavez took a half-second, saw the AK-47 slung across the man's chest, then put a round above his right ear. Ding pivoted on his heel, brought his left arm up, and grabbed the man across the chest as he fell. Bianco was already moving up, going through the door, looking for more targets. Chavez eased his man to the ground.

"Clear," he radioed five seconds later, then came out and helped Chavez drag the body into the room. They closed the door behind them, got themselves restacked, and crouched down to wait. If his shot had attracted any attention, they'd know in short order. Nothing moved. "At second door, north wall," he radioed.

"Don't see any more movement," Johnston replied.

Ding and Bianco cleared the room and came back out.

"Command, Blue Actual. Upstairs clear," Ding called. "Heading to main floor."

"Roger," Stanley replied.

Twenty feet down the hall lay an arch and a sharp right turn to what Chavez knew was the stairway to the first floor. The stairs were open, twenty feet wide, bordered on the right by a wall, and open on the left, overlooking what they'd decided was probably the embassy's main work area—and the most likely place the terrorists had bunched the hostages.

This had advantages and disadvantages, Ding knew. If the hostages were bunched together, there was a good chance most of the bad guys were as well. This would make Rainbow's job easier, having targets concentrated like that, but it also meant the hostages, sitting cheek by jowl, were fish in a barrel should the terrorists open fire.

Then we just don't give 'em that chance, mano.

He crept forward, moving slowly on flat feet until he reached the arch. A quick glance around the corner revealed the ground floor. Down the stairs and to the right was the front wall, windows still shuttered. At the bottom of the stairway would be that short hall and the four unknown rooms.

Chavez tracked his eyes back to the northwest corner of the room, then mentally measured four feet down the wall. Give or take half a foot, that's where Weber would be coming through. Farther to the left, just visible over the railing, he could see two figures standing together. Each held a compact submachine gun, but not up and ready. Dangling at their sides. *Fine by me,* he thought. A few feet away on a desk, a green-shaded banker's lamp cast a pool of light on the wall.

Chavez pulled back and returned to where the rest of the team was waiting. He gestured: *Layout confirmed; move as planned.* Chavez and Bianco, joined by Weber and his team once they were through the wall, would take the heavy side of the main room. Showalter and Ybarra would go right at the bottom of the stairs, taking the hallway. He got nods from each man.

"Command, Blue Actual, over."

"Go, Blue."

"In position."

"Roger."

From Weber: "Red Actual, roger."

"Moving in ninety seconds," Chavez said.

"Standing by," Weber replied.

"Start the count," Ding radioed.

"Five and counting." This from Weber. Five seconds to Gatecrasher.

Each of Chavez's men had a flashbang in hand, pin pulled. Four . . . three . . . two . . .

In unison, Ding and Bianco tossed the flashbangs over the

railing and started down, MP5s up and tracking, looking for targets. Ding heard the first flashbang skitter across the floor below, followed a quarter-second later by the Gatecrasher going off. A gout of smoke and debris whooshed across the room. Chavez and Bianco kept moving, Ybarra and Showalter passing them on the right, moving fast for the right-hand hallway that led to the east side of the building.

The second flashbang exploded. Bright light bounced off the ceiling and over the walls. Ding ignored it.

Target.

Over the railing a figure was turning toward them. Ding laid the MP5's sight over the man's chest and fired twice. He dropped, and Ding kept moving. To his left he saw another figure but knew Bianco was covering it, and as if on cue, he heard a *pop-pop*. To Chavez's right he saw the first of Weber's team coming through the four-foot-tall oval hole created by the Gatecrasher, followed by a second, third, and fourth.

Ding veered left, moving toward the center of the room. Screams now. A mass of huddled bodies on the floor. *Target.* He fired twice and kept moving, MP5 tracking. Behind him he heard Showalter call, "Target, left," followed by a series of overlapping pops.

Weber and his team had caught up with Chavez and Bianco now and were fanning out, each man covering a sector.

"Down, down, down! Everybody down!" Ding shouted.

To the right: *pop, pop, pop.*

Chavez kept moving, pushing through the center of the room, Bianco on his left doing the same, looking for movement. . . .

"Clear," he heard Weber call out, followed by two more.

"Clear on the left!" Bianco answered.

"Hall clear!" This from Showalter. "Checking the rooms."

"On my way," Ybarra called.

From Showalter's hallway came a woman's scream. Chavez

spun. Ybarra, who had reached the entrance to the hallway, sidestepped right and pressed himself against the left wall. "Target." Chavez sprinted to the hall and took position opposite Ybarra. Down the hall, a figure had emerged from the last room, dragging a woman along with him. The man had a pistol pressed to her neck. Ding peeked out. The man spotted him and turned the woman a bit, shielding himself. He shouted something in panicked Arabic. Ding pulled back. "Showalter, say position," he whispered.

"Second room."

"Target's just outside the third door. Ten, twelve feet. He's got a hostage."

"I hear her. How's my angle?"

"Half a head shot open."

"Roger, say when."

Chavez peeked out again. The man turned ever so slightly, squaring off with Chavez. Showalter, his MP5 shoulder-tucked, stepped up to the threshold of his door and fired. The bullet entered the man's right eye. He crumpled, and the woman started screaming. Showalter stepped out and moved toward her.

Chavez let out a breath, then slung his MP5 and turned to scan the main room. *Done and done.* Twenty seconds, no more. *Not bad.* He keyed his radio. "Command, this is Blue Actual, over."

"Go."

"We're secure."

Once Chavez did his final walk-through and judged the embassy to be fully locked down, he radioed Clark and Stanley a firm "all clear." From there, events moved rapidly as the report went from Tad Richards to his People's Militia liaison, Lieutenant Masudi, then up the Libyan chain of command to a major who insisted that Chavez and his team exit the front door and escort the hostages out the main gate. In Rainbow's temporary command center, Clark and Stanley, misunderstanding the demand, balked until Masudi explained in broken English that there would be no television cameras. The Libyan people simply wanted to express their gratitude. Clark considered this and gave his shrugged approval.

"International goodwill," he muttered to Alistair Stanley.

Ten minutes later Chavez, his team, and the hostages emerged from the embassy's main entrance amid the glare of klieg lights and applause. They were met at the gate by a contingent of Swedish Security Service (Säkerhetspolisen) and Criminal Investigation Department (Rikskriminalpolisen) officers, who took custody of the hostages. After two solid minutes of handshaking and hugs, Chavez and his team moved out onto the street, where a gauntlet of People's Militia brass and soldiers offered yet more backslapping.

Richards appeared at Chavez's side as they pushed through the crowd toward the command center. "What the hell's going on?" Chavez shouted.

"Hard to catch the words," Richards replied, "but they're just impressed. No, *amazed* would be a better description."

Behind Chavez, Showalter yelled, "At what, for Christ sake? What the fuck were they expecting?"

"Casualties! Lots of dead people! They didn't expect any of the hostages to make it out, let alone all of them. They're celebrating!"

"No shit?" Bianco called. "What're we, amateurs?"

Richards replied over his shoulder, "They haven't got the best track record with hostage rescue."

Chavez smiled at this. "Yeah, well, we're Rainbow."

Had he been in an objective frame of mind, Nigel Embling might have recognized his current mood as nothing more than self-indulgent crap, but at that moment it was his considered decision that the world was in fact going quickly and directly to hell. Later he would likely reevaluate that decision, but right now, sitting at his kitchen table over a cup of tea and reading the morning's *Daily Mashriq,* one of Peshawar, Pakistan's half-dozen daily newspapers, nothing he saw improved his mood.

"Bloody idiots," he grumbled.

His houseboy, Mahmood, magically appeared in the kitchen's doorway. "Something, Mr. Nigel?" Mahmood, eleven, was too happy and eager by half—especially at this time of day—but Embling knew his household would be a shambles without him.

"No, no, Mahmood, just talking to myself."

"Oh, that's not good, sir, not good at all. Touched, that's what people will think. Please, if you would, be certain to save your talking for at home, yes?"

"Yes, fine. Go back to your studies."

"Yes, Mr. Nigel."

Mahmood was an orphan, his mother, father, and two sisters having died in the rash of Sunni-on-Shia violence that had plagued Pakistan following the assassination of Benazir Bhutto. Embling had all but adopted the boy, giving him food, board, a small stipend, and, unbeknownst to Mahmood, a steadily growing trust fund he'd inherit when he turned eighteen.

Another mosque burned, another faction leader found murdered, another rumor of rigged elections, another ISI intelligence officer arrested for stealing state secrets, another call for calm from Peshawar. It was a damned shame, all of it. Not that Pakistan had ever been the model of peace, mind you, but there had been some periods of mostly calm, though even that was just a sham, a thin film covering the cauldron of violence always boiling just under the surface. Still and all, Embling knew there was no place else for him on earth, though he'd never quite understood why. Reincarnation, perhaps, but whatever it was, Pakistan had certainly wormed its way into his life, and now, at age sixty-eight, he was firmly and irrevocably rooted in his adopted home.

Embling knew that most men in his position would be, and perhaps should be, afraid—an Anglo-Saxon Christian from England, birthplace of the British Raj, or "rule" in Hindi. For the better part of ninety years, from the mid-1850s to just after World War Two, Great Britain had held sway over what it called the "Indian Subcontinent," which had at various times during its history included India, Pakistan, Bangladesh, Somaliland, Singapore, and Lower and Upper Burma, today known as Myanmar, though Embling still and always would call it Burma, political correctness be damned. Though memories of the British Raj in Pakistan had faded with time, its impact had never completely disappeared, and Embling could see it and feel it every day he went out, in the stares from the old-timers in the market and in the whispered conversations between policemen who'd heard the stories from their parents and grandparents. Embling did nothing to hide his heritage, and he couldn't have if he'd wanted to anyway, what with his perfect but ever-so-slightly accented grasp of Urdu and Pashto. Not to mention his white skin and six-foot-four-inch frame. Not a lot of natives with those traits.

Still, he was mostly shown respect, and that had nothing to do with lingering deference to the Raj but rather his own history. He had, after all, been in Pakistan longer than many of the people you might find in the Khyber Bazar market on any given day. *How many years, exactly?* he thought. Give or take holidays or brief assignments to Pakistan's neighbors . . . Say, forty-plus years. Long enough for his former (and sometimes current) compatriots to have long ago labeled him as "gone native." Not that he minded. For all its shortcomings and all the near misses and dodgy spots he'd seen, there was no place for him but Pakistan, and in his secret heart he took it as a point of pride that they thought him so well integrated that he was "more Paki than Brit."

Embling, at the tender and naive age of twenty-two, had been one of MI6's many postwar Oxford recruitments, having been approached by the father of a schoolmate who Embling had thought worked as a bureaucrat in the Ministry of Defence but who was in fact a scout for MI6—one of the few, in fact, who had warned his superiors that the infamous traitor Kim Philby was a less-than-stellar catch who would in time either muck up so badly he would cost lives or be tempted and slip over to the other side, which he did, working as a mole for the Soviets for many years before being exposed.

After surviving the rigors of MI6 training at Fort Monckton on the Hampshire Coast, Embling was assigned Pakistan's North-West Frontier Province, or NWFP (or Pakhtunkhwa or Sarhad, depending on who you were talking to), which abutted Afghanistan, at the time just becoming a playground for the Russian KGB. Embling had spent the better part of six years living in the mountains along the border, making inroads with the Pashtun warlords who ruled the gray area of overlap between Pakistan and Afghanistan. If the Soviets put out feelers in Pakistan's direction, it would likely come over the mountains and through the lands of the Pashtuns.

Save the occasional trip home to the UK, Embling had spent his career in the Central Asian Stans—Turkistan, Kazakhstan, Turkmenistan, Uzbekistan, Kyrgyzstan, and

Tajikistan—all of which fell in varying degrees and in various times under the rule or at least the sway of the Soviet Union. While the American CIA and his compatriots in MI6—officially known as the Secret Intelligence Service or SIS, a term Embling had never taken to—were fighting the Cold War in the fog-shrouded streets of Berlin and Budapest and Prague, Embling was traipsing the mountains with the Pashtun, living on *quabili pulaw dampukht* (rice with carrots and raisins) and bitter black tea. In 1977, unbeknownst to his superiors in London, Embling had even married into a Pashtun tribe, taking as his bride the youngest daughter of a minor warlord, only to lose her two years later in a Hind airstrike when the Soviets invaded Afghanistan. Her body had never been recovered. He often wondered if that was why he'd stayed in Pakistan long after he'd retired. Was some sad part of his heart still hoping to find Farishta still alive somewhere? Her name, after all, when translated into English, meant "Angel."

A pipe dream, Embling now thought.

A pipe dream, just like the idea of a stable Pakistan.

Seven thousand miles away in Silver Spring, Maryland, Mary Pat Foley was having a similar thought over a similar beverage— her one cup of half-caf/half-decaf reheated and salted coffee she allowed herself in the evening—but on a wholly different topic: the Emir, and the two questions that had plagued U.S. intelligence for the better part of a decade: where he was and how to catch the bastard. With few and only fleeting exceptions, and despite being the White House's Public Enemy Number One, a position with which Mary Pat mostly disagreed. Certainly the guy needed to get caught or, better yet, put down for good and scattered to the winds, but killing the Emir wasn't going to solve America's problem with terrorism. There was even some debate over how much, if any, operational intelligence the Emir possessed; Mary Pat and her husband, Ed, now retired, tended to fall on the "not a hell of a lot" side of the argument. The Emir knew he was being hunted, and while he was a grade-A sonofabitch and a mass murderer, he sure as hell wasn't stupid enough to put himself in the operational need-to-know loop, especially nowadays, with terrorists having stumbled onto the beauty of compartmentalization. If the Emir was an acknowledged head of state sitting in a palace somewhere, he would likely be getting regular briefings, but he wasn't—at least no one thought so. He was, as best the CIA could tell, holed up somewhere in the badland mountains of Pakistan, along the border with Afghanistan. But that was the proverbial needle-in-a-haystack scenario, wasn't it? Still, you never knew. Someday someone would get lucky and find him, of that she was certain. The question was, Would we get him alive or otherwise? She didn't really care either way, but the idea of standing toe to toe with the bastard and looking him in the eye did hold a certain appeal.

"Hi, honey, I'm home. . . ." Ed Foley called out cheerily, coming down the stairs and into the kitchen in his sweatpants and T-shirt.

Since retiring, Ed's commute consisted of thirty or so feet and a half-dozen stair steps to his study, where he was working on a nonfiction history of the U.S. intelligence community, from the Revolutionary War to Afghanistan. His current chapter, a damned good one if she said so herself, was about John Honeyman, an Irish-born weaver and perhaps the most obscure spy of his time. Tasked by none other than George Washington with infiltrating the ranks of Howe's fearsome Hessian mercenaries stationed around Trenton, Honeyman, posing as a cattle dealer, slipped through the lines, scouted the Hessians' battle order and positions, then slipped out again, giving Washington the edge he needed for an all-out rout. For Ed, it was a dream chapter, that little bit of unknown history. Writing about Wild Bill Donovan, the Bay of Pigs, and the Iron Curtain was all well and good, but there were only so many twists you could put on what had become old chestnuts of the espionage nonfiction genre.

Ed had certainly earned his retirement many times over, as had Mary Pat, but only a handful of Langley insiders—including Jack Ryan Sr.—would ever know to what degree the Foleys had served and sacrificed for their country. Ed, Irish by birth, had graduated from Fordham and started his career in journalism, serving as a solid if undistinguished reporter for *The New York Times* before slipping into the world of bad guys and spies. As for Mary Pat, if ever a woman had been born to do intelligence work, it was her, the granddaughter of the riding tutor to Czar Nicholas II and the daughter of Colonel Vanya Borissovich Kaminsky, who in 1917 had seen the handwriting on the walls and slipped his family out of Russia just before the revolution that would topple the Romanov dynasty and cost the lives of Nicholas and his family.

"Hard day at the office, dear?" Mary Pat asked her husband.

"Grueling, absolutely grueling. So many big words, such a small dictionary." He leaned in to give her a peck on the cheek. "And how are you?"

"Fine, fine."

"Pondering again, are we? About you know who?"

Mary Pat nodded. "Got to go in tonight, in fact. Something hot in the pipeline, maybe. I'll believe it when I see it."

Ed frowned, but Mary Pat couldn't tell if it was because he missed the action or because he was as skeptical as she was. Terrorist groups were growing more intel-savvy by the day, especially after 9/11.

Mary Pat and Ed Foley had both earned the right to be slightly cynical if it suited them, having witnessed firsthand the CIA's internal workings and convoluted history for nearly thirty years, and having served at Moscow Station as husband-and-wife case officers back when Russia was still ruling the Soviet Union and the KGB and its satellite agencies were the CIA's only real bugaboo.

Both had risen through the ranks of Langley's directorate of operations, Ed ending his career as DCI, or director central intelligence, while Mary Pat, once the deputy director for operations, had requested a sub-lateral transfer to the NCTC— the National Counterterrorism Center—to serve as its deputy director. As expected, the rumor mill had gone into overdrive, speculating that Mary Pat had in fact been demoted from her DDO post and that her position at the NCTC was merely a waypoint on the road to retirement. Nothing could be further from the truth, of course. The NCTC was the tip of the spear, and Mary Pat wanted to be there.

Of course, her decision had been helped by the fact that their old home, the DO, wasn't what it used to be. Its new name, the Clandestine Service, while it grated on both of them (although neither was under the illusion that the term *director-ate of operations* fooled anyone, *Clandestine Service* seemed just a tad too flashy for their tastes), they also knew it was just another moniker. Unfortunately, the change had come at roughly the same time they felt the directorate had become less about covert operations and intelligence gathering and more about politics. And while Mary Pat and Ed each had his and her own unique—and frequently contrary—political views, what they both agreed on was that politics and intelligence were a bad mix. Too damned many in the CIA's upper echelons were simply civil servants looking for a ticket punch on their way to bigger and better things, something the Foleys had never fathomed. As far as they were concerned, there was no higher calling than to serve in defense of your country, whether in uniform on the battlefield or behind the curtain of what CIA Cold War spymaster James Jesus Angleton had dubbed the "Wilderness of Mirrors." Never mind that Angleton had very likely been a delusional paranoid whose witch hunts for Soviet moles had eaten Langley from the inside out like so much cancer. As far as Mary Pat was concerned, Angleton's nickname for the world of espionage was dead-on.

As much as she loved the world in which she worked, the "Wilderness" took its toll. Over the last few months, she and Ed had started chatting about her eventual retirement, and while her husband had been characteristically tactful (if not subtle), it was clear what he wanted her to do, going as far as leaving copies of *National Geographic* open on the kitchen table, turned to a picture of Fiji or a history piece on New Zealand, two places they'd put on their "someday" list.

In those rare moments when she allowed herself introspection about something other than work, Mary Pat had found herself dancing around the critical question—*Why am I staying?*—without really tackling it head-on. They had plenty of money to retire on, and neither would lack for things to keep them occupied. So if money wasn't the issue, what was? It was simple really: Intel work was her calling, and she knew it—had known it from day one with CIA. She'd done some real good in their time, but there was no denying the CIA wasn't what it used to be. The people were different and their motivations obscured by ambition. Nobody seemed to be "asking not what their country could do for them." Worse still, the tentacles of Beltway politics had wound their way deeply into the intelligence community, and Mary Pat feared this was an irreversible condition.

"How long will you be?" Ed asked.

"Hard to say. Midnight, maybe. If it's going too much past that, I'll give you a call. Don't wait up."

"You hear anything juicy about the Georgetown business?"

"Not much beyond the newspaper stuff. Lone gunman, got a single shot to the head."

"I heard the phone ring earlier. . . ."

"Twice. Ed Junior. Just called to say hi; said he'd call you tomorrow. And Jack Ryan. He wanted to see how the book was coming. Said to call when you got a chance. Maybe you can squeeze some details out of him."

"Not holding my breath."

Both men were writing recollections of a sort: Ed a history, former President Ryan a memoir. They commiserated and cross-referenced memories at least once a week.

Jack Ryan's career, from his rookie days at the CIA to his being thrust into the presidency by tragedy, was intertwined with Mary Pat's and Ed's. Some wonderful times and some downright shitty times.

She suspected Jack and Ed's weekly phone sessions were ninety percent war-story talk and ten percent book-related. She had no complaints. They both had earned the right—in spades. Ed's career she knew by heart, but she felt certain there were portions of Jack Ryan's career only he and a couple of others knew about, which was saying something, given her access. *Oh, well,* she consoled herself. *What is life without some mystery?*

Mary Pat checked her watch, then downed the last of her coffee, scrunched up her face at the tang of it, then stood up. She kissed Ed on the cheek.

"Got to run. Feed the cat, huh?"

"You bet, babe. Drive safe."

22

Mary Pat doused her headlights and pulled up to the guard shack and rolled down her window. A grim-faced man in a blue windbreaker stepped out of the shack. Though he was the only one visible, she knew half a dozen other eyes were on her, along with just as many security cameras. Like the rest of the facility's protection force, the gate guards were drawn from CIA's internal security division. Nor did the lone Glock 9-millimeter pistol on the man's belt fool Mary Pat. Under the man's windbreaker, within easy reach of his well-trained hands, would be a specially designed lumbar pack containing a compact submachine gun.

The National Counterterrorism Center, which had until 2004 been named the Terrorist Threat Integration Center and was now known to its employees as Liberty Crossing, sits nestled in the quiet suburbs of McLean in northern Fairfax County, Virginia. Composed of a whole lot of glass and gray concrete, it was more James Bond than CIA drab, something that had taken Mary Pat some time to get used to. Still, the walls were blast-resistant and the windows bulletproof, rated to stop sustained .50-caliber rounds. Of course, if things ever went so far south that bad guys were taking potshots at the building with a .50-cal, they would likely have bigger problems to worry about. All in all, though, despite the NCTC's six-story exterior being a tad conspicuous for her taste, she had to admit it was a damned nice place to come to work every day. The on-site restaurant was top-notch, too, which drew Ed to Liberty Crossing every Wednesday for their standing lunch date.

She held up her ID for the perusal of the guard, who studied it carefully, matching it against both her face and the access sheet on his clipboard. Night had fully fallen, and in the bushes she could hear the croaking of frogs.

After a long ten seconds the guard nodded to her, clicked off his flashlight, and waved her through. She waited for the barrier to come up, then pulled through the checkpoint and into the parking lot. The security procedure she'd just undergone was the same for every employee at the NCTC, at all hours, every day, from the lowest-grade analyst to the director himself. The fact that she was the number two at Liberty Crossing was immaterial to the security guards, who seemed to develop amnesia for faces and vehicles and names within seconds of their passing through the checkpoint. It was not a good idea to get friendly with the guards. They were paid to be suspicious, and they took the onus seriously. Nor were they known for their sense of humor. The whole thing vaguely reminded Mary Pat of the *Seinfeld* "Soup Nazi" episode: step forward, place your order, step right, pay, take soup, leave. In this case it was pull forward, show badge, speak only if spoken to, wait for nod, then pull ahead. Deviate at your peril.

It was a hassle sometimes, especially on days when she had gotten a late start and wasn't able to make her usual Starbucks pit stop, but Mary Pat wasn't about to complain. What they did was important, and woe be the idiot who thought otherwise. In fact, a few morons had over the years made the mistake of taking lightly what the guards did—usually some jackass trying to do a rolling stop and quick badge-flash—and had gotten a weapons-drawn, police-style felony stop for their trouble. A few had even made the mistake of later complaining about the treatment. Not many of those still had jobs at Liberty Crossing.

She pulled into her personal parking space, which was separated from the rest by only a special hash mark on the curb. More security: Names were personal details, and personal details were potential tools for bad guys. Again, not a likely scenario, but here it wasn't about odds but rather comprehensiveness. Control what you can, because there's a hell of a lot you can't.

She walked through the lobby and made her way to the heart of the NCTC and her "office," as it were, the operations center. While the rest of the NCTC was all warm wood furniture and pleasant earth-toned carpeting, the operations center was something straight out of the television show *24*—an oft-joked-about subject here.

At ten thousand square feet, the operations center was

dominated by a handful of wall-sized display screens, on which were projected the hot threat or incident or raw data of the minute or hour—given the NCTC's mission as an intelligence clearinghouse, it was more often than not the former.

Dozens of computer workstations with ergonomic keyboards and multiple wraparound flat-screen LCD monitors manned by analysts from the CIA, FBI, and NSA filled the center space, and at either end sat a raised and glassed-in watch center, one for the FBI's Counterterrorism Division, one for the CIA's Counterterrorism Center. In any given calendar day the NCTC could see upward of ten thousand cables come across its electronic desk, any one of which could be a piece of a jigsaw puzzle that, if left unassembled, could cost American lives. Most pieces turned out to be trivial, but all were analyzed with equal care.

Part of the problem was translators, or a lack thereof. A good chunk of the data they looked at every day came to them raw, in Arabic, Farsi, Pashto, or any of a half-dozen other dialects that were just different enough from their root language to require a specialist translator, which were hard enough to find themselves, let alone translators who could pass the kind of vetting necessary to work at the NCTC. Add to that the sheer volume of traffic the operations center saw and you got a recipe for data overload. They'd developed a pigeonhole program for categorizing incoming intercepts so high-priority stuff got reviewed first, but that was more art than science; often they found important nuggets only after they'd filtered down through the system, having lost their relevance and context along the way.

The translator problem was just one side of the same coin, Mary Pat believed. Coming from the collection side of CIA, she knew human assets were what really made the intelligence world turn, and developing assets in Arab-centric countries had proven a tough nut to crack. The sad truth was that the CIA had in the decade leading up to 9/11 let agent recruitment slip down its list of priorities. Technical collection—satellites, audio intercepts, and data mining—was easy and sexy, and could, within certain parameters, produce great results, but old hands like Mary Pat had long ago learned that most intelligence battles were won and lost on the strength of HUMINT—human intelligence, i.e., agents and the case officers who ran them.

Langley's crop of case officers had grown in relative leaps and bounds over the last seven years, but they still had a long way to go, especially in countries such as Afghanistan and Pakistan, where religion, ancient rivalries, and cutthroat politics made the recruitment of reliable agents a daunting task.

As visually impressive as the operations center was—even to a veteran like Mary Pat—she knew the real triumph of the place was an intangible that would be lost on the casual observer: cooperation. For decades the albatross around the U.S. intelligence community's neck was at best a crippling lack of cross-pollination and at worst overt internecine warfare, most notably between the two agencies tasked with keeping the country safe from terrorist attacks. But as the TV pundits and Beltway pols had pointed out ad nauseam, the events of 9/11 had changed everything, including how the U.S. intelligence community went about the business of keeping America safe. For Mary Pat and many intelligence professionals, 9/11 hadn't been so much a surprise as it had been a sad confirmation of what they'd long suspected: The U.S. government hadn't been taking seriously enough the threat of terrorism, and not just in the few years leading up to 9/11 but perhaps as far back as the 1979 Soviet invasion of Afghanistan, when the Taliban and the mujahideen—then convenient but ideologically incompatible allies—had shown what determined but woefully outnumbered and outgunned fighters could accomplish against one of only two superpowers on the planet. For many—the Foleys and Jack Ryan included—

the war in Afghanistan had been a preview of sorts, a movie they feared would be played out against the West once the mujahideen had finished with the Soviets. Effective as the CIA's alliance with the mujahideen had been, the relationship had been tenuous at best, always overshadowed by the chasm between Western culture and sharia law, by radical Islamic fundamentalism and Christianity. The question, born from the Arabic proverb "the enemy of my enemy is my friend" became "How soon would the friendship end?" For Mary Pat the answer had been simple: the moment the last Soviet soldier left Afghan soil. And depending on who was writing the history, she had been either dead-on right or nearly so. Either way, by the mid- to late '80s the Taliban, the mujahideen, and eventually the Emir's URC had turned their scornful and now battle-tested eyes toward the West.

What's done is done, Mary Pat thought, looking over the balcony railing at the operations center. Whatever tragedy it had taken to get them here, the U.S. intelligence community was more on its game than it had been since the early days of the Cold War, and the NCTC was owed a lion's share of the credit. Staffed as it was by analysts from virtually every branch of the intelligence world who sat side by side seven days a week twenty-four hours a day, cooperation was now the rule rather than the exception.

She made her way down the stairs and through the rows of workstations, nodding at colleagues as she went, until she reached the CIA's Counterterrorism Center. Waiting for her inside were two men and a woman: her boss and the director of the NCTC, Ben Margolin; the Chief of Operations, Janet Cummings; and John Turnbull, the head of Acre Station, the joint task force dedicated to tracking down, capturing, or killing the Emir and the leadership of the URC. The frown on Turnbull's face told Mary Pat all was not rosy at Acre Station.

"Am I late?" Mary Pat asked, and took a seat. Beyond the glass wall, the staff of the operations center silently went about its business. Like virtually every conference room at Liberty Crossing, the Counterterrorism Center was an EM tank—isolated from virtually all electromagnetic emissions, both inbound and outbound, save encrypted data streams.

"No, we're early," Margolin said. "The package is on its way down."

"And?"

"We missed him," Turnbull grumbled.

"Was he ever there?"

"Hard to say." This from Operations Chief Janet Cummings. "We've got product from the raid, but how good we don't know. Somebody was there—probably a higher-up—but beyond that . . ."

"Nine dead," Turnbull said.

"Prisoners?"

"Started with two, but during the exfil the team was ambushed and they lost one; lost the second when their LZ took an RPG. Lost some Rangers, too."

"Ah, shit."

Ah shit, indeed, Mary Pat thought. The Rangers would, of course, be mourning the loss of one of their own, but these guys were the best of the best; consequently, they took the hazards simply as part of the job. They were consummate professionals, but whereas their civilian counterparts might know how to unclog a drain or rewire a house or build a skyscraper, Rangers specialized in something completely different: killing bad guys.

"The team leader"—Cummings paused to check her file—"Sergeant Driscoll, was wounded, but he made it. According to Driscoll's after-action report, the prisoner stood up during the firefight. On purpose."

"Christ," Mary Pat muttered. They'd seen that before with URC soldiers, preferring death over capture. Whether that was born of pride or an unwillingness to risk talking during interrogation was a point of heated debate in the intelligence and military communities.

"The second one tried to make a break for it when the helo went down. They dropped him."

"Well, not exactly a dry hole," Turnbull said, "but not the result we wanted."

The problem hadn't been the radio transmission, of that Mary Pat was certain. She'd read both the raw data and the analysis. Somebody had been transmitting from that cave using recognized URC plain-speak code packets. One of the words—*Lotus*—is something they'd seen before, both in asset debriefs from case officers and in NSA Driftnet intercepts, but what it meant no one had been able to determine.

They'd long suspected the URC had gone old school for its encrypted communications, employing onetime pads, essentially a point-to-point protocol where only the sender and receiver had the pad required to decrypt the message. The system was ancient, dating back to the Roman Empire, but reliable and, provided the pads were in fact fully randomized, nearly impossible to break unless you got your hands on a pad. On a Tuesday, say, Bad Guy A would send a series of key words—*dog, cabbage, chair*—to Bad Guy B, who, using his own pad, would convert the words to their alphanumeric value, so *dog* would translate into 4, 15, and 7, which in turn would translate into a different word altogether. Special Forces teams in Afghanistan had in raids captured a number of onetime pads, but none were current, and so far neither the CIA nor the NSA had been able to glean a pattern from which they might extrapolate a key.

There were downsides to the system, however. First, it was cumbersome. For it to work properly, senders and receivers had to be working on the same physical pads, switching to a new one at the same intervals, the more often the better, which in turn required couriers to move between Bad Guy A and Bad Guy B. Whereas the CIA had Acre Station dedicated to hunting down the Emir, the FBI had a working group called Clownfish, dedicated to intercepting a URC courier.

The big question, Mary Pat knew, was: What had prompted whoever had been living in the cave to bug out shortly before the team hit the ground? Dumb coincidence or something more? She doubted it was human error; Rangers were too good for that. She had, in fact, read the after-action report earlier that day, and in addition to a broken wheel suffered by the team's CO and Driscoll's own injury, the op had been costly: two dead and two wounded. All that for a dry hole.

Barring coincidence, the most likely culprit was word of mouth. Rare was the day a helo could lift off from bases in either Pakistan or Afghanistan without a URC soldier or sympathizer taking note and making a call, a problem that had partially been solved by Special Forces teams making short, random hops around the countryside in the hours and days leading up to an op as well as using offset waypoints en route to the target, both of which helped keep prying eyes guessing. The rugged and unforgiving terrain made this problematic, though, as did the weather, which often made certain routes impassable. Just as Alexander the Great's Army and the Soviets after them had learned, the geography of Central Asia was a foe unto itself. *And an unconquerable one at that,* Mary Pat thought. You either learned to live with it or work around it, or you failed. Hell, both Napoléon and Hitler had learned that lesson—albeit belatedly—each during a bold, if ill-advised, wintertime invasion of Russia. Of course, each of them had been certain of a quick victory, long before the snow started flying. And, hell, in Russia the land was nice and flat. Add mountains to the mix . . . Well, you've got Central Asia.

A courier appeared at the glass door, punched in the cipher code, and entered. Without a word he laid a stack of four brown, red-striped folders and an accordion folder before

Margolin and then departed. Margolin passed out the folders, and for the next fifteen minutes the group read in silence.

Finally Mary Pat said, "A sand table? I'll be damned."

"Woulda been nice if they'd brought it back whole," Turnbull said.

"Look at the dimensions," Cummings said. "No way to get it outta there on foot. Not without compromising the team. Right call, I think."

"Yeah, I suppose," the Acre Station chief mumbled, unconvinced. Turnbull was under incredible pressure. While the official line was that the Emir wasn't at the top of the United States' Most Wanted List, he indeed was. However unlikely his capture was to turn the tide in the war on terrorism, having him on the loose out there was at best embarrassing. At worst, dangerous. John Turnbull had been hunting the Emir since 2003, first as Acre Station's deputy, then as its head.

As good as Turnbull was at his job, like many current career CIA officers, he suffered from what Mary Pat and Ed called "operational disconnect." He simply had no idea what an op looked like or felt like, in person, on the ground, and that disconnect led to a plethora of problems, which generally fell into one category: unrealistic expectations. In planning an op, you expect too much, either from the people working it or from the scope of the mission. Most ops aren't home runs; they are base hits that slowly and steadily put points on the board that eventually add up to a big win. As Ed's literary agent once told him, "It takes ten years to become an overnight success." The same was generally true with covert ops. Sometimes intelligence, preparation, and good luck come together in the right way at the right time, but most times they're out of sync just enough to keep that long ball from sailing over the left-field fence. *And sometimes,* she reminded herself as she continued scanning the report, *you don't know you've got a home run until well after the fact.*

"You see this business about the Koran they found?" Cummings asked the group. "No way that belonged to anybody in that cave."

No one responded; there was no need. She was right, of course, but barring an inscription and a "return to" address on the front cover, an antique Koran wasn't going to do them much good.

"They got plenty of pictures, I see," Mary Pat said. The Rangers had meticulously photographed all the URC faces in the cave. If any of them had been nabbed or tagged in the past, the computer would spit out the details. "And samples of the table. Smart guy, this Driscoll. Where are the samples, Ben?"

"Somehow they missed the helo out of Centcom Kabul. They'll be here in the morning."

Mary Pat wondered what, if anything, the samples would tell them. Langley's Science and Tech wizards were miracle workers, as were the FBI labs at Quantico, but there was no telling how long that thing had been in the cave, nor was there any guarantee the mock-up would hold any peculiar traits. Crapshoot.

"Pictures we got now," Margolin said.

He picked up a remote control from the table and pointed it at the forty-two-inch flat screen on the wall. A moment later an 8 × 10 grid of thumbnail images appeared on the monitor. Each was annotated by a date and a time stamp. Margolin clicked the remote and enlarged the first photo, which showed the sand table in situ from a distance of about four feet.

Whoever had actually taken the shots had done a thorough job, Mary Pat saw, photographing the sand table from the macro to the micro, using a miniature measuring tape for scale in each shot. Despite it being a cave, they'd taken care with the lighting, too, which made a big difference. Of the 215 shots Driscoll and his team had taken, 190 were variations on a theme—same view but close up or at a different angle—and Mary Pat wondered if there was enough for Langley to create a 3-D rendering of the thing. Something to pursue. Whether animating the damn thing would make any difference she had no idea, but better to try it and fail than later regret not trying. Somebody in the URC had gone to a lot of trouble to make this thing, and it'd be nice to know why. You don't make a goddamned sand table on a whim.

According to the report, the remaining twenty-five pictures were repeats of three separate spots on the sand table, two on the front and one on the back, all displaying some kind of marking. Mary Pat asked Margolin to call these up on the monitor, which he did, setting it for slideshow. When it was done, Mary Pat said, "The two on the front look like manufacturer's marks. Driscoll said the base was heavy-duty plywood. Might be able to use the marks to track something down. The other mark, on the back . . . Tell me if I'm wrong, but that looks handwritten."

"Agreed," Margolin said. "We'll turn the translators loose."

THE SAND TABLE

"And what about the million-dollar question?" Cummings said. "Why make the sand table, and where's it supposed to represent?"

"The Emir's vacation spot, I hope," Turnbull said.

They all laughed.

"If wishes were horses . . ." Margolin mused. "Mary Pat, I can see the gears cranking in your head. Got an idea?"

"Maybe; lemme get back to you."

"How about the documents in the ammo box?" Turnbull asked.

"Translators estimate tomorrow afternoon," Margolin said. He opened the accordion file, withdrew the map from the cave, and unfolded it on the table. Everyone stood up and leaned over it.

Cummings read the legend: "Defense Mapping Agency . . . 1982?"

"Left behind by the CIA advisers," Mary Pat said. "They wanted the mujahideen to have maps, just not the best maps."

Margolin turned the map over, displaying the Baedeker's Peshawar side.

"Got some markings here," Mary Pat said, tapping the paper and leaning closer. "Dots. Ballpoint pen." They scoured the map and in short order found nine marks, each a cluster of either three or four dots.

"Who's got a knife?" Mary Pat asked. Turnbull handed her a pocketknife, and she slit the masking tape along all four edges, then turned the Baedeker's over. "There you are. . . ." she murmured.

Inscribed in the upper-right-hand corner, no larger than a quarter-inch, was an upward-pointing arrow followed by three dots, and a downward-pointing arrow followed by four dots.

"Legend," Margolin whispered.

23

It started in the Department of Justice. Forwarded by the Pentagon, it was First Sergeant Driscoll's written report of his takedown in the Hindu Kush cave. The report—only three pages long, and simply written—detailed what Driscoll and his men had done. What flagged it for the attorney who reviewed the report was the body count. Driscoll reported having killed nine or so Afghan fighters, four of them with a silenced pistol at zero range. Direct shots to the head, the attorney saw, which made his blood run a little cold. It was the nearest thing he'd ever read to a confession of cold-blooded murder. He'd read his share of such confessions but never written so directly. This Driscoll fellow had violated some rules or laws or something, the attorney thought. It wasn't a battlefield action, not even a sniper's account of kill-ing people at a hundred yards or so as they stuck their heads up like ducks at a shooting gallery. He'd taken care of the "bad guys" (so he called them) while they slept. Slept. Totally harm-less, the lawyer thought, and he'd killed them without as much as a thought and reported it straightforwardly, like an account of cutting the grass in his front yard.

This was outrageous. He'd had "the drop" on them, as they said in Western movies. They'd been unable to resist. Hadn't even known their lives were in danger, but this Driscoll guy had taken out his pistol and dispatched them like a kid stomp-ing on insects. But they hadn't been insects. They'd been human beings, and under international law, they'd been enti-tled to capture and to be transformed into prisoners of war protected by the Geneva Protocols. But Driscoll had killed them, totally without mercy. Worse still, the knuckle-dragger seemed to have given little thought to whether the men he'd killed could have been milked for information. He'd decided, quite arbitrarily, it seemed, that the nine men were worthless, both as human beings and as sources.

The lawyer was young, not yet thirty years of age. He'd graduated Yale at the top of his class before taking an offer to work in Washington. He'd almost clerked for a Supreme Court justice, but had been knocked out of that slot by a hick from the University of Michigan. He wouldn't have liked it anyway, he was sure. The new Supreme Court, in place for five or so years now, was full of conservative "strict construc- tionists" who worshipped the letter of the law as if it were Zeus of ancient times. Like Southern Baptists in their coun- try pulpits or on TV on Sunday mornings, which he saw only in glimpses while surfing the channels for the morning talk shows.

Damn.

He reread the report and was again shocked at the bare facts of the third-grade language. A United States Army soldier had killed without mercy, and without regard to international law. Then he wrote a report on the event, outlining the process in stark terms.

The report had come to his desk from a friend and class- mate working in the office of the Secretary of Defense, with a cover note saying that nobody in the Pentagon had taken much note of it, but that he, the other attorney, had found it outrageous. The new SecDef had been captured by the bloated bureaucracy on the other side of the river. A lawyer himself, he'd spent too much time with those creatures in uniform. He hadn't been alarmed by this bloody report, and that despite the fact that the sitting President had issued directives on the use of force, even on the battlefield.

Well, he'd see about this, the attorney thought. He wrote up his own summary of the case, with a blistering cover note that would go to his section chief, a Harvard graduate who had the President's ear—well, he might; his father was one of the President's foremost political supporters.

This First Sergeant Driscoll was a murderer, the attorney thought. Oh, in a court of law the judge might take pity on him, noting that he was a soldier on what was a battlefield, sort of. It wasn't really a war, the attorney knew, since Congress had not declared war, but it was commonly assumed to be so, and the attorney for Driscoll would point that out, and the Federal District Court judge—who would have been selected by the defense for his equanimity to soldiers—would take pity on the killer for that reason. It was a standard defense tactic, but even so, this killer would be slapped down rather hard. Even if acquitted (which was likely, given the composition of the jury that the attorney for the defense would work hard to select, not a difficult task in North Carolina), he'd learn a lesson, and the lesson would be learned by a lot of other soldiers who'd much rather shoot guns on a hillside than sit in a law court.

What the hell; it would send a message, and it was a message that needed to be sent. Of the many things that distinguished the United States from Banana Republics was the military's unwavering obedience to its civilian leadership. Without that, America was no better than Cuba or frickin' Uganda under Idi Amin. The scope of Driscoll's crime, while admittedly small, was beside the point. These people needed to be reminded who they answered to.

The attorney drafted his endorsement to the document and e-mailed it to his section chief with a return-receipt feature allowed on the in-house computer network. This Driscoll guy needed to be slapped down, and he was the man to do it. The young attorney was sure of that. Okay, fine, they'd been after the Emir, but they hadn't got him, and there was a price for failure in the real world.

*

After a five-hour journey by car, he boarded a plane in Caracas for the flight to Dallas and points beyond. Shasif Hadi's carry-on bag held a laptop that had been duly checked at the gate to make sure it was real. Also checked were the nine CD-ROMs in the bag with various games for him to play on the hop across the ocean. Except for one. Even if that one had been examined, it would have been shown to contain gibberish, robustly encrypted data written in C++ computer code that made no sense at all, but unless the TSA had programmers or hackers on staff at the checkpoints, there would be no way of distinguishing it from a regular computer game. He'd been told nothing of the contents and had merely been given a meeting place in Los Angeles to hand it over to someone he would know only by the exchange of carefully scripted recognition phrases.

Once that was done, for appearances' sake he'd spend a few days in California, then fly to Toronto, and from there back to his semipermanent home base to await another assignment. He was the perfect courier. He knew nothing of genuine value and could therefore betray nothing of value.

He desperately wanted to be more directly involved with the cause, and he'd made this desire known to his Paris contact. He'd been loyal; he was capable and ready to lay down his life if asked. Admittedly, he'd had only rudimentary military training, but there had to be more to this war than pulling a trigger, didn't there? Hadi felt a pang of guilt. If Allah, in all his wisdom, saw fit to ask more of him, then he would gladly oblige. Similarly, if his destiny was to play only this small role, he should accept that as well. Whatever Allah's wish, he would obey.

He proceeded through the checkpoint with little trouble beyond the supplemental search most Arab-looking men got nowadays, then made his way to the gate. Twenty minutes later he was aboard the aircraft and belted in.

His total time in transit would be only twelve hours, and that included his automobile ride to his airport of origin. And so he sat in the aft-most first-class seat on the right side of the airbus airliner, playing his mindless shoot-'em-up game and thinking about a movie on the mini-screen provided for free with the cost of the ticket. But he was close to a personal record on the game, and he passed on the movie for the moment. He found that a glass of wine helped his score. Must have relaxed him just enough to steady his hands on the laptop's trackpad . . .

24

Chief of Staff Wesley McMullen hurried down the hall, got the nod from the secretary, then pushed through the door and into the Oval Office. He was late, not quite by a minute, but the President was a stickler for timeliness. The group had already assembled, with Kealty in the wingback chair at the head of the coffee table and Ann Reynolds and Scott Kilborn seated on the couches on either side. McMullen took the chair opposite the President.

"Car wouldn't start this morning, Wes?" Kealty joked. The smile seemed genuine enough, but McMullen knew his boss well enough to recognize the warning.

"My apologies, Mr. President." As he was every day except Sunday, McMullen had been in the office since five a.m. Sundays he worked a half day, from nine until three. Such was life in the Kealty administration and the rarefied atmosphere of the executive branch.

It was a Tuesday, the day of Kealty's biweekly meeting with Director of Central Intelligence Scott Kilborn. Unlike the previous President, Kealty wasn't hands-on when it came to intelligence, trusting Kilborn to keep him up to speed.

Kilborn, a supporter of Kealty's since the President's days in the Senate, had left his post as chairman of the political sciences department at Harvard to serve as Kealty's foreign affairs adviser before being nominated for the slot at Langley. Kilborn was competent enough, McMullen knew, but the DCI was overcompensating for the previous administration's foreign policy platform, which both he and Kealty had proclaimed wrongheaded and counterproductive. McMullen agreed, at least marginally, but Kilborn had swung the pendulum too far in the opposite direction, pulling back from some of the CIA's overseas operational initiatives that had finally started bearing fruit, something that McMullen knew had infuriated the Clandestine Service. Case officers who had been living overseas, away from their families, for six to eight months at a time and risking their lives where a white face was as good as a bull's-eye had recently been told, "Thanks for all your hard work, but we've decided to go in a different direction." The rumor was that in the next few months Langley was going to be seeing an exodus of retirement- and near-retirement-age case officers putting in their papers. If so, it would set the Clandestine Service back nearly a decade.

Worse still, with Kealty's tacit approval, Kilborn often side-stepped into the state department's turf and poached issues that lay in that arguably gray area between diplomacy and intelligence.

As for Ann Reynolds, Kealty's National Security Adviser, she, too, was smart enough but painfully inexperienced. Plucked by Kealty from the House of Representatives during her first term, Reynolds had little background in security matters, save a junior membership on the House Intelligence Committee. She was, Kealty had told McMullen at the time of the decision, a "demographic necessity." He had badly mauled his challenger for the Democratic nomination, Vermont Governor Claire Raines, winning the party nod but losing a good chunk of his female base in the process. If he had any hopes of a second term, he had to win it back.

Reynolds was well spoken and had a good academic mind, of that there was no question, but after nearly a year on the job, she was still far, far down the wrong side of the learning curve and realizing, McMullen suspected, that the real world and the world of textbooks had little in common.

And what about you, Wes, old buddy? he thought. A black man, under thirty, a Yale-graduated lawyer with half a dozen years of quasigovernmental think-tank service under his belt. He had no doubt the media and gossip mavens said the same thing about him: He was an affirmative-action choice and in way over his head, which was partially true, at least the last part. He was in over his head but learning to swim quickly. The problem was, the better his backstroke got, the dirtier the pool seemed. Kealty was a decent enough man, but he was too concerned with the big picture—about his "vision" for the country and its place in the world—and less focused on the "how" of making it happen. Worse still, he was so worried about reversing the course his predecessor had set that he, too, like Kilborn, often sent the pendulum swinging danger-ously in the other direction, too lenient in his stand against enemies and too forgiving of allies who failed to follow through on their commitments. The economy was warming again, though, and with it the President's approval ratings were rising, and Kealty took this as a blanket indicator that God was in his heaven and all was well with the world at large.

And why are you staying, he asked himself for the umpteenth time, *now that you've seen the emperor's new clothes?* He didn't have a ready answer to the question, which worried him.

"Okay, Scott, what's happening in the world today?" Kealty said, starting the meeting.

"Iraq," Kilborn began. "Centcom has submitted a final drawdown plan for our forces. Thirty percent over the first one hundred twenty days, then ten percent each sixty-day period to follow until we reach nominal force status."

Kealty nodded thoughtfully. "And the Iraqi Security Forces?" The training and outfitting of the new Iraqi Army had progressed in fits and starts over the past eight months, leading to a debate in Congress about when, if ever, the ISF would be ready to take over completely. The problem wasn't skill but rather unit cohesion. For the most part the ISF soldiers absorbed the training well enough, but like most Arab nations, Iraq was little better than a collection of sects and extended families, both secular and religious alike. The concept of nationalism came in a distant second to tribe loyalty or Shia/Sunni affiliation. For a time Centcom had toyed with the idea of organizing units and commands based on such familial and religious alignments, but the plan was quickly abandoned as the analysts realized the United States would be doing nothing more than creating well-armed gangs who were already predisposed to internecine warfare. The question was: Could rival clan or sect members stand side by side and fight for the larger good of their country?

Time, McMullen decided, would be the judge of that.

The fact that Kilborn was giving Kealty this drawdown news rather than the chairman of the joint chiefs, Admiral Stephen Netters, told McMullen that the President had already made up his mind about the drawdown in Iraq. At last week's Thursday meeting, Netters had argued against the ambitious pace of the withdrawal, citing the universally dismal reports on the ISF's readiness from the Army's brigade commanders. The ISF was certainly not ready now, and they certainly wouldn't be ready in three months, when the first U.S. forces were scheduled for withdrawal.

For his part, Kealty had to get it done, McMullen knew,

having centered much of his campaign on troop reduction. Whether Netters was right or not was irrelevant to Kealty, who ordered his Chief to get it done and make it work.

"There's debate between brigade and division commanders about the readiness figures, but the data seem to support our plan. Four months isn't much time, but the initial drawdown will be gradated over three months, so it'll be a full seven months until the ISF will really start to feel any pressure."

Crap, McMullen thought.

"Good, good," Kealty said. "Ann, get the draft from Scott and run it through the NSC. If they don't find any problems, we'll move forward. Next, Scott."

"Brazil. There are indications their expansion plan for their refinery infrastructure is more ambitious than we'd projected."

"Which means?" Kealty asked.

Reynolds answered. "Their Tupi fields are richer than they either thought or were letting on."

At least on the surface, the ever-growing scope of the Santos Basin's potential had been as much a surprise to Brazil as it had been to the United States. There'd been not a whisper of it until Petrobras's press release, and that was not the kind of news you could keep secret for long.

"Sons of bitches," Kealty growled. Shortly after he won the general election and even before he had taken the oath, Kealty had ordered his presumptive Secretary of State to reach out to the Brazilian government. Along with getting the United States out of Iraq, a reduction in gas prices had been a cornerstone of Kealty's campaign. The oil importation deal with Brazil, set to go into effect at the end of the month, would go a long way to fulfilling that promise. The downside was that the Brazilian government, friendly as it was now, had in its hands a lever of considerable strength. The question that no one seemed to be able to answer at this point was whether Brasília would remain benevolent or go the way of Saudi

Arabia—one hand outstretched in friendship, the other clutching a dagger.

"We don't know one way or another whether there's intent there, Mr. President," McMullen said, trying to head Kealty off at the pass. "When their expansion plans changed or to what degree they will change is still a question mark." McMullen looked hard at Kilborn, hoping he'd take the cue, which he did.

The DCI said, "That's true, Mr. President."

"Wes, when we're done here, I want to talk to Ambassador Dewitt."

"Yes, sir."

"What else?"

"Iran. We're still working a few sources, but there are indications Tehran's going to be ramping up its nuclear program again."

Ah, shit, McMullen thought. Among Kealty's many campaign promises had been to resume direct diplomacy with Iran. Bringing Iran into the wider community of nations and working on areas of mutual interest, Kealty had proclaimed, was the best way to convince Tehran to halt its nuclear ambitions. And until now, it seemed to have been working.

"Define 'ramping up.'"

"Centrifuges, refinement plants, some back and forth with Moscow."

"Sons of bitches. What in God's name are they up to?" This question Kealty directed at his National Security Adviser.

"Hard to say, Mr. President," Reynolds replied.

McMullen thought, *Translation: I have no fucking idea.*

"Then make it easy," Kealty barked. "Get on the goddamned phone with State and get me some answers." Kealty stood up, calling the meeting to an end. "That's all. Wes, Scott, stay for a moment."

Once Reynolds was gone, Kealty strolled to his desk and

sat down with a sigh. "What do we know about this Ryan thing?"

"The Secret Service is still working the case," DCI Kilborn replied. "But it looks like there was only one shooter—no ID on him yet, but dental work says he's Jordanian. The gun came from a stolen shipment of Egyptian military sidearms—it matched two found after the Marseille bombing last month."

"Refresh my memory."

"Bus attack. Fourteen dead, including the shooters."

"Suspected URC."

"Yes, sir."

McMullen knew his boss well enough to read the expression he now wore: In choosing Jack Ryan as a target, the URC had focused the media spotlight on the former President. Half of the cable networks were rerunning biography pieces on Ryan, who had so far been downplaying the incident, releasing a brief press statement and declining interview requests. For his part, Kealty had handled the incident with a prearranged questioning during a press conference: glad that former President Ryan was uninjured, etc. The words had come out sincerely enough, McMullen admitted, but he had no doubt they'd burned his boss's throat during trainsit.

Kealty moved on: "Wes, this business with Netters . . ."

Uh-oh, McMullen thought. "Yes, Mr. President."

"I think we're nearing a time for a change."

"I see."

"You disagree?"

McMullen chose his words carefully. "I'd like to suggest, Mr. President, that a little dissent can be a healthy thing. Admiral Netters is plain-spoken, perhaps to a fault, but he's widely respected, not only in the services but in Congress as well."

"Christ, Wes, I'm not going to keep him on board just because he's popular."

"That's not my point—"

"Then what is?"

"He's respected because he knows his business. My dad used to say, 'You don't ask directions from somebody who hasn't been where you're going.' Admiral Netters has been where we're going."

Kealty turned down his mouth, then flashed a smile. "That's good, really good. Mind if I use it? Okay, we'll see where it goes. I'm making this happen, though, Wes. We're getting out of that damned country, one way or another. Is that understood?"

"Yes, sir."

"You look like your dog just died, Scott. Let's hear it."

Kilborn laid a file folder on Kealty's desk, then said, "Last week, a raid on a cave in the Hindu Kush mountains—a Ranger team looking for the Emir."

"Ah, Jesus, that guy?" Kealty said, flipping through the file. "We're still wasting resources on him?"

"Yes, Mr. President. Anyway, the team's CO was injured, so his first sergeant took over—Driscoll, Sam Driscoll. Got to the cave, took out a couple guards, but when they went inside there was nothing."

"No big surprise there."

"No, sir, but if you'll take a look at page four . . ."

Kealty did so, his eyes narrowing as he read.

Kilborn said, "As far as we can tell, none of them were armed, per se, but they were certainly sleeping."

"And he just shot 'em all in the head," Kealty grumbled, shoving the file aside. "It's sickening."

McMullen said, "Mr. President, I'm clearly a little behind here. What're we talking about?"

"Murder, Wes, plain and simple. This sergeant, this Driscoll, murdered nine unarmed men. Period."

"Sir, I don't think—"

"Listen, my predecessor let the military run rampant. He got them all jazzed up and let them off their leashes. It's high time we put the collar back on. We can't have U.S. soldiers going around shooting sleeping men in the head. Scott, can we do it?"

"There's precedent both ways, but I think a case can be made to stick. We'd have to start the ball at the Pentagon, then have it bumped to justice, then bring in Army CID."

Kealty nodded. "Do it. Time to let the grunts know who's in charge."

A damned fine day for fishing, Arlie Fry decided, but then again, just about any day was a fine day for fishing—at least here, that was. Not like Alaska, where they shot that show, *Deadliest Catch*. Fishing there had to be hell on earth.

The fog was thick, but it was a Northern California morning, after all, so a little muck was to be expected. Arlie knew it would lift within a couple of hours.

His boat, a twenty-one-foot Atlas Acadia 20E with a Ray Electric outboard motor, was just three months old, a retirement gift from his wife, Eunice, who'd chosen the inshore saltwater launch model in hopes of keeping him close to dry land. And there the blame lay again at the feet of the boob tube, specifically that George Clooney movie, *The Perfect Storm*. In his younger days he'd had dreams of sailing across the Atlantic, but he knew the stress of that would outright kill Eunice, so he satisfied himself with biweekly coastal fishing trips, most often alone, but today he'd talked his son into coming along. Chet, now fifteen, was more interested in girls, his iPod, and when he could get his learner's permit than he was in catching yellowtails and lingcods—though he did perk up when Arlie mentioned having seen a shark on his last outing. The story had been true, but the shark was only two feet long.

Currently Chet sat in the bow, earbuds in his ears, as he leaned over the gunwale and trailed his hand in the water.

The sea was mostly flat, with a slight chop, and high above Arlie could see the sun, a fuzzy pale circle, trying to burn its way through the clouds. Be bright and hot within the hour, he thought. Eunice had packed them plenty of soft drinks, half a dozen baloney sandwiches, and a plastic Baggie filled with Fig Newtons.

Suddenly something thumped against the Acadia's hull. Chet jerked his hand out of the water and stood up, causing the boat to rock. "Whoa!"

"What is it?"

"Something hit the side. . . . There, see it?"

Arlie looked where Chet was pointing, just off the stern, and caught a glimpse of something orange just before the fog swallowed it.

"You get a look at it?" Arlie asked.

"Not really. Scared the shit—heck—out of me. Looked like maybe a life jacket or bumper float."

Arlie briefly considered continuing on, but the object, whatever it was, hadn't been just orange but international orange, which was generally reserved for distress and emergencies. And life jackets.

"Sit down, son, I'm coming about." Arlie turned the wheel and brought the Acadia back on a reverse course, slowing as he did so. "Keep an eye out."

"Yeah, Dad, I am. Jeez."

Thirty seconds later Chet called out and pointed off the port bow. Just visible through the fog was an orange blob about the size of a soccer ball.

"I see it," Arlie said, and steered that way, bringing the object alongside. Chet leaned over and snagged it.

It wasn't a life jacket, Arlie saw, but a diamond-shaped rubber float. Attached to it was a two-foot painter line, and attached to that was a black metal box, roughly four inches wide, eight long, and about as thick as a good-sized paperback book.

"What is it?" Chet asked.

Arlie wasn't sure, but he'd seen enough movies and television shows to have a hunch. "Black box," he muttered.

"Huh?"

"Flight data recorder."

"Whoa . . . You mean like from a plane?"

"Yeah."

"Cool."

The facility's security was decent enough, Cassiano knew, but three things were working in his favor: One, he'd been working for Petrobras for eleven years, long before the discovery of Tupi. Two, the industry was unique above all others, so hired security personnel could competently check only so much of the facility's inner workings. The rest had to be done by workers who knew what they were looking at and how things worked, and so while such double-duty provided a good paycheck and ensured the smooth running of the facility, it also gave Cassiano unfettered access to high-security areas. And three, the demographics of Brazil itself.

Of Brazil's estimated population of 170 million, less than one percent is Muslim, and of that number only one percent are made up of Brazilian-born Islamic converts. The rising tide of Islamic radicals so feared in other Western hemisphere countries was in Brazil a virtual nonissue. No one cared what mosque you went to or whether you hated the war in Iraq; those subjects rarely came up and certainly had no bearing on your job fitness, whether it be at a restaurant or at Petrobras.

Cassiano kept his thoughts to himself, prayed in private,

was never late for work, and rarely took sick days. Muslim or not, he was the ideal worker, for both Petrobras and for his new employer, which certainly paid much better.

The details they'd asked him to provide made their intentions fairly transparent, and while Cassiano didn't particularly like the idea of playing the role of industrial spy, he took comfort in their assurances that the only damage his actions and information would cause would be monetary. Besides, he told himself, with the extent of the Santos Basin find growing by leaps and bounds, the government of Brazil, which was a majority shareholder in Petrobras, would have money to burn for decades to come.

There was no reason he shouldn't share in that boon, was there?

25

"Carpenter is inbound," the radio chirped next to where Andrea was sitting.

"Want me to get him, boss?" she asked.

"No, I'll get it." Ryan got up from his computer and walked to the front door. "He'll be staying for dinner, by the way."

"Sure, boss."

Arnie van Damm had never been one to stand on ceremony. He'd rented a car at BWI Airport and driven himself down. Still wore those L.L.Bean shirts and khaki pants, too, Jack saw, as he got out of his Hertz Chevy.

"Hey, Jack," the former Chief of Staff called in greeting.

"Arnie, it's been a while. How was the flight?"

"Slept for most of it." They headed inside. "How's the book coming?"

"It's kinda hard on the ego to write about yourself, but I'm trying to tell the truth."

"Whoa, boy, that ought to confuse the reviewers at the *Times*."

"Well, hell, they never did like me much. I wouldn't expect them to change now."

"Hell, Jack, you just fought off an attempt on your life—"

"Bullshit, Arnie."

"Perception, my friend. The public hears about that kind of thing, all they absorb is that somebody tried to kill you and paid the price."

"So what, omnipotence by proxy?"

"You got it."

By this time they were in the kitchen and Jack was pouring the coffee. It'd be an hour before Cathy got home, and Jack still had time for a little unauthorized afternoon caffeine. "So give me the gossip. I heard the Supreme Court's giving Kealty fits."

"You mean not being able to make appointments? Yeah, he's going quietly nuts about it. During the campaign he promised a seat to Professor Mayflower at Harvard Law."

"That guy? Christ, he wants to rewrite the Gospel of Saint Matthew."

"God didn't go to Harvard. Otherwise He would have been better informed," van Damm offered.

Ryan chuckled at this. "So: Why this visit?"

"I think you know, Jack. Moreover, I think you've been thinking about it yourself. Tell me I'm wrong."

"You're wrong."

"Another thing I always loved about you, Jack: You never could tell a lie worth a damn."

· Ryan grumbled.

"Being a bad liar ain't a bad thing," Arnie said. "Kealty is already heading off the rails, Jack. Just my opinion, but—"

"He's a crook. Everybody knows that, but the papers won't say it."

"He's a crook, but he's their crook. They think they can control him. They understand him and how he thinks."

"Who says he thinks at all? He doesn't think. He has a vision of the way he wants the world to be. He's willing to do anything to make the world conform with that idea—if you can call it an idea."

"What about your ideas, Jack?"

"It's called principle; there's a difference. You sell the principle as best you can and hope the public understands. Anything more than that and you're a used-car salesman."

"A famous politician once said that politics is the art of the possible."

"But if you limit yourself to what's possible—to what's already been done—how the hell does progress happen? Kealty wants to bring back the thirties, with FDR and all that goes with that."

"Thought much about this, Jack?" Arnie said with a hint of a smile.

"You know I have. The Founding Fathers would turn over in their crypts over what that bonehead is doing."

"So replace him."

"And go through all that again—to what end?"

"Edmund Burke, remember? 'All that is required for the triumph of evil is for good men to do nothing.'"

"I should have seen that coming," Jack responded. "I served my time. I fought two wars. I set up my own line of succession. I did everything a man is supposed to do."

"And you did it well," the former Chief of Staff admitted. "Jack, here's the bottom line: The country needs you."

"No, Arnie. The country doesn't need me. We still have a good Congress."

"Yeah, they're fine, but they haven't generated a real leader yet. Owens, from Oklahoma, he has possibilities, but he has a way to go yet. Not seasoned enough, too small-town and too idealistic. He's not ready for major league ball yet."

"You could say the same thing about me," Ryan pointed out.

"True, but you listen, and mostly you know what you don't know."

"Arnie, I *like* the life I have now. I have work to keep me busy, but I don't have to run my ass off. I don't have to watch every single word I say for fear of offending people who don't like me anyway. I can walk around the house without my shoes on, and without wearing a tie."

"You're bored."

"I've earned the right to be bored." Ryan paused, took a sip of coffee, then tried to change the subject: "What's Pat Martin doing now?"

"He doesn't want to be AG again," van Damm responded. "He's teaching law at Notre Dame. He does seminars for newly frocked judges, too."

"Why not Harvard or Yale?" Ryan wondered.

"Harvard wouldn't have him. They'd like the idea of a former Attorney General there, of course, but not yours. Pat wouldn't go there anyway. He's a football fan, big-time. Harvard plays football, but not like the Dame."

"I remember," Jack admitted. "They wouldn't even play us upstart Catholics at Boston College." And the BC Eagles occasionally got to beat Notre Dame, when the Fates allowed.

"Willing to think about it?" Arnie asked.

"The United States of America chooses her own Presidents, Arnie."

"That's true, but it's like a restaurant with a short menu. You can only choose from what the cook's cooking, and you can't leave and go to Wendy's if you're not happy with the selection."

"Who's sending you?"

"People talk to me. Mostly of your political persuasion—"

Jack cut him off with a raised hand. "I'm not a registered anything, remember?"

"That ought to make the Socialist Workers Party happy. So run as an Independent. Start your own party. Teddy Roosevelt did."

"And lost."

"Better to try and fail than—"

"Yeah, yeah."

"The country needs you. Kealty is already shitting himself. He has his opposition research people digging into you right now. Haven't you heard?"

"Bullshit."

"They've been at it for almost a month. Georgetown's got them worried. I'm telling you, Jack, we need to grab this thing while we can." Ryan started shaking his head. "Listen, you didn't plan it. People are all over the story because your numbers are still high."

"Goddamn sympathy votes—"

"It won't play out that way, believe me, but as far as grand entrances go, this one is golden. So: Got any dirty laundry out there?"

"Nothing you don't know about." But Jack managed to pull off that lie. Only Pat Martin knew about that particular legacy Ryan had left behind. He'd never even told Robby. "I'm too dull to be a politician. Maybe that's why the media never liked me."

"Those opposition research people will have access to everything, Jack, even CIA documents. You must have left some nasty things behind," van Damm persisted. "Everybody does."

"Depends on interpretation, I suppose. But revealing any of it would be a federal felony. How many political pukes would risk that?"

"You're still a babe in the woods, Jack. Aside from being videotaped raping a girl or diddling a young boy, there isn't much a politician would not risk for the Presidency."

"That brings up a question I can't quite get my head around: Does Kealty like being President?"

"He probably doesn't even know himself. Is he doing a good job? No, not really. But he doesn't even know that. He thinks he's doing as well as any man could, and better than most. He likes playing the game. He likes answering the phone. He likes having people come to him when they have a problem. He likes being the guy who answers the questions, even when he doesn't have a clue what the answer is. Remember what Mel Brooks said? 'It's good to be the king,' even if the king is a total fuckup. He wants to be there, and for nobody else to be there, because he's been a politician all his life. It's Mount Everest, and he climbed up it because it's there, and so what if you get to the top and there's nothing you can do there? It's there, and you're on top of it, and nobody else is. Would he kill for the job? Probably, if he had the guts. But he doesn't. He'd have one of his troops do it, deniably, with no written records. You can always find people who do that sort of thing for you, and you kiss them off if they get caught."

"I never—"

"That guy John Clark. He's killed people, and the reasons for it would not always have stood the test of public scrutiny. You have to do that sort of thing when you run a whole country, and fine, maybe it's technically legal, but you keep it secret because it wouldn't look good on the front page of the paper. If you left anything like that behind, Kealty will make it public, through intermediaries and carefully structured leaks."

"If it came to that, I could handle it," Ryan said coolly. He'd never reacted well to threats and had rarely issued them, not without a lot of gun in his holster. But Kealty would never let that happen. Like too many "great" men, and like very many political figures indeed, he was a coward. Cowards were the first to resort to a show of force. It was the sort of power that some men found intoxicating. Ryan had always found it frightening, but Ryan had never had to pull that gun out of the holster without grave cause. "Arnie, I'm not afraid of anything that bastard can throw at me, if it comes to that. But why should it come to that?"

"Because the country needs you, Jack."

"I tried to fix it. I had the best part of five years, and I failed."

"System's too corrupt, eh?"

"I got a decent Congress. Most of them were okay—the ones who've gone back home because of campaign promises. Hell, those were the honest ones, weren't they? Congress is much improved, but the President sets the national tone, and I couldn't change that. Christ knows I tried."

"Callie Weston wrote you some good speeches. You might have made a good priest." Arnie leaned back and finished his coffee. "You did make an earnest effort, Jack. But it wasn't enough."

"So you want me to try again. When you bash your head against a stone wall, the squishy sound gets kinda depressing after a while."

"Have Cathy's friends found a cure for cancer yet?"

"No."

"Have they stopped trying?"

"No," Jack had to admit.

"Because it's worth doing even if it's impossible?"

"Playing with the laws of science is easier than amending human nature."

"Okay, you can always just sit here and watch CNN and read the paper and bitch."

And I do a lot of that, Jack didn't have to admit. The thing about Arnie was that he knew how to manipulate Ryan the same way a four-year-old girl could manipulate her father. Effortlessly and innocently. About as innocently as Bonnie and Clyde in a bank, of course, but Arnie knew how it was done.

"I'll say it again, Jack. Your country—"

"And I'll ask you again: Who sent you?"

"Why do you think somebody sent me?"

"Arnie."

"Nobody, Jack. I mean it. I'm retired, too, remember?"

"Do you miss the action?"

"I don't know, but I'll tell you this: I used to think that politics was the highest form of human activity, but you cured me of that. You have to stand for something. Kealty doesn't. He just wants to be the President of the United States because he figures he was in the line of succession, and it was his turn. At least that's how he sees it."

"So you'd jump with me?" Ryan asked.

"I'll be there to help, and to advise you, and maybe you'll listen to the voice of reason a little better this time around."

"This terrorism thing—it's too big a job for four years."

"Agreed. You can reestablish your program for rebuilding the CIA. Beef up the recruitment program, get operations back on track. Kealty has crippled it, but he hasn't completely destroyed it."

"It would take a decade. Maybe more."

"Then you get it back on track, step aside, and let somebody else finish it."

"Most of my cabinet members won't be coming back."

"So what? Find new ones," Arnie observed coldly. "The country's full of talented people. Find some honest ones and work your Jack Ryan magic."

Ryan Senior snorted at this. "It'll be a long campaign."

"Your first real one. Four years ago you were running for

coronation, and it worked. It was disgustingly easy, flying around and giving speeches to uniformly friendly crowds—most of whom just wanted to see who they were voting for. With Kealty, it'll be different. You'll even have to debate him—and don't underestimate him. He's a skilled political operator, and he knows how to hit low," Arnie warned. "You're not used to that."

Ryan sighed. "You're a son-of-a-bitch, you know that? If you want me to commit to this, you're going to be disappointed. I'll have to think it over. I do have a wife and four kids."

"Cathy will agree. She's a lot tougher and a lot smarter than people realize," van Damm noted. "You know what Kealty said last week?"

"What's that?"

"On national health care. Some local TV crew in Baltimore interviewed her. She must have had a weak moment and said that she didn't think government health care was a very good idea. Kealty's reaction was, 'What the hell does a doctor know about health-care issues?'"

"How come that didn't make the papers?" It was delightfully juicy, after all.

"Anne Quinlan is Ed's Chief of Staff. She managed to talk the *Times* out of putting it in print. Anne is no dummy. The managing editor up in New York is an old friend of hers."

"How is it that they always bagged me when I put my foot in it?" Ryan demanded.

"Jack, Ed is one of them. You, on the other hand, are not. Don't you ever cut your friends some slack? So do they. They're human beings, too." Arnie's demeanor was more relaxed now. He'd won his main battle. It was time for magnanimity.

Having to think of reporters as human beings was enough of a stretch for Ryan at the moment.

26

Nearly a quarter of the world's supply of heavy-lift cranes, Badr thought, staring out over Port Rashid. Thirty thousand of the world's 125,000 cranes, all gathered in one place and for one purpose—to turn Dubai into the jewel of the planet and a paradise for the wealthiest of its inhabitants.

From where he stood he could see offshore the Palm and World islands—vast man-made archipelagoes, one in the shape of the tree itself, the other the earth—as well as the Burj Al Arab hotel, a 1,000-plus-foot-tall spire in the shape of a giant sail.

Inland, the city was a sea of skyscrapers and crisscrossing highways and construction equipment. And in another five years, attractions would continue to pop up across the landscape: the Dubai Waterfront, a crescent extending some fifty miles into the ocean; the Hydropolis Underwater Hotel; the Sports City and ski dome complexes; Space Science World. In less than a decade, Dubai had gone from what many considered little more than a desolate backwater speck on the map to one of the world's top resort destinations, a playground for the super-rich. Before long, Badr thought, Dubai's amenities and attractions would outpace even those of Las Vegas. Or perhaps not, Badr reminded himself. The global economic crisis had hit the UAE as well. Many of the cranes looming over the city were, in fact, still, as construction projects had ground to a halt. Badr suspected this was the hand of Allah. Such decadence in an Arab country was unthinkable.

"Magnificent, isn't it?" Badr heard behind him, and he turned around.

"My apologies for being late," the real-estate agent said. "As you've probably noticed, construction can be something of a nuisance. Mr. Almasi, yes?"

Badr nodded. It was not his name, of course, and the agent probably suspected as much, but another of Dubai's many admirable traits was a universal respect for discretion and anonymity among its army of bankers, brokers, and agents. Business was business and money was money, and each was held in greater esteem than arbitrary and wholly subjective codes of conduct.

"Yes," Badr replied. "Thank you for meeting me."

"Not at all. This way, please."

The agent walked to a nearby electric golf cart. Badr got in, and they started down the pier.

"You probably noticed the dock is not concrete," the agent said.

"I did." In fact, the surface had a slightly terra-cotta hue to it.

"It's a composite material—something akin to synthetic decking material, I'm told, but much stronger and durable, and the color will hold for a lifetime. The designers thought it a more attractive alternative to standard gray concrete."

They stopped before a warehouse at the far end and got out. "You mentioned the need for privacy," the agent said. "Will this do?"

"Yes, I think so."

"As you can see, it's a corner unit, with water-access points at the front and the side. Enough to accommodate two ships of three hundred feet each. Of course, tracked derricks are available for lease, should you require them."

The truth was, Badr knew little about his client's requirement beyond the size and layout of the warehouse and the period of time it would be needed. Access and privacy, he'd been told, were paramount.

"May I see the inside?" he asked.

"Of course."

The agent produced a card key and slid it through a reader beside the door. There was a soft beep. The agent pressed his thumb onto a pad beside the reader. A few moments later the lock clicked open.

"The card keys and biometric reader are fully programmable by the lessee. You and you alone would control who has access to the facility."

"How is that done?"

"Through our secure website. Once your account is created, you simply log on, program the cards, and scan in the fingerprint records. All the data is encrypted with what's called TLS, or Transport Layer Security, and digital certificates."

"Very good. And the police?"

"In the last ten years I can count on one hand the number of times the police have asked for warrants to search our facilities. Of those, all but one were denied by the courts. We pride ourselves on providing security and anonymity—both within the legal bounds of the Emirates, of course."

They stepped inside. The space, which measured two thousand square feet, was empty. The floor and walls were made of the same composite material as the dock but tinted off-white. No windows, either, which had been an item on his client's wish list. Not a must but certainly a plus. The air was cool, hovering in the low seventies, he judged.

"Comfortable, yes?" the agent asked.

Badr nodded. "Fire- and theft-control systems?"

"Both. Monitored by our control center less than a mile away. In case of fire, a halon suppression system is activated. In case of unauthorized breach, the lessee is contacted for further instructions."

"Not the police?"

"Only on the lessee's approval."

"What about your company? Surely you have access to—"

"No. If a lessee's rent is found to be overdue by seven days, we make every attempt to contact them. At the fourteen-day mark, if contact still hasn't been established, the card reader and biometric scanner are removed and the locking system dismantled—an expensive and time-consuming process which would, of course, be charged to the lessee's account, as would any reinstallation of these systems. Similarly, all contents of their warehouse would be forfeit."

"You won't have that problem with us, I assure you," Badr replied.

"I have no doubt. We do have a minimum one-year contract, with six-month increments beyond that."

"A year should do." A month would do, actually, he'd been told. The warehouse would sit empty after that, its purpose— whatever that was—having been served. In fact, within days of his client's departure, the financial artifices put in place to affect the lease would be the only thing left for the authorities to find, and even those would lead only to more closed accounts and front companies. The "money trail," which the American intelligence community was so good at following, would be ice-cold.

"We can also provide assistance in streamlining the customs process, should you have cargo to offload," the agent said. "Export licenses would be your responsibility, however."

"I understand," Badr replied with a barely suppressed smile. Something told him the last thing his clients were concerned about was export licenses. He took a final look around, then turned to the agent. "How soon can you have the lease drawn up?"

Though Adnan would never know it, his counterparts were not only further along in their mission but were riding in the relative comfort of a charter boat—albeit a converted Russian landing craft.

For days Adnan and his men had been traveling up the coast road along the Kara Sea, through fishing hamlets and abandoned settlements and the whited-out desolate landscape, seeing only the occasional vehicle on the road, and none heading in their same direction—a fact that Adnan was doing his best to not take as an omen. He had trouble imagining anyone living here voluntarily. At least in the desert you could take cheer in the sunlight. Here, gray overcast skies seemed more the rule than the exception.

As he'd expected, finding shelter for their nightly stops wasn't hard, but finding shelter that was little more than a shack was something altogether different. On the first night they'd been lucky enough to find an abandoned wall tent with a working woodstove, and while the canvas walls were pitted and had lost their waterproofing, the support poles were buried deep in the ground and the support wires were still taut, so they'd spent the night in relative comfort while outside near-gale-force winds whipped the snow and ice against the canvas like shrapnel and the waves roared against the rocks. The second night they'd been less fortunate, having to huddle together in their sleeping bags in the rear of the truck as the sieve-like canvas sides rippled in the wind. After several hours of trying to sleep, they'd given up and spent the reminder of the night drinking tea brewed on their portable camp stove and waiting for the first signs of dawn.

And now, after three days of travel, they were within a day or a day and a half of their destination—or so said the map, which Adnan consulted warily, taking care to double-check its markings and measurements against the readings on his own handheld GPS unit. *Destination* wasn't quite the right word, though, was it? *Stepping-stone,* perhaps. Providing their charter captain was as good as his word and he wanted to earn the remainder of his fee, they'd be one step closer to their goal, an idea that caused Adnan no small amount of trepidation. From what little he'd read about the place, their current surroundings, bleak as they were, would soon prove to be comparatively luxurious. And then there was the disease. They had pills for that, but the doctor who had provided the doses had been unsure about the efficacy. They would help, Adnan was told, but there were no guarantees. Their best protection would be speed and caution. The longer they spent there, the higher the risk. The worst of it was that none of them would know whether they were safe until many years had passed, never knowing until too late that invisible death was eating away at them. *No matter,* he told himself. Death was death, simply a bridge to paradise, and his men knew that as well as he did. To doubt that was an insult to Allah.

Despite the brutal cold and meager rations, not one of them had uttered the slightest complaint. They were good men, faithful to both Allah and the cause—which were, of course, one and the same. And while he was reasonably confident they would remain steadfast when he finally revealed the purpose of their journey, he knew he couldn't let down his guard. The Emir had personally chosen him for this mission, and their job was too important to let fear turn them away.

But what about the task itself? Adnan asked himself. His instructions were detailed and clear, and readily accessible in his pack—several dozen laminated pages—but what if there were complications? What if their tools were inadequate for the job? What if they cut in the wrong place or the winch system could not support the load? And what if, God forbid, the security measures had changed since they received the information?

Stop, he commanded himself. Like fear, self-doubt was a trick of the mind, a weakness to be overcome through faith in Allah, and in the Emir. He was a wise man, a great man, and he'd assured Adnan that their prize would be there waiting for them. They would find it, do whatever was necessary to secure it, then return.

Three more days, then five more back.

<h1 style="text-align:center">27</h1>

Jack Junior shut his computer down and left his cubbyhole, heading out to the parking lot and his yellow Hummer H2, one of his few guilty pleasures in life. Still, with gas prices and the general state of the economy where they were, he felt a pang of guilt every time he turned the ignition key on the damned thing. He was no tree hugger, that much was certain, but maybe it was time to think about scaling back. Damn, his annoyingly eco-aware little sister was rubbing off on him. He'd heard Cadillac was making a pretty decent Escalade Hybrid. Might be worth a trip to the dealership.

He had a rare dinner with Mom and Dad scheduled for tonight. Sally would be there, too, probably full of ideas from her medical school. She had to think about picking her specialty, and for that she'd be bending Mom's ear. And Katie would be as charming as ever, doting as she did on her big brother, which could be a pain in the ass, but SANDBOX wasn't all that bad for a little sister. Family night, steak and spinach salad, baked potato, and corn on the cob, because that was his father's favorite supper. Maybe a glass of wine now that he was old enough.

The life of a presidential son had its drawbacks, Jack had long ago learned. His protective detail was gone, thankfully, though he was never entirely sure that he didn't have covert coverage on him. He'd asked Andrea about it and been told that he no longer had troops assigned, but who was to say that she was entirely truthful about it?

He parked on the street in front of his apartment, and went inside to change into slacks and a flannel shirt, then out again. Before long he was on I-97 for the ride down to Annapolis and thence to Peregrine Cliff.

His parents had built a sizable house before entering government service. The bad news was that everyone knew where it was. Cars would drive by the narrow country road and stop to stare at it, not knowing that every tag was recorded and computer checked by the Secret Service via a gaggle of concealed TV cameras. They might guess that a concealed structure within seventy yards of the main house held a minimum of six armed agents in case someone tried to pass through the gate and motor up the driveway. He knew his father found it oppressive. It was a major production even to go to the local Giant to get a loaf of bread and a quart of milk.

The prisoner in the gilded cage, Jack thought.

"SHORTSTOP, coming in," he told the gatepost, and a camera would make sure of his identity before the gate opened. The Secret Service disliked his choice of car. The bright yellow of his Hummer was conspicuous, that much was certain.

He parked, got out, and walked to the door, beside which he found Andrea.

"Didn't get a chance to talk to you afterward," she said to him. "It was a hell of a thing you did, Jack. If you hadn't caught it . . ."

"Then you just would've had a longer shot, that's all."

"Maybe. Still, thanks."

"You bet. We know anything about the guy? Heard a rumor he might be URC."

Andrea considered this for a moment. "I can neither confirm nor deny," she said with a smile and a distinct emphasis on *confirm.*

So the Emir tried to take out Dad, Jack thought. *Un-fucking-believable.* He quashed the impulse to return to his computer at The Campus. The Emir was out there, and sooner or later he'd run out of running room; sadly, though, Jack wouldn't be there when it happened.

"Motive?"

"Shock value, we're thinking. Your dad might be a 'former,' but he's still damned popular. Plus, the logistics are more manageable—easier to kill a retired President than a sitting one."

"Maybe easier, but sure as hell not easy. You proved that."

"*We* proved that," Andrea said with a smile. "You want an application?"

Jack smiled at this. "I'll let you know how the trading business goes. Thanks, Andrea." He pushed through the door. "Hey, I'm home!" he called.

"Hi, Jack," Jack Junior's mom said, emerging from the kitchen with a hug and a kiss. "You look pretty good."

"So do you, Professor-of-surgery lady. Where's Dad?"

She pointed to his right. "Library. He's got company. Arnie."

Jack headed over there, up the short steps and turning left into Dad's workplace. Dad was sitting in his swivel chair, with Arnie van Damm sprawled in a club chair nearby. "What are you guys conspiring on or for?" he asked on his way into the room.

"Conspiracies don't work," his father said tiredly. There'd been a lot of that talk during his presidency, and his father detested all of it, though he'd once joked of having the presidential helicopter fleet painted black just to annoy the idiots who believed that nothing happened on planet earth without a dark conspiracy's having brought it about. It didn't help that John Patrick Ryan Sr. was both wealthy and a former employee of the Central Intelligence Agency, of course—a combination sure to create a conspiracy buzz, real or imagined.

"Ain't that a shame, Pop," Jack offered, coming over for a hug. "What's Sally doing?"

"Went to the store for the salad fixings. Took Mom's car. What's new?"

"Learning currency arbitrage. It's kinda spooky."

"Making any moves yourself?"

"Well, no, not yet, no big ones anyway, but I advise people."

"Theoretical accounts?"

"Yeah, I made half a million virtual dollars last week," he said.

"You can't spend virtual dollars, Jack."

"I know, but you have to start somewhere, right? So, Arnie, trying to get Dad to run again?" he asked.

"Why do you say that?" van Damm asked.

Maybe it was the setting, Jack thought. His eyebrow went up a little, but he didn't press the issue. And so everyone in the room knew something the other two didn't know. Arnie didn't know about The Campus and his father's part in setting it up, didn't know about the blank pardons, didn't know what his father had authorized. Dad didn't know his own son worked there. And Arnie knew more political secrets than anyone since the Kennedy administration, most of which never left his lips, even to the sitting President.

"D.C.'s a mess," Jack offered, wondering what it might break loose.

Van Damm wasn't buying: "Usually is."

"Makes you wonder what people were thinking in 1914, how the country was going to hell in a basket back then—but nobody remembers that now. Is that because somebody fixed it, or was it because none of it really mattered?"

"The first Wilson administration," Arnie responded. "War breaking out in Europe, but nobody saw how badly it would all turn out yet. Took another year before reality sank in, and by then it was too late for anyone to figure a way out of it. Henry Ford tried, but he got laughed out of town."

"Is that because the problem was too big, or the people were too small and too dumb?" Jack wondered.

"They didn't see it coming," the senior Ryan said. "They were too busy dealing with the day-to-day stuff to step back and see the big historic trends."

"Like all politicians?"

"Professional politicians tend to focus on the small issues rather than the large ones, yes," Arnie agreed. "They try to maintain continuity because it's easier to keep the train on the same tracks. Trouble is, what do you do when the tracks come unglued around the next turn? That's why it's a hard job, even for smart men."

"And nobody saw terrorism coming, either."

"No, Jack, we didn't, at least not entirely," the former President admitted. "Some did. Hell, with a better intelligence service we might have, but that damage was done thirty years ago, and nobody ever really made it right."

"What does work?" Jack asked. "What would have made the difference?" It was a sufficiently general question that it might generate a truthful answer.

"Signals intelligence—we're still the best at that, probably—but there's no substitute for HUMINT—real field spooks, talking to real people and finding out what they really think."

"And killing some?" Jack asked, just to see what would result.

"There's not much of that," his father responded. "At least, not outside Hollywood."

"Not what it says in the papers."

"They still report Elvis sightings, too," Arnie replied.

"Heck, maybe it would be good if James Bond were real, but he isn't," the former President observed. It might have been the undoing of the Kennedy administration, which had started to buy in to the 007 fiction, except for an idiot named Oswald. So did history take its major turns at accidents, assassins, and bad luck? Maybe a decent conspiracy was possible once, but not anymore. Too many lawyers, too many reporters, too many bloggers and Handycams and digital cameras.

"How do we fix it?"

That caused Jack Senior's head to look up—rather sadly, his son thought. "I tried once, remember?"

"So then why is Arnie here?"

"Since when did you become so curious?"

"It's my job to look into stuff and figure it all out."

"The family curse," van Damm observed.

That's when Sally walked in. "Well, look who showed up."

"Finished dissecting your cadaver yet?" Junior asked.

"The hard part's putting it back together and having it walk back out the door," Olivia Barbara Ryan shot back. "It beats handling money—dirty stuff, money, full of germs."

"Not when you do it by computer. Nice and clean that way."

"How's my number-one girl?" the former President asked.

"Well, I got the lettuce. Organic. The only way to go. Mom told me to tell you it's time for you to grill the steaks."

Sally didn't approve of steak, but it remained the one thing her father knew how to cook, along with burgers. Since it wasn't summer, he had to do it on a gas grill in the kitchen instead of outside over charcoal. It was enough to get her father to stand up and head toward the kitchen, leaving Junior and Arnie together.

"So, Mr. van Damm, is he going to do it?"

"I think he has to, whether he accepts it yet or not. The country needs him to do it. And it's Arnie now, Jack."

Jack sighed. "That's one family business in which I have no interest. It doesn't pay enough for all the heartbreak that comes along with it."

"Maybe so, but how do you say no to your country?"

"I've never been asked," Jack responded, lying to a minor degree.

"The question is always internal. And your father is hearing it now. What's he going to do? Hell, you're his son. You know him better than I ever will."

"The hard part for Dad is us—Mom and the kids. I think his first loyalty is to us."

"As it should be. Tell me: Any nice girl in your life?" van Damm asked.

"Not yet."

This wasn't entirely true. He and Brenda had been dating for a month or so, and she was special, but Jack wasn't sure she was *that* kind of special. Bring-home-to-the-parents special.

"She's out there, waiting to be found. The good news is that she's looking for you right now, too."

"I'll take your word for it. Question is, will I be old and gray before it happens?"

"You in a hurry?"

"Not especially."

Sally appeared in the doorway. "Dinner, for those who want to devour the flesh of some harmless and inoffensive creature, murdered in Omaha, probably."

"Well, he had a fulfilling life," Jack observed.

Arnie chimed in, "Oh, yeah, they brought the food right to him, lots of friends, all his own age, never had to walk too far, no wolves to worry about, good medical care to handle any diseases he might have had to worry about . . ."

"Just one thing," Sally shot back, leading them down the steps. "They made him climb up a steep ramp into a one-critter cage and zapped his brains with an air hammer."

"Has it ever occurred to you, young lady, that a head of lettuce might scream when it's cut off the stem?"

"It's hard to hear them," Jack chimed in. "They have small vocal cords. We're carnivores, Sally. That's why we have so little enamel on our teeth."

"In that case, we are maladapted. Cholesterol kills us as soon as we're past reproductive age."

"Christ, Sally, you want to run around the woods naked with a stone knife to live? What about your Ford Explorer?" Jack demanded. "And the steer that made our dinner also made the leather for your designer shoes. You can push the eco-freak stuff too far, remember?"

"It becomes religion, Jack," Arnie warned, "and you can't hassle a person over religion."

"A lot of that going around. And not all of it's expressed in words."

"True," Arnie conceded. "But no sense in our adding to it."

"Okay, fine. Sally, tell us about the ozone hole," Jack invited. He'd win that one. Sally liked having a tan too much.

28

As Vitaliy had predicted, his charters didn't drink vodka. He'd purchased four full liters to stock his own cupboard, but though they all smoked, they didn't drink. It only confirmed what he suspected about them. Not that it mattered one way or another. Their money spent the same as anyone else's.

He'd beached his landing craft on a gentle gravel sloping shore, what passed for a beach here. The landing ramp he kept in the up position, lest a bear wander aboard. They were even heading toward prime hunting country, though the hunting season was now closed. While his charters had firearms, they were not of the type fit for big game. He'd thought about shooting one for his own purposes. It would make a good decoration for his wheelhouse, something for clients to remember him by. But he'd never found the time.

The charter party was camped out in the cargo area. Vitaliy had set out plastic mattresses and some folding chairs. They sat there and smoked and talked quietly among themselves, not bothering him much at all. They'd even brought their own food. Not a bad idea. Vanya was not a gourmet cook by any means, and mainly fed himself on Russian Army rations, which he bought for cash from a supply sergeant at Arkhangel'sk.

It was eerily quiet here. Airplanes flew too high to hear them, and even seeing their anticollision lights was difficult and rare enough, so remote from civilization was this part of Russia, home to the occasional adventurer or naturalist, as well as the local fishermen trying to wrest a meager living from the sea. To call this part of Russia an economic backwater was generous. Except for the moribund Russian Navy, there was nothing here for men to do, and half of that was cleaning up a mess or disaster that had gotten sailors killed, the poor sods.

But that, he remembered, was what had brought him here, and for some reason he liked it. The air was always fresh, and the winters were beyond brisk, something a true Russian had in his blood, what made him different from the lesser European breeds.

He checked his watch. The sun would rise at an early hour. He'd shake his charter party loose in five hours or so, let them drink their wake-up tea and eat their buttered bread for breakfast. He had bacon to supplement it but no eggs.

In the morning he'd go out to sea and watch the merchant traffic. There was a surprising amount of that. It made more economic sense than either trucks or the rail line into the new oil fields and the gold-mining complex at Yessey. And they were building an oil pipeline to transport the oil into European Russia, funded by mostly American oil concerns. Locals called it the "American invasion."

Call it a day, he thought. He took a last slug of vodka and settled down on the mattress he'd laid on the deck of the wheelhouse, anticipating five or six hours of sleep.

Save some extra scrutiny at Dallas customs, which Shasif had been told to expect, given his name and face, the plane change had gone smoothly. As instructed, he'd booked a round-trip flight and was carrying luggage commensurate with a week's stay in the United States. Similarly, he had arranged a rental car, booked himself into a hotel, and was well armed with brochures to local attractions, as well as e-mails from friends in the area. Shasif assumed they were real people; either way, it was highly unlikely that the authorities would check.

All the red-flag issues had been covered. Still, the inspection had been nerve-racking, but in the end, it was uneventful. He was waved through the checkpoint and beyond to the gate.

Seven hours after leaving Toronto, he touched down at Los Angeles International Airport at 10:45 in the morning, a little more than two hours' difference on his watch, having essentially traveled backward in time as he crossed the country.

After clearing customs once again, this time under the even unfriendlier eyes of LAX's TSA agents, Shasif made his way to the Alamo counter and waited patiently in line for fifteen minutes. Ten minutes after that he was in his Dodge Intrepid and heading east on Century Boulevard. The car came equipped with one of those navigation computers, so he pulled over at a gas station, punched the address into the computer, then pulled back out and started following the arrows on the computer's screen.

By the time he pulled onto the 405 heading north it was nearing the lunch hour, so the traffic was getting heavier. By the time he reached Highway 10, the Santa Monica Freeway, cars were moving at a sporadic thirty miles an hour. How people lived in such a place, Shasif couldn't imagine. Certainly it was beautiful, but all the noise and commotion . . . How could anyone hope to hear the quiet voice of God? It was no wonder America was in such a state of moral confusion.

The Santa Monica Freeway was moving at a steadier clip, so he reached his turn onto the Pacific Coast Highway within ten minutes. Another seven miles brought him to his destination, Topanga Beach. He pulled into the parking lot, which was three-quarters full, found a spot nearest the beach trail, and pulled in.

He climbed out. The wind was brisk off the ocean, and in the distance he could hear the cawing of seabirds. Over the dunes he could see surfers, five or six of them, carving their way through the surf. Shasif walked through the parking lot and over a small rise covered with scrub brush and onto the service road. Fifty feet down the dirt tract a lone figure stood, staring out over the ocean. The man was of Arab descent. Shasif checked his watch. On time. He walked over to the man.

"Excuse me," Shasif said, "I'm looking for the Reel Inn. I think I may have missed it."

The man turned. His eyes were shielded by a pair of sunglasses. "You did," he replied. "By about three hundred feet. If you are looking for chowder, though, I would try Gladstone's. The prices are higher, but the food's better."

"Thank you."

That done, Shasif didn't know what else to say. Just hand him the package and leave? The man made the decision for him, holding out his hand. Shasif drew the CD-ROM case from his jacket pocket and gave it to the man, noticing as he did the scars on his contact's hands.

Fire, Shasif thought.

"You're staying for a while?" the man asked.

"Yes. Three days."

"Which hotel?"

"The Doubletree. City of Commerce."

"Stay by your phone. We may have something for you. You've done well. If you're interested, we may ask you to play a larger role."

"Of course. Anything I can do."

"We'll be in touch."

And then the man was gone, walking back down the road.

29

Jack Ryan Sr.'s private phone rang, and he lifted it, hoping for a distraction from writing. "Jack Ryan."

"Mr. President?"

"Well, yeah, I used to be," Ryan said, leaning back in his chair. "Who's this?"

"Sir, this is Marion Diggs. They made me FORCECOM. I'm at Fort McPherson, Georgia—Atlanta, actually."

"Four stars now?" Ryan remembered that Diggs had made something of a name for himself a few years back in Saudi Arabia. Pretty good battlefield commander as Buford-Six.

"Yes, sir, that's right."

"How's life in Atlanta?"

"Not too bad. The command has its moments. Sir—" His voice became a little uneasy. "Sir, I need to talk to you."

"What about?"

"I'd prefer to do it in person, sir, not over the phone."

"Okay. Can you come here?"

"Yes, sir, I have a twin-engine aircraft at my disposal. I can be to BWI airport in, oh, two and a half hours or so. Then I can drive down to your home."

"Fair enough. Give me an ETA and I'll have the Secret Service pick you up. Is that agreeable?"

"Yes, sir, that would be fine. I can leave here in fifteen minutes."

"Okay, that puts you at BWI around, oh, one-thirty or so?"

"Yes, sir."

"Make it so, General. You'll be met at the airport."

"Thank you, sir. See you in a few hours."

Ryan hung up and buzzed Andrea Price-O'Day.

"Yes, Mr. President?"

"Got company coming, General Marion Diggs. He's FORCECOM from Atlanta. Flying into BWI. Can you arrange to have him picked up and driven here?"

"Certainly, sir. When's he getting in?"

"About one-thirty, at the general aviation terminal."

"We'll have somebody right there."

The General's twin-prop U-21 arrived and did the usual roll-out, right up to a Ford Crown Victoria. The general was easy to spot in his green shirt with four silver stars on the epaulets. Andrea had driven up herself, and the two didn't talk much on the ride south to Peregrine Cliff.

For his part, Ryan had set up lunch himself, including a pound and a half of corned beef from Attman's on Lombard Street in Baltimore. The drive down and the general's arrival had been handled fairly stealthily. Less than forty minutes after deplaning, Diggs was at the door. Ryan got it himself.

Ryan had met Diggs only once or twice before. A man of equal height, and black as a hunk of anthracite coal, everything about him said "soldier," including, Jack saw, a little bit of unease.

"Hey, General, welcome," Ryan said, taking the man's hand. "What can I do for you?"

"Sir, I'm—well, I'm a little uneasy about this, but I have a problem I think you ought to know about."

"Okay, come on in and build a sandwich. Coke okay?"

"Yes, thank you, sir." Ryan led him into the kitchen. After both men had assembled their sandwiches, Ryan took his seat. Andrea floated around on the periphery. General or not, he wasn't exactly a regular here, and Andrea's job was to keep Ryan alive against all hazards. "So, what's the problem?"

"Sir, President Kealty is going to try and prosecute a U.S. Army sergeant for alleged murder in Afghanistan."

"Murder?"

"That's what the justice department is calling it. They sent down an Assistant Attorney General to my command yesterday, and he questioned me personally. "As commander in chief of Forces Command, I legally own all the operational forces of the U.S. Army—other branches, too, but this is really an Army matter. The soldier involved is a Company First Sergeant (E-8) named Sam Driscoll. He's a special ops soldier, part of the 75th Ranger Regiment at Fort Benning. I pulled his personnel package. He's a very serious soldier, combat record is excellent, a poster-boy soldier and a hell of a good Ranger."

"Okay." Ryan thought about that addition. He'd been to Fort Benning and had gotten the standard VIP tour of the base. The Rangers, all spit and polish for that day, had impressed him as supremely fit kids for whom killing was at the top of their job description. Special operations types, the American counterpart to the British SAS regiment. "What's the problem?"

"Sir, a while back we got an intel blip that the Emir might be in one particular cave, and so we detailed a special operation to go in and try and bag him. It turned out he wasn't there. The problem, sir, is that Driscoll killed nine bad guys, and some people are upset about how he did that."

Ryan was two bites into his sandwich. "And?"

"And it came to the President's attention, and he directed DOJ to prosecute him for—that is, to investigate this incident for—a possible murder investigation, since it may or may not have violated an executive order for battlefield conduct. Driscoll took down nine people, some of them asleep."

"Murder? Awake or asleep, they were enemy combatants, right?"

"Yes, sir. Driscoll had an adverse tactical situation, and in his judgment as the senior NCO on the scene, he had to eliminate them before continuing the mission. And so he did. But the guys at Justice—all political appointees, if that matters—seem to think he should have arrested them instead of killing them."

"Where does Kealty come into this?" Jack asked, sipping some of his Coke.

"He read the report, and he was upset by it. So he brought it to the AG's attention, and then the AG sent one of his people down to me to commence the investigation." Diggs set his sandwich down. "Sir, this is hard for me. I swore an oath to uphold the Constitution, and the President is my commander in chief, but goddamn it, this is one of my soldiers, a good soldier, doing a tough job. I have a duty to be loyal to the President, but—"

"But you have a responsibility to be loyal to your sergeants," Ryan finished the statement.

"Yes, sir. Driscoll might not be much in the great scheme of things, but he's a fine soldier."

Ryan thought this one over. Driscoll was only a soldier to Kealty, a low form of life. Had he been a union bus driver it might be different, but the U.S. Army didn't have unions yet. For Diggs it was a question of justice, and a question of morale, which would suffer throughout the armed forces if this soldier went to prison, or even to a general court-martial over this incident.

"Where's the law on this?" Jack asked.

"Sir, it's a bit of a muddle. The President did send out

orders, but they were not terribly clear, and anyway, such orders do not generally apply to special operations. His mission was to locate and capture this Emir guy if they found him— or kill him if that's how it worked out. Soldiers are not policemen. They're not trained for it, and they're crummy at it when they try. From where I sit, Driscoll didn't do anything wrong at all. Under the rules of war, you don't have to warn an enemy before you kill him. It's *his* job to look out for his own safety, and if he screws up, well, that's his tough luck. Shooting a guy in the back is perfectly all right on a battlefield. That's how soldiers are trained. In this case, four bad guys were asleep in the racks, and Sergeant Driscoll saw to it that they didn't wake up. End of story."

"Is this going to go any further?"

"The Assistant AG seemed to be pretty worked up about it. I tried to explain the facts of life to him, but he just tried to explain the facts of life back to me. Sir, I've been a soldier for thirty-four years. I ain't never heard anything like this." He paused. "The President sent us there. Just like into Iraq, but he's running this like—like Vietnam was once, I suppose. We've lost a lot of people, good people, to their microman-agement, but this one—Jesus, sir, I just don't know what to do."

"Not much I can do about it, General, I'm not the President anymore."

"Yes, sir, but I had to go to somebody. Ordinarily I report directly to the SecDef, but that's a waste of time."

"Have you spoken with President Kealty?"

"Waste of time, sir. He's not very interested in talking to people in uniform."

"And I am?"

"Yes, sir. You were always somebody we could talk to."

"And what do you want me to do?"

"Sir, Sergeant Driscoll deserves a fair shake. We sent him

into the mountains with a mission. The mission was not accomplished, but that wasn't his fault. We've drilled a lot of dry holes there. This turned out to be just one more, but goddamn it, sir, if we send any more troops into those hills, and if we clobber this guy for doing his job, every hole we drill will be dry."

"Okay, General, you've made your point. We have to support our people. Anything this guy should have done different?"

"No, sir. He's a by-the-book soldier. Everything he did was consistent with his training and experience. The Ranger Regiment—well, they're paid killers, maybe, but sometimes that's a useful sort of thing to have in your bag. War is about killing. We don't send messages. We don't try to educate our enemies. Once we go into the field, our job is to kill them. Some people don't like that, but that's what we're paid for."

"Okay, I'll look into this and maybe raise a little hell. What are the ground rules?"

"I brought a copy of Sergeant Driscoll's report for you to read, along with the name of the Assistant AG who tried to ram it up my ass. Goddamn it, sir, this is a good soldier."

"Fair enough, General. Anything else?"

"No, sir. Thanks for lunch."

He'd had maybe one bite of his sandwich, Ryan saw. Diggs walked back out to the car.

30

The flight was uneventful. The rollout ended, and they'd been on the aircraft for eight and a half hours when the transfer bus pulled up to the left-front door of the 777. Clark didn't sit. He'd done enough of that to make his legs stiff. The same was true of his grandson, who looked excitedly out at his native land—he'd actually been born in the UK, but he already had a baseball and his first glove. He'd be playing T-ball in six months or so, and he'd be eating real hot dogs as an American boy was supposed to. On a roll, with mustard, and maybe some onions or relish.

"Glad to be home, baby?" Ding asked Patsy.

"I liked it over there, and I'll miss my friends, but home is home."

Despite urging to go on ahead from both Clark and Chavez, their wives had gotten off the plane at Heathrow, and no amount of argument had changed their minds. "We're going home together," Sandy had declared, firmly bringing the discussion to an end.

The Tripoli op had gone off without any significant hitches. Eight bad guys KIA with only minor injuries among the hostages. Within five minutes of Clark's "go" to Masudi, local ambulances pulled up to the embassy to treat the hostages, most of whom were suffering from dehydration but little else. Minutes after that, the Swedish Säkerhetspolisen and Rikskriminalpolisen arrived and took charge of the embassy, and two hours after that, Rainbow was back aboard the same Piaggio P180 Avanti they'd flown in on, heading north for Taranto, then London.

The official debrief of the operation with Stanley, Weber, and the others would come later, probably via secure webcam once Clark and Chavez had settled back into life in the United States. Including them in the debrief was as much a courtesy as it was a necessity, and probably a little more of the former. He and Ding were officially separated from Rainbow, and Stanley had been right there in Tripoli, so aside from the "lessons learned" postmortem they did for each mission, Clark had little to offer the official report.

"How you feeling?" John Clark asked his wife now.

"I'll sleep it off." Westbound jet lag was always easier to deal with. The eastbound kind could be a killer. She stretched. Even first-class seats on British Airways had their limitations. Air travel, while convenient, is rarely good for you. "Got the passports and stuff?"

"Right here, babe," Ding assured her, tapping his jacket pocket. J.C. must have been one of the youngest Americans ever to have a black diplomatic passport. But Ding also had his .45 Beretta automatic pistol, and the gold badge and ID card that said he was a deputy U.S. marshal, which was very useful indeed for an armed man in an international airport. He even still had his British carry permit—rare enough that the Queen practically had to sign it. The former allowed them to speed through customs and immigration.

After customs, they found in the public reception area a nondescript man holding a cardboard card with CLARK written on it, and the party of five moved to where he was.

"How was the flight?" The usual question.

"Fine." The usual answer.

"I'm parked outside. Blue Plymouth Voyager with Virginia tags. You'll be staying at the Key Bridge Marriott, two top-floor suites." *Which will have been fully swept,* he didn't have to add. The Marriott chain did a lot of government business, especially the one at the Key Bridge, overlooking Washington.

"And tomorrow?" John asked.

"You're scheduled for eight-fifteen."

"Who are we seeing?" Clark asked.

The man shrugged. "It'll be on the seventh floor."

Clark and Chavez traded an *oh, shit* look, but for all that it wasn't surprising, and both were ready for a lengthy night's sleep that would probably end about 0530 at the latest, but this time without the three-mile run and the daily dozen setting-up exercises.

239

"How was England?" The receptionist/driver asked on the way out.

"Civilized. Some of it was pretty exciting," Chavez told him, but then realized that the official greeter was a junior field officer who hadn't a clue what they'd been doing in Old Blighty. Probably just as well. He didn't have the look of former military, though you couldn't always tell.

"You catch any rugby while you were over there?" their escort asked.

"A little. You have to be nuts to play that without pads," Clark offered. "But they are a little peculiar over there."

"Maybe they're just tougher than we are."

The ride toward D.C. was uneventful, helped by the fact that they were just ahead of the evening rush hour and not going all the way into the city. The effects of jet lag struck even these experienced travelers, and by the time they got to the hotel, the presence of bellmen seemed a very good idea. Inside five minutes they were on the top floor in adjoining suites, and J.C. was already looking at the king-size bed he'd have to himself. Patsy gave the same sort of look to the bathtub—it was smaller than the monsters the Brits built, but there was room to sit down, and a limitless supply of hot water just on the other side of the tap. Ding picked a chair and got the remote, and settled in to get reacquainted with American television.

Next door, John Clark left the unpacking to Sandy and raided the minibar for a miniature of Jack Daniel's Old No. 7. The Brits didn't understand bourbon or its Tennessee cousin, and the first stiff shot, even without ice, was a rare delight.

"What's tomorrow?" Sandy asked.

"Have to have a meeting on the seventh floor."

"Who with?"

"He didn't say. Probably a deputy assistant director of

operations. I haven't kept track of the lineup at Langley. Whoever he is, he'll tell me about the great retirement package they have set up for me. Sandy, I think it's about time for me to hang it up."

He couldn't add that he'd never really considered the possibility of living this long. So his luck hadn't quite run out? Remarkable. He'd have to buy himself a laptop and get serious about an autobiography. But for the moment: stand up, stretch, pick up his suit jacket and hang it in the closet before Sandy yelled at him for being a slob again. On the lapel was the sky-blue ribbon and five white stars that denoted the Medal of Honor. Jack Ryan had arranged that for him, after looking into his Navy service record and a lengthy document written by Vice Admiral Dutch Maxwell, God rest his soul. He'd been away when Maxwell had checked out at eighty-three—he'd been in Iran, of all places, trying to see if a network of agents had been completely rolled up by Iranian security. That process had begun, but John had managed to get five of them out of the country alive, via the UAE, along with their families. Sonny Maxwell was still flying, a senior captain for Delta, father of four. The medal was for getting Sonny out of North Vietnam. It now seemed like something that had happened during the last ice age. But he had this little ribbon to show for it, and that beat a kick in the balls. Somewhere packed away were the mess jacket and black shoes of a chief bosun's mate, along with the gold Budweiser badge of a Navy SEAL. In most Navy NCO clubs he wouldn't have been allowed to buy his own beers, but Jesus, today the chiefs looked so damned young. Once they'd seemed like Noah himself.

But the good news was that he wasn't dead yet. And he could look forward to honorable retirement, and maybe doing that autobiography, if Langley ever let him publish it. Not very likely. He knew a lot of things that ought not to be known, and he'd done one or two things that probably ought not to have been done, though at the time his life had ridden on that particular horse. Things like that didn't always make sense to the people who sat at desks in the Old Headquarters Building, but for them the big part of the day was finding a good parking place and whether or not the cafeteria had spice cake on the dessert stack.

He could see Washington, D.C., out the window. The Capitol Building, the Lincoln Memorial, and George's marble obelisk, plus the surpassingly ugly buildings that housed various government departments.

To John Terrence Clark it was just a whole city composed of headquarters pukes for whom reality was a file folder in which the papers were supposed to be properly filled out, and if a man had to shed blood to make it that way, well, that was a matter of only distant interest. Hundreds of thousands of them. Most of them had wives—or husbands—and kids, but even so it was hard not to regard them with distaste—and, on occasion, with outright hatred. But they had their world, and he had his. They might overlap, but they never really met.

"Glad to be back, John?" Sandy asked.

"Yeah, sorta." Change was hard but inevitable. As far as where his life would go from here . . . time would tell.

The next morning Clark turned right off the George Washington Parkway, looping to the left and through the gatehouse, whose armed guard had his tag number on his list of "okay to admit" strangers. John was allowed to park in the visitors' area just in front and to the left of the big canopy.

"So how long before they tell us to find new employment, John?" Domingo asked.

"I give it maybe forty minutes. They'll be polite about it, I'm sure."

And with that assessment, they exited his rented Chevy and walked to the front door, there to be met by an SPO, or security and protective officer, whom they didn't know.

"Mr. Clark, Mr. Chavez. I'm Pete Simmons. Welcome home."

"Good to be back," John responded. "You are . . . ?"

"I'm an SPO, waiting for a field assignment. Got out of The Farm two months ago."

"Who was your training officer?"

"Max DuPont."

"Max hasn't retired yet? Good man."

"Good teacher. He told us a few stories about you two, and we saw the training film you did back in '02."

"I remember that," Chavez observed. "Shaken, not stirred." He had himself a brief laugh.

"I don't drink martinis, Domingo, remember?"

"Not as good-looking as Sean Connery, either. What did you learn from the film, Simmons?"

"Keep your options open, and don't walk in the middle of the street." Those were, in fact, two good lessons for a field spook.

"So who're we meeting?" Clark asked.

"Assistant Deputy Director Charles Sumner Alden, ADDO."

"Political appointment?"

"Correct. Kennedy School, Harvard, yeah. He's friendly enough, but sometimes I wonder if he really approves of what we do here."

"I wonder what Ed and Mary Pat are doing now."

"Ed's retired," Simmons told him. "Working on a book, I hear. Mary Pat's over at NCTC. She's a pistol."

"Best instincts in a field spook I ever encountered," Clark said. "What she says, you can take to the bank."

"Makes you wonder why President Kealty didn't keep her and Ed on the payroll," Chavez observed.

Unclean, unclean, Clark thought. "How's morale?" Clark asked on the way through the security card readers. Simmons handled that for them with a wave to the armed guard at the end of the gate line.

"Could be better. We have a lot of people running around in circles. They're punching up the intelligence directorate, but mine was the last class through The Farm for a while, and none of us have field assignments yet."

"Where'd you come from?"

"Cop, Boston city police. I was hired under Plan Blue. My degree is from Boston University, not Harvard. Languages."

"Which ones?"

"Serbian, some Arabic, and a little Pashtun. I was supposed to go out to Monterey to polish them up, but that got shelved."

"You're going to need the last two," John advised. "And work on the jogging. Afghanistan—I spent some time there back in the mid-'80s, and it'll wear out a mountain goat."

"That bad?"

"The people there fight wars for fun, and there ain't no good guys. I found myself feeling sorry for the Russians. The Afghans are tough people. I guess in that environment you have to be, but Islam is just an overlay on a tribal culture that goes back three-thousand-plus years."

"Thanks for the tip. I'll cross it off my list of preferences," Simmons said as the elevator reached the seventh floor.

He dropped them off at the secretary's desk. The plush carpet told them that the office was an important one—it looked fairly new. Clark took a magazine and paged through it while Domingo stared placidly at the wall. His former life as a soldier allowed him to tolerate boredom fairly well.

After forty minutes, Charles Alden came to the anteroom, smiling like a used-car salesman. Tall and thin like a runner, old enough to seem important to himself, whatever he'd done to earn this post. Clark was prepared to give him the benefit of the doubt, but the doubts were piling up rapidly.

"So you're the famous Mr. Clark," Alden said in greeting—and without an apology for keeping them waiting, Clark noted.

"Not too famous," Clark replied.

"Well, at least in this community." Alden led his guest into his office, not inviting Chavez to join them. "I just read through your file."

In fifteen minutes? Clark wondered. Maybe a speed-reader. "I hope it was illuminating."

"Colorful. Getting the Gerasimov family out of Russia was quite a job. And the mission in Tokyo, with a Russian cover . . . impressive. Ex-SEAL . . . I see President Ryan got you your Medal of Honor. Twenty-nine years with the Agency. Quite a record," Alden said, waving Clark to a chair; it was smaller than Alden's own chair and designed to be uncomfortable. *Power game,* Clark thought.

"I just did the jobs they gave me, best I could, and I managed to survive them all."

"Your missions tended to get somewhat physical."

Clark shrugged this off.

"We try to avoid that now," Alden observed.

"I tried to avoid it back then. Best-laid plans."

"You know, Jim Greer left behind a lengthy document about how you came to the Agency's attention."

"Admiral Greer was a particularly fine and honorable

gentleman," John observed, instantly on guard for what that file might say. James Greer had liked his written records. Even he'd had his weaknesses. Well, everybody did.

"He discovered Jack Ryan, too, correct?"

"And a lot of others."

"So I have learned."

"Excuse me, sir, doing research, are we?"

"Not really, but I like to know who I'm talking to. You've done some recruiting, too. Chavez, for example."

"He's a good officer. Even if you discount the stuff we did in England, Ding has been there when our country needed him. Got himself educated, too."

"Oh, yeah, he did get that master's degree at George Mason, didn't he?"

"Right."

"A little physical, though, like you. Not really a field officer, as most people understand the term."

"We can't all be Ed Foley or Mary Pat."

"They also have colorful files, but we're trying to get away from that as the world evolves."

"Is that so?"

"Well, it is today. The world's changed. The Romania job you and Chavez pulled off—that must have been exciting."

"That's one way to put it. Not often you find yourself in a foreign country in the middle of a revolution, but we got the job done before we skipped the country."

"You killed your subject," Alden said, somewhat distastefully.

"He needed killing," Clark said in reply, eyes locked on to Alden's face.

"It was against the law."

"I'm not an attorney, sir." And an executive order, even a presidential one, wasn't exactly statutory or constitutional law. This guy was a quintessential desk-sitter, John realized. If it wasn't written down, it wasn't real, and if it wasn't authorized in writing, then it was wrong. "When someone points a loaded firearm at you," Clark said, "it's a little late to start formal negotiations."

"You try to avoid such contingencies?"

"I do." *It's better to shoot the bastards in the back and unarmed, but that's not always possible,* Clark thought. When it's life and death, the concept of a fair fight went out the window. "My mission was to apprehend that individual and, if possible, to hand him over to appropriate authorities. Didn't work out."

"Your relations with law enforcement have not always been friendly," Alden said, flipping through pages of the classified file.

"Excuse me, does that file have my driving record in it?"

"Your friendship with senior people has been helpful to your career."

"I suppose so, but that happens with a lot of people. I generally accomplish my missions, and that's why I stayed around so long. Mr. Alden, what is the purpose of this interview?"

"Well, as deputy DO I have to be familiar with people in the Clandestine Service, and looking over this, I see that you've had a most colorful career. You're lucky you lasted this long, and you can now look back on a singular career."

"And my next assignment?"

"There is no next assignment. Oh, you can go back to The Farm as a training officer, but really my best advice would be for you to take your retirement. It's well earned. Your retirement papers are ready for processing. You've earned it, John," he said, with the cold hint of a smile.

"But if I were twenty years younger, you would not have a place for me?"

"Maybe an embassy posting," Alden said. "But neither one of us is twenty years younger. The Agency's changed, Mr.

Clark. We're getting out of the paramilitary business, except when we have people assigned directly to us from Delta Force, for example, but we're trying to get away from the hands-on stuff that you and Chavez have specialized in. The world is a kinder and gentler place."

"Tell that to New Yorkers, maybe?" Clark asked evenly.

"There are other ways to deal with things like that. The trick is finding out ahead of time and encouraging people to take a different path if they want to get our attention."

"How, exactly, does one do that—theoretically, of course?"

"That's an issue we address here on the seventh floor, on a case-by-case basis."

"Out in the field, issues like that one don't always arrive in your lap in a manner which allows referral to headquarters. You have to trust your people to take the initiative, and support them when they do so intelligently. I've been there. It can get awfully lonely out there in the field if you do not have confidence in the people behind you, especially when they're five thousand miles behind you."

"Initiative works well in the movies but not in the real world."

When's the last time you were out in the field in the real world? Clark wanted to ask but did not. He was not in here for an argument or even a discussion. He was here only to listen to the voice of God, and relayed from this academic asshole. It had happened before at the Agency, but back in the 1970s, when he'd avoided involuntary retirement for the first time, with the help of James Greer, he'd made something of a name for himself working in the Soviet Union on "special" missions. It had been nice, once, to have an enemy everyone believed in.

"So I'm out?"

"You will retire honorably, with the thanks of the nation, which you have served well, and at peril to your life. You know, reading through this, I wonder why you don't have a star on the atrium wall." He referred to the white marble wall with gold stars that memorialized the names of field officers who'd died in the service of the CIA.

The book that listed those names—it was in a glass-and-brass case—had many blank spaces showing only dates, because the names were themselves classified, even fifty years after the fact. In all likelihood, Alden took the executive elevators up from the security parking under the building, and so was not routinely forced to look at the wall—hell, not even to walk past it.

"What about Chavez?"

"As I told you, he's eligible for retirement in just ten more weeks, counting his time in the Army. He'll retire as GS-12, with full benefits, of course. Or if he insists, he can have a training post at The Farm for a year or two, before we send him off to Africa, probably."

"Why Africa?"

"Things are happening there—enough things to keep us interested."

Sure. Send him to Angola, where they'll take his Spanish accent for Portuguese and help him get whacked by some leftover guerrillas, right? Not that you'd care one way or another, Alden. These kinder and gentler people never really cared much for individuals. They were too interested in the big-picture issues of the day, forcing square reality pegs into the round theoretical holes of how the world was supposed to look and act. It was a common failing among the politically astute.

Clark said, "Well, that's up to him, I suppose, and after twenty-nine years, I guess I have my retirement pretty well maxed out, eh?"

"Pretty well," Alden agreed, with a smile about as genuine as a man about to close the sale on a 1971 Ford Pinto.

Clark stood. He did not extend his hand, but Alden did,

and Clark had to take it out of simple good manners, and good manners were always disarming to the assholes of the world.

"Oh, I almost forgot: Someone wants to see you. You know a James Hardesty?"

"Served with him once, yeah," Clark replied. "Isn't he retired by now?"

"No, not yet. He's working with operational archives, part of a project for the DO we've been running for about fourteen months—sort of a classified history project. Anyway, his office is on the fourth floor, past the kiosk by the elevators." Alden handed over the room number, scribbled on a blank sheet of paper.

Clark took it and folded it into his pocket. Jimmy Hardesty was still here? How the hell did he evade the attention of people like this Alden prick? "Okay, thanks. I'll catch him on the way out."

"They need me in there?" Ding asked when Clark came out the door.

"No, he just wanted me this time." Clark adjusted his necktie in a prearranged signal, to which Chavez did not react. And with that, they took the elevator down to the fourth floor. They walked past the kiosk staffed by blind vendors who sold such things as candy bars and Cokes—it always struck visitors as creepy and sinister, but for the CIA it was a laudable way to provide employment to the handicapped. If they were really blind. One could never be sure of anything in this building, but that was just part of the mystique.

They found Hardesty's office and knocked on the cipher-locked door. It opened in a few seconds.

"Big John," Hardesty said in greeting.

"Hey, Jimmy. What're you doing in this rat hole?"

"Writing the history of operations that nobody will ever

read, at least not while we're alive. You're Chavez?" he asked Ding.

"Yes, sir."

"Come on in." Hardesty waved them into his cubbyhole, which did have two spare chairs and almost enough room for the extra legs, plus a worktable that acted as an ersatz desk.

"What year are you in?" John asked.

"Would you believe 1953? I spent all last week on Hans Tofte and the Norwegian freighter job. That job had a real body count, and they were not all bad guys. Cost of doing business back then, I guess, and the sailors on the ship should have thought twice before signing on."

"Before our time, Jimmy. Did you talk to Judge Moore about it? I think he had a piece of that operation."

Hardesty nodded. "He was in last Friday. The judge must have been a handful in his younger days, before he took that seat behind the bench. Him and Ritter both."

"What's Bob Ritter doing now?"

"You didn't hear? Shit. Died three months ago down in Texas, liver cancer."

"How old was he?" Chavez asked.

"Seventy-five. He was at MD Anderson Cancer Center, down in Texas, so he had the best treatment available, but it didn't work."

"Everybody dies of something," Clark observed. "Sooner or later. Nobody told us about Ritter over in England. I wonder why."

"The current administration didn't like him much."

That made sense, John thought. He was a warrior from the worst of the bad old days who'd worked in Redland against the main enemy of the time, and cold warriors died hard. "I'll have to hoist a drink to his memory. We butted heads occasionally, but he never back-shot me. I wonder about that Alden guy."

"Not our kind of people, John. I'm supposed to do a full report on people we whacked along the way, what laws might have been violated, that sort of thing."

"So what can I do for you?" Clark asked his host.

"Alden pitched retirement to you?"

"Twenty-nine years. And I'm still alive. Kinda miraculous when you think about it," John observed with a moment's sober reflection.

"Well, if you need something to do, I have a number for you to call. Your knowledge is an asset; you can make money off it. Buy Sandy a new car, maybe."

"What sort of work?"

"Something you will find interesting. Don't know if it'll be your kind of thing, but what the hell. Worst case, they'll buy lunch."

"Who is it?"

Hardesty didn't answer the question. Instead he handed over another slip of paper with a phone number on it. "Give 'em a call, John. Unless you want to write your memoirs and get it through the people on the seventh floor."

Clark had himself a laugh. "No way."

Hardesty stood up, extended his hand. "Sorry to cut this short, but I have a ton of work to do. Give 'em a call—or don't, if you don't feel like it. Up to you. Maybe retirement will agree with you."

Clark stood. "Fair enough. Thanks."

With that, it was one more elevator ride and out the front door. For their part, John and Ding did stop and look at the wall. For some of the people at the CIA, those stars did represent the Honored Dead, no less than Arlington National Cemetery, though tourists were allowed to go there.

"What number, John?" Chavez asked.

"Some place in Maryland, judging by the area code." He

checked his watch and pulled out his new cell phone. "Let's find out where. . . ."

Jack's daily electronic traffic scan took up the first ninety minutes of his day and provided nothing of substance, so he grabbed his third cup of coffee, picked through the bagels, then returned to his office and began what he'd come to call his "morning troll" of the myriad intercepts the campus received from the U.S. intelligence community. Forty minutes into what was amounting to an exercise in frustration, a Homeland Security intercept caught his eye. *Now, that was interesting,* he thought, then picked up the phone.

He was in Jerry Rounds's office five minutes later. "Whatcha got?" Rounds asked.

"DHS/FBI/ATF intercept. They're looking for a missing plane."

This got Rounds's attention. The Department of Homeland Security had something of an event threshold system in place that generally did a good job of keeping trivial inquiries off its intelligence plate. The fact that such an inquiry had climbed this high on the food chain suggested that another agency had already done the routine legwork and confirmed that the plane in question hadn't simply been misplaced by a sloppy charter company in an administrative shuffle.

"ATF, huh?" Rounds muttered. Alcohol, Tobacco, and Firearms also specialized in explosive-related investigations. *Combine that with a missing plane . . .* Jack thought.

"What kind?" Rounds asked.

"Didn't say. Has to be small, noncommercial, or the news would have it." Missing 757s tended to generate buzz.

"How long ago?"

"Three days."

"We know the source?"

"The routing looked internal, so FAA or NTSB, maybe. I

checked yesterday and today; not a peep from anyone." Which meant somebody had clamped a lid on the subject. "Might be another way to go about this, though."

"Tell me."

"Follow the money," Jack said.

Rounds smiled at this. "Insurance."

32

It was 10:47 when his phone rang. Tom Davis had just finished a fairly large bond trade, one that would earn The Campus $1,350,000, which was not bad for three days' work. He grabbed the phone on the second ring. "Tom Davis."

"Mr. Davis, my name is John Clark. I was told to give you a call. Maybe do lunch."

"Told by whom?"

"Jimmy Hardesty," Clark replied. "I'll have a friend with me. His name is Domingo Chavez."

Davis thought for a moment, immediately cautious, but it was more an instinctive reaction than a necessity. Hardesty didn't hand out these introductions to hacks. "Sure, let's talk," Davis replied. He gave Clark directions and said, "I'll look for you about noon."

"Hey, Gerry," Davis said on entering the top-floor office. "Just got a call."

"Anybody we know?" the boss asked.

"Hardesty at Langley sent two guys to see us. Both slotted for retirement from the Agency. John Clark and Domingo Chavez."

Hendley's eyes went a little wide. "*The* John Clark?"

"So it would appear. He'll be here around noon."

"Do we want him?" the former senator asked, already half-knowing the answer.

"He's certainly worth talking to, boss. If nothing else, he'd be a hell of a training officer for our field people. I only know him by reputation. Ed and Mary Pat Foley love the guy, and that's a hard endorsement to ignore. He doesn't mind getting his hands dirty, thinks on his feet. Good instincts, plenty smart. Chavez is cut from the same cloth. He was part of Rainbow with Clark."

"Reliable?"

"We have to talk to them, but probably."

"Fair enough. Bring them over if you think it's worthwhile."

"Will do." Davis made his way out.

Christ on a bike, Hendley thought. *John Clark.*

"Left here," Domingo said as they got within a hundred yards of the light.

"Yeah. Must be that building there on the right. See the antenna farm?"

"Yep," Chavez observed as they took the turn. "Get a whole shitload of FM with that."

Clark chuckled at that. "Don't see any security. Good sign." Professionals knew when to play harmless.

He parked the rent-a-car in what seemed to be the visitors' lot, and they got out and walked in the front door.

"Good morning, sir," said a uniformed security guard. He was in a generic uniform, and his name tag said CHAMBERS. "Can I help you?"

"I'm here to see a Mr. Davis. John Clark and Domingo Chavez."

Chambers lifted his phone and punched some numbers. "Mr. Davis? Chambers here in the lobby. Two gentlemen here to see you. Yes, sir, thank you." The phone went back down. "He's coming down to see you, gentlemen."

Davis appeared in just over a minute. He was black, of average size, about fifty or so, Clark estimated. Well dressed, shirtsleeves rolled up, tie loosened. The busy broker. "Thanks, Ernie," he said to the security guard, then: "You must be John Clark."

"Guilty," John admitted. "And this is Domingo Chavez." And handshakes were exchanged.

"Come on up." Davis led them inside to the elevators.

"I've seen your face before. Other side of the river," Chavez clarified.

"Oh?" Davis reacted guardedly.

"At the operations room. Watch officer?"

"Well, once I was an NIO. Here I'm a lowly bond trader. Mainly corporate stuff, but some government issues."

They followed Davis to the top floor and then to his office—or most of the way. His office was right next to Rick Bell's, and someone was heading in there.

"Hey," Clark heard, and turned around to find Jack Ryan Jr. walking down the hall.

Clark took his hand, and for once his face showed surprise. "Jack . . . You work here, eh?"

"Well, yeah."

"Doing what?"

"Currency arbitrage, mostly. Swapping money back and forth, stuff like that."

"I thought the family business was stocks and bonds," Clark observed mildly.

"Not into that . . . yet," Jack responded. "Well, I've got to run. Catch you later, maybe?"

"Sure," Clark said. His brain wasn't exactly spinning, but he wasn't entirely oriented to the day's discoveries.

"Come on in," Davis said next, waving him through the door.

The office was a comfortable one and wasn't full of furniture made in a federal prison, such as they had at CIA headquarters. Davis waved them into seats. "So how long have you known Jimmy Hardesty?"

"For ten or fifteen years," Clark replied. "Good man."

"He is that. So: You want to retire?"

"I've never really thought about it."

"What about you, Mr. Chavez?"

"I'm not ready for Social Security, either, and I guess I have a few marketable skills. Wife and kid, with another one on the way. Till now I haven't had to give it much thought, but what you do here looks to be miles out of our skill set."

"Well, everyone here has to know the language anyway," Davis told them. "But beyond that . . ." Davis shrugged. "How're you fixed for clearance?"

"Top secret/special intelligence/poly—both of us," Clark replied. "At least until Langley puts our paperwork through. Why?"

"Because what we do here is not for public dissemination. You will sign some pretty tight NDAs," he said, referring to non-disclosure agreements. "Any problems with that?"

"Nope," John said at once. His curiosity had been well and truly piqued in a way he hadn't experienced in years. He noted that they hadn't asked him to swear an oath. That was passé anyway, and the courts had voided them a long time ago—if you spoke to the newspapers.

The signing took less than two minutes. The forms weren't anything they hadn't seen before, though the setting certainly was.

Davis checked the forms over, then slid them into a drawer. "Okay, here's the short of it: We get a lot of insider information through irregular channels. NSA keeps an eye on international trading for security reasons. Remember when Japan had that set-to with us? They clobbered Wall Street, and that made the Feds think they needed to keep an eye on such things. Economic warfare is real, and you can really mess up a country by clobbering its financial institutions. It works for us, especially for currency trading. That's where we make most of our money."

"Why is that important?" Chavez asked.

"We're self-funding. We're off the federal budget, Mr. Chavez, and therefore off the radar. No taxpayer money comes in the front door. We make what we spend, and what we don't spend ourselves, we keep."

Curiouser and curiouser, Clark thought.

You kept something secret by not having Congress fund it, and not having the Office of Management and Budget do the audits. If the government didn't fund it, to Washington it existed only as a source of taxes, and a good accounting firm could ensure that Hendley Associates—The Campus's official cover—kept a low profile: Just pay everything in full and on time. And if anyone knew how to hide money, it would have been these guys. Surely Gerry Hendley had enough contacts in Washington to keep the heat off his business. You mainly did that by being honest. There were enough high-priced crooks in America to keep the IRS and SEC interested, and like most government agencies, they didn't go freelance looking for new crooks without a solid lead. As long as you didn't get a reputation for being too good at what you did, or sailing too close to the wind, you didn't appear on the radarscopes.

"How many real clients do you have?" Chavez asked.

"Essentially, the only private accounts we manage belong to our employees, and they do pretty good. Last three years we've averaged a return of twenty-three percent, over and above salaries that are pretty decent. We've got some good benefits, too—especially educational perks for our employees who have kids."

"Impressive. What exactly do you have to do?" Ding asked.

"Kill people?" He'd thought he'd added that as a minor-league joke.

"Occasionally," Davis told him. "Kinda depends on the day."

The room got very quiet for a moment.

"You're not kidding," Clark stated.

"No," Davis said.

"Who authorizes it?"

"We do." Davis paused to let that sink in. "We employ some very skillful people—people who think first and handle it carefully. But yes, we do that when the circumstances call for it. We did four in the last couple of months, all in Europe, all terrorist affiliates. No blowback on any of them yet."

"Who does it?"

Davis managed a smile. "You just met one of them."

"You have to be shitting us," Chavez said. "Jack Junior? SHORTSTOP?"

"Yeah, he bagged one in Rome just six weeks ago. Operational glitch; he kind of fell ass-backward into it but did a decent job. The target's name was Mohammed Hassan Al-din, senior ops officer for the terrorist group that's been giving us a headache. Remember those mall shootings?"

"Yeah."

"His handiwork. We got a line on him and took him down."

"Never made the papers," Clark objected.

"He died of a heart attack, so said the forensic pathologist of the Rome city police force," Davis concluded.

"Jack's dad doesn't know?"

"Not hardly. As I said, his role had been planned differently, but shit happens, and he handled it. Had we known, we would probably have done something else, but it didn't work out that way."

"I'm not going to ask how Jack gave your subject a heart attack," Clark said.

259

"Good, because I'm not going to tell you—not now anyway."

"What's our cover?" Clark asked.

"As long as you're in the United States, you're covered completely. Overseas is something else. We'll take proper care of your families, of course, but if you're bagged overseas, well, we'll hire you the best lawyer we can find. Other than that, you're private citizens who got caught doing something naughty."

"I'm used to that idea," Clark said. "Just so my wife and kids are protected. So I'm just a private citizen abroad, right?"

"That's correct," Davis confirmed.

"Doing what?"

"Making bad people go away. Can you handle that?"

"I've been doing that for a long time, and not always on Uncle Sam's nickel. I've gotten into trouble at Langley for it sometimes, but it was always tactically necessary, and so I—we—have always gotten clear. But if something happens over here, you know, like conspiracy to commit murder—"

"You have a presidential pardon waiting for you."

"Say again?" John asked.

"Jack Ryan is the guy who persuaded Gerry Hendley to set this place up. That was Gerry's price. So President Ryan signed a hundred blank pardons."

"Is that legal?" Chavez asked.

"Pat Martin said so. He's one of the people who knows that this place exists. Another is Dan Murray. So is Gus Werner. You know Jimmy Hardesty. Not the Foleys, however. We thought about getting them involved, but Jack decided against it. Even the ones I named only know to recruit people with special credentials, to go to a special place. They have no operational knowledge at all. They know a special place exists but not what we do here. Even President Ryan doesn't have any operational information. That stays in this building."

"Takes a lot for a government type to trust people that much," Clark observed.

"You have to pick your people carefully," Davis agreed. "Jimmy thinks you two can be trusted. I know your background. I think he's right."

"Mr. Davis, this is a big thought," Clark said, leaning back in his chair.

For more than twenty years he'd daydreamed about how nice it would have been to have a place like this. He'd been dispatched by Langley to eyeball the head of Abu Nidal in Lebanon once, to determine *if* it might be possible to send him off to see God. That had been as dangerous as the actual mission itself, and the sheer insult of such a mission assignment had boiled his blood at the time, but he'd done it, and had come home with the photograph to show that, yes, it was possible to take the bastard down, but cooler heads or looser bowels in Washington had voided that mission, and so he'd put his life on the line for nothing, and so later the Israeli Army had killed him with a Hellfire missile fired from an Apache attack helicopter, which was altogether messier than a rifle from 180 meters and had also caused considerable collateral damage, which didn't really trouble the Israelis all that much.

"Okay," Chavez said. "If and when we go out on a mission, we're supposed to take down somebody who needs to be taken down. If we get caught, it's tough luck for us. As a practical matter, chances are fifty-fifty we get killed on the spot, and that's the ante, I get it. But it's kinda nice to have a government blue blanket around us when we do that sort of thing."

"More than one way to serve your country."

"Maybe so," Ding conceded.

Clark said, "There's a guy at Langley who's doing a background check on me, guy named Alden, in the DO. Evidently Jim Greer left behind a dossier on me and the things I did before I joined up. I don't know what's in it exactly, but it could be problematic."

"How so?"

"I took down some drug dealers. Never mind why, but I took down a whole drug ring. Jack Ryan Sr.'s father was a police detective, and he wanted to arrest me, but I talked him out of it and faked my own death. Ryan knows the story—at least part of it. Anyway, the Agency might have some of it in writing. You need to know that."

"Well, if any trouble develops from it, we have that presidential pardon to look after you. You think this Alden guy might want to use it against you?"

"He's a political animal."

"Understood. You two want some time to think it over?"

"Sure," Clark answered for both of them.

"Sleep on it, then come back tomorrow. If this goes further, you can meet the boss. Just a reminder: What we discussed—"

"Mr. Davis, I've been keeping secrets for a long time. Both of us. If you think we need a reminder, you've read us wrong."

"Point taken." Davis stood up, concluding the meeting. "See you tomorrow."

They didn't exchange words until they were outside, walking to the car. "Man, oh, man, Jack Junior whacked somebody?" Chavez asked the sky.

"Sounds like it," Clark replied, thinking it might be time to stop thinking of him as Junior. "Looks like he's in the family business after all."

"His father would shit himself."

"Probably," John agreed. *And that's nothing compared to how his mother would react.*

A few minutes later in the car, Chavez said, "Got a confession to make, John."

"Speak to me, my son."

"I fucked up—and royally." Chavez leaned forward in his seat, withdrew an object from his back pocket, and laid it on the car's center console.

"What's that?"

"A USB drive. You know, for a computer—"

"I know what it is, Ding. Why're you showing it to me?"

"Took it off one of the gomers in the Tripoli embassy. We did a quick shakedown, frisked 'em, all that. Found that on the lead guy—the one I dropped near the laptop."

Despite having a 9-millimeter round from Chavez's MP5 buried in his side, one of the tangos had managed to stumble to a laptop and hit a key combo that had fried the hard drive and wireless card, both of which were now in the possession of the Swedes, for all the good they would do them.

The consensus was that the bad guys had been using the laptop to communicate with someone on the outside. Such was the curse of the digital age, Clark knew. The state of wireless Internet technology was such that signals had not only greater reach but more robust encryption technology as well. Even if the Libyans had been fully cooperative, the chances Rainbow could have monitored and/or throttled every hot spot around the embassy were virtually nonexistent, so unless the Swedes were able to salvage either the drive or the card, they'd never know who the tangos in the embassy had been talking to.

Or maybe not, Clark thought.

"Christ, Ding, that's a hell of an oversight."

"Put it in my pocket and didn't think about it until we got back and unpacked. Sorry. So what d'you wanna do?" Ding asked, smiling evilly. "Hand it over to Alden?"

"Let me give it some thought."

It was well into the afternoon before Jack found what he wanted. While by law aviation insurance carriers were required to make claims available to the public, there were no regulations regarding ease of access. Consequently, most carriers made sure digital claim searches were painstakingly convoluted.

"XLIS—XL Insurance Switzerland," Jack told Rounds. "Does a lot of aviation stuff over there. Three weeks ago a claim was filed on a Dassault Falcon 9000. It's a small executive jet. Built by the same people who do the Mirage fighter. The claimant is a woman named Margarite Hlasek, co-owner of Hlasek Air with her husband, Lars—who also happens to be a pilot. It's based out of Zurich. Here's the kicker: I cross-referenced our intercepts, mixed and matched some keywords, and got a hit: Two days ago the FBI contacted its legal attachés in Stockholm and Zurich. Somebody's looking for info on Hlasek Air."

"Why Stockholm?"

"Just a guess, but they'd want to look into Hlasek's home base, and maybe the last airport the Falcon visited."

"What else do we know about Hlasek?"

"They're dicey. I found four separate complaints forwarded to either the Swedish Civil Aviation Administration or the Swedish Civil Aviation Authority—"

"What's the difference?"

"One handles state-owned airports and air traffic control; the other deals with commercial aviation and safety. Four complaints in the last two years—three about irregularities in customs forms and one about a misfiled flight plan."

"Fly the friendly terrorist skies," Rounds murmured.

"Could be. If so, that kind of service doesn't come cheap."

"Let's go talk to Gerry."

Hendley was in with Granger. The boss waved them in. "Jack may have something," Rounds said, and Jack laid it out.

"Long shot," Granger observed.

"Missing plane, ATF involvement, the FBI putting out feelers on the ground in Sweden, and a shady charter company," Rounds countered. "We've seen this before, okay? Hlasek Air's moving people who either don't *want* to fly commercial or they *can't* fly commercial. This probably won't lead us to who we're looking for, but maybe it's a thread we can pull. Or a trigger on some miscellaneous mutts."

Hendley considered this, then looked to Granger, who shrugged and nodded. Hendley said, "Jack?"

"Doesn't hurt to get out and shake some trees once in a while, boss."

"True enough. What're the Caruso boys up to?"

33

Having to deal with an intermediary wasn't common, but it wasn't so uncommon that it gave Melinda cause for concern. Usually it meant the customer was married and/or a luminary in a prominent position, which in turn usually translated into more money, which was the case here. The intermediary—a Mediterranean type named Paolo with burn scars on his hands—had given her half of the $3,000 fee up front, along with the address of the corner on which she should be waiting for pickup—again, not her usual modus operandi, but money was money, and this money was far beyond her usual fee.

The most likely danger she faced was that the john was into something kinky she didn't want to do. Then the problem became how to misdirect him without losing the date. Most men were easy that way, but once in a while you'd come across one with his sights stubbornly set on something perverse. In those cases—it had happened twice to her—discretion, she'd found, was the better part of business. Say thanks but no thanks, and get the hell out of there.

Statistically, there weren't that many serial killers around, but about half of them killed hookers—all the way back to Jack the Ripper in London's Whitechapel district. Ladies of the evening, in the elegant phrase of nineteenth-century England, took their johns to secluded places for a "knee trembler," where a murder was easier than it was in the middle of a busy street, and so she and some of her colleagues had evolved a simple system of mutual security, sharing with one another the details of their dates.

In this case the car was a Lincoln Town Car with tinted windows. It pulled up to the curb, and Melinda heard the rear door unlock. The windows did not roll down. After a moment's indecision, she climbed in.

"Why the tinted windows?" she asked the driver, trying to sound casual.

"To protect against the sun," he replied.

Reasonable enough, Melinda had thought, keeping her hand near her purse, where she had a very old .25-caliber Colt pocket model automatic, nearly weightless at thirteen ounces. She'd hardly ever fired it, but it was fully loaded with seven rounds, with the safety on. Not exactly a .44 Magnum, but not a kiss on the cheek, either.

She checked her watch. They were thirty minutes out of town, she figured. Good news and bad news. A really private place was a good place to kill a whore and dump the body. But she wasn't going to worry about everything, and her purse was only an inch from her right hand, and Little Mr. Colt was right in there. . . .

The car took a hard left turn into an alley, and then another left into a condominium parking garage. A private garage rather than a communal one, which meant a private entrance to the condo. At least it wasn't a trailer park. The people who lived in those frightened her, though they did not constitute her normal clientele. Melinda charged a thousand or two a pop, and $4,500 for overnight. The remarkable part was that so many were willing to pay it, which was a fine supplement to her regular job, receptionist at the headquarters of the Las Vegas public school system. The man got out of the car, opened her door, and offered her his hand as she climbed out.

"Welcome," called an adult voice. She walked toward it and saw a tallish man in the living room. He smiled pleasantly enough. She was used to that. "What is your name?" he asked. He had a nice voice. Melodic.

"Melinda," she replied, walking toward him, putting a little extra sway into her hips.

"Would you like a glass of wine, Melinda?"

"Thank you," she responded, and a nice crystal glass was provided. Paolo had disappeared—where to, she had no idea—but the atmosphere had disengaged her alarm systems. Whoever this was, he was rich, and she had ample experience with those. She could relax a little now. Melinda was excellent at reading men—what else did she do for a living?—and this guy was not threatening in any way. He just wanted to get his rocks off, and that was her business. She charged so much because she was good at it, and men didn't mind paying because she was worth the money. It was a perfectly laissez-faire economic system well known in this area, though Melinda had never voted Republican in her life.

"This is very good wine," she observed after a sip.

"Thank you. One tries to be a good host." He waved in a courtly gesture to a leather couch, and Melinda took her seat, putting her purse at her left side but leaving it unzipped.

"You prefer to be paid the remainder beforehand?"

"Yes, if you don't mind."

"Certainly." He reached into his back pocket and pulled out an envelope, which he handed over. Twenty $100 bills, which took care of business for the evening. Maybe more, if he was particularly pleased with how things turned out.

"May I ask your name?" Melinda asked.

"You will laugh—my name really is John. It does happen, you know."

"That's fine, John," she responded, with a smile that would melt the chrome off the bumper of a 1957 Chevy. She set her wine down. "So . . ." And business commenced.

Three hours later, Melinda had taken the time to shower and brush out her hair. It was part of her après-sex routine, to make her client feel as though he had touched her soul. But that was a long reach for most men, and it was too long a reach for John this night. It would also wash away the smell he'd had all over him. The odor was vaguely familiar, though she couldn't place it. Something mediciney, she thought, dismissing it. Probably athlete's foot and something similar. Still and all, he wasn't a bad-looking man. Italian, maybe. Mediterranean or Middle Eastern for sure. Plenty of those around, and his manners certainly suggested he wasn't hurting for money.

She finished dressing and walked out of the bathroom, smiling coquettishly.

"John," she said in her sincerest voice, "that was wonderful. I hope we can do this again sometime."

"You are very sweet, Melinda," John answered, and then he kissed her. He was, actually, rather a nice kisser. All the more so that he produced another envelope with a further twenty $100 bills. For that he got a hug.

This could be something, she thought. Maybe, just maybe, if she'd done her job right, she'd be invited back. Rich, exclusive clients were the best kind.

*

"She was adequate?" Tariq said after returning from dropping Melinda off.

"Quite," the Emir said, reclining on the sofa. *More than adequate, in fact,* he thought. "A vast improvement over the first."

"My apologies for that mistake."

"No apology necessary, my friend. Ours is a unique situation. You were being cautious—as I expect you to be." The other woman—Trixie—had been ill-mannered and too practiced in bed, but those were traits the Emir could forgive. Had she not asked so many questions, not been so curious, she would have been safely returned to her street corner to continue her pathetic life—her only punishment not being asked for a return engagement. *Unfortunate but necessary,* the Emir thought. And a necessary lesson. Bringing Trixie directly to the house had been a mistake, one that he'd had Tariq correct by leasing the condominium; it would serve as a buffer, should they need to dispose of another harlot.

"Anything before I go to bed?" he asked. They would spend the night here before returning to the house. Cars coming and going in the night tended to attract the attention of nosy neighbors.

"Yes, four items," Tariq replied, sitting down in the opposite chair. "One, Hadi is on his way back to Paris. He and Ibrahim will be meeting tomorrow."

"You reviewed Hadi's packet?"

"Yes. Four facilities in particular look promising. Our agent has worked at each of them within the last two years, and it appears security has changed dramatically at only one of them."

"Paulinia?"

"Correct."

This made sense, the Emir thought. Petrobras's facility there had been tasked with accommodating the new influx, which in turn required new construction—and this, he knew, was where the vulnerability lay. They'd seen it happen outside Riyadh in the '70s and '80s, a deficit of trained, competent security personnel to keep pace with expansion. Such was the price of greed.

"It'll be a year before their security has caught up."

"You're probably right, but we are not going to wait to find out. Recruitment?"

"Ibrahim is almost done," Tariq concluded. "He reports he'll be ready within two weeks. He's proposed that Hadi be recruited for the team."

The Emir considered this. "Your thoughts?"

"Hadi is reliable, that much we know, and there's no question about his loyalty. He's had some training in fieldwork, but little real-world experience beyond what he's done in Brazil, which has been solid. If Ibrahim thinks he is ready, I tend to agree."

"Very well. Give Ibrahim my blessing. What else?"

"An update from the woman. Their relationship is well established and she's making progress, but she doesn't think he's quite ready to be reeled in yet."

"Did she offer a timeline?"

"Three to four weeks."

The Emir mentally projected that on the calendar. Her information was the cornerstone. Without it, he would have to consider postponing for another year. Another year for the Americans to whittle away at their networks and for tongues to wag. And for someone somewhere to get lucky and stumble onto that one thread that would unravel the entire spool.

No, he decided, it had to be this year.

"Tell her we'll expect it no later than three weeks. Next."

"A message from Nayoan in San Francisco. His men are in place and awaiting orders."

Of all of Lotus's myriad parts and pieces, Nayoan's had

proven the easiest, at least the infiltration and preparatory phases. Student visas were relatively easy enough to come by, and easier still to acquire by someone in Nayoan's position. Besides, as ignorant as Americans were about the world outside their own borders, Indonesians were for the most part seen simply as Asians or "Orientals" rather than as members of the single greatest concentration of Muslims on the face of the earth. Bigotry and narrow-mindedness, the Emir thought, were weapons the URC was only too happy to employ.

"Good," the Emir said. "Tomorrow let's review the targets again. If there are changes to be made, we should make them sooner rather than later. Next?"

"Last item: You saw the news about the Tripoli embassy?"

The Emir nodded. "Idiotic business. A waste."

"The planner was one of ours."

The Emir sat up, his eyes hard. "Pardon me?" Eight months earlier, word had been sent to all URC affiliates that cell-level missions were forbidden until further notice. Their current operation was too delicate, too intricate. Smaller operations— mostly near misses and low-casualty events—had their place in creating the illusion of disorganization and business as usual, but something like this . . .

"What's his name?" the Emir asked.

"Dirar al-Kariim."

"I don't recognize it."

"A Jordanian. Recruited from the Hussein mosque in Amman three years ago. A soldier, nothing more. The same mission was proposed last year by our people in Benghazi. We declined it."

"How many dead?"

"Six to eight of ours. None of theirs."

"Praise God for that." With no hostages killed, the Western press would quickly forget about the incident, and often where

271

the press's attention went, so, too, did intelligence agencies'. Such was the burden of fighting their "global war on terror." They were the proverbial Dutch boy with his finger in the dike.

"Do we know who he recruited?"

"We're looking into it. Also, we don't know whether anyone survived the raid—except for al-Kariim himself," Tariq added. "He didn't participate, in fact."

"Imbecile! So this . . . nothing plans a mission without our approval, then botches it and doesn't have the good sense or honor of dying in the attempt. . . . Do we know where he is now?"

"No, but he shouldn't be hard to find. Especially if we extend our hand. He'll be on the run, looking for safe haven."

The Emir nodded thoughtfully. "Good. Do that. Offer him an olive branch, but at a distance. Have Almasi handle it."

"And when we have him?"

"Make him an example for the others."

34

In Paris's Montparnasse Arrondissement Shasif Hadi sat, sipping his coffee and doing his best not to appear nervous.

As promised, his connection at Topanga Beach had made contact the day after their meeting and given him instructions where he should pick up the return packages, each of which he'd found at rented mailboxes in the Los Angeles area. He was unsurprised to find each package contained an unlabeled CD-ROM but was surprised to find a typewritten note attached to one of them—"Indiana Café, Montparnasse, 77 Av Maine"—along with a date and time. What Hadi didn't know was whether this was simply another courier mission or something more.

Algerian by birth, Hadi had emigrated to France in his early teens as his father sought gainful employment. Hadi spoke good French, with the accent of a *pied-noir*, a "black foot," the name applied two hundred years before to French colonial citizens of what had been the French colony on the North Coast of Africa, erased in the early 1960s after a bloody and prolonged colonial/civil war that the French Republic had more left than lost. But Algeria had not exactly flourished, and so the Arabs had exported millions of its citizens to Europe, where they had been marginally welcomed, all the more so in the last decade of the twentieth century, when they'd discovered their Islamic identity in a country that still held to the idea of the melting pot. Speak the language (pronounce the words properly), adopt the customs, and you were French, and the French race didn't particularly care what color your skin might be. Though nominally a Catholic country, the French didn't care what church you might attend, since they were not a nation of churchgoers, either. But Islam had changed that. Perhaps remembering the victory of Charles Martel at the Battle of Tours in 732, they knew that they'd fought wars with Muslims, but mostly they objected to the fact that Muslim immigrants rejected their culture, adopting modes of dress and customs that did not fit in with the wine-drinking bons vivants, and thus leaped out of the melting pot. *And why would any man or woman* not *wish to be French?* they asked themselves. And so the myriad French police agencies kept an eye on such people. Hadi knew this, and therefore made an effort to fit in, in the hope that Allah would understand and forgive him out of His infinite mercy. And besides, he was hardly the only Muslim who imbibed alcohol. The French police took note of this and consequently ignored him. He had a job, as a salesclerk in a video store, got along well with his workmates, lived in a modest but comfortable flat on rue Dolomieu in the 5th Arrondissement ("district" in Paris), drove a Citroën sedan, and made no trouble for anyone. They did not notice that he lived somewhat in excess of his means. The cops here were good but not perfect.

Nor did they notice that he traveled a little, mostly within Europe, and occasionally met people from out of the country, usually at a comfortable bistro. Hadi particularly enjoyed a light red from the Loire Valley, not knowing that the vintner was a Jew who was a vigorous supporter of the State of Israel. Anti-Semitism was regrettably alive in France once again, rather to the pleasure of the five million Muslims who now lived there.

"Mind if I join you?" a voice said near Hadi's shoulder.

Hadi turned. "Be my guest."

Ibrahim sat down. "How was your trip?"

"Uneventful."

"So what do you bring me?" Ibrahim asked.

Hadi reached into his coat pocket and withdrew the CD-ROM disks, which he passed over without attempting to hide the transfer. Trying to appear inconspicuous was often conspicuous in and of itself. Besides, if the casual stranger— or even a seasoned customs official, for that matter—were to see the contents of either CD, they'd find themselves looking at a digital slideshow of someone's summer vacation.

"Did you look at these?" Ibrahim asked.

"Of course not."

"Any problems with customs?"

"No. I was surprised, actually," said Hadi.

"There are five million of us here. They cannot watch us all, and I keep a low profile. They think that a Muslim who drinks alcohol is not a danger to them."

Keeping a low profile meant that he never attended a mosque and didn't frequent places used by Islamic fundamentalists, called "Integrists" by the French because "fundamentalist" was a term locally applied to Christian religious fanatics, who were probably too busy getting drunk to be a threat to him, Hadi thought. *Infidels.*

"They mentioned a possibility of my role changing," Hadi prompted.

They were at a sidewalk table. There were people within three meters, but there was traffic noise, and the usual bustle of a big-city environment. Both men knew not to hunch over the table in a conspiratorial manner. That had gone out with 1930s movies. Much better to drink wine anonymously, smoke, and turn heads to look at the women passing by in their chic dresses and bare legs. The French could understand that readily enough.

"If you're interested," Ibrahim replied.

"I am."

"It will be different than what you're used to. There is some risk."

"If God wills it."

Ibrahim looked hard at him for five seconds, then nodded. "Your trip to Brazil . . . How many times have you been there?"

"Seven in the last four months."

"You enjoyed yourself?"

"It was nice enough, I suppose."

"Nice enough to return if you are asked?"

"Certainly."

"We have a man there. I'd like you to meet with him and arrange accommodations."

Hadi nodded. "When do I leave?"

"Got him," Jack said, handing the pages over.

Bell took them and leaned back in his swivel chair. "France?" he asked. "The birth announcement?"

Exploring his suspicions about the URC's sudden communication protocol change, Jack had backtracked and cross-referenced until he managed to strip away one of the alphanumeric handles, revealing a new name on the e-mail distribution list.

"Yep. His name is Shasif Hadi. Apparently lives in Rome, not sure where exactly, but he's a Muslim, probably Algerian in origin, and probably doing his best to stay under the radar. Been spending a lot of time in Paris."

Bell chuckled. "Probably the Italians have no idea he exists."

"How good are they?" Jack asked.

"The Italians? Their intelligence services are first-rate, and historically they don't mind doing some heavy lifting. Their police are pretty good, too. They don't have as many restrictions on them as our guys do. They are better at tracking people and investigating background stuff than we allow our people to be. They can do wiretaps administratively, without a court order, like our guys have to do it. I wouldn't go out of my way to attract their attention if I were breaking the law. It's the old European way, they like to know as much about people and what they do as possible. If your nose is clean, they'll leave you alone. If not, they can make your life pretty miserable. Their legal system is not like ours, but on the whole it's pretty fair."

"They keep an eye on their Muslim population because there've been some rumbles, but not much more than that. You're right, though: If this fellow's a player, he'll know to keep his head down, drink his wine, eat his bread, and watch TV like everybody else. They've had terrorism problems, but not too bad. If you go back to the OAS in the 1960s, yeah, that was a real problem once, and a scary one, but they handled it pretty efficiently. Pretty ruthlessly, too. The Italians know how to do business when they have to. So this Hadi—is he static?"

"No, been traveling a lot in the last six months or so—here, Western Europe, South America. . . ."

"Where specifically?"

"Caracas, Paris, Dubai . . ."

"Aside from that and the e-mail, what makes you think he's hot?" Bell asked. "You know, I got a call once from Comcast. It seems I'd been accidentally piggybacking on my neighbors' Internet Wi-Fi. I had no idea."

"That's not the case here," Jack countered. "I checked it and double-checked it; it's Hadi's account. It originates from a German ISP based in Monte Sacro, a Rome suburb, but that doesn't mean anything. You can access it from anywhere in Europe. The question is, why send it encrypted over the Internet when he could do it over the phone or meet the guy at a restaurant? Obviously the sender thinks it's sensitive. Maybe he doesn't know Hadi by sight, or doesn't want to make a phone call or a dead drop—or maybe he doesn't know how. These guys are wedded to the Internet. That's an operational weakness that they try to turn into a virtue. They have a relatively small organization that is not professionally trained. If these guys were the KGB from the old days, we'd be in deep shit, but they're using technology to make up for their structural weaknesses. They're small, and that helps them hide, but they have to use Western electronic technology to communicate and coordinate their activities, and that's fine, but we know they're outside Europe, too. Crossing technology boundaries can be dicey. All the more reason to use couriers for the high-end stuff.

"If they were a nation-state, then they'd have better resources, but then we'd be able to target them and their chain of command more efficiently. Good news and bad news. You can use a shotgun on a vampire bat but not against a mosquito. The mosquito can't really hurt us badly, but it can make our lives pretty miserable. Our vulnerability is that we value human life more highly than they do. If we didn't, then they couldn't hurt us at all, but we do, and that's not going to change. They try to use our weaknesses and our fundamental principles against us, and it's hard for us to use those assets against them. Unless we can identify these birds, they will continue to sting us, hoping to drive us mad. Meanwhile, they're going to try to leverage their skills—plus our technology against us."

"So: recommendations?"

"We pull apart his ISP account if we can, get some financials on him. Follow the money. In an ideal world, we'd cross-deck this to German BND, but we can't do any of that. Hell, we can't even have the Agency do it for us, can we?"

And with that question, Jack had identified the real problem at The Campus. Since it didn't exist, it couldn't broadcast its hits to the official intelligence community and thereby follow things up via conventional channels. Even if they discovered oil in Kansas and got people rich, some bureaucrat or other would backtrack the notice just to find out who'd done it, and thus blow The Campus's cover. Being supersecret could be as much a handicap as an advantage. Or even more. They could transmit a query to Fort Meade disguised as an Agency question, but even that was dangerous, and had to be approved by Gerry Hendley himself. Well, you took the bitter with the sweet. In a world where two or more heads were in fact better than one at problem solving, The Campus was alone.

"I'm afraid not, Jack," Bell replied. "Well, unless this Hadi's on someone's list by accident or the e-mail itself is innocuous, I'd say we're looking at a courier."

While not the fastest means of communication, couriers were the most secure. Encrypted data and messages, easily hidden in a document or on a CD-ROM, aren't something airport security folks were trained to ferret out. Unless you had a courier's identity—which they might now have—the bad guys could be planning the end of the world and the good guys would never know it.

"Agreed," Jack said. "Unless he's working for *National Geographic,* there's something there. He's operational or he's playing support."

The kid thought operationally, and that, too, was not a bad characteristic, Rick Bell thought to himself. "Okay," Bell told Jack. "Put it at the top of your list and keep me up to speed."

"Right," Jack said, then stood up. He turned for the door, then turned back.

"Something on your mind?" Bell asked.

"Yeah. I want to have a sit-down with the boss."

"What about?"

Jack told him. Bell tried to keep the surprise off his face. He steepled his fingers and looked at Jack. "Where's this coming from? The MoHa thing? Because that ain't real life, Jack. Fieldwork is—"

"I know, I know. I just want to feel like I'm doing something."

"You are."

"You know what I mean, Rick. Doing something. I've given it a lot of thought. At least let me put it on the table in front of Gerry."

Bell considered this, then shrugged. "Okay. I'll set it up."

Nine thousand fucking miles and still no beer, Sam Driscoll thought, but only for a moment as he reminded himself yet again he could have just as easily made the hop home in a rubber bag. A couple of inches either way, the docs had said, and the splinter would've shredded either his brachial, cephalic, or basilic vein, and he might have bled out long before reaching the Chinook. *Lost two along the way, though.* Barnes and Gomez had taken the full brunt of the RPG. Young and Peterson had caught some minor leg shrapnel but had managed to climb aboard the Chinook on their own. From there it had been a short hop to FOB Kala Gush, where he parted company with the team, save Captain Wilson and his shattered leg, who accompanied him first to Ramstein Air Base, then on to Brooke Army Medical Center at Fort Sam Houston. As it turned out, both needed the kind of orthopedic surgery in which Brooke specialized. And Demerol. The nurses here were real good with the pain meds, which had gone a long way to helping him forget that five days earlier he'd had a hunk of Hindu Kush granite sticking out of his shoulder.

The mission had been a bust, at least in terms of their main objective, and Rangers weren't in the business of failing, their fault or not. Providing the intel had been right and their target had ever been in the cave at all, he'd slipped away, probably less than a day before they'd arrived. Still, Driscoll reminded himself, given the shit storm they came through on the way back to the LZ, it could have been a lot worse. He'd lost two but had come back with thirteen. *Barnes and Gomez. Goddamn it.*

The door opened, and in rolled Captain Wilson in a wheelchair. "Got a minute for a visitor?"

"You bet. How's the leg?"

"Still broken."

Driscoll chuckled at that. "Gonna be that way for a while, sir."

"No pins or plates, though, so I got that going for me. How about you?"

"Don't know. Docs are being cagey. Surgery went fine, no vascular damage, which woulda been bad mojo. Joint and bone's a lot easier to fix, I guess. You hear from the guys?"

"Yeah, they're good. Sitting on their asses, and rightly so."

"Young and Peterson?"

"Both fine. Light duty for a few weeks. Listen, Sam, something's going down."

"Your face tells me it ain't a visit from Carrie Underwood."

"'Fraid not. CID. Two agents back at Battalion."

"Both of us?"

Wilson nodded. "They've pulled our after-actions. Anything I should know about, Sam?"

"No, sir. Got a parking ticket outside the gym last month, but other than that I've been a good boy."

"All kosher in the cave?"

"Standard shit, Major. Just like I wrote it."

"Well, anyway, they'll be up this afternoon. Play it straight. Should work out."

It didn't take more than a couple of minutes for Driscoll to realize what the CID goons were after: his head. Who and why, he didn't know, but somebody had pointed the bone at him for what went on in the cave.

"And how many sentries did you encounter?"

"Two."

"Both killed?"

"Yes."

"Okay, so then you made your way into the cave proper. How many of the occupants were armed?" one of the investigators asked.

"After we policed everything up, we counted—"

"No, we mean upon your entry into the cave. How many of them were armed?"

"Define 'armed.'"

"Don't be a smart-ass, Sergeant. How many armed men did you encounter when you entered the cave?"

"It's in my report."

"Three, correct?"

"That sounds right," Driscoll replied.

"The rest were asleep."

"With AKs under the pillows. You guys don't get it. You're

talking about prisoners, right? It doesn't work that way, not out in the real world. You get yourself into a firefight inside a cave with just one bad guy, and you end up with dead Rangers."

"You didn't attempt to incapacitate the sleeping men?"

Driscoll smiled at that. "I'd say they were thoroughly incapacitated."

"You shot them in their sleep."

Driscoll sighed. "Boys, why don't you just say what you came to say?"

"Have it your way. Sergeant, there's sufficient evidence in your after-action report alone to charge you with the murder of unarmed combatants. Add to that the statements of the rest of your team—"

"Which you haven't officially taken yet, right?"

"Not yet, no."

"Because you know this is a load of crap, and you'd prefer it if I lay my head on the block nice and gentle and not make a fuss. Why're you doing this? I was doing my job. Do your homework. What we did up there is standard procedure. You don't give gomers a chance to draw down on you."

"And apparently you didn't give them a chance to surrender, did you?"

"God almighty . . . Gentlemen, these idiots don't surrender. When it comes to fanaticism, they make kamikaze pilots look downright spineless. What you're talking about doing would've gotten some of my men killed, and that I won't have."

"Sergeant, are you now admitting you preemptively executed the men inside that cave?"

"What I'm saying is we're done talking until I see a TDS lawyer."

35

"Goose chase," Brian Caruso said, staring out the car's passenger window at the scenery. "Worse places to do it, though, I guess." Sweden was damned pretty, with lots of green and, as far as they'd seen since leaving Stockholm, spotless highways. Not a scrap of trash to be seen. They were ninety miles north of the Swedish capital; twelve miles to the northeast, the waters of the Gulf of Bothnia sparkled under a partially overcast sky. "Where do you suppose they keep the bikini team?" the Marine asked now.

Dominic laughed. "They're all computer-generated, bro. Nobody's ever seen them in person."

"Bullshit; they're real. How far is this place? What's it called? Söderhamn?"

"Yeah. About a hundred fifty miles."

Jack and Sam Granger had given them the briefing, and while the Caruso Brothers agreed with the chief of ops's "long shot" assessment of the job, they also liked the idea of beating the bushes. Plus, it was a good way to sharpen their tradecraft. So far most of their work at The Campus had been in Europe, and the more time one got to train in a real operating environment, the better. They both felt more than a little naked without guns, but this, too, was an operational reality: More often than not, when overseas, they would find themselves unarmed.

How exactly Jack had found Hlasek Air's connection to Söderhamn's tiny airport neither of them knew, but wherever the missing Dassault Falcon had ended up, its last known touchdown had been there. It was, Dominic explained, a lot like tracking down a missing person: Where were they last seen, and by whom? How exactly they'd go about answering those questions once they reached Söderhamn was another matter altogether. Jack's suggestion, which had been offered with a sheepish grin, would probably turn out to be prescient: *Improvise.* To that end, The Campus's documents people, who lived in some cubbyhole office in the bowels of the building, had provided them with letterheads, business cards, and credentials from the claims-investigation division of Lloyd's of London, XL Insurance Switzerland's parent company.

It was early afternoon when they reached the southern outskirts of Söderhamn, population 12,000, and Dominic turned east off the E4, following aircraft pictograph signs for five miles before pulling into the mostly empty airport parking lot. They counted three cars. Through the eight-foot hurricane fence they saw a line of four white-roofed hangar buildings. A lone fuel bowser tooled across the cracked tarmac.

"Good idea to come on a weekend, I guess," Brian observed. The theory was that the airport would be lightly manned on a Saturday afternoon, which meant, they hoped, less chance of them coming across anyone with real authority. With greater luck they'd find the office staffed by a part-time minimum-wager who just wanted to pass the afternoon with a commensurate minimum of fuss. "Score another one for cuz."

They got out, walked over to the office, and went inside. An early-twenties blond kid sat behind the counter, his feet propped on a filing cabinet. In the background a boom box blasted the latest version of Swedish techno-pop. The kid stood up and turned down the music.

"God middag," the kid said.

Dominic laid his credentials out on the counter. *"God middag."*

*

It took but five minutes of cajoling and oblique threats to talk their way into the airport's daily flight logs, which showed only two arrivals of Dassault Falcons in the last eight weeks, one from Moscow a month and a half ago and one from Zurich-based Hlasek Air three weeks ago. "We'll need to see the manifest, flight plan, and maintenance record for this aircraft," Dominic said, tapping the binder.

"I don't have that here. It would be in the main hangar."

"Let's go there, then."

The kid picked up the phone.

The on-duty flight mechanic, Harold, was barely older than the desk clerk and even more unsettled by their appearance. *Insurance investigator, missing aircraft,* and *maintenance records* was a trio of phrases no flight mechanic wanted to hear, especially when combined with Lloyd's of London, which had for nearly three hundred years enjoyed and wielded cachet like few other companies in the world.

Harold showed them into the maintenance office, and in short order Dominic and Brian had before them the records they'd requested and two cups of coffee. Harold loitered in the doorway until Brian gave him a *you're dismissed* stare that only a Marine officer can generate.

The flight plan Hlasek Air filed listed the Falcon's destination as Madrid, Spain, but flight plans were just that: plans. Once outside Söderhamn's airspace, the Falcon could have gone anywhere. There were complications to this, of course, but nothing insurmountable. The maintenance records seemed similarly routine until they got past the summary and read the details. In addition to a topping off of the Falcon's fuel tanks, the on-duty flight mechanic had performed a diagnostics scan of the aircraft's transponder.

Dominic got up, tapped on the office's glass window, and waved Harold over. He showed the mechanic the maintenance report. "This mechanic—Anton Rolf—we'd like to talk to him."

"Uh, he's not here today."

"We assumed as much. Where can we find him?"

"I don't know."

Brian said, "What's that mean?"

"Anton hasn't been to work in a week. No one's seen him or heard from him."

The Söderhamn police, Harold further explained, had come to the airport the previous Wednesday, following up on a missing-person report from Rolf's aunt, with whom Anton lived. Her nephew had failed to return home after work a week ago Friday.

Assuming the police would have already done the customary legwork, Brian and Dominic drove into Söderhamn, checked into the Hotel Linblomman, and slept until six, then found a nearby restaurant, where they ate and killed an hour before walking three blocks to a pub called Dålig Radisa—the Bad Radish—which, according to Harold, was Anton Rolf's preferred hangout.

After doing a walk-around survey of the block, they pushed through the bar's front door and were struck by a wave of cigarette smoke and heavy metal, and engulfed in a sea of blond-haired bodies either jostling for position at the bar or dancing wherever free space was to be found.

"At least it isn't that techno shit," Brian yelled over the cacophony.

Dominic grabbed a passing waitress and used his halting Swedish to order two beers. She disappeared and returned five minutes later. "You speak English?" he asked her.

"Yes, English. You are English?"

"American."

"Hey, American, that's great, yeah?"

"We're looking for Anton. You seen him?"

"Which Anton? There are many that come here."

"Rolf," Brian replied. "Mechanic, works at the airport."

"Yes, okay, Anton. He has not been here for a week, I think."

"You know where we can find him?"

The waitress's smile faded a bit. "Why are you looking for him?"

"We met him on Facebook last year. Told him next time we were over here we'd look him up."

"Oh, hey, Facebook. That's cool. His friends are here. They might know. Over there, in the corner." She pointed to a table surrounded by half a dozen twentysomethings in jerseys.

"Thanks," Brian said, and the waitress turned to go. Dominic stopped her. "Hey, just curious: Why'd you ask why we were looking for Anton?"

"There were others. Not nice like you."

"When?"

"Last Tuesday? No, sorry, Monday."

"The police, maybe?"

"No, not the police. I know all the police. Four men, not white but not black. From Middle East, maybe?"

Once she was gone, Dominic shouted in Brian's ear, "Monday. Three days after Rolf's aunt said he didn't come home."

"Maybe he doesn't want to be found," Brian replied. "Shit, man, it just had to be footballers."

"So?"

"You never watched the World Cup, bro? These guys like fighting more than they like drinking."

"Shouldn't be too hard to get a reaction, then."

"Dom, I ain't talking about boxing. I'm talking about rip-your-ear-off, stomp-on-your-guts street brawling. Add that whole group together and you know what you get?"

"What?"

"A mouthful of teeth," Brian replied with an evil grin.

"Hey, guys, we're looking for Anton," Dominic said. "Waitress said you're his friends."

"Don't speak English," one of them said. He had a lattice-work of ropy scars on his forehead.

"Hey, fuck you, Frankenstein," Brian said.

The man scooted his chair back, stood up, and squared off. The rest of them followed suit.

"Speak English now, huh?" Brian shouted.

"Just tell Anton we're looking for him," Dominic said, raising his hands to shoulder height. "Otherwise, we're going to pay a visit to his aunt."

Brian and Dominic stepped around the group and headed for the alley exit. "How long, you figure?" Brian asked.

"Thirty seconds, no more," Dominic replied.

Out in the alley, Brian grabbed a nearby steel garbage can and Dominic picked up a piece of rusted rebar as long as his forearm, and they turned in time to see the door swing outward. Brian, standing behind the door, let three of the footballers come out and go for Dominic in a rush, then kicked the door shut on the fourth and stepped in, swinging the garbage can like a scythe. Dominic took out the lead footballer with a shot to the knee, then ducked a punch from the second and brought the rebar down on his extended elbow, shattering it. Brian turned as the door swung back open, rammed the garbage can's rounded bottom edge into the bridge of the fourth man's forehead, waited for him to go down, then tossed the can at the knees of the last two charging across the threshold. The first went down at Brian's feet, then pushed up to his hands and knees, but Brian heel-kicked him in the head, dropping him back down. The last footballer, fists clenched and arms windmilling, was charging Dominic, who kept backing up,

288

staying out of range, letting him come, before sidestepping and backhanding the rebar into the side of the man's head. He crashed into the alley wall and slumped down.

"You okay?" Dominic asked his brother.

"Yeah, you?"

"Anybody awake?"

"Yeah, here, this one." Brian knelt down beside the first footballer through the door. He was groaning and rolling from side to side while holding his shattered knee. "Hey, Frankenstein, tell Anton we're looking for him."

They left the footballers in the alley and walked across the street from the bar into a park, where Dominic took a seat on a bench. Brian jogged back to the hotel, retrieved their rental car, then returned, parking on the opposite side of the park.

"No police?" Brian asked, approaching Dominic's bench through the trees.

"Nah. Didn't strike me as the police-loving kind."

"Me neither." They waited five minutes, then the front door opened and two of the footballers came out and shuffled toward a car parked down the block. "Good friends," Brian observed. "Gullible but good."

36

They followed the footballers' car, a dark blue Citroën, through downtown Söderhamn to the eastern outskirts of the city, then into the countryside. After four miles they pulled into a town, this one a quarter the size of Söderhamn. "Forsbacka," Brian read from the map. The Citroën pulled off the main road, then took a series of lefts and rights before pulling into the driveway of a mint-green saltbox house. Dominic passed the house, took a right at the next corner, and pulled to the curb beneath a tree. Out the back window they could see the saltbox's front door. The footballers were already on the porch. One of them knocked. Thirty seconds later the porch light came on and the door opened.

"What do you think? Go in now or wait?" Dominic asked.

"Wait. If it's Rolf, he's been smart enough to stay out of sight for a week. He's not going to bolt before giving it some thought."

After twenty minutes, the front door opened again and the footballers emerged. They got back into the Citroën, pulled out, and headed down the block. Brian and Dominic waited until the taillights disappeared around the corner, then got out, crossed the street, and walked down to the saltbox. A hedge of overgrown lilac bushes separated the house from its neighbor. They followed the hedge, passing two darkened windows, until they reached a detached garage, which they circled until they could see the rear of the house: a back door flanked by two windows. All were dark except one. As they watched, a male figure walked past the window and stopped before a kitchen cabinet, which he opened, then closed. Ten seconds later the man emerged carrying a suitcase. Brian and Dominic ducked back. The garage's side door opened, followed by a car door opening and closing. The garage door closed again, then the house's back door slammed shut.

"Taking it on the road. Better assume Anton's a footballer like his buddies."

"I was thinking the same thing, too. Doubtful he has a gun—Swedish laws are kind of a bitch on that count—but better safe than sorry. We swarm him, put him down hard."

"Right."

*

They took positions on either side of the back door and waited. Five minutes passed. They could hear the man moving about inside. Brian opened the back screen door and tried the inside doorknob. Unlocked. He looked back at Dominic, gave him a nod, then turned the knob, eased open the door, stopped. Waited. Nothing. Brian stepped through and held the door for Dominic, who followed.

They were in a narrow kitchen. To the left, past the refrigerator, was a dining room. To the right, a short hall leading toward the front of the house into what looked like a living room. Somewhere a television was playing. Brian sidestepped and peeked around the corner. He pulled back and signaled to Dominic: *Eyes on one man. I'm going.* Dominic nodded.

Brian took a step, paused, then another, then he was halfway down the hall.

The plank floor beneath his feet creaked.

In the living room, Anton Rolf, standing in front of the TV, looked up, saw Brian, and bolted for the front door. Brian rushed ahead, bent over, and placed both hands against the long wooden coffee table and bulldozed it, pinning Rolf against the partially opened front door. Rolf lost his balance and fell backward. Brian was already moving, up on the coffee table and across it. He caught Rolf's head by the hair and slammed his forehead into the doorjamb once, then twice, then a third time. Rolf went limp.

They found a roll of quarter-inch clothesline in a kitchen drawer and tied up Rolf. While Brian watched over him, Dominic searched the house but came up with nothing unusual, save the suitcase Rolf had been packing. "He did a quick pack job," Brian said, sorting through the clothes and toiletries that had been shoved into the case. It seemed clear that Rolf's decision to leave had been precipitated by his friends' visit.

Outside they heard the squeal of brakes. Brian went to the

front window, looked out, then shook his head. Dominic went into the kitchen. He reached the sink window in time to see a woman come around the corner from the driveway and head for the back door, which opened a moment later, just as Dominic slipped behind it. The woman stepped inside. Dominic swung the door shut, stepped to her, clamped his right hand over her mouth, and twisted her head so it lay tight against his shoulder.

"Quiet," he whispered in Swedish. "Do you speak English?"

She nodded. Most Swedes did, they'd found, which seemed to be the case in most European countries. Americans were unique in that respect, having largely remained literate in English only—and sometimes then only marginally so.

"I'm going to take my hand away. We're not going to hurt you, but if you scream, I'll gag you. Understand?"

She nodded.

Dominic took his hand away and gently shoved her into one of the dining room chairs. Brian came in. "What's your name?" Dominic asked her.

"Maria."

"Anton's your boyfriend?"

"Yes."

"People are looking for him, you know."

"You're looking for him."

"Other than us," Brian replied. "The waitress at the Radish told us some Middle Eastern guys were asking about him." Maria didn't answer. "He didn't tell you, did he?"

"No."

"Probably didn't want to worry you."

Maria rolled her eyes, and Brian chuckled. "We're kinda stupid that way sometimes."

This brought a smile to Maria's lips. "Yes, I know."

Dominic asked, "Did Anton tell you why he's hiding?"

"Something to do with the police."

Brian and Dominic exchanged glances. Had Anton assumed the police were looking for him for another reason? Something other than his aunt's missing-person report?

"Where were you two going?" Dominic asked.

"Stockholm. He has friends there."

Okay, listen: If we'd meant you harm, we would've done it by now. Do you understand?"

She nodded. "Who are you?"

"Doesn't matter. We need you to make Anton understand. If he answers our questions, we'll see what we can do to help him. Okay? If not, things go bad."

"Okay."

Brian got a pitcher of cold water from the kitchen and dumped it over Anton's head. Then he and Dominic retreated to the far side of the living room while Maria knelt before Anton's chair and started whispering to him. After five minutes, she turned around and nodded to them.

"My aunt filed a report," Anton said a few minutes later.

Dominic nodded. "She hadn't seen you. I guess she was worried. You thought it was about something else? Something to do with that plane?"

"How did you know about that?"

"A hunch," Brian replied. "Until now. You did something with the transponder?"

Anton nodded.

"What?"

"Duplicated the codes."

"For another plane, a Gulfstream?"

"Right."

"Who hired you?"

"The guy—the owner."

"Of Hlasek Air. Lars."

"Yes."

Brian asked, "Not the first time you've done this for him, is it?"

"No."

"How's he pay you?"

"Money . . . cash."

"Were you there the night the Dassault came in and took off?"

"Yes."

"Tell us about it," Dominic said.

"Four passengers, Middle Eastern, came in a limousine. They got aboard, and the plane took off. That's it."

"Can you describe any of them?"

Rolf shook his head. "It was too dark. You said something about the Radish. Someone else looking for me?"

Brian said, "According to the waitress. Four Middle Eastern men. Any idea why they're looking for you?"

Rolf glared at him. "Are you trying to be funny?"

"No, sorry."

Dominic and Brian left Maria with Anton and stepped into the hall. "You think he's telling the truth?" Brian asked.

"Yeah, I do. He's scared shitless, and happy as hell we were white faces coming through the door."

"Doesn't change much, though. He's got nothing we can use. No name, no faces, no paper trail—just Middle Eastern-ers traveling incognito to who knows where. If DHS or the FBI had Hlasek or his pilot, they wouldn't have asked Zurich and Stockholm to beat the bushes."

"Probably right," Dominic replied.

"What about those two?"

"Best we can do is get them to Stockholm. If Anton's smart, he'll turn himself in to the Rikskriminalpolisen and pray they're interested in his story."

Dominic watched over Anton and Maria as they gathered their things. Brian left through the back to retrieve the car. He returned three minutes later, panting. "Problem. Tires on our rental are slashed."

Dominic turned to Anton. "Your friends?"

"No. I told them not to come back."

From outside came the squelch of brakes. Dominic shut off the table lamp. Brian locked the front door and peered through the peephole. "Four men," he whispered. "Armed. Two coming to the front, two going around back."

"You were followed," Dominic told Maria.

"I didn't see anyone—"

"That's sort of the point."

"You have a gun?" Brian asked Anton.

"No."

Dominic and Brian exchanged glances. Each knew what the other was thinking: too late to call the cops. And even if it wasn't, their involvement would bring more problems than it would solutions.

"Get in the kitchen," Dominic ordered Anton and Maria. "Lock the door, then get on the floor. Stay quiet." Dominic and Brian followed them there. "Knives?" Brian whispered to Anton, who pointed to a drawer. Hunched beneath the level of the window, Brian walked over, slid the drawer open, and found a pair of five-inch stainless-steel steak knives. He handed one to Dominic, then pointed to himself, then the living room, then moved that way. Dominic followed, and together they shoved the couch, the coffee table, and a side chair up against the door. It wouldn't stop whoever was coming, but it would slow them down and, they hoped, even the odds. Though unavoidable, Brian and Dominic had, in fact, brought knives to a gunfight. Dominic gave his brother a good-luck wave, then returned to the kitchen. Brian took up station at the end of the hall, eyes fixed on the front door.

From the floor, Maria whispered, "What—"

Dominic held his palm up, shook his head.

Outside the kitchen window came a pair of hushed voices. Ten seconds passed. The doorknob on the back door turned, creaking, first one way, then the other. Dominic crab-walked around Anton and Maria, then pressed himself against the wall beside the door on the knob side.

Silence.

More hushed voices.

From the side of the house came shattering glass. Dominic heard what sounded like a rock thump against the floor. A feint, he decided, knowing Brian would have reached the same conclusion. The screen door creaked open.

Something bulky crashed against the door. Then again. The wooden jamb beside Dominic's head splintered. On the third crash, the door flew inward. A forearm and a hand holding a revolver appeared first, followed a second later by a face. Dominic waited for his target—the soft spot just beneath the earlobe—to appear, then straight-armed the knife, burying it to the hilt in the man's throat, then using it as a lever to bring him farther in the doorway. The man dropped the gun. Dominic kicked it down the hall, where Brian scooped it up. Dominic withdrew the knife, then reached across, grabbed the door, and slammed it shut, driving the man back outside.

From the front came two gunshots. The windows shattered. Brian crouched down and pointed the revolver at the front door. Dominic stepped around Maria and Rolf, ducked down, then peeked through the kitchen window. Outside, two men were kneeling over their partner. One of them looked up, saw Dominic, and fired two shots through the window.

On his hands and knees now, Dominic asked Maria, "Cooking oil?" She pointed to the opposite lower cabinet. Dominic ordered them into the living room with Brian, then retrieved the oil and dumped the bottle on the linoleum floor five feet from the door, then headed for the living room. As he stepped around Brian, the back door burst open again. A figure rushed through, followed by a second. The first hit the oiled floor and went down, taking his partner with him. Revolver outstretched, Brian stepped down the hall, right shoulder pressed to the wall, then opened fire. He put two rounds into the first man and three into the second, then grabbed their guns and tossed one to Dominic, who was already heading down the hall, pushing Maria and Rolf before him.

Careful to avoid the oil, Dominic stepped over the bodies, peeked out the back door, then pulled back. "Clear—"

From the living room the front door crashed inward, followed by the grating of furniture legs on the hardwood floor.

"Go for the car," Dominic told Brian. "Start it up, make some noise."

"Got it."

As Brian ushered Maria and Rolf out the back door, Dominic looked down the hall in time to see a figure push through and begin crawling over the stacked furniture. Dominic ducked out the back door and sprinted across the lawn and around the back corner of the garage; inside it, Brian had Rolf's car started and was revving the engine. Dominic dropped to his knee and peeked around the corner; the fence at his back was dark and covered in shrubbery. It would make his outline all but invisible.

The last man appeared in the doorway. Having seen his dead comrades in the kitchen, this one was more cautious, looking this way and that before stepping out. He paused again, then slid down the wall and checked the driveway before starting across the lawn. Dominic waited until his hand had almost touched the knob of the garage door, then rasped, "Hey!" He let the man turn ever so slightly, just enough for a good solid-mass shot, then fired twice. Both shots took the man in the sternum. He stumbled backward, dropped to his knees, then toppled over.

37

Time to land a new job, Clark told himself after breakfast. He called ahead and arranged to arrive at 10:30, then woke up Chavez, and they met at the car at half past nine.

"Well, we'll see what they pay," Ding observed. "I'm ready to be impressed."

"Don't get too enthused," Clark warned as he started the car. "Hell, I never expected to see a hundred grand from Langley when I started there. My starting salary was nineteen-five a year."

"Well, the guy said their IRA plan—whatever you call it—works pretty well, and I saw all the Beemers in the parking lot. I'll let you do the talking," Chavez suggested.

"Yeah, you just sit there and look menacing." John allowed himself a laugh.

"You suppose they really want us to whack people?"

"I guess we'll have to find out."

The traffic on the American Legion Bridge wasn't too bad with the approaching end of rush hour, and soon enough they were northbound on U.S. 29.

"You decide what you're going to do about my fuckup?"

"Yeah, I think so. We're going down the rabbit hole, Ding—a lot farther than we've been before. Might as well go all the way. We'll hand it over to them and see what they can make of it."

"Okay. So this Hendley guy—what do we know about him?"

"U.S. Senator from South Carolina, democrat, served on the Intelligence Committee. They liked him at Langley—smart, straight shooter. Ryan liked him, too. Hendley lost his family in a car accident. Wife and two boys, I think. He's very rich. Like Ryan, he made a pile of money in the trading business. He's good at seeing things other people don't."

Both men were properly dressed, in decent suits both had bought in London during their Rainbow tour, with Turnbull & Asser ties and nicely polished shoes. Actually, this was something Chavez still did every day, from his time in the U.S. Army, though Clark occasionally had to be reminded.

They parked in the visitors' lot and walked inside. Ernie Chambers still had the desk duty. "Hi. We're here to see Mr. Davis again."

"Yes, sir. Please have a seat while I call upstairs."

Clark and Chavez took a seat, and John picked up a current copy of *Time* magazine. He'd have to get used to reading the news four days late. Davis appeared in the lobby.

"Thanks for coming back. You want to follow me?"

Two minutes after that, all three were in Tom Davis's office, looking out at some Maryland horse country.

"So are you interested?" Davis asked.

"Yes," Clark replied for them both.

"Okay, good. Rules: First, what happens here stays here. This place does not exist, and neither does any activity that may or may not happen here."

"Mr. Davis, we both know about secrecy. Neither one of us talks much, and we don't tell tales out of school."

"You'll have to sign another round of NDAs on that. We can't enforce anything with statutory law, but we can take all your money away."

"Are we supposed to have our personal attorneys review them?"

"If you wish, you can. There's nothing compromising in the agreements, but then you could tear it up. We can't have any lawyers wondering what we do here. It's not all, strictly speaking, legal."

"How much travel?" John asked next.

"Less than you're used to, I suspect. We're still figuring that out. You'll spend most of your time right here, looking over data and planning ops."

"Source of the data?"

"Langley and Fort Meade, mostly, but skim a little from the FBI, Immigration and Customs, DHS . . . Those kinds of places. We've got a damned good technical team. You probably noticed the hedgehog on our roof."

"We did."

"We're the only building on a direct line of sight from CIA to NSA. They swap data by microwave, and we download all their interagency transmissions. That's how we do our financial trading. NSA keeps a close eye on domestic and foreign banks. They can also tap into the bank computer systems and internal communications."

"What you said the other day about wet work . . . ?"

"We've only run one real operation to date—the four people I mentioned yesterday. Truth be told, we were halfway curious about what would happen. In fact, nothing much happened. Maybe we covered our tracks too well. All the killings looked like heart attacks, the victims were posted, and the autopsy reports all said 'natural causes.' We think the opposition bought that story and kept going. The fourth one—MoHa—netted us a laptop with encryption keys, so we're reading some of their internal mail at the moment—or were, until recently. Looks like they might have switched up their communication protocols last week."

"Out of the blue?" Clark asked.

"Yep. We intercepted a birth announcement. Big distribution list. Within hours, everyone went quiet."

"Switching channels," Chavez said.

"Yep. We're working on a lead that may get us back in."

"Who else will be operating like us?"

"You'll meet them in due course," Davis promised.

"And the pay?" Ding asked.

"We can start you both at two-fifty a year. You can partici-pate in the office investment plan with as much or as little of your salary as you wish. I told you already about the rate of return. We also pay for reasonable educational expenses for any kids. Up to one Ph.D. or professional degree. That's the limit."

"What if my wife wants to go back to medical school for some additional work? She's a family practitioner now, but she's thinking about getting trained up for OB/GYN."

"We'll cover it."

"If she asks what I'm doing here, what do I say?"

"Security consulting for a major trading house. It always works," Davis assured him. "She must know you were an Agency guy."

"She's his daughter." Chavez pointed to Clark.

"So she'll understand, won't she? And your wife, Mr. Clark?"

"Name's John. Yeah, Sandy knows the drill. Maybe this way she can tell people what a real job I have," he added with a thin smile.

"So how about we meet the boss?"

"Okay with us," Clark said for them both.

"The pardons are real," Hendley assured them a few minutes later. "When Ryan pitched me the idea of setting this place up, he said it would be necessary to protect such field person-nel as we sent out, and so he signed a hundred. We've never had to use one, but they're an insurance policy should they ever become necessary. Anything you're curious about that Tom didn't cover?"

"How are the targets selected?" Clark asked.

"You'll be part of the process for the most part. We have to be careful how we choose the people we want to go away."

"Do we also pick the methods?" Clark asked delicately.

"You tell them about the pens?" Hendley asked Davis.

"This is one of the tools we use." Davis held up the gold pen. "It injects about seven milligrams of succinylcholine. That's a sedative used in surgical procedures. In stops the breathing and voluntary muscle movement. But not the heart. You can't move, can't speak, and you can't breathe. The heart keeps beating for a minute or so, but it's starved of oxygen, and so death happens from what appears on postmortem examination to be a heart attack. It evidently feels like it, too."

"Reversible?" Clark wondered.

"Yeah, if you get the victim on a respirator immediately. The drug wears off—metabolizes—in about five minutes. It leaves nothing in the way of traces unless the victim is posted by a really expert ME that knows what they're looking for. Damned near perfect."

"I'm surprised the Russians didn't come up with something like this."

"They surely tried," Davis responded. "But succinylcholine didn't make it to their hospitals, I guess. We got it from a doc friend up at Columbia's College of Physicians and Surgeons who had a personal score to settle. His brother—a senior broker with Cantor Fitzgerald—died on Nine-Eleven."

"Impressive," Clark said, eyeballing the pen. "Might be a good interrogation tool, too. It would be a rare customer who'd want to go through that experience twice."

Davis handed it over. "It's not loaded. You twist the tip to swap out the point. It writes perfectly well."

"Slick. Well, that answers one question. We're free to use more conventional tools?"

"If and as the job calls for doing so," Davis confirmed with a nod. "But we're all about not being there, so always keep that in the back of your mind."

"Understood."

"And you, Mr. Chavez?" Hendley asked.

"Sir, I just try to listen and learn," Ding told the boss.

"Is he that smart, John?" the former Senator asked.

"More so, actually. We work well together."

"That's what we need. Well, welcome aboard, gentlemen."

"One thing," Clark said. He withdrew Ding's flash drive from his pocket and laid it on the desk. "We took that off one of the bad guys in Tripoli."

"I see. And why is it sitting on my desk?"

"An oversight," Clark replied. "Call it a 'senior moment.' I figure we can give it to the Swedes or to Langley, but I suspect we'd put it to better use here."

"Have you looked at it?"

Chavez answered, "JPEG image files—a dozen or so. Looked like vacation shots to me, but who knows."

Hendley considered this, then nodded. "Okay, we'll take a look. Tom, do we have an office for them?"

"Right down with the Caruso boys."

"Good. Have a look around, guys, then we'll see you first thing tomorrow morning."

Hendley stood, encouraging the others to do the same. Davis headed toward the door, followed by Chavez and Clark.

"John, can you hang back for a moment?" Hendley asked.

"Sure. Ding, I'll catch up."

Once they were alone, Hendley said, "You've been around the block a few times, John. I wanted to get your take on a couple things."

"Shoot."

"We're pretty new, this whole concept, in fact, so a lot of it is trial and error. I'm beginning to think our work flow's a little convoluted."

Clark chuckled. "No offense, Gerry, but using words like *work flow* for an outfit like this tells me you're right. What's the chain like?" Hendley described The Campus's organizational structure, and Clark said, "Sounds like Langley. Listen, intelligence work is mostly organic, okay? Analysis is something you can't do without, but trying to shove the process into some artificial structure is a cluster-fuck waiting to happen."

"You don't pull any punches, do you?"

"Did you want me to?"

"No."

"Too many good ideas get lost making their way up a chain. My advice: Get your principals in a room once a day and brainstorm. Might be a cliché, but it works. If you've got people who're worried about whether their creative thinking will make the cut, you're wasting talent."

Hendley whistled softly, smiling. "Don't take this the wrong way, John, but you sure as hell aren't your average knuckle-dragger, are you?"

Clark shrugged but didn't reply.

"Well," Hendley continued, "you kind of hit it on the head. I'd been thinking the same thing. Nice to get a second opinion, though."

"Anything else?"

"Yeah. Jack Ryan came to me the other day. He wants more fieldwork."

Junior ain't so junior anymore, Clark reminded himself.

"Tom told you about the MoHa thing?" Hendley asked.

"Yeah."

"Well, I heard secondhand the Caruso brothers took Jack to Hogan's Alley for a little stress relief. He did damned good, or so they say. Got a little banged up, made some rookie mistakes, but damned good all the same."

So he's got some talent, Clark thought. Genetics, maybe, if you buy into that sort of thing. He'd seen Jack's dad at work, and he was a fair trigger, too. And cool under pressure. Both can be taught, but the latter was more about mind-set and temperament. It sounded like Jack had both, plus a steady hand.

"Where's his head on it?" Clark asked.

"No illusions, I don't think. Doesn't strike me as a glory hound, anyway."

"He isn't. His parents raised him right."

"He's a damned good analyst, got a real knack for it, but he feels like he's spinning his wheels. He wants to get in the weeds. Problem is, I don't think his dad would—"

"If you're going to make decisions about him based on what his dad would say or think, then . . ."

"Say it."

"Then you need to be worrying about where your head is, not his. Jack's an adult, and it's his life. You need to make the decision based on whether he'd be good at it and whether it'd help The Campus. That's it; that's all."

"Fair enough. Well, I need to mull it over some more. If I decide to send him out, he'd need a training officer."

"You have one of those."

"I could use another, or two. Pete Alexander is damned good, but I'd want you to take Jack under your wing."

Clark considered this. *Time to practice what you just preached to the boss, John.* "Sure, I'll do it."

"Thanks. We're always on the lookout for more like you and Chavez, too, if you've got any thoughts on that. We've got our own talent scouts, but it's always better to have a surfeit of candidates."

"True. Let me think about it. I may have a name or two."

Hendley smiled. "Some recently retired operators, maybe?"

Clark smiled back. "Maybe."

38

"Dead drops," Mary Pat Foley announced, pushing her way through the NCTC conference room's glass door. She walked to the corkboard to which they had tacked both the DMA chart and the Baedeker's Peshawar map and tapped one of the dot clusters.

"Come again?" John Turnbull said.

"The legend on the back—up and down arrows combined with dot clusters—their dead-drop locations. The up arrow is the pickup signal, the down arrow the drop box location. The location of the first tells you which box to check for the package. A three-dot cluster for the pickup signal location, a four-dot cluster for the box location."

"That's some nitty-gritty Cold War shit right there," Janet Cummings said.

"It's tried and true—goes back to ancient Rome."

The fact that her colleagues seemed surprised by this turn of events told her that they—and perhaps the CIA at large— were still working with a perceptual deficit when it came to the URC's intelligence capability. Providing the agents working the dead drops were careful, the system was an effective way to make secondhand exchanges.

"No way to know if they're still active, though," she said. "Not without boots on the ground."

The phone at Ben Margolin's elbow trilled. He picked up the handset, listened for thirty seconds, then hung up. "Nothing so far, but the computers are chewing away at it. The good news is, we've eliminated a sixty-mile radius around the cave."

"Too many variables," John Turnbull, head of Acre Station, said.

"Yep," Janet Cummings, the NCTC's Chief of Operations, replied.

Mary Pat Foley's idea for solving the "Where in the world is this?" riddle surrounding the sand table Driscoll and his team had recovered from the Hindu Kush cave involved a CIA project code-named Collage.

The brainchild of some mathematician in the Langley science and technology directorate, Collage had been out of Acre Station's frustration in answering a question to Mary Pat's, in their case, "Where in the world is he?" The Emir and his lieutenants had long been fond of releasing photos and videos of themselves traipsing about the wilds of Pakistan and Afghanistan, giving the U.S. intelligence community plenty of hints about the weather and terrain of their locations but never enough to be of any help to UAVs or Special Forces teams in the area. Without larger context, points of reference, and reliable scale, a rock was a rock was a rock.

Collage hoped to solve that by collating every available piece of raw topographical data, from commercial and military Landsat images to radar imaging satellites such as Lacrosse and Onyx, to family photo albums on Facebook and travelogues on Flickr—as long as the image's location could be solidly fixed and scaled to some point on earth, Collage put it into the hopper for digestion and spit it out as an overlay of the earth's surface. Also into this mix went a dizzying array of variables: geological characteristics, current and past weather patterns, timber-use plans, seismic activity. . . . If it involved the earth's surface and how it might look at any given time, it was fed into Collage.

Questions no one thought to ask, such as, "What does the granite in the Hindu Kush look like when it's wet?" and "In what direction would a certain shadow lean with thirty percent cloud coverage and a dew point of x?" and "With ten days of twelve- to fourteen-mile-per-hour winds, how high is this sand dune in Sudan likely to get?" The permutations were daunting, as was the mathematical modeling system buried within Collage's code structure, which ran far into the millions of lines. The problem was that the math wasn't based solely on known variables but also imaginary ones, not to mention probability threads, as the program had to make assumptions about not only the raw data but also what it was seeing in an image or a piece of video. In, say, a thirty-second 640×480 video, Collage's first pass would identify anywhere from 500,000 to 3,000,000 points of reference to which it had to assign a value—black or white or grayscale (of which there were sixteen thousand)—relative size and angle of the object; distance from its foreground, background, and lateral neighbors; intensity and angular direction of sunlight or thickness and air speed of cloud cover, and so on. Once these values were assigned, they were fed into Collage's overlay matrix, and the hunt began for a match.

Collage had had some successes, but nothing of real-time tactical significance, and Mary Pat was beginning to suspect the system was going to come up short here, too. If so, the failing wouldn't lie with the program but rather with the input. They had no idea if the sand table was even a true representation of anything, let alone whether it was to scale or within a thousand miles of the Hindu Kush.

"Where do we stand with Lotus?" Mary Pat asked. The NSA had been scouring its intercepts for any references to Lotus, in hopes of finding a pattern with which the NCTC could start back-building a picture. Like the model on which Collage was built, the number of questions they would have to answer to assemble the puzzle was daunting: When did the term first come into use? In what frequency? From which parts of the world? How was it most often disseminated—by e-mail, by phone, or through websites, or something else they hadn't yet considered? Did Lotus precede or follow any major terrorist incidents? And so on. Hell, there were no assurances Lotus meant anything. For all they knew, it could be a pet name for the Emir's girlfriend.

"Okay, let's play worst-case scenario," Margolin said, bringing things back on track.

"I say we double-cover our bets," Cummings replied. "We know where the cave is, and we know the signal had a fairly short reach—a few dozen miles on either side of the border. Assuming Lotus means anything at all, the chances are halfway decent that it caused some kind of movement—personnel, logistics, money. . . . Who knows."

The problem, Mary Pat thought, was that personnel and logistics were often better tracked with HUMINT—human intelligence—than they were with signals intelligence, and right now they had virtually none of those assets in the area.

"You know what my vote would be," Mary Pat told the NCTC's director.

"We've all got the same wish list, but the resources just aren't there—not in the depth we'd like."

Thanks to Ed Kealty and DCI Scott Kilborn, she thought sourly. Having spent the better part of a decade rebuilding its stable of case officers—much of it through Plan Blue—the Clandestine Service had been ordered to scale back its overseas presence in favor of ally-generated intelligence. Men and women who had risked their lives building agent networks in the badlands of Pakistan and Afghanistan and Iran were being reeled back into the embassies and consulates with not so much as an attaboy.

God save us from the shortsighted politicalization of intelligence.

"Then let's think out of the box," Mary Pat said. "We've got tappable assets there—just not ours. Let's reach out for some good old-fashioned ally-generated intelligence."

"The Brits?" Turnbull asked.

"Yep. They've got more experience in Central Asia than

anyone else, including the Russians. Couldn't hurt to ask. Have somebody check the dead drops, see if they're still viable."

"And then?"

"We cross that bridge when we get there."

At the end of the conference table, Margolin tilted his head back and stared at the ceiling for a moment. "The problem isn't the asking; the problem is getting permission to ask."

"You have got to be fucking kidding me," Cummings said.

He wasn't, Mary Pat knew. While Kilborn's deputies in intelligence and Clandestine hadn't guzzled the Kool-Aid like the DCI had, they were certainly imbibing. In choosing Kilborn, President Kealty had ensured that the CIA's upper echelons would toe the executive branch's new line, regardless of the consequences to the agency or to the intelligence community at large.

"So don't ask," Mary Pat said simply.

"What?" replied Margolin.

"If we don't ask, we can't get a no. We're still spitballing here, right? Nothing's operational, nothing's funded. We're just fishing. It's what we do; it's what they pay us to do. Since when do we have to ask anyone about a little chat with an ally?"

Margolin looked hard at her for a few moments, then shrugged. The gesture said nothing and everything. She knew her boss well enough to know she'd struck a chord. Like her, Margolin loved his career but not at the expense of doing his job.

"We never talked about this," Margolin said. "Let me run it up the flagpole. If we're flamed, we'll do it your way."

This was the real Russia, Vitaliy thought, with the harshest winters in a nation famous for bitter weather. The polar bears here were fat now, covered in a thick layer stored up for insulation, enough to allow them to sleep the months away in caves hollowed out amid the pressure ridges and seracs on the ice, waking occasionally to snatch a seal that ventured too close to a breathing hole.

Vitaliy stood up and shook himself awake, then shuffled into the galley to get the water started for his morning tea. The temperature was just above freezing—what passed for a warm fall day. No new ice had formed overnight, at least nothing his boat couldn't crush or bypass, but the decks were coated in an inch-thick layer of frozen spindrift, something he and Vanya would have to chop free, lest the boat grow top-heavy. Capsizing in these waters meant almost certain death; without immersion suits, a man could expect to be unconscious within four minutes and dead within fifteen, and while he had enough suits aboard for everyone, his passengers had shown little interest in his explanation of their use.

His charter party was awake, struggling to stamp their feet and fling their arms across their chests. They all lit their cigarettes and moved aft to the boat's primitive head facilities. All ate the bread and ice-hard butter set out for breakfast.

Vitaliy gave it an hour to get the day started, then he fired up his diesels and backed off the gravel beach on which they'd spent the night. His charts were already laid out, and he headed east at ten knots. Vanya spelled him at the wheel. They listened to an old but serviceable AM radio, mostly classical music beamed out from Archangel. It helped pass the time. There were ten hours of steaming remaining to their destination. About 160 kilometers. Ten hours at ten knots, so said the chart.

"That doesn't look good," Vanya said, pointing off the starboard bow.

On the eastern horizon was a line of swollen black clouds, so low they almost seemed to merge with the ocean's surface.

"Not good at all," Vitaliy agreed. And it would get worse, he knew. To reach their destination they would have to pass through the storm—either that or go far out of their way, or even ground the boat and wait it out.

"Ask Fred to come up, will you?" Vitaliy said.

Vanya went below and returned a minute later with the leader of the charter group. "A problem, Captain?"

Vitaliy pointed through the window at the squall line. "That."

"Rain?"

"It doesn't rain here, Fred. It storms. The only question is, to what degree? And that mess there, I'm afraid, is going to be bad." *Worse still for a T-4 slab-sided landing craft with one meter of draft,* he didn't add.

"How long until we reach it?"

"Three hours—a little longer, maybe."

"Can we weather it?"

"Probably, but nothing is certain out here. Either way, it's going to be rough going."

"What are our alternatives?" asked Fred.

"Return to where we just overnighted or head south and try to get around the edge of the storm. Either option will cost us a day or two of travel time."

"Unacceptable," Fred replied.

"It will be dicey, going through that—and you and your men are going to be miserable."

"We will manage. Perhaps a bonus for your trouble will make the inconvenience more palatable?"

Vitaliy shrugged. "I'm game if you are."

"Proceed."

Two hours later he saw a ship on the horizon, heading west. Probably a supply ship, coming back from delivering her cargo of oil-drilling equipment to the new oil field discovered farther east, up the Lena River, south of Tiksi. Judging by the ship's wake, she was making her best speed, obviously trying to outpace the very storm into which they were headed.

Vanya appeared at his side. "Engines are fine. We're locked down tight." Vitaliy had asked him to prepare the boat for the impending weather. What they couldn't do was either prepare their guests for what was to come or prepare for what the sea might do to the boat. Mother Nature was fickle and cruel.

Earlier, Vitaliy had asked Fred to have his men lend a hand in de-icing the boat, something they did despite their unsteady legs and seasick green pallor. While half of them chopped at the ice with sledgehammers and axes, the other half, under the supervision of Vanya, had used grain shovels to scoop the loosened chunks of ice overboard.

"How about after this we move to Sochi and run a boat there?" Vanya asked his captain after releasing the passengers to go below and rest.

"Too hot there. That's no place for a man to live." The usual arctic mentality. Real men lived and worked in the cold, and boasted how tough they were. And besides, it made the vodka taste better.

Ten miles off their bow the storm loomed, a roiling gray-black wall that seemed to visibly surge forward before Vitaliy's eyes. "Vanya, go below and give our guests a refresher course on the immersion suits."

Vanya turned toward the ladder.

"And make sure they pay attention this time," Vitaliy added.

As a captain, he had a professional responsibility to ensure the safety of his passengers, but more important, he doubted whoever his party worked for would be forgiving, should he get them all killed.

An idiotic exercise, Musa Merdasan thought, watching the gnomelike Russian man unfold the orange survival suit on the deck. First, no rescue ships would reach them in time, suit or no suit; second, none of his men would be donning the suits in any event. If Allah saw fit to give them over to the sea, they would accept their fate. Moreover, Merdasan didn't want any of them being fished from the sea at all; if they were, he prayed it would be in an unidentifiable state. That was something to consider, how to ensure neither the captain and his deckhand survived any such catastrophe, lest the nature of the trip and their passengers be scrutinized. He couldn't count on a gun if they went into the water. Knife, then, preferably before they abandoned ship. And perhaps slit open their bellies to make sure they sank.

"First you lay the suit flat on the deck, unzipped, and then you sit down with your rear end just above the lowermost point of the zipper," the Russian was saying.

Merdasan and his men were, of course, following along, doing their best to appear attentive. None of them appeared well, though, the building seas having leached the color from their faces. The cabin stank of vomit and sweat and over-cooked vegetables.

"Legs go in first, followed by each arm in turn, followed by the hood. Once that's done, you roll to your knees, pull the zipper fully closed, and close the Velcro flaps over the lower half of your face."

The Russian went from man to man, making sure each one of them was following his instructions. Satisfied, he looked around and said, "Any questions?"

There were none.

"If you go overboard, your EPIRB—"

"Our what?" asked one of the men.

"Emergency Position-Indicating Radio Beacon—the thing attached to your collar—will activate automatically as soon as it is submerged."

"Any questions about that part?"

There were none.

"Okay, I suggest you get in your bunks and hold on."

Though Vitaliy knew what to expect, the speed and ferocity with which the storm hit was jarring nevertheless. The sky went night-black around them, and within five minutes the sea went from relative calmness, with six- to eight-foot swells, to a roiling surface and twenty-foot waves that crashed into the bow ramp like the hand of God itself.

Great plumes of spray and foam billowed over the slab sides and pelted the wheelhouse windows like handfuls of hurled gravel, obliterating Vitaliy's vision for ten seconds before the wipers could compensate, only to clear in time to give him a glimpse of the next wave. Every few seconds, tons of seawater broke over the starboard rail and surged knee-deep across the deck, overloading the scuppers, which couldn't keep up with the volume. Hands clenched tightly around the wheel, Vitaliy could feel the helm growing sluggish as the trapped water crashed from beam to beam against the gunwales.

"Get below and mind the engines and the pumps," Vitaliy told Vanya, who lurched to the ladder.

Joggling the dual throttles, Vitaliy struggled to keep the bow pointed into the oncoming waves. To let the boat swing broadside into the surge was to invite a fatal roll that would capsize them. The flat-bottomed T-4 had virtually no ability to snap itself upright beyond anything more than a fifteen-degree roll. Capsized in a trough, the boat would go under within a minute or two.

On the other hand, Vitaliy was too aware of the bow ramp's structural limitations. Though he and Vanya had worked hard to ensure that the ramp was secure and water-resistant, there was no way around its design: It was meant to drop flat on a beach to disgorge soldiers. With each crashing wave, the ramp shuddered, and even over the roar of the storm, Vitaliy could hear the metal-on-metal hammering of the inch-thick securing pins.

Another wave loomed over the rail and broke, half of it shearing off and cascading over the deck, the other half slamming into the wheelhouse windows. The boat lurched to port. Vitaliy lost his footing and pitched forward, his forehead slamming into the console. He regained his feet and blinked rapidly, vaguely aware of something wet and warm running down his temple. He took his hand from the wheel and touched his forehead; his fingers came back bloody. Not too bad, though, he decided. A couple stitches.

From the intercom, Vanya's muffled voice: "Pump . . . failed . . . trying restart . . ."

Damn. One pump they could do without, but Vitaliy knew most boats sank not from a single catastrophic incident but from a domino effect of them, one after the other, until the boat's vital functions were overwhelmed. And if that happened out here . . . It didn't bear thinking about.

Sixty seconds passed, then Vanya again: "Pump restarted!"

"Understood!" Vitaliy replied.

From below he heard a voice shout, "No, don't! Come back!"

Vitaliy scooted to his right and pressed his face to the side window. Aft he saw a figure stumble through the cabin door and onto the pitching deck. It was one of Fred's men.

"What the devil . . ."

The man stumbled, fell to his knees. Vomit spewed from his mouth. He was panicked, Vitaliy now saw. Trapped belowdecks, the man's instinct to escape had overwhelmed the logical part of his brain.

Vitaliy reached for the engine-room intercom. "Vanya, there's a man on the afterdeck—"

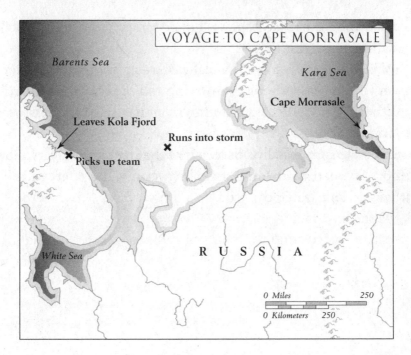

VOYAGE TO CAPE MORRASALE

Barents Sea

Kara Sea

Cape Morrasale

Leaves Kola Fjord

Runs into storm

X Picks up team

White Sea

R U S S I A

0 Miles   250

0 Kilometers   250

The boat's stern was tossed up in the air. As it dropped back down, a rogue wave struck the starboard quarter. The man, already airborne, was tossed sideways and slammed into the gunwale. He hung there for a moment, draped over the side like a rag doll, legs on deck, torso hanging in space, then tipped over and disappeared.

"Man overboard, man overboard!" Vitaliy shouted over the boatwide intercom. He peered through the windows, looking for a gap in the crests so he could come about.

"Don't," he heard a voice say behind him.

He turned to see Fred standing at the top of the ladder, both hands clenching the safety railing. The front of his shirt was vomit-stained.

"What?" Vitaliy asked.

"He's gone; forget him."

"Are you insane? We can't—"

"If you turn the boat around, we risk being capsized, yes?"

"Yes, but—"

"He knew the risks, Captain. I'm not going to let his mistake jeopardize the rest of us."

Vitaliy knew Fred was logically correct, but to abandon a man to the sea without even trying to recover him seemed inhuman. And to do it without the slightest trace of emotion on one's face . . .

As if sensing Vitaliy's indecision, the man known as Fred said, "My men are my responsibility; yours is the safety of the boat and its passengers, true?"

"True."

"Then we continue."

39

"Hello?" former President Jack Ryan said. He still liked to answer his own phone, at least this one.

"Mr. President?"

"Yeah, who's this?" Whoever it was, he had access to Jack's private line. There weren't many of those.

"John Clark. Just got back from the UK day before yesterday."

"John, how're you doing? So they did it, huh? Sent the Yankee packing."

"Afraid so. Anyway, Ding and I are home. Reason I called, well, maybe we both owe you a courtesy call. Is it okay?"

"Hell, yes. Come on over for lunch. Tell me when."

"Maybe an hour and a half?"

"Okay, lunch is fine. See you about eleven?"

"Yes, sir."

"The name's still Jack, remember?"

Clark chuckled. "I'll try to remember."

And the phone went dead. Ryan switched lines and beeped Andrea.

"Yes, Mr. President?"

"Two friends coming over about eleven. John Clark and Domingo Chavez. Remember 'em?"

"Yes, sir. Okay, I'll put them on the list," she replied in a studiously neutral voice. These two people, she remembered, were of the dangerous sort, though they seemed loyal enough. As a special agent of the United States Secret Service, she trusted nobody at all. "For lunch?"

"Probably."

It was a pleasant drive east on U.S. Route 50, then south before reaching Annapolis. Clark found that re-adapting to driving on the right side of the road after several years driving on the left was almost automatic. Evidently the programming of a lifetime easily overcame the adjustments he'd made in the UK, though he occasionally had to think about it. The green signs helped. The corresponding signs in England and Wales had been blue, and had been a convenient reminder that he'd been in a foreign land, albeit one with better beer.

"So what's the plan?" Chavez asked.

"We tell him we've signed on."

"And about Junior?"

"What you decide is up to you, Ding, but here's how I see it: What father and son tell one another is their business, not ours. Jack Junior is an adult. What he does with his life is his business, and who he includes in that loop is his business, too."

"Yeah, I hear you, but man, if he got hurt . . . Christ almighty, I wouldn't want to be around for that shit storm."

Neither would I, Clark thought.

"But then again, what could you have said?" Ding continued. "The man asks you to train him, you can't hardly say no."

"You got that right." The truth was, Clark felt bad about

not telling Ryan Senior—they went back a long way, after all, and he owed the former President a lot—but he'd built a big part of his life on keeping other people's secrets. This was personal, of course, but Jack was a big boy with a decent head on his shoulders. That didn't mean he wasn't going to try to convince Jack to tell his father about working at The Campus.

After forty minutes they turned right onto Peregrine Cliff Road, doubtless under TV surveillance from this point on, and Secret Service agents would be on their computers to check out his license plate numbers, then to determine that he was driving a rental car, and they couldn't access Hertz's computer quickly enough to identify the renter. That would get them slightly worried, though only in an institutional sense, something the USSS did well. Finally came the stone pillar that marked the entrance to Ryan's quarter-mile driveway.

"Please identify," said the remote-control voice in the pillar's speaker.

"Rainbow Six inbound to see SWORDSMAN."

"Proceed," the voice replied, followed by an electronic tone and the hydraulic sound of the gate controls being told to open.

"You didn't tell them about me," Chavez objected.

"Just keep your hands in the open." Clark chuckled.

Andrea Price-O'Day stood on the porch as they drove up. The detail chief herself, Clark noted. Maybe they thought he was important. Being a friend of the boss had its uses.

"Hello, Chief," she said in greeting.

She likes me? Clark thought. Only his friends called him Chief.

"Good morning, ma'am. How's the boss doing?"

"Working on his book, like always," Andrea answered. "Welcome home."

"Thanks." He took her offered hand. "You know Domingo, I believe."

"Oh, sure. How's the family?"

"Great. Glad to be home. Got another one on the way, too."

"Congratulations!"

"How's he doing?" Clark asked next. "Climbing the walls?"

"Go see for yourself." Andrea opened the front door.

They'd both been here before, the large open living room, the Potlatch decking that formed the ceiling, and the large expanse of windows revealing the Chesapeake Bay, plus Cathy's Steinway grand piano, which she probably played every other day. Andrea led them up the carpeted steps, right to Ryan's library/office, and left.

They found Ryan tapping on his keyboard with strokes heavy enough to kill one every two years or so. Ryan looked up as they entered.

"Heavy thoughts, Mr. President?" Clark asked with a smile.

"Hey, John! Howdy, Ding. Welcome!" Steps were taken and handshakes exchanged. "Sit down and take a load off," Jack commanded, and his orders were followed. Old friend or not, he was a former President of the United States, and they'd both worn uniforms in the not-so-distant past.

"Glad to see you're in one piece," Clark said.

"What, Georgetown?" Ryan shook his head. "Not even a close call. Andrea dropped him as pretty as you please. With a tip-off from Jack, that is."

"Come again?"

"He was there. He gave Andrea the nod. He spotted something about the janitor that didn't sit right."

"Such as?" asked Clark.

"He was using a screwdriver on a buffer; should have had a crescent."

"Sharp kid," Chavez observed. "Gotta make Dad proud."

"Bet yer ass," former President Ryan said, not hiding it. "Want some coffee?"

"That's one thing they don't do well in England, sir," Chavez said in agreement. "They got Starbucks, but that doesn't quite do it for me."

"I'll fix you up. Come on." He rose and walked down to the kitchen, where there was a pot full of Kona and mugs close by. "So how was life in Britain?"

"Good people. Our base was out near the Welsh border— nice people out there, good pubs, and the local food was pretty good. I especially like their bread," Clark reported. "But they think corned beef is something that comes out of a can."

Ryan laughed. "Yeah, dog food. I worked in London nearly three years, and I never found decent corned beef. They call it 'salt beef,' but it isn't quite the same. Rotated out of Rainbow, huh?"

"I guess we just wore out our welcome," Clark said.

"Who'd you leave behind?" President Ryan asked.

"Two go-teams, all trained up, about half SAS members from the British Army. They're pretty good," Clark assured him. "But the other European contingents are backing off. Too bad. Some of them were ace operators. The intel backup is also pretty well up to snuff. Rainbow will still work, if they let it. But the local—by which I mean mainly European— bureaucrats, they kinda wet their pants when my boys deploy."

"Yeah, well, we have them here, too," Ryan replied. "Kinda makes you wonder where Wyatt Earp went to."

That got a chuckle from his guests.

"What's SHORTSTOP doing now?" Clark asked. It was a natural question to ask among friends who'd been apart; failing to ask would have been noted.

"Trading business, like I did. I haven't even asked where. Having a President for a father can be disabling at his age, y'know?"

"Especially the chase cars on a date," Chavez suggested with a grin. "Not sure I would have liked that."

They spent ten minutes chatting and catching up on their

respective families, on sports, and on the general state of the world, then Ryan said, "What are you guys going to do? I imagine CIA has suggested you both retire. If you need a letter of reference, let me know. You've both served your country well."

"That's one of the things we wanted to talk to you about," Clark said. "We ran into Jimmy Hardesty at Langley, and he put us in touch with Tom Davis."

"Oh?" Ryan said, setting his cup down.

Clark nodded. "They offered us a job."

Former President Ryan considered this for a moment. "Well, it's not like I hadn't bounced that around in my head before. You two are suited for it, no doubt about that. What'd you think of the setup?"

"Good. Some growing pains going on, I think, but that's to be expected."

"Gerry Hendley's a good guy. I wouldn't have signed off on it otherwise. You know about the pardons?"

Chavez answered that one. "Yeah, thanks in advance. Pray we won't need one, but nice to know they're there."

Ryan nodded. "How's lunch grab you?"

And thus endeth the conversation, Clark noted. Brainchild of Ryan's or not, The Campus was something best kept at arm's length.

"Thought you'd never ask," Clark said, not missing a beat. "Can I hope for corned beef?"

"Place called Attman's up in Baltimore. One nice thing about the Secret Service: They don't let me do anything, and so they run a lot of errands."

"In the old days I bet they'd fly it down from the Carnegie in New York," Chavez speculated.

It was Ryan's turn to smile. "Occasionally. You have to be careful with that sort of stuff. You can get spoiled, and you can start believing you deserve it. Hell, I miss not being able to wander around shopping myself, but Andrea and her troops have a conniption fit when I try to do it." The Secret Service had insisted, for example, that his house have a sprinkler system. Ryan had submitted and footed the bill himself, though it could have been billed to the Department of the Treasury. He didn't want to start feeling like a king. With that decided, he led his guests into the kitchen, where the corned beef was already laid out, along with kaiser rolls and deli mustard.

"Thank God for an American lunch," Clark said aloud. "I love the Brits, and I like having a pint of John Smith's with it, but home is home."

In the car, Ryan said, "Now that you're free men, tell me: How's the new Langley?"

Clark answered, "You know me, Jack. How long have I been screaming about building up the DO?" he asked, meaning the CIA's Clandestine Service, the real spies, the field intelligence officers. "Plan Blue got off the ground just long enough to be shot down in flames by this jack-off Kealty."

"You speak Arabic, right?"

"Both of us," Chavez confirmed. "John's better than I am, but I can find the men's room when I need to. No Pashto, though."

"Mine's pretty rusty," Clark said. "Haven't been there in twenty years or so. Interesting people, the Afghans. They're tough but primitive. Thing is, the whole place is about the poppy."

"How big a problem?"

"There are some no-shit billionaires over there, all from opium. They live like kings, spread the money around in the form of guns and ammo, mostly, but all the hard drugs you can buy on the street in Southeast Washington come from Afghanistan. Nobody seems to recognize that. All of it, or damned near. It generates enough money to corrupt their culture, and ours. They don't need the help. Until the Russians came in '79, they were killing off each other. So they got their act together and gave Ivan a major bellyache, took maybe two weeks off after the Red Army bugged out, and then they started killing each other again. They don't know what peace is. They don't know what prosperity is. If you build schools for their kids, they blow the schools up. I lived there for over a year, climbing the hills and shooting at Ivan, trying to get them trained up. There's a lot to like about them, but don't turn your back on 'em. Toss in the terrain. Some places too high to fly a helicopter. Not your basic vacation spot. But their culture is the hard part. Stone-age people with modern weapons. They seem to have genetic knowledge of anything you can kill a guy with. They're not like anybody you've ever met. The only thing they won't do is eat your body after they kill you. They're Muslim enough for that. Anyway, as long as the poppy brings in money, that's the engine that drives the country, and ain't nothing gonna change it."

"Sounds grim," Ryan observed.

"*Grim* ain't the word. Hell, the Russians tried everything they knew—building schools, hospitals, and roads—just trying to make it an easy campaign, to buy them off, and look how far that got 'em. Those people fight for fun. You can buy their loyalty with food and stuff, and, yeah, try building hospitals and schools and roads. It ought to work, but don't bet the ranch on it. You have to figure a way to erase three thousand years of tribal warfare, blood feuds, and distrust of outsiders. Tough nut to crack. Hey, I served in Vietnam, and Vietnam is like fucking Disneyland compared to Afghanistan."

"And somewhere in the Magic Kingdom the Emir is playing hide-and-seek," Chavez observed.

"Or maybe not," Clark countered. "Everybody's assuming he's still there."

"You know something we don't?" Ryan asked with a smile.

"No, just trying to think like the guy. In SEALs, that was rule number one in evasion and escape training: Go where the bad guys ain't. Yeah, his options are limited, but they've got a decent infrastructure and plenty of cash."

"Maybe he's in Dubai," Ding offered, "in one of those luxury villas."

Former President Ryan laughed at that one. "Well, we're looking hard. Problem is, without a DI to ask the right questions, and a DO deep enough to go get them, you're just spinning your wheels. All the guys Kealty's put in are big-picture thinkers, and that just isn't gonna get the job done."

Two hours later, Clark and Chavez were heading back to Washington, digesting lunch and contemplating what they'd learned. Though Ryan hadn't given the subject more than a passing comment, it was clear to Clark that another run for the White House was weighing heavily on the former CINC.

"He's going to do it," Chavez observed.

"Yep," Clark agreed. "He feels trapped."

"He is trapped."

"So are we, Domingo. New job, same shit."

"Not exactly the same. Going to be interesting, that's for sure. Wonder how much—"

"Not too much, I'd think. Dead bodies are generally bad for business, and dead bodies don't tell you much. We're in the information business now."

"But sometimes the herd needs culling."

"True. At Langley, the problem's always been to get somebody to sign the order. Paper lasts forever, you know? In Vietnam, we had a real war, and orders could be verbal, but when that ended, the desk-sitters kept getting their panties in a wad, and then the lawyers raised their ugly heads, but that's not entirely a bad thing. We can't have government employees giving that sort of order whenever the mood strikes them. Sooner or later, person A is going to get carried away, and person B is going to have a conscience attack and rat you out for it, no matter how much the bad guy needed to meet God. It's amazing how dangerous a conscience can be—and usually at the wrong time. We live in an imperfect world, Ding, and there ain't no rule that says it has to make sense."

"A blank presidential pardon," Chavez observed, changing directions. "And it's legal?"

"Well, that's what the man said. I remember when *Dr. No* came out. I was in high school. The promo for the film said, 'The double-oh means he has a license to kill who he wants, when he wants.' That was cool back in the '60s. Before Watergate and all that, the Kennedy administration liked the idea, too. So they initiated Operation Mongoose. It was a total fuckup, of course, but it's never been revealed how big a fuckup it was. Politics," Clark explained. "I guess you've never heard the stories."

"Not on the syllabus down at The Farm."

"Just as well. Who'd want to work for an agency that did dumb shit like that? Taking down a foreign chief of state is really bad juju, son. Even if one of our Presidents thought it was cool to be a sociopath. Funny how people don't like to think things all the way through."

"Like us?"

"Not when you take out people who don't matter all that much."

"What's that shit about the Ranger?"

"Sam Driscoll," Clark replied. Ryan had told them about Kealty's push for the CID investigation. "Humped a few hills with Driscoll in the '90s. Good man."

"Anything being done to stop it?"

"Don't know, but Jack told us about it for a reason."

"New recruit for The Campus?"

"It sure would soften Driscoll's fall, wouldn't it?"

"Yeah, but still, to watch your career get flushed because some dickhead wants to make a point—it just ain't right, *mano.*"

"In so many ways," Clark agreed.

They drove in silence for a few minutes, then Chavez said, "He looks worried. Tired."

"Who, Jack? I would be, too. Poor bastard. He just wants to write his memoirs and maybe work on his golf game, play daddy to the kids. You know, he really is a good guy."

"That's his problem," Chavez pointed out.

"Sure as hell." It was nice to know that his son-in-law hadn't wasted his time at George Mason University. "A sense of duty can take you into some tight places. Then you have to figure your own way out."

Back at Peregrine Cliff, Ryan found his mind drifting, fingers poised over the keyboard. *Fucking Kealty* . . . Prosecuting a soldier for killing the enemy. It was, he thought sadly, a perfect testament to the character of the current President.

He glanced at the multiline phone. He started reaching for it twice, only to have his hand stop, seemingly of its own accord, in contradiction to Saint Augustine's dictum on will and resistance. But then he picked it up and punched the buttons.

"Yeah, Jack," van Damm's voice answered. He had caller ID on his private line.

"Okay, Arnie, pull the trigger. And God help me," he added.

"Let me make some phone calls. Talk to you tomorrow."

"Okay. See ya." And Ryan hung up.

What the hell are you doing? he asked himself.

But he knew the answer all too well.

40

They had to practice not being conspiratorial, to seem like ordinary people having an ordinary lunch in a Parisian café on a drizzly day, which worked in their favor. Aside from themselves, there were only two patrons, a young couple, at a nearby umbrella-covered table.

Ibrahim had told them how to dress—like middle-class Frenchmen—and to do it all the time from now on. They all spoke French, and while all were Muslims, none of them attended mosque on a regular basis, doing their daily prayers at home, and definitely not attending the sermons of the more radical and assertive imams, all of whom were kept under regular observation by the various French police agencies.

In sticking to public places and chattering like normal people, they avoided conspiratorial meetings in small rooms that could be bugged by clever policemen. Open-air meetings were easy to observe but nearly impossible to record. And nearly every man in France had regular lunch mates. However large and well funded the French police were, they could not investigate everybody in this infidel country. With regular visibility came anonymity. Quite a few others had been caught or even killed by taking the other route. Especially in Israel, where the police agencies were notoriously efficient, largely because of the money they so liberally spread on the street. There were always those willing to take money for information, which was why he had to choose his people so carefully.

And so the meeting did not begin with religious incantations. They all knew them anyway. And they spoke exclusively in French, lest someone take note of a foreign language. Too many Westerners were learning what Arabic sounded like—

and to them it always sounded conspiratorial. Their mission was to be invisible in plain sight. Fortunately, it wasn't all that hard.

"So what is this mission?" Shasif Hadi asked.

"It's an industrial facility," Ibrahim answered. "For now that's all you need to know. Once we're on the ground, you'll be fully briefed."

"How many?" Ahmed asked. He was the youngest member of the team, clean-shaven with a well-groomed mustache.

"The goal isn't casualties—at least not human casualties."

"Then what?" This was Fa'ad. He was a Kuwaiti, tall and handsome.

"Again, you'll know more when it becomes necessary." He drew a piece of paper from his pocket and unfolded it on the table before them. It was a computer-printed map, altered with some image-editing software so all the place names were missing.

"The problem will be selecting the best point of entry," Ibrahim said. "The facility is fairly well guarded, both within and along the perimeter. The explosive charges necessary will be trivial, small enough to carry in one backpack. The guards inspect the area twice daily, so timing will be critical."

"If you'll get me the explosive specifications, I can start planning," Fa'ad said, pleased to have his education being used in Allah's Holy Cause. The others thought him overly proud of his engineering degree from Cairo University.

Ibrahim nodded.

"What about the police and intelligence services there?" Hadi asked.

Ibrahim waved his hand dismissively. "Manageable."

His casual tone belied his thoughts. He had a genuine fear of police investigators. They were like evil djinns in the way they could inspect a piece of evidence and turn all manner of magical information from it. You could never tell what they knew and how they could tie it all together. And his primary job was not to exist. No one was to know his name or his face. He traveled as anonymously as a desert breeze. The URC could stay alive only if it remained hidden. For his part, Ibrahim traveled on numerous unknown credit cards—cash, unfortunately, was no longer anonymous at all; the police feared those who used cash, and searched them out rigorously. He had enough passports in his home to satisfy a nation-state's foreign ministry, each of them expensively procured and used only a few times before being burned to ashes. And he wondered if even this was precaution enough. It took only one person to betray him.

And the only people who could betray him were those whom he trusted absolutely. Thoughts like that turned over and over in his mind. He took a sip of coffee. He even worried about talking in his sleep on an aircraft during an overwater flight. That's all it might take. It wasn't death he feared—none of them feared that—but rather failure.

But were not the Holy Warriors of Allah those who did the hardest things, and would not his blessings be in proportion to his merit? To be remembered. To be respected by his compatriots. To strike a blow for the cause—even if he managed to do that without recognition, he would go to Allah with peace in his heart.

"We have final authorization?" Ahmed asked.

"Not yet. Soon, I expect, but not yet. When we separate here, we won't see each other again until we're in country."

"How will we know?"

"I have an uncle in Riyadh. He's planning on buying a new car. If my e-mail says it is a red car, we wait; if a green car, we move to the next stage. If so, five days after the e-mail we will meet in Caracas, as planned, then drive the rest of the way."

Shasif Hadi smiled and shrugged. "Then let us all pray for green car."

*

The office already had their name tags on the doors, Clark noticed. Both he and Chavez had medium-sized adjoining offices, with desks, swivel chairs, two visitor chairs each, and personal computers, complete with manuals on how to use them and how to access all manner of files.

For his part, Clark was quick to figure out his computer system. Inside of twenty minutes, rather to his amazement, he was surfing through the basement-bedrock-floor level of CIA's Langley headquarters.

Ten minutes later: "Holy shit," he breathed.

"Yeah," Chavez said from the door. "What do you think?"

"This is a director-level compartment I just surfed into. Jesus, this lets me into damned near everything."

Davis was back. "You're both fast. The computer system gives you access to a lot of stuff. Not quite everything, just the major compartments. It's all we need. Same thing with Fort Meade. We have a road into nearly all of their SigInt stuff. You have a lot of reading to catch up on. Keyword EMIR will let you into twenty-three compartments—all we have on that bird, including a damned good profile; at least we think so. It's labeled AESOP."

"Yeah, I see it here," Clark replied.

"A guy named Pizniak, professor of psychiatry at Yale medical school. Read it over and see what you think. Anyway, if you need me, you know where my shop is. Don't be afraid to come up and ask questions. The only dumb question is the one you don't ask. Oh, by the way, Gerry's personal secretary is Helen Connolly. She's been with him for a long time. She is not— repeat not—cleared into what we do here. Gerry does his own drafting of reports and stuff, but mostly we do it verbally at his level of decision-making. By the way, John, he told me about your restructuring idea. Glad you said it; saved me from bringing it up."

Clark chuckled. "Always happy to be the bad guy."

Davis left, and they got back to work. Clark went first to the photos they had of the Emir, which weren't many and were of poor quality. The eyes, he saw, were cold. Almost lifeless, like a shark's eyes. No expression in them at all. *Isn't that interesting?* Clark thought. Many said the Saudis were a humorless people—*like Germans but without the sense of humor* was the phrase a lot of people used—but that hadn't been his experience there.

Clark had never met a bad Saudi. There were a few he knew well from his life in the CIA, people from whom he'd learned the language. They'd all been religious, part of the conservative Wahhabi branch of Sunni Islam. Not unlike Southern Baptists in the thoroughness of their devotion. That was fine with him. He'd been to a mosque once and watched the exercise of the religion, careful to stay inconspicuously in the back—it had been a language lesson, for the most part, but the sincerity of their religious beliefs was evident. He'd talked religion with his Saudi friends and found nothing the least bit objectionable in it. Saudis were hard to make as close friends, but a true Saudi friend would step in front of the bullet for you. Their religion's rules on such things as hospitality were admirable indeed. And Islam prohibited racism, something Christianity had unfortunately left out.

Whether the Emir was a devout Muslim or not Clark didn't know, but the man was no fool, that much AESOP made clear. He was patient by nature but also capable of being decisive in his decision-making. *A rare combination,* Clark thought, though he'd been that way himself on occasion. Patience was a hard virtue to acquire, all the more so for a true believer in whatever cause he might have chosen as his life mission.

His computer manual had a directory of the Agency's in-house computer library, and he also had references from the keyword EMIR access point. So Clark started surfing. How much did Langley have on this mutt? What field officers had worked with him? What anecdotes did they write down? Did anyone have the key to this guy's character?

Clark shook himself out of his reverie and checked his watch. An hour had gone by. "Time flies," he muttered, and reached for the phone. When the other end picked up, Clark said, "Gerry, John. Got a minute? Tom, too, if he's handy."

He was in Hendley's office two minutes later. Tom Davis, The Campus's recruiter, walked in a minute later. "What's up?"

"Got a candidate, maybe," Clark said, then, before either of them could ask the obvious question, continued: "This came from Jack Ryan—Senior, that is."

This got the attention of Hendley, who leaned forward in his chair, hands clasped on his desk blotter. "Go on."

"Don't ask me how, because I don't know all the details, but there's a Ranger, an old hand named Driscoll, who's landed in some hot water. Rumor is, Kealty is looking to make an example of him."

"Over what?"

"A mission in the Hindu Kush. Killed a handful of bad guys in a cave while they were sleeping. Kealty and his AG want to hang murder on Driscoll."

"Good Christ," Tom Davis muttered.

"You know this guy?" Hendley asked.

Clark nodded. "About ten years ago, just before Rainbow started, I had a little job in Somalia. Had a team of Rangers working overwatch for me. Driscoll was one of them. We've stayed in touch, had a beer now and again. Solid guy."

"How far's this thing with the AG gone?"

"The Army CID has it. Preliminary investigation."

Hendley sighed and scratched his head. "What's Jack say?"

"He told me for a reason. He knows I'm on board here."

Hendley nodded. "First things first: If this is coming from the White House, Driscoll's not getting out of this unscathed."

"I'm sure he knows that."

"Best case, he's separated. Maybe keep his pension."

"He knows that, too, I'm sure."

"Where is he?"

"Brooke Army Medical down in San Antonio. He got a little souvenir in the shoulder during the exfil."

"Serious?"

"Don't know."

"Okay, go have a chat with him. Feel him out." Then to Davis: "Tom, in the meantime, get a jacket started on Driscoll. Full background and all that."

"Right."

"Come on in," Ben Margolin told Mary Pat. "Shut the door."

Another day at NCTC. More intercept traffic, more leads that could be something big or nothing at all. The volume was overwhelming, and while this was nothing new to any of them, most were worried they were missing much more than they were catching. Better technology would help, but who knew how long it would take to get the new systems up and running. The Trailblazer fiasco had made the powers-that-be gun-shy of another failure, so they were beta testing the hell out of the thing. In the meantime, Mary Pat thought, she and the rest of the NCTC scrambled, trying to keep the dike plugged while looking for new cracks.

Mary Pat closed the door as instructed and took a seat across from Margolin's desk. Outside, the operations center hummed with activity.

"They shit-canned our outreach idea," Margolin said without preamble. "We won't be using any of the Brits' assets in Pakistan."

"For God's sake, why?"

"Above my pay grade, Mary Pat. I took it as far as I could, but no go. My best guess: Iraq."

The same thought had occurred to Mary Pat just before

her boss said the word. Up against pressure from its citizens, the UK had been steadily distancing itself, both in policy and in combat resource allocation, from the Iraq War. Rumor was, despite his conciliatory tone in public, President Kealty was furious with the Brits, who had, he felt, left his administration holding the bag. Without the UK's even nominal support, any plan to withdraw U.S. troops would be slowed, if not jeopardized. Worse still, Britain's arms-reach attitude had in turn emboldened the Iraqi government, whose calls for a U.S. departure had gone from polite but firm to strident and belligerent, a trend American citizens could not help but notice. First our closest ally, then the very people we'd shed blood to rescue. Having run his campaign on the promise to disentangle the United States from Iraq, Kealty was slipping in the polls, and some of the TV pundits had gone as far as accusing Kealty of stifling the withdrawal to put pressure on Congress, which had itself been wishy-washy on some of their new President's pet projects.

The fact that their request to enlist the Brits in following the Peshawar-map angle was denied shouldn't have surprised Mary Pat, a veteran of more intragovernment political squabbles than she could remember, but it did nonetheless. This damned cave was the best lead they'd had on the Emir in years. To see it slip through their fingers over what amounted to a presidential tantrum was infuriating. Of course, it didn't help that their DCI, Scott Kilborn, was himself a weasel.

Mary Pat shook her head and sighed. "Too bad Driscoll lost his prisoners."

"A little water inhalation tends to loosen the lips," Margolin said.

A popular view, Mary Pat thought, *but of little use in the real world.* She was neither squeamish nor such a Pollyanna that she thought torture did not have its merit, but generally those techniques fell far short on producing reliable and verifiable information. More often than not, it was a waste of time. During and shortly after World War Two, MI6 and the OSS got more information from captured German generals with a game of Ping-Pong or checkers than they did with a pair of pliers or electrodes.

The "ticking bomb" scenario so casually batted about was a near myth. Most plots against the United States since 9/11 had been broken in their infancy, as the bad guys were recruiting, or moving money, or putting logistics into place. The image of a terrorist with his finger hovering over a button somewhere while the good guys tried to squeeze info from his compatriot was beyond rare, a Hollywood concoction, and bore about as much similarity to real-world intelligence work as James Bond did. In fact, there'd been only one instance of the "ticking bomb" during her entire career, and John Clark had settled that in a matter of minutes by breaking a few fingers and asking the right questions.

"Clichés are clichés for a reason," Ed had told her once. "It's because they're usually so true, people overuse them." As far as Mary Pat was concerned, when it came to interrogation, the cliché "You catch more flies with honey than you do with vinegar" was dead right. Morality was only one facet in the pros-and-cons argument. What really mattered was effectiveness. You do what gets you the best results. Period.

"So," she said to her boss, "back to square one?"

"No fucking way. That old friend across the pond you mentioned . . . Give him a call, have an informal chat."

Mary Pat smiled but shook her head. "This is what they call a job killer, Ben."

He shrugged. "You only live once."

Melinda was pleasantly surprised to see him again. He'd taken her out for a drive to see "John" a week before. He had paid nicely and done nothing overtly kinky, and all that was fine with her, especially the money part.

This guy—well, he was properly turned out, or what passed for it here. It was unusual for her to appear in public this way. She was a call girl, not a streetwalker, but this hotel had a particularly fine dining room, and the maître d' knew and liked her. A freebie took a girl a long way in her business, and truth be told, he was a decent chap, married, like so many of her clients, and therefore dependably nice. Well, almost dependably. You could never be sure, but men in his position, the ones who lived around here, generally knew what the rules were. And if that failed, she still had Little Mr. Colt in her purse.

Eye contact. A knowing smile. He was cute, this procurer. A very short beard, like something Errol Flynn might have worn in a pirate movie. But she wasn't Olivia de Havilland. She was prettier, Melinda thought, not the least bit self-consciously. She worked hard to stay slim. Men liked women whose waists they could encompass with their hands. Especially the ones with nice tits overtop of them.

"Hello," she said pleasantly. A smile that was merely friendly on its face, but the recipient knew that there was much more that came behind the smile.

"Good evening, Melinda. How are you this warm evening?"

"Just fine, thank you." A little teeth with the smile.

"Are you busy this evening?"

"No, not at the moment." More teeth. "I never did get your name."

"Ernest," he replied with a gentle smile. The man had a certain charm, but of the foreign sort, Melinda thought. Not European. Somewhere else. His English was okay, some accent . . . He'd learned English in a different place. That was it. Learned it well, and . . . and what? What was different about him? she wondered. She started cataloging him more fully.

Slim, taller than she, lovely dark eyes, rather soulful. Soft hands. Not a construction worker. More a money type, this Ernest, which was surely not the name he'd been born with. His eyes were evaluating her. She was used to that. The *How good is she in the sack?* look. Well, he had reason to know she was pretty good. His boss had not complained, had even overpaid her. She was used to that. Yeah, she was *that* good. Melinda had lots of repeat customers, some of whom were known to her by their real names—or what they said were their real names. She had her own names for her regulars, frequently related to their dick size. *Or color, in this case,* she thought with a suppressed chuckle and a not-suppressed smile that Ernest might take for himself. That was something she did almost on instinct. In any case, she was already counting the money.

"Would you like to come with me?" he asked, almost shyly. Men knew by instinct—the smart ones anyway—that shyness is a major turn-on for all women.

"I'd like that." And being demure worked just as well in the other direction. "To see your friend?"

"Perhaps." His first mistake. Ernest would not be displeased to sample these goods himself. Filthy whore though she might be, she was a good lover, with much practice in her trade, and his drives were the same as those of most men. "Would you please come with me?"

"Surely."

It was only a short drive, rather to Melinda's surprise. A place right in town, an upscale condo with its own underground parking garage. "Ernest" got out of the car and gallantly opened the door for her. They walked to the elevator bank, and Ernest hit the button. She didn't know the building, but the outside was distinctive enough to remember the image of it. So John had a place in town? More convenient for her, and for him? she wondered. Or maybe he remembered her fondly. That happened quite a lot in her experience.

"John" was standing at the entrance to the kitchen, holding a nice glass of white wine.

"Well, hello, John, what a pleasant surprise," she said in greeting, with her best smile. It was a particularly good smile, sure to warm the cockles of a man's heart, and the other cockles, too, or course. Then she walked over, kissing him sweetly before taking the offered glass. Then a tiny sip. "John, you have the best taste in wine. Italian?"

"Pinot grigio," he confirmed.

"They do the best food, too."

"Is your ancestry Italian?" John asked.

"Hungarian," she admitted. "We do good pastry, but the Italians do the best veal in the world." Another hello kiss. John was a little odd but a really good kisser. "How have you been?"

"Travel is such a problem for me," he admitted, falsely at the moment.

"Where did you have to go?" Melinda asked.

"Paris."

"Do you like the wine there?"

"Italian is better," he replied, a little bored with the conversation. She wasn't here for her talking ability. All women had that, but Melinda's talents went to other areas. "You are nicely dressed," he observed.

It comes off quickly enough, she didn't say. She selected her business clothing with that in mind. Some men like their women nude, but a surprising number liked the partially clothed quickie: skirt hiked up, bent over a table or couch, bra on but tits out. . . . John liked on-the-knees oral, too, something she didn't mind as long as he didn't get carried away. "Just something I threw together. So this is a nice apartment."

"It is convenient. I like the view."

Melinda took the opportunity to look out the plate-glass window. *Okay, good.* Now she knew exactly where she was.

There were a lot of people on the street, insofar as they had streets here, ways to walk from one lavish hotel to another, for those too cheap to get a taxi. Not much in the way of sidewalks, though. You didn't make money from the sidewalks. John just stayed back and looked at her.

"Melinda, you are a vision," he said with a smile. It was a smile she was used to—the "wannafuckyou" smile. Polite on the surface, yearning underneath. A brief glance below John's belt line confirmed her guess.

It was time to walk toward him for another kiss. Could have been worse.

"Mmm," she murmured. *Okay, time for business, John.* His arms went around her. Rather strong arms, maybe to let her know that she was his property. Men were that way. Then, gently, he led her to the bedroom.

Wow, she thought. Whoever had decorated this room had been one who knew what the condo was for. Probably not his/her first such commission, Melinda was sure, down to the cute little chair for her to disrobe on, by the window. At sunset it would have been fucking perfect, she thought. She sat down and first of all removed her Manolo Blahnik shoes. Pretty though they were, taking them off was more pleasant than putting them on. They were made for looking, not for walking, and she had cute, girly feet. Men always liked them. The wraparound top came off and was laid on the dressing table, and she stood. She never wore a bra while at work, which was fine with her. No sagging yet on her B+ (almost C) chest. Men always liked that. A moment later she was nude, and she walked to see John more closely.

"May I help?" she asked. Men *always* liked to have her undress them, especially if you threw in a little "do me" urgency.

"Yes, please," John replied, with a dreamy smile. Wherever he came from, he wasn't used to this sort of worship. Well, he paid top dollar to get it, which was one of the things she was good at. In a minute she saw the reason she remembered him. Red, a perfect moniker for him. Of course, she delivered a kiss.

And, of course, he reacted favorably to it. At what he paid, she wanted him to become a regular. She was thinking about a new car. A BMW, or maybe all the way to a Mercedes. He could help her with that. As with business, she liked to pay cash for things. Well, a certified check for the right car. An E-Class Benz, she was thinking. She liked the solidity of the German car. You felt safe in one of those. She liked feeling safe. She stood.

"John, is this all night? That costs more, two and a half."

"So much?" he asked, with a smile.

"There's an old saying: You get what you pay for."

"Not tonight. I must be off later."

You don't overnight here? she wondered. *Is this just your fuck pad?* He must have a ton of money to throw around. This place must have set him back a million, maybe a million and a half. If he were a man who enjoyed sex that much, then she sure as hell wanted him to be a regular customer. Men never appreciated how women like her evaluated men, and in what depth. Men were such fools, Melinda thought, even the rich ones. *Especially the rich ones.* She watched him reach for an envelope. This he handed over.

As always, Melinda opened the envelope and counted the bills. It was important that men knew that this was a business transaction, even one delivered with the best simulated love that money could buy. Quite a few men had leaned toward wanting their relationship to be more than that. She had a supremely charming way of steering the conversation in other directions.

The envelope went into the Gucci purse, next to Little Mr. Colt with his mother-of-pearl handle. When she arose, it was with the best of smiles. The business part was over. Now love could begin.

41

Was it a mistake? the Emir wondered. Things were rarely entirely clear at his level of operational responsibility. The target country was inconsequential, actually, but the target itself of great significance—or potential significance. The effects of the attack would spread like ripples in a pond, lapping soon enough at the shores of their true target.

Of all his worries about the current operation, his commander on the ground did not count among them. Ibrahim was ambitious but also careful and thorough, and he'd kept his team small and well organized in every detail. Then again, the real test would come when the plan went operational, which was the decision that he presently faced. Timing was everything, along with the ability to focus on the "big picture," as the Americans called it. There were a number of pieces moving about the board, and each had to move in the right direction and at the right pace, lest any one of them get caught alone and without support. If that happened, the rest would fall in turn, and Lotus would collapse. And he would likely die before seeing Lotus come to fruition. If he moved too fast, his life could end before it bloomed; too slow, the same result.

So he'd let Ibrahim continue with his on-scene reconnaissance, but he'd withhold final approval on the operation until he knew the disposition of the other pieces.

And if Ibrahim succeeds? he asked himself. *And what then?* Would this Kealty react as they expected? Their profile of him—code-named CASCADE—seemed certain of it, but the Emir had long ago learned to be wary of the vagaries of the human mind.

CASCADE . . . an apt title. He found both it and the concept behind it amusing. Certainly the Western intelligence agencies had psychological profiles of him—he'd read one, in fact—so he found it entertaining to be largely basing their most ambitious operation on a profile of their own.

Kealty was the consummate politician, which in American politics was taken as synonymous for leader. How and when this ignorance had started he didn't know. Nor did he care. The American people had chosen for themselves the politician who had most ably portrayed himself as a leader, never asking whether the image matched the character behind it. CASCADE said it did not, and the Emir agreed. Worse still—or better still, depending on your perspective—Kealty had surrounded himself with sycophants and favor-holders who did nothing to improve his credentials.

So what happens when a weak man of flawed character is faced with a cascade of catastrophes? He crumbles, of course—and with him, the country.

As promised, their charter boat was waiting for them. The captain, a local fisherman named Pyotor Salychev, sat in a lawn chair at the end of the deserted plank pier, smoking his pipe. Bobbing in the black, cold water was a twelve-meter wide-beamed British Halmatic trawler. Salychev grunted as he rose to his feet.

"You're late," he said, then stepped off the pier onto the afterdeck.

"Bad weather," Adnan replied. "You're ready?"

"Wouldn't be here if I wasn't."

During their first negotiations, Salychev had asked few questions about who they were or why they wanted to go to

344

the island, but Adnan, playing the role of an ecological zealot, had dropped several hints during their conversation. Watchdog groups had long been coming here to document the ravages of the Cold War, Salychev had replied with a shrug. As long as they paid and as long as they didn't hazard him or his boat, Salychev was happy to take anyone to that godforsaken place. "No accounting for stupidity," he'd told Adnan.

"It's smaller than I'd imagined," Adnan said, nodding at the boat.

"You were expecting a battleship? She's tough enough. One of the only good things the British ever built, the Halmatic. I've had her lying on her beam and she still snaps to. You worry about yourself. Come on, then, we push off in ten minutes."

The rest of Adnan's men finished unloading their gear from the truck, then hurried down the pier and started loading it onto the afterdeck as Salychev barked orders about where and how to place everything. Once satisfied all was in order, Salychev cast off the lines, propped a foot on the pier, and pushed the Halmatic off. Seconds later he was in the wheelhouse, turning over the engine. With a belch of black smoke from the manifolds, the diesel engine roared to life and water frothed at the stern.

"Next stop," Salychev called over his shoulder, "hell."

Two hours later the island's southern headlands appeared through the fog off the starboard bow. Adnan stood amidships, watching the coastline through a pair of binoculars. Salychev had assured him military patrols would be no trouble, and Adnan could see none.

"They're out there," he called from the pilothouse, "but they're not so bright. You could set your watch by 'em. Same patrol routes, every day at the same time."

"What about radar?"

"Where?"

"On the island. I heard there was an air base. . . ."

Salychev chuckled. "What, you're talking about Rogachevo? Not really, not anymore. Not enough money. Used to have an interceptor regiment there, the 641st, I think, but nowadays it's just a few cargo planes and helicopters.

"As for the boat patrols, they got dinky navigation sets, and like I said, they're predictable anyway. Once we're inshore, we're safe. As you might imagine, they try to keep their distance."

Adnan could understand why. While his men knew little about the nature of their mission or their destination, Adnan had been fully briefed.

Novaya Zemlya was indeed a hell on earth. According to the last census, the island was home to 2,500 people, mostly Nenetses and Avars living in Belushya Guba settlement. The island itself was in reality two islands—Severny in the north, and Yuzhny in the south—each separated from the other by the Matochkin Strait.

It was a shame, really, Adnan thought, that all the world knew of Novaya Zemlya was its Cold War history. The Russians and Europeans had known about it since the eleventh century, first through Novgorod traders, then through a steady string of explorers—Willoughby, Barents, Liitke, Hudson. . . . They'd all visited here hundreds of years before it was annexed by the Soviets in 1954, renamed the Novaya Zemlya Test Site, and divided into zones: A, Chyornaya Guba; B, Matochkin Shar; and C, Sukhoy Nos, where the fifty-megaton Tsar Bomba was detonated in 1961.

During its lifespan, Novaya Zemlya had been home to nearly three hundred nuclear detonations, the last one in 1990. Since then it had become many things to many people—a curiosity, a tragedy, a grim reminder. . . . But for the cash-poor Russian government after the dissolution, the island had become a dumping ground, a place to abandon their abominations.

What was that American phrase? Adnan wondered. Ah, yes ... One man's trash is another man's treasure.

They were interested in the new line, Cassiano saw. Where it crossed roads, how far off the ground it was, how many support pylons per mile ... An interesting request, and of course he would do his best to acquire the information.

They were also interested in trains, which puzzled him. It was true that trains came and went on a daily basis, but their entry into the facility was strictly limited and monitored. If they were looking to gain access to the facility, there were easier ways. Perhaps that was the answer. They weren't interested in the trains as a means of infiltration but rather as a measurement tool. The facility's output was a closely kept secret, but if the trains coming and going were monitored and their specifications known, one could make a good guess as to the output levels.

Very smart, he thought. And it did fit with what he knew about his employers. Competition was a healthy thing, he'd been told, and nothing could be done about a newly discovered oil field. What could be controlled, however, were prices and output capacity, which is what he suspected his employer planned to do. The OPEC nations (Islamic nations) had been the world's largest supplier of oil for decades upon decades, and if Cassiano could help maintain that supremacy, he would happily do so.

42

In retrospect, Jenkins realized he should have seen it coming, this "promotion" that was in fact nothing more than a grade-A pain in the ass. The facility got regular visits from a plethora of government agencies and officials, from the Environmental Protection Agency and Homeland Security to the U.S. Geological Survey and the Army Corps of Engineers, all of which had thus far been handled by a Department of Energy spokesperson. The recently reheated battle in Washington over the future of the facility had changed all that, and it seemed every pol or bureaucrat who could find his or her way here was showing up, armed with probing questions generated by underpaid staffers and a deep desire to understand every nuance of the facility.

"What they want, Steve," his boss had told him, "is a peek behind the curtain, and you're just unpolished enough to make 'em think they're getting it."

Backhanded compliment notwithstanding, Steve had to admit he knew the facility inside and out, backward and forward, having started here just three years out of college, which was, in the lifespan of the project, nineteen years after the site had been initially identified as a possible candidate, along with ten others in six states; twelve years after it was nominated for intensive "site-characterization" studies; and ten years after it was crowned the winner of the beauty contest. He'd worked at this not-so-little patch of desert for most of his adult life, and at a current cost of $11 billion, it was one of the most extensively studied chunks of land in the world. And depending on who won the battle in Washington, that $11 billion might be written off as a loss. How did one do that? he wondered. In what column on the federal balance sheet did such a sum fall?

The project's completion had become a point of pride for the nine hundred or so members of the team, and while opinion varied from employee to employee whether they would want to live next to it, their collective investment in its success was enormous. Though only thirty-seven, Steve was considered one of the site's old hands, along with a hundred or so others who'd been here since the project had gone from a notion on a piece of paper to a shovel-in-the-dirt concern. Unfortunately, he could tell no one much about what he did, a restriction he hadn't minded until he'd met Allison. She was keenly and genuinely interested in his work, about how he spent his days, a trait neither of his previous two girlfriends had displayed. God, he was a lucky man. To find a woman like her, and to have her attracted to *him* . . . And the sex. God almighty. Admittedly, his experience was somewhat limited, but the things she did to him, with her hands, with her mouth . . . Every time they were together, he felt like he was living a *Penthouse* Forum letter.

His musings were interrupted by a telltale plume of dust appearing over the hill opposite the main tunnel entrance, indicating vehicles approaching. Sixty seconds later, two black Chevy Suburbans appeared on the north road and pulled into the parking lot. Afternoon work had been halted, and all the trucks and equipment pallets moved to the perimeter of the lot. The Suburbans slowed to a stop about fifty feet away and sat idling. None of the doors opened, and Steve imagined the occupants dreading the idea of leaving the air-conditioned interiors. And it wasn't even hot, he thought, not summer-hot, at least. Funny how delegation visits like this one tended to taper off in June, July, and August.

Now the doors opened, and out climbed the ten staffers who had been dispatched by their respective governors. Two for each of the five bordering states. Having already rolled up their shirtsleeves and loosened their ties, the group stood for a moment, blinking and looking around, before seeing Steve waving his arm at them. En masse, they walked over to him and gathered in a semicircle.

"Afternoon, and welcome," he said. "My name is Steve Jenkins, and I'm one of the senior on-site engineers here. I'll do my best to learn your names before we're through, but for now I'll leave it to you to sort out your visitor badges."

He held out a shoebox, and one by one each delegate came forward and found his or her badge.

"Just a couple quick reminders, and then we'll get out of the heat. I'll be passing out information sheets that will cover everything we're going to talk about this afternoon, and everything I'm allowed to say."

This got a few chuckles. Steve relaxed a bit. Might not be so bad after all.

"That said, I'll ask you not to take notes, either on paper or on a PDA. Same with voice recorders and cameras."

"Why is that?" one of the delegates, a blond California-type woman, asked. "There are plenty of pictures on the Internet."

"True, but only the ones we want there," Steve replied. "Believe me, if I can answer a question, I'll do it. Our goal is to give you as much information as we can. One last thing before we step inside: This contraption next to me that looks like part rocket booster, part mobile home, and part oil pipeline is our TBM, or tunnel boring machine, known affectionately as the Yucca Mucker. For those of you that love facts and figures, the Mucker is four hundred sixty feet long, twenty-five feet wide, weighs seven hundred tons, and can cut through solid rock at up to eighteen feet an hour. To put that into perspective, that's about the length of one of the Suburbans you arrived in."

There were appreciative murmurs and chuckles from the delegation.

"Okay, if you'll follow me to the tunnel entrance, we'll get started."

"We're now standing in what we call the Exploratory Studies Facility," Jenkins said. "It is shaped like a horseshoe, about five miles long and twenty-five feet wide. In several places in the ESF we constructed eight alcoves about the size of pole barns, in which we store equipment and conduct experiments, and six weeks ago we completed the first experimental emplacement drift."

"Which is what?" one of the delegates asked.

"It's essentially where deposits will be stored when and if the site goes active. You'll see the entrance to the drift in a few minutes."

"We're not going inside?"

"No, I'm afraid not. We're still conducting tests to ensure its stability." This was a vast understatement, of course. The digging of the emplacement drift had taken a relatively short time. Testing and experimentation would take another nine months to a year. "Let's talk a little geography," Steve continued.

"The ridge above us was formed about thirteen million years ago by a now-extinct caldera volcano, and is comprised of alternating layers of rock called welded tuff—also known as 'ignimbrite'—nonwelded tuff and semiwelded tuff."

A hand went up. "Did I hear you right? You said 'volcano.'"

"I did. But it's long extinct."

"You've had earthquakes, though, right?"

"Yes, two of them. One measuring five on the Richter and one measuring 4.4. The first caused some minor damage to the surface buildings, but not so much as a crack down here. I was here—in here—for both of them. Barely felt a thing."

There were, in fact, thirty-nine earthquake faults and seven baby volcanoes in various stages of activity in the desert surrounding the facility. This was in the information sheet he'd handed out, but if no one brought it up, he certainly wasn't going to. When people heard the words *volcano* and *fault,* their brains tended to switch into caveman mode.

"The truth is," Steve continued, "this particular chunk of geology has been under close study for almost twenty-five years, and there's a mountain of evidence that the three kinds of stuff here is aptly suited for the storage of nuclear waste."

"How much waste, exactly?"

"Well, that's one of those questions I'm not allowed to answer."

"On whose orders?"

"Take your pick. Homeland Security, the FBI, the DOE . . . Suffice it to say, this facility will be the country's primary storage site for spent nuclear fuel."

The best estimate put the facility's eventual maximum capacity at around 135,000 metric tons, or 300 million pounds, some of which would degrade to "safe" levels in decades, and some of which could potentially remain lethal for millions of years. The poster child for nuclear waste, the one most often quoted by journalists—plutonium-239, which had a half-life of about twenty-five thousand years—was far from the longest-lived, Steve knew. Uranium-235, used in both reactors and weapons, had a half-life of about 704,000,000 years.

"By what method would the waste be transported?" This from one of the Oregon delegates.

"By rail and truck, both purpose-designed for the task."

"What I meant was, I assume we're not talking about fifty-five-gallon drums."

"No, sir. You'll find detailed information about the transportation vessels on the sheets I gave you, but I've seen the things up close and watched the stress testing they go through. They're about as close to indestructible as you can get."

"They said the same thing about the *Titanic*."

"Which I'm sure General Atomics has kept well in mind as they've worked on these things for the past ten or twelve years."

This had the desired effect: If one of the project contractors had spent a decade working on the transport cask alone, how much time and care and expense had been spent on the facility itself?

"How about security, Mr. Jenkins?"

"If the facility goes online, primary security will be handled by the DOE's National Nuclear Security Administration Protective Forces—the NNSA for short. There would, of course, be . . . supplemental forces on quick standby, should an emergency arise."

"What kind of supplemental forces?"

Steve smiled. "The kind that give bad guys nightmares."

More laughter.

"Okay, let's move on to what you all came for. If you'll board the little rail carts to the right, we'll get going."

The trip took fifteen minutes, but frequent questions brought the convoy to a halt. Finally they slowed beside an opening in the main tunnel wall. The delegates climbed out and gathered around Steve at the mouth. "The shaft you see sloping downward is six hundred feet long and connects to the emplacement drift, which is a horizontal grid of smaller tunnels that, in turn, lead to waste-storage areas."

"How does the waste get from the truck or train down to the storage level?" one of the Utah staffers asked. "Does it stay inside the transport vessel?"

"Sorry, that's hush-hush territory again. What I can tell you about is how the waste will be stored down in the drift. Each 'packet' will be encased in two nested canisters, one made of almost an inch of a highly corrosion-resistant metal called Alloy 22, then a two-inch-thick second canister made of something called 316NG—essentially, nuclear-grade stainless steel. Overhanging the nested canisters will be a titanium shield designed to protect them from seepage and falling rocks."

"Is that something you're worried about?"

Steve smiled. "Engineers don't worry. We plan. We try to model every possible scenario and plan for it. These three components—the two nested canisters and the titanium shield—form what we call a 'defense-in-depth.' The packets will be stored horizontally and commingled with different grades of waste, so each chamber maintains a uniform temperature."

"How big are these packets?"

"About six feet in diameter and ranging in length from twelve to eighteen feet."

"What happens if the packets get . . . misplaced?" the other California candidate asked.

"Couldn't happen. The number of steps involved to move a packet and the people that have to sign off on it make that a virtual impossibility. Think of it this way: We've all lost our car keys, right? Imagine a family of eight. Each person in the family would have a duplicate set of keys; three times a day, each person would have to sign a form stating the keys are either in their possession or in the agreed-upon key-collection area; three times a day each person would have to verify that their particular set of keys in fact works in the car's locks and ignition; and finally, three times a day each person would have to go around to the other family members and verify that *that* person has taken all of the above steps. Are you starting to get the picture?"

Nods all around.

"All of that and more would be going on here every shift of every day of the year. And it would be backed up by computer oversight. I promise you, as sure as the sun will rise tomorrow, nothing is going to get misplaced in this facility."

"Talk to us about corrosion, Mr. Jenkins."

"Our corrosion testing is done at the LTCTF—sorry, the Livermore's Long-Term Corrosion Test Facility."

"As in Lawrence Livermore National Laboratory?"

Thanks for the softball, Jenkins thought but didn't say. Lawrence Livermore was a household name, and while most people couldn't tell you exactly what LLNL did, it was nevertheless held in high regard. Again, if Lawrence Livermore was on the job, what was there to worry about?

"Right," he said. "The testing process involves aging and stressing metal samples called 'coupons.' Right now they're testing eighteen thousand coupons representing fourteen different alloys in solutions common to this area. As of now, the average corrosion rate on the coupons is twenty nanometers a year. A human hair is *five thousand* times wider than that. At this rate, the Alloy 22 used in the nested canisters would hold up for about a hundred thousand years."

"Impressive," said a man in a cowboy hat, one of the Idaho delegates, Jenkins assumed. "What say we talk worst-case scenario. What if something leaks and starts seeping into the earth."

"The chances of that are—"

"Humor us."

"First of all, what you need to know is the water table beneath our feet is unusually deep, running at an average of fifteen hundred feet, which would be eleven hundred feet below this emplacement drift."

This was another point of heated debate, Steve knew. While what he'd just told the delegates was true, some of the project scientists were lobbying for deeper emplacement drifts—some three hundred feet below this one. The truth was, there was no firm answer to the percolation question. How fast various liquids would seep through the rock beneath the facility was an unknown, as were the effects an earthquake might have on percolation rates. Then again, he reminded himself, the best estimates put the chances of a catastrophic earthquake affecting the storage levels at one in seventy million.

If anything was going to be the inescapable death knell for the facility, it would be the nature of the water table. Up until ten months earlier, it was uniformly believed that the area beneath the facility was what's known as a *closed hydrologic basin,* an inward-sloping formation that offered outlets to neither oceans or rivers. Two exhaustive studies, one by the EPA and one by the USGS, now contradicted that belief. If accurate, aquifers might extend as far as the West Coast and the Gulf of California. Until the matter was settled, however, Steve's orders were clear: The closed hydrologic basin model was the gold standard.

He said, "For waste to even begin seeping into the rock, dozens of systems and subsystems—both human and computer—would have to fail. Again, we need to put this into perspective: Compared to the security protocols this facility would operate on, sneaking into an ICBM silo and launching a missile would be a stroll in the park."

"Is any of this material fissionable?"

"You mean can any of it explode?"

"Yes."

"Well, it would take someone with a couple Ph.D.s at the end of their name to answer the whys, but the answer is no."

"Say someone managed to sneak through security and get down to the storage levels with a bomb—"

"By 'someone,' I assume you mean Superman or the Incredible Hulk?"

This got outright laughter.

"Sure, why not? Let's say they did. What kind of damage could they do?"

Steve shook his head. "Sorry to rain on your parade, but the logistics alone make that incredibly unlikely. First of all, you'll notice this diagonal tunnel is ten feet wide. The amount of conventional explosives it would take to do any significant damage to the storage levels wouldn't fit into a moving truck."

"And nonconventional explosives?" asked the Idaho delegate.

Then, Steve thought, *we'd have a problem.*

43

"Okay, people, time to change up the game," Gerry Hendley announced as he filed into the conference room and found a seat.

It was another morning at The Campus, and the conference table was laid out with carafes of steaming coffee and platters of pastries and doughnuts and bagels. Jack poured himself a cup of coffee, grabbed a whole-wheat bagel—no cream cheese—and found an empty spot at the table. Also present were Jerry Rounds, chief of analysis/intelligence; Sam Granger, chief of operations; Clark and Chavez; and the Caruso brothers.

"It's time we start taking a focused approach. From this point on, every person in this room is going to have nothing else on his plate except for the Emir and the Umayyad Revolutionary Council—except for myself, Sam, and Jerry, of course. We'll also be keeping the lights on and the doughnuts fresh, but the rest of you start shifting your workload. We're going to live, breathe, and eat Emir twenty-four-seven until he's caught or dead."

"Hoo-yah," Brian Caruso said, getting a round of laughter.

"To that end, we've given the group a fitting name: Kingfisher. The Emir thinks he's a king of sorts, fine. We're going to fish him out. From now on, this is your workspace, and everyone's door is always open—that means me, it means Sam, and it means Jerry."

Holy crap, Jack thought. *Where's this coming from?*

"First things first. Dom and Brian were tracking down leads in Sweden," Hendley said, then recounted Jack's discovery of the DHS/FBI intercept about Hlasek Air.

"We're going to keep pulling at that thread, but nothing jumped out. Mechanic's turned himself into the Swedish national police, but he's got nothing to give. Cash transaction for a little work on a transponder and a charter full of maybe Middle Easterners."

"Kingfisher," Hendley continued. "If you've got an idea, tell someone. If you want to try something new, ask. If you just want to brainstorm or play what-if, get together and do. The only dumb questions or ideas are the ones we don't ask or put out there. We're going organic, people. Forget the way we were doing things and start thinking outside the box. You can bet your ass the Emir is. So: Questions?"

"Yeah," Dominic Caruso said. "Why the change?"

"Got a piece of good advice recently."

Jack saw Hendley give John Clark a barely perceptible glance, and then it made sense.

"We're too small a shop to be running it like a bureaucracy," Jerry Rounds added. "The three of us will be rotating through here regularly to make sure we're still on the rails, but the bottom line is this: The Emir is an extraordinary character, and we have to change our tactics accordingly."

"What does this mean for the operational side of things?" Chavez asked.

Sam Granger answered, "More business, we hope. A lot of the new stuff we'll be generating won't be verifiable in the hypothetical. That means beating the bushes and running down leads. A lot of it might be scut work, but it adds up. Don't get me wrong, we'd all love a home run, but you don't stumble ass-backward into them. You've got to work for them."

"When do we start?" Jack asked.

"Right now," Hendley replied. "First order of business is making sure we're all on the same page. Let's lay out what we know, what we suspect, and what we still have to find out."

He checked his watch. "We'll break for lunch, then meet back here."

Jack popped his head into Clark's office. "Whatever you did, John, you sure as hell got Hendley's attention."

Clark shook his head. "I didn't do anything but nudge him where he was already headed. He's sharp. He would've gotten there eventually. Come on in. Got a minute to sit?"

"Sure." Jack took a seat across the desk.

"Heard you want to get your hands dirty."

"What? Oh, yeah. He told you, huh?"

"Asked me to train you."

"Well, that'd be fine with me. More than fine, really."

"Why do you want to do this, Jack?"

"Didn't Hendley tell—"

"I want to hear it from you."

Jack shifted in his chair. "John, I sit here every day, reading traffic, trying to make sense of information that could be something, or nothing, and sure, I know it's important and it's got to be done, but I want to do something, y'know?"

Clark nodded. "Like MoHa."

"Yeah, like that."

"It's not always clean like that."

"I know."

"Do you? I've done it, Jack—face-to-face and hand to hand. Most of the time it's ugly and messy, and you never forget. The faces fade, so do the places and circumstances, but the act—the deed itself—sticks with you. If you're not ready to deal with that, it can eat you up."

Jack took a deep breath, eyes on the floor. Was he ready? He could sense the truth of what Clark was saying, but at this point it was an abstract. He knew none of it was like the movies, or in novels, but knowing what something was not like was useless, kind of like describing the color red by saying

359

it didn't look like blue. *No point of reference—or almost no point of reference,* he reminded himself. There'd been MoHa.

As if reading his mind, Clark said, "And make no mistake: MoHa was an aberration, Jack. You fell into that, didn't have a chance to think about it, and you were sure the guy was bad. It's not always that cut-and-dried. In fact, it's rarely that way. You have to get comfortable with uncertainty. Can you do that?"

"To tell you the truth, John, I don't know. I can't give you an answer. I know that's not the right answer, but—"

"Actually, that's exactly the right answer."

"Huh?"

"When I was going through the entry process into BUD/s—Basic Underwater Demolition School—everybody had to meet with a psychologist. I was in the lobby waiting, and a buddy of mine came out. I asked him what it was like. He said the doctor had asked him if he thought he could kill a man. My buddy, anxious to kick ass, said, 'Hell, yes.' When my turn came and the doctor asked me the same question, I told him I thought so but I wasn't a hundred percent sure. One of us made it in; the other didn't."

I'll be damned, Jack thought. Thinking of John Clark as some fresh-faced raw recruit rather than a godlike special operator was a hard concept to wrap your head around. Everyone started somewhere.

Clark continued, "You show me a guy who answers 'Hell, yes' to those kinds of questions and I'll show you a nutcase, a liar, or someone who hasn't given it enough thought.

"Tell you what: Ask Ding sometime. First time he had to put someone down, it'd been a near thing right up until the moment he'd pulled the trigger. He knew he could do it, and he was ninety-nine percent sure he was going to do it, but until he dropped the hammer there was still a little voice in his head."

"And what about you?"

"The same."

"That's hard to believe," Jack replied.

"Believe it."

"So what're you saying? I should stick to my keyboard and computer monitor?"

"That's your choice. I just want to make sure you're straight in your head about it. If not, you're a danger to yourself and to everyone else."

"Okay."

"One more thing: I want you to think about telling your dad."

"Jesus, are you kidding—"

"No, I'm not. I'll keep the secret, Jack, because you're an adult and the choice is yours, but it might be time to step out on your own, and you can't do that while you're still afraid to stand in front of him. Until then, you're not your own man."

"You don't pull any punches, do you?"

Clark smiled at this. "I've been hearing that a lot lately." He checked his watch. "Almost time to get back. Give it another day's thought—both things. If you still want to go out, I'll teach you what I can."

Mary Pat's contact at Legoland—Britain's Secret Intelligence Service headquarters at Vauxhall Cross on the River Thames was colloquially known as either Legoland or Babylon because of its chunky, ziggurat-like architecture—had offered only one name in response to her query. Nigel Embling, she was told, was a retired old hand in the Stans and had forgotten more than most people knew about the region. Mary Pat assumed the Brits had active assets there, but whether or not Embling was one of these, she couldn't be sure. Probably not. Her back-channel inquiry had likely made clear to her contact that she was slightly off the reservation, in which case the

Brahmins at SIS wouldn't look kindly at him handing over a genuine agent.

Of course, being armed with a contact was only half the battle. Embling was an older man and well past his fieldwork days, which meant they'd need to put someone else on the ground to do the legwork. Mary Pat didn't have to think very hard about that one. Two names immediately came to mind, and if the scuttlebutt was true, these particular individuals might be interested in a little contract work. The NCTC had some discretionary funds, and both she and Ben Margolin agreed this might be a worthy expenditure.

It took only two phone calls to confirm the rumors, and another two to nail down a current phone number.

Clark's cell phone, tucked into the top drawer of his desk, trilled once, then again. He grabbed it on the third ring. "Hello."

"John, Mary Pat Foley here."

"Hey, Mary Pat, you were on my to-do list."

"That so?"

"Me and Ding just rotated out of Rainbow. Wanted to touch base and say hi."

"How about we do that in person? I've got something I want to run by you."

Clark's internal radar chirped. "Sure. When and where?"

"As soon as possible."

Clark checked his watch. "I can shake loose for lunch right now."

"Good. You know Huck's in Gainesville?"

"Yeah, just off Linton Hall Road."

"Yep. Meet you there."

Clark shut down his computer, then headed up to Sam Granger's office. He recounted the phone call for The Campus's ops chief. "I'm guessing this isn't a social lunch," Granger said.

"Doubt it. She had her game voice on."

"She know you're cycling out of the Agency?"

"Not much escapes Mary Pat."

Granger considered this. "Okay, check in when you get back."

Clark had passed by Huck's but had never gone inside. Best pies in Virginia, he'd been told. *Not that you could tell from the outside,* he thought, as he pulled into the diagonal parking space in front. Two large glass windows flanked a single door shaded by a faded red-and-white canvas awning. A neon light in the window advertised "ucks." *Bad omen?* Clark wondered. *Probably not.*

Truth was, he had nothing but good memories of Gainesville, having spent many hours walking its streets, teaching CIA case officers surveillance/countersurveillance techniques. There was only so much you could learn in the classrooms of Camp Perry. Unbeknownst to the fine citizens of Gainesville and a dozen other cities in Maryland and Virginia, at any given time their streets were being strolled by spooks playing at staying alive before they had to do it in the real world.

He pushed through the door and found Mary Pat sitting on a stool at the counter. They embraced, and Clark sat down. A portly man with thinning red hair and flour-dusted hands walked down to them. "What can I get you?"

"Apple," Mary Pat said without hesitation. "To go."

Clark shrugged and ordered the same. "How's Ed?"

"Okay. Got a little cabin fever, I think. He's writing a book."

"Good for him."

When the pies came, she said, "Feel like a walk?"

"Sure."

Once outside, they strolled down the sidewalk, chitchatting until they reached an acre-sized park covered in green grass and neat box hedges. They found a bench and sat down.

"I've got a problem, John," Mary Pat said after they'd both had a few bites of pie. "Thought you and Ding might be able to help."

"If we can. First things first, though: You know we're—"

"Yeah, I heard. Sorry. I know the honorable Charles Sumner Alden. He's a jackass."

"Seems to be a lot of that going around Langley these days."

"Sadly, yes. Starting to feel like the Dark Ages over there. Tell me: How do you feel about Pakistan?"

"Nice place to visit . . ." Clark offered with a smile.

Mary Pat laughed. "It's a pretty simple op, five or six days, maybe. We've got a few things that need chasing down, but nobody on the ground there—at least nobody that we can use. The new administration's stripping the ops directorate like they're having a fire sale. We've got a guy—a Brit—who knows the area, but he's a little past his prime."

"Define 'things that need chasing down.'"

"Should be straight intel gathering. Legwork."

"I assume we're talking about something peripheral to the big fish?" This got a nod from Mary Pat. "And you've already tried to source this through Langley?" Another nod. Clark took a breath, let it out. "You're getting pretty far out on the limb with this."

"That's where the fruit is."

"What's your timeline?"

"Sooner the better."

"Give me the afternoon."

He was back at The Campus an hour later. He found Granger in Hendley's office. He knocked on the doorjamb, got a come-in wave from Hendley, and took a seat. "Sam told me," Hendley said. "You try the pie?"

"Apple. Might not be the best, but it's damned close. She

pitched me a contract job. Pakistan." He outlined their conversation.

"Well, hell," Granger said. "She's NCTC, so it's not too tough to figure out what's on their radar. What'd you tell her?"

"That'd I'd call her later with an answer. It's a no-brainer, really, but here's the rub: If we take it, I'm not inclined to keep her in the dark."

"About The Campus?" Granger said. "I don't—"

"Sorry," Clark said. "Mary Pat and I go back a long way, and she's risking a lot on this. I'm not going to play her. Look, you guys know her reputation; you know what Jack Ryan thinks of her. If that's not bona fides enough, I don't know what is."

Hendley mulled this over for half a minute, then nodded. "Okay. Tread carefully, though. When would she need you?"

"Yesterday, I suspect," Clark replied.

44

What we know for sure about the Emir and the URC is limited," Jerry Rounds said, restarting the meeting. "Let's talk about what we're *pretty* sure about."

"Up until recently, the URC's relied heavily on the Net for communication, but we can't track them down to an ISP because it's always something different, and we depend on NSA to pick it up from the encryption method, and even then we can't always identify the ISP, but they know they skip from one country to another."

Dominic picked up the thread. "Unless we're missing a whole bunch of e-traffic—which is always possible—it's a safe bet he's having important stuff physically transmitted from one place to another, which means couriers. Maybe carrying CD-ROMs or some other portable media they can use on a laptop, or can hand to somebody else in their outfit who has a desktop machine that's hooked into a phone or cable line. Or a Wi-Fi hot spot."

"Hot spots ain't very secure," Brian suggested.

"Might not matter," Chavez countered. "Wasn't one of the ideas that they're using onetime pads?"

"Yeah," Rounds said.

"With those you can say just about anything you want. To anybody picking it up, it'd look like a whole bunch of random numbers or letters or words."

"Which begs the question," Jack said, "are the couriers carrying just messages, or onetime pads, too—if that's what they're using—"

Rounds interrupted. "Jack, bring everyone up to speed on this guy. . . ."

"Shasif Hadi," Jack replied. "He was on an e-mail distribution list we've had our eye on. His ISP account wasn't as well insulated as the others. We're trying to peel back his financials. Whether that'll lead to anything but which grocery store he shops at, I don't know."

"About the couriers," Chavez said. "Doesn't the FBI look at frequent travelers on the airlines? Any way of sorting a pattern that way? Find some link between URC e-mail traffic and travel patterns."

Dominic answered this. "You have any idea how many people regularly hop the Atlantic? Thousands, and the Bureau's looking at all of them. It'll take a long time to check out as many as a quarter of them. It's like reading through a phone book eight hours a day. And for all we know, the bastard's sending his CD-ROMs by FedEx or even regular mail. A mailbox is a great place to hide something."

366

Jerry Rounds's laptop chimed, and he checked the screen. He read for a full minute, then said, "This complicates things."

"What?" Jack said.

"We got an info dump from the Tripoli embassy thing. Ding inadvertently pocketed a flash drive from one of the tangos. The drive had a bunch of JPEG files on it."

"Pictures of the Emir's bolt-hole?" Brian asked.

"Not so lucky. The bad guys are upping their game. They're using steganography."

"Come again?"

"Steganography. Stego, for short. It's a method of encryption—essentially, hiding a message inside an image."

"Like invisible ink."

"More or less, but it's even older than that. In ancient Greece they used to shave a portion of a servant's head, tattoo a message on the skull, then wait for the hair to grow back and send him through enemy lines. Here we're talking about digital pictures, but the concept is the same. See, a digital image is nothing more than a whole bunch of colored dots."

"Pixels," Chavez offered.

"Right. Each pixel is assigned a number—a red, blue, and green value, usually ranging from zero to two fifty-five, depending on the intensity. Each of these are, in turn, stored in eight bits, starting at one twenty-eight and jumping down to one, halving as they go, so one twenty-eight to sixty-four to thirty-two, and so on. A difference in one or two or even four in the RGB value is imperceptible to the human eye—"

"You're losing me," Brian said. "Bottom-line it."

"You're essentially hiding characters inside a digital photo by slightly altering its pixels."

"How much information?"

"Say, a six forty by four eighty image . . . half a million characters, give or take. A good-sized novel."

"Damn," Chavez muttered.

"That's the hell of it, though," Jack said. "If they're using stego, they're probably smart enough to keep the messages short. We're talking about a dozen or so altered pixels in an image containing millions. It's the proverbial needle in a haystack."

"So how hard is it to do the encoding?" Chavez asked. "Any way we can track it that way?"

"Not likely. There are tons of shareware and freeware programs out there that can do it. Some are better than others, but it's not a specialized thing. Doesn't have to be, when only the sender and recipient have the decryption key."

"How about pulling the messages out? Can it be done? What's that involve?"

Rounds answered, "It's essentially reverse-engineering each image—deconstructing it, figuring out which pixels have been altered and by what amount, then pulling out the message."

"This sounds right up the NSA's alley," Brian said. "Can we tap—"

"No," Rounds replied. "Love to, believe me, but intercepting their traffic is one thing. Trying to hack into their systems is another. Anyway, we might not need something that strong. Jack, are there commercial programs out there?"

"Yeah, but whether they've got the horsepower we need, I don't know. I'll start looking around. If nothing else, we might be able to model our own program. I'll check with Gavin."

"So the Tripoli thing," Dominic asked. "I assume we're thinking it was a URC op?"

"Right. All of the tangos were from URC affiliate groups— half of them from a Benghazi cell, the other half a mixed bag."

"A pickup game," Jack said. "From everything I've read, that's pretty unusual for a URC job. Usually they're keen on cell integrity. That's got to mean something."

"Agreed," Rounds said. "Let's start a thread and see where it goes. Why did they break routine?"

"And where are the other Benghazi members?" Brian added.

"Right. Okay, back to the stego: Unless this is an aberration, we have to assume it's standard URC practice and may have been for a long time, which makes our job a whole lot tougher. Every message board and website the URC has ever used or is currently using is a potential source now. We need to scour them for image files—JPEGs, GIFs, bitmaps, PNGs. Anything."

"Video?" This from Chavez.

"Yeah, it can be done, but it's harder. Some of the compression stuff can mess with image pixels. Better to concentrate on still images and screen caps for now. So we grab everything we can and start dissecting for embedded messages."

"We should make sure we have a benign IP base, in case anyone's keeping track," Jack suggested.

"How about giving me that in English?" Brian said. "You know me, big dumb Marine."

"IP is Internet protocol—you know that string of numbers you see on your home network . . . like 67.165.216.132?"

"Yeah."

"If we bombard these sites with the same IP and somebody's watching, they'll know they're getting probed. I can have Gavin set us up on a random rotation so we'll just look like regular visitors. Maybe even ghost them to other Islamic websites."

"Good," Rounds said. "Okay, let's keep going. What else? Toss it out there."

"Any way to check when pictures are posted on a website?" Dominic asked.

"Maybe," Jack replied. "Why?"

"Match the post dates against e-mails, known operations, that kind of thing. Maybe a picture being posted prompts an e-mail, or vice versa. Maybe there's a pattern we can start to build on."

Jack made a note. "Good idea."

"Let's talk assumptions," Chavez offered. "We've been assuming the Emir's still somewhere in Pakistan and Afghanistan. When's the last time he's been confirmed there?"

"A year ago," Jack replied. "We've tossed that around, the idea of him having relocated or even changed his appearance, but there's no evidence of it."

"Pretend there is. Why would he move?"

"Either operational reasons or we were getting too close to his bolt-hole for comfort," Rounds said.

"Where would he go?"

"My vote is Western Europe," Dominic said.

"Why?"

"Borders, for one thing. A lot easier to move around."

The Schengen Agreement had seen to that, Jack knew, having standardized border controls and entry requirements among most EU nations, making travel between them almost as easy as moving between states in North America.

"Don't forget currency," Brian added. "The euro's accepted just about everywhere. It would make moving money and setting up house a whole lot easier."

"Assuming he hasn't changed his appearance, it'd be a lot easier for him to blend in somewhere in the south, the Med—Cyprus, Greece, Italy, Portugal, Spain . . ."

"A whole lot of territory," Brian observed.

"So how do we triangulate?" Rounds said.

"Follow the money," Dominic offered.

"Been doing that for a year; so has Langley," Jack replied. "The URC's financial structure makes the Knossos Labyrinth look like a place-mat maze at Denny's."

"Nice obscure reference, cuz," Brian said with a grin.

"Sorry. Catholic education. The point is, without a corner

to peel back, I think the financial angle is a nonstarter. At least by itself."

"Anybody modeled it?" Chavez asked. "Take what we know about their money handling, tie it to e-mail traffic and website announcements, and cross-reference those with incidents?"

"Good question," Rounds replied.

"I'd be surprised if the NCTC and/or Langley hasn't already tried that. If they'd had any luck, the guy would be in the bag."

"Maybe," Rounds said, "but *we* haven't tried it."

"If The Campus ain't done it, it can't be done?" Brian offered.

"Exactly. Let's assume they haven't tried it. Or let's assume they did try it but in the wrong way. What would it take to do it right?"

"A custom-made software application," Jack replied.

"We've got the people and the money. Let's explore it."

"Gavin's gonna start hating us," Dominic said with a smile.

"Buy him a case of Cheetos and Mountain Dew," Brian shot back. "He'll be fine."

"How about we put some boots on the ground in Tripoli?" Dominic said, changing directions. "This embassy job didn't happen in a vacuum. Let's go down there and shake the tree. Maybe Benghazi, too."

Rounds considered this. "I'll put it to Sam and Gerry."

They kicked the ball around for another hour before Rounds brought the meeting to a close. "Let's break up and get to work. Meet again tomorrow morning."

Everyone filed out, save Jack, who'd rotated his chair to stare out the window.

"I can see the gears turning," Chavez said from the doorway.

"Sorry . . . what?"

"Same look your dad gets when his brain is on overdrive."

"Still playing what-if."

Ding pulled out a chair and sat down. "Shoot."

"The question we didn't ask is why. If the Emir has left Pakistan or Afghanistan for points unknown, why? Why now? As far as we can tell, he hasn't left the area for maybe four years. Were we getting too close to him, or was it something else?"

"Such as?"

"Don't know. Just trying to think like him. If I had something cooking, a really big operation, I might be tempted to pull up stakes and find another bolt-hole, to make sure I didn't get caught and give away the farm to interrogators."

"Risky move."

"Maybe, but maybe not as risky as sticking around the same place, knowing the odds were probably catching up to me. If you move and set up shop somewhere else, you not only stay free, but you're also able to keep your hands in the pot."

Chavez was silent for a few moments. "You've got a good head, Jack."

"Thanks, but I kinda hope I'm wrong on this. If I'm not, something big may be coming down the road."

They'd managed to survive the storm, but it had been too close for comfort, the boat having been nearly battered to its breaking point. Four hours after they'd entered the squall, they broke through its western limits, finding themselves in calm water and blue skies again. Vitaliy and Vanya had spent the remainder of the day and part of the evening after they'd put ashore checking the boat for damage but finding nothing that would require them to return to port. And even if they had, Vitaliy wondered if Fred would have permitted it. His sacrifice of his man had been a shock to Vitaliy—not so much the decision itself but rather the lack of emotion it had evoked in Fred. These were serious, serious men.

The lighthouse was their objective, though he still had no idea why anyone would want to go there. Situated atop Cape

Morrasale on the Gulf of Baidaratzkaya, it wasn't a particularly important navigation aid—not anymore, at least. There had once been a settlement here, probably a monitoring station for the nuclear tests on Novaya Zemlya, and some commercial fishermen had tried to make a go of it, but that had lasted only four seasons before the men and the boats had moved west to better grounds. The charts showed ten to twelve fathoms of water, and so there was little danger of running aground, and besides, most boats had Western-made GPS navigation to keep them in safe waters.

His passengers were checking with their truck now, testing the engine and the A-crane. It should have offended him, what they planned to do, but he didn't fish here, and nobody he knew did.

He could just see the light, blinking away every eight seconds, just as the chart said it did. Once they reached their destination beach, the lighthouse would be less than a kilometer away, up a spiral switch-backed road that led to the top of the cliff. That was going to be the worst part, Vitaliy knew. No more than three meters across, the roads were barely wide enough to accommodate the GAZ.

Why come here? he again wondered. The seas alone were daunting enough, but the journey by truck over this wasteland was a job for neither the fainthearted nor the irresolute. While it would take Fred and his men only ten minutes to reach the lighthouse, he'd told Vitaliy to expect they would be gone for the day, if not overnight. What could they be doing that would take so long? Vitaliy shrugged off the question; not his job to wonder. It was his job to drive the boat.

Sea conditions looked glassy-flat, and the slapping of shore waves against the steel sides of his landing craft was hard to hear. On deck, his charter party was brewing up coffee on a small, gasoline-powered stove they'd brought with them.

With a throaty rumble from the diesels, Vitaliy shifted the

engines to reverse and increased the throttle, grinding away from the gravel beach. After a hundred meters, he turned the wheel to bring his boat about, and then consulted his gyro-compass before turning again, this time on a heading of zero-three-five.

Vitaliy lifted his binoculars and swept the horizon. Not a thing in sight that God didn't Himself put here, except for a buoy or two. The winter ice often swept them away or ground them into pulp, sending them to the bottom, and the Navy didn't trouble itself to replace them as they should, because nobody came here in a deep-draft ship. Another indicator of just how far into the wildlands they were.

Four hours later he opened the side window and called out, "Attention! Landing in five minutes." He pointed to his watch and held five fingers out. He got a wave from Fred in reply. Two members of the party went to the truck to start the engine, while two others started throwing their duffel-bagged gear in the back.

Peering through the window, his eye picked a spot to aim his boat for, and he came in at about five knots, enough to be properly beached but not so hard as to jam his bow hard on the stones.

About fifty meters out he unconsciously braced for the impact and stopped his propeller. He hardly had to bother. The T-4 hit bottom, not too hard, and quickly came to a stop with the mild grinding sound of gravel on steel.

"Set the anchor?" Vanya asked. There was a fair-sized one on the stern for hauling the boat loose of a sticky shore.

"No. It's low tide, isn't it?" Vitaliy answered.

They throttled the diesels down to idle, moved to the ramp-control lever, and bled the hydraulics. The ramp dropped under its own weight and crashed down on the beach. The beach gradient was fairly steep, it appeared. Hardly a splash of water when the ramp went down. One of the men climbed into the GAZ's cab and pulled it forward, brake lights flashing as he navigated the ramp, then pulled onto the gravel, the chain waving off the end of the crane like the trunk of a circus elephant. The truck ground to a stop. Fred and the rest of the men walked down the ramp and onto the beach—save one, Vitaliy now saw, who stood at the top of the ramp.

Vitaliy left the wheelhouse and walked forward. "You're not taking this one?" he called to Fred.

"He'll stay behind to lend a hand if you need it."

"No need. We'll manage."

In reply, Fred simply smiled and lifted his hand in a wave. "We'll be back."

45

Clark took it as a sign of his advancing age that he'd grown increasingly intolerant of air travel. The cramped seats, the bad food, the noise . . . The only thing that made it remotely tolerable were the Bose noise-canceling headphones and a horseshoe neck pillow he'd gotten for Christmas, and a few tablets of Ativan Sandy had given him for the trip. For his part, Chavez sat in the window seat, eyes closed as he listened to his iPod Nano. At least the seat between them was empty, which gave each of them a little more elbow room.

After his discussion with Hendley and Granger, he'd found Ding, brought him up to speed, then called Mary Pat's cell and arranged to meet her at home later in the afternoon. At her urging, he arrived early and shot the breeze with Ed for an hour before she arrived. While Ed started dinner, Clark and Mary Pat retreated to the back deck with a pair of beers.

Ignoring Hendley's "tread carefully" warning, Clark laid his cards on the table. They'd known each other too long for anything less. Mary Pat didn't bat an eye. "So Jack did it, huh? Always wondered if he'd gone through with it. Good for him. Well, they didn't waste much time snatching you two up, did they? Who tapped you?"

"Jimmy Hardesty, about ten minutes after Alden canned us. The thing is, Mary Pat, I think we're working on the same puzzle. If you're not okay with cross-decking whatever intel we dig up . . ."

"Why wouldn't I be?"

"For starters, we'll be breaking at least three federal laws. And be risking the wrath of the Aldens at Langley."

"If we can get this asshole—or even get a little closer to getting him—I'll be fine with that." Mary Pat took a sip of her beer, then glanced sideways at Clark. "Does this mean Hendley's footing the bill?"

Clark chuckled. "Call it a gesture of goodwill. So what's it going to be? A onetime deal, or the beginning of a wonderful friendship?"

"Share and share alike," Mary Pat replied. "Bureaucracy be damned. If we have to put our heads together to get our man, so be it. Of course," she added with a smile, "we'll have to take credit, seeing as how you guys don't exist and all."

Half a tablet of Ativan and a beer helped Clark pass the last five hours of the flight in a deep, untroubled sleep. As the plane's wheels bumped and squelched on the Peshawar airport's tarmac, he opened his eyes and looked around. Beside him, Chavez was stuffing his iPod and paperback into his carry-on.

"Time to work, boss."

"Yep."

*

Surprising neither of them, their passage through the airport's customs and immigration line went slowly but without incident. An hour after entering the terminal, they were outside at the ground transportation curb. As Clark raised his hand for a cab, an accented voice behind them said, "I would advise against that, gentlemen."

Clark and Chavez turned to see a lanky white-haired man in a powder-blue summer suit and a white plantation hat standing behind them. "The cabs are death traps here."

"You would be Mr. Embling," Clark said.

"Indeed."

Clark introduced himself and Chavez, using first names only. "How did you—"

"A friend e-mailed me your flight information. After that, it was simply a matter of looking for two chaps with the appropriate air about them. Nothing obvious, mind you, but I've developed something of a . . . radar, I suppose you would call it. Shall we?"

Embling led them to a green Range Rover with tinted windows parked beside the curb. Clark got in the front passenger seat, Chavez in the back. Soon they were pulling out into traffic.

Clark said, "Forgive me, but your accent—"

"Dutch. A throwback to my service days. There's a significant Muslim population in Holland, you see, and they're fairly well treated. Much easier to make friends—and stay alive—as a Dutchman. A matter of self-preservation, you see. And your covers?"

"Canadian freelance writer and photographer. Spec piece for *National Geographic*."

"That'll do in the short term, I suppose. The trick to blending is to look as though you've been here awhile."

"And how do you do that?" This from Chavez.

"Look scared and disheartened, my boy. As of late, it's the Pakistan national pastime."

*

"Care for a quick tour of the hot spots?" Embling asked a few minutes later. They were driving west on Jamrud Fort Road, moving toward the heart of the city. "A little who's who of Peshawar?"

"Sure," Clark replied.

Ten minutes later they pulled off Jamrud and headed south on Bacha Khan. "This is the Hayatabad, Peshawar's version of your South Central Los Angeles. Densely populated, impoverished, very little police presence, drugs, street crime . . ."

"And not much in the way of traffic laws," Chavez said, nodding through the windshield at the zigzagging stream of cars, trucks, man-hauled carts, and mopeds. Horns honked in a nearly continuous symphony.

"No laws at all, I'm afraid. Hit-and-runs are almost a sport here. In years past, the city's made some effort to lift the neighborhood, mind you, but they never seem to get any traction."

"Bad sign when the police stop showing up," Clark observed.

"Oh, they show up. Two or three cars pass through twice a day, but unless they see a murder in progress, they rarely stop. Just last week they lost one of their cars and two officers. And when I say 'lost,' I mean they vanished."

"God almighty," Chavez said.

"Not around here," Embling muttered.

For the next twenty minutes they drove ever deeper into the Hayatabad. The streets grew narrower and the homes more ramshackle until they were passing huts of corrugated tin and tarred-over cardboard. Vacant eyes watched Embling's Range Rover from darkened doorways. On every corner, men stood clustered, smoking what Clark assumed wasn't tobacco. Garbage lined the sidewalks and blew down the streets, pushed along by dust devils.

"I'd be a whole lot more comfortable armed," Chavez murmured.

"No worries, my boy. As luck would have it, the Army's

Special Service Group is fond of Range Rovers with tinted windows. In fact, if you look behind us right now, you'll see a man running across the street."

Chavez turned around. "I see him."

"By the time we reach the next street, doors will be slamming."

John Clark smiled. "Mr. Embling, I can see we've come to the right person."

"Kind of you. It's Nigel, by the way."

They turned yet again and found themselves on a street lined with a mixture of cinder-block stores and multistoried homes of unbaked brick and wood, many of whose façades were either fire-blackened or pockmarked with bullet holes, or both.

"Welcome to extremist heaven," Embling announced. He pointed at buildings as they drove past, reciting as they went the names of terrorist groups—Lashkar-e-Omar, Tehreek-e-Jafaria Pakistan, Sipah-e-Muhammad Pakistan, Nadeem Commando, Popular Front for Armed Resistance, Harkat-ul-Mujahideen Alami—until he turned yet again, where the list continued. "None of these are official headquarters, of course," he said, "but rather something akin to clubs, or fraternities. Occasionally the police or the Army will come in and conduct a raid. Sometimes the targeted group goes away altogether. Sometimes they're back here the next day."

"How many in all?" Clark asked.

"Officially . . . almost forty and counting. The problem is, the ISI is doing the counting," he replied, referring to the Directorate for Inter-Services Intelligence, Pakistan's version of the CIA. "Military intelligence to some extent as well. It's the proverbial fox-guarding-the-henhouse scenario. Most of these groups either receive funding, or resources, or intelligence from the ISI. It's become so convoluted that I doubt the ISI is counting wickets anymore."

"That damage back there," Chavez said. "From police raids?"

"No, no. That's the work of the Umayyad Revolutionary Council. They are without a doubt the biggest dog on the block. Any time one of these guppies swims in the wrong pond, the URC comes in and swallows them up, and unlike with the local authorities, when that happens, the group stays gone."

"That's telling," Clark replied.

"Indeed."

Through the windshield, a few miles away, they could see a plume of smoke gushing into the sky. They felt the *crump* of the explosion in their bellies a few moments later. "Car bomb," Embling said lightly. "Average three a day here, plus a couple mortar attacks for good measure. Nightfall is when things get truly interesting. I trust you can sleep through gunfire, yes?"

"We've been known to," Clark replied. "I have to tell you, Mr. Embling, you paint a bleak picture of Peshawar."

"Then I've given you an accurate portrayal. I've been here on and off for nearly four decades, and in my estimation Pakistan is at a tipping point. Another year or so should tell the tale, but the country's about as close to being a failed state as it's been in twenty years."

"A failed state with nuclear weapons," Clark added.

"Right."

"Why do you stay?" Chavez asked.

"It's my home."

A few minutes later Chavez said, "Back to the Hayatabad . . . What I'm wondering is who *doesn't* live there?"

"And a good question it is," Embling said. "Though it's a subjective measure the three big players here—the URC, Lashkar-e-Taiba, and Sipah-e-Sahaba, formerly Anjuman—are

380

generally clustered around the Peshawar cantonment—the Old City—and the Saddar area. The closer to the cantonment they are, the more dominant they are. The URC currently holds that title."

"As luck would have it, we're primarily interested in those areas," Clark said.

"Imagine that." A smile from Embling. "My house is just outside the cantonment, near Balahisar Fort. We'll have a spot of lunch and talk shop."

Embling's houseboy—a term Clark had trouble wrapping his head around, despite knowing it was common here—Mahmood served them a lunch of *raita,* a yogurt and vegetable salad; lentil stew; and *kheer,* a rice pudding, to which Chavez took a ravenous liking.

"What's the boy's story?" Clark asked.

"His family was killed during that bad business following the Bhutto assassination. He'll be going to Harrow in Middlesex next year."

"That's a good thing you're doing, Nigel," Chavez said. "You don't have any—"

"No." Curt.

"Sorry. I didn't mean to stick my nose in your business."

"No apology necessary. I lost my wife in '79, when the Soviets invaded. Wrong place, wrong time. Who's for tea?" Once he'd poured everyone a cup, he said, "What's it going to be, gentlemen? Person, place, or thing? What you're after, I mean."

"For starters, a place. Places, plural, actually," Clark replied. From his briefcase he pulled out a digitally enhanced copy of the Baedeker's map, then pushed aside the cups and saucers and unfolded it on the table. "If you look close—"

"Dead letter drops," Embling interrupted. He saw Clark's and Chavez's astonished expressions and smiled. "In the ancient days of espionage, gentlemen, dead drops were our bread and butter. Three-dot cluster for drop-off; four for pickup?"

"Reverse that."

"How recent is this map?"

"No idea."

"So we have no way of knowing whether the drops are still active. Where did you—"

"In the mountains," Chavez replied.

"A dark and dank place, I'm guessing. The previous owners—were they present?"

Clark nodded. "And did their damnedest to destroy it."

"That's a point in our favor. Unless I'm off the mark, the three-dot clusters aren't intended so much as a pickup location as they are a pickup signal."

"Our thought as well," Clark replied.

"Is your interest in what's being dropped off and picked up, or who's doing either or both?"

"The who."

"And do you know the signal?"

"No."

"Well, in all probability, that's the least of our worries."

Chavez asked, "How so?"

"We're not so much interested in the signal's correctness as we are in identifying who takes an interest in it. In that case, we'll have to chose our location carefully." Embling went silent, clicking his tongue and staring at the map. "Here's my suggestion: We take the afternoon on doing a little recce—"

"Come again?" This from Chavez.

"Reconnaissance."

"Must have missed that over there."

"We spent a little time at Hereford," Clark explained to Embling.

"There's a grim-faced bunch," Embling replied. "Nice to

see you haven't lost your smiles. Okay, then, we'll get you gentlemen comfortable with the territory, then start laying bait tomorrow. Otherwise, I fear we'll run out of daylight today."

While the majority of the drops were well outside the cantonment, they decided to concentrate on the four within the Old City, first driving around its perimeter, roughly following the wall that enclosed the cantonment until the mid-'50s. "Used to be sixteen gates here along the wall, complete with turrets and ramparts for archers," Embling said, pointing out the passenger window. "In fact, in Persian, *Peshawar* means 'The High Fort.'"

Clark liked Embling, partially because during his Rainbow tour he'd come to understand the British mind-set a little better, and partially because he was a genuine character—emphasis on the former. Given the way Embling waxed on about Peshawar, Clark half wondered if the man had been born a hundred years too late. Nigel Embling would have been right at home during Britain's rule of the area.

Embling found a parking space near Lady Reading Hospital, and they got out and walked west into the Old City. The streets of the cantonment buzzed with activity: bodies, moving elbow to elbow, darted in and out of alleys and beneath canvas awnings; on overhanging balconies, children peeked curiously through wrought-iron bars. The scent of roasted meat and strong tobacco filled the air, along with an overlapping babble of voices speaking in Urdu, Punjabi, and Pashto.

After a few minutes walking, they entered a large square. "Chowk Yadgaar," Embling announced. "All the drop-offs are within a half-mile of the square."

"Probably chose it for the crowds," Chavez said. "Hard to be seen, easy to get lost."

"Another astute observation, young Domingo," Embling said.

"I have my days."

Clark said, "Let's split up and check 'em out. Meet back here in an hour." They decided who would take which, then parted company.

They regrouped and compared notes. Two of the spots—one in a small courtyard between the jeweler's bazaar and the Mahabbat Khan mosque, and one in an alley near the site of the Kohati Gate—showed the faintest traces of a single chalk mark, the gold standard for dead-drop pickup signals since the Cold War. Chalk weathered well and was easily dismissed as a child's doodling. Clark got out his map, and Embling checked the two locations. "Kohati Gate," he said. "Easiest to surveil, and closest exit out of the cantonment."

"Done," Clark said.

"It's early yet," Embling said. "How do you chaps feel about cricket?"

46

Not wanting to risk being seen placing the pickup mark, Clark and Chavez woke well before sunrise the next morning to find Embling already up, making coffee and putting together a cooler of rations for the day. So armed, they set out for the cantonment, this time in Embling's other car, a shabby blue 2002 Honda City, and arrived at Chowk Yadgaar fifteen minutes later, where they split up in the predawn gloom—Clark and Chavez taking a walk to refamiliarize themselves with the area and to test the new earpiece/mic/push-to-talk portable radios with which Gavin Biery had equipped them; Embling surveying the Kohati Gate location and placing their mark. Forty minutes later, they met back at Chowk Yadgaar.

"Bear in mind," Embling said, "there's a police station a couple hundred yards down the square. If you're stopped—" He paused and laughed. "Listen to me prattling on. I imagine you two have done this sort of thing before."

"Once or twice," Clark said. *Or a hundred.* Working dead drops wasn't all that common a task, but the universal surveillance/countersurveillance methods still applied. As they were waiting for their quarry rather than already tailing him, boredom would be their most potent enemy. Get bored, lose focus, miss something. In the back of Clark's mind was a ticking clock; how long did they stay in Peshawar waiting for someone to service the drops before deciding the network was dead?

"Right, then," Nigel said. "I'm going to move the car closer to Kohati Gate. I'll be about with my mobile."

As the day's first vendors arrived to lift their awnings and put out their kiosks and carts, Chavez took up the first shift. "In position," he radioed.

"Roger," Clark replied into his collar mic. "Let me know when you see Nigel pass by."

Ten minutes passed. "Got him. Just passed Kohati Gate. Parking now."

Now we wait, Clark thought.

As the Old City came to life and the tourists and locals began streaming in, Clark, Chavez, and Embling rotated through the Kohati Gate area, smoothly and without so much as a glance, transferring surveillance to the next man, who did his best to loiter without making it obvious: stopping at nearby kiosks to haggle with the owners over a bead necklace or carved wooden camel, taking pictures of the architecture, and chatting with the occasional local who was interested in where he was from and what had brought him to Peshawar—all the while, keeping half his attention focused on the chalk-marked clay brick in the alley wall opposite the gate.

At 11:15, Clark, who had the watch, felt a tap on his shoulder and turned to see a cop. "American?" he asked Clark in broken English.

Clark gave him a disarming smile. "No, Canadian."

"Passport." Clark handed it over. The cop studied it for thirty seconds, then snapped it closed and handed it back. He nodded to Clark's digital camera. "What pictures?"

"Pardon?"

"You photograph. What?"

Clark waved his arm at the nearby buildings. "Architecture. I'm with *National Geographic*. We're doing a story on Peshawar."

"You have permit?"

"I didn't know I needed one."

"Permit."

Clark understood. *Baksheesh*. In the Muslim world, the term could mean either charity to beggars, tipping, or flagrant bribery, which was the case here. "How much is the permit?"

The cop looked Clark up and down, assessing his worth. "Fifteen hundred rupee."

About twenty dollars. Clark pulled a wad of crinkled bills from his "light" pocket and gave him three five-hundred-rupee bills.

"Only day be here?"

"I might be back tomorrow," Clark said with a friendly smile. "Can I pay for that permit in advance?"

This offer brought a smile to the cop's face, which had so far remained stony. "Of course."

"Is there a discount for paying in advance?" Most commerce-minded Pakistanis were slightly insulted if their marks didn't haggle a bit.

"Fourteen hundred rupee."

"Twelve."

And then, predictably, "Thirteen." Clark handed over the notes, and the cop nodded and walked off.

"What'd he want, boss?" Chavez radioed from some unseen location.

"Shaking me down. We're good."

Embling's voice: "We have a nibbling fish, John."

Clark raised his camera to his eye and turned slowly, a tourist looking for a good shot, until the alley and Kohati Gate were in frame. A boy of seven or eight, wearing filthy white canvas trousers and a blue Pepsi T-shirt, was stooped beside the chalked brick. After a moment he spit into his hand and vigorously rubbed the brick clean.

"He bit," Clark reported. "He's heading out the gate. White pants, blue Pepsi T-shirt."

"On my way." This from Chavez.

"Moving to the car," Embling reported. "Meet you outside."

Chavez reached Clark, who had moved just outside the gate, in less than sixty seconds. "He's walked down the street. Our side, just passing that blue Opel."

"I see him."

Embling pulled up in the Honda, and they climbed in. The Brit pulled out, swerved to miss a delivery truck approaching the gate, accelerated hard for five seconds, then coasted back to the speed limit as they drew even with the boy and passed him. Embling took the next right, drove thirty meters down a side street, then did a quick U-turn and pulled back to the intersection, stopping ten feet short. Through the windshield they could see the boy turn left onto his own side street, then trot diagonally across the street and into a tobacco shop.

"I'll go," Chavez said from the backseat, and reached for the door handle.

"Wait," Embling muttered, eyes fixed on the shop.

"Why?"

"Whoever he's working for probably has a few at his disposal. It's a practice here, little runners to do one's trivial errands."

Sixty seconds later the boy reappeared on the sidewalk. He looked both ways, then called out to a man sitting on a bench two doors down. The man said something back and pointed directly at Embling's Honda.

"Distressing turn," Embling said.

Clark replied evenly, "Not if he comes this way. If we're burned, he'll go in the opposite direction."

He didn't. Running at a sprint now, dodging a stream of honking and swerving cars, the boy crossed the street and ran past them. From the backseat, Chavez said, "One block up. Turned east."

Nigel put the car in gear and pulled up to the stop sign, waiting for a break in traffic. When it came, he turned right. "This will run parallel to him for two blocks." At the next stop sign he turned right, then left, then pulled to a stop beside a school playground.

"Got him," Clark said, eyes fixed on the side mirror.

The boy turned into a doorway covered in a red awning and reemerged a few seconds later with another boy, this one in his early teens, with curly black hair and a leather jacket. As the first boy talked and gesticulated, the teenager walked to a nearby streetlamp and began working a cable lock around a lemon-yellow moped.

"Well played, Nigel," Clark said.

"We'll see. Moped kids here think they're bloody off-road bikers."

This one, they quickly realized, was no exception. Though his top speed never exceeded twenty-five miles per hour, the teenager weaved through traffic with a seeming irregularity that reminded Clark of a kite on a gusty day. For his part, Nigel did not follow the moped's every lane change but rather continued straight, always keeping the yellow moped within sight and changing lanes only when necessary.

The teenager headed southeast away from the cantonment, first on Bara Road, then northwest onto the Ring Road Bypass. The street signs, written in Urdu, were indecipherable to Clark and Chavez, but Embling kept a color commentary of their route.

"Crossing Kabul Canal," he announced.

Chavez asked, "Closing in on the Hayatabad, aren't we?"

"Good eye. Yes, we are. Another two miles. Coming up on Gul Mohar."

At the last second the moped swerved right across two lanes and took the exit. Embling, already in the far right lane, simply put on his blinker and followed.

For the next twenty minutes the teenager took them on what could only be a dry-cleaning run—and did a fairly decent job of it, Clark had to admit. They passed the University of Peshawar, the Department of Tourism offices, and the British Cemetery, until finally their subject headed north on Pajjagi Road, passed the Peshawar Golf Club, and again crossed the Kabul Canal. Soon they were on the outskirts of the city. Squares of green irrigated fields appeared on their left and right. Embling dropped back until the moped was a speck of bright yellow.

After six miles, the moped turned west and followed a winding, tree-lined road before pulling into a narrow driveway. Embling stopped a few hundred yards down the road, did a U-turn, then shut off the engine. They waited. This far from Peshawar proper, there were no honking horns and no revving of engines. The minutes ticked by until a half-hour had passed.

Down the road came the sound of a puttering engine.

Embling started the car and accelerated for a quarter-mile to the next driveway and pulled in, coasting down the sloping dirt tract until the main road was barely visible through the back window. Ahead was an old barn, its roof partially caved in. Chavez turned around in his seat. A moment later, the top of the boy's head drove past.

"Your call, John."

"Let him go. I think we've found what we're looking for. If the boy's going to check the pickup spot, he'll be back soon enough."

And he was, forty minutes later, flashing by their driveway. Moments later the moped's engine went silent.

"I'd say you've found your quarry," Embling said.

Clark nodded. "Let's drive past and see what we can see."

An hour later, back at Embling's house, Clark and Chavez sat and sipped tea while their host made three phone calls in rapid-fire Urdu. He hung up and said, "It's a private security firm."

"Wonder who he's afraid of?"

What they'd seen as they'd passed the driveway was a white van bearing a white-and-red placard sitting in the dirt turn-around, and next to it a two-story white farmhouse.

"That I don't know, nor was I able to find out the client's name. The firm is a fairly recent hire, however. Last week, in fact. Two men per shift, round-the-clock coverage."

Clark checked his watch. Nightfall was in five hours. He looked at Chavez, who'd already read his partner's mind. "Let's go get him."

"Nigel, I don't suppose you have any hardware—"

"I do. An alarming array, in fact."

47

Two hours after sunset, Clark turned Embling's Honda into the abandoned barn's driveway. He shifted into neutral, shut off the engine, and allowed momentum to carry them down the slope and into the shadow along the barn's wall. When the car came to a halt, he shifted into park, Chavez turned off the dome light, and they climbed out.

Nigel hadn't been exaggerating the extent of his weapon's cache, which he kept in an old steamer trunk in his closet. They chose a pair of noise-suppressed SIG Sauer P226 9-millimeter pistols. Standard-issue sidearm for the British SAS. They'd both spent many hours on the range with the P226. At Embling's urging, they each grabbed a lead-and-leather cosh. "Never can tell when you'll have a merciful moment," he told them with a smile.

Now Chavez whispered, "What's the plan?"

"Probably be one guard outside, either static or roving, and another inside. We'll take down the first, then deal with the other when the time comes. Ding, try the cosh first. The fewer bodies we leave, the better."

"Fine by me."

They split up, Clark moving west through the trees behind the barn and Chavez following the drainage ditch bordering the main road. "In position," Clark heard through his earpiece.

That was fast, Clark thought. *Ah to be young again.* "Stand by."

He took his time moving through the underbrush, checking for telltales underfoot and low-hanging branches too dark to see. After a quarter-mile the trees began thinning out, and he soon found himself at the north end of the turnaround, thirty yards opposite the driveway entrance.

"In position," he whispered. "Where are you?"

"End of the drainage ditch, against the driveway berm."

"I see one sentry. Sitting in a lawn chair at the van's front bumper."

"Come again?"

"Sitting in a lawn chair, smoking, facing my direction." Whoever had hired them was not getting his money's worth. "Got a Type 56 leaning against the bumper on his right." The 56 was a Chinese copy of the AK-47. Not the same quality, but certainly enough to worry about.

Chavez said, "I'm seeing one light on, lower level, my side."

"Dark here. No movement. Go when you're ready."

"Roger."

Even though he knew Ding was coming, Clark didn't spot him until he was within ten feet of the van's rear bumper. *Ninjas own the night* had been Chavez's old unit's motto. And he still did, Clark knew.

Chavez reached the bumper, took a peek around the quarter panel, then dropped into a crouch and waited.

"Still nothing," Clark whispered after a minute.

He got a double-click *roger* in reply.

Chavez eased back now, moving around the other side of the van and out of sight. Ten seconds later, a shadow appeared behind the seated guard. Chavez's arm cocked back and came forward. The guard slumped forward, leaning sideways against the van's grille. Chavez pulled him back upright and crushed out the fallen cigarette.

"Down and out."

"Roger. Moving."

They met in the shadows along the house's south wall. The porch and front door lay to their left. With Clark in the lead, they slid down until the entrance was in view. The inside door stood open, but the screen door was closed. They mounted the porch and got stacked on either side of the door. Now they could hear the faint sounds of television from inside the house. Clark, on the latch side, reached up and tested it. Locked. He reached into his back pocket, thumbed open his knife, and gently, carefully, inserted the tip into the mesh and drew the blade down until he had created a six-inch slit. He closed the knife and returned it to his pocket, then reached through and felt around until he found what he was looking for. There was a soft *snick*. He withdrew his hand and then sat still for a full minute.

Clark nodded at Chavez, who returned it, then crab-walked across the doorway and slid into position behind Clark, who reached up and depressed the door handle. He opened the door an inch, stopped, then tried another couple of inches. No matter their age or condition, screen doors seemed prone to creaking. Maybe it was the exposure to the elements.

This door didn't disappoint. At the halfway point the hinges peeped. Clark froze. Chavez scooted forward until he could see beneath Clark's outstretched arm into the house. He pulled back and signaled *clear*. Inch by slow inch, Clark opened the door the rest of the way. With his gun leading, he stepped inside. Chavez took control of the door, then followed, easing it shut behind him and getting nothing worse than another metallic peep.

They were in a kitchen. Wooden countertops, cabinets, and a sink to the left; round dining table in the center. An arched doorway in the right-hand wall led to another room. Chavez checked it and gave a thumbs-up. They moved through into what was clearly a sitting room. To the right, a set of stairs led to the second floor. Ahead, a short hall. This is from where the television sounds were emanating. Each taking a wall, they moved into the hall, stepping and pausing, stepping and pausing, until they were within ten feet of an open door. Inside, Clark could see the blue-gray light of a television flashing off the walls.

Clark closed the remaining distance and took up position beside the doorjamb. He nodded at Ding, who came up the right wall until he had an angled view through the door. He stepped back a couple of feet and gestured: *Two men in chairs. One nearest the door armed.* Clark signaled back: *I'll take him; you sweep through.*

Chavez nodded.

Clark switched his gun to his left hand and drew the cosh from his belt. With a curt nod, he leaned around the corner, picked his target, and wrist-whipped the cosh into the man's temple. Even as he slumped sideways, Chavez was in the room, gun up. He stopped. His brow furrowed. He crooked his finger at Clark, who stepped through the door.

Their man was asleep.

Chavez woke him up with a light tap of the gun's barrel across the bridge of his nose. As his eyes flittered open, Chavez said, "English?"

The man pressed himself as far back in his chair as he could.

"English?" Chavez repeated.

"Yes, I speak English."

Clark said, "Make sure this one and Mr. Lawn Chair are out of action. I'll take him." Chavez shoved the guard to the floor, then grabbed his wrist, dragged him down the hall into the sitting room, and headed outside.

"What's your name?" Clark asked their host.

No reply.

"If you're not even going to give me your name, we're in for a long, ugly night. Let's start with your first name. No harm in that."

"Abbas."

Clark pulled the now-empty guard's chair out, spun it around, and sat down so they were knee to knee.

The screen door opened and banged shut. Chavez came in with the first guard over his shoulder in a fireman's carry. He unceremoniously dumped him beside his partner. "Found some duct tape in the van," he told Clark, then went to work with it. Once done, he joined Clark.

"Let's make sure we're getting off on the right foot," Clark told Abbas. "You know what that means?"

"Yes."

"I don't think your name is Abbas. I'm going to have my friend look around your house for anything with a name on it. If it doesn't say Abbas, we're going to start hurting you."

"My name is Obaid. Obaid Masood."

"Good." Clark nodded at Ding, who went out and started rummaging around. "Do you want to change your answer while there's still time?"

"My name is Obaid Masood. Who are you?"

"Depends on how you answer my questions. Cooperate and we're friends. Don't cooperate . . . Tell me about your security detail. Why do you think you need them?"

Masood shrugged.

"Listen, if your worry was about the police or the Army, they probably would have already been here, which suggests to me you've fallen into some bad company. Somebody you worked for, maybe?"

Chavez reappeared. He nodded: *He's telling the truth.*

"Somebody you worked for?" Clark repeated.

"Perhaps."

"The Umayyad Revolutionary Council?"

"No."

"Do you watch baseball?"

Masood's brows furrowed. "I have, yes."

"We're going to call your 'no' strike two," Clark said. "One more and I'm going to shoot you in the foot. Have you bothered to ask yourself how we found you?"

"The dead drops?"

"Right. And who do you suppose we got those from?"

"I see."

"I don't think you do. We found you. They can find you."

"You're American."

"That's true. What you need to decide is whether you hate us more than you fear them. Because if we don't start getting some answers, we're going to drive you into the Hayatabad and dump you out of the car."

This got Masood's attention. "Don't do that."

"Convince me."

"I used to work for ISI. I . . . moved people. Relocated them."

"Like a black-market travel agent?" Chavez observed.

"Yes, I suppose. Eight months ago I was approached."

"By whom?"

"I didn't know him, and I've never seen him again."

"But URC, correct?"

"I found that out later. He offered me a lot of money to move someone."

"How much money?"

"Two hundred thousand, U.S."

"Did you ever meet this person?"

"No."

"What exactly did you do for them?"

"Passports, documentation, private planes. Making sure the right customs and immigration people are paid. It took me five months to put everything together. They were meticulous in their demands, having me double- and triple-check every arrangement."

"When did you hand over everything?"

"Two months ago."

Chavez asked, "Did you give them everything?"

"What do you mean?"

"Did you keep copies?"

"Paper copies?"

Clark put a little steel in his voice. "*Any* kind of copies, Obaid."

"There is a hard drive."

"Here?"

Masood nodded. "Taped to the underside of the kitchen sink in a plastic bag."

Chavez headed out the door. He was back a minute later carrying a Ziploc bag. Inside was a drive about the size of a deck of cards. "Eight gigs," Chavez said.

"English, Ding."

"A lot of storage space." He held the bag up toward Masood. "Everything you did for them is in there?"

"Yes. Digital scans, e-mails . . . everything. Can you get me out? Out of the country?"

"Might take a little time," Clark said, "but we'll get it done. Until then, we'll get you out of sight. Stand up."

Masood did so. Clark clapped him on the shoulder. "Welcome to the good guys' team." He pushed Masood toward the door. Ding grabbed Clark's elbow. "A minute?"

"Go ahead, Obaid. Wait for us in there."

Chavez said, "You're thinking about stashing him with Nigel."

"I was."

"Fifty-fifty chance somebody will track him down. If they do, that's it for Nigel and his kid."

"You got a better idea?"

Chavez paused. "We got the drive. Maybe we cut our losses and—" Chavez tipped his head to the side, looking over Clark's shoulder. "Shit."

Footsteps pounded in the other room.

"He heard me! Goddamn it!"

Chavez darted out the door, through the sitting room, and into the kitchen just as the screen door slammed closed. "Ah, fuck me!" He was halfway to the screen when a *crack* brought him to a halt. In a crouch, he backtracked into the sitting room. Clark was already there, peeking his head above the windowsill. In the driveway a pair of headlights cast stripes in the dirt. Lying in one of the beams was Masood. A figure carrying a pistol walked up to him, knelt down, and fired two rounds into his head, then stood up and walked back into the headlights. A door slammed shut, followed by the crunch of tires on gravel.

Silence.

"What the hell just happened?" Chavez whispered.

"He got the visit he was worried about."

"And us?"

"They must've assumed he was running from them. Let's get out of here before they think twice."

48

Jack heard his computer chime, indicating a new e-mail message. He scanned it once, then again. "Hello there. . . ." He picked up the phone, called Rick Bell, told him what he had, and a few moments later they were on a conference call with Sam Granger.

"Tell him, Jack," Bell prompted.

"You know the guy we think might be a URC courier?"

"Hadi?"

"Right. Got something on his financials—a credit card. He's moving—right now. An Alitalia 747 from da Vinci in Rome to Pearson outside Toronto."

"And from there?"

"Chicago, but nothing beyond that on his credit card yet."

"It's either his destination or a dry-cleaning stop," Bell said, using the old CIA tradecraft term for an SDR, or surveillance detection run. "Chicago's a hub; he could be going anywhere, in country or out again."

"How long do we have?" Granger asked.

"Four hours," Jack replied.

Granger asked, "Rick, how solid are we on this guy?"

"Seventy-thirty. He's on a known URC distribution list, does a lot of shuttling: here, Europe, South America. Best guess: He's either a full-fledged courier or a stringer doing logistics for them. Either way, I think he's worth the effort. We've got him on a plane, with a known destination and time. Doesn't get much better than that."

Granger was silent for a few moments, then: "Okay, get Kingfisher in the conference room. I'm coming down."

"So what's happening?" asked Dominic Caruso, walking into the conference room. Save Clark and Chavez, the others were already assembled: Brian, Rick Bell, Jerry Rounds.

Jack explained briefly.

"Holy shit."

"My words exactly."

"When's the plane get in?"

"Three-twenty, the schedule says," Jack replied.

Sam Granger walked in and took his seat at the head of the conference table. "Okay, it's eight-forty here, figure seventy, seventy-five minutes to Toronto. We don't have much time to do anything. Not without official support anyway. When are Clark and Chavez due in?"

Rick Bell checked his watch. "'Bout forty minutes."

"Let's see if we can get them in on this. Jack, you got Hadi's pedigree?"

"Yeah."

He handed out the documents, and there was sixty seconds of silence as everyone flipped through the pages. Brian asked, "Do we have a photo of this guy?"

"Nope," Jack answered. "No description at all."

"Rome to Toronto—on from there to Chicago and then . . . No information, right?"

"Correct," Jack confirmed with a nod.

"If this was a Bureau op," Dominic said, "we'd contact the RCMP and flood plainclothes guys into the airport and try to ID the guy, then follow him to wherever he's going. But we can't do that, can we?"

"Fly to Toronto," Jack said. "Use the Mark-1 eyeball and pray for luck. Let's assume we can ID the bird. Then what can we do?"

"Covert surveillance," Dominic said. "Try to follow him to wherever the hell he's going. Ain't gonna be easy. Even if we succeed, we can't arrest him, can't interview him, can't do much of anything, unless somebody wants to green-light a takedown."

"No chance," Granger said. "He's the only shot at a bird dog we've ever had with the URC. We either tail him, tag him, or snag him—in that order."

"We gather information," Bell told them. "Whatever we get, it's more than we have now. Small steps, guys."

"Let's go see the boss," Granger said.

"We have a bird in the air," Jack told Hendley a few minutes later. "Subject name is Hadi, on his way to Toronto. His plane arrives after three Eastern Time."

"Want to try to eyeball the guy?" Hendley asked.

"It's a potential curveball hanging over the plate," Rounds said. "But our subject information is a little thin," he had to admit.

"What, exactly, do we have?" Hendley asked. Jack handed

400

over the printout, and Hendley set it on his desktop to read. "Good catch," he said, looking up briefly. "Okay. Let's send everybody—"

"Clark and Chavez are almost wheels-down. Gonna see if we can intercept them."

"Good. Jack, Dom, Brian, draw credit cards and cell phones from the second floor."

They all drove together to BWI Airport in Brian's Mercedes C-Class sedan. There was a 737 scheduled to leave for Canada in seventy-five minutes, Rounds told them via phone. Tickets were waiting for all of them. Once inside the terminal, they picked up their tickets, located Clark and Chavez's flight on the board, and headed out.

Brian asked Dominic, "How're the Canadian cops?"

"Brit tradition, and some of their own. The RCMP—the Mounties—go way back, and they're pretty good at investigations, but I've never interacted with them."

"Bright red coats," Brian said. "But that can make easy targets, especially on the back of a horse."

"They're good guys, too," Dominic reminded his brother.

Brian chuckled. "Just a random observation."

Clark and Chavez came off the jetway, saw Jack and the others, and walked over. "Door-to-door service?" Clark asked.

"We got something cooking. You guys up for a little tag?"

Chavez said, "As long as you find me Starbucks first."

Jack explained the situation as they exited the security checkpoint and returned to the ticketing desk for Clark and Chavez's passes. "So how do we do this?" Jack asked Clark, as they went back through security.

"Look for a guy who looks like he doesn't belong. He's sort of a trained spook. He presumably knows how to be invisible.

You look for that. He won't be looking around like most tourists do, won't be doing anything to call attention to himself, but he probably also will not be overly familiar with the location. So a business type who doesn't know the turf. When he looks around, he'll be doing it carefully. He'll probably be careful—looking for surveillance. You've been taught how to do that. Look for somebody else who's doing what you were taught. It's more art than science."

"So what the hell do we do?" Brian demanded.

"Look like an American tourist. Turn everything off, all the training. Just be a normal schlub. Nobody notices them. Unless you're in Redland—in the old USSR, for example. You especially never smile. The Russians almost never smile, weird thing about their culture. It ain't easy, I know. But I been doing it for almost thirty years. It's a little easier to remember when your ass is on the line," he concluded with a smile.

"How many times?"

"Russia? More than once, and I was scared every time. You went in naked, no gun, no place to run to, just a 'legend,' a little backstopped cover if you were lucky."

"'Backstopped.'"

"Background that would stand up to light scrutiny. The hotel you stayed at in the last city, employer's phone number . . . Stuff like that."

"Been meaning to ask you," Dominic said. "What about these guys, the current class of enemies?"

Clark thought this over. "Part of me says they're all the same—different motivation, different outlook, all that, but doing the same shit. But the other part of me isn't so sure. This bunch at least believes in God, but then they violate the rules of their own religion. Sociopathic personalities? Hell, I don't know. They have their version of the world, and we have ours, and the twain don't meet."

*

402

The flight was called, and they went aboard together. Five seats abreast, separated by the aisle, all in coach. Chavez, with his short legs, didn't mind, though Clark did. As he grew older, he got stiffer. The usual safety routine. Clark had his belt on and snugged in. He'd learned over the years not to dismiss safety rules in any of their manifestations. The 737-400 taxied out and rotated off the ground as routinely as if the pilot were driving a car. Clark lifted the in-flight magazine and started flipping through the catalog section. He stopped, looking at a toolbox ad.

"So how exactly are we going to do this?" Jack asked Clark.

"Play it by ear," Clark replied, then turned back to his catalog.

The landing was almost as smooth as the takeoff, followed by the rollout and taxi trip to the terminal, and deplaning, and the usual shuffling walk-off. And the terminal was as nondescript as all the others around the world. They turned left and walked down the wide, anonymous concourse. Signs directed them to international arrivals, and it was just enough of a walk to get the blood flowing in their legs. Information TV monitors told them that the Alitalia flight was still ninety minutes out. A quick check of the area told them that it was easily surveilled. So much the better, there was a casual eatery in direct line of sight, with the usual plastic chairs surrounding plastic tables.

"Okay, guys, we have maybe two hours, counting processing the mutt through customs," Clark thought aloud.

"That's all?" Jack wondered.

"Maybe they'll have a dog wander past the bags, sniffing for drugs, but not much more than that. The Canadians aren't being all that careful. Bad guys transit Canada. They don't stay here to do mischief. Good luck for them, I guess. It allows them to save money on security expenditures."

"If the bad guys are casual here, you could bag a few fairly easily and put them on a boat to Buffalo."

"And then," Dominic continued the thought, "they'd make enemies they really don't need. It's business."

"Good point," Chavez said. "Business is business, and you let a sleeping dog alone, until you get bit. I wonder when they'll have that happen to them."

"Depends on the bad guys, but making enemies gratuitously is not good for business. Remember, a terrorist is a business-man whose business is killing people. Maybe they're ideologically driven, but business is still business."

"How many have you bagged?" Dominic asked Clark.

"A few, all in Europe. They're not well trained. Alert, and they can be sly like a fox, but that isn't the same as training. So you just exercise caution and take them down. Helps to shoot them in the back. Hard for them to return fire that way."

Dominic frowned. "Huh."

"Ain't supposed to be fair. This isn't the Olympics."

"I suppose."

"But it goes against your grain, doesn't it?"

Dominic gave this a moment's thought, then shrugged. "I don't know about grain—just a different mind-set."

Clark smiled grimly. "Welcome to the other side of the looking glass." He checked his watch. The flight would be descending now.

It struck Hadi that the ground under an airplane always looked the same—but different. Distant but inviting as you came back down. Like America, all the roads and cars coming into view. He gauged height by whether or not he could see individual cars and trucks. The "Air Show" setting on his mini-TV said that altitude was 4,910 feet and dropping, ground speed 295, well down from their cruising height and speed over the ocean. They'd land soon. Ten minutes, according to the computer.

Time for him to wake up all the way. The stewardess took his coffee cup away. Italian coffee was much like that of his distant youth in its acidity, and truth be told, he much enjoyed Italian food, though they served pork far too much, and though he drank wine, he drew the line well short of pig flesh. He'd get off, waltz through customs and immigration, spot his greeter, and get his ticket on to Chicago from him, who'd drive him also to his connecting flight for United Airlines Flight 1108, and he'd have a cigarette but not much of a chat.

He had to be alert coming through customs and immigration. He had nothing to declare, of course, not even a bottle of Italian wine. Business traveler, he was supposed to be, for whom such a trip was routine. Jewel dealer, that was his cover. He knew enough to have a brief conversation on the subject. Not enough to impress or fool a real Jewish diamond merchant, of course, but he knew how to deflect any conversation, even to fake an accent. Well, he was a business traveler of sorts, and this sort of trip was routine, though this was his first-ever visit to Canada. One more infidel country, with simple and gentle rules for people in transit, and they'd be just as happy to see him on his way, taking no notice of him as long as he didn't carry a firearm or commit a crime.

The touchdown was a little rough. Perhaps the flight crew was weary as well. What a terrible life they had, Hadi thought. Sitting down all day, not walking around, constantly changing their body clocks to different places and times. But all men had their places in the world, and theirs was well paid, just unpleasant, even for infidels. His job and his cover compelled him to be pleasant to all he met. That included infidels who routinely ate pig. It was hard, but it was required by his place in life. The airliner stopped, and with the other 153 people aboard, he stood, collected his carry-on bag, and stumbled to the door.

You could tell the Canadian officials in their navy-blue

visored caps, blank expressions, and scanning eyes. Greeters who didn't care a whit about those whom they greeted to their infidel country. There were probably mosques within a mile or so, but he would not go near one of those. The local government might permit Muslims to worship Allah in a place of their own, but surely they were all watched, and the entrants photographed. His job was to be invisible.

"It's down," Clark said, looking at the TV monitor hanging twenty feet away.

"All we know is that he takes a piss standing up," Dominic reminded them.

Where's the nearest head? Clark thought. A lot of people made a head call soon after deplaning, after being too nervous to use the one on the airplane. Wouldn't be a bad idea to camp out on that possibility. Spooks were not robots. Every one had his own peculiarities, and those, once identified, made them vulnerable. It struck him that he'd never been a counterspy. Identifying spooks was something he'd always worked to prevent . . . but maybe that gave him the resources needed to do the job? He'd see. They were after an Arab, probably late thirties to middle forties, male. Height, weight, hair color, and eye color were all unknowns. He was a trained operator. He'd probably act like a trained operator.

Well, he was being met. They knew that much. Somebody to hand him a ticket for a connecting flight. Probably not as well trained. Probably a stringer. Maybe somebody hoping to earn a promotion in whatever organization he belonged to. Maybe as smart but not as experienced or as well trained. Somebody who knew his inbound asset by sight? Maybe, maybe not. Probably a driver. He'd be looking to make the pickup. Scanning the faces for recognition. Holding a sign? *Yeah, maybe THE EMIR SENT ME,* Clark thought with a snort. He'd seen some dumb ones in his time, but never that dumb. Might as well eat a gun outside the terminal with TV cameras watching. These guys might not be pros the way he thought of the term, but neither would they be stupid. Somebody had trained them or instructed their organization on how to teach them fieldcraft. It wasn't that hard. The nuances came with experience, but the basics were things a half-smart guy could figure out on his own. The four of them were standing in line. That wasn't smart. He shuffled over to Dominic.

"Break into pairs, opposite sides of the railings. Dominic, you and Brian. Jack, you're with Ding and me."

Dominic and Brian moved down the escalator and away, curling back to a place opposite Clark and Chavez. John tapped his nose, and the twins repeated the signal.

"What are you thinking, Domingo?" John asked.

"Who, them? Good instincts, a little rough around the edges, but that's natural. If trouble develops, I think they'll handle it okay."

"Fair enough for a ninja," Clark responded.

"We own the night, baby." That had been quite a while ago, but it was part of Domingo's core identity. He was a hard one to spot. Short as he was, people often overlooked him. His eyes could give him away, but only if you took the time to scan his face, and he really wasn't big enough for any tough guy to worry about, until you were on your back, wondering how the hell you got there. Times had changed since his SEAL days. Third SOG had had a few John Wayne types, but the new ones looked more like marathon runners, short and skinny. They tended to live longer, being harder to hit. But their eyes were different, and that's where the danger was. If you were smart enough to notice.

"Little nervous," Jack admitted.

"Nice and casual," Clark replied. "Don't try too hard. And never look directly into the subject's eyes, except maybe to check out the way he was looking around, but only briefly and carefully."

Who are you, Hadi? Clark thought. *Why are you here? Where are you going? Whom do you want to meet?* None of which was he likely to ask or have answers for. But the mind did its own thing all the time, the more so for a fairly intelligent and active mind.

49

Hadi could have been the first in line, but he manufactured a false delay to avoid that possibility. He didn't have to pretend to be tired. Counting the feeder flight from Marseille and the layover at Milan, he'd been in the air for fifteen hours, and the reduced partial-pressure of oxygen had taken its toll on his body. One more reason to wonder about the flight crew and their miserable jobs.

"Hello, Mr. Klein," the immigration clerk said with what appeared to be a smile.

"Good day," Hadi replied, reminding himself again of his false identity. Fortunately, no one had tried to speak with him on the flight, except the flight attendant, who kept his wine-glass fully attended. And the food had been tolerable, a pleasant surprise.

"The purpose of your visit?" the clerk asked, studying Hadi's face.

"Business." It was even true.

"Duration?"

"Not sure yet, but probably four or five days. Is that important?"

"Only to you, sir." The clerk scanned the passport, ran the

cover through the barcode reader, wondering if the red light would go on—but they almost never did, and it didn't this time. "Nothing to declare?"

"Nothing at all," Hadi replied.

"Welcome to Canada. The exit is that way," the clerk said, pointing.

"Thank you." Hadi took his passport back and walked to the multiple doors. Western countries were so self-destructively welcoming to their enemies, he noted yet again. He supposed they just wanted the money to be had from tourists. They couldn't really have such hospitality in their infidel hearts, could they?

"Heads up," John said. The first two people through the doors were women, and Hadi wasn't one of those . . . unless the intel was really bad, Clark thought. He'd had that happen to him more than once.

Okay, what are we looking for? Male, thirty-five to forty-five, average height, maybe a little less by American standards. Dark eyes, not looking around very much, feigned relaxation, but still looking around. Curiosity, but controlled curiosity. He'd be a little tired from the journey. Flying usually tired people out. A little wrung-out from the drinks he'd probably had . . . but he would have slept some, too.

They saw a tan camel-hair coat, mid-thigh in length. It looked Italian. *Hadi was supposedly based in Italy—in Rome—right?* Five-eight or so, medium build, a little on the skinny side. Dark eyes. *Dark as hell, almost black,* John thought. Looking studiously forward, not to the side, pushing a wheeled dolly with one large bag and one small one. They didn't look that heavy, and the big one had wheels on it . . . lazy or tired? His hair was as black as the eyes were; nondescript haircut. Clean shaven. No beard, perhaps—probably?—deliberately so. Two more people came out behind him, obviously Canadians, fair-skinned and ginger-haired. One waved to somebody to Clark's right. Wave off. Back to the camel coat. His eyes were moving left and right, but his head remained still. *Good fieldcraft,* John thought at once, on noting that. Then they locked on something: Clark's head turned and saw somebody in a black suit, like a chauffeur but without the cap, holding a white cardboard sign with KLEIN written on it in Magic Marker.

"Bingo," he whispered to himself. To Chavez: "Link up with the brothers and watch the flanks. I'm taking a walk. Jack, you're with me."

They headed down the concourse.

"See something I didn't?" Jack asked.

"His name isn't Klein. I'd bet the wad on that."

No trip to the head, Clark saw. So much for that idea. They followed forty yards back. The subject, they saw, didn't seem to speak with his pickup man. *Too disciplined, or did they know each other?*

"Got a camera?" John asked.

"Yeah, digital one. Ready to run. I might have a shot of our friend, but I haven't checked yet."

"If he gets into a car, let's make sure—"

"Yep. Make, model, and tag. How're we doing?"

I don't think he's seen us—damned sure didn't look at where we were, either side. Either he's one very cool customer or he's as pure as the driven snow. Take your pick."

"Looks kinda Jewish," Jack said.

"There's an old joke in Israel. If he looks Jewish, and he's selling bagels, he's an Arab. Not always true, but good enough for a joke."

"Except for the hair, I can see him in a cowboy hat and long black coat, on Forty-seventh Street in New York, handling diamonds. Not a bad disguise. But he's about as Jewish as I am."

Past the magazine stands, past the beer bar, past the one-way exit by the metal detectors, out to the main concourse. Not down the escalator to baggage recovery, but he'd already done that, of course. Toward the main door in the glass wall, and out into the cool air of a Canadian autumn. Past the taxi traffic for arrivals, across the street to the parking lots. Whoever the greeter was, he'd parked in the hourly lot, not the daylong-or-later lot. Okay, this was a scheduled pickup, all right. And not one called ahead for from the plane phone. Into the lot, and then Clark had to slow his tailing routine . . . and right to a parked car.

"Camera," Clark said sharply, hoping that Jack knew how to flash a photo covertly.

Actually, he did it pretty well, with the lens telescoped out to 2- or 3X zoom. It was a new-model black Ford Crown Victoria, of the sort used by a low-end car service. Everything was nominal to profile, Clark thought, as they started to close the gap.

"Here's your ticket from Chicago west," the driver said, handing the ticket folder back over the bench seat.

Hadi opened the folder and studied the ticket. He was surprised to see the destination. He checked his watch. The timing was almost perfect. It had helped that first-class passengers were quicker to get to immigration.

"How long to the other terminal?"

"Just a couple of minutes," the driver answered.

"Good." And Hadi lit a cigarette.

The car pulled out. Clark noted this but kept walking. Until the car was a hundred yards away, then he doubled back to the arrival traffic and hailed a cab.

"Where to?" the driver asked.

"I'll tell you in a minute. Jack: Eyeballs?"

"Got it," Jack assured him. The Crown Vic had pulled into

a line to pay the parking toll. He took two more shots to catch the tag number, which he already had memorized. Just to be sure, he scribbled it down on the notepad he always kept in his coat pocket.

"Okay," Clark told the driver. "See that black Ford up there?"

"Yes, sir."

"Follow it."

"Is this a movie?" the driver asked lightheartedly.

"Yeah, and I'm the star."

"I've done that, you know? Real movies. They pay pretty well for driving a car."

Clark took the hint, fished out his wallet, and handed the driver a pair of twenties. "Fair enough?"

"Yes, sir. I'll bet he's going to Terminal Three."

"Let's see," Clark responded. Now he had eyes on the Crown Vic, which did the usual rigmarole common to airports, whose roadways were doubtless designed by the same soulless idiot who did the architecture for the terminals. Clark had been in enough airports to be fairly certain all the architects went to the same school.

The taxi driver was right. The Crown Vic pulled to a stop at the UNITED AIRLINES sign and angled right to the curb. The driver's door opened, and the driver climbed out and moved to the passenger door.

"Good call—what's your name?" Clark asked.

"Tony."

"Thank you, Tony. You have a good one." Clark and Jack hopped out. In Jack's hand was the camera, well concealed but ready for action.

"He smokes," Clark observed. More to the point, he also posed pretty well. Sometimes luck worked in your favor. "Okay, shoot me," Clark said, posing. This Jack duly did, and afterward Clark came over to say something innocuous, followed by, "Got him?"

"Dead on. Now what?"

"Now I try to get a ticket to Chicago. You follow him to the gate and call me when you ID the flight."

"Think you can get a ticket fast enough?"

"Well, if I fail, we're no worse off than we are now."

"Gotcha," Jack agreed. "I got your number." And he hopped to it, taking position fifty yards from their friend Hadi, who enjoyed every possible puff from his smoke before turning to walk into the terminal. He had a good photo of the mutt, Jack realized, checking the preview screen.

Clark walked toward the United desk, pleased that there wasn't much of a line to fight through.

Hadi finished his smoke and flipped the butt onto the curb, took one deep breath of non-airliner air, and walked inside. Dominic followed at a discreet distance, holding his secure cell phone in his left hand. Hadi walked directly toward the proper concourse and checked a monitor for the right jetway. He walked out just like any normal person trying to catch a flight. It took under ten minutes, and then he took his seat at D-28. Brian made his call.

"Clark," the voice said on the other end.

"Jack here. Gate D-Twenty-eight, flight one-one-zero-eight."

"Got it. Does it look crowded?"

"No, but the bird's pulled up to the jetway, and the posted departure time is in twenty-five minutes. Better get a move on."

"On my way." John walked to the desk, had to wait for one business puke to get his ticket, then smiled at the desk clerk. "Flight one-one-zero-eight to Chicago, please. First-class, if possible, but I'll take coach." He handed over his gold Master-Card.

"Yes, sir," the clerk said politely. She proved to be wonderfully efficient, and the computer printer spat out the cardstock ticket in just three minutes.

"Thank you, ma'am."

"To the right." She pointed in case he didn't know where right was. John walked evenly. Twenty minutes to make the flight. *No problem.* That came at the metal detector. It pinged, rather to John's surprise. Then a uniformed rent-a-cop waved the magic wand over him and it pinged at his coat pocket. John reached in and found that his U.S. marshal's badge had tripped it. This metal detector was really turned up.

"Oh, okay, sir."

"I'm not even here on official business," Clark said, with a shy smile. "Is that it?"

"Yes, sir. Thank you."

"Right." Next time he'd toss it on the conveyor, John thought, and let the whole world think he was a cop. It had *not* pinged on the pen in his pocket. Wasn't that interesting, or could be, if he had the Magic Pen. But he didn't. Too bad.

It was a Boeing 737. Seattle must have sold a lot of them, Clark thought, looking around the uncomfortable lounge. Same architect, same crummy chairs. *The same company who did the airliner seats?* he wondered. *Was that a conflict of interest, maybe?*

There was Hadi, sitting in the nonsmoking sitting area. Not trying to call attention to himself? If so, good fieldcraft. Just sitting there reading a magazine, *Newsweek,* with cursory attention. Ten more minutes and they called the flight. Clark had lucked out and gotten a first-class seat, 4C. On the aisle, which was useful. He thought back to a recent commercial flight, but he'd had a pistol back then, unbeknownst to the British Airways cabin crew; would have alarmed them about as much as a carry-on bag full of dynamite sticks. Well, flight attendants were pretty girls for the most part, and it wouldn't do to annoy them in any way. They worked hard for their lowly salaries. Hadi walked aboard with three people ahead of him, John saw, and ended up in 1A, the most forward window seat on the left side, maybe fifteen feet ahead of Clark and to the left. Three steps and he could snap the guy's neck like a twig. He hadn't done that, exactly, since Vietnam, where the men often had scrawny little necks. But that had been a long time ago, and even back then, he'd nearly blown it. Memories of old days. More to the point, fifteen feet to the forward head. The older he got, the more he needed to keep track of that kind of thing.

The usual safety briefing. The seat belt is just like the one on your car, dummy, and if you really need it, Mommy will come buckle it up for you—but no booze for you! The bathrooms are fore and aft, and they're marked with pictures if you're too dumb to read. Dumbing down society was happening in Canada, too. *A pity,* John thought. Unless United flew only American citizens.

The flight was grossly ordinary, with nary a bump, taking hardly an hour before they touched down at O'Hare, named for a World War Two naval aviator who'd won the Medal of Honor before getting splashed, probably by friendly fire, which could kill you just as dead as the other sort. Clark wondered how hard it was for the pilot to find the right jetway, but then he'd probably made this flight before, maybe a hundred times. Now came the hard part, John realized. Where was Hadi going, and could he bag a seat on the same flight? A pity he couldn't just ask the bastard. He had to go through immigration, because America had gotten serious about controlling who came into the country. Really that meant tough enough that the bad guys had to devote maybe a whole minute of thought before sneaking in, but maybe it was something to stop the really dumb ones. But the dumb ones weren't much of a threat, were they?

That was far above his pay grade, however, and those who made such decisions rarely consulted the worker bees who live out where one's ass was on the betting line. That fact had started for Clark in Vietnam, when his name had been Kelly. So maybe stuff like that never changed. That was a frightening thought, but frightening things came with the territory, and he'd signed on to that more than thirty years earlier. The entry procedures were not even perfunctory. His passport wasn't even stamped, a considerable surprise. Another procedure change? Keep the ink from staining the clerk's hand, maybe?

"Okay, what's happening?" Granger asked over the secure line.

"Clark took the same flight as our friend," Jack replied. "We got a couple photos of him. With luck, he'll shadow him to where he's going."

Not likely, the operations boss at the other end thought. *Not enough troops, not enough resources.* Well, you couldn't do everything as a private corporation, and it kept the overhead down. "Okay, keep me posted. When will you guys be back?"

"We're booked on a flight into D.C. National; leaves in thirty minutes. Be back in the building about five-thirty or six, probably." Which amounted to a complete wasted day, unless you counted a couple of photos as a success, Jack thought. What the hell, it was more than what they'd had.

50

Clark was in the subterranean walkway from one terminal complex to another. Mostly moving walkways, like conveyor belts; it certainly looked long enough. He'd watched Hadi step out into the open air and have another smoke before coming back in, running through the metal detectors—miraculously, his marshal's badge did not trip it here—down into this lengthy tunnel, and then up the escalator to the outboard terminal, where it was time to go to work. Hadi turned left at the top. He'd gotten his gate assignment from an information monitor—without checking his ticket for the flight number. Did that make him a trained pro or just a guy with a good memory or a surfeit of confidence? Clark wondered. You pays your money and you takes your choice. At the top, Hadi turned left onto Concourse F. He was walking briskly. *Maybe in a hurry?* Clark wondered. If so, bad news for him. Sure enough, the subject turned to check a monitor, oriented himself, and angled to the left for Gate F-5, where he took a seat, looking as though he needed to relax. F-5 was a flight for . . . Las Vegas? McCarran International was a sizable airport with a huge number of connecting flights to Christ knew how many other destinations. Just one cutout for Hadi? Was that prudent? John wondered. *Hmm.* Who, if anyone, had trained this bird? A KGB type, or someone internal to his organization? Whatever the answer, the flight was leaving in fifteen minutes, not enough time for John to get back to the desk at Terminal 1 and get a ticket to allow him to follow. The tracking exercise would end at this point. *Damn.* He couldn't even make the effort to eyeball the guy too obviously, even to observe very closely. Hadi may have looked around, and might, therefore, recognize his face. He might have been trained by a pro, and he might have the ability Clark had for remembering faces that appeared and disappeared in the course of life. For a field spook, that was a survival skill of considerable importance. Clark walked to a gift shop and bought a PayDay candy bar, along with a Diet Coke, just allowing his eyes to trace around the concourse. Hadi was sitting, not even looking around for a smoking booth where people could indulge their bad habit behind glass. Maybe he could control his passions, John thought. Such people could be dangerous. But the flight was called then, first-class tickets first, and Hadi stood, walked to the jetway gate, and showed his ticket. He even smiled at the male clerk, who checked his ticket and waved him aboard the elderly DC-9 for a wide leather seat and free booze for his trip to Vegas, where people could indulge in all manner of bad habits to their hearts' content. John finished his candy bar and walked back to the tunnel entrance. As before, the down escalator seemed to go halfway to hell, and he blessed whatever architect had specified the moving walkways. Clark was old enough to appreciate it. He remembered not to frown at what he thought of as a blown mission. Partially blown, anyway. They knew things about this subject that they hadn't known before, including a photo. He liked to travel under a Jewish cover, almost clever but a little obvious. Jews and Arabs were genetic cousins, after all, and their religious beliefs were not all that disparate—furious as both were even to consider such a thought, of course. Christians, too, all People of the Book, so his Saudi friends had explained it to him once upon a time. But religious people generally did not commit murder. God might not agree. In any case, his current job was to fly back to The Campus. He waited for the jetway door to be closed and watched the twin-engine airliner back away from the terminal, then turn under its own power for the taxi out to the runway. Three hours to Vegas? Maybe a little less, over Iowa, Nebraska, and Wyoming, to the city that celebrated sin. *And on from there to where?* John wondered. Wherever it was, he wouldn't be finding out anytime soon. Well, this whole mission had been on the iffy side, and he couldn't be too disappointed that it had turned into a washout. And what the hell, they had some photos of the mutt. He found a counter that offered him a ticket back to BWI in ninety minutes. He called ahead to make sure someone would be waiting with a car.

Hadi, in seat 1D of his flight, considered the menu as he sipped his complimentary white wine—it was better in Italy, but that was no surprise—and he chided himself for an unseemly discrimination in his nose for wine. The ground below was mostly flat, with a few strangely green bull's-eyes, which, he'd learned, marked the rotary irrigation systems American farmers used in the prairie states. This area had once been called the Great American Desert by explorers. It was the world's breadbasket today, though other deserts, real ones, lay ahead, beyond the mountains. Such a large, strange country this was, full of strange people, most of them unbelievers. But they were people to be wary of, and so he had to watch himself and his conduct every minute, even more than he had in Italy. It was hard on a man never to relax, never to let down his guard. With luck he'd be able to relax when he met his friend, depending on the next stop in his flight. How strange that he'd never learned where the Emir lived. They'd been friends for many, many years. They'd even learned to ride horses together, at the same time and place, at a very young age, attended the same school, played and run together. But the wine took its toll, and he'd suffered through a long day. His eyes grew heavy, and he drifted off to sleep as night overtook the aircraft.

Clark boarded another airliner, took his first-class seat, and closed his eyes, not to sleep but to run his mind over the events of the day. What had he done? What things had he done wrong? What had he done right, and why had it not mattered?

The short version was manpower. The Caruso boys seemed competent enough, and Jack did fine, but that was no big surprise. The kid had some good instincts. Heredity, maybe. All in all, not a bad op, given how hastily it had been assembled. They'd known he was headed to Chicago. Better to have split into teams of two and then forwarded the photo electronically to make it easier to carry forward? Could they have done that? Technically possible, maybe, but just because it might have been possible didn't mean it would have worked. Stuff like this, you wanted multiple backups, because random chance could not be depended on to do anything but screw things up. Hell, carefully planned stuff could not be depended on, even with ample manpower composed of trained professionals. The enemy didn't even have to be professionals for random events to screw up the best-laid plans. Might be a good idea, he thought, to walk through the European missions with the twins, just to see how good their fieldcraft was. They looked good, but looking good was something fashion models could do. It came down to training and experience. Heavy on experience. You grew your own training out in the field, and experience was something he'd tried hard to teach new CIA officers down at The Farm in the Virginia Tidewater. He'd never learned how well that had gone. Some came back and quaffed beers with him and Chavez. But what about the kids who had *not* come back? What lessons were to be learned from them? You rarely heard those stories, because not coming back meant never coming back, a gold star on the right-side wall in the CIA atrium, and usually a blank spot in the book.

Improve intrateam communications, for starters, he thought. If they didn't have the experience to read minds, they damned well should have solid comm protocols. Hiring more troops would be a good idea, but that wasn't going to happen. The Campus was supposed to run small and smart. Maybe they had the ability to do that, but damned sure there were times when a lot of people could solve a lot of problems. But that wasn't going to happen.

Clark's plane landed softly at Baltimore-Washington International Airport. It took five minutes to taxi to gate D-3, allowing Clark to walk off quickly. He made a head call and walked down the concourse, hoping that someone would be waiting for him. It turned out to be Jack, who waved.

"I know what you look like," Clark said. "You don't have to let other people know that you know me."

"Hey, I mean—"

"I know what you mean. You never break fieldcraft until it's over your first beer at home, kid. Don't ever forget that."

"Got it. What did you learn?"

"He flew on to Vegas, and he's probably there now. Mainly I learned that we don't have enough troops to do anything important at The Campus," he concluded crossly.

"Yeah, well, we can't do what we do if we have government oversight, can we?"

"I suppose not, but there are advantages to being part of a larger organization, y'know?"

"Yeah. I guess we're kinda parasites on the body politic."

"I suppose. Was there any attempt to track the bird to where he went?"

Jack shook his head as they walked out of the concourse. "Nope."

"I'd bet he kept on going—maybe two or three more stops, but there's no telling."

"Why?"

"Complexity. Make it as hard for your adversary as possible. That's a basic principle in this life."

Outside McCarran International, Hadi was saying exactly the same thing to Tariq, who said, "We've discussed this at length. There is no danger that we know of. Our communications are as secure as money can buy, and no one has penetrated us, else we would not be here, would we?"

"What about Uda bin Sali and the others?" Hadi demanded.

"He died of a heart attack. We have all reviewed the official autopsy report."

"And the others?"

"Men die every day from heart trouble, even the elect of Allah," Tariq pointed out.

"Perhaps the Jews killed him, but the doctors in Rome said he died from a heart attack."

"Perhaps there is a way—a drug, perhaps—to make it appear that way."

"Perhaps." Tariq turned left to go into town. "But in that case, we need not fear the Israelis here."

"Perhaps," Hadi conceded. He was too tired from his long travel day for a serious disagreement. Too much time in the air, too much wine, and too little decent sleep for him to summon the intellectual energy. "Your car is clean?"

"We wash the car every three days. When we do that, we search it for listening devices of every sort."

"So how is he?"

"You will see for yourself in a few minutes. You will find him healthy and quite well, physically speaking. But you will also find it difficult to recognize him. The Swiss surgeons worked a miracle with his appearance. He could, if he wished, walk the streets here without fear of recognition."

Hadi took the opportunity to look out of the car. "Why here?" he asked tiredly.

"No one ever admits to living here, except for the thieves who own the hotel/casinos. The city is notably corrupt, rather as Beirut once was—or so my father liked to tell me. Much gambling, but his highness doesn't gamble with money."

"I know, just his life. More dangerous in its way, but all men die, don't they?"

"The local infidels act as though they have no fear of that. It is strange how many Christian churches there are here. People like to get married in this city—I do not understand why this is so, but it is. The Emir selected this city because of its anonymity. I think he was wise to do so. So many people come here to gamble and to sin against Allah. There is enough crime of the sort that keeps the local police concerned."

Tariq made a right-hand turn for the final approach to the Emir's country home, and Tariq thought of it. It was far more comfortable than the caves of Western Pakistan, much to Tariq's personal pleasure, and that of the remainder of the staff, Allah be praised. He slowed and flipped his turn signal to turn left. He and his colleagues obeyed every law that they knew of in America.

"This is it?"

"Yes," Tariq confirmed.

He'd chosen well, Hadi didn't say. The Emir might have chosen a better-defended dwelling, but that might well have attracted the interest of his neighbors, and been counterproductive in this age of helicopters and bomb-laden aircraft. On the approach to Las Vegas, the pilot had called attention to a large U.S. Air Force base just north of the city. Another clever move on his friend's part, to settle close to a major American military installation—on the face of it, not a good idea, but brilliant for that very reason. *His desire to live in the Infidel West but writ large,* Hadi thought in admiration. How long had he planned it? How had he arranged it? Well, that was why he'd come to lead the organization: his ability to see that which others could not see. He'd earned his place in the world, and in that place he had the ability—the right—to have his way with men . . . and women, according to the man behind the wheel. *All men have their needs, and their weaknesses,* Hadi told himself. That one wasn't particularly disabling. For his part, Hadi had partaken in some of the joys of Rome. Often enough that he felt no guilt for it. So his friend did the same. No surprise there.

The car pulled into the garage. One space was empty, he noted. So did he have another servant? He got out of his car, fetched his bag from the trunk, and walked toward the door.

"Hadi!" boomed the voice from the door to the house. The garage doors were already coming down.

"Effendi," Hadi called in return. The men embraced and kissed in the manner of their culture.

"How was your flight?"

"All four were fine but tiring." Hadi took the time to look him in the face. The voice made him more recognizable. The face did not. Saif Rahman Yasin was transformed. The nose, the hair, even the eyes somewhat— *Or were they?* he asked himself. Only the expression in them. Clearly he was pleased to see his childhood friend, and the mirth they contained was so different from his formal face seen on TV and in the newspapers. "You are well, my friend," Hadi said.

"It is a gentle, comfortable life I live here," the Emir explained with a rare smile. "Praise Allah, we have no hills to climb. There is much happiness in living under their noses, as they say."

"When I learned of this, I thought you mad, but now I can see your wisdom."

"Thank you." The Emir pulled him into the house. "You choose to travel as a Jew, do you not? That is well. There are many of them here."

"Is this city as corrupt as they say?"

"Much more so. The population is very transient. People here do not recognize anyone, except perhaps their closest friends; it is as Lebanon used to be."

"Or Bahrain still is?"

"That is far too close to home." He didn't have to explain. Many Saudis drove there in their chauffeured cars to enjoy the pleasures of the flesh, but too many of them might recognize his voice, if not his new face. The Saudi royal family wanted him as dead as the Americans did. Indeed, they'd set up viewing stands in Chop Chop Square in Riyadh for the infidels to see his last minutes with their mini-cams and other recording systems. There were many prices on his head. . . . And the American one was not nearly the highest. "Come. Let us find you a proper bed."

And Hadi followed him through the kitchen and into the house, thence left toward the bedroom wing.

"You are secure here?" Hadi asked.

"Yes, but in a few minutes I can be away. It is not perfect, but it is the best a man can arrange."

"Do you test your escape route?"

"Weekly."

"So it is for me in Italy."

"Rest!" the Emir said, opening the door to the bedroom. "Do you require anything?"

Hadi shook his head. "I could eat, but I need sleep. I will see you in the morning."

"Good night, my friend." A shake of the shoulder, and the Emir closed the door. The man had flown almost six thousand miles. He'd earned the right to be exhausted.

51

Bell and Granger were waiting in Hendley's office when Jack and Clark walked in. "Washed out in Chicago," Clark told them, falling into a swivel chair. "He flew as far as Las Vegas. After that, who can say? McCarran has flights to everywhere. Maybe L.A., San Francisco, hell, back to the East Coast, maybe."

"His traveling name?" Bell asked.

"Joel Klein. Jewish, would you believe? Makes sense, I suppose. I suppose we can surf the computers to see if he booked a flight on from there, but who's to say he doesn't have numerous other identities?"

"Already being checked," Granger assured him. "No hits yet. I'm fresh out of ideas."

"If I had to bet, I'd say he's bedded down somewhere, maybe scheduled to continue his travel regimen tomorrow. Not enough manpower, Rick. We need more bodies and more eyes to do this."

"We got what we got," Bell said.

"Yeah."

"There is another possibility," Jack said. "What if Las Vegas was his destination? Then what?"

"Damned scary thought," Granger replied. "It means we've got an operational URC cell here."

"Tell us about Peshawar," Hendley said a few minutes later.

Clark dug into his carry-on and laid Masood's drive on the desk. He gave the *Reader's Digest* condensed version of the trip. "Why they didn't toss the house I don't know," he said. "According to Masood, he copied everything he did for the URC. Have to assume the guy who helped them move was the Emir."

"For now we will." Hendley nodded to Bell. "Rick, can you get that down to Gavin? Have him send up the contents asap?" To Clark: "You want to call Mary Pat?"

"Already did. She's on her way."

Hendley picked up the phone and called the lobby. "Ernie, Gerry here. Got a visitor coming. Mary Pat Foley. Right, thanks."

Mary Pat appeared in Hendley's doorway forty minutes later. "Nice digs," she said. "Looks like I'm in the wrong business." She walked across the carpet and shook Hendley's hand. "Good to see you again, Gerry."

"You too, Mary Pat. This is Rick Bell and Sam Granger. And I think you know Jack Ryan." More handshakes, and a surprised look from Mary Pat. "Keeping up the family legacy?" she asked Jack.

"It's early days yet, ma'am."

"Mary Pat."

Hendley said, "Have a seat." She took the chair next to Clark. "You look tired, John."

"I always look this way. It's the lighting."

"Let's get on the same page," Hendley said.

Clark gave Mary Pat the same recap. When he was done, she let out a low whistle. "A mover. That tells us something. You don't need somebody like Masood unless you're leaving the region."

Granger said, "We should have the hard drive contents shortly."

"It's not going to tell us where he is," Mary Pat predicted. "The Emir's too slippery for that. Probably used more than one mover. Used them to hopscotch himself somewhere he could drop off the radar. Best we're going to get is close."

"Which is a damned sight closer than we are now," Rick Bell observed.

While Biery and his geeks dug into Masood's drive and Clark and Chavez caught a power nap on the break-room couches, Jack turned his attention to the flash drive Ding had taken off one of the Tripoli tangos. Having determined that it contained stego-encoded images, he and Biery had decided to try a brute-force algorithm crack, with a free steak dinner for whoever got there first. Busy as he was with Masood's drive, Jack felt confident in his head start.

After two hours of crunching, one of the algorithms struck gold and an image began depixelating on his screen. It was a large file, almost six megabytes, so the decoding would take a few minutes. He picked up the phone and called Granger. Two minutes later Jack had an audience of eight standing over his shoulder, watching the monitor as the photo resolved.

"What the hell is that?" Brian asked, leaning in.

The photo was blurred and desaturated of color. Jack imported it into Photoshop and washed the file through some filters, working the contrast and brightness until the image came clear.

There was ten seconds of silence.

The 8×10 image was done in 1940s pinup style: a dark-haired woman in a white cotton peasant skirt, sitting on a bale of hay, her legs crossed demurely. She was naked from the waist up, her impossibly massive breasts drooping to her thighs.

"Tits," Sam Granger said. "My God, Jack, you've discovered tits."

"Oh, shit," Jack muttered.

Everyone burst out laughing.

Dominic said, "Jack, you little pervert . . . I had no idea."

Then Brian: "So, Jack, exactly how much 'depixelation' do you do in your spare time?"

More laughter.

"Very funny." Jack groaned.

Once the laughter died down, Hendley said, "Okay, let's break it up and let Mr. Hefner carry on. Nice work, Jack."

At four o' clock, Jack woke up Clark and Chavez. "Showtime, guys. Conference room in five minutes."

They showed up in four minutes, both armed with an extra-large cup of coffee. Everyone else was already seated: Hendley, Granger, Bell, Rounds, Dominic, and Mary Pat. Clark and Chavez took their seats. Rounds took the lead. He looked up from the summary Biery had sent up a few minutes earlier.

"A lot of this is nuts-and-bolts stuff that may help us down the road. The big-picture items are three. He picked up the remote and aimed it at the forty-two-inch wide-screen TV. The frontspiece of a passport appeared on the screen. "That's what our guy looked like at some point in the last six to nine months."

There was ten seconds of silence around the table.

"Bears a resemblance to the few pics we've got of him," Bell said.

Rounds said, "Forged French passport. High-quality work. The stamps, the backing, the threading—all perfect. According to Masood's hard drive, the Emir used this three months ago. Peshawar to Dushanbe, Tajikistan, then to Ashgabat, Volgograd, then Saint Petersburg. Then nothing."

"That's as far as Masood took him," Dominic added.

"Can't be his final destination," Jack replied. "Another mover took over, maybe?"

Clark said, "If you average out his hops, he was heading generally northwest. Extend that a little and you're into Finland or Sweden."

"Sweden," Mary Pat said. "The plastic-surgery thing?"

"Maybe," Granger said.

"The Hlasek Air thing?" Chavez wondered aloud.

"That, too, maybe. If Saint Petersburg was as far as Masood took him, that means he dumped the French passport for a new one. If he went into Sweden or Finland on a new one, he wouldn't be able to land anywhere after that—at least not legitimately."

"Explain that." This from Hendley.

"He couldn't use his old face for the next passport, and there's no way he gets one all bandaged up, so he sits still until all the swelling and bruising are gone, *then* gets the passport."

"Let's back up a second," Jack said. "Who took over as the mover in Saint Petersburg? That's the question we need to ask."

"Needle in a haystack," Bell said.

"Maybe not," Mary Pat came back. "Masood was ex-ISI. The URC chose him because he was a pro at it. They'd want the same thing in Russia. Maybe we're looking for ex-SVR, or ex-KGB."

"Or GRU," Rounds added. "Military intelligence."

"Right."

"Any way to narrow down the list, Mary Pat?" Clark asked.

"Maybe. It's a pretty specialized skill. Probably would take somebody who handled illegals. Lot of those still around, though."

"How many of them are dead, though?" Jack said. "In Saint Petersburg. And in the last four months. They probably would've killed Masood a lot earlier if he hadn't gone to ground. He was a loose end. The Russian mover would be, too."

"Good thinking, Jack," Hendley said. "Think you can work with that?" he asked Mary Pat.

"Give me a few hours."

She was back from the NCTC in two. "Wasn't all that hard, really. Jack, you nailed it. Last month in Saint Petersburg, Yuriy Beketov, former KGB officer, Directorate S—Illegals—of the First Chief Directorate. Shot dead in a Chechnyan restaurant. The Saint Petersburg cops put it on the Interpol wire. I've got a couple people trying to tease out some more details, but Beketov seems to fit."

"Until then, let's play with it," Hendley said. "Say he goes to Switzerland, or Sweden or Finland, for surgery."

"Sweden gets my vote, too," Rounds said. "He'd want something high-end, very private, with select clientele. A lot more of those in Sweden than Finland. It's a place to start."

"Google," Jack said.

It was nearly nine at night when they found what they needed. Jack pushed back from his laptop and ran his hands through his hair. "Well, I'll give them this. They're consistent. Ruthless and consistent."

"Enlighten us," Clark said.

"Three weeks ago, the Orrhogen Clinic in Sundsvall. Burned to the ground with the managing director inside. Something else: Sundsvall is only about seventy-five miles north of Söderhamn. If Brian and Dominic hadn't shown up, it's a safe bet Rolf the mechanic would be dead right now."

"Okay, so the Emir has the surgery, spends a few days recuperating, then leaves," Granger said. "Chances are halfway good he hasn't got a passport. He'd need a private charter, a private airport, and a pilot who doesn't mind getting a little dirty." Hendley considered this. "How exactly would he do it?"

"Rolf gave us the answer," Dominic replied. "Duplicate transponder code."

"Right," Jack replied. "Hlasek switches off the first transponder code, drops off the radar, turns on the second transponder code, and they've got themselves a new plane."

"That kind of thing would certainly get written down somewhere," Rounds observed. "Do we have an in with the FAA or Transport Canada?"

"No," Granger replied. "Doesn't mean we can't, though." He picked up the phone, and two minutes later Gavin was in the conference room.

Jack explained what they were looking for. "Doable?"

Gavin snorted. "The FAA's firewalls are a joke. Transport Canada's not any better. Give me a half-hour."

Good as his word, thirty minutes later Biery called up to the conference room. Hendley put him on speakerphone. "In the time frame you gave me, eighteen flights dropped off radar in either U.S. or Canadian airspace. Sixteen were nothing—operator error—one was a Cessna that crashed outside Albany, and one, a Dassault Falcon 9000, that dropped off altogether. The pilot reported a problem with its landing gear on its way into Moose Jaw. A couple minutes later they lost it on radar."

"Where's Moose Jaw?" Dominic asked.

"Canada. Due north, about where North and South Dakota meet," Jack said.

"There's something else," Biery said. "I did a little cross-hacking keyword search between Transport Canada, the FAA, and the NTSB. Three days after Moose Jaw lost the Falcon, a fisherman off the coast of California found an FDR—flight data recorder. According to the NTSB, the box belonged to a Gulfstream—the one that's supposedly still sitting in a hangar outside Söderhamn. Problem is, Dassault planes are equipped with prototype FDR. It's designed to break free of the airframe when it detects a certain kinetic threshold. And it's got a float and a beacon—Gulfstream boxes only have a beacon. The box they found belonged to Hlasek's Falcon."

Hendley let out a breath and looked around the table. "He's here. The sonofabitch is hiding right under our noses."

Clark nodded. "The question is, what? It would have to be something big to bring him out."

52

"Our friend arrived safely?" Ibrahim asked. Digital clicks occasionally interrupted his subordinate's voice.

"Yes," the Emir replied. "He left again yesterday. I've read the details of your plan. Tell me where things stand."

"We're ready. Simply give the word and we can be in country within seventy-two hours."

Talking directly to the commander of his ground team had

been an impromptu decision on his part, and certainly dangerous, especially given his own precarious circumstances, but
the risk was warranted. The communication method was as
secure as any, a homemade encryption package they had
married to the house's VoIP—Voice over Internet Protocol—
computer-to-computer Skype account.

Having decided to proceed with Ibrahim's operation, the
Emir wanted a final discussion, as a measure of reassurance
not only for himself but also for Ibrahim. If he should lose
his life on the mission his true reward would come in paradise,
but here on earth he was still a soldier going into battle, and
soldiers often needed praise and encouragement.

"How many times have you been there?" the Emir asked.

"Four times. Twice for recruitment and twice for reconnaissance."

"Tell me more about your contact."

"His name is Cassiano Silva. Brazilian by birth, raised in the
Catholic faith. He converted to Islam six years ago. He is one
of the faithful, of that I'm sure, and he's never failed to
provide what I've asked of him."

"Tariq tells me your recruitment of him was nicely done."

"Western intelligence calls it a 'false flag.' He believes I'm
with Kuwait's intelligence service, with connections to OPEC's
Market Analysis Division. I thought he would find the idea
of industrial espionage more . . . palatable."

"I'm impressed, Ibrahim," the Emir said, meaning it.
"You've shown good instincts."

"Thank you, sir."

"And your plan . . . you're confident it is feasible?"

"I am, but I'd like to remain cautious until I am on the
ground. On the surface, all the parts fit together nicely."

So he'd let Ibrahim go forward with his plan and know it
would be the first domino in a series, at the end of which
awaited a truly world-changing event. But that was in the

future—not far in the future but far enough that focusing on it to the exclusion of the smaller pieces could harm the whole.

"How many casualties do you expect?" the Emir asked.

"That is impossible to say at this time. Hundreds, perhaps. As you said, though, those numbers are largely irrelevant."

"True, but dead bodies on television have a fearsome effect, which is something that will work to our benefit later. How long will your final reconnaissance take?"

"Five to six days."

"And after that?"

"Forty-eight to seventy-two hours to the event itself."

The Emir brought his mental calendar to the forefront of his mind. Juggling more than one operation as he was, he would have to hold off on final approval until they heard back from the Russian teams at least. The other pieces in Dubai and Dakar were in place and standing by. The cornerstone, of course, their lovely Tatar girl, could be hurried only so much. Tariq was confident she was moving at an appropriate pace, and that would have to do for now, but in the back of his mind he had to consider alternatives should she fail. Still, they had to be ready to step in. A dangerous gambit, that. They might be able to disguise their actions or put in place some delaying tactics, but violence—especially the kind of violence that would likely be required—would without a doubt draw the attention of the authorities.

If such action became necessary, could they stay far enough ahead of the authorities to complete Lotus?

"You have final approval," the Emir said.

Their hunch that the Emir was in all likelihood already in the United States, hiding somewhere between the Dakotas and California, was quickly followed by the realization that there was little they could do to confirm the hypothesis. True, they knew Shasif Hadi, flying under the alias Joel

434

Klein, had been headed for Las Vegas when they lost his trail, but that meant nothing. The Klein passport hadn't subsequently shown up in the system, which could mean he went no farther than Las Vegas, or it could mean he'd simply followed the rules of tradecraft and dumped Klein for yet another alias. Jack's peel-back of Hadi's activities had shown a lot of travel to the Persian Gulf states, Western Europe, and South America—which would necessitate a number of CONUS layovers. Short of distributing Hadi's photo to Las Vegas law enforcement, there was little they could do but continue to work the problem with what they had in hand.

"Whoa!" Jack Ryan Jr. said from his cubicle.

"What?" Dominic called from the conference room, where the daily skull session had just started.

"Hang on, I'm coming in." He tapped a few keys, sending the file to the conference room's AV node, then walked in and picked up the remote from the table.

"You look like a teenager who's seen his first boob," Brian said. "What's up?"

"I was trolling one of the URC websites when I came across this." He aimed the remote at the forty-two-inch monitor on the wall. After a few seconds, three side-by-side images appeared on the flat screen, the first showing a man hanging from the neck in a featureless room; the second showing the same man lying on the floor, his severed head sitting beside him; in the third, the man's severed head was bracketed by his severed feet.

"Jesus Christ, that's some serious shit," Brian said.

"Which website, Jack?" Rounds asked.

He recited the URL, then said, "It's a URC hub, but up until now it's been all propaganda—'rah-rah, stick it to the infidel, we've got them on the run' kind of stuff."

"Well, this sure as hell ain't a pep talk," Ding Chavez said.

"It's punishment," Clark said, staring at the screen.

"What're you thinking?"

"Hanging is a pretty standard execution technique for them, and the beheading is a little extra humiliation—something out of the Koran, as I recall—but the feet . . . That's the real message?"

"What, he tried to run?" Dominic asked. "Leave the URC?"

"No, he made a move and the higher-ups weren't happy about it. Saw this in Lebanon in '82. Some offshoot of Hamas, I can't remember the name, blew up a bus in Haifa. A week later the leaders were found the same way: hanged, beheaded, their feet chopped off."

"Hell of a way to make your point," Chavez said.

Rounds asked, "Jack, where's the site run out of?"

"That's the kicker," he responded. "It's Benghazi."

"Bingo," said Dominic. "This thing coming so close on top of the Tripoli embassy . . . How much you wanna bet we're looking at the fallout from an unsanctioned mission?"

There were no takers at the table.

"What if it's more than punishment?" Jack offered.

"Explain," Rounds said.

Clark answered, "It's a warning. That Lebanon thing . . . Two weeks later, Hamas tried to ram a car bomb into the British embassy about a block from the bus explosion. It fell through because their intel people were still cranking away on the bus bombing."

"Same principle could be at work here," Jack said. "They're telling the other cells to mind their manners."

"Yeah, but in favor of what?" Chavez asked.

53

The gravel roadway leading away from the beach looked almost pristine, probably because there was little, if any, traffic on it, and not even much in the way of animals to trample on it, and the harsh weather either killed or stunted anything that tried to grow.

Musa gave their captain, Vitaliy, a final wave, then nodded solemnly at Idris, whom he'd ordered to stay behind. However unlikely, if the captain tried to leave before they returned, Idris would kill the two Russians. Piloting the boat back to port without them would be a challenge, but Allah would show them the way.

Musa climbed into the cab's passenger seat. Fawwaz, already behind the wheel, started the engine while Numair and Thabit climbed into the bed.

"Go," Musa ordered. "The sooner we finish what we came to do, the sooner we can leave this cursed place."

Fawwaz shoved the gearshift into drive and started up the hill.

The lighthouse and its neighboring hut were only a kilometer away, maybe five hundred meters uphill. Vitaliy and Vanya sat in the wheelhouse swivel chairs and watched their progress through binoculars, drinking tea and smoking cigarettes, and wishing for more food, while the music on the radio got worse. Fred's watchdog stood at the rail, watching them both. To the east was kelly-green tundra, and the view was as featureless as what a mouse might see when contemplating a green carpet.

Vitaliy watched as two of the charter party stepped out of

437

the truck, then used hand signals to direct the driver to back up to the steel shed.

Vitaliy had never seen one of the generators that ran the lighthouses. He'd heard they contained radioactive material, though how they worked was beyond his knowledge. He'd heard also that some had disappeared, but if so, it hadn't happened to an important lighthouse on his part of the coast. As far as he knew, they might well be small diesel generators. The lightbulb on the house was usually a small one, hardly ever more than one hundred watts, a fact that surprised—indeed, amazed—those who didn't know about it. The Fresnel lenses focused the light into a small, pencil-thin beam whose effective range was determined by the height of the house, and any light showed up brightly on a dark night. Lighthouses, he told himself, were an obsolete leftover from earlier times, hardly necessary anymore in the age of electronic aids. So what damage might he be doing, really? His charter party would themselves finance his acquisition of a modern GPS system, probably one of the new Japanese ones that sold for five or six hundred euros, cheaper than the new car he coveted. And what the hell did it matter?

That this could kill thousands of people never occurred to him for a moment.

It took four hours, far less than Fred had suggested. It might have gone faster still if they'd simply demolished the corrugated shed, but evidently they didn't want to do that. The lighthouse would look entirely normal in daylight (with the sun fully up and out, it was difficult to tell if the light was on or off), and at night, few came into this gulf to notice. And even if they did, so many things in Russia didn't operate as designed that one more would hardly be seen as headline news. Two cups of tea and five cigarettes after they'd started, the truck rumbled back to life and started driving down the gravel driveway to the boat. It wasn't until they reversed direction to back in that Vitaliy saw something dangling from the crane, about a meter, roughly rectangular, but with curved edges that suggested a cylinder inside, maybe the size of an oil drum. So that was a lighthouse battery? He'd wondered what they looked like, and wondered how they worked. It seemed awfully large to power such a small lightbulb. That made it typically Soviet, of course: large, clunky, but generally functional.

One of the party walked backward behind the crane truck, guiding it back onto the boat, and after three hours, when the tide was again right, it was time to raise the ramp and depart. The man in the truck's cab worked the crane controls to lower the generator to the deck. The colleagues didn't secure it in place. They were not seamen, but they had a lot of euros.

Vitaliy set the engines in reverse and backed away into deeper water, then spun the wheel to head back northwest for the Kara Strait. So he'd earned his two thousand or so euros. In the process he'd burn perhaps a thousand of that in diesel fuel—actually less, but his charter party didn't know that—and the rest was wear and tear on his T-4 landing craft, and his own valuable time, of course. So a task halfway completed. On getting back to port, he'd unload them and let them go wherever it was they wanted to go. He didn't even wonder where that might be. He didn't care enough to want to know. He checked his chronometer. Fourteen hours exactly. So he'd not make port before the end of the day, one more day to bill them for, and that was fine with him.

Unaware that there was a complementary mission under way three hundred miles away, Adnan and his men were preparing to leave the relative comfort of the boat. The captain, Salychev, was maneuvering the Halmatic into a cove on the island's western coast. Adnan stood on the afterdeck, watching the snow-encrusted arms of the inlet close in around them until the passage was no wider than a kilometer. The fog continued to build over the water's surface until Adnan could catch only fleeting glimpses of the cliffs, erosion-slashed brown escarpments studded with scree and boulders.

The Halmatic's diesel engine chugged softly while in the wheelhouse Salychev whistled to himself. Adnan walked forward and stepped inside.

"How far are we from the settlement—"

"Belushya Guba," Salychev finished for him. "Not far. Just up the coast—a hundred, hundred-fifty kilometers. Don't worry yourself. The patrols don't come into the coves; they stick to the shoreline. Might hear them if the wind is right, but this close to land, their navigation radars get jumbled. Couldn't see us unless they bumped into us."

"Were there detonations in this area?"

"Some, but that was back in '60 or '61. Small ones, too. No more than fifteen kilotons. Just babies, nothing to worry about. Now, up the coast, maybe three hundred kilometers north of Belushya Guba, is Mityushev. That's where they did a lot of them. Dozens upon dozens, all in the hundreds of kilotons, a couple of megatons, too. If you want to see what the moon looks like, that's the place to go."

"You've been there?"

"Offshore I have. Not enough money in the world could get me into those bays and channels. No, this place we're headed is paradise compared to Mityushev."

"It's a wonder anything lives here."

"Everything is relative. You've heard of the Pak Mozg, yes?"

"No."

"The English translation is 'brain crab.' It's supposed to be about half a meter tall, with a shell that's split along the bottom and its nervous system exposed, sort of hanging out the gap in the shell."

"You're joking with me."

Salychev shrugged. "No. I've never seen one, but I've got a friend who swears he did."

Adnan waved his hand dismissively. "Nonsense. How long until we reach the shipyard?"

"Two hours, give or take. Going to be dark not long after that, so you'll have to wait until morning. Don't want to be stomping around in the dark."

"No."

"You never did say exactly what you're after. Samples, right?"

"Excuse me?"

"Soil and rock samples. That's what most of you types come here for: dirt. Testing it for whatever."

"That's right," Adnan replied. "Dirt."

54

The one drawback might be that people would notice the cars coming in and out.

Arnie came in first. Former President Ryan met him and walked him into the living room.

"Ready?" the former Chief of Staff asked.

"Not sure," Jack admitted.

"Well, Jack, if you have any doubts, you'd better exorcise them today. Do you want four more years of Ed Kealty in the White House?"

"Hell, no," Jack replied almost automatically. Then he thought it over again. Was he so arrogant that he thought *he* was the projected savior of the United States of America? Such moments of introspection came quickly to him. He wasn't one to measure his ego on the Richter scale or power-of-ten notation. The campaign to come would not be fun in any respect. "Here's the problem: My strength is national security matters," Ryan said. "I'm not an expert on domestic affairs."

"Kealty is—or at least that's the image he projects. He's got chinks in his armor, Jack, and we'll find them. And all *you* have to do is to persuade two hundred million American voters that you're a better man than he is."

"You're not asking much," Ryan groused. "A lot of things to fix." *A hell of a lot of things to fix,* he added to himself. "Okay, who's first?"

"George Winston and some of his Wall Street friends. George'll be your finance chairman."

"What will this cost?"

"North of a hundred million dollars. More than you can afford, Jack."

"Do these people know what they're buying?" Ryan asked.

"I'm sure George explained it to them. You'll have to back that up, of course. Hey, look on the bright side. Your administration didn't have much in the way of corruption. Reporters sniffed around plenty looking, but nobody ever found much."

"Jack, this guy's a loser," George Winston announced, to general agreement around the dining room table. "The country needs somebody different. You, for example."

"Question is, will you come back in?" Ryan asked.

"I've served my time," the former Secretary of the Treasury replied.

"I tried saying that, too, but Arnie isn't buying."

"Goddamn it, we got the tax system all fixed until that dickhead went and fucked it all up again—and he chopped revenue doing it!" Winston emphasized in some disgust. Raising tax rates invariably decreased revenues as soon as accountants got to work on the new code. The new and "fair" tax code was a godsend to the tax-avoidance community.

"What about Iraq?" Tony Bretano asked, changing directions. The former CEO of TRW had been Ryan's chosen Secretary of Defense.

"Well, like it or not, we're stuck with it," Ryan admitted. "Question is, can we smart our way out of it? Smarter than Kealty's being, at least."

"When Mary Diggs gave his speech two years back, he damned near got himself shot." General Marion Diggs had clobbered the military of the United Islamic Republic during his tour as Army chief of staff, but his observations about more recent conflicts had been totally ignored by the new administration. Diggs's successors in the Pentagon had bowed to White House orders and done what they'd been told to do. It was a common-enough failing of senior military officers and wasn't the least bit new. The price for many of the fourth star was to have your balls removed. Most of them were not old enough to have served in Vietnam. They hadn't seen friends and classmates die for political misjudgment, and the lessons inflicted on the previous class of officers had been lost in the process of something called "progress." That Ed Kealty had dissolved two complete light-infantry divisions, then walked into a conflict that cried aloud for light-infantry formations, was something the news media had almost totally ignored. Besides, tanks were pretty things to photograph.

"I'll say this for you, Tony. You always listened to advice," Ryan told him.

"Helps to know what you don't know. I'm a good engineer, but I don't know it all yet. This guy who took my old office is occasionally wrong, but he's never in doubt." Former Secretary Bretano had just described the most dangerous person on the planet. "Jack, I have to tell you now, I won't be coming back.

443

My wife's sick. Breast cancer. We're hoping they caught it early enough, but the jury's still out on that."

"Who's your doc?" Ryan asked.

"Charlie Dean. UCLA. He's pretty good, they tell me," Bretano answered.

"Wish you luck, pal. If Cathy can help, let us know, okay?" Ryan had used his wife for numerous medical referrals over the years, and unlike most political figures, he didn't figure that everybody with an M.D. after his name was the same, at least in treating other people.

"I will, thanks." The news had a sobering effect on the meeting, in any case. Valerie Bretano, a vivacious mother of three, was well liked by just about everyone.

"What about the announcement?" van Damm asked.

"Yeah, gotta do that, don't I?"

"Unless you want a stealth campaign. Kinda hard to win that way," Arnie observed. "Want me to get Callie Weston to gin up a speech for you?"

"She's good with words," Ryan acknowledged. "When will I have to do it?"

"Sooner the better. Start framing the issues."

"I agree," Winston said. "He doesn't know how to hit above the belt. Any bad baggage, Jack?"

"Nothing I know of—and that doesn't mean nothing I remember. If I've ever broken the law, they'll have to prove it to me, *and* a jury."

"Good to hear that," Winston observed. "I believe you, Jack, but remember the devil's advocate. Lots of them in Washington."

"What about Kealty? What dirty laundry does he have around?"

"A lot," Arnie answered. "But you can only use that weapon with care. Remember, he has the ear of the press. Unless you have a videotape, they'll apply a hellacious reality test to it, and they'll try to ricochet it back on you. I can help a little with that. Leave the leaks to me, Jack, and the less you know about the process, the better."

Not for the first time, Ryan found himself wondering why van Damm was so faithful a vassal to him. He was so far into the political system that he did and said things Jack would never really understand. If he were the babe in the woods, then Arnie van Damm was his nanny. Useful things, nannies.

55

The diesels chugged monotonously away as the landing craft headed back west. Vitaliy stood at the wheel, keeping a loose eye on the gyrocompass, watching the water slide by the blunt bow and down the sides. Not another ship or even a fishing boat in sight. It was mid-afternoon. The truck was back in its place. The beige-colored gadget they'd taken—*stolen?* he wondered. *Well, probably yes*—sat on the rusted steel deck. He'd have to scrape and paint it before the weather got too cold for that. Painting in freezing air was time wasted. Even if it dried, it would just flake off. *Have to paint soon,* he told himself. Vanya would bitch about it. As a former seaman in the Soviet Navy, he regarded such maintenance as an insult to his manhood. But Vanya didn't own the boat, and Vitaliy did, and that was that. The charter party was relaxing, smoking their cigarettes and sipping at their tea. Strange that they didn't drink vodka. He troubled himself to get the good stuff, not the bootleg trash made from potatoes. Vitaliy indulged himself in his drinking. Only proper vodka, made from grain. Sometimes he went overboard and drank Starka, the brown vodka once drunk only by the Politburo and local party bosses. But that time was gone—forever gone? Only time would tell, and for now he would not trouble his insides with bootleg liquor. Vodka remained the one thing his country still did well—better than any other country in the world. *Nasha lusche,* he told himself—*Ours is best*—an ancient Russian prejudice, though this one was factual. What these barbarians didn't drink, he'd account for by himself soon enough.

The chart table showed his position. He'd really have to get that GPS navigation system. Even up here, there was no substitute for knowing your exact position at all times, because the flat, black waters did not reveal what lay only a meter beneath . . . *Too much daydreaming,* he chided himself. A seaman was supposed to be alert at all times. Even when he was aboard the only vessel in view on a flat, calm sea.

Vanya appeared at his side.

"Engines?" the owner asked his mate.

"Purring like kittens." Rather loud kittens, of course, but smooth and regular for all that. "The Germans designed them well."

"And you maintain them properly," Vitaliy noted approvingly.

"I would not want to lose engine power out here. I am here as well, Comrade Captain," he added. Besides, the job paid well enough. "Want me to spell you at the wheel?"

"Fair enough," Vitaliy said, stepping back.

"What did they want that thing for?"

"Maybe they have large flashlights where they come from," Vitaliy suggested.

"Nobody's that strong," Vanya objected, with a belch of laughter.

"Maybe they want to set up their own lighthouse where they live, and that battery thing is too expensive to buy."

"What do you suppose it costs?"

"Not a thing, if you have the right truck," Vitaliy observed.

"It doesn't even have any warning stickers on it. Not about taking it anyway."

"I wouldn't want it under my pillow. That's an atomic generator."

"Is that so?" Vitaliy had never been briefed on how the generator operated.

"Yes. It has the triple-triangle sign on the right side. I'm not going near the damned thing," Vanya announced,

"Hmph," Vitaliy grunted from the chart table. Whatever it was, the charter party must have known, and *they* were close enough to it. How dangerous could it be, then? But he decided not to get overly close to it. Radioactive stuff. You couldn't see or feel what it did. That's what made it frightening. Well, if they wanted to play with it, it was up to them. He remembered the old Soviet Navy joke: *How do you tell a Northern Fleet sailor? He glows in the dark.* Certainly he'd heard all manner of stories about the men who'd been sent to serve on the atomic submarines. Miserable work, and as the crew of *Kursk* had discovered to their sorrow, they were still dangerous. *No, what sort of madman goes to sea on a ship that's* supposed *to sink?* he asked himself. Plus a power plant that sent out invisible poisons. It took much to make him shudder, but this thought managed to do it. A diesel engine might not be as powerful, but it didn't try to kill you just for walking by it. Well, fifteen meters away from that battery. It ought to be safe. His charter party was only five meters away, and they looked comfortable enough.

"What do you think, Vanya?" the owner asked.

"That battery thing? I'm not going to worry. Too much, at least." His sleeping accommodations were aft and below the wheelhouse. Not an educated man, Vanya was clever enough with machines and their personalities.

Vitaliy looked at the steel bulkhead forward of the wheel. It was steel, after all, and seven or eight millimeters thick.

Enough to stop a bullet. Surely that was enough to stop radiation, wasn't it? Well, you couldn't worry about everything.

It was just past sunset when they arrived in the harbor, where things were shutting down. At the big-ship quay a ro-ro ship was about half loaded with cargo boxes for the oil fields to the east, and the longshoremen were walking back to their homes in anticipation of finishing up loading the next day, and waterfront bars were cleaning tables for the usual evening business. All in all, a normal sleepy evening for what was, mostly, a sleepy port. Vitaliy eased his boat into the dock, the one with a ramp for loading trucks and trailers onto boats such as his. The dock looked unattended, as was normal, the dockmaster doubtless on his way to one of the bars to drink his dinner.

"Days getting shorter, Captain," Vanya observed, standing left of the wheel. In another few weeks, they'd hardly see the sun at all, and it would be their winter maintenance period, with nobody chartering their craft. Even the polar bears would be looking for dens in which to sleep out the bitter winter, while humans did much the same, helped along the way by vodka. And one lighthouse would be dark all through the winter, not that it mattered all that much.

"So we can sleep longer, eh, Vanya?"

Always a good way to spend your time, the deckhand thought.

The charter party was still in the well deck, standing by their truck. Not overly excited about getting back to port, Vitaliy saw. Well, they were businesslike, and that was fine with him. He had half his charter fee in his pocket, and the rest of the cash would join it soon enough, and maybe he would buy the GPS system to ease his navigation, if he could get a good deal for it. Yuriy Ivanov should have a goodly supply of the gadgets at his chandlery, and for a bottle of Starka, maybe he could get a decent bargain in what was still largely a barter economy.

"Stand by the engines, Vanya."

"As you say, Comrade Captain," the deckhand responded, heading aft and below.

He'd just beach his craft, Vitaliy decided. The ramp was concrete covered with dirt, and his boat was made for that sort of thing. He carefully lined up and moved it at three or four knots, just about right. The light was fading, but not that fast.

"Stand by," he said over the intercom.

"Standing by," Vanya replied the same way.

Vitaliy's left hand found the throttle but didn't move it quite yet. *Thirty meters, approach gently,* he told himself. *Twenty meters.* His peripheral vision showed only a fishing boat, sitting idle alongside, with nobody in sight. *Just about . . . now.*

It was an awful noise, the sort to set a man's teeth on edge, and his steel bottom grated on the ramp, but soon enough the noise stopped, and Vitaliy chopped the throttles back to zero/idle. And the trip and charter were complete.

"Finished with engines, Vanya."

"Yes, Comrade Captain. Shutting down." And the rumble stopped.

Vitaliy pulled the wheelhouse ramp-release handle, and the bow ramp fell slowly to the dock. With that done, he walked down to the well deck. The charter party walked to him.

"Thank you, Captain," their leader said with a smile. He spoke in English, which was accented, though Vitaliy didn't really notice.

"All is satisfactory?"

"Yes," the foreigner answered. He spoke in another language to one of his friends, but Vitaliy didn't understand it. It wasn't English and wasn't Russian. It's hard to identify a language you don't speak yourself, and as the old joke went, it was Greek to the captain. One party member got into the truck and started it up, then backed it ashore, its cargo dangling from the A-frame crane on the flatbed. In the diminishing light, the triple-triangle radiation-warning label was unusually bright, which was probably intentional. A moment later another truck appeared on the dock, and the former Army truck backed to it. Another member of the charter party activated the crane controls, lifting, then lowering the cargo into the second truck's cargo area. Whoever these people were, they were reasonably efficient. One must have used a cell phone to call ahead, Vitaliy speculated.

"So here is your money," the leader said, handing over an envelope.

Vitaliy took it, opened it, and counted off the bills. Two thousand euros, not a bad compensation for what had been a simple enough job. And enough to buy the GPS system, plus some Starka, and a hundred for Vanya, of course.

"Thank you," Vitaliy said politely, taking his hand. "If you need me again, you know how to contact me."

"I may come by tomorrow, say, about ten in the morning?"

"We'll be here," Vitaliy promised. They'd have to start painting the deckhouse, and tomorrow was as good a day as any other.

"Then I will see you," the leader promised. Then they shook hands, and he walked ashore.

Onshore, he talked to a companion, speaking now in his native language. "Tomorrow at ten," he told his most senior subordinate.

"And if the port is busy?"

"We'll just do it inside," he explained.

"What time do we meet the plane?"

"Tomorrow at noon."

"Excellent."

They showed up just before ten a.m., Vitaliy saw. With the rest of his money, he hoped. Drove a different car this day. A

Japanese one. They were taking Russia over. Too many of his countrymen still disliked German hardware, a lingering attitude that probably came less from history than from the war movies that the Russian film industry turned out like cigarette packs.

He was wearing a parka, loose enough for a sweater underneath, and he walked up to the boat with a smile. So, yes, maybe he did have a bonus for him. People usually smiled before giving money over.

"Good morning, Captain," he called, coming into the wheelhouse. He looked around. Not much activity to be seen, except over at the big-ship pier, where they were on-loading cargo boxes, half a kilometer away. "Where is your mate?"

"Below, tinkering with the motors."

"Nobody else around?" he asked with some surprise.

"No, we maintain our own craft," Vitaliy said, reaching for his cup of tea. He didn't make it. The 9-millimeter round went into his back without warning and transited his heart, back to front, before exiting the chest and his coat. He dropped to the steel deck, hardly grasping what had happened, before he lost consciousness for the last time.

Then the leader of the erstwhile charter party walked down the ladder to the engine room, where Vanya, as reported, was working on the manifold for the starboard engine. He hardly looked up from his tools and never saw the gun come up and fire. Two shots this time, right into the chest, from a range of three meters. When he became certain that his target was dead, Musa pocketed the pistol and walked back up. Vitaliy's body was facedown on the deck. Musa checked the carotid pulse, and there was nothing, and with his mission completed, he walked out of the wheelhouse and down the ladder, pausing to turn and wave to the body in the wheelhouse in case anyone saw him alight, then forward and down the ramp to where his rented car was waiting for him. He had a map to guide him to the local airport, and soon enough his time in this infidel country would be at an end.

56

They were up shortly after six the next day, gathering their equipment on deck while the grizzled old Salychev sipped his coffee and looked on. The previous day's wind had died away, leaving the bay flat and calm, save a soft lapping against the rocks half a kilometer away. The sky hadn't changed from the day before, however, remaining the same leaden color it had been since they'd arrived in Russia.

When all the gear was assembled, Adnan double-checked it against his mental list, then ordered everything packed into four large external-frame backpacks. Next came their two rafts, inflated. They were black and looked ancient, but the transom-mounted trolling motors were in good repair and there were neither patches nor leaks, of this Adnan had made sure when he'd purchased them. Once the rafts were up to full pressure, the men began inserting the deck planks into their notches.

"Wait, wait," Salychev said. "That's the wrong way." He walked over and removed one of the planks and flipped it around, matching its end curve with the raft's deck flange. "Like that, see?"

"Thank you," Adnan said. "Does it make a difference?"

"Depends on whether you want to live or die, I suppose," the captain replied. "The way you had it, the bottoms would've folded up on you like a clam. You would've been in the water before you knew it."

"Oh."

Five minutes later, the rafts were fully assembled. The men dropped them over the side, then tied off the bow painters to the Halmatic's stern cleats. Next came the motors, then the equipment bags, then the men. Adnan climbed over gunwale last. "We'll be back before dark," he told Salychev.

"And if you're not?"

"We will."

Salychev shrugged. "Don't want to get caught out there at night—not unless you got arctic gear hidden away in those bags."

"We'll be back," Adnan repeated. "Make sure you're here."

"That's what you're paying me for."

If not for the drifting growlers and barely submerged pancake ice, the trip to shore would have taken ten minutes, but it was nearly forty minutes before the nose of the lead raft scraped on the pebble-strewn beach. The rafts were pulled onto higher ground and the backpacks unloaded. In turn, Adnan helped each man don his pack, then shouldered his own.

"Inhospitable," one of the men said, looking around.

Aside from a line of smooth brown cliffs four kilometers to the east, the ground was flat, covered in stones, clumps of brown grass, and a thin crust of snow that crunched under their boots.

"What about the rafts?" another man asked.

"We'll tow them," Adnan said. "The stones are smooth enough."

"How far is it?" another asked.

"Six kilometers," Adnan answered. "Let's go."

They set off, following the shoreline north and east, keeping the bay on their left until it narrowed to a mere hundred meters and curved south around the headland, where the channel turned parallel to the cliffs they'd spotted from their landing site. Up close, Adnan could see that the cliffs were actually sharply sloped hills, their faces grooved by centuries or millennia of snow runoff and wind. After another two kilometers of walking, the channel suddenly widened into a second bay, this one a rough oval measuring two square kilometers.

The ships had been moored with neither care nor order, Adnan could see, some listing against their neighbors, others with bows and sterns abutting one another at odd angles, while still others had been grounded by tugboats to make room for new arrivals. All were civilian in origin, mostly dry cargo carriers and tenders and repair vessels, but they ranged in size from thirty to two hundred meters, some so old their hulls were rusted through in spots.

"How many are there?" one of the men asked, staring.

"Eighteen, give or take," Adnan replied.

It was a rough estimate to be sure, based on their own intelligence, but probably as close as the Russian government could itself come. This bay had become an unofficial graveyard in the mid-'8os as the arms race with the West began to take its toll on the Soviet financial infrastructure and more and more corners were trimmed in favor of military expenditures. It was cheaper to strip and abandon decommissioned ships than it was to properly scrap them. This was just one of dozens of maritime graveyards in the Barents and Kara seas, most of them full of ships that had simply been recorded in a ledger somewhere along with the notation "moored, pending dismantling." Adnan hadn't been told how the graveyards had come to the attention of his superiors, nor did he know the details of what would soon be seen as the most costly administrative error in modern history.

The ship probably had a name and a designator, but those particulars had also been excluded from Adnan's briefing report. What he did have was a map with the ship's anchorage coordinates and a roughly sketched blueprint of the cargo hold and deck entrances; clearly, the blueprint had come from neither Atomflot nor the manufacturer, but rather a firsthand source, likely one of the crew. Adnan also knew the vessel's history and how it had come to rest here.

Commissioned in 1970 as an Atomflot nuclear tender, it had been designed to offload spent fuel and damaged components from nuclear-powered civilian vessels at sea and transport them back to shore for disposal. In July of 1986, overburdened with high-level reactor rods from a damaged icebreaker, the ship lost steerageway in heavy seas and foundered, spilling seawater into the cargo hold and breaking loose the reactor rods. So severe and immediate was the contamination that the ship's crew, forty-two in all, died before rescue vessels could reach the scene. Anxious to avoid revealing to the world another Chernobyl-level disaster, which had happened just three months earlier, Moscow ordered the ship towed to a secluded cove on the eastern coast of Novaya Zemlya and abandoned in place.

The error that had allowed other vessels to be deposited here was monumental, but such was the nature of bureaucracy, Adnan reasoned. Surely at some point the government had realized its error, but by then little could be done. The bay was designated a restricted area, and the secret was kept. On occasion, teams were likely sent into the bay to check the ship's hull for leaks or signs of intrusion, but as time passed and priorities changed, the incident would have faded into the secret pages of Soviet Cold War history.

Out of sight, out of mind was the phrase, Adnan believed.

The ship was anchored on the north side of the cove, fifty meters offshore and sheltered from view by a pair of bulk carriers. It took them another forty minutes to circumnavigate the cove.

They began unpacking their equipment. First came the rubber-impregnated L1 chemical protection suits, followed by the rubber boots and gloves. Like most of their equipment, the suits were Army-issue: olive drab and stiff, and stinking of new dye. After making sure zippers and snaps were sealed, each man donned a Soviet-era GP-6 rebreather mask.

"How much good will these do?" asked one of the men, his voice muffled.

"They are rated for short-term exposure," Adnan replied. Part of him regretted the lie, but there was nothing to be done about it. Even if the suits hadn't been twenty-plus years old, they would be of little use against anything other than chemical and biological agents.

If told the true extent of the danger before them, the men would likely go anyway, but it was a chance he couldn't afford to take. "As long as we're out within an hour, there will be no long-term damage." This, too, was a lie.

They pushed the rafts into the water, then piled in and set off across the water, heading for the ship's midships accommodation ladder, which was extended, coming to within a foot or two of the water. Why this was Adnan didn't know; none of the crew had made it off. Perhaps the government had performed some sort of inspection in the past.

They tied the rafts to the ladder, then started upward. The ladder shook and clanked beneath their feet. At the top they found the railing gate closed, but after a few smacks of his palm, Adnan was able to dislodge the latch and push through.

"Stay together and watch your step for weak spots in the deck," Adnan said. He checked his sketch, then faced aft to orient himself. *Second hatch down,* he thought, *down one ladder, turn right . . .*

They set out, walking stiffly and slightly bowlegged, the fabric of their suits rasping at armpits and thighs. Adnan kept his head moving, checking both the deck beneath his feet and the overhang above. He tried not to think of the invisible particles bombarding his suit and penetrating his skin. Like the railing gate's latch, the dogging lever on the hatch was rusted and resisted his first tug. Another member of the team joined him, and together they heaved back on the lever until it screeched open.

Each man clicked on his flashlight, and one by one they stepped through the hatch and started downward. At the next deck they turned left down a passageway. They passed three side passages, each lined with cabin doors or hatches. Pipes and electrical conduits crisscrossed the ceiling like veins. At the fourth intersection, Adnan turned left and stopped at a door. There was a porthole window at eye level. He peered through but could see nothing.

He turned around. "There will likely be water on the deck. That will be our biggest risk. Don't rely too much on the handrails or catwalk. If something starts to give way, you must freeze and not panic. Is that understood?"

He got nods all around.

"What does it look like, this container?"

"An oil drum, but only half as tall. If Allah wills it, it will still be secured to the wall of the containment vault." *Better that Allah will that the containment door still be shut and locked,* Adnan thought. Otherwise, they had no chance of finding what they came for before the radiation killed them. "Any other questions?" he asked.

There were none.

Adnan turned back to the door and tried the knob; largely protected as it was from the salt air, it turned freely. He slowly pushed the door open until it was wide enough to accommodate him but kept a hold of the knob so the door wouldn't swing shut as they entered. He took a tentative step forward, placing his foot flat on the catwalk and slowly shifting his weight forward until certain it would hold him. He took another step, then turned left, then two more steps. He looked over his shoulder and nodded. The next man entered.

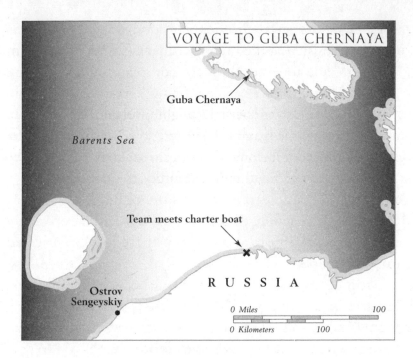

VOYAGE TO GUBA CHERNAYA

Guba Chernaya

Barents Sea

Team meets charter boat

RUSSIA

Ostrov
Sengeyskiy

0 Miles   100
0 Kilometers   100

As cargo spaces went, this one was small, measuring roughly one hundred square feet and twenty feet deep. The catwalk on which they stood extended the length of the bulkhead and ended at a ladder. Once the rest of the men were through the door, Adnan started down the catwalk. At the halfway point, he stopped and stepped to the railing, taking care not to bump it. He shined his flashlight at the overhead and could see the twenty-foot by twenty-foot square outline of the loading hatch; along one edge he could see a sliver of gray light. This is where the seawater had entered, he knew. The loading hatch had torqued during a starboard roll and the seal had given way. He shined his flashlight downward. As he'd feared, the deck was awash, a slurry of black seawater and radioactive dust and chunks of spent fuel rods, several of which he could see floating on the surface. Somewhere down there were the lead-lined containment "sarcophagi." How many of the lids had broken free during the accident? he wondered. How many fuel rods remained locked in the caskets?

They proceeded to the ladder.

"Is that it?" one of the men asked, shining his light down the steps.

At the bottom, across six feet of flooded deck, was a bank vault–style door secured by eight dogging levers, three to each side and one at the top and bottom. At waist height along the left-hand jamb was a latching mechanism secured by a padlock.

"Allah be praised," Adnan murmured.

57

The international airport outside Archangel mainly handled domestic flights, and few enough of those, except in the summer. More took the train south, which was cheaper and more accessible to the local citizens. Aeroflot hadn't quite shaken its long-held reputation for substandard flight safety. But there was a rather more active air-freight terminal, used largely for fish that needed swift transport to various international restaurants. And so the package was loaded into the forward cargo hatch of a forty-year-old DC-8 belonging to Asin Air Freight. It would fly to Stockholm, and from there, with a new crew, it would fly farther south, stopping at Athens before its final leg to Dubai International Airport in the United Arab Emirates.

"What's this?" a customs officer asked, looking at the recently painted "battery" casing.

"Scientific gear, X-ray equipment, something like that," his partner replied.

The official saw that the paperwork was properly filled out, and that was, really, all he cared about. It wasn't a bomb. Those required different forms. So he signed on the long green line and affixed a stamp that made it official. Nobody even had to bribe him for this. For munitions, they would have, but this was not obviously any sort of weapon. He didn't ask, and they didn't offer. To their relief, and his indifference. A gas-powered forklift hoisted the package—it weighed about seven hundred kilos—and drove it to the platform sitting outside the cargo hatch. There it was manhandled aboard and tied down firmly to the aluminum deck.

The pilot and copilot were preflighting the aircraft, walking around, checking for fluid leaks, visually inspecting the airframe for anything amiss. The air-freight business was not known for the quality of its maintenance procedures, and the flyers, whose lives rode on the flight deck, did their best to make up for that troubling fact. The left outboard main-gear tire needed replacement in ten or so cycles. Aside from that, the airplane looked as though it would fly for the next eight hours. They walked back inside to the crew lounge to try some of the (miserable) local coffee and (pretty decent) bread. Their box lunches were already aboard, already stacked by their flight engineer, who was busily prepping the engines.

They walked back out thirty minutes later and climbed up the old-fashioned boarding ladder to get under way. That took another fifteen minutes, and then they taxied to the end of runway one-eight to start their takeoff roll. The old aircraft had thirty-seven thousand hours on the airframe—it had begun life as a passenger liner for United Airlines, mostly on cross-country runs from the East Coast to the West, along with a few stints as a Freedom Bird out of Saigon, which the aircraft, if it had a memory, would recall with a smile. It climbed to its assigned cruising altitude of thirty-two thousand feet, and headed west before turning south over Finland, slowing as it crossed the Baltic Sea, then descended to land at Stockholm. It was all entirely routine, ending on runway two-six and turning left for the cargo terminal. A fuel bowser pulled up at once to refuel the wing tanks, and a minute later came the relief crew, asking how things went and how the aircraft was. All answers were within acceptable limits, and the inbound crew walked down the steps to a car that would take them to the local hotel that flight crews used. It had a pub, they were pleased to see, with cold beer on tap. The relief crew had the DC-8 back in the air before they'd finished their first pint.

Back in Russia, Musa was at Moscow's Domodedovo Airport in the main terminal building, the one that looks like an alien spacecraft (but it was an improvement on Stalin's beloved wedding-cake school of design), on an international call to a friend in Berlin. When the connection was made, he told his friend that the car had been properly fixed, and that he would accept payment when next they met. His friend agreed, and the call was terminated. Musa and his men then walked to an airport bar, where they indulged freely in overpriced shots of Russian vodka, which was, at least, of a premium brand, as they waited two hours for their KLM flight to the Netherlands. The bar also served them cucumber slices and bread to accompany the vodka into their stomachs. They paid the bar bill in euros, leaving a niggardly tip for the bartender before boarding the KLM 747, in the first-class cabin, where the liquor was free, and they indulged themselves there, too. For his part, Musa's thoughts did not linger on the two murders he had committed. It had been necessary. He'd accepted that part of the mission before traveling to Russia and chartering the infidel's boat. Looking back, he was surprised that he and his friends had not indulged in drink while aboard, but there was an old adage about not mixing business with pleasure, and not mixing alcohol with business was surely even a more intelligent rule. Had that Vitaliy fellow remarked on his charter with some local friends? Impossible to know. But since he didn't know their names or addresses, and no one had taken any photographs, what evidence had he left behind? Northern Russia had looked to him like old movies of the American West, and things there were manifestly too casual for a proper police investigation. The pistols used had been disposed of, and that, he figured, was that. With this decided, he rocked his seat back and let the alcohol take him off to sleep.

The 747 landed at Berlin's Templehoff International at 0100 local time. Musa and the others deplaned separately, went through the rigmarole of immigration, using their Dutch passports, then walked to collect their baggage, and from there out to the taxi stand, where a German in a Mercedes took directions, delivered in English, to a certain street location. It was in what was locally called Dish City, called that for the plethora of satellite-TV receiving dishes. These allowed the mainly Arabic residents to watch TV in their own native language.

His host was already expecting him, flagged by a friend in Amsterdam, and so it took only one knock. Hands were taken and kisses exchanged, and Musa went into the living room of the small apartment. Mustafa, the host, held a finger to his lips and then to his left ear. The apartment might be bugged, he thought. Well, you had to take precautions in an infidel country. Mustafa turned on the TV to a same-day repeat of a game show.

"Your mission was successful?" Mustafa asked.

"Completely."

"Good. Can I get you anything?"

"Wine?" Musa asked. Mustafa went into the kitchen and produced a tumbler full of a white Rhine wine. Musa took a long pull on it, then lit a cigarette. He'd had quite a long day, plus the two murders, which, he found, tended to unsettle him for no reason he could understand. In any case, sleep came quickly once Mustafa had rolled out the sleeper bed, and he'd finished off his Rhine wine. Tomorrow he'd go to Paris, await word that the package had arrived safely, then follow. Once in Dubai, he could enjoy some leisure time; the engineer assigned to the package was reliable and competent, and would need little supervision. Then again, Musa thought, what supervision could he offer? What had to be done with the package was beyond his skill level.

It was a strange name for a town, Kersen Kaseke thought. The site of Napoleon's final defeat at the hands of Wellington. Perhaps an apt metaphor: a divinely ordained reversal of fortune for a tyrant who had kept much of the world under his thumb. Still, to find such a place here, in the middle of the "corn belt," had been a surprise, as had much of America. The people here seemed decent enough and had treated him well, despite his funny name and heavily accented English. It had helped, he was sure, that he'd managed to pass himself off as a Christian, the adopted son of Lutheran missionaries who had died two years earlier during a mortar attack outside Kuching. Repugnant as he found it to overtly deny Islam and the One True Prophet, the story had, in fact, softened the hearts of the most suspicious of the town's residents, most of whom were blue-collar workers or farmers. No, it wasn't the people he despised but rather their government, and sad as it might be, citizens had been paying the price for flawed and brutal policies for millennia. For the people here, it was simply a matter of fate finally catching up with them. Fate and Allah's will. Besides, he reminded himself, what was coming for these people was but a fraction of what his own country had suffered. While the tragic tale of his missionary parents was technically false, it was, in spirit, true enough. The streets of Zagreb and Rijeka and Osijek and dozens of others had been awash in the blood and misery of Muslims for decades, while the West did nothing to help. What would have happened, Kaseke wondered, if it had been blond-haired and blue-eyed Christian children being slaughtered in the streets of London or Los Angeles? What then?

As the e-mail instructed, Kaseke drove his 1995 Ford Ranger to the Trailways bus station on Sycamore between Third Street and Park Avenue. He pulled the Ranger into the parking lot of Doyle's Pub, then walked back down the block to the bus station and went inside. The key he'd received in the mail a week earlier fit locker number 104. Inside he found a thick cardboard box wrapped in brown kraft paper. It was heavy, nearly thirty pounds, but reinforced with filament tape. There was no writing on the paper. He removed the box, placed it on the floor between his feet, then looked around to ensure that no one was watching before using the sleeve of his sweatshirt to wipe off the locker key. Had he touched anything else? Left fingerprints anywhere nearby? No, just the key.

Kaseke picked up the box and walked outside, then back down the block to his truck. The box went in the passenger-side door and on the seat. He got in on the other side and turned the ignition key, then paused, briefly wondering if he should put the box on the floorboards. If he got in an accident . . . *No,* he thought. *Not necessary.* He knew what was in the box, or at least he had a good idea, given the training curriculum he'd been put through in the camp. They'd trained him well to do one thing and one thing only.

This cargo was perfectly harmless. For now.

58

Their leads into what, if anything, the Emir and the URC were planning were three: old e-mail intercepts, which had yielded little of use, save a birth announcement that seemed to have pushed every URC cell into radio silence, as well as perhaps moving some URC pieces around the board; Hadi, a courier and a fresh face on the scene; and the flash drive Chavez had inadvertently liberated from one of the tangos at the Tripoli embassy takedown. So far the fact that the URC was using steganography had given them nothing but hundreds of gigabytes of photos from URC-affiliated websites dating back eight years. Finding a five-kilobyte message embedded in a JPEG that was two hundred times that size was not only time-consuming but daunting.

Their fifth and most promising lead happened by accident, a finger that had kept a camera's shutter button pressed down for a few seconds longer than intended.

Of two dozen or so pictures Jack had taken of Hadi in Chicago, three were keepers, showing the courier's face either in profile or on the oblique, and in good enough light. As it turned out, though, it wasn't Hadi's face that became of interest to The Campus but rather his hands. When it came to intel work, Jack knew, it wasn't always about finding what you were looking for but rather seeing what's in front of you.

"This one here," Jack said, touching the forward button on the remote. The next photo slid onto the conference room's LCD TV screen. It showed Hadi stepping up on the curb and sidestepping a fellow pedestrian on the way to the door. Near the bottom of the frame, barely visible in shadow, Hadi's hand and the stranger's hand were pressed together, and between them, an indistinguishable object.

"Brush pass," Clark said, leaning closer. "Clean, too."

"Good catch, Jack," Hendley said.

"Thanks, boss, but it was dumb luck."

"No such thing, *mano*," Chavez said. "Luck is luck. Take it as it comes."

"So we've got a second face," Sam Granger said. "What's it do for us?"

"Nothing. Not by itself," Jack said. "But this might get us somewhere." He touched the forward button again. "The guy's suitcase, blown up and sharpened. I had Gavin work a little Photoshop magic. Check the upper-right-hand corner—that curled white square." Jack hit forward again, and the white square expanded and resolved. "It's a luggage claim sticker."

"I'll be damned," Brian Caruso muttered. "Gotta love that computer shit."

Hendley turned to Dominic. "Special Agent Caruso, this might be right up your alley."

"On it, boss."

Armed with the claim-check number, a rough time frame, and his FBI badge number, it took less than an hour for Dominic to come back with a name: Agong Nayoan, Vice Consul for Economic Affairs at Republic of Indonesia's Consulate General in San Francisco.

"Nothing outstanding on him," Dominic said. "Flight from Vancouver to Chicago to San Francisco the same morning as Hadi. The Frisco FO did its due diligence on him a few years back. Nothing popped. No known ties to extremist groups, politically moderate, no criminal history—"

"As far as Jakarta would admit to," Granger said. "It's either that or he's covered his tracks well. We've got him brush-passing a known URC courier. Somebody messed up on a background check somewhere."

With a population of nearly two hundred million Muslims, Indonesia was, according to many intelligence communities, Western and otherwise, quickly becoming the central recruiting front for extremist terrorist groups, the most powerful of which—Jemaah Islamiah, Islamic Defenders' Front (FPI), Darul Islam, and Laskar Jihad—had not only both operational and financial ties with the Emir's URC but also sympathizers at every level of the Jakartan government. The idea that Agong Nayoan, staff member of the Indonesian consulate, had such leanings didn't surprise Jack, but the fact that Nayoan had chosen to become a cutout for a URC courier meant they were dealing with a whole different kettle of fish altogether.

"Whatever brought Nayoan out to play has to be big," Jack said. "If he's caught, all he'd probably get from us is a PNG." This was persona non grata, a bureaucratically couched term for "no longer welcome." Expulsion. "Jakarta's a different story, though. That'd be a welcome to remember."

Indonesia's Agency for Coordination of Assistance for the Consolidation of National Security, or BAKORSTANAS, had the broad and disturbingly vague mandate to ferret out and eliminate threats to the republic, which was, in turn, coupled with little legal restrictions and oversight. If expelled from the United States under accusations of aiding the URC, the best Nayoan could hope for was a dark hole in Cipinang Prison and years to consider his crimes. The government in Jakarta had in recent years been trying to get out from behind the economic shadow of China and sell itself to the West as a market counterbalance. Hard to do that with a reputation as a terrorist petri dish.

"Thoughts?" Hendley asked, looking at Clark.

"Track back the cat," Clark replied. "We know Hadi headed to Las Vegas and maybe points beyond. We know where Nayoan is and where he came from. Let's put eyes on him and see where it takes us."

Hendley considered this; he looked at Granger, who nodded. "You and Chavez," Granger said. "Start in San Francisco, then Vancouver. Dissect him."

"How about Jack?" Clark suggested. "Good op to get his feet wet."

Again, Hendley and Granger exchanged glances. The boss looked at Chavez and the Caruso brothers. "Gentlemen, can

467

we have the room for a few minutes?" Once they'd filed out, Hendley said to Jack, "You're sure this is what you want?"

"Yeah, boss."

"Tell us why." This from Granger.

"I already—"

"Tell us again."

"I can do some good, I think—"

"You're doing good right where you are. Plus, we don't run the risk of burning you—of getting a former President's son killed. You're a face, Jack."

"An average face. I can count on one hand the number of times I've been recognized in the last two years. Out of sight, out of mind. John and I have had this conversation already, okay? I don't have any grand visions about fieldwork."

Hendley looked to Clark, who spread his hands. "Either he's a good actor or that's the truth."

Jack smiled. "Hey, worst case, I see how the other half lives and it makes me a better analyst, right? It's a win-win."

"Okay, you're on the team. Mind your manners, though. No jabbing folks with needles this time around, understood?"

Jack nodded. "Understood."

"John, where are you with Driscoll?"

"Talked to him this morning, put out some feelers. I think it's sunk in that CID wants his head. He's taking it in stride— better than most would be. He likes the work. I think if he had a chance to get out from under and still have his hand in the pot, he'd be interested. Any luck on your end?"

"I think we might have enough horsepower to get the AG to back down but not enough to keep Driscoll in uniform. When you get back from Chicago, go pitch him."

Clark nodded.

"Call them back in, Sam."

As Chavez and the Carusos reentered, Brian said, "Hey, since we're finally getting proactive about this shit . . . The

URC had that Dirar mutt killed for a good reason. Any more thoughts on us going to Tripoli and shaking the tree?"

"What do you expect to fall out?" Granger asked.

Dominic answered this one. "Either Dirar got whacked by the URC directly, or they had an affiliate do it. Either way, we find who did it and we've got another piece of the puzzle—maybe a peek at communication protocols, funding routes. . . . Who knows?"

Hendley nodded. "Draw your documents and get Travel working on itineraries. We'll see if you can scare up a contact in Tripoli—somebody at the embassy who doesn't mind having a hats-off chat. Also see if we can get Brian and Dominic a briefing—Jack, maybe that new deal you and Gavin have been working on?"

"Can do, boss."

Hendley stood up and looked around the table. "Okay, gents, do your thing. We need a corner, something we can peel back and turn into leverage."

Each man would need a motel room of his own, Hadi knew, all within an hour's driving distance of the facility and none lavish enough that a ten- to fourteen-day stay would arouse curiosity. Foreigners coming to a new country looking for work didn't have enough money for fancy accommodations, and while it might make sense for friends to stay together on such a trip, four Arabic-looking males staying in one place together might pique the interest of local law enforcement.

There were plenty of two-star motels in São Paulo; Hadi wasn't worried about finding those, but this was his first foray into fieldwork and he wanted to leave nothing to chance—just as they'd left nothing to chance with their cover stories.

Each of them had studied or knew enough about the industry that their arrival and subsequent job inquiries would draw little attention, at least for the short time they planned to be in the country. Brazil's new boom had seen an influx of workers, many of them from the Middle East and tired of being paid poverty-level wages for exhausting and dangerous work. No, Hadi thought, as long as they did nothing to distinguish themselves, four more Arabs going about the business of finding work would not be noticed.

The difficult part would be reconnaissance. There were many miles of track and hundreds of cars to survey; there were schedules and routes to double- and triple-check; topography and infrastructure to study. The facility itself, while far from impregnable, did have its own security force, and Ibriham's preparatory research had suggested that the facility routinely conducted drills that involved both the military and the police, each of which maintained a quick-reaction force. Of course, such forces would be useful only up to a point. If he and the others planned well and remained steadfast under Allah's guiding hand, nothing could stop them.

59

Steve had passed the most recent test with flying colors, Allison decided. She had at the last minute canceled their rendezvous in Reno, claiming that her boss had asked her to take his place at a pharmaceutical-rep conference in Sacramento. The conference was real enough, as were her business cards and the drug samples and the literature she carried in her leather briefcase whenever they met for sex, but that's as far as it went. She liked him well enough, but in her business, such things were gauged on a sliding scale. Steve wasn't repulsive, or abusive, so that put him nearer to the upper end of the scale. Not that that would have mattered to her performance, but it certainly made their meetings tolerable.

As predicted, Steve had been upset and disappointed at her last-minute cancellation, and just as predictably, he'd immediately offered a solution: He would take time off from work and fly to Sacramento for the weekend so they could spend time together. She could attend the conference during the day, and they would have the nights to themselves. Allison showed the appropriate level of surprise and gratitude at his suggestion, and promised to make their first weekend getaway something to remember. At some point during the weekend, she would set the hook a little deeper, coyly suggesting that he introduce her to his family. Perhaps she might even arrange for him to catch her tearing up, after which she would confess that she was somewhat taken aback by the "special connection" she felt with him.

As she'd known from the beginning, the tricky part would be the pitch. Her "handler"—a Russian term she had never liked—the man with the fire-scarred hands, had proposed an angle she thought was worth exploring, but it would involve exposing herself with an unbackstopped story that Steve could check into, if so inclined. Then again, if by the time she made the pitch Steve wasn't completely under her thumb, she would back off and try another tack. Steve wasn't stupid, but when it came to matters of the heart, men were just as irrational, if not more so, than women. Sex, for all its power, was simply a stepping-stone, and if she judged her mark correctly, she was but a few stones away from the prize.

The question that Allison didn't let herself wonder too much about was the nature of the information her employer was seeking. Why in the world, she wondered, did they care about groundwater in the middle of a desert?

As Panamax "box ships" went, the *Losan* was small, a "twelve abreast" 2,700 TEU—twenty-foot equivalent units—vessel measuring 542 feet, whose capacity had long since been surpassed by Post Panamax descendants, but Tarquay Industries of Smithfield, Virginia, was less interested in modernity than it was in cutting its losses.

Of the 120 five-hundred-gallon propane tanks it had sold to the government of Senegal, forty-six had proved defective, having slipped through quality control with improperly welded lifting lugs. By itself this was not an insurmountable problem, one that Tarquay had offered to fix at no cost and on-site, but an examination by both Senegalese government inspectors and Tarquay's lead engineer in Dakar had revealed that the welds had compromised the shell integrity; none of the tanks could have withstood the mandated 250-pounds-per-square-inch pressure capacity.

As this was Tarquay's initial contract with Senegal and in fact its first overseas deal, a quick refund was issued, along with an official apology from the board of directors, and replacement tanks were dispatched immediately. In Dakar, the defective tanks were listed on the bill of entry with the code R3001c—"Re-exportation of quality-rejected non-petroleum products following storage warehousing"—then transported to a government customs warehouse in Port Sud and offloaded in a vacant weed-filled lot surrounded by a four-foot-high hurricane fence.

Eight months later, arrangements were made to have the defective tanks returned to Smithfield. The *Losan*, making its final port of call before crossing the Atlantic to the United States, had the requisite space to take the cargo.

Two days before departure, the tanks were loaded by forklift onto platform railcars, locked into place, and transported two miles down the tracks to the *Losan*'s berth, where the tanks were offloaded by crane into open-top "bulktainers"—four tanks to a container—then hoisted to the *Losan*'s deck and stacked twelve abreast.

Having been inspected upon entry, the tanks, which had been under the control of customs since their arrival, were neither weighed nor examined before being loaded aboard the *Losan*.

The headache and nausea had been getting progressively worse for the last ten hours, which somewhat surprised Adnan; he hadn't expected symptoms this soon. His hands were trembling and his skin felt clammy. Clearly the stories about the vessel's toxicity hadn't been exaggerations. *No matter*, he thought, it was almost time. According to Salychev's chart, they were only twenty kilometers from the drop-off point.

By Allah's grace they'd found the containment drum precisely where it should have been, still resting in its bulk-head-mounted rack. It had been lighter than Adnan had anticipated, which was both a blessing and a curse. He knew the approximate weight of the core, so it was relatively easy to estimate the weight of the containment drum; it was obviously lead-shielded but not as thickly as their intelligence had suggested. This meant the vault itself had been intended as the primary shield, but that wouldn't help them. However, the drum was still sealed and seemed to have suffered no damage during the incident those many years ago.

They'd unlatched the rack enclosure, lifted the drum up and out by its four welded D-shaped handles, then walked it out of the vault and across the flooded deck to the ladder. Here they'd moved slowly, cautiously, one step at a time, to the catwalk, then out into the main passageway. The last two major obstacles—the ladder up to the weather deck and the accommodation ladder down to the rafts—passed without incident, and soon they were back on shore. They gratefully shed their protection suits and gas masks, then stuffed them in one of the backpacks, which was weighted down with a stone and tossed into the cove.

The walk back to the headland took an hour. Adnan ordered the men to put down the drum and rest, then he walked to the shoreline and peered through the mist toward the bay. He could just make out the outline of Salychev's boat. He pulled a flare from his backpack, popped off the ignition cap, and waved the sparking tube over his head. Thirty seconds passed, and then from the boat there came the double wink of a flashlight. Adnan turned to the others and waved them ahead.

Thirty minutes later they were back aboard the boat and returning the way they'd come. By the time they reached the main bay, the containment drum was sealed inside the second, more heavily shielded, drum they'd brought along. Salychev eyed the container suspiciously but said nothing as he steered the boat toward open water.

Now Adnan stood beside Salychev in the pilothouse. It was nearly midnight, and nothing but blackness showed through the windows. "You've certainly earned your fee, Captain," Adnan said. "We're grateful."

Salychev shrugged, said nothing.

Beside his hip, Adnan could feel the square outline of the radio jutting from the wooden helm console. Moving slowly, he withdrew the small knife from his jacket pocket and thumbed open the blade, which he pressed against the radio's power cable. It made a barely perceptible *snick* as it parted.

"I'm going to check on the men," Adnan said. "Can I bring you a cup of coffee? Something stronger?"

"Coffee."

Adnan went down the ladder into the main salon, then down another short ladder into the sleeping compartment. It was dark, save what little light filtered down from the salon. The men were asleep, one to a bunk, all lying on their backs. Earlier he'd passed out what he'd told them was another dose of potassium iodide; it was in fact three grams of lorazepam stuffed into a generic cellulose capsule. At three times the standard dose, the anti-anxiety medication was enough to put the men into a profoundly deep sleep. *A blessing,* Adnan thought.

For the last four hours he'd wrestled with what he had to do next—not the necessity of it but the method. These men were already dying, and nothing could change that; he was dying, and nothing could change that, either. It was the cost of war and the burden of the faithful. He took some consolation that they would never awaken, never feel any pain. The only other consideration, then, was noise. Salychev was old, but he was tough and hardened by a life at sea. Safer to take him by surprise.

Adnan went to the workbench mounted on the aft bulkhead and opened the top left-hand drawer. Inside was the knife he'd found during his earlier search. It was J-shaped, with a needle-sharp point and a finely honed edge, used, he assumed, to gut fish.

He gripped the wooden haft, blade angled up, then stepped to the first bunk. He took a deep breath, then placed his left hand on the man's chin, turned the head toward the mattress, then jammed the tip of the blade into the hollow beneath his earlobe and drew the knife up, following the edge of his jawline. Blood gushed from the severed carotid; in the darkness, it looked black. The man gave out a soft moan against Adnan's palm, then spasmed once, twice, and went still. Adnan moved to the second man, repeated the process, then to the third. In all, it took ninety seconds. He dropped the knife onto the deck, then went up into the salon and washed the blood from his hands. He knelt down beside the sink, opened the bottom drawer, and withdrew the 9-millimeter Yarygin pistol he'd secreted there. He drew back the slide an inch to ensure that a bullet was chambered, then cocked the hammer, flipped off the safety, and stuffed the pistol into the side pocket of his jacket. Finally, he grabbed a plastic coffee cup from the drying rack.

He climbed back up the ladder and into the pilothouse.

"Coffee," he said, handing the cup to Salychev with his left hand. The captain turned, reached for it. Adnan drew the Yarygin from his pocket and shot him in the forehead. Blood and brain matter splattered against the side window. Salychev slumped backward and slid down the bulkhead. Adnan flipped the autopilot switch on the helm console, then grabbed Salychev by the ankles, dragged him to the ladder, and rolled him down into the salon.

Back at the helm, Adnan took a minute to recheck their position with the ancient Loran-C unit, then he flipped off the autopilot and adjusted course.

The linear dark streak of the island appeared on the horizon an hour later, and an hour after that, Adnan slowed the engines and came about following the shoreline east until the Loran-C's display showed the correct coordinates.

The island was known as Kolguyev and was, according to Adnan's chart, part of the Nenets Autonomous Okrug, an almost perfect circle of wetlands, bogs, and low hills measuring eighty kilometers across and home to one lonely settlement called Bugrino on the southeastern coast, populated by a few hundred Nenets, who fished, farmed, and herded reindeer.

Adnan throttled back to idle and turned off the ignition. He checked his watch: ten minutes late. He pulled the portable spotlight from the bulkhead rack and walked onto the deck. The coded blink of his spotlight was immediately followed by the correct response from shore.

Five minutes later he heard the soft rumble of an outboard motor. A speedboat appeared out of the darkness and pulled alongside the port gunwale. Four men were aboard; each was armed with an AK-47. Adnan didn't recognize any of them. Not that it mattered; the spotlight code matched, and if it was a trap, there was nothing to be done about it now.

"You are Abdul-Baqi—Servant of the Creator?" one of the men, the leader, Adnan assumed, asked.

"No. Servant of the Everlasting," Adnan replied. "It's good to see you here."

"And you, brother."

"Toss me your bowline and come aboard. It will take at least two of you to lift."

While Adnan wrapped the line around the gunwale cleat, two of the men climbed aboard, unchained the containment vessel from its position on the deck, and carried it back to the gunwale, where the two men aboard the speedboat took it and set it on the deck. The last two men joined their partners.

"Any problems?" the leader asked.

"None. Everything went as planned."

"Can we help you any further?"

Adnan shook his head. "No, thank you. It's almost done. It's deep here, almost three hundred meters. The sea will do the rest."

60

This, Admiral Stephen Netters knew, was going to be an unpleasant meeting, and it had as much to do with who wasn't attending as it did with who was. By all rights, the man sitting on the other side of the desk from him should have been Robby Jackson, but it wasn't. Some redneck with a heart full of hate had seen to that. Instead, they had Edward Kealty. The wrong man for any season. Netters and Jackson had come up together, starting at the Naval Academy, their careers intersecting now and again as they climbed the ladder until finally, in the waning days of the Ryan administration, Netters had been appointed chairman of the JCS. He'd taken the job for a variety of reasons, ambition being the lowest among them, respect for Ryan being paramount.

It'd been hard not to quit after that, and especially after it became clear that Kealty was going to win the Oval Office not on merit but by dumb fate and tragedy. But even as the votes were being counted and the electoral map inexorably tipped in favor of Kealty, Netters knew he'd stay on, lest the new President appoint one of the Pentagon's "perfumed princes." One only had to look at the depth (or lack thereof) of Kealty's cabinet to know what the man expected from his people. And therein was the rub. Contradict the king too often or with too much zeal and a more amenable prince would be found. Fail to contradict the king and the kingdom goes to the barbarians.

"Tell me what I'm looking at, Admiral," President Kealty said with a grunt, and shoved the satellite photo back across the desk at Netters.

"Mr. President, what we're seeing is a large-scale movement of tanks and mechanized infantry moving west toward the border."

"I can see that, Admiral. What kind of numbers are we talking about, and what the hell are they up to?"

"As for the first question, we've identified an armored division consisting of three tank brigades with a mix of older Soviet T-54s, T-62s, and Zulfiqar main battle tanks; four artillery battalions; and two mechanized infantry divisions. As for what they're up to, Mr. President, we can't think in those terms yet. We need to concentrate on what they're capable of, then work forward to intention."

"Explain that," National Security Adviser Ann Reynolds said.

Translation: *I don't know what the hell you're talking about.* Like Scott Kilborn, the Democratic congresswoman from Michigan was unqualified in the extreme, but both her demographically friendly gender and her seat on the House Intelligence Committee had made her a shoo-in for Kealty's cabinet. As the CEO of a Detroit-based social-networking website company, Reynolds had been savvy and capable, skills she assumed were easily transferable to the role of politician and legislator. Netters suspected it hadn't quite sunk in that she was in over her head, a fact that scared the living hell out of him. The National Security Adviser was white-knuckling it, hoping her Donna Karan power suits, severe glasses, and rapid-fire speaking style would keep the wolves at bay.

"Say I intend to beat the Olympic record for the marathon. That's my intention. Problem is, both my legs are broken and I've got a heart condition. That's my capacity. The latter dictates the former."

Reynolds nodded sagely.

Scott Kilborn, the DCI, said, "Mr. President, Tehran is going to call it an 'exercise,' but we can't ignore the obvious: First of all, the force is moving toward the Ilam salient—as the crow flies, it's as close to Baghdad as any point in Iran. Eighty or so miles. Second, we just put into motion our draw-down plan in Iraq. Best case, they're sending a warning to the Sunnis to mind their manners. Worst case, this is the real deal and they're planning an incursion."

"To what end?"

Kealty had asked the question, which was good, Netters thought, but there was no curiosity behind it. When it came to Iraq, the President was solution-focused to a fault. From day one, he'd made it clear that he intended to withdraw U.S. forces as quickly as possible, with only token regard paid to tactical safety. Kealty lacked two critical ingredients for good leadership: flexibility and curiosity. He had each in abundance in the political arena, but that was about power, not genuine leadership.

"Testing the waters, see how we react," Kilborn replied. "The longer we delay in drawing down, the more time Tehran has to work behind the scenes with the Shia militias. If an incursion doesn't reverse our drawdown now they've got a preview."

"I disagree," Admiral Netters said. "They've got nothing to gain and everything to lose by crossing the border. Moreover, they're light on triple-A."

"Explain."

"They're fielding only token antiair elements. That's not an oversight. They know if we come at them, it'll be from carriers in the Gulf first."

Kealty's National Security Adviser, Ann Reynolds, said, "A message?"

"Again, Ms. Reynolds, that falls into the 'intentions' category, but I'll tell you this much: For all their shortcomings, the Iranians aren't blind, and they're big believers in the Soviet order of battle model, which is big on mobile antiaircraft systems. They saw what we did during Gulf One and Two, and they haven't forgotten it. You don't strip out your antiair elements just for the hell of it."

"What about air cover?" This from NSA Reynolds. "Fighters?"

"No change," Netters replied. "Nothing moving but routine patrol flights."

President Kealty was frowning. *A fly in his soup,* Netters thought. He'd promised the country he'd get the United States out of Iraq, and the clock was ticking, but not on the troops or America's strategic welfare but rather on Kealty's chances for a second term. Of course, Netters had from the outset his own reservations about the Iraq War, and he still did, but those were dwarfed by the very real possibility of getting it wrong over there. Like it or not, the United States was up to its eyeballs in the Middle East, more so than it had in perhaps its entire history. A painless withdrawal was a pipe dream

Kealty had sold to an understandably war-weary nation. While the current drawdown plan would never succeed, it was measured enough that Iraq would slowly slip into chaos rather than fall headfirst into it, in which case he hoped Kealty would have the good goddamned sense to regroup and listen to the theater commanders.

In one respect, Scott Kilborn was correct: This business on the border may well be a preview of Kealty's endgame for Iraq without American troops, though whether Iran would actually put troops on the ground once U.S. forces were gone was anyone's guess. If they did, however, they'd use soaring Sunni-on-Shia violence to justify it.

It was a perplexing game the Iranians were playing. A delay in U.S. troop withdrawal seemed contrary to Tehran's interests—or at least those visible from Washington.

Kealty leaned back in his chair and steepled his fingers. "So, Admiral, since you're not willing to talk about intentions, I'm going to do it for you," Kealty said. "The Iranians are saber rattling. Testing our resolve. We ignore them, keep to the drawdown plan, and give them a message of our own."

"Such as?" Admiral Netters said.

"Another carrier group."

A message. Another mission without a goal. While it was true enough that carrier groups were all about projection of power, the concept was analogous to basic firearm safety: Never point a gun at anything you don't intend to shoot. In this case, Kealty just wanted to wave the gun around.

"What assets do we have available?" Kealty demanded.

Before Netters could answer, Kilborn said, "The *Stennis*—"

Netters interrupted. "Sir, we're stretched thin as it is. *Stennis* group was just relieved on station ten days ago. It's long overdue for a—"

"Goddamn it, Admiral, I'm getting tired of hearing about what we can't do, is that understood?"

"Yes, Mr. President, but you need to understand the—"

"No, I don't. That's what you're paid to do, Admiral. Get it done, and get me the plan, or I'll find someone who will."

Tariq walked into the living room, where the Emir was reading, and picked up the television remote control. "Something you should see." He turned on the TV and changed the channel to a cable news station. The pretty blond-haired, blue-eyed anchor was in mid-sentence.

"—again, a Pentagon spokesperson just confirmed an earlier BBC report of an Iranian Army exercise being conducted on its border with Iraq. While the Pentagon admitted the government in Tehran failed to announce the exercise, it went on to say such events are not uncommon, citing a similar movement of troops and equipment in early 2008. . . ."

Tariq muted the television.

"Strange bedfellows," the Emir murmured.

"Pardon?"

While Tehran had been generally unsupportive of the URC's cause, neither had it been a hindrance, knowing well that one never knew where interests might intersect. In this case, the Iranian Ministry of Intelligence and National Security, or VEVAK, had in recent years turned its attention to how a postoccupation Iraq might look. Though well represented by several militias and bolstered by both Hezbollah and Pasdaran aid, the Iraqi Shia population was still a minority, and therefore vulnerable to Sunni persecution, an imbalance of power that Tehran despised and the URC was only too happy to exploit. Even as the United States had begun banging the drum for war in 2002, the Emir had conducted his own cost-benefit analysis and developed a strategy to further the URC's aim. The fact that the strategy was obliquely based on the American economic model was something that would likely never occur to Washington.

The United States would eventually leave, or at least decrease its presence to a nominal level, at which time Iran would begin its play for domination in Iraq, a feat it couldn't hope to accomplish without an advantage over the Sunni majority. In this, Iran had a need. It was a customer-in-the-making.

The URC's involvement in Iraq had begun in August of 2003 with an influx of men, matériel, and expertise, all of which were freely offered to Sunni extremist groups. Based on a mutual hatred of the U.S. occupiers, resources were shared and goals intertwined, and by 2006 the URC held sway over great portions of Baghdad and most of the Sunni Triangle. This was the good or service for which Tehran was willing to pay.

As Mary Pat Foley and the NCTC well knew and Jack Ryan Jr. had recently realized, information availability in the digital age could be as much a hindrance to intelligence work as it could be a blessing. Computers can categorize, collate, and disseminate massive amounts of information, but the human mind can absorb and use only so much of it. The application of information is the pivot on which decisions—good, bad, and neutral—are made, a fact that engineers, game wardens, casinos, and hundreds of other seemingly unrelated disciplines had long ago recognized. Who does what, and where and when do they do it? To a city planner, a list of intersections prone to traffic gridlock was virtually useless; a dynamic map on which he or she could see hot spots and trends, invaluable. Sadly, as was too often the case, the U.S. government was playing catch-up in the fields of Data Visualization and information architecture, having to outsource such services to private cyber-savvy firms while the federal bureaucracy threw millions of dollars and lost time at the issue.

For Jack and Gavin Biery, the project they eventually dubbed PLOWSHARE began as a technical challenge: how to take the flood of open-source information on the Internet and beat it into something useful—a sword with which they could pare down the overload. The slightly overwrought metaphor notwithstanding, they made rapid progress, starting with a software program designed to gather obituaries from the eastern seaboard and map them according to various group- ings: age, location, cause of death, vocation, etc. Many of the patterns that emerged were predictable—such as elderly deaths clustered around retirement homes—but some were not, such as the recent raising of the drinking age in one state preceding more young-adult deaths on highways leading to a nearby state with a lower drinking age. This, too, was some- what predictable, they admitted, but seeing the clusters on the map was the proverbial picture that paints a thousand words.

The other surprise was the depth and scope of open-source information. The truly useful data, while not inaccessible, were tucked away deep within local, state, and federal govern- ment websites, available to anyone with enough patience and technological literacy to find it. Second and Third World countries, the ones in which most terrorist incidents took place, were the easiest prey, often failing to close the gap between online record-keeping and online database security. Otherwise confidential information such as arrest reports and investigatory case files were stored in unsecured servers with- out so much as a firewall or password between them and government website portals.

And such was the case with Libya. Within four hours of getting the go-ahead from Hendley, Jack and Gavin had PLOWSHARE chewing on gigabytes of data from both open- source and government databases. Two hours after that, PLOWSHARE regurgitated the information onto Gavin's hacked copy of Google Earth Pro. Jack called Hendley, Granger, Rounds, and the Caruso brothers into the dimmed conference room. The PLOWSHARE-enhanced satellite view of Tripoli was overlaid with crisscrossing multicolored lines, clusters, and squares. Jack stood by the LCD screen with remote in hand; Biery sat in the back against the wall, his laptop open on his legs.

"Looks like a Jackson Pollock painting," Brian observed. "You trying to give us a seizure, Jack?"

"Bear with me," Jack replied, then touched a button on the remote. The "data tracery," as he and Gavin had come to call it, disappeared. Jack gave the group a five-minute primer on PLOWSHARE, then touched the remote again. The image zoomed in on the Tripoli airport, which was now overlaid with what looked like the head of a flower, its center a stigma divided into colored pie slices, its petals squared off and of various lengths.

"The stigma represents average arrival volume per day. Mornings are busiest; afternoons the slowest. The petals represent average number of special searches conducted at airport checkpoints. As you can see, there's a spike in the mornings, from seven to ten, and a drop-off the closer you move toward noon. Translation: Thursdays between ten-thirty and noon are the best times to try to sneak something through the screeners."

"Why?" asked Granger.

"The checkpoints are fully manned in the morning, but personnel are rotated through lunch breaks in late morning; less staff plus more transitions equals less security. Plus, almost two-thirds of the screeners and security guards work Sundays through Thursdays."

"So Thursdays are their Fridays," Dominic said. "Already thinking about the weekend."

Jack nodded. "That's what we thought. We've also got a corresponding departures graph. Might be of more use to you."

Jack cycled through a series of colored overlays depicting traffic patterns, acts of violence, kidnappings, raids conducted by both police and military units, anti-Western demonstrations . . . all categorized by dates and times, demographics, neighborhoods, ethnicity, foreign involvement, religious and political affiliations, until finally summarizing the data into a "do's and don'ts" for Brian and Dominic: areas to avoid, and at what times of the day, neighborhoods in which they were likely to find strong URC support, streets on which military checkpoints and police raids were most common.

"Jack, this is great stuff," Brian commented. "Kind of our own bizarro Frommer's guidebook."

"How much does the data vary?" This from Dominic.

"Not by much. There's some fluctuation on and around major Islamic observances, but unless you stay more than ten days or so, you won't encounter any of it."

Granger asked, "Can they access this in the field?"

"Gavin's hacked a couple of Sony Vaio VGNs—eight-inch screen with Ubuntu OS and a one-point-three—"

"English, Jack," said Rounds.

"Tiny laptop. It'll have all the data on it in Flash format. You can change and review the PLOWSHARE overlays on the fly. We'll give you a walk-through when we're done here."

Hendley said, "Nicely done, Jack . . . Gavin. Any questions, guys?"

Brian and Dominic shook their heads.

"Okay, safe travels."

61

Jack Ryan Senior knotted his tie and looked in the mirror. He decided he looked good enough. His lucky suit, a plain white button-down shirt, a red tie. He got a haircut the previous day, and his hair showed enough gray to make certain he wasn't exactly a kid anymore, but he looked youthful enough for a man in his early fifties. A test smile showed that he'd brushed his teeth properly. *Game time.*

It would start in an hour, in front of twenty or so TV cameras and the hundreds of reporter/commentators behind them, few of whom had any real affection for him. But they didn't have to. Their job was to report the facts as they saw them, fairly and honestly. Most, or at least some, of them would, God willing. But Ryan had to deliver his lines properly, not throw up or fall down in front of the cameras, however entertaining that would be to Jay Leno later this day.

There was a knock on the door. Ryan walked to answer it. He didn't have to be overly careful. His Secret Service detail had this whole floor guarded like an Air Force nuke locker.

"Hey, Arnie, Callie," he said in greeting.

Arnie van Damm looked him over. "Well, Mr. President, good to see you still know how to dress."

"Got a different tie?" Callie Weston asked.

"What's wrong with red?" Ryan asked in reply.

"Too in-your-face."

"What would you prefer?"

"Sky-blue is better."

"Callie, I love your work, but, please, let me dress myself, okay?"

Callie Weston growled but let it slide.

"All ready?" Arnie asked.

"Too late to run away," Ryan answered. And it was. From now on he was a willing, fire-in-the-belly candidate. Blood in his eyes and steel in his spine.

Van Damm said, "Sure I can't talk you into—"

"No." He and Arnie and Callie had batted around Georgetown—whether or not to include the assassination attempt in his announcement speech. Predictably, they'd argued for inclusion, but Ryan would have none of it. The incident would be raised during the campaign, but not by him. Nor would he avoid it.

"How's the audience?" Ryan asked, closing the subject.

"All wired up," Arnie replied. "It is otherwise a slow news day out there, and so they'll be glad to see you. It gives them almost five minutes of airtime to fill. You will sell a lot of toothpaste for them, Jack. Hell, some of them actually like you."

"Really? Since when?" Ryan asked.

"They're not the enemy. They're the press. They're neutral observers. You ought to hang out with them, off-the-record talks. Have a beer with them. Let them come to like you. You're a likable guy. Let it work for you."

"I'll think about it. Coffee?"

"They do it good here?"

"No complaints from me," Jack told them. He wandered over to the room-service tray and sat down to pour another cup. His third. That would be his limit, lest the caffeine make him jumpy. At the White House, presidential coffee was all Jamaican Blue Mountain, from the former British colony, widely regarded as the best in all the world. *That* was a cup of coffee. Maybe it was the bauxite in the beans, Jack thought.

Again Ryan's mind came back to the central question: *If* he won, how to put the country back on course? Governing so complex a country as the United States of America was an effective impossibility. Too many interests, each of them matters of life and death to somebody, and that somebody would be on TV or in the papers to make sure that his/her views got their proper—preferably loud—attention. The President might or might not pay attention. He/she had a staff to make sure that only the important stuff made it to his/her desk. But that made the President a hostage to the staff, and even a good man could be misdirected by the people that

488

he or she had chosen for the job—and as a practical matter, selection of the staff was delegated to more senior staffers, all of whom had a sense of self-importance about them, as though a desk in the White House West Wing or the Old Executive Office Building was a personal gift from God's Own Hand. Such people could and did shape the ideas of their President just by selecting the things he saw. *And you're going to fight for four more years of this?* Ryan asked himself. *You fucking idiot.*

"I know that look," Arnie said. "I know what you're thinking. What can I say, Jack, except that I think you really are the best man for the job, and it's necessary. I believe that down to my bones. How about you?"

"I'm getting there," Ryan said.

"You see the business about Iran?" Arnie asked.

"Which part? Their nuclear program or the border exercise?"

"Both."

"Same houses, different paint," Jack said. "Tehran knows all it has to do is rattle a little saber and Kealty will react—or overreact. What's he got Netters sending over there, a whole battle group?"

"Yep. *Stennis*. Pulled it back from a rotation home."

"Idiot. They've got the President of the United States dancing on a string." He checked his watch. "How much more time do I have?"

"Ten minutes," Callie replied. "Can I talk you into some TV makeup?"

"No way in hell!" Ryan thundered in reply. "I'm not a ten-dollar hooker on Sixteenth Street."

"They cost more than that now, Jack. Inflation, remember?"

Ryan stood and made his way to the bathroom. Losing bladder control was something else to be avoided, and not something he could do in front of cameras. As Ryan grew older, he found himself liking less to wait in line to take a leak. Part of the aging process, he figured. Well, he took his leak, zipped up, and walked back out to don his jacket.

"Off we go, guys?"

"Into the lion's den, Mr. President." Arnie called him Jack only in private. Callie Weston had the same privilege, which made her uncomfortable. On walking out of the room, Andrea Price-O'Day was there, along with other members of Jack's detail, guns securely holstered.

"SWORDSMAN is moving," Andrea told the rest of her team over her lapel microphone.

Jack walked to the elevator, which was, as usual, held for him, with yet another armed agent inside.

"Okay, Eddie," Andrea said, and Eddie released the key he'd been holding, and the elevator went down to the second floor, which had the meeting room reserved for today's announcement.

Forty seconds and the doors slid open, and the Secret Service team went out to lead the parade. There was a funnel of spectators, some of them ordinary citizens, remarkably enough, but the majority of them reporters of various flavors, and their TV cameras. Jack smiled at them—candidates had to smile all the time—waving to a few he knew by name from four years earlier. The smile threatened to make his face crack, Jack thought.

"Mr. President, please follow me," the hotel manager said, shepherding the party to the back of the room. There was the lectern. Ryan went to it at once. Gripping the wood panel hard enough to make his hands hurt a little. It was his normal practice, and helped synchronize him with the task at hand.

"Ladies and gentlemen," Jack began. "Thank you for coming. I am here to announce my candidacy to run for the Presidency of the United States in this coming year.

"Since I left the Presidency three years ago, I've watched

the current President's term of office with disappointment. President Kealty has not responded well to the challenges our country has faced. In Afghanistan and Iraq, soldiers have died needlessly, victims of a rudderless policy of withdrawal. Even when a war is ill conceived, when you have a war, you are stuck with it, and you must play it out. Running away from a conflict is not a policy. President Kealty, as a United States Senator, was not a friend of our military services, and he has compounded his earlier errors to utilize those forces inefficiently, micromanaging their field activities from the Oval Office in such a way as to get our people killed instead of listening to the commanders on the ground.

"Moreover, President Kealty has also mismanaged our national economy. When I left office, America had a growing and healthy economy. In his first two years, President Kealty's misguided tax policy has stopped that cold. In this last year, the economy bounced off the bottom and is now starting to grow again, but that is in spite of government policy, not because of it. Under my administration, we simplified tax policy. That put a lot of lawyers and accountants out of business—by the way, you might remember that I am still a CPA, and the new tax codes are to the point that *I* can't comprehend them anymore. Maybe President Kealty is happy that, in his words, everybody pays his fair share of taxes, but revenues to the federal government have gone *down,* not up, and the resulting deficit is harming America every day.

"I can only regard Kealty's first three years in the White House as a mistake for our country, and for that reason, I am here to try to get back there myself to correct the mistakes.

"On the issue of national security, our country needs a new and efficient look at where we are in the world. Who our enemies are, and how we need to deal with them. For starters, we need a better intelligence service. Fixing it will be a task of years, but the work must begin soon. You can't deal with your enemies unless you know who they are, and where they are. You fight against enemies by supporting and then using your military assets efficiently. President Kealty has manifestly not done that well. National security is the first task of the federal government. Life, as Thomas Jefferson put it, comes before liberty and the pursuit of happiness. Protecting the nation's life is the job of the Army, the Navy, the Air Force, and the Marine Corps. To that end, they must be properly supported, trained to perfection, and then allowed to do their job in accordance with the wishes and expertise of their professional officers, under strategic direction from the sitting President. President Kealty doesn't seem to recognize that simple fact.

"Ladies and gentlemen, I am here because someone has to replace the President, and that person, I think, is John Patrick Ryan. I call on your support, and the support of our citizens. America deserves better than what he's done, and I offer myself, and my vision, to fix the problems that have been created in the last three years. My mission is to return America to the old truths that have stood us in good stead for two hundred years. Our people deserve better. I am here to give the people the things they need. And what is that?" he asked rhetorically.

"Freedom from fear. The people need to know they are safe in their homes and places of work. They need to know that their government is alert, looking for those who would wish to hurt our country, and ready to bring justice to those who attack Americans in America or anywhere else in the world.

"Freedom to live their lives without interference from people who live in Washington and seek to enforce their will on everyone else, whether they live in Richmond, Virginia, or Cody, Wyoming. Freedom is the common birthright of every American, and that birthright is something I will protect to the best of my ability.

"Ladies and gentlemen, it is not the job of government to be the national nanny. The average citizen can look after his or her own needs without assistance from somebody who works here in Washington. America was founded because our citizens two-hundred-plus years ago didn't want to live under the distant rule of people who didn't know and didn't especially care for their welfare. America is about freedom. Freedom to make your own decisions, freedom to live in peace with your neighbors. Freedom to take our kids to Disney World in Florida, or a trout stream in Colorado. Freedom means deciding what *you* want to do with *your* life. Freedom is the natural state of nature. That's how God wanted us to live. The job of the President of the United States is to preserve, protect, and defend our country. When the President does that job, the citizens can live any way they wish. That is the objective of the President: to protect the people and then to leave them alone.

"That is what I propose to do. I will rebuild the military, allow it to train its uniformed members, give it proper support, and turn it loose to deal with our enemies. I will rebuild our intelligence community so that we can identify and counter those who want to hurt our country and our citizens before they can begin to take destructive action against us. I will reestablish a rational tax system that takes from the people only the money which the country needs to fulfill its proper functions, not suck the life out of its citizens while it tells them how they must live.

"One other thing recently came to my attention. President Kealty has turned the full weight of the United States Department of Justice loose on a distinguished soldier of the United States Army. That soldier was in Afghanistan looking for the Emir, Saif Rahman Yasin. The mission to apprehend him failed, probably due to poor intelligence, but in carrying out that mission, this soldier killed several enemy combatants.

Now the Department of Justice is investigating him for murder. I've looked in to this particular incident. This soldier did exactly what soldiers have been doing since the beginning of time: He killed enemies of our country. Clearly President Kealty and I have very different ideas about what the armed forces of our country are supposed to do. This prosecution is a gross injustice. The government is supposed to serve the citizens, and a soldier in the United States Army is, in fact, a uniformed citizen. I call upon President Kealty to put an end to this outrage immediately.

"So thanks for coming. My campaign starts here and now. It will be a long one and probably a hard one, certainly harder than my first. But I am in the race, and we'll see what the American people decide in November. Again, thanks for coming."

Ryan stepped back from the lectern and took a deep breath. He needed a sip of water. This he got from a glass on the lectern. He looked over at Arnie and Callie, and got thumbs-up from both. Okay, that was done. The race was on. God help him.

"Motherfucker!" Edward Kealty snarled at the TV. "Goddamned Dudley Do-Right riding to the rescue of a beleaguered nation! The worst part is, millions of sheep out there are buying his shit."

McMullen and his staff had known Ryan's announcement was coming and had been prepping Kealty for it; clearly, their efforts had failed. Kealty's reaction was mostly anger, McMullen knew, but there was genuine worry there, too. Much of the American public was still uneasy with Kealty, due in large part to the way the election played out. The phrase "victory by forfeiture" had been common fodder on the political shows for a month following Kealty's election, and while the polling numbers couldn't quite encapsulate the country's mood,

McMullen suspected most people felt as though the election had been missing an essential ingredient—namely, a long and hard-fought contest between two candidates who'd bared their souls for the voters. Kealty had done this, or mostly done this, but his opponent hadn't had the chance.

"How the hell did he find out about this thing with the Ranger?" Kealty demanded. "I want to know."

"Impossible to know, sir."

"Don't give me that shit, Wes! Find out."

"Yes, sir. We're going to have to drop the prosecution."

"Of the grunt? Yeah, I know, dammit. Dump it into Friday's news cycle. Get rid of it. Where are we on opposition research?"

"Still working on it. Nothing we can sink our teeth into; the problem is Langley. A lot of stuff Ryan did there is still compartmentalized."

"Get Kilborn—"

"There'll be leaks. If the press finds out we're digging into Ryan's CIA past, it'll backfire on us. We'll have to find another way."

"Whatever you need to do. This dickhead wants back in, fine, but I want it to hurt."

"Holy shit," Sam Driscoll said from his hospital bed. "Here's a face from the past. What the hell're you doing here?"

John Clark smiled. "Heard through the grapevine you fucked up your shoulder playing badminton."

"I wish. Sit down, man."

"I come bearing gifts," Clark said, then set his briefcase on the bed and opened it. Inside were two bottles of Sam Adams beer. He handed one to Driscoll, then opened his own.

Driscoll took a gulp and sighed. "How'd you know? The beer, I mean."

"Remembered you talking about it after Somalia."

495

"Some memory you got there. Got a little more gray, too, I see."

"Look who's talking."

Driscoll took another long pull. "So what's the real reason?"

"Mostly just wanted to check in, but I heard about the CID bullshit, too. Where's that stand?"

"No idea. They've interviewed me three times. Best my lawyer can figure is some dickhead behind some desk is trying to figure out what to charge me with. It's a cluster-fuck, John."

"You got that right. Damned if you do the job, damned if you fail. What do the docs say about your shoulder?"

"Need one more surgery. The rock missed the big vessels in there but fucked up the tendons and ligaments. Figure three months' recovery, then another three for rehab. They're pretty confident, but I don't think I'll be swinging from the monkey bars again."

"What about a humping rucksack?"

"Probably not that, either. The doc that cut on me guesses I won't be able to lift by elbow much above my ear."

"I'm sorry, Sam."

"Yeah, me, too. Gonna miss it. Gonna miss the guys."

"You got your twenty, right?"

"And then some, but with this CID shit . . . Who knows?"

Clark nodded thoughtfully. "Well, you went out with a bang. Got some good intel from that cave. Hell, you could have glided down the mountain on that sand table."

Driscoll laughed, then: "Wait a second. How do you know about that? Oh, yeah, scratch that. You're still in, aren't you?"

"Depends on what you mean by 'in.'"

A nurse walked into the room carrying a clipboard. Driscoll slipped his beer beneath the sheet; Clark lowered his out of sight. "Afternoon, Sergeant Driscoll. I'm Veronica. I'll be with you until midnight. How're we feeling?"

"Just fine, ma'am, and you?"

Veronica dutifully checked boxes on her clipboard and scribbled a few notes. "Can I get you anything? How's your pain level, on a scale of one to—"

"Six-ish and holding steady," Driscoll shot back with a smile. "Maybe a little ice cream with dinner?"

"I'll see what I can do."

Veronica flashed a smile, then turned and headed for the door. Over her shoulder, she said, "Just make sure those bottles disappear when you're done with them, gentlemen."

After Clark and Driscoll got done laughing, Driscoll asked, "What I mean by 'in' is government."

"Then no. I came to offer you a job, Sam." Here Clark knew he was overstepping his bounds a tad, but he doubted he'd have any trouble selling Driscoll's qualifications.

"Doing what?"

"Sort of what you've been doing, but no rucksack and better wages."

"You getting me into something illegal, John?"

"Nothing you won't be comfortable with. Nothing you haven't done before. Plus, it comes with a get-out-of-jail-free card. You'd have to relocate, though. Winters are colder than Georgia."

"Washington?"

"Thereabouts."

Driscoll nodded slowly, chewing on Clark's offer. Then: "What's this?" He grabbed the remote from the bedside table and unmuted the wall-mounted TV.

". . . Kealty has turned the full weight of the United States Department of Justice loose on a distinguished soldier of the United States Army. That soldier was in Afghanistan looking for the Emir, Saif Rahman Yasin. The mission to apprehend him failed, probably due to poor intelligence, but in carrying out that mission, this soldier killed several enemy combatants. Now the Department of Justice is investigating him for

497

murder. I've looked in to this particular incident. This soldier did exactly what soldiers have been doing since the beginning of time: He killed enemies of our country. . . ."

Driscoll muted the TV. "What the fuck . . . How the hell?" Clark was smiling. "What?" Driscoll said. "You did that?"

"Shit, no. That's all General Marion Diggs and Jack Ryan."

"Your timing is damned incredible, John."

"Dumb coincidence. I had a hunch he was going to do something like that, but beyond that . . ." Clark shrugged. "I'd say that about takes care of your CID problem, wouldn't you?"

"How do you figure?"

"Ryan's running for President, Sam, and he just bitch-slapped Kealty on national television. He can either let this bullshit prosecution eat up a few weeks of news cycle or he can dump it and hope people forget about it. As of right now, Kealty's shit pile of worry just got a lot bigger, and you've become small potatoes."

"I'll be damned. Thanks, John."

"Didn't do anything."

"My chances of getting Jack Ryan or General Diggs on the phone are pretty slim, so you'll have to do."

"I'll pass it along. Think about my offer. We'll keep it open till you're back on your feet, then bring you up for a meet and greet. What do you say?"

"Sounds good."

Forty-three hours after Adnan opened the seacocks on Saly-chev's Halmadic trawler and sunk it along with his three comrades beneath the surface of the Barents Sea 700 feet below, the second package arrived at the Dubai warehouse.

Since Musa's arrival, the engineer had been hard at work, setting up the lead-lined containment tent on the warehouse's floor and checking his inventory list of component parts. Like the tent itself, which had been manufactured in Malaysia based on specifications stolen from the online curriculum for Fort Leonard Wood's Operational Radiation Safety (OPRAD) course, the component parts had been laser-milled and lathed in Morocco-based Ukrainian schematics.

The beauty of simplicity, Musa thought.

Each of the device's components was born either from benign dual-use technology or from plans that had long ago been discontinued, considered obsolete according to modern standards.

The component he and his team had recovered existed only because of what most environmental groups considered Russia's lax attitude toward nuclear material, but Musa knew that was only part of the equation, the others being the Russian government's love affair with innovative nuclear-power programs and its tendency toward circumspection when it came to telling the world about those programs.

Spread along Russia's northern shipping routes were some 380 RTG—radioisotope thermoelectric generator—lighthouses, the vast majority of which were powered by strontium 90 cores, a low-level, heat-producing radioisotope with a half-life of twenty-nine years and an output capacity ranging from a few watts to eighty watts. Distributed among the four RTG models—Beta-M, Efir-MA, Gorn, and Gong—were a handful designed to use a core of a wholly different sort: plutonium-238, a material that, unlike strontium, which could at worst be used in the construction of a dirty bomb, was of fissionable quality. However, the amount of salvageable core material alone would not be sufficient for their purposes. A second source was required. This had been Adnan's task. One for which he and his men had given their lives. The prize they'd recovered from the abandoned icebreaking ship on that godforsaken island had been the final piece of the puzzle: an OK-900A pressurized water reactor core containing 150 kilograms, or some 330 pounds, of enriched uranium-235.

Both elements free for the taking, Musa thought. Nominal security and virtually nonexistent record-keeping. Would the fools even notice the loss, and if so, how long would it take them? he wondered. In any case, it would be too late.

However complex the processes and theories behind the device's actual function, the construction of it was no more complex than building a four-cylinder automobile engine from scratch, the engineer had told him. The fittings had to, of course, be of exacting standards, down to the micrometer scale, which made the assembly process painstaking, but Musa's choice of the Dubai warehouse would assure them of privacy and anonymity. The Emir's timetable would assure them ample time to allow proper assembly.

The engineer emerged from the zippered door of the tent's work area, stripped off his protective gear in the change room, then stepped out into the warehouse. "Both assemblies were packed correctly," he announced, accepting a bottle of water from Musa. "Aside from trace residual radiation on the exterior of the containers, there are no leaks. After lunch I will extract the contents. My biggest worry is the second package."

"Why is that?"

"The fittings where the control-rod drive actuators enter the vessel could be problematic. They were likely sealed off during the original rescue operation, but by what method and how well is the question. Until I see them, there's no way of telling if they've maintained their integrity."

Musa thought about this, then nodded. "And the yield?"

"Again, once I've dismantled them."

"You understand the minimum output we require, yes?"

"I do, and I suspect we'll have no trouble reaching that, but I cannot promise anything. This is important: You are certain neither of them came from military platforms, correct?"

"Why does that matter?"

"It matters a great deal. It is everything, my friend. We are, in essence, reverse-engineering the device. To complicate matters, we're dealing with very different sources, used for very different purposes. How we go about disassembly is almost as important as how we go about assembly. Do you understand?"

"I understand. They were obtained just as we told you. The schematics you have are for these two devices."

"Good, that's good. Then I don't foresee any insurmountable problems."

"How long will it take?"

"Disassembly another day. Assembly . . . two to three days. Say, four days until it is ready for departure."

62

The Consulate General of the Republic of Indonesia sat on Columbus Avenue, a few blocks south of the Embarcadero, flanked by Telegraph Hill and Lombard Street and within sight of Alcatraz Island. Clark found a parking spot on Jones Street, one block south of the consulate, and parked their rented Fort Taurus.

"Ever been to Frisco, Jack?" Chavez asked from the backseat.

"When I was a little kid. All I remember is Fisherman's Wharf, that museum submarine—"

"USS *Pampanito*," Clark said.

"Right. And Treasure Island. As my dad tells it, I cried when he told me it wasn't the same Treasure Island from the book."

Clark laughed. "Was that before he broke the news about the Easter Bunny and Santa Claus?"

Jack laughed in return. "Same day, I think."

Clark pulled out his cell phone, one of three sanitized pay-as-you-go push-to-talk models they'd picked up at the airport. He dialed a number and said after a moment, "Yes, good morning, is Mr. Nayoan in this morning? Yes, thanks." Clark hung up. "He's in. Let's take a walk, get a lay of the land."

"What're we looking for?" Jack asked.

"Nothing and everything," Clark responded. "The map isn't the territory, Jack. You're acclimatizing. Find out where the coffee shops are. ATMs, alleys and side streets, newspaper vendors, pay phones. Where're the best places to catch taxis or hop a cable car? Learn to feel like you live here."

"Oh, is that all?"

Chavez answered that one. "No. How do the people move, how do they interact? Do they wait for Walk lights, or do they jaywalk? Do they meet one another's eyes on the sidewalks or exchange pleasantries? How many cop cars do you see? Check for parking. Is it metered or free? Nail down the BART entrances."

"Bay Area Rapid Transit," Clark added before Jack could ask. "Their subway."

"That's a lot of shit to absorb."

"That's the job," Clark replied. "Wanna go home?"

"Not on your life."

"It's a mind-set, Jack. Change the way you see the landscape. Soldiers look for cover and ambush spots; spooks look for dead drops and surveillance boxes. Two questions you should always be asking: How would I follow somebody here, and how would I lose somebody here?"

"Okay."

Clark checked his watch. "We'll take an hour, then meet back at the car and see if Nayoan's ready for lunch. Jack, you head south; Ding and me will take northeast and northwest."

"Why that coverage?" Jack asked.

"Gets more residential to the south. At least during the day Nayoan will be on the clock—meetings, lunch, that sort of thing. Use the stroll to acclimatize."

As instructed, Jack walked south down Jones Street, then west up Lombard, getting a workout on the steep and winding pavement, until he reached the tennis courts at the top of Telegraph Hill, where he turned south again. The houses here were tightly packed and colorfully painted, many with balconies and porches overflowing with flowers. Jack had seen plenty of pictures of the 1906 earthquake here, and it was hard to mentally overlay that with what he was seeing now. The earth's crust slips along a seam a couple of feet, maybe inches, and a city is ruined. Truly, you do not mess with Mother Nature. Hurricane Katrina had reminded America of that most recently, though nature had only costarred in that one. The rest was bad logistics and inadequate supplies. Made you wonder what things would be like if something worse befell the country, natural or man-made. Were we really ready for something like that? Jack pondered. Better question: Was there such a thing as being truly ready? China and India and Indonesia had been dealing with tsunamis and earthquakes since time immemorial, and still when it happened today the response and recovery looked like barely controlled chaos. Maybe the problem was the definition itself. All systems, whether they be governments or fire departments or police departments, had breaking points where circumstances outdistanced manpower and resources. Come to think of it, humans were probably different, and if so, doesn't the concept of readiness become a matter of life and death, of survival or extinction? If after the catastrophe you find yourself alive, were you then ready for it?

Mind back in the game, Jack commanded himself.

At the forty-minute mark, he turned back north at the

Feusier Octagon House and returned to the car. Clark and Chavez weren't back yet, so he found a bench across the street under a tree and read the newspaper he'd picked up during his walk.

"Smart not to get back in the car," Jack heard behind him. Clark and Chavez were standing there. "Why?"

"On a nice day like this? Who'd do that except for cops, detectives, or stalkers?"

"Attaboy. Stand up, come over here. Same principle: Three guys don't just sit around on a bench together unless they're waiting for a bus or they're bums." Jack joined them under the tree and they stood in a semicircle. "Okay, we're business schmucks," Clark said, "standing around talking about the game last night or our asshole boss. So what'd you see?"

"The vibe's more laid-back than New York or Baltimore," Jack replied. "People don't seem to be in as big a hurry. More eye contact and smiles."

"Good, what else?"

"Good mass-transit system, plenty of stops. Saw five cop cars but no lights and sirens. Just about everyone is wearing or carrying a jacket or sweater. Not a lot of honking. A lot of compact cars and hybrids and bicycles. A lot of little shops and cafés with back entrances."

"Not bad, Jack," Chavez said. "Maybe a little spook in the boy's DNA, huh, John?"

"Could be."

After ten minutes more of the businessmen routine, Clark said, "Okay, almost lunchtime. Ding, you're driving. Jack and I'll roam a bit. Main entrance to the consulate is on Columbus and Jones, but there's a side entrance, farther south down Jones."

"Saw a vending delivery truck pull up there during our walk," Chavez said. "And a couple staff outside there smoking."

"Good. Let's move."

*

Twenty-five minutes later, Jack was on the phone: "Got him. Coming out the main entrance. On foot, heading south down Columbus."

"Ding, stay put. Jack, stay on him, twenty yards back at least. I'm a block east of you, coming up on Taylor."

"Roger." A minute later: "Passing the Motor Coach Inn. About thirty seconds from the corner of Taylor."

"I'm there, heading south," Clark replied. "No matter what he does at the corner, cross the street and head west down Chestnut. I'll pick him up."

"Gotcha. He's at the corner now. Turning north up Taylor."

"I see him. Break off, keep going."

Jack strolled through the crosswalk to Chestnut and kept going. In the corner of his eye he could see Nayoan. "Losing him . . . now," Jack called.

Clark: "He's heading right at me. Stand by." A moment later, Clark's voice changed. "No, no, I'm telling ya, their pitching roster is for shit. They got no depth. Man, you're wrong. Ten bucks they tank the first game. . . ." A few seconds passed. "Just passed me. He's stepping into a restaurant—Pat's Café, east side of the street. Jack, let's have some lunch. I'll get us a table."

Ding chimed in: "I'll take a pastrami on wheat."

Jack turned north at the corner of Chestnut and Mason, then north again to Taylor. He found Clark at a table near the door, facing the window. The place was getting busy, catching the early lunch crowd. Jack sat down.

"At the counter," Clark said. "Third from the end."

"Yep, saw him."

"Who's sitting on either side of him?"

"What?"

"Keeping track of your principal is only half the battle, Jack. He talk to anybody while you were on him, make any stops?"

"No, and no close passes, either."

Clark shrugged. "Even mutts gotta eat."

Jack ordered a tuna fish on rye, Clark a BLT and a doggie bag for Ding. "He's finishing up," Clark said. "I'll get the tab. We shake hands at the door, say, 'See you next month,' then you head back to the car. I'll take our boy home, then meet you at the Starbucks on Bay."

Thirty minutes later they were sharing three cups of Gold Coast dark roast at a booth near the window. Outside, pedestrians and cars slipped by in the bright sunlight. On the TV mounted in the corner, Jack Ryan Sr. was standing behind a podium speaking. The sound was muted, but all three of them knew what was going on. So did the rest of the customers and the baristas, most of whom were either staring at the set or catching glimpses of the news ticker as they went about their business.

"Man, he's really doing it," Chavez said. "Your dad's got some brass ones, Jack."

Jack nodded.

Clark asked, "He told you about it, I assume?"

Another nod. "I don't think he's overjoyed at the whole idea, but it's the call of duty, you know? To whom much is given, much is asked."

"Well, he's given a lot already. Okay, to business: What'd we learn?"

Jack took a sip of coffee, then said, "Nayoan likes pea soup, and he's a bad tipper."

"Huh?" Chavez said.

"He had pea soup and a club sandwich. Twelve bucks, give or take, according to the menu. He left a few quarters. Besides that, I'm not sure what we learned."

"Not much," Clark agreed. "Didn't expect much. If he's in the bag for the URC, it could be a once-in-a-while thing. The odds of us catching him dirty in one day were nil."

"So what next?"

"According to the consulate website, they've got a reception at the Holiday Inn Express tonight. Some kind of joint benefit party with the Polish consulate."

"Left my tux at home," Chavez said.

"Not going to need it. Point is, we know where Nayoan's going to be tonight, and it ain't at home."

Eight thousand miles away, the engineer emerged from the tent's changing room and used a rag to wipe the sweat from his forehead and neck. On wobbly legs, he walked to a nearby stool and sat down.

"Well?" Musa asked.

"It's done."

"And the yield?"

"Seven to eight kilotons. Smallish by today's standards—for example, the Hiroshima bomb was fifteen kilotons—but it will be more than sufficient for what you're planning. It should give you, say, fifteen pounds per square inch out to a distance of five hundred meters."

"That doesn't sound like much."

The engineer smiled wearily. "Fifteen psi is enough to demolish reinforced concrete. You said the floor is mostly earthen?"

"That's correct. With some underground hardened structures."

"Then you have no worries, my friend. This enclosed space you've mentioned . . . You're certain of its volume?"

"Yes."

"And the overstructure? What's its composition?"

"I'm told it is something called ignimbrite. It is—"

"Yes, I'm familiar with it. Also called volcanic pyroclastic or welded tuff—essentially, compacted layers of volcanic rock. That's good. Providing the overstructure is thick enough, the shock wave should be directed downward with minimal attenuation. The penetration requirements you gave me will be met."

"I'll take your word for that. Is it ready for transport?"

"Of course. It has a relatively low output signature, so passive detection measures won't be your worry. Active measures are a different story altogether. I assume you've taken steps to—"

"Yes, we have."

"Then I'll leave it in your good hands," the engineer said, then stood up and headed toward the office at the rear of the warehouse. "I'm going to sleep now. I trust the remainder of my fee will be deposited by morning."

63

Their contact met them near Al Kurnish Road on the east side of Sendebad Park, within a stone's throw of the Australian consulate. Hendley had declined to explain to Brian and Dominic the nature of his relationship with the Aussie, nor had their boss felt it necessary to share the man's name, but neither brother thought it a coincidence their bogus passports and visas bore Australian seals.

"Afternoon, gents. I assume you're Gerry's boys, yes?"

"I suppose we are," Dominic said.

"Archie." Hands were shaken all around. "Let's take a stroll, what say?" They waited for a break in traffic, then jogged across Al Kurnish to a dirt parking lot beside the wagon wheel–shaped Al Fatah building, then down to the water's edge.

"So I understand you're on a little snipe hunt?" Archie said over the rush of the waves.

"Guess you could call it that," said Brian. "Guy got murdered here last week. Hung first, then decapitated and feet chopped off."

Archie was nodding. "Heard about that. Nasty bit of work, that. Call that the 'naughty no-step' around here. You think this bloke got out of line, did a little freelancing?"

Dominic nodded.

"The Swedish embassy, yes?"

Another nod.

"And you're after the whos and whats, I take it?"

"We'll take anything we can get," Brian said.

"Well, first thing you need to know about Tripoli is that it's a damned safe city, all things considered. Average street crime is pretty low, and neighbors watch after one another. The police don't get overly concerned about this group killing a member of that group unless it spills over onto the streets or one of them does something to draw attention to itself. The last thing the Curly Colonel wants is bad international press, not after all the public-relations work he's done. The truth is the URC has been rather quiet for eight or nine months. In fact, there's some spin on the street that the Swedish embassy business wasn't URC."

"Not sanctioned, at least," Dominic said.

"Ah, I see. A lopped head and chopped feet tends to send a strong admonishment, doesn't it? Still, could be worse. Usually the family jewels are involved, too. Well, the apartment where your fellow got clipped is off Al Khums Road. Pretty tight-knit place. As I understand, that particular apartment was empty at the time."

"Where'd you hear that?"

"I know some French ex-pats that are pretty friendly with the cops."

"They just used the apartment for convenience, you think?" Dominic asked. "A studio?"

"Yeah. Poor dill was probably killed somewhere else. You saw it on a website? URC or LIFG?" Archie said, referring to the Libyan Islamic Fighting Group.

"URC," Brian replied. "Anyone else the URC might have farmed the job out to?"

"Plenty. Wouldn't even have to be a group. There're crims in the Medina—the Old City—that'd slit your throat for twenty U.S. Not robbery per se, but murder-for-hire, mind you. But that video . . . Seems a tad highbrow for your average ape."

"So why didn't they just do the deed somewhere in the Medina?" Brian asked. "Kill him, then tape it, then dump the body on the street."

"Then the cops'd have to go into the Medina, see? This way everybody gets to pretend it happened somewhere else and the natural balance remains. How many sites did this video go up on?"

"Six that we found." This from Dominic.

"Well, there're plenty of Internet service outfits around, but the groups that run those sites usually do the hosting themselves, with a dedicated server so they can pick up and move—physically and electronically. If the URC farmed out the killing, then you're probably out of luck; if they did it themselves, it means the message came from high up the ladder. The kind of job you don't leave to chance. If that's the case, then there's going to be some overlap—some local URC captain in touch with one of the mobile hosts."

"I take it this ain't something you look up in the yellow pages," Brian said.

"You take it correctly. I may know a man. Let me make some calls. Where are you staying?"

"The Al Mehari."

Archie checked his watch. "I'll meet you there by five; we'll have a drink."

*

He was an hour early and came with his own car, a mid-'80s forest-green Opel; as was almost everything else in Tripoli, the car was covered in a fine layer of red-brown dust.

"You have a rental car?" Archie asked as they pulled west onto Al Fat'h Street amid a cacophony of horns and squealing of brakes.

"Whoa!" Brian shouted from the backseat.

"Traffic laws here are nonexistent. Call it Darwinism at its most basic. Driver survival of the fittest. So: the rental car?"

"No, we don't have one."

"Once we're done, you can drop me back at the embassy and use this. Mind that second gear, though. It's wonky."

"Just as long as you don't expect it back in one piece."

"This is rush hour. It'll quiet down in another couple hours."

Tripoli's modern-day walled and labyrinthian Medina was born during Ottoman occupation and had served for centuries as much as a deterrent to invaders as it did a center of commerce. Situated beside the harbor and bordered on four sides by Al Kurnish Road, Al Fat'h Street, Sidi Omran Street, and Al Ma'arri Street, the Medina was a warren of narrow streets, blind, winding alleys, arched walkways, and small courtyards.

Archie found a parking spot near the Bab Hawara gate, along the southeastern wall, and they got out and walked two blocks south to a café. A man in black slacks and a tan short-sleeved shirt stood up from his table as Archie approached. They shook hands, embraced, and Archie introduced Brian and Dominic as "old friends."

"This is Ghazi," Archie said. "You can trust him."

"Sit, please," Ghazi said, and they settled at the table beneath the umbrella. A waiter appeared, and Ghazi fired off something in Arabic. The waiter left and reappeared a minute later with a pot, four small glasses, and a bowl of mints. Once tea was poured, Ghazi said, "Archie tells me you have an interest in websites."

"Among other things," Dominic said.

"There are many men who provide the services Archie mentioned, but one in particular might be worth your time. His name is Rafiq Bari. The day after that Web video went up and a day before that man's body was discovered, he moved his business—quite suddenly and during the night."

"Is that all?" Brian said.

"No. There are rumors that he's done work for certain people. Websites that appear and disappear—proxy servers, redirects, rotating domain names, all of that. That's Bari's specialty."

"How about ISPs?" Dominic said, referring to Internet service providers. "Any chance these people are creating their own rather than using commercial companies?"

Archie answered this one. "Too much hassle, I expect. There's not a lot of oversight with that sort of thing here. A name and a credit card number is all it takes. Domain names can be registered in bulk and changed at the drop of a hat. No, the way this Bari fella does it is the way to go, at least here."

Dominic said to Ghazi, "Who's he living with? Any family?"

"Not here. A wife and daughter in Benghazi."

"What're the chances he's going to be armed?"

"Bari himself? Very unlikely, I would think. When he moves about, he sometimes has protection."

"URC?"

"No, no, not directly, I do not believe. Perhaps hired by them, perhaps, but these are just Medina people. Thugs."

"How many?" This from Brian.

"The times I have seen him . . . Two or three."

"Where do we find him?" said Brian.

*

By the time they dropped Archie back at the consulate, the sun's lower rim was nearly touching the sea's surface to the west. All across the city, streetlamps, car headlights, and neon signs were flickering to life. They'd decided that Dominic, who'd undergone the FBI's defensive driving course, would be behind the Opel's wheel. True to Archie's prediction, the traffic had slackened somewhat, but the roads still bore more of a resemblance to racetracks than to urban thoroughfares.

Archie climbed out from the backseat and leaned his arms against the passenger door. "That map of the Medina you've got is a fairly good one but not perfect, so keep your heads about you. Sure this can't wait till morning?"

"Probably not," Brian said.

"Well, then loosen up and smile. Act like tourists. Window-shop; haggle a bit; pick up some swag. Don't march through the place like diggers—"

"'Diggers'?"

"Soldiers. You can park on one of the side streets near the Corinthia—that monstrosity of a hotel we passed on the way here."

"Got it."

"It's visible from pretty much everywhere in the Medina. If you get lost, head for it."

Brian said, "Damn, man, you make it sound like we're walking into the lion's den."

"Not a bad analogy. All in all, the Medina's safe at night, but word'll spread if you stand out. Two more things: Dump the car if you have to. I'll report it stolen. Second, there's a brown paper bag under the tire in the boot with some goodies inside."

Dominic said, "I assume you're not talking about snacks."

"That I'm not, mate."

64

Nayoan left the embassy at five p.m., took the bus to a park-and-ride lot off Columbus, and got into a blue Toyota Camry. With Clark at the wheel, they followed him to a first-floor apartment on the southwestern edge of San Francisco's famous Tenderloin district, between the City Hall and Market Street. It was arguably the city's worst neighborhood, with more than its fair share of poverty, crime, homelessness, ethnic restaurants, dive hotels, and fringe clubs and art galleries. There could be only one reason Nayoan had chosen this area in which to live, Clark and the others decided: The Tenderloin had a fairly healthy Asian-American population, which would allow him to move about in relative anonymity.

After a couple of hours at home, Nayoan emerged from the apartment in a somber black suit and got back in the Camry. This time with Jack in the driver's seat, they followed him back downtown to the Holiday Inn. They watched him enter the lobby, waited ten minutes, and headed back to the Tenderloin.

"Why's it called the Tenderloin?" Chavez asked as Clark turned off Hayes Street and started looking for a parking spot. The car's headlights skimmed over tipped-over garbage cans and shadowed figures sitting on front stoops.

"Nobody knows for sure," Jack said. "Sort of an urban legend. Stories range from it being the soft underbelly of the city to it once being a hazardous-pay neighborhood for cops, who could buy better cuts of meat with the extra money."

"Been reading the Frommer's, Jack?"

"That and a little Sun Tzu. Know thine enemy, right?"

"The place has got character, that's for damned sure."

Clark found a spot under a tree between two streetlamps

and pulled in. He doused the headlights and shut off the engine. Nayoan's apartment building was one block down and across the street.

Clark checked his watch. "Eight o'clock. Nayoan should be at the reception. Change," Clark said.

They traded their downtown garb—khaki pants, sweaters, windbreakers—for the Tenderloin attire they'd picked up earlier at a secondhand shop: sweatshirts, flannel shirts, ball caps, and knit beanies.

"Twenty minutes, then back here," Clark said. "Three-block radius. Same drill as before. It's a shitty neighborhood, so look the part."

"Which is?" Jack said.

Chavez answered, "You don't fuck with me, I don't fuck with you."

They met back at the car, then walked south half a block and stood together beside an empty stoop. Chavez started: "Only saw one police cruiser. Looked like a mandatory drive-through. Didn't do a lot of looking around."

"Jack?"

"Didn't see any lights on in the apartment. There's an alley on the back side and a crappy wooden fence with an unlocked gate leading to a concrete patio. Dogs two yards down on either side. They barked as I walked by, but I didn't see any faces come to the windows."

"Back porch light?" Clark asked.

Jack nodded. "Bare bulb. And no screen door."

"Why's that important?"

Jack shrugged. "Screen doors squeak; they rattle."

"Man gets a gold star."

Thirty seconds apart, they circled the block, then met in the alley. Chavez went through the gate first, up the steps, then unscrewed the lightbulb and stepped down. Clark and Jack came through. Clark went up the steps and spent ninety seconds crouched by the door, working the knob lock, then the deadbolt. He gave them the wait signal, then slipped through the door. He was back sixty seconds later and waved them in.

The apartment's interior was a mirror image of the architecture: long and narrow, with cramped hallways, narrow-plank hardwood floors covered in worn carpet runners, and dark baseboards and crown molding. Nayoan wasn't much on interior decoration, Jack saw: a utilitarian kitchen and bathroom done in checkerboard porcelain tile, and a front room with a sectional sofa, a coffee table, and a thirteen-inch television. Probably didn't expect to be here for long, Jack thought. Why bother with anything but the necessities? Could that mean something? Might be worth checking how long Nayoan had left on his tour at the embassy.

"Okay, let's toss it," Clark ordered. "Everything back in its place when we're done."

They clicked on their flashlights and went to work.

Almost immediately Chavez found a Dell laptop on a card-table desk in Nayoan's bedroom. Jack powered it up and started sifting through the folders and files, the Web browser history, and the e-mail backlog. Clark and Chavez let him work, spending thirty minutes dissecting the apartment room by room, checking the obvious hiding spots first.

"Okay," Jack said. "No password protection, no key logging software . . . Aside from a standard firewall and an antivirus program, this thing is wide open. Lot of stuff here, but nothing that jumps out. Mostly unclassified embassy business and e-mails—some of it personal. Family and friends back home."

"Address book?" Clark asked.

"Same there, too. Nothing we've seen from URC distribution

lists. He cleans his Web browser history almost daily, right down to the temporary files and cookies."

"'Cookies'?" Chavez asked.

"Little bits of data websites leave on your computer every time you visit. Pretty standard practice, for the most part."

"How deep can you dig?" Clark asked.

"Here? Not very. I can copy all his files and folders and mailboxes, but to duplicate his hard drive would take too long."

"Okay, grab what you can."

Jack plugged a Western Digital Passport hard drive into the Dell's FireWire port and started copying files while Clark and Chavez kept hunting. After another forty minutes, Chavez whispered from the kitchen, "Gotcha."

He came into the bedroom carrying a zip-top sandwich baggie. "False bottom in his utensil drawer."

Jack took the baggie, looked at it. "Read-write DVD." He popped open the Dell's drive bay and slipped the DVD inside. He clicked on the appropriate drive letter, and the window popped up on the screen. "Lotta data here, John. About sixty gigabytes. A lot of them are image files."

"Pull some up."

Jack double-clicked a folder open and brought up the pics in thumbnail sizes. "Look familiar?"

"They do indeed," Clark said.

Jack tapped his index fingernail on three pictures in turn. "For sure those are from URC websites."

"Where's there's smoke . . ." Chavez said.

Clark checked his watch. "Copy it. Ding, let's police it up. Time to get out of here."

They were back at their hotel, a La Quinta Inn near the airport, an hour later. Jack used a secure FTP—file transfer protocol—to upload some of the images to The Campus's server, then called Gavin Biery, their info-tech wunderkind, and put him on speakerphone.

"We've seen these before," Biery said. "From the Tripoli flash drive?"

"Right," Jack said. "We need to know if they've got stego embedded."

"I'm putting the finishing touches on the decryption algorithm; part of the problem is we don't know what kind of program they used for the encryption—commercial or homemade. According to the Steganography Analysis and Research Center—"

"There's such a place?" asked Chavez.

"—to date there's seven hundred twenty-five stego applications out there, and that's just the commercial stuff. Anybody with halfway decent programming skills could make one up and fit it on a flash drive. Just carry it around, plug it into a computer, and you're in stego mode."

"So how do you break it?" This from Clark.

"I put together a two-part process: First check for discrepancies in the file—be it video, or image, or audio. If that finds an anomaly, then the second part of the program starts running the file through the most common encryption methods. It's a brute-force process, but chances are the URC has its favorite methods. Find that and we can start speeding up the dissection."

"How long?" Jack asked.

"No idea. I'll start feeding the monster and get back to you."

At three a.m. the phone rang. The three of them were awake instantly. "Biery," Jack said, rubbing his eyes and squinting at the cell phone's ID screen. He put the call on speakerphone.

"I might be popping the cork a little early," Biery said, "but I think we've hit the mother lode. That's the good news. The bad news is it looks like they're using three different encryption methods, so it's going to take some time."

"You have our attention," Clark replied.

"First thing: The banner image we saw on the URC website showing Dirar's murder—I think it's a digital onetime pad. Essentially a decoding grid for plain-speak messages. Whether it's outdated or current I don't know yet."

This was no surprise to Jack. What was old is new again, he knew. The OTP system was ancient—how ancient was a topic of debate among cryptography scholars, but its birth into the modern age was in 1917 with an AT&T engineer named Gilbert Vernam—and while there were a variety of OTP flavors, at its core it is a substitution cipher, most simply arranged in the form of a random alphanumeric grid: combing a character from the left-hand margin with a character from the top margin, and where they intersect in the grid's body is the single character substitution. Encoding and decoding was time-consuming, but providing the OTP was restricted to only the sender and the receiver; it was virtually unbreakable. In this case, certain URC members would know to check certain websites on certain days and download certain images, which would then be steganographically decrypted, revealing a onetime pad with which plain-speak phone calls, letters, and e-mails could be securely transmitted.

The question was, Jack thought, how often did the URC rotate its online OTP? The only way to find that out was to try to match known URC messages with onetime-pad images in the same time frame.

"This could explain why the baby announcement e-mail has dead-ended," Jack said. "They switched pads and we've been a step behind."

Clark nodded and said, "Go ahead, Gavin."

"Second: One of the larger image files on Nayoan's DVD—didn't have a match on any we pulled off URC sites. The algorithm's still chewing on it, but based on what I'm seeing so far, we've got a whole lot of credit card and bank routing numbers."

"Nayoan's a URC treasurer," said Chavez. "Sure as shit."

"You're checking the numbers?" Clark asked Gavin.

"Not yet. Which do you want first?"

"Credit cards. Easier to get and easier to dump than a bank account. Start with stuff in San Francisco and West Coast accounts. Might as well make hay while we're out here."

65

If their entry into the Medina caused any curiosity it was well disguised, the Caruso brothers decided. It was not yet dark, of course, so there were plenty of obviously white and Western tourists still milling around vendors' stalls and wandering through the switchback narrow alleyways; their presence was of little consequence. The sun was dropping below the horizon, however, and with the dimming light the Medina would slowly empty of outsiders, leaving behind only locals and those few-and-far-between tourists who were either familiar enough with Tripoli or ignorant of its hazards. There were few murders of tourists in the Medina, Archie had assured them, but nocturnal muggings and purse snatchings were almost considered a sport here. Thieves had a discerning eye for the unmindful and the weak. Brian and Dom would appear neither, Archie had observed, so they had little to worry about. The Aussie's brown-bag present in the trunk— a pair of Browning 9-millimeter Hi-Power Mark III semiautomatics, sans serial numbers, and four magazines of low-velocity hollow-points—made doubly sure of this. The noise suppressors Andy had provided were bench-made from

PVC piping, each about the size of two soda cans stacked atop each other and spray-painted black. Neither would last more than a hundred rounds before losing its effectiveness, but since they had only forty rounds between them, the point was moot.

For twenty minutes they wandered through the stucco- and brick-walled alleys, stopping at portable vendor stalls and shops to look at the merchandise, all the while following Archie's map, which Brian folded in his hand. Archie had given them several routes to Rafiq Bari's apartment, and several routes out, including two E&E—escape and evasion—paths, an addition that had solidified their hunch that their contact was ex-military, probably Australian SASR, or Special Air Service Regiment. It was an insight of no small comfort: The Aussie's mind-set was aligned with their own.

"Something smells good," Dom said, sniffing.

The air was full of scents: burning charcoal, broiled meat, spices, as well as the stink of a thousand sweating bodies packed into enclosed spaces. The noise, too, was at first disorienting, a cacophony of Arabic, French, Maghrebi, and heavily accented English. The throngs seemed to move as if guided by some unseen traffic cop, sidestepping around one another and into and out of alleys with only the occasional eye contact or hesitation.

"Dog meat, maybe?"

"That's Asia, bro, and less common than you'd think. Maybe a little horse here, but mostly lamb, I'd bet."

"Been reading brochures again?"

"When in Rome."

"Something tells me cleanliness ain't high on their list of priorities," Brian said, nodding at a vendor who was cutting up raw chicken on a cutting board; his canvas apron was speckled with blood.

Dominic laughed at this. "Hell, didn't they have you eating

bugs at SERE?" referring to Survival, Evasion, Resistance, and Escape school.

Like all Marines, Brian had been through recruit, entry-level A SERE, but he'd also been pushed through the remaining B and C levels, reserved for forward operating combat units and aircrews.

"Yeah, bugs at Bridgeport, snakes at Warner."

Navy and Marine Corps B and C SERE was held at a number of sites, including the Mountain Warfare Training Center in Bridgeport, California, and Naval Air Station in Warner Springs, California.

"So what's a little horse meat?"

"Maybe on the way out, okay? We getting close or what?"

"Yeah, but we got time to kill. We'll make a pass of Bari's place at dusk, get the lay of the land. Wait for dark to go in."

"Sounds good. What time is—"

As if on cue, a loudspeaker down the alley crackled to life and emitted the muezzin's call to prayer. Around them, the alleys slowly went silent as locals stopped what they were doing, unfurled their prayer rugs, and knelt for the ritual. Along with the other non-Muslims, Brian and Dominic stepped aside and remained quiet and still until the ritual was completed and normal activity resumed. The Carusos started walking again. Dusk was fading quickly, and lights were glowing to life in windows and outdoor cafés.

"Can't say Islam is my cup of tea," Dominic said, "but I'll give them this: They're dedicated."

"Which is the problem when it comes to the radicals. That kind of dedication is the first step toward suicide bombing and flying planes into buildings."

"Yep, but I can't help wondering sometimes if we're talking about the bad-apple theory."

"Say what?"

"One bad apple in the barrel. In this case, there are plenty of really bad apples, but probably still a pretty small minority."

"Maybe so, maybe not. Kinda above our pay grade, though."

"I mean, think about it: How many Muslims in the world?"

"Billion and a half, I think. Maybe two."

"And how many of them go around blowing themselves up? Better question: How many are radical terrorists?"

"Twenty or thirty thousand, probably. I get your point, bro, but I don't worry about the good apples. Who and how you worship is your own business—up until you start getting divine messages to blow the shit out of innocent people."

"Hey, no argument here."

They'd had this discussion before: Was broad-brushing a whole people or religion merely a mistake of morality, or was it also a tactical mistake? When you see whole chunks of a demographic as the enemy, does that keep you from not only spotting the real bad guys but also recognizing an ally? Like almost every country on earth, America had had enemies turn to friends, and friends into enemies. The Afghan mujahideen was a case in point that Dominic had often cited. The same rebels the CIA had helped drive the Soviets out of Afghanistan had morphed into the Taliban. The history books would forever be debating how and why that had happened, but there was little arguing the truth of the thing itself. One issue the Caruso brothers agreed on was the similarities between a soldier's perspective and a cop's perspective: Know your enemy as best you can, and be flexible in your tactics. Plus, both of them had seen enough shit in their lives to know there was no such thing as black-and-white in the real world—and that was especially true of their roles at The Campus, where gray was the norm. There was a good reason why spooks and special operators were often referred to as "Shadow Warriors."

"Don't get me wrong," Dominic added. "I'm only too happy to pull the trigger on any mutt who threatens my country. I'm just saying, the guy who fights the smart war is usually the winner."

"Amen to that. There's probably a few million Soviet soldiers who'd argue that, though. Stalin shoved them into the meat grinder of the Eastern Front like they were cattle."

"Always an exception to the rule."

Brian stopped to check their map. "Almost there. Next left, then right down an alley. Bari's apartment is the third door on the left. Painted bloodred, according to Ghazi."

"Let's hope that ain't a bad omen."

They found the right alley ten minutes later and ducked through the arch. Soldier that he was, Brian's night vision was better tuned than that of his brother, so he was the first to realize the man walking toward them down the alley was none other than Rafiq Bari. He was not alone but rather was flanked by a pair of men, each dressed in dark slacks and long-sleeved white shirts open at the neck and untucked at the waist.

"Local heavies," Dominic muttered.

"Yep. Let's let them pass."

Bari was walking fast, as were his bodyguards, but both Bari's body language and that of the two bodyguards told the Carusos that Bari wasn't under duress. The relationship was clearly of an employee-employer nature.

Brian and Dom reached the red door first and kept going, letting Bari and his party pass on their left. Brian cast a quick glance over his shoulder and saw Bari slipping a key into the door's lock. Brian turned back forward. The door opened, then slammed shut. The Carusos turned left at the next corner and stopped.

"Never gave us a second look," Dominic said. Bari's bodyguards were probably street-level thugs who assumed a familiarity with violence was training enough for the job, and they'd probably be right in most circumstances.

"Bad luck for them, good for us," Brian replied. "He was moving quick, though. He's either in a hurry to catch *Wheel of Fortune* or he's on the move."

"Better assume the latter. Time to improvise."

"The Marine way."

Twenty feet down the alley, they found an open archway on their left and stepped through into a small courtyard with a dry circular fountain in the center. It was almost fully dark now, and the corners were cast in deep shadow. They took a few moments to let their eyes adjust. Leaning against the far wall was a trellis covered in dried vines. They walked over and tested the wood; it was brittle.

"Boost," Brian said, then stepped to the wall and formed a saddle with his hands. Dominic stepped into it, reached high, and snagged the top of the wall. He scrambled up, then looked down and gave Brian the *wait* one-hand signal and crawled away. He was back in three minutes. He gave an *all okay* nod, then leaned over and helped Brian up.

"Bari's door leads to an inner courtyard. Open doorway on the east wall. One bodyguard there. Bari and the other one are inside. I can hear them banging around. Sounds like they're in a hurry."

"Let's do it."

They loaded their Brownings, affixed the suppressors, and started across the roof. To their left, in the alley, there came the sound of a dog barking, then a dull thump. The dog yelped and went silent. Brian held up his closed fist, calling a halt. They both knelt down. Brian crept across the roof, peeked over the edge, then returned.

"Four men coming down the alley," he whispered. "Moving like operators. Or police."

"Maybe the reason Bari's in a hurry," Dominic observed. "Let it play out?"

"If it's the police, we got no choice. If not . . ."

Dominic shrugged, nodded. They'd come a long way for Bari; they weren't going to give him up unless they had no other option. The question was, if these new players had come to kill Bari, would they do it here or take him somewhere else?

Brian and Dominic moved closer to the eaves overlooking Bari's courtyard, then dropped to their bellies and eased forward until they could see. The lone bodyguard was still standing beside the door, a mere shadowed outline in the darkness. A cigarette's cherry tip glowed to life, then dimmed.

To their left the footsteps grew louder, scuffing along the sand-and-dirt alley before stopping—presumably at Bari's door. The Carusos knew the next few moments would tell them all they needed to know about their competitors. The police would go in shouting; anyone else would go in shooting.

Neither happened.

There came a soft knock at the courtyard door. Bari's bodyguard tossed his cigarette away and leaned into the opened doorway, said something, then headed toward the courtyard door. His body showed no signs of tension; he made no move to draw the weapon that Brian and Dominic assumed was tucked into a belt holster. They exchanged glances: *Bari expecting company?*

The bodyguard threw back the sliding latch and pulled open the door.

Pop, pop.

The gunshots were soft, no louder than a palm being slapped on a wooden tabletop. The bodyguard stumbled backward and sprawled onto the ground. Three figures rushed past him toward the inner doorway. A fourth followed, paused beside the bodyguard's body to put a final round in his forehead, then kept walking.

Two more muffled pops came from within the house, then a shout, then silence. Ten seconds later Bari came out with his hands clasped behind his head, being shoved from behind by the three intruders. He was pushed to his knees before the fourth man—the leader, it seemed—who bent at the waist and said something to Bari. Bari shook his head. The man slapped him.

"Looking for something," Dominic whispered.

"Yeah. URC, you think?"

"I'd say. Unless he's freelancing for someone else."

The questioning went on for another two or three minutes, then the leader gestured to the other men, who pinned him to the ground. His hands were bound with duct tape, and a rag was stuffed into his mouth. They dragged him back into the house.

"Mr. Bari's going to lose some fingernails," Brian observed.

"If he's lucky. Best we get to him before they fuck him up too much."

"Give it a few minutes. He'll be all the happier when the cavalry arrives." This Brian said with a grin Dominic decided was halfway evil.

"Shit, Bri, that's hard-core."

"That's leverage."

The muffled screams from inside the house started almost immediately. At the five-minute mark, Dominic looked up from his watch and nodded. Brian went over the edge first, hanging from the eaves, then dropping lightly to his feet. Hunched over and Browning pointed at the door, he side-stepped to the far wall, then knelt down and gave his brother a nod. Dominic was down ten seconds later and crouched beside the near wall.

Together they started forward, sliding along the wall in the shadows until Dominic gestured for a halt. He crept forward until his angle allowed him a glimpse through the door. He gestured to Brian: *Three men visible; room to left through the door. Short hall straight through the door. Two unaccounted for.*

Brian nodded, then signaled back the entry plan and got a nod in return. Dominic crossed the last ten feet to the doorside wall, then sidestepped along it until he was pressed flat beside the doorjamb. Brian moved forward and crouched beside the other jamb. Dominic took one last look, leaning out just enough to see through the door. He nodded.

Brian nodded one . . . two . . . three, then stood up, stepped through the door and turned left, the Browning up and leading him. Dominic was a step behind.

Two of the men had Bari pressed face-first into a wooden trestle table; the surface was slick with blood, which glistened blackly under the glow of a floor lamp in the corner. The leader sat across from Bari, a paring knife in his right hand; the blade and his hand were wet.

One of the men holding Bari looked up, saw Brian as he sidestepped into the room. Brian's first shot struck the man in the throat, the second in the center of the forehead. Brian adjusted aim, put down the second man. The leader spun around, a gun in his hand. Dominic was already there. He slammed the butt of the Browning into the man's temple, and he slumped sideways to the floor.

"Clear."

"Clear," Brian whispered. "Him?"

"Give him a nap."

Brian rapped Bari behind the ear with the Browning's butt, then checked him. "Good."

They both turned, stalked back down the hall, glanced right through the open door and saw nothing, so they turned left, down the short hall. A silhouette appeared in the doorway at the end. Dominic fired twice. The man went down. From the room they heard the screeching of wood on wood.

"Window," Dominic said.

"Got it."

Brian was at the threshold in three steps. He peeked around

the corner and saw a man climbing through a window on the other side of the room. He fired. The 9-millimeter hollow-point slammed into the man's hip. His leg collapsed beneath him, and he fell backward into the room. In his left hand was a pistol. Dominic stepped forward and double-tapped the man in the chest.

"Clear."

"Clear."

The rest of the apartment consisted of a bathroom and a second bedroom, both off the short hall. Both rooms were empty, as were the closets. They found Bari's second bodyguard in the bathtub, fully clothed, with a neat hole in the back of his head. They returned to the front room, which they realized was in fact a living room/kitchenette. Bari lay where they'd left him, face-first on the table, arms spread.

"Christ," Brian said. "What the fuck . . ."

In the short five minutes in which Bari's visitors had worked on him, they'd managed to cut two fingers off his left hand.

"Somebody green-lit this guy," Dominic said.

"Yeah. The question is why?"

66

Whatever his effectiveness as a bureaucrat, one thing about Agong Nayoan became quickly apparent to Clark, Jack, and Chavez: As an intelligence operative, either the man was untrained in the ways of fieldcraft or he'd chosen to ignore the rules, and nowhere was this more acutely obvious than his choice of online passwords, which Gavin Biery cracked within hours of Clark and company leaving Nayoan's home. The Web browser on Nayoan's laptop had the normal array of bookmarks—from shopping sites to reference sites and everything in between—but he also maintained several online e-mail accounts, one at Google, one at Yahoo!, and one at Hotmail. Each mailbox contained dozens of messages, mostly from friends and family, it seemed, but also junk mail and spam, these heavily laden with banner images that Biery would be scanning for traces of stego.

Nayoan was also an avid user of Google Maps, which Jack found heavily annotated with digital pushpins. Most of these turned out to be restaurants, cafés, or similar San Francisco hot spots within walking distance of both the embassy and his home. One pushpin, however, caught Jack's attention, a private home in San Rafael, about fifteen miles north of the city across the Golden Gate Bridge.

"What's the pushpin called?" Clark asked.

"Sinaga," Jack replied.

"Sounds like a last name."

"Checking," Jack said, before Clark could make the suggestion. He had Biery on the phone a minute later. "Need you to scan Nayoan's accounts for a name: Sinaga."

Biery was back ten minutes later. "Kersan Sinaga. Nayoan has written him seven checks in the last two years, ranging from five hundred to a couple thousand bucks. One of the check abstracts I pulled up at his bank's website has a notation: 'computer consultation.' Here's the interesting part, though: I ran his name through Immigration; they've got him flagged. He was supposed to show up for a hearing eight months ago and never showed. He's also flagged on the watch list."

"Double whammy," Chavez said. "Skipping an ICE hearing doesn't get you a place on the list all by itself."

"No chance," Clark agreed. "What else?"

"He's wanted by the Indonesian POLRI," Biery replied, referring to the Polisi Negara Republik Indonesia. The Indonesian national police. "Seems your Kersan Sinaga is a top-notch forger. They've been looking for him for four years."

The drive north out of the city took thirty minutes. According to Jack's own Google map, Sinaga lived on the eastern outskirts of San Rafael, in a sparsely populated mobile-home park. They drove through once, then circled back and parked a hundred yards north of Sinaga's trailer, a double-wide surrounded by a rusted waist-high hurricane fence and hedges.

"Ding, there's a legal pad in my briefcase back there," Clark said over his shoulder. "Grab it for me, will you?"

Chavez handed it over. "Whatcha thinking?"

"A little neighborhood survey. Be back in ten minutes."

Clark climbed out, and Jack and Chavez watched him walk down the lane to the nearest trailer, where he mounted the steps and knocked on the door. A woman appeared a few seconds later, and Clark chatted with her for thirty seconds before moving on to the next house, where he repeated the process until he reached Sinaga's trailer. When he reappeared, he walked to three more trailers before walking back to the car and climbing in. He handed the legal pad to Jack. It was covered in names, addresses, and signatures.

"Care to clue us in?" Jack said.

"I told him I was trying to open a restaurant down the road and I needed five hundred signatures from nearby residents to apply for a liquor license. Sinaga's not home. According to his neighbor, he works part-time at the Best Buy off one-oh-one. He gets off at two."

Chavez checked his watch. "An hour. Not enough time."

"We'll wait for dark," Clark said.

"And then?" Jack asked.

"We're going to kidnap the sonofabitch."

*

Clark's reasoning was sound. Nayoan rarely contacted Sinaga, and even then only by e-mail, so the man's disappearance wasn't likely to raise an alarm. Better still, if they worked the scam correctly, they might be able to parlay their electronic association into an information dump from Nayoan. Worst case, they would have a warm body who had, more than likely, forged documents for the URC, perhaps both here and overseas. Whether Gerry Hendley would like the idea of The Campus having custody of a URC stringer none of them knew.

"Easier to ask forgiveness than permission," Clark observed.

They drove to the Best Buy and waited for Sinaga to emerge, then followed him to a nearby grocery store, then home. They waited thirty minutes, then Clark reprised his bar-owner role, this time taking the houses on the opposite side of the street before crossing over to Sinaga's trailer. He was back five minutes later.

"He's alone. Playing Xbox and drinking beer. I didn't see any feminine touches, so it's a good bet he's a bachelor," Clark reported. "He's got a dog, though, an old cocker spaniel. Didn't bark until I knocked on the door."

They killed time until nightfall, then drove back to the trailer park and circled the block once. Sinaga's car, a five-year-old Honda Civic, was parked under the carport awning, and lights showed in the trailer's windows. A bare bulb cast the porch in white light. Clark doused the Taurus's headlights and killed the engine, then scanned the legal pad.

"His neighbor—the one that knew he was at work—is a guy named Hector. Looks a bit like you, Ding."

"Let me guess: I'm borrowing a cup of sugar."

"Yep. There's no screen door, so he'll have to open the door. When he does, you bulldoze him and I'll grab the dog and put it in the bathroom. Jack, you go through the side gate and cover the back windows. Not much of a chance he'll have time to get to them, but better safe than sorry."

"Okay."

"Don't skulk around. Walk like you've got purpose. The neighbors were pretty friendly, so if somebody sees you, just wave or say hi like you belong. Let's do it."

They got out and started down the street, chatting quietly and occasionally chuckling, a trio of residents walking back from somewhere. When they drew even with the trailer, Clark and Chavez turned toward it. Jack stepped into the shadows beside the gate and watched as Clark pressed himself against the wall beside the door and Chavez mounted the steps. Clark turned and nodded to Jack, who gently pushed open the gate and stepped into the yard. There wasn't much grass, but there were plenty of weeds and brown spots and piles of dog crap. He reached the rear of the trailer and squatted down so he could see the length of the trailer. There were two windows, but one was too small for an adult; the window closest to him was the only exit.

From the front, Jack heard Chavez's knock, followed a few seconds later by a "Yeah, who's there?"

"Hector, from next door. Hey, man, my phone's disconnected. Can I use yours for a second?"

Footsteps clicked on the trailer's floor. Hinges squeaked. "Hey!"

A door slammed, followed by the pounding of footsteps. Jack looked up, on alert now. *Shit . . . what . . .*

"Coming your way!" Clark called. "Back window!"

Even as Clark said the words, the window slid open and a figure appeared, diving out headfirst. He landed with a grunt, then rolled over and jumped to his feet.

Jack froze momentarily, then said, "Stop, right there!"

Sinaga spun on him, head darting first left, then right. He

charged Jack, and in the light filtering from the window Jack saw a glint of steel in Sinaga's hand. *Knife,* some distant part of his brain told him. Then Sinaga was on him, knife slashing sideways. Jack backpedaled. Sinaga kept coming. Jack felt the fence railing slam into his back, then saw Sinaga bringing his arm around. He jerked his head sideways, felt an impact on his right shoulder. Slightly off balance by the wild swing, Sinaga stumbled sideways. Jack caught his arm, left hand on his wrist, and gave it a jerk, then wrapped his right arm around Sinaga's neck, his larynx in the crook of Jack's elbow. Sinaga bent his head forward, then butted backward. Jack sensed it coming but was able to only tilt his face sideways. The back of Sinaga's head slammed into Jack's cheekbone. Pain burst behind Jack's eyes. Sinaga flailed, trying to free himself, and slammed Jack back against the fence again, but losing his own footing in the process. Legs splayed out before him, Sinaga dropped straight down and landed on his butt. Jack held on, felt himself tipping forward over Sinaga's head. *Don't let go, don't let go. . . .* Arm still wrapped around Sinaga's throat, Jack somersaulted. He heard a muffled crunch-pop. He landed in a heap, rolled sideways, sure Sinaga would be on him.

"Jack!" Chavez's voice. Ding appeared, running through the gate. Without breaking stride, he kicked the knife away from Sinaga's hand. He wasn't moving. His head was cocked strangely to one side. His eyes blinked several times, but they were fixed, staring. His right arm was jerking, rapping softly on the ground.

"Christ . . ." Jack whispered. "Christ almighty."

Clark ran through the gate, stopped short, then knelt down beside Sinaga. "His neck's broken. He's gone. Jack, you okay?"

Jack couldn't take his eyes off Sinaga. As he watched, the man's arm stopped twitching.

Clark said, "Jack, wake up. You okay?"

Jack nodded.

"Ding, get him inside. Quick."

Once inside the trailer, Ding sat Jack on the couch, then walked down the hall to the bedroom and helped Clark manhandle Sinaga's body back through the window. They met back in the front room. From the bathroom, the cocker was barking.

"Nothing moving outside," Clark reported, shutting the front door. "Ding, check the fridge, see if a little food'll quiet down Fido."

"Got it."

Clark stepped over to Jack. "You're bleeding."

"Huh?"

Clark pointed at Jack's right shoulder. The material of his shirt was dark with blood. "Take off your shirt." Jack did so, revealing a two-inch gash on his collarbone at the base of his throat. Blood trickled down his chest.

"Huh," Jack mumbled. "Didn't know. Felt something hit my shoulder, but I didn't realize."

"An inch or two higher and you'd be done, Jack. Put your thumb on it. Hey, Ding, see if Sinaga's got some superglue."

From the kitchen came sounds of drawers opening and closing, then Chavez walked out and tossed a tube to Clark, who handed it to Jack. "Put a line of that in the cut."

"You're kidding."

"No. Better than stitches. Do it."

Jack tried, but his hands were shaking. He looked at them. "Sorry."

"Just adrenaline, *mano,*" Chavez said, taking the tube. "Don't sweat it."

"He's really dead?" Jack asked Clark.

Clark nodded.

"Shit. We needed him alive."

"His choice, Jack, not yours. You can feel bad about it if you want. That's natural. But don't forget: He was trying to open your throat."

"Yeah, I guess. I don't know."

Chavez said, "Don't overthink it. You're alive; he's dead. Would you rather have it the other way around?"

"Hell, no."

"Then chalk it up as a win and move on." Chavez capped the superglue tube, stood up.

"Just like that? Move on?"

"Might take a little time to process it," Clark replied. "But if you can't, you need to stick to your desk."

"Jesus, John."

"If you carry this dirtbag around in your head, it's going to get you or somebody else killed. I guarantee it. This job isn't for everyone, Jack. There's no shame in that. Better you figure that out now than later."

Jack exhaled, rubbed his forehead. "Okay."

"Okay, what?"

"Okay, I'll think about it." Clark smiled at this. "What?" Jack asked.

"That was the right answer. You just killed a man. I'd be worried if you didn't have a little soul-searching to do."

From the kitchen, Ding called, "Got something, John."

Three days after it left on a charter flight from Dubai, the device touched down at Vancouver International Airport in British Columbia. Having landed the day before, Musa was waiting for the flight. His business card and letter cleared him into the customs warehouse, where he met the inspector.

"Silvio Manfredi," Musa introduced himself, handing over his documentation.

"Thanks. Phil Nolan. Your package is over here."

They walked to a nearby pallet on which the plastic crate sat.

Neither the card nor the letterhead had been difficult to create using Photoshop and a high-end desktop publishing program. Of course, the inspector would care little about a letter from the University of Calgary's veterinary medicine department chair, but the psychological effect couldn't be ignored. The inspector was dealing with a fellow citizen and a renowned Canadian university.

What Musa's fourteen months of study had taught him was that customs inspectors the world over were overworked and underpaid, and lived by checklists and forms. For this particular type of shipment—radioactive materials—the inspector would be concerned with three forms of documentation: an invoice and bill of lading for the device; the stamps and seals from the International Air Transport Association (IATA) agent in Dubai, stating the origin of the shipment; and the myriad paperwork demanded by the Canadian Nuclear Safety Commission, Transport Canada, the Nuclear Substances and Radiation Devices license, the Canadian Nuclear Substances Act, and the Transportation of Dangerous Goods Act. While none of these documents had proven difficult to reproduce, the intelligence groundwork Musa and his men had conducted had alone taken eight months.

"So what is it?" the customs inspector asked.

"It's called a PXP-40HF portable equine imager."

"Come again?"

Musa chuckled. "I know. Quite a mouthful. It's a portable X-ray machine for horses. A friend of the university president lives in Dubai. Has this prized Arabian stallion worth more than either of us will make in a lifetime. Horse got sick, friend complains to president, the university puts the machine on loan."

The inspector shook his head. "Must be nice. Did the horse make it?"

"Yes. Get this: It was just colic. Spent a week over there babysitting an X-ray machine because the guy's vet didn't recognize a simple case of indigestion."

"Well, at least you got some sun. Okay . . ." the inspector said, flipping through the paperwork. "I need radioisotope code, activity level, dose rate, contamination limits. . . ."

"Page four. And page nine. Pretty low across the board."

"Yeah, okay, I see it. So how dangerous is this thing?"

"Pretty harmless unless you manage to take a couple hundred X-rays of your balls. Then you'd have problems."

The inspector laughed at this. "Not exactly a WMD, is it?"

Musa shrugged. "Rules are rules. Better to be a little overcautious than the opposite, I suppose."

"Yeah. Hey, how come they didn't fly you straight into Calgary?"

"Couldn't get a flight in there until Wednesday. Thought it'd be easier to come in here and rent a car. With luck, I'll be home before nightfall."

The inspector signed where he needed to sign and affixed adhesive seals on the crate. He had Musa countersign in the appropriate places, gave the paperwork once last glance, then handed it back. "You're good to go."

"My rental car is in the parking lot. . . ."

"Just pull up to the gate. I'll tell them to wave you through."

Musa shook his hand. "Thanks."

"Sure thing. Travel safe."

67

After staunching the blood pulsing from Bari's severed fingers, they sat him in a chair in the living room and duct-taped his feet to the legs. The leader of the group they duct-taped to the trestle table. Both men were still unconscious. Finally, they policed up the bodies and piled them into the bathtub, atop Bari's second bodyguard.

"I'm going to take a walk around the block," Dominic said. "See if the natives are restless. Don't think we attracted any attention, but . . ."

"Sounds good."

"Be back in five."

Brian sat in the living room, studying their captives and doing a mental postmortem of their takedown. *Pretty damned good job,* he thought. Dominic had always been good with a gun, and a pro at Hogan's Alley, but this had been the first time they'd really gotten into the shit together. Sure, there'd been that mall thing, but that wasn't quite the same, was it? Here they'd taken on genuine URC bad boys on their home turf. Not really accustomed to taking prisoners, though; he'd have to change mental gears on that point. The butt of the Browning had laid both mutts out, sure enough, but not very efficiently. Maybe a lead-and-leather sap might do the trick. Have to look into that.

He heard the courtyard gate open. He got up, walked to the door, peeked around the corner. "Just me, bro," Dominic said, walking inside.

"How's it looking?"

"Quiet. The place really dies down after dark. Another couple hours and it'll probably be a ghost town."

"Which brings up a good point."

"These two?" Dominic replied, nodding at Bari and the other one.

"Yeah. If they've got info, we can either try to wring them out here or try to get them out."

"Well, one thing's for sure, we're not getting them out of Libya on our own. Maybe a run for Tunisia."

"How far?"

"Hundred miles west, give or take. Let's not get ahead of

ourselves. Let's have a chat with Bari and see where it takes us."

With a cold glass of water poured over his head and a few light slaps to the face, they were able to rouse Bari. He blinked several times, then looked around the room, then at Brian and Dominic.

He barked a few words in Arabic, then said in heavily accented English, "Who are you?"

"The cavalry," Brian said.

Bari squeezed his eyes shut and groaned. "My hand."

"Just two fingers," Dominic said. "We stopped the bleeding. Here." He handed Bari half a dozen aspirin from a bottle they'd found in the bathroom. Bari shoved the tablets into his mouth, then accepted a glass of water from Brian.

"Thank you. Who are you?"

"But by the looks of it, we're the only friends you've got left in the Medina," Dominic said. "Who were they?"

"They're all dead?"

"Except for the fella with the paring knife," Brian replied. "Who were they?"

"I can't . . ."

"Our guess is URC. Somebody pushed the button on you, Mr. Bari."

"What does that mean?"

"Somebody ordered you murdered. What were they asking you about?"

Bari didn't reply.

"Look, without help, they're going to get you. You might be able to hide for a while, but they'll find you. Probably your family in Benghazi, too."

Bari's head jerked up. "You know about them?"

Dominic nodded. "And if we do . . ."

"You're Americans, aren't you?"

"Does it matter?"

"No, I suppose it doesn't."

Brian said, "Help us and we'll help you—try to get you out of the country."

"How?"

"Let us worry about that. Who were they?"

"URC."

"The same ones who did Dirar al-Kariim?"

"Who?"

"Web video. Guy with no head and no feet . . ."

"Oh. Yes. That's them."

Dominic asked, "What's his name, the one with the knife?"

"I know him as Fakhoury."

"What's he do?"

"What you saw here. Murder. Punishment. Very low-level type of person. He bragged about al-Kariim. Talked about it."

"Why was he after you?"

"I don't know."

"Bullshit," Brian said. "You and your bodyguards were in a hurry. You knew Fakhoury was on his way. How?"

"Word on the street was that I was talking to the police. It wasn't true. I don't know who said it, but with these people . . . security is everything. Killing me was a precaution."

"What'd they want from you? You're their Web nerd, right?"

"Yes. Fakhoury wanted to know if I'd kept any data."

"Such as?"

"Domain names. Passwords. Graphics . . ."

"Like banner images?"

"Yes. Yes, he asked about those."

Dominic looked at Brian and muttered, "Stego."

"Yep."

"What are you talking about?" Bari asked.

"So what's the answer?" Dominic asked. "Did you keep any data? A little insurance, maybe?"

Bari opened his mouth to speak, but Brian cut him off: "You lie to us and we're going to cut Fakhoury free and leave."

"Yes, I kept data. It's on an SD card—secure digital, like for a camera. It's under a tile behind the toilet."

Brian was already moving. "Got it." He was back two minutes later with a thumbnail-sized card.

Dominic asked Bari, "Who gives Fakhoury his marching orders?"

"I've only heard rumors."

"Fine."

"A man named Almasi."

"Local?"

"No, he's got a house outside Zuwarah."

Dominic looked at Brian. "About sixty miles west of here."

"How high up is this guy? Could he have okayed al-Kariim's execution?"

"It's possible."

They left Bari alone and walked out into the courtyard. "What'dya think?" Brian asked.

"Bari's a good catch, but it'd be nice to grab a fish higher up the food chain. If this Almasi has enough juice to green-light one of their own, it might be worth a try."

Brian checked his watch. "Almost ten now. Figure a half-hour to get back to the car, then two hours to Zuwarah. Hit him by two, then back on the road."

"So we take Bari, grab Almasi if we can."

"Which leaves Fakhoury."

"Dead weight, bro."

Dominic thought it over and sighed.

Brian said, "He's a stone-cold murderer, Dom."

"No shit. Having trouble throwing the switch in my head, you know?"

"You threw it once. The kiddie-raper thing."

"That was a little different."

"Not much different. Bad guy that wasn't going to stop on his own. Same thing here."

Dominic considered this, then nodded. "I'll do it."

"No, bro, this one's mine. Go get Bari ready to move. I'm going to police up."

Five minutes later Dominic and Bari were in the courtyard. Brian came out, dropped a canvas shopping tote at Dominic's feet. "Half a dozen semiautos and ten magazines. Be right back." Brian went back inside.

"What's he doing?" Bari asked.

From inside came a dull clap, then a second.

"Fakhoury?" Bari said to Dominic. "You killed him."

"Would you rather he be alive to come after you?"

"No, but who's to say you won't do the same to me when you're done?"

"I am. Worst case, we'll let you walk away."

"And best case."

"That depends on how helpful you are."

Brian walked out ten minutes later. He and Dominic walked to the far wall, and Brian boosted Dominic onto the roof. He was back ten seconds later with their backpacks. The three of them moved to the courtyard door.

Brian turned to Bari. "Just so we're clear: You run, or draw attention to us, we'll put a bullet in your head."

"Why would I do such a thing?"

"Don't know, don't care. You put us in a jackpot, you'll be the first one to die."

"I understand."

Forty minutes later they emerged from the Medina on Sidi Omran and walked two blocks east toward the Corinthia, where they'd parked the Opel. Five minutes after that, they were on Umar al Mukhtar and heading west toward the outskirts of the city. Overhead the sky was clear, showing a quarter-moon and a diamond field of stars.

They drove in silence, with Bari lying flat on the backseat until they were past Sabratah, forty miles up the coast from Tripoli. "You can sit up," Dominic told him from the passenger seat. "How's the hand?"

"Very painful. What did you do with my fingers?"

"Flushed them down the toilet," Brian replied.

This was the easiest of his tasks inside Bari's home. In turn, he had checked Fakhoury and his men for tattoos and identification. He found none of the former but plenty of the latter; these he put in the tote bag. Next he fired three rounds into the back of each man's head. The hollow-points did their job, turning each face into so much unrecognizable hamburger. The police would probably be able to eventually identify them, but by the time the URC realized it had lost one of its own, he, Dominic, and Bari would be out of the country.

"You flushed my fingers down the toilet?" Bari repeated. "Why?"

Dominic answered this one. "So there's no trace of you. The more unknowns they have, the better. Where's Almasi's house?"

"East of the city. I'll recognize the turnoff. It's across from an old refinery." Twenty minutes later, Bari said, "Slow down. This next road on the left."

Brian slowed down and turned onto the dirt tract. Almost immediately the grade increased; ahead, the road wound its way in a series of low, scrub-covered hills. After five minutes the road turned sharply right. Bari, looking out the driver's-side window, tapped the glass. "There. That house with the lights on. That's Almasi's."

A quarter-mile away down an eroded slope, Brian and Dominic could make out the two-story adobe structure surrounded by a shoulder-high mud-brick wall. Fifty yards away to the west was a cluster of four adobe huts. Directly behind the house sat a barn.

"Old farm?" Dominic asked.

"Yes. Goats. Almasi bought it as a retreat home three years ago."

Dominic said, "See the antennas on the roof, Bri?"

"Yeah. The guy's wired for some serious comms."

They continued on for another half-mile, losing sight of the farmhouse behind a hill, then slowed at a crossroads. On impulse, Brian turned left. The dirt road narrowed for fifty yards before opening into what looked like a gravel quarry.

"This ought to do," Dominic said.

Brian doused the headlights, coasted to a stop, then killed the engine. They turned in their seats and looked at Bari. "What else do you know about this place?" Brian asked.

"Just where it is, that's all."

"Never been here?"

"Once. Just to drive by it."

"How'd that happen? Just curiosity?"

Bari hesitated. "In my business, it pays to know who you're dealing with. I knew Fakhoury answered to Almasi. I thought it might be smart someday to deal directly with him, so I made some inquiries."

"Industrious," Dominic remarked. "So you've never been there, never been in the house?"

"No."

Brian: "What about bodyguards?"

"I'm sure he has them, but I don't know how many." Brian and Dominic stared hard at him. "It's the truth, I swear on my children."

"Dogs?"

"I don't know."

"Give me your hands," Brian said. "Put them on the head-rests."

Tentatively, Bari did so. Together Brian and Dominic duct-taped his hands to the headrests. "Is this really necessary?"

"We're not quite to the trust stage yet," Dominic explained. "Don't take it personally. We'll be back."

"And if you're not?"

"Then you're shit out of luck," Brian said.

They climbed out, retrieved the tote from the trunk, and sat down in the dirt to sort through their arsenal. In addition to their Brownings, they had four French-made MAB P15 9-millimeter semiautos, and two snub-nosed .32 revolvers.

"Got sixty rounds from the P15s," Brian said. "Nine-mil Parabellum. Good fit for our Brownings. If we need more than sixty, it means we've fucked up anyway."

They reloaded the Brownings' magazines, then divided up the remaining loose P15 rounds and stuffed them into the thigh pockets of their cargo pants. Finally, they stuffed some odds and ends into their backpacks. Dominic walked to the Opel's back window. Bari said, "I need some more aspirin."

Brian fished the bottle from his backpack and tossed it over. Dominic dropped half a dozen into Bari's mouth, then gave him a swig from their canteen.

"Don't go anywhere, and don't make any noise," Dominic ordered. He turned to Brian. "Ready?"

"Damn straight. Let's go bag us a big fish."

68

"How're you holding up?" Gerry Hendley asked, as Jack sat down across from the desk. Sam Granger stood to one side, leaning against the window, arms folded.

"Aside from getting asked that too many damned times, just

fine," Jack replied. "It was just a nick, Gerry. Nothing a little superglue couldn't handle."

"That's not what I'm talking about."

"I know what you're talking about."

"Jack, less than twelve hours ago you killed a man. If you tell me it's not bugging you, I'm chaining you to your desk."

"Boss—"

"He's serious," Granger said. "Like it or not, you're President Jack Ryan's son. If you don't think that gives us pause, think again. And if for a second we don't think you've got your head screwed on right, you're benched."

"What do you want from me? The truth is, my hands still shake a bit and my stomach's churning. I pushed the plunger on MoHa because he deserved it. This Sinaga guy . . . I don't know. Maybe he deserved it, maybe not. He came at me, tried to kill me. . . ." Jack hesitated, cleared his throat. "Did I want to kill him? No. Am I glad it's him and not me? You bet your ass."

Gerry considered this for a few moments, then nodded. "Give it some thought and let me know tomorrow. Whatever you want to do, you've got a place here."

"Thanks."

"Sam, ask them in, will you?"

"Hang on a second," Jack said. "I already ran this by John and Ding. . . . Remember the birth e-mail we got?" Hendley nodded. "It never went anywhere. No replies, no follows. Just dead air, pretty much across the board. I'm thinking that e-mail was a 'change the channel' order."

"Explain," said Granger.

"We know the URC's using steganography to communicate. Probably in the banner images on their websites, and they've probably been doing it awhile. What if the e-mail was a signal telling cells to switch to some stego-only protocol—call it their version of radio silence."

"To what end?"

"Special ops guys go radio-silent when they're getting ready to jump off. Maybe the Emir gave the go signal on an operation."

"We saw a drop in chatter before Nine-Eleven," Granger observed. "Bali and Madrid, too."

Hendley nodded. "Jack, I want you to glue yourself to Biery. Tear down the dump from Nayoan."

"Okay."

"Call them in, Sam."

Granger opened the door, and Clark and Chavez walked in and took their seats next to Jack. Hendley said to Clark, "You hear?"

"What?"

"The charges against Driscoll are gone."

"Imagine that," Clark said with a grin.

"Kealty's press secretary announced it yesterday at close of business. Just in time to slide into the weekend. Sam talked to an old friend at Benning. Driscoll's clear. Honorable discharge, full pension plus disability. His shoulder going to be a problem?"

"Not unless you're hiring him to drywall your office, Gerry."

"Good. Okay, let's hear it."

"Didn't find anything in Sinaga's trailer but a digital SLR camera," Clark said. "Nikon, medium price range. It had an SD card inside it with a few hundred images. Mostly landscape stuff, but maybe a dozen were head shots."

"Passport head shots," Chavez added. "All men, mostly Middle Eastern or Indonesian, looks like. And one we've seen before. Remember the courier we tailed—Shasif Hadi."

"No shit?" said Granger.

"But get this," Jack replied. "In the head shot Sinaga had, Hadi's clean shaven. When we were tailing him, he had a beard and mustache. Shave it off, use the new passport, and you're good to go."

Clark said, "That might answer the question of where he went after Las Vegas—at least partially. He left the country."

Hendley nodded. "Where and why, though? Sam, what else do we know about Sinaga?"

"He's high on the hit parade in Jakarta. I talked to a friend of a friend who's the station chief in Surabaya. The guy was good. Had a real eye for passports."

"Where are we with facial recognition?"

Jack answered this one. "Biery's got his system in beta testing, but we don't know much about the system ICE and Homeland Security is using. Their parameters might be different than ours."

"FBI?" Granger offered.

"Probably the same system. If not, they'll all be cross-pollinating anyway."

"When Dom gets back, let's have him run up a trial balloon. Since Hadi's our only known quantity, let's focus on him first. Find out where he was heading from Vegas. Mr. Clark, where did you leave things in San Francisco?"

"We're clean with Nayoan. Left everything as is but downloaded a lot of data. Gavin's massaging it right now. One thing's for sure, Nayoan was a big logistics operator for the URC. Money, documentation . . . Who knows what else. As for Sinaga, we staged a break-in. He lost the fight with the burglar and got killed. Took his DVD player, some cash, to flesh it out."

"We'll keep an eye on the news out there, see if it's playing. It should. We were careful."

"Okay, so we wait until our über-nerd has something. Thank you, gentlemen. Mr. Clark, can you stay for a minute?" Once Jack and Chavez were gone and the door was closed, Hendley said, "So?"

Clark shrugged. "He's okay. Whether he's got a taste for fieldwork only time will tell, but he's dealing with it. He's a smart kid."

"What's smart got to do with it?" Granger asked.

"Okay, then, he's even-keeled. Just like his dad."

"You'd take him out again?"

"In a New York minute, boss. He's got good instincts, good observation skills, and learns damned fast. Plus, he's got a little gray in him, too, which doesn't hurt."

"'Gray'?" Hendley asked.

"The gray man," Clark answered. "The best spooks know how to fade into the background: how they walk, how they dress, how they talk. You pass them on the street and you never notice them. Jack's got that, and it's natural."

"More Ryan genetics?"

"Maybe. Don't forget, he grew up under the microscope. Without even knowing it, he probably picked up a lot from his environment. Kids are savvy. Jack figured out early what those guys with dark suits and guns were doing hanging around all the time. Got his antennae working."

"You think he'll tell his dad?"

"About The Campus? I do. It's nobody's fault, really, but Jack's living under his dad's shadow—a damned big shadow at that. Once he figures out what he wants to do here, he'll find a way to bring it up."

With the help of a customs worker, Musa loaded the container into the rear of his rented Subaru Outback, then gave the inspector a wave and drove out the gate. Musa, of course, did not begin his long journey back to Calgary as he'd told the customs inspector, but rather drove fifteen miles east to the suburb of Surrey and pulled into the parking lot of the Holiday Inn Express. He found a parking space directly outside his ground-floor room, then went inside and spent the remainder of the day napping and flipping from one inane television show to another until finally settling on CNN. His room was equipped with wireless Internet access, so he had to resist the urge to log on with his laptop and look for an update. He had a flash drive with the latest onetime pads and steganographic decryption software—neither of which he fully understood—but logging on to one of their satellite sites this late in the operation was unwise. Tomorrow at noon was the next scheduled check-in, and even that would be brief. Failing word to the contrary, he would assume the other pieces of the plan were falling into place.

Musa stared at the ceiling, let the babble of the television fade into the background, and tabbed through his mental checklist. He knew the distances and routes by heart, and his documentation would stand up to all but the most intense scrutiny. True, the customs inspector at the airport had been a hurdle, but they were nothing compared to security measures within the United States. There police were curious and thorough and hypervigilant. Then again, Musa reminded himself, in a matter of days both state and federal American security forces would find their plates very full indeed, and he would be at his destination.

He dozed until his watch alarm woke him at seven p.m. He sat up and rubbed his eyes. Through the drawn curtains he could see the last remnants of daylight were fading. He clicked on the bedside lamp. On the television, one of the anchors was questioning some Wall Street type, hashing and rehashing the American economy. "Has it hit bottom?" the anchor was asking. "Is the country moving into recovery mode?" *Idiots. America had yet to see the bottom. Soon.*

Musa went into the bathroom, splashed water onto his face, then put on his jacket. He stood in the center of the room, thinking, then went back into the bathroom and pulled a washcloth from the towel rod. Moving backward, he wiped down every surface he had touched: counter, toilet seat, toilet handle, light switch. . . . He finished with the bedside table, the remote control, and the lamp. He had already paid for the room, so there was no need to stop at the front desk. The receptionist had told him he could leave the card key in the room, which he did, first wiping it down, then placing it on top of the television. He stuffed the washcloth into his front pants pocket. What else? Had he forgotten anything? No, he decided. He stepped outside, closed the door behind him, then walked to the rear of the Subaru. The container was still in place. He unlocked the doors, got in, and started the engine.

Once out of the parking lot, he got onto Highway 1 and headed southeast for twenty-two miles to the Fraser Highway turnoff, which he took east for seven miles to 264th Street. Here he turned south and drove for four minutes. Soon he saw the glow of stadium lights ahead. This was the 13/539 crossing, a cloverleaf-shaped compound sitting astride the U.S.-Canadian border. Musa felt his heart rate increase. He kept going.

A few hundred yards north of the compound the road split, the left-hand lane heading into the crossing, the right-hand lane curving until it merged with what his map called Zero Avenue and turned west. He pushed the odometer's trip reset button and glanced in his rearview mirror. No one behind him. He brought the Subaru up to the speed limit, then backed off a tick, then set the cruise control.

Strange, he thought, that this nondescript two-lane road bracketed on both sides by copses of trees and farmers' fields was the border between two countries. The only evidence Musa saw of this was a waist-high hurricane fence on the south side of the road. The Americans were fond of their fences, weren't they?

He drove for eight miles, watching the sun set and the stars rise. His headlights skimmed over the gray asphalt, the yellow lane dividers disappearing beneath the car, until after what seemed like hours, his headlights picked out a road intersection. As he approached it, he read the sign: 216th Street. Good. He was close now. Next came 212th Street, then 210th. He flipped off the cruise control and let the car coast. Ahead and to his right he saw some house lights behind a screen of trees. He peered out the driver's window, watching, letting the car continue to slow . . . *There.*

Beside a stand of pine trees, a gap in the hurricane fence. A sign read, PRIVATE PROPERTY. KEEP OUT. Musa looked ahead, saw no headlights, then checked the rearview mirror. Clear. He doused his headlights, tapped the brake, then swung left, across the opposite lane, and through the gate.

He was in America.

The road almost immediately angled downward, smooth dirt turning to washboard ruts. To his right, an acre of pine stumps jutted from the landscape. Some logging company had bought up this stretch of forest and had decided to clear-cut it.

The road grew rougher, but the Subaru's all-wheel drive handled the ruts well enough. The logging road meandered south and east, downward through the wasteland for another half-mile before reaching a tri-intersection of dirt roads. Musa turned left. The road smoothed out and within minutes merged with another intersection. Here he turned left, heading east again for a few hundred yards before turning south once more. Five minutes later a blacktop road appeared. This would be H-Street Road. He let out a breath. If he was going to get caught during the crossing, it would have happened by now. He was clear. For now.

He clicked on his headlights and turned right onto the road. Five more miles would bring him to Highway 5, just north of Blaine, Washington. From there he would head south. Three days of easy travel on major highways.

69

Almasi's house backed up to a low scrub pine–covered hill, the downslope of which led directly to the gravel quarry. Dominic and Brian took their time, keeping to the rock-strewn gullies that wound their way up the hill. After thirty minutes they reached the ridge. They dropped to their bellies and wriggled forward.

Down the slope, perhaps twenty yards away, was the rear wall of the barn; to the right of that, the cluster of adobe huts. They saw no lights in the windows. To their left and front was the rear porch of the farmhouse. A single light showed in an upstairs window.

"Almost three," Brian whispered. "Let's hunker down. If Almasi's got patrols out, we'll see them eventually."

Ten minutes passed, then twenty. They saw no movement.

"Shake the trees?" Dominic suggested. "Barn first?"

"Why not?"

Brian scooted back from the ridge, gathered a handful of stones, then returned. He tossed the first stone in a high arc. It smacked into the barn's roof, then clattered down the shingles and thumped to the ground.

Nothing moved. No sounds.

Brian tossed another stone, this time in a flat trajectory. The stone thunked against the barn's wall. Five minutes passed.

"Been a half-hour."

"The barn first, then the huts?" asked Dominic.

"Yeah. If there are any reinforcements, that's where they'll be."

They backed away from the hilltop and crawled to their right until they were directly behind the barn, then went back over the top of the hill and picked their way down the slope to the barn's rear wall. The wood planking was old and brittle and widely gapped. Brian and Dominic looked inside but saw nothing moving. Brian gestured: *On to the huts. I'm on point.*

Hunched over, they moved out from behind the barn and crept along the base of the hill, keeping their heads below the top of the scrub brush. After fifty feet they reached a narrow dirt path. Directly across it lay the adobe huts. Twenty yards with no cover. A hundred feet to their left stood the farmhouse. Above the back porch, the window was still lighted.

Brian gestured: *You go; I'll cover.*

Dominic nodded, took one more look around, then sprinted on flat feet across the road to the westernmost hut's outer wall. He checked both corners, then signaled Brian to cross over. He was there ten seconds later. Dominic tapped his ear, then tapped the wall. A few feet above their heads was a horizontal slit window. Through it they heard sounds of snoring.

I'll take the two on the north, Dominic gestured.

They met back up two minutes later. Brian cupped his hand around Dominic's ear and whispered, "Two men, one to a hut. AK-47 each."

Dominic nodded his agreement, held up two fingers, then four. Four total. He drew his thumb across his throat, shrugged his shoulders: *Take 'em down?*

Brian shook his head and pointed to the farmhouse. Dominic nodded. With Brian in the lead, they followed the contour of the hut walls to the eastern side, the closest point of approach to the farmhouse's back porch. More open ground, but only twenty feet this time.

Browning up and tracking right, left, up, down, Brian crossed the distance, then dropped into a crouch beside the steps. After two minutes, he gestured Dominic across. Brian pointed at the wooden steps and drew his thumb across his throat. *Too old, too noisy.* Dominic nodded. He crab-walked to the edge of the porch and tested the railing. He turned and gave a thumbs-up to Brian. Three minutes later they were over the railing and on the porch. They moved to the door, each taking a jamb. Brian tested the knob. It was unlocked. He swung it open two inches, then stopped. Waited. He pushed it open the rest of the way, peeked around the corner, and pulled back. He shook his head.

They stepped across the threshold, Brownings up and tracking for movement. They were in a tiled foyer. Ahead and to the right, a set of stairs led up to a balcony hall lined with doors. To their left and right, sitting rooms. The walls were painted stark white stucco, seemingly glowing in the darkness. Dominic pointed to himself. *On me.* Brian nodded and sidestepped over, and together they moved into the sitting room and into a dining room beyond, off which they found a kitchen. Out the opposite kitchen door they found themselves back in the sitting room to the left of the foyer.

Brian pointed at the stairs and got a nod in return. Dominic backed into the corner of the foyer to act as overwatch as Brian mounted the stairs; once at the top, he took overwatch, and Dominic climbed up to join him.

There were four doors along the hall and one on the far wall. They started with the first door. A bedroom. Empty, bed made. The air was musty, as though the room hadn't been occupied for some time. They moved to the second and third doors and found two more empty bedrooms. Behind the fourth door was what looked like a home office, complete with an oak desk, a multiline phone, a fax/scanner/copier, and a flat-screen computer monitor. Brian stepped inside and looked around. Built into a credenza opposite the desk was a wall safe.

They moved to the last door. Dominic pressed his ear to the wood, then pulled back and mouthed, *Snoring.* He gestured: *I'll go for Almasi; you clear the room.*

Brian nodded.

Dominic turned the knob, eased the door open an inch, and put his eye to the gap. He turned back, gave Brian a nod, then swung open the door. He was at Almasi's four-poster bed in three strides. Almasi was lying on his back, his arms by his sides. Brian was moving through the room, checking the corners and the master bedroom. He nodded at Dominic, who grabbed Almasi's opposite arm, jerked him onto his stomach, pressed his face into the pillow. Almasi was instantly awake, arms flailing. Dominic jammed the Browning's suppressor into the base of his neck.

"One sound and you're dead. Nod once if you understand."

Almasi nodded.

"We're leaving, and you're coming with us. Make life hard for us and I'll make sure you die badly. You've got a computer and a safe in your office. You're going to give us the password and combination, yes?"

Almasi nodded again.

Brian handed Dominic a roll of duct tape; he bound Almasi's hands, then tossed back the roll. He backed away from the bed and gestured for Almasi to stand. He did so. With Brian in the lead, they moved back into the hall, then into the office.

Dominic powered up Almasi's computer, a high-end Dell tower. The Windows Vista logo came up, followed by a log-in screen. He found a pad and pen in the desk drawer and shoved it across the desk to Almasi. "User name and password."

Almasi didn't move.

Brian pulled a nearby chair across the room and shoved Almasi down in it. He pressed the Browning against Almasi's right knee. "That's where I'll start. Knees, then ankles, then elbows." He picked up the pad and pen from the desk and dropped them in Almasi's lap. "User name and password."

This time Almasi didn't hesitate. When he finished, Brian handed the pad to Dominic, who logged in and began scanning

557

the computer's directories. "Get him started on the safe," Dominic said. "I'll start downloading, then toss his bedroom." He inserted a flash drive into the tower's USB port and began transferring files.

Brian got Almasi to his feet and prodded him toward the safe. "Open."

"My hands."

"You'll manage."

Almasi dropped to his knees and began turning the dial.

"Be right back," Dominic said, and left the room.

Almasi looked up at Brian. "Done."

"Open it, then move back."

Almasi did so, sidling backward on his knees. Brian knelt before the safe. Inside, it was empty, save a single CD-ROM in a paper sleeve. He reached inside. In the corner of his eye, he saw Almasi's bound hands moving toward the shelf beside him. He turned, saw the pistol in his hands, spun, brought the Browning up while sidestepping. There was a crack. The room flashed orange. From the hip, Brian snapped off a shot, hitting Almasi in the center of the sternum. Almasi toppled sideways.

"Brian!" Dominic came through the door, took two strides, and kicked the gun from Almasi's hand. He knelt down, checked his pulse. "He's gone."

"He came up with a gun," Brian panted. "Took my eyes off him for a second. Goddamn it."

"Whoa, sit down, Brian, sit down."

"What?"

"You're bleeding."

"Huh?"

Dominic pushed him into the chair, grabbed his right hand, and pressed it against his upper belly. Brian felt the wetness and took his hand away and looked at his fingers. "Aw, shit."

"Keep the pressure on it."

"We're gonna have company. Better check."

Dominic moved to the window and parted the curtains. Below, lights were coming on in the adobe huts. "They're coming." He turned back to Brian, who had his shirt open. There was a pinkie-tip-sized hole about four inches below his right nipple. He pressed his fingertips around the wound and winced. Blood gushed from the wound.

"Rib broken?" Dominic asked from the window.

"Yeah, I think so. Slowed the bullet down. Ah, Jesus, that hurts. Shit, shit, shit! Get that CD I dropped, will you? It was in the safe."

Dominic grabbed his backpack from the floor, fished inside, came up with a half a dozen maxi-pads. He handed them to Brian, then returned to the window. "We should have brought the real deal."

"These are better, man, really absorb the blood." He tore open a pad and pressed it to his chest. "See anything?"

"Lights are on. They'll be coming. Can you move?"

"Yeah."

"Gonna see if I can slow them up."

Dominic grabbed Almasi's pistol—a Beretta .32 Tomcat semiauto—from the floor.

"What kind of rounds?" Brian asked.

Dominic ejected the magazine and checked. "Hollow-point."

"Huh. Okay. Get moving."

Dominic dashed out the door, down the stairs, then out the door. He dropped to a crouch beside the steps, took aim on the westernmost hut, and fired three rounds through the window. Shouts came from inside. The lights went off. Dominic sprinted back into the house, locked the door, then turned right and ran to the corner window. He opened it and fired four shots at the east-side hut, then put five rounds through the front door. The pistol's slide locked open. He dropped it, ran back upstairs. Brian was on his feet and steadying himself against the desk.

"I'm good. Bleeding's slowing down. You got a plan?"

"Yep." Dominic scooped up the CD-ROM from the floor, shoved it into his backpack, then leaned across the desk and jerked the flash drive from the tower's USB port. "The porch is right below us. Once they make their move, you're going out the window. Lay flat on the roof. When you hear things start in here, get to the ground and go for the barn. If you feel up to it, go for the car. I'll meet you along the way. Gimme your gun."

"Dom—"

"Shut up and give me your gun. Can you handle your pack?" Brian nodded. Dominic handed it to him. "You're looking green, bro. Sure you're okay to move?"

"We have a choice?"

"No."

"Watch the window, give me the play-by-play."

"Got it."

Dominic laid both Brownings on the desk, looked around the room. He grabbed Almasi's desk chair and shoved it toward the door, then did the same with a nearby side table. He bulldozed them through the door, down the hall, then tipped them down the stairs. They tumbled to the bottom and landed in a heap.

"How're we doing?" he called.

"Nothing yet—wait. Got a body coming out, circling west. He's got the AK."

Dominic went into the first guest bedroom and grabbed a nightstand, a floor lamp, and a chair, all of which he shoved down the stairs.

"What the hell are you doin', Dom?"

"Homemade barricade."

He repeated the process with the next guest bedroom, then returned to the office. He grabbed his backpack and slipped it on, then grabbed up the Brownings and removed the noise suppressors, then shoved them into his belt.

At the window, Brian said, "You go, cowboy. The other three just came out. . . . Two heading for the porch, another around the front. First one's coming around the east side now. Hey, I found a surprise in the closet." He pointed to the corner, where a shotgun was leaning. "Twelve-gauge Mossberg 835. Six rounds loaded."

Dominic stepped to Brian and gently opened the window. He helped Brian out and held on until he was splayed across the shingles. Dominic said, "I'm going to wait until they're all in the house. I'll yell for more ammo. You hear that, you go. How long will you need?"

"Two minutes."

"I'll be right behind you. We can't have them on our tails."

Dominic closed the window, turned around, snatched up the shotgun, and headed into the hall. From the west-side sitting room came the sound of breaking glass. Down in the foyer, something pounded into the door. Then again, then a third time. The doorjamb cracked, bulged inward. Dominic pumped the shotgun and dropped to his belly and eased the shotgun's barrel an inch through the banister uprights. In the sitting room he heard a chair leg squelch on wood. A head peeked around the corner, pulled back, then returned. Dominic froze. He held his breath. *Nothing to see here, asshole.* The pounding on the door became louder, more insistent. The man in the sitting room took one last peek around the corner, then sidestepped, his AK up and tracking along the balcony. He sidestepped one of the toppled nightstands, then went back to the door. He took his left hand off the AK, reached for the doorknob.

Dominic adjusted the shotgun, laid the front site over the man's chest, and fired. The man staggered backward and slammed into the door and slumped down. Footsteps pounded across the porch and faded away. A few moments later came the sound of breaking glass. *One down, three left,* Dominic thought. A thought popped into his head. He got up, ran back to the office, and opened the window. He handed one of the Brownings to Brian. "In case they decide to climb." He closed the window and returned to the hall.

Downstairs, nothing was moving. A full minute passed, then somewhere to Dominic's right he heard a whispered voice. To the left a hand appeared around the corner and tossed something up the stairs. *Grenade,* Dominic thought even as it bounced onto the balcony. The shape told him it wasn't a frag but a flashbang. They didn't want to risk killing Almasi. *Too late, boys.* Dominic pushed himself up, rolled right through the office door, and clapped his hands over his ears and squeezed his eyes shut. There was a ringing boom. White light flashed through Dominic's eyelids. He felt the floor beneath him tremble. He rolled back onto his belly and wriggled back to the door. To his left, a figure was charging up the stairs, firing as he went. Bullets pounded into the wall. The man reached the top of the stairs and stopped, crouching behind the corner post. Dominic drew the Browning from his belt, took aim, and fired. The bullet tore through the man's exposed kneecap. He screamed and tumbled backward down the stairs. Dominic changed back to the shotgun, got up, raced down the hall. He fired at a head peeking around the sitting-room entrance. *Miss.* He pumped another round into the chamber, swiveled right, and fired from the hip, hitting the tumbling man center-mass. He landed on the foyer floor and was still. Dominic spun left, ducked into the first guest bedroom, dropped to his belly.

"Almost out of ammo!" he shouted. "Get me some!"

Dominic checked his watch. Two minutes. He took stock. Almost two full mags for the Browning and six rounds left in the shotgun. He rolled left, then got to his feet and peeked around the corner. In the foyer, nothing moved. He took a step out, keeping behind the corner post. He checked once more, then spun and sprinted down the hall. Bullets peppered the wall behind him. He hunched over, covered the last eight feet, and ducked into Almasi's master bedroom.

"Bro, where's that damned ammo!" Dominic shouted.

He counted to ten, then stepped out, fired two blasts into the foyer, then closed the office door before stepping back into the bedroom. He slammed the door shut loud enough that it wouldn't be missed. Once they made it up the stairs, they'd have to clear the guest bedrooms, then the office, leaving Almasi's bedroom for last. The question was, how long would that take? How long before one of them went back outside to cut off the window exits?

He locked the door and pressed his ear to the wood. One minute passed, then two. From the foyer he heard the scrape of furniture on tile. Then the creak of a stair tread. Brian crept to the window, opened it, and climbed out onto the roof. He left the window open. He looked around, saw no one. He crouch-walked to the edge. It was a ten-foot drop. He stuffed the shotgun between his pack and his shoulder blades, then rolled onto his belly and let his legs and torso dangle. He let go. As soon as his feet impacted the ground, he bent his knees and rolled. He climbed to his feet and sprinted around the house to the east side, then mounted the porch and found the broken window. He slipped inside and crept across the sitting room to the foyer. He peeked around the corner. On the balcony, only one figure was visible. He stood, back toward Dominic, at the threshold of the second guest bedroom. Dominic stepped out, picked his way through the jumble of furniture to the center of the foyer. He drew the Browning, took aim, and shot the man in the back of the head. Even as he was falling, Dominic sidestepped and ducked beneath the stairs. He holstered the Browning, drew the shotgun.

Footsteps pounded on the balcony above, then stopped. The footsteps resumed, this time moving cautiously. With a splintering crack, a door flew open. *Office*, Dominic thought.

Thirty seconds passed. Footsteps came out of the office, then paused. The master-bedroom door was kicked open.

See the window, dickhead. . . .

Another thirty seconds passed.

"Yebnen kelp!" a voice barked.

Dominic's Arabic was mediocre, but the tone told him the phrase was a curse, somewhere along the lines of *shit* or *sonofabitch*.

Footsteps pounded down the hall, then down the stairs, then onto the tiled foyer. He heard the rattle of a lock being disengaged. Dominic crab-walked two steps, brought up the shotgun, and blasted the man in the back of the legs. The impact shoved him against the door. His AK clattered to the tiles as he slumped sideways. Dominic stood up and tossed away the shotgun. He drew the Browning and walked over to the man, who lay writing and groaning on the floor. He saw Dominic and put up his hands. "Please . . ."

"Too late for that."

Dominic shot him in the forehead.

He found Brian sitting on the ground behind the barn, his back resting against the slope. He saw Dominic and raised his hand in greeting. "Get 'em?"

"Every last one. How're you doing?"

Brian gave a wobbly shake of his head. His face was ashen and glistening with sweat. "Got a confession to make."

"What?"

"Bullet missed my ribs, went clean through. It's in my liver, Dom."

"Jesus, are you sure?" He moved to open Brian's shirt, but Brian waved him off.

"The blood's really dark, almost black. Hollow-point probably shredded my liver. I can barely feel my legs, too."

"I'll get you to the hospital."

"No. Too many questions."

"Fuck you. Zuwarah's ten miles away."

Dominic knelt down, grabbed Brian's opposite arm, and pulled him across his shoulders. He got his feet under him and straightened up. "You okay?"

"Yep," Brian grunted.

The slog back up the hill took ten minutes, then ten more minutes for Dominic to pick his way down the opposite slope. When he reached the quarry floor, he started jogging toward the Opel. "You still with me?" Dominic asked.

"Uh-huh."

He reached the Opel, then dropped to his knees and lowered Brian to the ground. From the backseat, Bari called, "What happened?"

"He's shot. Is there a hospital in Zuwarah?"

"Yes."

Dominic opened the back door and used his pocketknife to cut Bari free. Together they lifted Brian into the backseat.

"You know where it is?" Dominic asked Bari, who nodded. "Then you drive. Take one wrong turn and I'll blow you away, understood?"

"Yes."

Bari climbed into the driver's seat and started the engine. Dominic ran around the car and got into the backseat with Brian. "Go, go!"

70

Their target was not in São Paulo proper but eighty miles north of the city and the center of Brazil's exploding petro-economy. The largest refinery in all of Brazil, the Paulinia

REPLAN facility processed nearly 400,000 barrels of oil per day, some twenty million gallons. Enough, Shasif Hadi had read, to fill more than thirty Olympic-sized swimming pools. Of course, as Ibrahim had told him during their initial briefing, sabotaging such a facility was no easy task. There were myriad safety redundancies to be considered, not to mention the physical security measures. Getting onto the refinery grounds would be no hurdle at all (the highest perimeter fence was ten feet tall), but once inside, there was little they could do. Explosives could destroy collection tanks, but these were spaced too far apart to hope for a domino effect. Similarly, the facility's hundreds of control valves (officially known as ESDs, or emergency shutdown devices), which regulated the flow of chemicals to the labyrinth of distillation columns, fractionation towers, cracking units, and blending and storage tanks, were virtually invulnerable, having been recently refitted with something called a Neles ValvGuard system, which was, in turn, regulated from the refinery's control center, which from their earlier reconnaissance trips they knew was below-ground and heavily fortified. Shasif understood none of these particulars, but the essence of Ibrahim's point was clear: The odds against causing a catastrophic leak within the Paulinia REPLAN were astronomical. But that word—*within*—Shasif reminded himself, was pivotal, wasn't it? There were other ways to start the dominoes falling.

As planned, each of them had his own separate hotel, as well as his own rental car. Leaving at staggered times throughout the morning, each man took the SP-348 Highway out of São Paulo and drove north to Campinas, twenty miles south of Paulinia. At noon they met at a restaurant called the Fazendão Grill. Shasif was the last to arrive. He spotted Ibrahim, Fa'ad, and Ahmed sitting in a corner booth, and made his way over to them.

"How was the drive?" Ibrahim asked.

"Uneventful. And you?"

"The same."

"It's good to see all of you," Shasif said. He looked around the table and got nods in return.

They'd been in country for five days, each with his own tasks to complete in São Paulo. The explosives—Czech-made Semtex H—had been shipped by commercial carriers into the country piecemeal, two ounces at a time, in order to lessen the chances of interception. Reliable as Semtex was, it also carried with it a dangerous flaw: a chemical taggant added during the manufacturing process to make its presence more detectable to "sniffers." Prior to 1991 no such taggant was added, but these odorless batches had a maximum shelf life of ten years, so while the year 2000 was a societal milestone, it was also a watershed for terrorists, who either had to manufacture their own non-taggant explosives or devise special handling techniques for newer batches, which were perfused with either glycol dinitrate or a compound known as 2,3-dimethyl-2,3-dinitrobutane, or DMDNB, both of which were "slow-rate vaporizers" that were perfume to a sniffer's nose.

Luckily for Shasif and the others, they needed only sixteen ounces of explosives for their purposes, so the piecemeal shipments had taken only a few weeks. From this pound of Semtex they had formed six shaped charges—five each of two ounces, and one of six ounces.

"I performed my last survey of the facility yesterday. As we'd hoped, the diversion berm and canal aren't finished yet. If we do our job correctly, there will be nothing they can do to stop it."

"How many gallons, do you think?" This from Ahmed.

"Hard to say. The line is fully functional, and the capacity is almost three-point-two billion gallons a year—almost nine million gallons a day. From there the calculations become complex. Suffice it to say, it will be enough for our purposes."

"No change in the exfiltration plan?" asked Fa'ad.

Ibrahim looked hard at him. He lowered his voice. "No change. Do not forget, though: Live or die, we must succeed. Allah's eyes are upon us. If He wills it, all of us or some of us will survive. Or not. Those concerns are secondary, is that understood?"

One by one, each man nodded.

Ibrahim checked his watch. "Seven hours. I'll see you there."

After the initial excitement of their first getaway weekend and the flush of lovemaking faded, she began distancing herself from him, staring out the window, declining his suggestion that they go out, allowing just the right amount of pout to her lips. . . . After thirty minutes of this, Steve asked, "What's wrong?"

"Nothing," Allison replied.

"It's something. I can see it on your face. You're doing that thing with your lip." He sat down beside her on the bed. "Tell me."

"It's stupid. It's nothing."

"Allison, please. Have I done something wrong?"

This was the question she'd been waiting for. Kindhearted Steve. Wimpy Steve, so worried about losing her. "Sure you won't laugh?"

"I promise."

"I was talking to my sister Jan yesterday. She said she saw this documentary, something on the Discovery Channel or National Geographic, I think. It was all about the geology of—"

"Of where I work? Allison, I told you—"

"You promised you wouldn't laugh."

"I'm not laughing. Okay, go ahead."

"She said a lot of scientists are against the whole thing. There are protests all the time. Legal stuff, trying to shut it down. They saw there are earthquake faults all around that area. And they were talking about the groundwater, if there's a leak."

"There's not going to be any leaks."

"But what if?" Allison insisted.

"The slightest leak would be detected. They've got sensors everywhere. Besides, the water table is a thousand feet down."

"But the soil—isn't it soft or something? Permeable?"

"Yes, but there are redundant systems, levels upon levels, and the stuff will be sealed in casks. You should see these things, they're like—"

"I'm worried about you. What if something happens?"

"Nothing's going to happen."

"Can't you get another job? If you and I . . . I mean, if we keep going . . . I'd worry all the time."

"Listen, right now it's not even operational. Hell, we're just now getting around to doing a mock delivery."

"What's that?"

"Just a simulation. A trial run. A truck comes in, we offload the cask. You know, check all the procedures to make sure everything's working like it should."

Allison sighed, folded her arms.

Steve said, "Hey, I'm not going to lie. I think it's kinda cool you're worried about me, but there's nothing to worry about."

"Really? Here, look at this." Allison walked to the nightstand, grabbed her purse, and came back. She rummaged inside for a moment, then pulled out a folded sheet of paper. "Jan e-mailed me this." She handed it to him.

Though only an artist's cutaway rendering, it was detailed enough to show the facility's main level, two sublevels, and far below that, through layers of brown and gray "rock," a blue horizontal stripe labeled "water table."

"Where did she get this?" Steve asked.

"She Googled it."

"Ally, there's a lot more to the place than this . . . cartoon."

"I know that. I'm not stupid." She got up, walked to the balcony window, and stared out.

"I didn't mean that," Steve said. "I don't think you're stupid."

"So is Jan wrong? Are you telling me nobody at that place worries about this stuff?"

"Of course we do. It's serious business. We all know that. The DOE has—"

"The what?"

"Department of Energy. It's done years of research on this. Spent tens of millions just on feasibility studies alone."

"But that documentary—it kept talking about these rifts in the ground. Weak spots."

Steve hesitated. "Ally, I can't really talk about—"

"Fine, forget it. I'll just stop worrying. How's that?"

Allison could feel him standing there, staring at the back of her head. He would be wearing that scolded-puppy-dog look and have his hands stuffed into the pockets of his jeans. She let the silence hang in the air. After thirty seconds, he said, "Okay, if it's that important to you—"

"It's not that that's important to me. It's you."

Arms still folded, she turned to face him. She forced some tears into her eyes. He held out his hand to her. "Come here."

"Why?"

"Just come here."

She stepped over to him, to his hand. He said, "Just don't tell anybody I talked about this stuff, okay? They'd throw me in jail."

She smiled and wiped a tear from her cheek. "Promise."

The Panamax cargo ship *Losan* was three days from its destination, having made the bulk of the Atlantic crossing on calm seas and under clear skies. *Losan*'s captain, a forty-seven-year-old German named Hans Groder, had been the box ship's master for eight years, having spent ten months out of every one of those years at sea. A tougher schedule than his previous job—captain of a German Navy Type 702 Berlin-class replenishment oiler—but the pay was much better and the stresses much fewer. Better still, *Losan* was a blue-water ship, a nice change for Groder after twenty-two years of navigating the labyrinthian waters around Eckendorf and Kiel Naval Bases. Such a pleasure to simply point one's bow into the Atlantic and steam away with hundreds and thousands of feet beneath your keel and not a speck of land on your radar. Of course, on his more introspective days Groder indulged that sense of melancholy all sailors and soldiers felt once they've left military life behind, but on balance he enjoyed his life and the autonomy it allowed. He answered to only one man, the owner, not a chain of stuffed-shirt flag officers who wouldn't know the difference between a chock and a cleat.

Groder strolled across the bridge and glanced at the radar. There wasn't another vessel within twenty miles. Their nav radar wasn't the most powerful in the world but was sufficient for their purposes. For a watchful captain and crew, twenty miles was plenty of time to adjust course and give fellow travelers a wide berth. Groder walked to the windows and stared out across the foredeck, going through his instinctive scan of the stacked bulktainers. They'd experienced some shifting, most of the time due to those damned propane tanks. Packed four to a container, they were secure enough, but their shape lacked the user-friendly geometry of crates and pallets. It could be worse, Groder knew. At least the damned things were empty.

71

Later, Gerry Hendley would reflect that the hardest part of the whole damned affair—aside from the event that prompted it, that was—was simply finding a private place to bring them in. Former President Ryan had finally stepped in, making one phone call to the chief of staff of the Air Force, CSAF, who in turn called the commander of the 316th Wing, the host unit at Andrews Air Force Base.

They arrived in two black Chevy Tahoes, Hendley, Jerry Rounds, Tom Davis, Rick Bell, Pete Alexander, and Sam Granger in the first; Clark, Chavez, and Jack Ryan Jr. in the second. Both vehicles turned left onto C Street and coasted to a stop beside a hangar at the edge of the tarmac. Former President Ryan arrived five minutes later in a Town Car flanked by the Secret Service detail in two Suburbans.

The Gulfstream V touched down eleven minutes later, three minutes behind schedule, and taxied to a stop fifty yards away. The engines spooled down, and the scaffold stairs were rolled out and locked onto the plane's main door.

Jack Ryan Jr. climbed out of the Tahoe, followed by the rest, who stood a few feet behind him.

The Gulfstream's door opened, and thirty seconds later Dominic Caruso appeared at the threshold. He blinked at the sunlight, then started down the stairs. His face was drawn and showed five days' worth of stubble. Jack walked out and met him halfway. They embraced.

"I'm so sorry, man," Jack whispered.

Dominic didn't respond but broke the hug and nodded. "Yeah" was all he said.

"Where is he?"

"Cargo hold. They wouldn't let me take him in the cabin."

After leaving the quarry, Bari had driven as fast as possible with the Opel's headlights off, making it back to the main highway in less than ten minutes. Brian drifted in and out of consciousness as they raced west along the coast, as Dominic gripped his hand and cradled his head in his lap. He kept his other hand pressed to the bullet wound, which kept oozing dark blood, coating Dominic's hand and forearm and soaking the seat beneath his legs. Seven miles from Zuwarah, Brian started coughing, lightly at first, then spasmodically, his body heaving off the seat as Dominic lay across his torso and whispered for him to hang on. After a few minutes, Brian seemed to relax and his breathing steadied. Then stopped. Dominic wouldn't realize it until much later, but he'd felt that moment, that too-slight gap between Brian being alive and dead. Dominic straightened up in his seat and found Brian's head lolled to one side, his sightless eyes staring at the back of the seat.

He told Bari to pull over and stop the car, which he did, then Dominic took the keys from the ignition, got out of the car, and walked ten yards away. To the east, the first faint rays of pink sunlight were showing over the horizon. Dominic sat in silence, watching the sunrise and not wanting to look at Brian, half hoping that when he did he'd find his brother breathing again and looking at him with a stupid, goofy smile. Of course, that didn't happen. After ten minutes, he got back into the car and ordered the Libyan to get off the main highway and find them a place to hole up. After thirty minutes of driving, Bari found a shaded grove of palm trees and pulled in.

Dominic called Archie's cell phone; help from The Campus would take too long. In two curt sentences, he told the Aussie what had happened, then handed the phone to Bari, who gave Archie directions to their location. It took two hours. Archie arrived in a Range Rover, and without a word pulled Dominic out of the Opel, put him the Rover's backseat, then retrieved a plastic body bag from the hatch and returned to the Opel, where he and Bari carefully slid Brian's body from the backseat and sealed him in the bag. After placing the bag in the Rover's cargo area, he returned to the Opel and cleaned it out, dumping all the gear and weapons into the trunk. Once he was sure the car was clean, Archie doused the Opel's interior with the contents of a five-gallon gas can and lit it on fire.

They were back in Tripoli by noon. Archie bypassed the consulate and drove straight to what Dominic assumed was a safe house off Bassel el Asad near the stadium. Bari, bound hand and foot, was locked in the bathroom, then Archie made sure the landline's scrambler was running, then left Dominic alone to make the call home.

"Who else knows?" Dominic now asked his cousin.

"No one," Jack replied. "Just who's here. I figured you'd want to do it. Or if you want, I can—"

"No."

Jack asked, "You wanna go home?"

"No. We got some stuff. You guys are going to want it. Let's go back to the office. Hendley or somebody needs to get with Archie in Tripoli. If we want Bari back here, we're going to have to—"

"Dom, you don't have to worry about that stuff. We'll handle it."

Former President Ryan walked up, and he and Dominic embraced. "Sorry doesn't quite seem to do it, son, but I am."

Dominic nodded. To Jack: "Let's just go, okay."

"Sure."

Jack turned and signaled to Clark and Chavez, who walked up and escorted Dominic back to the second Tahoe. Jack asked his dad, "Get a ride with you?"

"Of course."

Jack gave Hendley a nod, then followed his dad to the Town Car.

They rode in silence until the cars cleared the main gate, then Ryan Senior said, "The hell of it is, we'll probably never know what happened. As much as I want to, I'm not going to ask Gerry."

"Ask me," Jack said.

"What?"

"They were in Tripoli, Dad, chasing down something."

"What're you talking about? How do you know that?"

"How do you think?"

Ryan Senior didn't answer right away but simply stared at his son. "You're serious."

"Yes."

"Jesus, Jack."

"You've always told me I gotta make my own way in life. That's what I'm doing."

"How long?"

"Year and a half. I kind of put two and two together and figured out there was more to Gerry's shop than met the eye. I went in and talked to him. Talked my way into a job, I guess."

"Doing what?"

"Mostly analysis."

"'Mostly.' What does that mean?" Ryan Senior's voice was harder now.

"I've been doing a little field stuff. Not much, just getting my feet wet."

"No way, Jack. That's done. I'm not going to have you—"

"Not your decision."

"The hell it isn't. The Campus was my idea. I went to Gerry and—"

"And it's his show, right? I'm halfway sharp, Dad. I don't need you watching over me. We've done some good work there. Same kind of stuff you used to do. If it was okay for you, then why not me?"

"Because you're my son, goddamn it."

Here Jack offered a half-smile to his father. "Then maybe it's in my blood."

"Bullshit."

"Look, I did the financial world, and it was okay, but it didn't take me long to realize I didn't want to do it the rest of my life. I want to do something. Make a difference, serve my country."

"So go teach Sunday school."

"Next thing on my list."

Ryan Senior sighed. "You're not a kid anymore, I guess."

"Nope."

"Well, it doesn't mean I have to like it, and I probably never will, but I suppose that's my problem. Your mom, though, that's going to be a different story."

"I'll talk to her."

"No, you won't. I will, when the time's right."

"I don't like lying to her." Ryan Senior opened his mouth to speak, but Jack quickly added, "And I didn't like lying to either of you. Hell, if not for John, I might not have ever told you."

"John Clark?"

Jack nodded. "He's sort of my de facto training officer. Him and Ding."

"Nobody better at this stuff than those two."

"So you're okay with this?"

"Sorta-kinda. I'll tell you a secret, Jack. The older you get, the less you like change. Last week, Starbucks stopped selling my favorite roast. Threw me off for days."

Jack laughed. "I'm a Dunkin' Donuts kind of guy."

"That's good, too. You're careful, right?"

"With the coffee. Yeah—"

"Don't be a smart-ass."

"Yeah, I'm careful."

"So what's he got you working on?"

Another smile from Jack. "Sorry, Dad, your need to know expired a while ago. If you win the election, we'll talk again."

Ryan Senior shook his head. "Fuckin' spooks."

Frank Weaver had spent four years in the Army, so he was well familiar with the maddening ways in which the government often went about its business, but he'd thought he'd left that all behind when he got his honorable discharge and went to truck-driving school. He'd spent ten years doing that, doing long hauls from coast to coast, sometimes taking his wife along, but mostly eating up the miles while listening to classic rock. *God love XM satellite radio,* he thought, and thank God the government was going to let him keep it for this new job. He hadn't relished the idea of working for the government again, but the pay had been too good to pass up, what with the hazardous-duty bonuses and all. They didn't call it that, exactly, but that's what it amounted to. He'd gone through a special training program and background checks by the FBI, but he had nothing to hide and he was a damned good driver. In truth, there was nothing extraordinary about what they had him doing—except for the cargo, that was, but he never had to touch the stuff. Just show up, let someone else load it, then get it safely to its destination and let someone else unload it. Mostly they drilled him on emergency procedures: what to do if someone tried to hijack the load; what to do if he got into an accident; what to do if a UFO came down and beamed him out of the cab . . . The Department of Energy and Nuclear Regulatory Commission trainers had "what-if" drills for everything you could think of, then a hundred more you'd never imagine. Besides, he'd never be driving the route alone. They hadn't told him yet whether his escorts would be in marked or unmarked cars, but you could bet they'd be armed to the teeth.

There'd be no guards this time, though, which surprised Weaver a bit. Yeah, it was only a trial run and his load would be empty, but given the way the DOE played everything as if it was real, he'd expected an escort. Then again, maybe they were lying; maybe he'd have an escort he wasn't supposed to see. Still didn't change his job.

Weaver downshifted and braked, swinging the rig into the entrance drive of the Callaway Nuclear Power Plant. A hundred yards ahead he could see the guard shack. He braked to a stop and handed his ID card down to the guard. The entrance was blocked by five steel-core concrete pillars.

"Engine off, please."

Weaver complied.

The guard looked over his ID, then slipped it into his front shirt pocket and had him sign in on the clipboard. Weaver's flatbed was empty, but the guard did his job, first walking a complete circle around the rig, then checking the undercarriage with one of those rolling mirror-cart things.

The guard reappeared below the window.

"Please step out of the truck." Weaver climbed down. The guard again examined Weaver's ID, taking a good ten seconds to check to make sure the faces matched. "Please stand beside the guard shack."

Weaver did so, and the guard climbed into the truck's cab and spent two minutes searching the interior before climbing down. He handed Weaver his ID card.

"Dock number four. You'll be directed along the way. Speed limit is ten miles an hour."

"Got it."

Weaver climbed back into the cab and started the engine. The guard lifted his portable radio to his lips and said something. A moment later, the concrete pillars retracted into the ground. The guard waved Weaver through.

Dock four was only a hundred yards away, on the back side of the plant. At the halfway point a hard-hatted man in coveralls waved him on. Weaver did a Y-turn, backed up to the dock, and shut off the engine.

The dock foreman walked up to Weaver's door. "You can wait in the lounge, if you want. Take us about an hour."

It took almost ninety minutes. Though Weaver had seen pictures of the thing during training, he'd never seen one in person. He and the other drivers had nicknamed it "King Kong's Dumbbell," but the DOE people had gone to a lot of trouble drumming the particulars into their brains. Officially known as the GA-4 Legal Weight Truck (LWT) Spent Fuel Cask, the container was an impressive piece of engineering. How they'd settled on the dumbbell shape Weaver didn't know, but he assumed it had something to do with durability. According to the trainers, the GA-4's designers had torture-tested the thing, subjecting it to dead-fall drops, incineration, puncture hazards, and submersion. For every ton of nuclear waste—fuel assemblies from either pressure water reactors or boiling water reactors—four tons of shielding went into the GA-4's shell.

Hell, Weaver thought, *you could no more get into the damned thing than you could steal it with anything short of a truck, a crane, and perhaps a heavy-lift chopper.* It would be like those idiots you occasionally see on television who hook a chain to an ATM, drag it off, then dump it somewhere because they can't break it open.

"Never seen one up close," Weaver told the dock foreman.

"Looks like something from a sci-fi movie, doesn't it?"

"Sort of is, in a way."

Per protocol, the two of them walked around the flatbed, checking "preflight" items off their forms as they went. Each tie-down chain was new, and had been stress-tested at the plant, as had the ratchets, each of those secured by dual padlocks. Satisfied the cask wasn't going anywhere before it reached its destination, Weaver and the foreman signed and countersigned the forms, each taking his own copy.

Weaver waved good-bye and climbed into his cab. Once the engine was going, he powered up the GPS nav system affixed to his dash, then scrolled through the touch-screen menu and selected his route; the unit had been preprogrammed with dozens of them by the DOE. Another safeguard, he'd been told. No driver would be given his until leaving a pickup facility.

The route popped up on the screen as a purple line overlaid on a map of the United States. *Not bad,* Weaver thought. Major highways for most of the trip, 1,632 miles total. Four days.

72

"Text message from our Russian girl," Tariq said, striding into the living room. The Emir stood at the window, staring out at the desert. He turned.

"Good news, I trust."

"We will know in sixty seconds."

Tariq powered up his laptop, opened his Web browser, and went to a website called storespot.com, one of dozens of free online file-storage sites available on the Internet. All that was required to open an account was a user name, a password, and an e-mail address, and for that there were sites that offered throwaway "self-destructing" e-mail addresses.

Tariq logged in to the account, clicked on three links, and found himself in the upload/download area of the site. There was one item waiting, a plain text file. According to the annotation, the file had been uploaded twelve minutes ago. Tariq opened the file, copied the contents to his clipboard, then deleted the file from the account. Next he opened the laptop's built-in text program and pasted the contents into a new file. He took two minutes to scan the contents.

"It's all here. Everything we need."

"Which entrance?"

"The south."

The Emir smiled. Allah was with them. Of the two, the facility's southern entrance saw less activity than the northern main entrance. This meant fewer security personnel. "Where exactly?"

"The third drift layer, five hundred meters in and three hundred meters below the surface. According to Jenkins, that's the area the engineering department is most concerned about. Next week they're having a meeting with the Department of Energy and Nuclear Regulatory Commission to discuss backfilling and capping the entire drift before they start accepting shipments."

There was, however, a drawback to using the south entrance, the Emir knew. Within minutes of the truck turning onto the service road from Highway 95, sensors and cameras would likely record its passage and alert the monitoring center at the facility's main entrance. Once the staff realized the truck was headed toward the south entrance, how would they react? It seemed unlikely an alarm would be immediately raised; this was, after all, only a trial shipment, and the first of its kind. More likely, the staff would assume the driver had taken a wrong turn. Calls would be made, perhaps a vehicle sent to the south entrance to collect the wayward truck. Musa and his men would take care of it.

Of all the feasibility studies the URC had done in the early stages of Lotus, the most troubling and nebulous question had involved the facility's on-site security, an issue that neither the DOE nor NRC had publicly addressed, either because of security concerns or because of internal indecision. As planning for Lotus progressed, it became clear to the Emir that they had to assume the worst-case scenario, which, in the case of nuclear facilities, involved the presence of NNSA protective forces, a well-trained and well-equipped paramilitary force under the control of the DOE.

As it had many facets of American government and society, 9/11 had brought into sharp focus the need for more robust material control programs, and to its credit the DOE had spared no expense in pursuit of that goal. NNSA Protective Forces were trained in small-unit antiterrorist tactics and equipped with armored vehicles and heavy-caliber weapons, including grenade launchers, armor-piercing rounds, and at select sites, mobile and fixed Dillon M134D Gatling Gun systems.

None of the URC's intelligence suggested the NNSA was manning the facility this far in advance, but the Emir had been clear with Musa: *Assume you will meet with heavy resistance. Assume you have only minutes to complete your mission.*

"Where are we with the other elements?" the Emir asked Tariq. "The truck."

"It left the plant this afternoon. Transit time is four days. Ibrahim and his team are on the ground. Unless we send him the abort, they should be moving in"—Tariq checked his watch—"three hours. The ship is two days out; our people in Norfolk are ready. As it stands, the ship will probably have to overnight at anchor before being assigned a berth."

"Good. And Mr. Nayoan's men?"

"In place and ready. They will not move until you give the order. They'll need twenty-four hours' notice." The Emir nodded, and Tariq asked, "What do you want to do with the girl?"

"Let her go. She knows nothing about us, and Beketov is dead. The link between us and her people is gone. Even if she's picked up, the only leads she can offer will either go nowhere or go where we want them to go. She's earned her money."

"She knows about the facility."

"What of it? She was hired by some fringe environmental group to dig up damaging information about the facility. That's all. She's a mercenary, Tariq. She'll take her money and move on."

Tariq considered this, then nodded. "Very well."

"One last detail: I'll be joining Musa on his mission."

"Pardon me?"

"I'll record a message before I leave. Once we've succeeded, you will make sure it reaches the right hands." Tariq opened his mouth to speak, but the Emir waved him off. "Old friend, you know this is necessary. My death, and what we do here, will fuel our war for generations to come."

"When did you decide this?"

"It's been the plan from the start. Why else would we have come here—to this forsaken place?"

"Let me join you."

The Emir shook his head. "It's not your time. You must trust me on this. Promise me you'll do as I ask."

Tariq nodded.

73

Pulling into the town of Paulinia just after sunset, Shasif Hadi could see the lights of the refinery, still some four miles away, long before he could see the complex itself. Seventeen hundred acres of distillation columns, fractionation towers, and high-voltage wires, all festooned with blinking red lights designed to warn off low-flying aircraft, and all unnecessary, as far as Hadi was concerned. If any pilot managed to miss seeing the dozens of pole-mounted stadium lights illuminating the complex's work areas, he deserved to crash.

The main highway from Campinas, the SP-332, wound along the northern outskirts of Paulinia before swinging back first to the west, then to the north, before finally passing the refinery complex on the left. Hadi drove past it and continued north for another mile before reaching his turnoff, a two-lane asphalt road heading due east. This he followed exactly one and a half miles to where the road curved yet again and the blacktop gave way to gravel. A hundred yards ahead, his headlights picked out what looked like a bridge spanning the road. Hadi felt his pulse quicken. This was not a bridge, he knew, but rather an ethanol pipeline. As he passed under the line, he glanced out his passenger window and could see a grass-covered clearing barricaded by a cattle gate. Sitting in front of the gate, hood facing out, was a white pickup truck. Hadi kept going, making one more turn, this time south, onto a dirt road. After fifty yards he slowed, scanning the tree line to his left. He spotted the gap between the trees and pulled in and shut off his headlights as he coasted to a stop. He checked his watch: on schedule.

He got out, locked the door, then walked out of the trees to the edge of the road. He looked right. A half-mile down the road a pair of headlights appeared around a corner. Ibrahim's blue Volkswagen Fox slowed beside Hadi, its brakes squealing slightly.

"No trouble?" Ibrahim asked.

"None."

Hadi climbed into the backseat. Fa'ad sat beside him, Ahmed in the front passenger seat. As part of their exfiltration plan,

Fa'ad and Ahmed had parked their cars on back roads to the southeast and northeast of the refinery, where they were picked up by Ibrahim. If for some reason the group became separated, they would rendezvous at one of these cars and make their way back to the coast.

Ahmed handed Hadi a pistol, a 9-millimeter Glock 17 equipped with a noise suppressor. "The truck is there," Hadi said. "I couldn't be sure, but I think I saw two figures sitting in it."

"Good. Ahmed, you will do it."

Headlights off, Ibrahim put the car in gear and drove on, retracing Hadi's inbound route. Fifty yards from the pipeline, he stopped the car. Ahmed climbed out, crossed behind the car, and walked into the trees. They sat in silence, Ibrahim keeping track of the time on his watch. After two minutes, he turned on the headlights and started out again. "Down in the back," he told them. Hadi and Fa'ad hunched down below the windows. As the car drew even with the pickup truck, Ibrahim slowed the car and got out. He had a map in his right hand.

"Excuse me," he called in Portuguese, as he walked toward the truck. "I'm lost. Can you give me directions back to Paulinia?"

No one responded.

"Excuse me, I need help. Can you—"

A hand appeared out of the driver's-side window and waved him forward. Ibrahim walked up to the window. The decal on the door said PETROBRAS SECURITY. "I think I missed a turn somewhere. How far away is Paulinia?"

"Not far," said the guard. "Follow this road west until it runs into the highway, then turn left."

Through the truck's open passenger window, Ibrahim could see Ahmed's outline emerge from the trees and start toward the truck.

Ibrahim asked, "How far is it?"

Before the driver could answer, Ibrahim took a step back. The first muffled shot went into the temple of the passenger-side guard; the second went into the neck of the driver, who slumped sideways. The noise suppressor, made from steel soup cans and fiberglass insulation, had worked well. The shots had been no louder than a muted hand-clap.

"One more each," Ibrahim ordered.

Ahmed fired another round into the first guard. He then extended the gun into the cab, took aim, and fired a round into the driver's ear. Ibrahim turned and signaled to the Volkswagen. Hadi climbed into the driver's seat and pulled the car into the clearing. Ibrahim and Ahmed already had the guards' bodies out of the truck.

"Key ring," Ahmed said, and tossed it to Ibrahim.

They started dragging the bodies toward the tree line. Hadi pulled out a pair of white towels he'd taken from his hotel, tossed one to Fa'ad, and together they wiped down the cab. The Glock's soft-nosed hollow-points had disintegrated inside the guards' skulls, leaving no exit wounds, so there was more blood than brain matter. Once done, Hadi tossed his towel to Fa'ad, who jogged into the trees and tossed them away.

Ibrahim returned to the clearing, unlocked the cattle gate, then tossed the key ring to Hadi. He and Fa'ad got in and backed the truck through the gate, followed by Ibrahim and Ahmed in the Volkswagen. Hadi shut and locked the gate as Ibrahim pulled the Volkswagen into the trees and out of sight.

The service road ran alongside the pipeline, which sat atop five-foot support pylons, spaced every fifty feet or so. Bracketed on both sides by trees and heavily rutted, the road had been built to accommodate construction equipment during the pipeline's construction and now served as an access road for the refinery's maintenance and security staff.

After a mile, the road veered, going right as the pipeline went left. In the median stood a grove of trees, over the top of which the lights of the refinery were visible. Ibrahim stopped the truck, and they got out. "Change clothes," he ordered.

The navy blue coveralls had been chosen not so much for stealth but for anonymity. Most of the refinery workers wore similar coveralls. If spotted, from a distance Ibrahim and his team would, they hoped, be mistaken for maintenance personnel. They were now less than a half-mile from the refinery's perimeter road and fence.

Once in their coveralls, they walked through the grove to a clearing. Here the pipeline zigzagged before straightening again, crossing over the road, and then, after another five hundred yards, passing through the security fence and into the refinery itself.

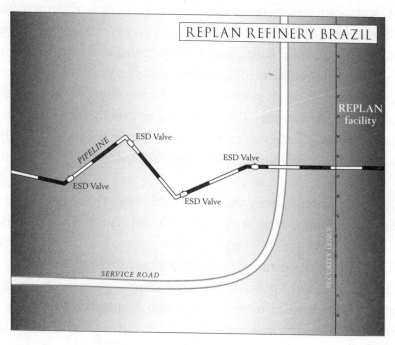

REPLAN REFINERY BRAZIL

REPLAN facility

PIPELINE

ESD Valve

ESD Valve

ESD Valve

ESD Valve

SECURITY FENCE

SERVICE ROAD

The ethanol pipeline running above their heads was less than a year old and ran from Goiás, five hundred miles to the north, through Paulinia before continuing on to the Japeri Terminal in Rio de Janeiro two hundred miles to the northeast. Three-point-two billion gallons of ethanol per year through a pipeline spanning a quarter of Brazil's breadth.

While the URC had been unable to discover the pipeline's precise flow rate, the averages had been enough to convince the Emir that the plan was feasible. With a reported "up time" of eighty-five percent, the pipeline was pumping its 3.2 billion gallons over a span of 310 days, which in turn meant that for every operational day, 10.3 million gallons were flowing from Goiás to Rio. At any given hour of the day, in any given ten-mile stretch of pipeline, there was enough ethanol to fill twenty tanker trucks.

"Four ESD valves between here and the perimeter," Ibrahim whispered. "One charge to disable each valve, one for the midpoint between the last pylons, and one for detonation. Those two I'll handle myself. Ahmed, you have the first valve; Fa'ad, the second; Shasif, you have the third and fourth. When I've planted my charge, I'll step out and scratch my head. Start your timers. Four minutes exactly. Remember: Walk back to the truck. Do not run. Anyone not back by the time the first charge goes off, they get left behind. Any questions?" There were none. "Allah be with us," Ibrahim said.

They took off together, walking casually and chatting, as would any maintenance crew trying to make the best of a night shift. Two hundred yards from the grove, they reached the first ESD. Ahmed peeled off and knelt down behind the barrel-sized valve, then Fa'ad, then finally Shasif.

"See you back at the truck," Ibrahim said, and kept walking.

The perimeter road was fifty yards ahead. To the right, a

white pickup truck appeared, moving slowly as the passenger-side guard shined a spotlight on the fence. Ibrahim checked his watch. *Early. Fifteen minutes early!* Their agent, Cassiano, had been sure of the facility's security routes and schedules. He'd either been wrong or the security schedule had changed. If the latter, why? Routine, or something else? This security truck, Ibrahim knew, would make its way along this perimeter road, then exit through the facility's west gate before swinging north again and eventually pass the cattle gate through which Ibrahim and the others had entered. When the guards saw no pickup truck there, how would they react? Ibrahim decided it was best not to find out.

They had twelve minutes. Say four more minutes to set the charges and eight minutes to run the mile back to the cattle gate. It would be very close. Or, he thought, there was another option.

Heart pounding, he slowed his pace. So did the truck, coming to a near halt. Ibrahim waved his arm in greeting and called out in Portuguese, *"Boa tarde!"* *Good evening.* He arched his back ever so slightly to check that the Glock was still in place.

After a long five seconds, the driver waved back. "How's it going?" he asked.

Ibrahim shrugged. *"Bem."* *Fine.* Casually, he began walking toward the truck. *How close?* he wondered. To kill both men before they had a chance to reach their radio, he would have to get within ten or twelve meters. Would they become suspicious of his face or uniform before then? Charge them and start firing? *No,* he decided. The truck would race away. Ibrahim stopped walking.

"What're you up to?" the driver asked.

"Weld checks," Ibrahim answered. "Our boss decided we needed something to do."

The driver chuckled. "I know the feeling. See you later."

The transmission shifted into gear, and the truck rolled forward. Then stopped. The reverse lights popped on, and the truck backed up until it was again even with Ibrahim. "You came in from the cattle gate?" the driver asked.

Heart in his throat, Ibrahim nodded.

"Was there a truck there?"

"Didn't see one. What's the problem?"

"Paiva and Cabral aren't answering their radio."

Ibrahim jerked his thumb toward the others spread out along the pipeline behind him. "Ours have been acting up tonight, too."

"Sunspots or something, probably," the driver said. "Interesting accent you've got."

"Angola. Lived there until about a year ago."

The driver shrugged. "Okay. Take it easy."

The truck drove on and disappeared down the road. Ibrahim waited until he could no longer hear its engine, then let out his breath. *Almost there. Allah guide me.* He crossed the road, picked his way down into the drainage ditch, then back up the other side. The fence was in sight now, a hundred yards away. He passed the final pylon and began counting steps. At the halfway point, he stopped and knelt down. The pipe was directly over his head. He could hear the gurgling rush of fuel through the steel.

The first of his two charges, the largest of the six, weighed eight ounces but still easily fit in the thigh pocket of his cargo pants. The second charge, at two ounces, fit in the palm of his hand. He set the main charge's digital timer to four minutes, ten seconds; the second charge to five minutes. He squeezed his eyes shut, said a quick prayer, then stood up, affixed the main charge to the pipe's underside, then started the timer. He watched two seconds click off, then walked into the open, turned around, and scratched his head. He waited long enough to ensure that all three of them had seen his signal, then started the timer on the last charge and stuffed it into its duct tape and Bubble Wrap cocoon.

He heaved the bundle over the fence, then turned around and started walking.

74

Hendley, Granger, and Rick Bell spent part of the afternoon and early evening debriefing Dominic in the conference room. Jack Junior and John Clark sat in a pair of chairs along the wall and listened; Jack was family and a good friend, and while Dominic seemed to be holding it together, Hendley had thought Jack's presence might be helpful. As for Clark, Hendley wanted his professional eye.

Jack watched his cousin carefully as he walked Hendley and the others through the Tripoli mission: their initial meeting with Archie, their foray into the Medina to snatch Bari, their trip to Almasi's house, and finally Brian's death. At every step, Dominic answered their questions curtly but thoroughly, never losing his patience and never hesitating. And not showing a trace of emotion, Jack realized. His cousin showed no affect in either his face or his body language. He was flat.

"Tell us again about Fakhoury," Sam Granger said.

"According to Bari, he was low-level, just an enforcer. We decided Almasi was a better target. We didn't want any witnesses to Bari's disappearance, so we talked about what to do with him."

"Whose decision was it to kill him?"

"We both decided. I wasn't so sure, but Brian . . . His argument made sense."

"Did you do it?"

Dominic shook his head. "Brian."

"Counting Fakhoury, how many dead?" This from Bell.

"Six. Four by us."

"Let's fast-forward to Almasi's house," said Hendley.

Dominic went through it again: parking in the quarry . . . infiltrating Almasi's house . . . the computer and the safe . . . Brian getting shot . . . the firefight and their exfiltration. Dominic trailed off there. "The rest you know."

"Body count?" asked Granger.

"Five."

"No wounded?"

Dominic shrugged. "Not when I left the house."

"What does that mean?" asked Rick Bell.

"It means I made sure there were no witnesses. No way for the URC to know who or what happened. That's kind of the point of what we're doing, right?"

Hendley nodded. "True." He looked to Bell and Granger. "Anything else?" Both men shook their heads. "Okay, Dom, thanks."

Dominic stood up to leave.

Hendley said, "Dom, we're sorry about Brian."

Dominic simply nodded.

"I'll get a car to take you home."

"No, I'm just going to find a couch and crash."

Granger said, "If you'd like us to make arrangements for Brian—"

"I'll do it."

Dominic left, shutting the door behind him. Hendley said, "Jack?"

"Hard to say. I've never seen him like this, but then again, it's not exactly common. For anybody. I think he's just numb. He's exhausted; he watched his twin brother die in his lap; and, right or wrong, he's probably feeling pretty damned guilty about it. Once it all sinks in he'll fall apart, then pull himself back together."

"You agree, John."

Clark took a moment to answer. "For the most part, but he's a changed man, that's for sure. Some switch got flipped."

Bell said, "Explain."

"He was on the fence about taking out Fakhoury. Brian had to talk him into it, and probably did the job himself because he knew Dom wasn't ready for it. Three hours later, they're at Almasi's house. Brian gets shot, and before Dom leaves the house, he's finishing off wounded men. That's day to night in pretty short order."

"So assume you're right about the flipped switch," Hendley said. "Is that a bad thing?"

"Don't know. Depends on how or if he rebounds. Right now he's got that thousand-yard stare in his eyes. This is usually where operators take one of two paths: learn to deal with the job and put it into perspective, or let it eat you up."

"Is he okay for the field?"

"This isn't an exact science, Gerry. Everybody's different."

"Best judgment. Is he okay for the field?"

Clark thought it over. "Not by himself."

Hendley asked Rick Bell, "What do we know about what Dom brought home?"

"A flash drive full of Almasi's computer files, and one CD-ROM. The files are gonna take a while to sift through; the CD was a gold mine: three hundred sixty five JPEG images of onetime pads—nine square by nine square grids with alphanumeric substitution characters. I don't know how the math works out, but we're talking about millions of different combos."

"About a year's worth," Hendley said. "One for every damned day. Please tell me they're dated."

Bell smiled. "Bet your ass. They go back almost ten months, which means unless they pull the plug, we've two months of future OTPs in our hands."

"That's how they're doing it," Jack muttered.

"What?" Clark asked.

"They're doubling up. They use steganography to embed the OTP into website images. Recipients pull an image off the site, use a program to peel away the stego layer, and they've got the daily OTP. After that it's just numbers: Go into a forum on a URC website, find the post with a string of a couple hundred letter-number combinations, run them through your OTP, and you've got your marching orders."

"I'm with you on most of that," Granger said, "but not the forum idea. I don't think the URC would shotgun a message like that. They'd want to make sure it reached only the recipients they wanted. We know it's not e-mail, right?"

"Doubtful. URC traffic is all but dead."

"How about online e-mail?" Bell suggested. "Google, Yahoo! . . . Agong Nayoan had a Google account, didn't he, John?"

"Yeah, but the IT nerds sifted through it. Nothing there. My guess is, if the URC went radio-silent with its regular e-mail accounts, they probably banned online accounts as well."

"So what they'd need," Hendley said, "is a hub. Someplace a guy could check every day and get messages meant only for him."

"Holy shit," Jack said. "That's it." He started typing on his laptop. "Online file storage."

"Come again?" said Clark.

"They're websites that offer backup file storage. Say you've got a bunch of MP3 songs and you're worried about losing them if your computer crashes. You sign up at one of these sites, upload the files, and they sit there on the servers."

"How many of these sites are there?"

"Hundreds. Some you have to pay to use, but the majority of them are free if you're dealing with small file sizes—anything under a gigabyte of data."

"Which is how much?"

Jack thought this over for a moment. "Take a standard Microsoft Word file. . . . A gigabyte could hold maybe half a million pages."

"Damn."

"But that's the beauty of this. Some URC mutt in Tangiers logs in to one of these sites, uploads a text document with a string of a couple hundred numbers, then another mutt in Japan logs in, downloads the file, erases it from the site, then plugs the numbers into a stego-embedded onetime pad he got from a URC site, and he's got his message."

"What's it take to sign up on one of these sites?" This from Hendley.

"The free ones . . . an e-mail address, and those are a dime a dozen. Hell, there are places on the Internet that'll give you an address that self-destructs after fifteen minutes."

"Talk about anonymity," Rick Bell said. "Listen, I can buy all this. It makes sense, but what do we do with it?"

The conference door opened, and Chavez walked in. "There's something you're going to want to see." He grabbed the television remote, powered up the LCD flat screen, and switched to CNN. The anchor was in mid-sentence.

". . . Once again, this is a live television feed from Record News helicopter in Brazil. The conflagration started just after eight p.m. local time. . . ."

Jack leaned forward in his chair. "Christ almighty."

The helicopter appeared to be filming from a distance of five miles or more, but still two-thirds of the screen was filled with roiling flames and thick, black smoke. Through the smoke there were glimpses of some kind of vertical structures and crisscrossing pipes, and round storage tanks.

"That's a refinery," said John Clark.

The anchor was talking again: "According to Record News, the location of the fire is a refinery run by Petrobras, known as the Paulinia REPLAN. Paulinia is a town of sixty thousand people and is located some eighty miles north of São Paulo."

Hendley turned to Jack. "Can you—"

Jack already had his laptop open. "Working on it."

". . . The Paulinia REPLAN is the largest refinery in Brazil, covering almost eighteen hundred acres and with an output of almost four hundred thousand barrels a day. . . ."

"Accident?" Rick Bell suggested.

"Don't think so," Clark replied. "Eighteen hundred acres is almost three and a half square miles. The complex is almost totally engulfed. Look, back when I was still getting wet for a living, we war-gamed this stuff all the time. Refineries are juicy targets, but just about anything short of half a dozen Paveways wouldn't be enough to light up a whole complex. Hell, our refineries here are almost thirty-five years old and you can count on one hand how many accidents there've been. Too many backup emergency systems."

Typing at his laptop, Jack said, "Paulinia's pretty new. Less than ten years old."

"How many employees?"

"Could be as many as a thousand. Maybe twelve hundred. It's the night shift, so less staff on duty, but we're probably talking about at least four hundred people in there."

"There," Clark said. "Right there . . ." He stepped up to the television and tapped an area inside the refinery complex. "Those flames are moving; that's liquid, and a lot of it."

As they watched, the Record News helicopter moved closer to the blaze, swinging around the refinery until the north side came into view.

Jack said, "Okay, got it: Paulinia's also a terminal for an ethanol pipeline. Comes in from the north."

"Yeah, I see it," said Rick Bell. He walked to the television and pointed to a spot along the complex's northern perimeter. Just short of the fence, the pipeline was ripped open, emitting a geyser of flaming ethanol.

"Yeah," Clark said. "They would have had to knock out some shutdown valves. . . ." He traced his finger north along the pipeline until he reached an isolated pocket of flame. "That's one."

"And three more back down the line," Granger added. "How much pipeline is that?"

"Half-mile, give or take," Clark replied.

"About ten thousand gallons," Jack said, looking up from his laptop.

"What?" said Chavez.

"That pipeline puts through over three billion gallons a year. Break down the math and that section probably contained about ten thousand gallons—call it enough to fill a tanker truck. Some of it'll get soaked up by the soil, but you gotta figure seven, maybe eight thousand gallons were dumped into the complex."

"The whole thing'll go," Clark said. "The blending and storage tanks . . . the towers. They'll start to cook off."

Even as Clark said the words, the helicopter's camera caught a trio of explosions, each one sending a mushroom cloud of flames and black smoke a mile into the sky.

"They're going to have to evacuate the whole damned region," Sam Granger said. "So we're agreed: This is no accident."

Clark said, "No chance. A lot of planning went into this. A lot of groundwork and intelligence."

"URC," Chavez speculated.

"Why Brazil?" Hendley asked.

"I don't think it's got anything to do with Brazil," Jack said. "That's meant for us. Kealty just signed a deal with Petrobras.

Sub-OPEC-priced oil from Brazil. They've got it coming out of their ears—the Lara and Tupi block fields alone could put Brazil's reserves at around twenty-five billion barrels. That's part of the equation. The other part is how far behind Petrobras is in building refineries. Paulinia was their workhorse. The new complex up in Maranhão will run at six hundred thousand barrels, but it's not coming online for another year."

"So Brazil's got the oil but no way to process it," Hendley said. "Which means our deal is down the tubes."

"For a year at least. Maybe two."

Jack's e-mail chimed. He scanned the message. "Biery got facial-recognition hits on a couple of Sinaga's passport photos. Two are Indonesians that came into Norfolk two weeks ago—Citra and Purnoma Salim."

"Citra's a female name," Rick Bell said. "Husband and wife?"

"Brother and sister. Nineteen and twenty years old, respectively. According to their ICE forms, they're here on vacation. The third is none other than our mystery courier: Shasif Hadi. He's traveling as Yaseen Qudus. Two days after we lost him on the way to Vegas, Hadi caught a United flight from San Francisco to São Paulo."

"Hell of a coincidence," Sam Granger said.

"Don't believe in them," Hendley replied. "Mr. Chavez, how do you feel about a trip down there?"

"Fine by me."

"You okay with taking Dom?"

Chavez thought about this. He'd seen plenty of men in Dominic's condition: stunned, guilty, playing the "What could I have done differently?" game . . . Feeling guilty that the other guy's dead, and guilty for being glad you're still alive . . . It was a shitty place to be, but Chavez had looked into the former FBI man's eyes: Dominic was wound up and looking for payback but still under control.

"Sure," Chavez said. "If he's up for it, I am. One question, though: What do we do when we get down there? It's a big country, and Hadi and whoever he's with probably already went to ground."

"Or slipped out of the country," Clark added.

"Let's assume they're still there," Hendley replied. "Jack, let's get back to Rick's question: Assuming you're onto something with this online file-storage stuff. What do we do with it?"

"We do an end run," Jack replied. "Right now, Hadi's the biggest URC player we've got a bead on, correct?"

"Yep," Chavez said.

"And we know he went from Vegas to San Francisco before heading to São Paulo, probably to get his Qudus passport from Agong Nayoan, which means they were probably in direct contact—at the very least, so Nayoan could tell him to pick it up."

"Go on," Hendley said.

"Nayoan's lazy. When we tossed his place, we found he never cleaned out his Web browser history." Jack turned his laptop around so everyone could see it. The screen displayed a text file with hundreds of lines of website addresses. "While we've been talking, I've been sifting through these. Since the URC went radio-silent, Nayoan visited an online storage site every day, three times a day, and he rotated to a different site every second day."

"I'll be damned," said Sam Granger. "That's good work, Jack."

"Thanks. So far, Nayoan's rotated through thirteen storage sites. Ten to one we'd find the same ones on Hadi's computer."

"That only gets us part of the way there," Bell said. "We're going to need his user name and password."

"Statistics," Jack replied. "Eighty-five percent of surfers either use their e-mail as a user name or some variation of their e-mail prefix—the stuff before the 'at' sign. Let's have Biery throw together a script—we'll check each site and try different permutations of Hadi's e-mail. When we find the right one, we do a brute-force crack of his password. Once we're in, we use the OTPs Dom found at Almasi's house and we start pulling Hadi's strings."

"One problem," Hendley said. "The whole thing's predicated on Hadi checking his online storage site."

"Then let's give him a reason," John Clark said.

"What're you thinking?"

"Spook him. We drop an anonymous tip with Record News. A vague description of Hadi and a few sketchy details. He sees it, panics, and checks in for new orders. We make sure something's waiting for him."

"There's a downside," Rick Bell said. "If the Brazilian cops get their hands on him before we do, we're shit outta luck."

Clark smiled. "No balls, no blue chips."

Hendley was silent for a few moments. "It's a long shot, but it's worth it. Jack, you get Biery rolling on this."

Jack nodded. "How about the Norfolk Indonesians?"

"You and John."

"Hate to jinx things, but I got a bad feeling about all this," Chavez said.

"Like?" This from Granger.

"Like this refinery thing is just the first shoe."

75

Shortly before nine a.m., Musa passed through Yakima, Washington, and drove another few miles to Toppenish, where he got off the highway and drove into town. He found a restaurant, something called Pioneer Kitchen, and pulled in. The parking lot was only a quarter full. Americans, Musa had long ago learned, preferred everything quick and easy, especially their food. Though he hadn't seen one, he assumed Toppenish had its fair share of McDonald's and Burger Kings and Arby's. Always on the move, going about their important business, Americans did not sit down and eat unless it was on their couch in front of a television. A pill for every ailment, and disorders for every character flaw.

He found a parking spot near the front door and walked in. The sign at the register counter told him to seat himself. He found a booth by the window so he could keep an eye on the Subaru, and sat down. A waitress in a mustard-yellow apron and white blouse walked up. "Morning; can I get you some coffee?"

"Yes, please."

"Do you need a minute to look at the menu?"

"No. Toast, no butter, and a fruit cup of some kind."

"Sure, no problem. Be right back." She returned with a cup and a coffee decanter and left.

Behind him he heard a voice ask, "Hey, is that your car?"

Musa turned. A uniformed police officer was standing there. He was in his mid-fifties, with a crew cut and paunch. He had sharp eyes, though. A cop's eyes. Musa took a calming breath and said, "Pardon me?"

"That car. Is it yours?"

"Which one?"

"The hatchback there."

"The Subaru? Yes."

"Your dome light's on. Noticed it as I was walking in."

"Oh, thank you, I didn't notice. I won't be here long. I don't think it will hurt the battery."

"Probably not. Just out of curiosity, what's that thing in the back? Looks like a big bait box."

"You wouldn't believe me if I told you."

"Try me."

"It's a portable X-ray machine for horses."

The cop snorted. "Didn't know there was such a thing. Where're you headed?"

"School of vet medicine at UNLV—Las Vegas."

"Long drive."

"Paperwork got messed up; the airline wouldn't put it in the cargo hold. I decided a little road trip wouldn't hurt me. Plus, I'm getting fifty cents a mile."

"Well, good luck."

"Thanks."

The cop walked away and took a stool at the counter. A few minutes later, the waitress returned with Musa's toast and fruit cup. "Willie gettin' in your business?" she asked.

"Pardon?"

She jerked her thumb at the cop. "Willie's the chief of police. He does a good job, but he's nosy as hell. Last year I broke up with my boyfriend, and Willie knew about it before my mother did."

Go away, woman. Musa shrugged. "Small towns."

"I guess. Enjoy your breakfast. I'll come check on you in a few." She left.

Allah, give me patience, Musa thought. Truth be told, he usually found most Americans quite tolerable, if a tad garrulous. That probably wouldn't be the case if his skin was a little darker or if he had an accent. Fate was a strange thing. Otherwise decent people blithely moving through life, worshipping a false god, trying to make sense of an existence that had no meaning outside of Islam. Americans loved their "comfort zones." The vast majority of them had never and would never leave the confines of the United States, so sure the rest of the world had nothing to offer except for perhaps an intriguing vacation spot. Even the events of 9/11 had done little to open Americans' eyes to the real world outside their bubble. Quite the contrary. Encouraged by their own government, many of them had withdrawn deeper into their shells, taking comfort in their labels and platitudes: Islamo-Fascist. Extremist. Evildoers who hate our freedom. Those that would see to destroy America.

America could not be destroyed from without, of that Musa was certain. In that, the Emir had been prescient. Every fallen empire in history had rotted from within, and the same would be true for America. Fighting two intractable wars, an economy in shambles, banks and manufacturing giants going bankrupt . . . Those conditions might change over time, and perhaps even improve, but future historians would mark these events as the first signs of decay. The sad truth was America couldn't be destroyed, per se, from within or from without, and certainly not by mortal effort. If it was to happen at all, it would come from Allah's own hand, and at a time of His choosing. And unlike all the leaders that had come before him, the Emir knew the truth of this and had adjusted his strategy accordingly.

Four more days, Musa thought, and the terrifying world America fought so hard to keep at bay would come crashing in.

Clark and Jack were booked on a six a.m. US Airways flight out of Dulles to Norfolk; Chavez and Dominic a Northwest redeye to Rio de Janeiro. They would be touching down at their respective destinations at roughly the same time.

Ninety minutes after the Paulinia fire started and the skies over the coast began to blacken with smoke, São Paulo closed its airspace to all traffic. Hendley and Granger took this as a good omen: With luck, the perpetrators of the refinery attack hadn't made it out before the airport closed. Almost certainly they would have a backup exfiltration plan, but how quickly it would get them out of the country was unknown.

While the others sat in the conference room and watched the Paulinia news coverage, Jack found Dominic sitting in the break room, hands clasped on the table before him. He was staring into space. It wasn't until Jack was standing beside him that Dominic looked up.

"Hey, Jack."

"Ding bring you up to speed? São Paulo?"

"Yeah."

"If you're not up for the job, I'm sure—"

"Why wouldn't I be up to it?"

This question surprised Jack. "I don't think I would be, if I were in your shoes. Dom, he was my cousin and I loved him, but he was *your* brother."

"What's your point?"

"My point is, twentysome hours after Brian died, you're going back out, and when I ask you about it, you give me some off-the-cuff answer. It's just a little strange, is all."

"Sorry."

"I'm not looking for an apology. I want you to talk to me."

"Brian's dead, Jack. I know that, okay? I watched the spark go out of him." Dominic snapped his fingers. "Just like that. You know the first thing I thought after that?"

"What?"

"That if not for that Bari asshole, Brian would probably still be alive."

"You believe that?"

"Not really, but it took everything I had to not climb out of that car and put a bullet in the guy's head. I actually had my hand on the door handle. I wanted to kill him, then go back to Almasi's house and see if any of those motherfuckers were still alive so I could kill them, too."

"You were in shock. You still feel that way?"

"I don't feel much, Jack. That's what scares me."

"It's called shock. You might feel that way for a while.

Everybody's different. You'll deal with it how you deal with it."

"Yeah, what makes you an expert on this shit?"

"You heard about Sinaga?"

"The forger guy? What about him?"

"I was watching the back when John and Ding crashed his door. He jumped out the window, then all the sudden he's coming at me with a knife. We wrestled; I had a hold of his neck and tripped or something. When I looked up he was lying there twitching. Staring at me. I don't know how exactly, but I broke his neck."

Dominic took this, but his face remained impassive. "I guess it's my turn to ask you how you're doing."

"Okay, I guess. I don't think I'll ever get his face out of my head, but it was him or me. I feel bad about it, but I sure as hell don't feel bad about still being alive."

"Then you're one up on me, cuz. If I could trade places with Brian, I would."

"Are you trying to tell me something?"

"Like what?"

"Like I need to hide all the steak knives next time you come over to watch football."

"No, Jack. But I will tell you this: Before this is all over, I'm getting some payback for Brian, and I'm going to start in São Paulo."

Jack opened his mouth to respond but was halted by Dominic's raised hand. "Mission first, Jack. I'm just saying, if I get a gomer in my sights, I'm putting him down and notching it up for Bri."

Aside from odd looks from his fellow travelers who stared at the GA-4 cask as they passed him on the highway, Frank Weaver's first day on the road passed without incident. As this was a trial run, this particular cask was merely a shell containing none of the neutron and gamma shields the real thing would carry. Nor did the cask bear any decals or stencils. Nothing to give away its purpose. Just a giant brushed stainless-steel dumbbell riding on a flatbed truck. The little kids had been particularly funny, pressing their wide-eyed faces to the windows as they passed.

Four hundred eighteen miles and seven hours from the Calloway plant, Weaver took exit 159 off Highway 70 and turned south onto Vine Street. The Super 8 Motel was a quarter-mile down the road. He followed a sign, TRUCKS ENTER HERE, into the parking lot and braked to a halt between the yellow lines of a truck slot. Three other trucks had taken nearby spots.

Weaver hopped out of the cab and stretched.

Day one down, Weaver thought. *Three to go.*

He locked the truck, then did a walk-around, checking each of the padlocked ratchets, then testing each chain's tension. All were solid. He headed across the parking lot toward the lobby.

Fifty yards away, a dark blue Chrysler 300 pulled into its own spot. In the front seat, a man raised a pair of binoculars and watched Weaver step through the lobby doors.

As he had been doing four times a day for the past two weeks, Kersen Kaseke powered up his laptop, opened his Web browser, and went to the online file-storage website. He was surprised to see a file sitting in his inbox. It was a JPEG image of some kind of bird—a blue jay, perhaps. He downloaded the file to his hard drive's documents folder, then erased the picture from the site and closed his Web browser.

He found the file, right-clicked on it, and selected "Open with . . . Image Magnifier." Five seconds later a window popped up showing the blue-jay image, which flashed from color to black-and-white before going grainy. Slowly at first and then more rapidly, chunks of pixels began fading. After thirty seconds, all that remained were two lines of alphanumeric pairs—168 of them. Finally, Kaseke double-clicked on the day's onetime pad to open it up. The decoding was tedious, taking almost ten minutes, but when he was done, he had two lines of text:

Sunday. 8:50 a.m.
Open Heart Congregational Church

A Christian church, Kaseke thought. Much better than a library or even a school. He knew where the church was located and suspected that like almost every church in Waterloo, this one conducted several services throughout the morning. Eight-fifty would be about the time people were leaving the first service and arriving for the second. Give the members a few minutes to collect their things and head for the door . . . In his earlier reconnaissance, he'd studied the comings and goings of the church's members. They loved to congregate outside between services and shake hands and laugh and talk about whatever they talked about. Such frivolity. What passed for worship here was a disgrace.

8:50. Yes, it was perfect. There would be a hundred or more people standing on the steps and sidewalk. There would likely be children present, though, and Kaseke didn't especially like the idea of that, but Allah would forgive him. To sacrifice a few for a larger good was acceptable.

It was Friday night. He would use most of Saturday to scout the locations, then Saturday evening to make sure the device was in order. That wouldn't take long, he knew. His job would be simple: Plant the device, set the timer, walk away, and find a vantage point to watch the results.

76

The fire was magnificent, Shasif Hadi thought. Even from three miles away, the sky over the treetops was almost as bright as the sun. And then had come the explosions, great mushrooms of flame and roiling black smoke rising silently into the dark sky, followed a few seconds later by a rumble so strong Hadi could feel it rise up through the road, through the tires of his car, and shake his seat. *Through the four of us,* Hadi thought, *the hand of Allah has struck that refinery dead.*

After setting their charges, they had done as Ibrahim instructed and walked one by one back along the pipeline to the grove of trees in which they'd changed their coveralls. Offering no explanation, Ibrahim ordered, "Run!" then took off in a sprint. They were two hundred yards away from the cattle gate when the first charge went off.

Staring out the car's rear window, Hadi had watched the syncopated valve charges go off, followed by the larger main charge, then nothing for the next one minute and fifty seconds except for the refinery's alarm Klaxon. Emergency response crews had probably just reached the shattered pipeline when the final charge ignited the ethanol spreading like a tidal wave into the complex. Those men had probably died almost instantly. A largely painless end, Hadi hoped. Brazil was a mostly Christian country, which made them enemies of Islam, but that didn't mean they were undeserving of mercy. If they suffered, it was Allah's will; if they'd perished quickly, Allah's will also. Either way, he and the others had succeeded in their mission.

Once at the gate, they drove the truck into the trees, then got back into the Volkswagen and pulled through, locking the gate behind them. Ninety seconds later, they were back at Hadi's car. As per the plan, Hadi followed Ibrahim and the others to where Fa'ad had left his car on a dirt road a few miles away. When they pulled over, Ibrahim got out and waved for Hadi to walk up.

"We forgot to account for a significant detail," Ibrahim told them. "The weather."

"I don't understand," Ahmed said.

Ibrahim pointed west, back toward the refinery. The flames were hundreds of feet high now, and topped by a ceiling of thick, black smoke. As they watched, they could see the smoke drifting southwest.

"It's heading toward São Paulo. They'll close the airport soon, if they haven't already."

"He's right," Hadi replied. "Still, of all the mistakes we could have made, this one is the least worrisome. If we make it out, so be it. If not, we die knowing we've done our duty."

Fa'ad chuckled. "You're right, of course, but I'd rather be alive to see the fruits of our effort. May Allah forgive my vanity."

"What will be will be," Ibrahim replied. "We still have a chance. You all know the alternate route." He checked his watch. "We'll meet tomorrow at noon in Rio at the Botanical Garden. If for some reason anyone's delayed, we meet at the secondary location four hours later. Good luck."

Though neither of them had caught more than a couple hours' sleep before leaving the airport, their flight's departure time, on that cusp between the dead of night and dawn, left them both restless. The good news was that there'd been no coach seats available, so they were riding first class on The Campus's dime. And the coffee wasn't half bad, either.

"You know, I don't get it, John," Jack said.

"What's that?" Clark replied.

"The two we're after . . . the brother and sister. They're barely out of their teens. What made them want to go to another country and kill people they've never met?"

"First of all, we don't know anything except that they came in on false passports."

"Maybe so, but odds are they aren't here for beach volleyball."

"Agreed. My point is, in our line of work it's best to take things as they come to you. Hunches can be damned handy, but they can get you killed, too."

"I hear you."

"To answer your question, I don't think there is an answer. At least not a simple one. What you're asking is: How are terrorists made? Poverty, hopelessness, misplaced religious fervor, the need to feel like you belong to something bigger than yourself . . . Take your pick."

"Damn, John, you almost sound sympathetic."

"I am. Up until the point where those motivations lead somebody to pick up a gun or strap on a bomb. After that, all bets are off."

"So what, you just switch off the sympathy?"

"That's up to you, Jack, but part of doing this kind of work is the willingness to put on blinders. Deal with what's in front of you. Every terrorist has a mother and father. Maybe kids, maybe people that love him. Hell, six days out of seven he might be a decent citizen, but on that one day he decides to pick up a gun or plant a bomb, he's a threat. And if you're the guy standing between him and innocent lives, the threat is all you can afford to worry about. You get what I'm saying?"

Jack nodded. "Yeah, I think so." While the real world existed mostly in shades of gray, when the moment of truth came, there was only room for black-and-white. Jack smiled and toasted Clark with his coffee cup. "You're a wise man, John."

"Thanks. You get older, you get smarter. At least that's how

610

it's supposed to work. There's always exceptions, though. Your dad, for one. He's wise beyond his years. I knew that the first time I met him."

"Yeah, when was that?"

"Nice try, Jack. Have you talked to him yet?"

"About The Campus? Yeah, when we rode back together from Andrews. He was pissed at first, but it went a lot better than I thought it was going to go."

"Let me guess: He wants to be the one to tell your mom?"

Jack nodded. "And just between you and me, I'm damned glad. My dad's a tough SOB, but my mom . . . She's got that look—that look that only a mom can give, you know?"

"Yep."

They sat in silence for a while, sipping coffee. "Been thinking about Dom," Jack said.

"He'll pull out of it. You gotta remember, except for maybe you, his transition has been the toughest. He went from being an FBI agent to a spook. From an agency that runs on rules and regs to a fake brokerage house that hunts down bad guys outside the law. And now this thing with Brian . . ." Clark shrugged. "No matter how you look at it, it's a shitty deal."

"I'm just thinking it's too early for him to be going back out."

"Ding doesn't think so, and that's good enough for me. For Gerry, too. Plus, there's just four of us now, and a lot of bases to cover." Clark smiled. "Hell, remember who he's running with. I trusted the guy with my daughter, Jack, and never regretted it. He'll make sure Dom comes through."

Though separated by less than four hundred miles, both Raharjo Pranata and Kersen Kaseke had been following virtually the same routine for weeks: Go to school, draw no attention to yourself, and wait for orders. Pranata's had come only hours after Kaseke's, during his final message check of the day. He was so surprised to see the text file sitting in his file storage's inbox that he botched his first attempt to decode the message.

The location they had chosen for him was less than a mile from his apartment. He'd passed by it almost every day. As targets went, it was almost ideal: large enough to accommodate hundreds of people yet hemmed in on all sides by buildings. The timing of the attack made sense as well. Pranata had seen signs advertising the event in question all over town, though he'd paid little attention to the specifics. A dedication of some kind. A statue or fountain. Not that it mattered.

Of the three targets they'd told him to prepare for, this one offered the greatest potential for massive casualties. What was that American saying? A turkey shoot?

The maps he'd used in his preparations had been easy to obtain, and several of them he'd even gotten at the town's visitor center. The topographical map he'd downloaded from a popular hiking website, and while he had no interest in the local trails, the elevations and distances were clearly marked, and a stroll around town with his portable GPS unit had confirmed their accuracy.

Once he was sure he had all the necessary data, he'd simply punched the numbers into the appropriate equations and come up with the settings.

Now would come the hard part: waiting. He would pass the time by practicing setting up and dismantling his equipment.

Musa's second day of driving was relatively short, taking him from Toppenish, Washington, to Nampa, Idaho, whose only claim to fame, according to a sign on the outskirts, was that it was not only the largest city in Canyon County, Idaho, with a population of 79,249, but also the fastest-growing. Yet another sign along the road, less than a hundred yards from the first, proclaimed that Nampa was also "a great place to live!"

When planning his route from Blaine, Musa had decided his overnight stops must be in medium-sized towns—not too large that the police force was aggressive or particularly well trained, and not too small, lest the arrival of a dark-skinned stranger provoke any undue curiosity. Toppenish, with a population of only eight thousand, might have fallen in the latter category if not for its close proximity to Yakima. Of course, his encounter with Willie, Toppenish's nosy chief of police, had placed a seed of doubt in Musa's mind. The situation hadn't escalated, of course, nor would it have, even if the cop questioned him further. Like the non-burned bogus documentation he'd shown the customs inspector in Vancouver, Musa was now armed with business cards, letterhead, and forms bearing the seal of the University of Nevada, Las Vegas. His cover story was essentially the same: a wealthy and neurotic horse owner in Bellingham who didn't trust his local vet's X-ray equipment.

It was mid-afternoon when he pulled off Highway 84/30 and into the parking lot of the Fairfield Inn & Suites. He shut off the ignition, then opened the travel atlas sitting on the passenger seat. He'd written nothing down, nor made any marks in the atlas. There was no need; he knew the route and distances by heart.

Six hundred forty miles to go, Musa thought. If he wished, he could start out early tomorrow and probably cover the remaining distance to Beatty, Nevada, in one day. It was tempting, but he decided against it. The Emir had been adamant in his orders. He would follow the timetable.

77

Descending through twenty thousand feet on their way into Rio de Janeiro, Chavez and Dominic could see the pall of oily smoke hanging over São Paulo two hundred miles down the coast from Rio. North of São Paulo, the Paulinia fires were still raging. On the way to the airport the night before, they'd heard on the news that firefighters and rescue workers in the area had changed their strategy, focusing not on extinguishing the refinery inferno but on evacuation and containment. Ethanol had stopped spewing from the pipeline within an hour of the initial explosion, but in that time some ten thousand gallons of fuel had spilled into the refinery, and while some of that was still burning, it was now the dozens upon dozens of blending and storage tanks that were involved. The conflagration would eventually burn out, but experts both in Brazil and in the United States disagreed on how long that would take. Some predicted four days, others two weeks or more. What no one disagreed on, however, was the environmental toll the disaster was taking. Already oil soot was blanketing fields and homes as far south as Colombo. Emergency rooms were overflowing with patients complaining of respiratory problems.

"If that's not hell on earth, I don't know what is," Dominic said, staring out the window.

"No argument there. How you feelin'?" While Ding had dozed on and off for much of the flight, Dominic had been dead to the world until an hour ago.

"Better, I think. I was ass-kicked."

"In more ways than one, *mano*. I know I already said this, but sorry about Brian. He was a good troop."

"Thanks. So when we touch down, what's the plan?"

"Call home and check the news stations to see if Hadi's information has hit the airwaves. If it has, we go hunting. If not, we hunker down and wait."

Once off the plane and cleared through customs, they went straight to the Avis desk and checked in. Ten minutes later, they were standing at the curb, waiting for their Hyundai Sonata to be brought around. "Air-conditioning?" Dominic asked.

"Yeah, but manual transmission. Can't have everything."

The dark green Sonata came around the corner. The attendant climbed out, had Chavez sign a form, then nodded and walked away. They got in and pulled out. Dominic retrieved his sat phone from his carry-on and dialed The Campus.

"We're down," he told Hendley, and turned on the phone's speaker.

"Good. You're on speakerphone. Sam and Rick are here, too. Biery's on his way up." Dominic heard a door open, then the creaking of a chair. Biery said, "Dom, you there?"

"Yeah, both of us."

"We're in business. We cycled through ten online storage sites before we got a hit. He's using a site called filecuda.com. Just like Jack figured, Hadi was using a variation of his e-mail for the log-in. The password we cracked in ten minutes. There's nothing in the account's inbox right now."

Rick Bell said, "We've put together a message we think will get Hadi moving in our direction. Sam will give you the details."

Granger came on. "We're a little worried that the news leak will really spook Hadi, so we're going to go with baby steps, move him from one place to another. He'll be on guard, so we figure if he moves to the first spot and doesn't get ambushed, he'll start getting more comfortable with the idea.

Once we think we've got him hooked, we're going to tell him to meet a contact in the Rocinha—"

"The what?"

Ding answered. "It's Portuguese. It means 'Little Ranch.' Down here, slums are called *favelas,* and the Rocinha's the biggest one in Rio."

"We figure we'll move him two, maybe three, times before sending him to the Rocinha. Depends on the tone of his responses. I'll e-mail you a list and timetable."

"Why there?"

"The Rio police don't go in there unless they absolutely have to. Be easier for you to operate."

Dominic asked, "When are you dropping the dime on Hadi?"

"In about forty minutes, by fax to Record News. We put together our own sketch and description—hopefully, close enough that Hadi'll recognize himself but vague enough that he won't get nabbed right away."

"How sure are we they'll use it?" Chavez asked.

Hendley said, "Survival of the fittest. They're a news channel, and they're fighting for market share during the biggest disaster in Brazilian history. They'll take the tip like a gift from God."

"Gotta love cutthroat journalism," Ding replied.

"We're tuned in to all the channels here. As soon as it hits the airwaves, we'll call you."

Dominic hung up. To Chavez: "We hunting?"

"Damn straight we are. Need to make a stop first. I know a guy who knows a guy."

"Who knows where to get his hands on some guns?"

"You got it."

Frank Weaver woke up at five a.m., had two cups of coffee from the in-room brewer, then read the newspaper for twenty minutes before he showered and headed down to the lobby for the free continental breakfast. By seven-fifteen he was packed up and out the door.

His rig was exactly where he'd left it, as was the cask, but he knew they would be. The DOE had equipped his truck with an immobilizer. Start the engine without a key and the fuel system shuts down. Nice little feature. As for the cask, no one would run off with that thing. Maybe King Kong, who'd noticed he was missing one of his barbells, but no one else.

He did his usual inspection walk-around, checking the ratchets, padlocks, and chains, and, finding nothing out of order, he unlocked the driver's door and climbed up into the cab. He was reaching his key toward the ignition when he stopped.

Something . . .

At first he couldn't put his finger on it, but slowly it dawned on him: Someone had been in the truck. That couldn't be, though. Like everything else with his rig, the door lock was beefed up. It'd take more than some crackhead thief to pick it. Weaver looked around. Nothing seemed out of place. He checked the glove box and center console for missing items. Everything was there. Same with the sleeping compartment. Everything was as he'd left it.

Gun.

He reached under his seat. The .38 revolver was still there, snug in its leather holster affixed to the seat frame.

Weaver sat in silence for half a minute before shrugging off the eerie feeling. Maybe the hotel coffee was stronger than he thought. Made him jumpy.

He powered up the dashboard GPS unit and waited for it to cycle through the self-diagnostic check, then punched up his route. Day three of four. An easy 310 miles to Saint George, Utah.

*

Tariq found the Emir in his bedroom, collecting what few possessions he'd brought along into a box. "After I've recorded my testament and left to meet Musa, burn these things."

"I will. I have two pieces of news. Each of Nayoan's four men have acknowledged their go-signals. The first will be Waterloo on Sunday morning."

"Good."

"Second, our man intercepted the truck without incident. We have the driver's route, including rest and fuel stops. He's due to arrive at the facility between two-thirty and three, the day after tomorrow."

The Emir nodded and closed his eyes, mentally recalling the timeline. "That's perfect, my friend. Musa will be in place at least four hours early. Go set up the camera. It's time."

78

By the time Clark and Jack got off the plane and found their rental car, it was seven a.m. and time for breakfast and a phone call back home. Armed with only the siblings' names—Citra and Purnoma Salim—and the date of their arrival into Norfolk, Clark and Jack had no choice but to rely on The Campus to give them a starting point.

They found an IHOP about a mile south of the airport on Military Highway, took a booth, and ordered coffee, eggs, and pancakes. While they were waiting, Clark called Rick Bell.

"All we've got is the hotel the Salims listed on their entry form," he told Clark. "If they didn't check in, we'll have to get creative. The Indonesian embassy in Washington keeps a list of citizens traveling on vacation to the U.S., but since they came in on a bogus passport, it's a toss-up whether they'd be logged into the system."

"We'll start with the hotel," Clark said. "They have to be sleeping somewhere."

Bell gave him the name of the hotel and signed off.

"Econo Lodge in Little Creek," Clark told Jack. "Stuff your face. We might be doing a lot of running today."

They found the Econo Lodge about two miles from the Amphibious Base and a quarter-mile from the Little Creek channel. Jack asked, "SEALs at the amphib base, right?"

"Yep. SpecWar Group Two—Teams Two, Four, and Eight, plus an SDV team—swimmer delivery vehicle."

"You miss it?"

"Sometimes, but most days not. Miss the people, mostly, and the work, but there were some pretty ugly times, too."

"Care to elaborate?"

Clark looked sideways at him and smiled. "No. It's the nature of what SEALs do, Jack. They go places nobody else wants to go and do what nobody else can. Nowadays they call those spots 'denied areas.' Back then we called it 'Indian country.' SEALs get a lot more attention today than when I was in, and more's the pity, as far as I'm concerned. The less people talk about you, the better job you're doing."

"So what changed?"

"Don't know, really. I keep in touch with guys that are still in, and they can't quite figure it out, either. They get a lot of kids who come in thinking they'll jog on the beach, do some push-ups, and walk away with the Budweiser." Here Clark was referring to the SEAL Trident badge. "Those usually last less than a week."

"Chaff from the wheat," Jack observed.

"At about a seventy-five percent attrition rate. Here we are. . . ." Clark pulled off of Shore Drive and parked beside the lobby. "Might have to run a little con to get the info we need," Clark said.

"You lead, I'll follow."

They went in and walked up to the reception desk. An early-twenties blond girl with a spray-on tan said, "Morning."

"Morning." Clark pulled out his marshal's badge and flashed it. "U.S. marshal. Looking for a couple kids that checked in a couple weeks ago."

"Wow. What'd they do?"

"Depends how quick we find them. After midnight, we'll have to file a material witness warrant. We're just trying to cross some *t*'s for an old case. The names were Salim—Citra and Purnoma Salim."

"They sound Arab." She wrinkled her lip.

"What's your point?"

Clark had put a little steel in his voice. The girl shrank back and said, "Nothing. Sorry. Uh . . . so you just wanna know if they were here?"

"For starters."

The girl sat down at her computer and started tapping the keyboard. "You gotta date?"

Clark gave it to her. "Give or take a day or two."

"Okay, yeah, here they are. They stayed one night, then checked out."

"Cash or charge?" Jack asked.

"Paid with cash, but we took a credit card for damages."

"You have it on file?"

"I don't know if I can give that to you. I could get in trouble, couldn't I?"

Clark shrugged. "No problem, I understand." He turned to Jack. "Get the Deputy AG on the phone."

Jack didn't miss a beat. He pulled out his cell phone, hit speed-dial, and walked to the other side of the lobby.

The girl asked, "What's that?"

"Deputy Attorney General. Gonna need your name for the warrant."

"Huh?"

"We've gotta serve the warrant on a named individual. That's the way it works. Gonna need your boss's name, too. So what's your name?"

"Lisa."

To Jack, Clark called, "Lisa . . ." Jack nodded and said her name into the phone. Clark, back to the girl: "Gimme your last name and Social Security number."

"Uh, wait. Wait a second. . . . So you just need the credit card info?"

"Yeah. Don't worry about it, though. We'll have a team down here in about twenty minutes. What time do you get off?"

"Nine a.m."

Clark chuckled. "Sorry, not today you're not."

Lisa was tapping on the keyboard again. "They used a Visa. Card number . . ."

"Pretty slick," Jack said, as they climbed back into the car.

"Nobody wants the hassle. I call it the little-big theory. Make the favor you're asking seem real small and the consequences real big. So whatdya think? Your type?"

"Her? Cute enough, but something tells me she's not exactly a crossword-in-ink kind of girl."

Clark laughed at this. "So you're holding out for beauty and brains?"

"Anything wrong with that?"

"Not a thing. Call in the card, get Bell working on it."

It took twenty minutes. "No more motel charges, but the day they checked out I've got half a dozen—souvenir shops, McDonald's, Starbucks . . . Just incidentals, and just that one day. I'm e-mailing the details and a Google map."

"Why the map?" Jack asked.

"All the charges were inside a square mile of one another."

Jack hung up and brought Clark up to speed. "They switched credit cards, switched names," Clark said. "Good sign."

"Good how?"

"Stand-up citizens don't do that, Jack."

Jack's phone e-mail chimed, and he checked it. Clark asked, "Where're we going?"

"Virginia Beach."

"Okay, guys, we gotta make a decision," Sam Granger said. "Plain text or encoded?"

Granger, Hendley, and Bell had been arguing over it for an hour: With Hadi and his team having gone to ground after the Paulinia attack, and with the URC changing its onetime pads every day, did Hadi have the ability to decrypt messages? Better question: Did they have the ability to "de-stego" the images in which the OTPs were embedded? Granger and Bell didn't think so, but Hendley was worried.

In the past, the URC had run its big operations by the dead-man switch rule: Once the execute order is given, there's no turning back and no pulling the plug. This change had come after the failed URC bombing of the Berlin U-Bahn, when, shortly after the go-signal had been given, the URC's cell leader in Munich was captured by the BfV and persuaded to reel in the attackers. Of course, in the larger context, none of that mattered: Dead-man switch rule or not, either Hadi would get the message or he wouldn't. If he had the ability to decrypt, a plain text message would spook him and their chance would vanish.

"Listen, we have to risk it," Bell said. "We use our message to spook him but in our favor. Get him worked up enough and he might not even question the plain text."

Hendley considered this, then looked to Granger. "Sam?"

"Okay, let's do it. We'll move Hadi just once and tell him

it's dry-cleaning, then we'll move him to the Rocinha, and Chavez and Dominic will grab him up."

Bell stood up and headed for the door. "I'll get it uploaded." He left.

A minute later, Hendley's phone rang. It was Gavin Biery. "You guys upload the message yet?"

"Rick just went to do it."

"Shit. Stop him; get him back. I'm on my way up."

79

Biery was upstairs and walking into Hendley's office two minutes later. "I found a pattern," he announced. "You send that thing in plain text and Hadi will know it's bogus."

His last-second interception of Rick Bell had been the result of a marathon night of watching his newly written algorithm chew on the URC's onetime pads. Though by their very nature the letters within an OTP are meant to be random and therefore unbreakable by anyone not working off of the current pad, it was in Biery's nature to look for patterns where none seem to exist. It was, he'd once explained to Jack, sort of like the SETI (Search for Extra-Terrestrial Intelligence) project: "There's probably nothing out there, but wouldn't it be cool if there was?" In this case, what Biery had found was a pattern to the URC's onetime pads.

"OTPs are great, probably the simplest form of 'unbreakable' encryption in the world, though nothing's truly unbreakable," he'd explained once Rick Bell returned. "It's all a matter of probabilities, really—"

Granger cut him off. "Another time, Gavin."

"Right."

"Well, like you figured, the Emir, or whoever came up with this, was probably worried about their people in the field. Kinda stupid to carry an OTP on you, or have it on a laptop you're carrying around, so they came up with a system to re-create the day's pad while you're on the go. It's time-consuming but doable."

"Let's hear it," said Bell.

"They're using a formula called the middle-square method. It was created by some Hungarian mathematician named von Neumann in 1946. Essentially, what you do is take a seed number—length doesn't matter, as long as it has an even number of digits—then square it, then take the middle part of the resulting number—again, however many digits you want—and use it for your new seed number. Since these guys would probably be doing it on paper, they'd use small numbers and build on them. Here . . ."

Biery grabbed the legal pad on Hendley's desk and started writing:

$49 \times 49 = 2\text{-}4\text{-}0\text{-}1$. New seed number $= 40$

"Since you can't use zeros, you round up. So your new seed number is 41. Then you square that, and so on, until you've filled the OTP grid."

"And the numbers are random?" This from Granger.

"Pseudo-random, but you wouldn't be able to tell unless you had a whole bunch of OTPs to number-crunch. The more complicated the formula, the more random the numbers, but at some point you can't run the calculations with pencil and paper."

"So what formula are they using?"

"Month, day, and year, all added together. Take today, for example: May 21, 2010 . . ." He wrote:

$5 + 21 + 2010 = 2036$

"You'd just use the middle two digits. Rounding up the zero, of course."

"And thirteen is your new seed number," Hendley said.

"You got it."

"And all their OTPs use the same method?"

"All the ones we got from Almasi's safe."

"Damn nice work, Gavin."

"Thanks." He left.

"That boy just saved our ass," Granger said.

Knowing Allah would take it as a sign of faithlessness, Hadi had always resisted believing in omens, but the proximity of Rio's Botanical Garden to the O Cristo Redentor, or Christ the Redeemer statue, was unnerving. But then again, he reminded himself, in Rio everything seemed close to the O Cristo Redentor. Sitting at 2,300 feet atop Corcovado Mountain, gazing down at hundreds of square miles of jungle and urban sprawl, the 120-foot, 600-ton soapstone-and-concrete monolith was the city's most famous landmark—and a reminder to Hadi that he was in a largely heathen country.

Hadi had made good time after parting company with Ibrahim and the others, but he'd spent the first two hours of the journey with his hands clenched white on the wheel and looking in his rearview mirror every twenty seconds.

An hour after dawn he had pulled into the municipality of Seropédica, on the far eastern outskirts of Rio. Thirty miles to the east he could see Rio proper: five hundred square miles of city holding some twelve million souls—almost half the population of Saudi Arabia in just one city. São Paulo was larger still, but he'd landed there at night and driven around the northern edge of the city on his way to his hotel in Caieiras.

At the garden's entrance he bought a ticket and a brochure/map from the cashier. The brochure gave him the highlights of the gardens—350 acres, 7,000 species of tropical plants, research laboratories . . . He flipped through the pages until he found the listing for specific sites. The aviary was at the top of the list. He oriented himself on the map and started walking. It was a bright, sunny day, and the humidity was already unbearable. Far to the south, he could see the cap of black smoke over São Paulo, so dense that it looked like night had fallen over that section of the coast.

Halfway to his destination, he was passing an ice cream shop and glanced in the window. A small television mounted in the corner of the shop was tuned to Record News. Images of the refinery fire, some taken from the ground and some from a helicopter, were playing beside the anchorwoman's face. She turned to face another camera, a change of topic, and suddenly a sketch appeared on the screen. The likeness was not perfect but was close enough that Hadi felt his heart lurch in his chest.

This can't be, he thought. *Who saw me?* They'd left no witnesses, of that he was certain. The refinery security truck that had passed by while they were setting the charges had been too far away to see him. *A surveillance camera, perhaps?* No, that wasn't right. If they had a real image of him, they would have broadcast that, not a sketch.

He continued to watch the report, expecting to see his sketch followed by one of Ibrahim, then Fa'ad, then Ahmed, but his alone stayed on the screen.

Think, think . . .

He spotted a souvenir shop across the food court. He walked across to the shop and stepped inside. He checked for television sets or radios; there were none, so he browsed around, not wanting to appear in a hurry, before selecting a baseball cap emblazoned with the Botanical Garden's logo. He paid cash for it, declined a bag, then walked out and put on the cap, pulling it close to his eyebrows. He checked his watch. He was early for the rendezvous by almost seventy minutes. He walked over to a concrete ledge surrounding a fern bed and sat down.

Had Ibrahim and the others heard about the sketch? If so, they may not show up. They'd discussed contingencies for pursuit, for capture, and for the death of team members during the mission, but not this.

He sat for five minutes, staring into space and thinking, then made a decision. He paged through the brochure until he found what he needed.

The Internet café was on the eastern side of the gardens. He paid the barista for a half-hour, and she assigned him one of the terminals. He sat down in the cubicle and opened the Web browser. It took him a moment to remember the site URL. It was the fifth today, so he'd rotated to . . . bitroup.com.

When the site came up on the screen, he logged in and tabbed to the messages area. He was surprised to see a text file sitting in the "uploaded "section. He double-clicked on the file; it contained two lines of alphanumeric pairs. He jotted the pairs on the back of his brochure. There were 344. He signed off and left.

It took him thirty minutes to create the grid, and another twenty to decode and double-check the message:

Saw TV sketch. Suspect compromised, one of your team. Break contact. Proceed Tá Ligado Cyber Café on Rua Bráulio Cordeiro for instructions. 1400 hours. Acknowledge this message by encode: 9M, 6V, 4U, 4D, 7Z.

Hadi read the message twice. *Compromised?* His mind spun. It wasn't possible. Ibrahim or one of the others had betrayed him? Why? None of it made sense, but the message was authentic. *Break contact.* He checked his watch: 11:45. Hurrying now, he encoded the acknowledgment pairs, then returned to the café, typed the response into a text file, then uploaded it.

Ibrahim passed both Fa'ad's and Ahmed's cars as he pulled into the parking lot. He found a spot, pulled in, and shut off the engine. Fa'ad and Ahmed had parked one row behind him, separated by half a dozen cars. Out his passenger window he saw Hadi exiting the garden's main gate. His pace was hurried, his posture tense. *Police?* Ibrahim wondered. He kept watching, half expecting to see men running after Hadi, but nothing happened.

What's this?

Hadi reached his car and got in.

Ibrahim made a snap decision. He waited until Hadi's car was headed toward the entrance driveway, then backed out and followed. He slowed beside Ahmed's car and gestured for him to follow.

What are you up to, my friend?

80

"They hooked him," Chavez said, punching off the satellite phone. "Two o'clock, an Internet café on Rua Bráulio Cordeiro."

"Great, where the hell's that?" Dominic replied, swerving their car as a taxi swept them, the driver honking and yelling. "Not that it matters. We ain't gonna get there in one piece anyway."

Chavez was tracing his finger along a city map. "Keep heading east. I'll steer you."

"I assume we're not grabbing him there?"

"Nope. First we gotta make sure he's alone. We told him to break contact, but who knows? Plus, we're gonna need some privacy to get done what we gotta get done."

"Which is?"

"Whatever it takes."

Dominic smiled grimly.

They found the café and circled the block twice to get the lay of the land, then found a parking spot on the street fifty yards to the north on the other side of an intersection. They got out and walked south. Between a pharmacy and a tire repair shop they found a short alleyway that led to a makeshift junk-yard full of rusted washing machines, car axles, and stacks of old sewer pipes. Chavez led the way to the back of the yard and behind a trash heap. Through a wide-slatted fence they could see the Internet café across the street.

"Shit," Chavez said.

"What?"

"Just noticed that walkway to the right of the café."

"Back entrance, maybe," Dominic said. He checked his watch. Still twenty minutes to go. "I'll circle around, see if I can get a look."

Ten minutes later, Chavez's phone beeped. He pushed the talk button. "Go ahead."

"There's a back door, but there's a Dumpster pushed up against it," Dom said.

"Bad for fire code, good for us. Okay, come on back."

Chavez had no sooner taken his finger off the button than a green Chevrolet Marajó slowed down outside the Internet café. Though the angle was oblique, Chavez could see a lone man sitting behind the wheel. The Marajó continued on, then braked and began backing into a space.

"Dom, where are you?"

"Almost back to the intersection."

"Slow up. We might have our guy."

"Roger."

Up the street, the Marajó's driver got out and started toward the café.

Chavez pushed the button. "It's our guy." He gave Dominic a description of Hadi's car, then said, "Get back to the Hyundai. Shouldn't take him long."

Chavez got a double button click in response: *Roger.* He dialed The Campus. Sam Granger answered. Chavez said, "He's in."

"The message is uploaded. We're sending him to a pool hall at the corner of Travessas Roma and Alegria at the south end of the Rocinha."

"Time?"

"Seven."

Chavez hung up. Ten minutes passed, and then Hadi walked out of the café. He looked up and down the street, then walked to his car and got in.

"Moving," Chavez said. He sprinted back through the yard, down the alley, and emerged on the street. To his left, Hadi's Marajó pulled up to the intersection and stopped.

Dominic said, "I see him."

Hadi turned left.

"Coming to you," Dominic radioed.

"Negative. Stay there." Chavez sprinted up the street and reached the Hyundai in thirty seconds. "Okay, go. Left at the intersection, then turn left and pull up to the stop sign."

Dominic did as instructed. As they reached the stop sign, Hadi passed in front of them, heading north. Dominic let two cars pass, then pulled out.

Fifteen minutes later: "Someone's on us," Dominic said. "Or Hadi."

Chavez glanced in the side mirror. "Blue Lancia?"

"And two more behind that. Green Fiat compact, red Ford Corcel."

"What the fuck? You sure?"

"Saw the Fiat and the Ford circle the block twice while I was going around behind the café. Can't be the cops."

"Yeah, why?"

"Cops would be better at it. They're in a goddamned convoy."

Chavez checked their map. "Let's get a face."

Dominic slowed beside a parking spot and put on his blinker. Behind them, the Lancia honked its horn. Chavez stuck his hand out the window and waved him past. As the Lancia swerved and sped by, Chavez glanced over.

"Looked like the same ethnic persuasion as Hadi. His partners in crime, you think?"

"Could be. Maybe Hadi didn't make a clean break."

Dominic let the third car, the Corcel, pass, then waited five beats, then pulled out and fell in behind it.

Musa's third day of travel went as smoothly as his first two, and by late afternoon he reached his final overnight stop: Winnemucca, Nevada; population 7,030; 350 miles northwest of Las Vegas.

81

To his credit, Hadi did his best to dry-clean himself on the way to the Rocinha, skirting the slums for two hours as he drove in circles and doubled back, looking for signs of pursuit that should have been plain to him. The Lancia, the Fiat, and the Corcel remained in convoy formation, never changing places and never more than a hundred yards from Hadi's rear bumper.

"We've got a decision to make," Dominic said. "Better do it now, before it's made for us." If he and Chavez had a chance to snatch Hadi and his three partners, did they go for it or concentrate on Hadi alone?

"The more, the merrier," Chavez said, "but we gotta remember it's just you and me, and the Rio cops wouldn't see any difference between us and Hadi's group if things go sideways."

At 6:15 they broke off their pursuit and made their way back to the Rocinha's southern entrance. Leaving Hadi on his own was a risk, they knew, but neither knew anything about the meeting's location; they would have to hope Hadi's pursuers didn't decide to intercept him in the next forty-five minutes.

The sun was slipping behind the mountains to the west, casting the slums in golden light.

While the Portuguese translation of Rocinha was "Little Ranch," Dominic and Chavez saw nothing small about it. Covering roughly three-quarters of a mile from north to south and a quarter-mile from east to west, the slums were situated in a shallow, sloping valley bracketed on both sides by thickly forested hills and cliffs. Shaded by crisscrossing clotheslines and makeshift canvas awnings, the narrow streets meandered up slopes of densely packed and pastel-painted saltbox apartments, many so close that their balconies touched and their rooflines merged. Crumbling concrete and brick stairways covered in climbing vines rose up from the streets and disappeared behind buildings. Telephone and power poles festooned with hundreds of feet of exposed wires and cables extended in every direction. Lining every alley were dozens upon dozens of huts made from planks and corrugated tin. Sewage ran down shallow gutters filled with trash.

"Unbelievable," Dominic said.

"How many people in this place?"

"Hundred thousand at least. Maybe a hundred fifty."

They found a parking spot down the block from the pool hall and got out. "You take the back, I'll take the front. Gimme fifteen minutes, then come on in."

"Roger."

Dominic headed down the street and turned the corner. Chavez walked across the street, bought a bottle of Coke from a street vendor, then leaned against a wall beneath an awning. Down the block, a lone streetlamp flickered to life. Ten minutes passed. No sign of Hadi, the Lancia, the Fiat, or the Corcel. He finished his Coke, handed it back to the vendor, then walked across the street and into the pool hall.

It wasn't so much a hall as a double garage-sized room with two pool tables in the center, a bar on the right, and hard-back chairs lining the opposite wall. At the rear of the bar was a seating area with four round tables and chairs. In the corner, a set of three steps leading down to a door labeled "Exit" in Portuguese. Beneath plastic stained-glass hanging lights, he could see men clustered around the pool tables. The air was thick with smoke.

Ding took a seat at the bar and ordered a beer. Five minutes later the back door opened and Dominic walked in. He walked up to the bar, ordered a beer, then took it to the back, choosing a table.

At five after seven, the front door opened and Hadi walked in. He stood near the door, nervously looking about. Dominic raised his beer bottle to shoulder height and nodded at Hadi, who hesitated, then headed in Dominic's direction.

The front door opened again. The Lancia driver walked in. Like Hadi, he stood still for thirty seconds, scanning the interior. His shirt was untucked, and on his right hip Chavez could see a familiar-shaped bump. The man's scan stopped suddenly as he saw Hadi, who was just approaching Dominic's table. The man started after him. Dominic let him pass, then got off his stool.

"Where's my money, asshole?" Chavez said in Portuguese.

The man spun around, fists coming up. Chavez raised his hands to ear height. "Easy, easy—"

He slapped his right palm down on the man's face, shattering his nose. He staggered backward, and Chavez followed, delivering a thumb-punch to the hollow beneath his larynx. The man went down. The other patrons watched curiously but made no move to intervene. Debts were debts.

At the back of the room, Dominic was already out of his seat and marching Hadi out the back door.

Chavez walked up to Lancia and stepped on his gun hand, then jerked the gun from his belt. "You speak English?"

The man sputtered.

"Nod if you speak English."

The man nodded.

"Get to your feet or I'll shoot you dead right here."

Dominic was waiting in the alley. It was fully dark now. To the left, the alley ended in a wall, into which was set a stairway leading up into darkness; to their right, twenty yards away, the mouth of the alley.

Hadi stood against the brick wall beside a cluster of garbage cans. Dominic had his gun out and tucked behind his thigh. Chavez shoved Lancia from behind, and he stumbled into the wall beside Hadi.

"Who are you?" Hadi asked.

"Shut up," Dominic growled.

Chavez saw Dom's fingers curling and uncurling on the butt of his gun. "Easy, Dom." He picked up a wad of newspaper from the ground and tossed it to Lancia. "Wipe your nose."

"Fuck you."

The door burst open beside them. Silhouetted by the dim light from the pool hall, Chavez saw a figure standing a few feet back from the threshold. His hand came up, extended toward them. Chavez double-tapped him in the chest, and he fell back. Chavez kicked the door shut.

"Go, Dom." He leveled his gun with Hadi and Lancia. "Move."

At the mouth of the alley, a figure was running toward him. A gun muzzle flashed orange, then twice more. Chavez side-stepped behind the garbage cans and fired twice. The figure dodged to one side.

"Stairs," Chavez ordered.

Prodding Lancia and Hadi along, Dom headed for the stairs. Chavez back-walked with them until he felt his shoulders bump into the wall, then turned and followed.

Charging up the steps on the heels of Dominic, Chavez reached the top and looked around. An alley stretched to the left and to the right; above them, overhanging balconies. Behind them and to the right, another rectangle set into another brick wall. Chavez gestured toward it. Dominic nodded and shoved Lancia and Hadi up the steps. Behind, Chavez heard the scuff of a shoe and looked back down the steps. Their pursuer was there, head peeking around the corner. Chavez pulled back, went still. After ten seconds of silence, the scuff of a shoe echoed up the steps.

Chavez tucked his gun into his belt, took two steps to the right, then reached above his head and snagged the balcony's lower rail. He chinned himself up, then reached again, grabbing the upper rail and pulling himself over. He dropped flat on the balcony.

The footsteps continued coming: Step . . . pause. Step . . . pause . . . In the distance, sirens were warbling. Would gunshots be enough to get the police to come into the Rocinha? he wondered. He closed his eyes and listened, waiting for the echo to change.

Step . . . pause. The shoe scuffed again. No echo this time. The man passed beneath Chavez's balcony, obviously trying to decide. *Alley or stairs?* He chose the stairs. Chavez quietly rose to his knees, braced his gun on the railing, and fired, putting a single round into the back of the man's head.

He jumped down, ran to the body, did a hurried frisk, then charged up the stairs. Dominic was waiting at the top, crouched down behind a Dumpster with Lancia and Hadi. A hundred yards away, the alley opened into a parking lot faintly illuminated by streetlamps. From somewhere close by came the bouncing of a basketball and kids shouting back and forth.

"We're down to two," Chavez said.

"We'll make do with these."

Chavez dropped the items he'd taken from the dead man on the ground: passport, a wad of cash, a set of car keys. He picked up the keys and dangled them before Lancia and Hadi. "Which car, the Fiat or the Corcel?"

Neither man answered.

Dominic grabbed Hadi by the hair, jerked his head back, and jammed the barrel of his gun between his lips. Hadi resisted, clenching his teeth. Dominic took his opposite hand and slapped Hadi hard on the side of his windpipe. He gasped. Dominic jammed his gun into Hadi's mouth.

"Five seconds and I'll spray your brains down this alley." Hadi didn't respond. Dominic jammed the gun deeper. Hadi started retching. "Four seconds. Three seconds."

Chavez watched his partner, watched his eyes. Facial expressions can be manufactured when necessary, but the eyes were a little trickier to get right. The look in Dominic's eyes told Ding he was serious.

"Dom . . ."

"Two seconds . . ."

"Dom!" Chavez rasped.

Hadi was nodding, raising his hands in supplication. Dominic withdrew the gun, and Hadi said, "Ford Corcel."

Lancia growled, "You're a traitor."

Dominic pointed the gun at Lancia's left eye. "You're next. Where's it parked?"

Lancia didn't respond.

"This time you get three seconds," Dominic said, then shifted his gun, jamming it against Lancia's knee. "Then a cane for life."

"One block east of the pool hall, middle of the block on the south side."

Chavez said to Dom, "Go grab it. I'll babysit our friends."

Fifteen minutes later, Chavez heard a honk and looked down the alley. The Corcel was sitting there, side door open. He got Lancia and Hadi up and walking. At the car, he prodded them into the backseat. "Found this in the trunk," Dominic said, holding up a small coil of rusted baling wire.

Chavez leaned over the seat. "Gimme your hands."

Dominic started driving.

"We're gonna need some privacy," Chavez said. He sat sideways in the passenger seat, gun resting on the backrest.

"I think I've got the place. Saw it on the way here."

The building was nearly identical to all the others—four-story rectangle with one door and balconied windows—except that the windows and door were boarded up. On the side of the building, a set of steps overgrown with shrubbery rose into the darkness. An official-looking seal was plastered across the front door. In Portuguese it read "Condemned."

"Here," Dominic said. "Be right back."

He got out, shoved his way through the overgrown steps,

and disappeared. He was back in two minutes. He nodded at Chavez, who got out and fell in behind Lancia and Hadi as they followed Dominic up the steps. After about thirty feet, the shrubbery thinned out and the steps turned right onto a porch. Like the one below, the back door was emblazoned with the "Condemned" seal, but this one was hanging by only its bottom hinge. Dominic lifted the door free and set it to one side. Chavez ordered Hadi and Lancia inside.

Under the glow of Dominic's LED penlight, it quickly became clear why the building had been condemned. The walls, floor, and ceiling were covered in soot and in some places charred down to the supports. The floor was a checkerboard of melted linoleum tiles, charred plywood, and open holes, through which they could see the lower floors.

"Sit down," Chavez ordered them.

"Where?" Lancia snapped.

"Anywhere that isn't a hole. Sit."

They complied.

Dominic said, "I'm gonna have a look around."

Chavez sat down across from their prisoners, listening as Dominic rummaged through the other rooms. He came back with a tarnished kerosene lantern. He gave it a shake; fluid sloshed inside. He set it down in the corner and lit it. Hissing yellow light filled the room.

Chavez looked over to Dom and shrugged. Dominic said, "You're the boss; your show."

Chavez got up, walked closer to Lancia and Hadi, then knelt down again. "I'm gonna talk for a little bit. I want you to listen. Closely. I ain't gonna bullshit you, and I don't want you to bullshit me. If we get along, you two stand a much better chance of seeing sunrise. What're your names?"

Neither man answered.

"Come on, just first names, so we can talk."

"Hadi."

The other one hesitated, his lips pressed tightly together. Finally he said, "Ibrahim."

"Good, thanks. Listen, we know you two, and your two dead friends, did the Paulinia refinery. We know this, so let's not talk about that again. We're not cops, and we're not here to arrest you for the refinery."

"Then who are you?" Hadi asked.

"Someone else."

"What makes you think we were involved with that place?" Ibrahim asked.

"How do you think?" This Chavez said with a half-smile and a fleeting glance at Hadi.

"Why do you look at me?"

To Ibrahim, Chavez asked, "Why were you chasing Hadi?" Ibrahim didn't answer, so Chavez continued: "I'm going to take a wild guess at something: You did the refinery job but didn't count on the smoke closing down the São Paulo airport, so you went to plan B—come to Rio. You get here, then things go bad. Hadi goes on the run; Ibrahim, you chase after him. Why?"

"Why don't you care about the refinery?" Ibrahim pressed.

"Not our country, not our problem. Why were you chasing him?"

"He's a traitor."

Hadi snapped, "You're a liar. You're the traitor. You, or Ahmed, or Fa'ad. You leaked the sketch."

"What sketch?"

"The one on the television. I saw it; it looked like me. Who else could have given it to them?"

"Who told you all this?"

"The Em—when I saw the sketch, I made contact. There was a message waiting. It said you'd betrayed me and that I had to run."

"You were tricked."

"I authenticated it. It was genuine."

Ibrahim was shaking his head. "No, you're wrong. We didn't betray you."

Chavez said, "So you and your friends just wanted to catch up with him and chat, is that it?"

"Yes."

Chavez leaned closer to Hadi. "That's bullshit, and you know it. Whether that message was real or not, all they knew was you were running. Probably to the police. They weren't going to take that chance. You know it's true."

Hadi said nothing.

"Okay, so here's the deal," Chavez said. "As far as we're concerned—"

"We still don't know who you are."

"Don't our accents tell you something?"

"Americans."

"Right. As far as we're concerned, the refinery is off the table. What we want to know is who's operating in the U.S. How many cells, where they're located . . . All that."

"Fuck you," said Ibrahim.

Chavez heard Dominic standing up behind him. He turned to see him walking into the kitchen. He turned back to Hadi. "How about you? Just give us—"

He heard Dominic's footsteps returning, but at a faster pace and with purpose. He turned. His gun wrapped in a mold-encrusted dish towel, Dominic walked up to Ibrahim, put the gun against his left knee, and pulled the trigger. The towel muffled the shot to a muted pop. Ibrahim screamed. Dominic stuffed a second towel in his mouth.

Chavez said, "Dom, Jesus . . ."

Dominic shifted the gun again and fired a round into Ibrahim's right knee. Ibrahim thrashed, screaming into the towel, his head banging against the wall behind him. Dominic crouched down beside him and slapped his face hard, once, twice, then a third time. Ibrahim went quiet. Tears streamed down his face. Hadi had shrunk away from his partner, trying to slide himself down the wall.

Chavez pointed at him. "Not another inch." He grabbed Dominic's arm and tried to stand him up. Dominic didn't budge but just crouched there, slump-shouldered beside Ibrahim, staring into his face.

"Dom! Get up."

Dominic tore his eyes off Ibrahim and stood up. Chavez pulled him into the kitchen. "What the fuck was that?"

"The talk therapy wasn't working, Ding."

"Not your call to make. Christ, get ahold of yourself. He's useless to us now. A bullet in each knee . . . we'll be lucky if he can string two words together."

Dominic shrugged. "Hadi's our guy anyway. He was a courier. Ibrahim is a cell leader. He knows Paulinia and that's it."

"We don't know that. Let me do it my way?"

"Okay, sure."

"You hearing me?"

"Yeah, dammit, I said I was."

Chavez walked back into the room and knelt down again. To Ibrahim he said, "I'm going to take the towel out. If you scream, it goes back in."

Ibrahim nodded. His face was slick with sweat. Beneath each of his knees, Frisbee-sized puddles of blood were soaking into the plywood.

Dominic removed the towel. Ibrahim gasped but snapped his jaw shut and went quiet. His lower lip trembled. "My friend's a little touchy today. Sorry. Let's talk about the U.S.; give us something, and we'll get you to a hospital."

Ibrahim shook his head.

To Hadi: "How about you? Give us what we're looking for and we won't take you back with us."

Ibrahim rasped, "Don't, Shasif . . ."

Dominic walked over and knelt beside Chavez, gesturing *I'm okay* with his palm. "Hadi," he said. "Let me put this together for you: Did anyone see you during the refinery job?"

"No, I don't think so."

"So who knew what you looked like? Who could have leaked the sketch? Either Ibrahim or someone higher up. No one else."

"But why?"

"Loose ends. Maybe somebody thought you were unreliable. Think about it. Ibrahim gets the order from the higher-ups to kill you; the sketch and message gets you to run. Ibrahim uses that to convince the other two to join the hunt. Otherwise, Ibrahim has to convince them to kill their friend for no good reason. Which is easier?"

Hadi considered this for a few moments, then glanced sideways at Ibrahim, who was shaking his head. Saliva leaked from the corners of his mouth and dribbled down his chin. "It's not true."

Dominic said, "Hadi, he betrayed you, and now he's sitting right here beside you, lying about it. Doesn't that piss you off?"

Hadi nodded.

"I know it really pisses me off."

Dominic jerked his gun up, extended it toward Ibrahim, and shot him in the eye. Blood and brain matter sprayed over the wall. Ibrahim slumped sideways and went still, save his left arm, which twitched and flopped for ten seconds before stopping.

Chavez slapped Dominic's arm up and away. "Christ almighty! What the fuck!"

Dominic stood up and backed away a few feet. Hadi curled himself into the fetal position and started whimpering. Dominic took two strides to him and pressed his gun to Hadi's temple.

Chavez shouted, "Don't! Not an inch, Dom."

Dominic glanced sideways. Chavez had his own gun half raised in the direction of Dominic, who just shook his head and returned his attention to Hadi.

"Dom, don't do it. . . ."

Dominic leaned down and said to Hadi, "Unless you've got something to tell us, shithead, I'm done with you. I'm going to put a bullet in your ear. When I say go, you either nod or you die."

82

Jack and Clark made it to Virginia Beach in twenty minutes and found some public parking a block from the beach. All of the purchases the Salim kids had made were within three blocks.

"So what're you thinking?" Jack asked as they got out.

"They checked in at one of the hotels around here using a new card but did some shopping on the old one. We play marshal and deputy again, and show their photos around."

For the next hour, they walked from hotel to hotel, checking them off Jack's list as they went. They were walking into the parking lot of the Holiday Inn at Atlantic and 28th when Jack said, "They're here."

"Yeah, where?"

"Swimming pool. Two loungers near the diving board."

"I see 'em. Keep walking."

They stepped into the lobby. Clark stopped, pursed his lips. "Remember that flower shop we passed on Twenty-seventh? Go back there, buy some daisies or something. And one of those card envelopes, too."

"Huh?"

"I'll explain. Don't come back the same way. Meet me in the rear parking lot."

Jack was back in fifteen minutes. He found Clark in the rear parking lot, standing beside a Dumpster. "They're checked in under the same first names, last name Pasaribu. Their room is on the north side, facing away from the pool."

"So we pick the door, go in."

"Maids are up there. Flowers will work better."

Jack went up first, carrying the daisies. Clark went up the opposite stairwell and stopped at the top, out of view around the corner. When Jack reached the Salims' room door, he stopped and knocked, waited for ten seconds, then knocked again. Four doors down, a maid came out of another room and grabbed some towels off her cart. "Excuse me, miss," Jack said.

"Yes, sir?"

"I got these flowers for my girlfriend. I have to get back to the base, but I wanted to leave them for her. Problem is, I already turned in my card key. Think you could pop open the door? I'll put the flowers on the bed and be out in five seconds."

"I'm not supposed to—"

"In and out in five seconds."

A pause. "Well, okay."

She opened the door and stepped aside.

"Thanks," Jack said.

Clark took his cue and came around the corner. "Miss, hey, miss . . ."

"Yes, sir?"

"I need some towels." Clark walked up to the cart and began pawing through the supplies, knocking soap bars and shampoo bottles on the ground. The maid walked over. "Let me, sir."

Inside the Salims' room, Jack dropped the flowers on the bed and looked around. Card key, card key . . . He spotted it lying on the ashtray, snatched it up, and headed for the door. Back outside, he called, "Thanks," and headed for the stairs. Clark got his towels and headed in the opposite direction, circling back to Jack's stairs, where they met at the top. They waited until the maid stepped into the room she was cleaning, then walked to the Salims' door, swept the card, and slipped inside.

"How'd you know about the card?" Jack asked.

"They always offer couples two cards, and most people take both with them—but not to the pool."

"What're we looking for?"

"Credit cards and IDs. Past that, anything that catches your eye."

They were out in three minutes. Clark dialed The Campus as they walked back to their car. "They've got four more credit cards and three passports each," he told Rick Bell. "E-mailing the details to you now."

Aside from their new hotel in Virginia Beach and yet more meals from McDonald's and Frappuccinos from Starbucks, the Salims had only one other charge: a rental car from Budget. Jack and Clark drove back to the Holiday Inn and found the platinum Intrepid in the rear parking lot.

"Now we wait," Clark said.

Shortly before two p.m., Citra and Purnoma came down the hotel's back stairway and got into the Intrepid.

From Virginia Beach they got on the 264 heading east, through Norfolk, then into Portsmouth on the 460 before turning north and taking the tunnel across Hampton Roads Bay. On the far side, they got off at Terminal Avenue then Jefferson to King Lincoln Park at the southern tip of Newport News Point. Clark followed them into the parking lot and watched the Salims climb out and head into the park. They gave the Salims a hundred-yard head start, then got out, separated, and followed.

The park was only a quarter-mile long. At the halfway point, Clark and Jack met back up at the basketball courts, where a shirts-skins pickup game was going on.

"Where the hell are they going?" Jack asked. The park was bracketed on two sides by water. "They just traded the sun and surf capital of Virginia for this."

"Doesn't feel right," Clark agreed.

The Salims reached the far edge of the park where it formed an arrowhead between the beach and Jefferson Avenue. As they watched, the girl got out a camera and started taking pictures—not of the ocean but across the highway.

"The cargo terminal," Clark muttered.

"They're doing reconnaissance," Clark told Hendley and the others over the phone an hour later. They'd just followed the Salims' Intrepid back to the hotel; now they sat on Atlantic Avenue, a block away, where they could see every car coming and going. "The Newport News Marine Terminal. What exactly they're interested in, we don't know, but they took dozens of pictures."

"Any military ships berthed there? Chemicals, fuel depot?"

"Nothing," Clark said. "Already checked. Mostly box ships with dry cargo. We've been on them since this morning. Aside from the pool and the terminal, they haven't gone anywhere, and no one's come up to their room."

"If they're scoping out targets," Granger said, "this could go on for weeks. We're not really set up for extended stakeouts. I say we tip the FBI and let them have it."

"Give us another day," Clark said. "If nothing pans out, we'll pull the plug and come home."

*

At the Claridge Inn in Saint George, Utah, Frank Weaver was showering off a day's worth of grime and looking forward to a *Law & Order* mini-marathon on TNT when he heard a knock on his door. He wrapped himself in a towel and padded across the room. "Who is it?"

"Front desk, Mr. Weaver. We have a problem with your credit card."

Weaver unlatched the door and opened it a crack. The door flew open and banged against the wall. Two men stepped inside, one shutting the door, the other taking two quick strides at Weaver, who began backpedaling across the room but not fast enough. He felt something hard pressed against his solar plexus, then felt a hammer blow, then another. He felt himself falling backward. He bounced once on the edge of the bed, then rolled to the floor on his back. He lifted his head and looked down at his chest. Just below his sternum, two pencil eraser–sized holes were bubbling blood. The man who shot him walked forward and stood over him, one leg on either side of his chest. Frank Weaver saw the gun's muzzle lowering toward his face, and he shut his eyes.

83

The Salim siblings left the hotel at nine p.m., and almost immediately Jack and Clark realized they were retracing their earlier route to the Newport News Marine Terminal. In Portsmouth they turned off the highway and drove to a U-Haul Storage on Butler Street. Clark kept going past the entrance, turned onto Conrad, shut off the headlights, then did a U-turn and pulled to a stop ten feet short of the intersection.

Down the block, the Intrepid had pulled into the parking

lot and stopped beside the first row of storage units. Citra Salim climbed out and trotted up to a unit, which she opened with a key.

"Don't like this," Jack said. "What do two kids on vacation need with a storage unit?"

"No good reason," Clark replied.

Citra was back out. She closed and locked the unit, then returned to the Intrepid. She was carrying two small canvas backpacks.

Within minutes they were back on the highway and headed into the bay tunnel. Once through to the other side, the Intrepid continued to retrace the afternoon route, ending up once more at King Lincoln Park. They didn't pull into the parking lot, however, but drove past it, then turned right onto Jefferson and headed back in the same direction.

"Think they made us?" Jack asked.

"No. They're just careful. We're okay."

They were in an industrial-park area: trucking companies, gravel suppliers, scrap yards, and boat repair shops. The Intrepid took another right.

"Twelfth Street," Jack said. "Heading east again."

Clark let them get a little farther ahead, then shut off his headlights, made the turn, and pulled to the curb. Three hundred yards down the road, the Intrepid was turning left into an apartment complex.

"Visiting new friends?" Jack wondered.

"Let's find out."

Clark turned on the headlights and pulled out again. As they drew even with the apartments, two figures walked out of the parking lot and started down the sidewalk. The Salims. With their backpacks. Clark passed them and looked in the rearview mirror. They were heading back toward Jefferson. Clark turned the next corner, stopped again, headlights off.

648

"See them?" Clark asked.

"Yep, got 'em."

At Jefferson, the Salims crossed the street and disappeared down a grassy median behind a trucking company.

"Time to move," Clark said.

Lights still off, he did a U-turn and rolled down Twelfth to Jefferson. As they reached the intersection, they saw the Salims turn left and disappear behind the trucking company's fence.

"They're running out of room," Jack said. The trucking company backed up to 664, a raised, four-lane highway.

"Let's hoof it," Clark said.

They parked, got out, and trotted across the street to the grass median. At the rear of the trucking company, they found a marshy creek bordered by thick brush and a narrow trail. They were halfway down it when Clark realized where they were. "It's the Six sixty-four canal. Remember to the right, as we came out of the tunnel?" They'd seen dozens of motor yachts and speedboats berthed in the canal.

Down the trail, an engine gurgled to life. Clark and Jack sprinted forward. Fifty yards away at the end of a dock, the Salims were sitting in a speedboat. The boy sat down in the driver's seat and eased the throttle forward. The boat pulled away from the dock and headed into the canal.

Jack and Clark were back to their car a minute later. They pulled onto Jefferson and headed south. After a few blocks, the canal came into view through the passenger window. They could see the Salims' boat motoring toward the mouth of the canal.

"They're going for the terminal," Clark said.

"What about the harbor patrol?"

"Jack, once they get around the jetty, they're a quarter-mile from the first berth. We've got five minutes, if that."

Clark did a U-turn and headed in the other direction.

They crossed under the 664, turned south onto Terminal. At the bottom of the ramp the road forked at a tank farm. Clark veered right and followed the winding dirt road. Halfway down the tank farm, Clark braked to a stop. A hundred yards away was a lighted guard shack. A swinging gate blocked the road.

"Shit."

"Marshal's badge get us through?" Jack asked.

"Once inside, yeah, but main gates switched to TWIC in January—Transportation Worker Identification Credential. You don't have one, you don't get in."

"How do you know that?"

"Rainbow had an E-Six devoted to keeping up with ID protocols," Clark replied. "Bad guys are all about going where they don't belong. Figure out what they're trying to counterfeit, you're halfway to figuring out what they're targeting."

Clark backed down the road, arm draped over the seat as he steered through the back window, until they reached the fork. He veered left and pulled into a gravel turnaround beside the tank farm's fence.

"Back on foot," Clark said.

To their left, on the other side of the tank farm, they could hear the traffic rushing by on the 664. To their right, across the dirt road, was a dirt berm overgrown with underbrush. They jogged over and up the embankment, then pushed through the foliage, then down the opposite slope. They found themselves in a scrub field about the size of a football field. At the far end, they could see the guard shack they'd spotted earlier. They sprinted across the field, up another slope, and through some brush, and ended up on a dirt road. To the left lay a dirt parking lot with rows upon rows of boxcar-sized shipping containers and two Quonset huts. Clark and Jack were down the road and among the containers thirty seconds later. They stopped to catch their breath, then kept going.

They picked their way through the rows of containers to the edge of the parking lot. Two hundred feet away were the docks, three of them extending into the harbor, with a ship berthed on each side, for a total of six.

"A lot of open ground between here and there. And a lot of damned lights. Looks like a stadium. Which ship?"

"Just a hunch, but I'd say the one that's not unloaded yet." He pointed at a box ship berthed on the far right. Bulktainers crowded the foredeck. "Can you make out the name?"

Jack squinted. *"Losan."*

Three hundred yards away, Citra and Purnoma Salim were pulling their boat alongside the pier beneath the stern of the *Losan*. "You're sure this is the one?" Citra whispered.

"I'm sure. Here." She took the backpack and donned it.

Purnoma reached out, grabbed the steel maintenance ladder, and knotted the bow line to upright. He steadied the boat, and his sister started up the ladder. When she reached the top rung, she extended her arms above her head, snagged the bowline, then swung her feet up and hooked her ankles in place. Once she was halfway across, Purnoma followed. They were on deck a minute later.

"There should be no more than two crew members aboard. You take them, and I'll head for the tanks. When you're done, let me know and I'll start."

"Remember, act like you belong and you do," Clark said, then stood up and walked into the parking lot. Jack followed. A trio of men smoking outside one of the Quonset huts were watching them. Clark raised his arm. "Hey, guys. How's it going?"

"Okay. You?"

Clark gave an exaggerated shrug. "Another day, another buck-fifty."

The men laughed.

Clark and Jack kept walking, leaving the parking lot and walking down an alley of tractor trailers. They emerged on the wharf and turned right, passing the ships. They reached *Losan*'s pier.

"Can't be this easy," Jack muttered.

"Don't jinx it, boy."

They turned left down the pier. Fifty yards away, they could see that the *Losan*'s accommodation ladder was down, the base resting a few feet off the pier.

"They gonna have a guard?" Jack wondered.

"Watch, Jack. In the maritime world, we call them 'watches.' We're about to find out."

They started upward, their feet softly pinging on the steel treads. At the top, the rail gate was open but blocked by a length of cable. Clark unclipped one end, and they stepped through. To their right, forward, an arch led to the foredeck; to the left, the weather deck stretched to the stern. The bulkhead was broken up by three hatches. Clark drew his gun. Jack did the same. They headed for the first hatch, quietly undogged it, then swung it open. From belowdecks came what sounded like two Ping-Pong paddles being slapped together. Clark mimed a gun with his hand, and Jack nodded.

A second shot.

Then, from the foredeck, the soft beep-squelch of a radio or a push-to-talk cell phone.

Clark pointed at himself, then pointed down the ladder, then pointed at Jack and pointed to the foredeck. Jack nodded, and Clark disappeared inside.

Jack took two steps down the deck, then stopped. His heart was pounding. He took a calming breath. Switched his gun to his left hand and wiped his palm on his pant leg. *Easy, Jack. Breathe.* Just like Hogan's Alley. Of course, it wasn't just like that, and he knew it, but he did his best to push the thought to the back of his mind. *John will be fine; don't worry about John. Focus on what's in front of you.* . . . He kept walking, one careful pace at a time, his gun up in a two-handed grip, leading him down the deck, scanning the superstructure above his head. He reached the foredeck arch. Stopped. Corners were hell, Dominic and Brian had told him. No cop likes corners. *Never jump a corner,* Jack reminded himself. *Take a peek, get a picture, then pull back.*

He did that now, peeked and pulled back. To his left was a wall of steel forty or fifty feet tall. These were the bulktainers, Jack realized. Four to a stack and twelve abeam. Their front edges abutted the raised lip of the forward cargo hold. Jack peeked again, this time scanning the deck forward of the hold. He was about to pull back when he saw a figure dash from behind the other side of the bulktainer stack and kneel atop the hold hatch. The figure started undogging hatches. Once done, he cranked the hatch open a foot or two, then sprinted out of sight again.

From the starboard side, there came the squeal of a hatch opening, then closing. Footsteps clicked on the deck. Now murmured voices. Jack stepped out and slid down the bulkhead to the bottom bulktainer. He crept to its front, peeked around the corner. Nothing.

Then a ping, and another, then another. It took Jack a moment to place the sound: feet on steel ladder rungs. Jack looked up. A few feet above his head was a ladder rung. *What're you up to, pal?* One way to find out. He reholstered his gun, then grabbed the bottom rung and started climbing. At the top, the next bulktainer's ladder was offset by a foot and a half, so Jack had to reach sideways, grab the next rung, and let his feet swing free.

He heard something below him and looked down. Though the deck was too dark to see her face, Jack recognized Citra

Salim's long black hair. She raised her gun. Jack let go of the rung with his right hand and went for his gun. Off balance, he swung sideways even more. Citra's muzzle flashed orange. Jack felt something white-hot rake along his jawline then thunk into the steel beside his head.

From the other side of the bulktainer, a man's voice: "Citra?"

Jack tried for his gun again, but knew, even as his fingers touched the butt, it was too late.

Dumb to go this way, he thought.

Behind Citra, a figure stepped through the arch. John Clark took one quick stride, raised his gun, and shot Citra in the back of the head. She pitched forward to the deck.

"Citra! Are you there?"

Jack pointed to the port side. Clark nodded and started moving that way. Jack pressed his hand to his cheek; his fingers came away bloody. *No gushing,* he thought, which was good. He started climbing again, moving from the second level to the third. Halfway up the side of the uppermost container, he stopped, drew his gun, and kept going. At the top he paused. To his left, the pilothouse windows and eaves overhang were three feet above his head. He peeked over the lip of the container.

Four cylindrical propane tanks, stark white in the darkness, sat side by side, two each fore and aft. Five containers away, Jack saw a dull silver object sail through the air and clatter into his container. Jack craned his neck, trying to locate the object, when he saw a sputtering yellow glow beneath the forward edge of one of the tanks.

"John!"

"Here!"

"He's got something, a bomb, a grenade . . . something."

Another object arced up into the air. This time Jack got a better look at it. Pipe bomb. Jack boosted himself up onto the lip of the container, then sidestepped to the front and began edging across the containers, heel to toe. On the starboard side, he saw Clark's head appear above the container's rim.

Balanced on the front rim, Jack peered into each container, gun tracking for movement. Another pipe bomb arced through the air and clattered into a tank. Then another.

He leaped to the next tank, teetered, then regained his balance and leaped again. His foot slipped, and he slammed chest-first into the fourth container's rim. On the starboard side, Clark was up on the rim and coming to meet him.

"Fuses are going, John," Jack called.

He pushed himself up, hooked his leg on the rim, got to his knees.

"You see him?" Clark called, taking a step.

A torso popped up in one of the containers, fired a shot at Clark, then ducked out of sight again.

"Fuck it," Jack muttered, and started running, arms extended like a tightrope walker's. He was crossing the sixth container when Purnoma Salim appeared over the rim of the eighth tank and tumbled into the next. Then he was up again, turning toward Clark, who was in mid-leap between two rims. Purnoma raised his gun. Still running, Jack brought his own gun around, left arm still extended for balance, and started firing, trying to keep the sites on center mass. Purnoma went down. Jack stopped firing. Two containers behind him, there came a crump. The container stack trembled. *Crump.*

"John, get off!" Jack yelled, and kept running.

Crump.

The rim shifted beneath Jack's feet, and he stumbled sideways into the container. He saw the white curve of a propane tank rushing up to meet him. He turned his body sideways and took the impact on his arm and shoulder, then slid down the curve and found himself pinned against the container wall.

Somewhere in the terminal, an alarm Klaxon sounded.

"Jack?" Clark yelled.

"I'm okay!"

He heard a hissing sound. Looked around. Directly below him, from beneath the bottom edge of the tank, he saw a yellow glow. *Aw, shit.*

"John, move, go!"

One tank over, another crump.

Jack rolled onto his back and sat up, then rolled again so he was straddling the tank. He stood up, looked around. Nowhere to go. Fifty-foot fall on all sides, the nearest ladder another twenty feet away. *Pilothouse.* Jack sprinted down the tank, then leaped. He grabbed the overhang, swung his leg up, hooked his ankle, then chinned himself and rolled onto the pilothouse roof.

Crump.

Jack rolled over, looked down. From inside the tank came the sounds of sloshing. The odor struck him. His eyes started watering.

"John!" he shouted.

"Yeah, port side!"

"You smell that?"

"Yeah. Move your ass."

Jack got up, sprinted across the roof, found the superstructure ladder, then started down. Clark was waiting at the bottom. Jack asked, "What the hell is that?"

"Chlorine gas, Jack."

Forty minutes later, wet and exhausted, they reached their car and headed back down Terminal Avenue. In the rearview mirror they could see clusters of flashing red and blue lights from one end of the terminal to the other. Knowing their presence would create more problems than it would solve, they'd gone over *Losan*'s side, stroked to shore a few hundred yards away, then picked their way back through the terminal, dodging fire trucks and cop cars until they reached the tank farm.

Clark got back on the 664 and headed northeast into Newport News, where they found an all-night diner. Jack dialed The Campus. Hendley answered. "This shit in Newport News . . . That you?"

"It's already on the news?"

"Every channel. What happened?"

Jack recounted the events, then asked, "How bad is it?"

"Could be worse. So far, only thirty or so terminal workers at the hospital. No deaths. What were they, what kind of tanks?"

"Propane, I think, about fifty of them. They only got off half a dozen pipe bombs, but we're betting they had a lot more in their backpacks."

"They're both dead?"

"Yes."

"I need you to head to the airport. We've got you booked on a three-thirty back here."

"What's going on?"

"We got word from Chavez and Caruso: They got Hadi, and he's talking."

84

Hendley and Granger were waiting with a Suburban when they touched down at Dulles. "Where're we heading?" Clark asked.

"Andrews. Gulfstream waiting," Hendley replied. "We've got gear and clothes already aboard. First things first: the ship—*Losan*. You were right, Jack. The Salims had two dozen pipe bombs. On the manifest there were forty-six propane tanks listed, all defective and empty, and heading back from Senegal to the manufacturer, Tarquay Industries out of Smith-field."

"Well, we know they weren't empty," Clark said.

"Right. They won't be sure for a couple days, but the Hazmat teams out there are guessing there was a couple hundred gallons of ammonia or sodium hypochlorite in each tank."

"Bleach," Jack said.

"Yeah, looks like. Common everyday bleach. Mix them together and you get chlorine gas. You do the math and we're talking about at least thirty-five tons of chlorine gas precur-sors. As it stands, only a couple hundred gallons got mixed. They've got it contained."

"Holy shit," Jack said. "Thirty-five tons. What kind of damage could that have done?"

Granger answered. "Depends a lot on wind, humidity, and temperature, but we could have been looking at thousands of dead. Thousands more with skin and mucosa burns, pulmo-nary edema, blindness . . . It's ugly shit."

Hendley said, "Next piece of business. Chavez and Caruso grabbed Hadi."

"What about the others in his group?" Clark asked.

"Dead in the Rocinha. That might have had something to do with it, but once Hadi started talking, he didn't stop for a while."

"We've got him?"

"No, they bundled him up like a Thanksgiving turkey and dropped him at a police station with a note attached. He'll never see the outside of a Brazilian prison."

"We were mostly right about Hadi. He was a longtime URC

courier, and got tapped for the Paulinia operation at the last minute. His last courier job—Chicago to Vegas to San Francisco—he stopped on the way to visit an old friend."

Hendley's expression answered their next question before either Clark or Jack could ask it. "You're shitting us?"

"No. The Emir came in on a Dassault Falcon from Sweden about a month ago. He's been living outside Vegas ever since."

"And Hadi knew where—"

"Yeah."

"It's bullshit," Jack said. "He came here for a reason. The Paulinia thing, the *Losan* . . . Ding is right. Shoes are starting to drop."

"Agreed," Granger said. "That's why you're going to go snatch him up. Chavez and Caruso are already in the air. They'll touch down about an hour after you."

"So we grab him and drop him on the FBI's doorstep?" Clark said.

"Not right away, and not until we've had a chance to wring him out."

"That could take some time."

"We'll see."

This Hendley said with a smile that Jack could describe only as slightly evil.

At Andrews, the Gulfstream was prepped and ready, the door open and stairs extended for them. Jack and Clark collected their gear from the back of the Suburban, shook hands with Hendley and Granger, then boarded the plane. The copilot met them at the door. "Sit wherever you want." He pulled up the stairs, swung the door shut, and locked it down. "We're taxiing in five, wheels up in ten. Help yourself to the fridge and minibar."

Jack and Clark made their way to the rear of the cabin. Sitting in the last row was a familiar face: Dr. Rich Pasternak.

"Gerry didn't tell me much," Pasternak said. "Please tell me I'm flying across the country in the dead of night for a good goddamned reason."

Clark smiled. "Nothing's written in stone, Doc, but I think it'll be worth your time."

With the four-time-zone difference and a four-hour-and-twenty-minute flight, they technically landed at North Las Vegas airport only twenty minutes after leaving Andrews. It was a phenomenon Jack understood, of course, but thinking too much about the surreal flexibility of the temporal world could give a man headaches.

Between catnaps he and Clark had dissected the *Losan* mission, talked baseball, and rummaged through the fridge and minibar. For his part, Pasternak sat in his seat, occasionally dozing but mostly staring into space. A lot on the doctor's mind, Jack knew. The man had lost a brother on that ugly September morning, and now here he was eight years later, flying across the country to perhaps meet the man who'd planned it all. But then, "meet" wasn't quite the right word, was it? What Pasternak had in store for the Emir was something Jack wouldn't wish on anyone. Almost anyone.

The plane came to a stop, and the engines spooled down. Jack, Clark, and Pasternak collected their personal belongings and headed for the door. The copilot came out of the cockpit, opened the door, and unfurled the stairs. "Doctor, you want us to send your gear along to ground transportation?"

"No, we'll wait for it."

On the tarmac, Clark asked Pasternak, "What gear?"

"Tools of the trade, Mr. Clark."

Pasternak said it without a hint of a smile.

A shuttle bus dropped them at ground transportation, and ten minutes later they were in a Ford minivan heading south on Rancho Drive. They pulled into McCarran's short-term parking and found a spot. Jack dialed Dominic's cell; he answered on the second ring. Jack said, "You're down?"

"Five minutes ago. Where you at?"

"We'll pull up to arrivals."

Chavez and Dominic threw their bags into the cargo area and climbed in. There were greetings all around. Chavez said, "Damn, John, never thought I'd see you behind the wheel of a soccer-mom mobile."

"Smart-ass."

Clark pulled out and headed for the highway.

It took only fifteen minutes, but soon enough they were entering the upmarket development. Following Chavez's directions, Clark drove by the house without pausing, then turned the corner and headed back to the subdivision's entrance. At the stop sign, he put the van in park and shut off his headlights.

"We got about two hours before sunrise and no intel on what's inside, right, Ding?"

"Hadi saw the garage, the kitchen, and the living room. That was it."

"Alarm systems?"

"He didn't remember seeing any keypads. He knows for sure the Emir has one bodyguard, a guy named Tariq. Regular-looking guy, medium height, brown hair, but his hands are all burned. Hadi didn't know anything about that."

"So two inside for sure," Clark said. "It's probably been a while since the Emir did any soldiering, but assume they're both badasses. Questions?"

There were none.

"We'll go quiet in the side garage door, then into the kitchen. Two teams. Anybody see any need to mix things up?"

Chavez said, "Nope."

Jack noticed Dominic drop his head slightly and look out the side window. Clark asked, "Dom?"

"We did okay together. I kinda fucked up a bit, but we got it straightened out, right?"

Ding nodded. "Good to go."

"Okay," Clark said. "Two teams, standard house clearing. We need all the live bodies we can get our hands on, but the Emir's our primary target. It'd be best if we don't fire a shot. A neighborhood like this and we'd have cops in five minutes. Doc, I'm going to ask you to stay here and man the fort. We'll call you when we're done. If there's room in the garage, pull right in. If not, in the driveway."

They parked the van at the end of the block and walked the remaining distance. The sky was clear, with a full moon; the air was cold, the kind of cold only a nighttime desert can produce.

Clark took the lead, walking up the driveway, through the side gate to the side door. The lock was a turn-knob, so he had it picked and open in forty seconds. They filed into the garage. Dominic, bringing up the rear, eased the door shut. The garage was empty. No car. They stood still for a full minute, listening and letting their eyes adjust to the relative darkness.

Clark walked to the kitchen door and tried the knob. He looked back at the others and nodded. Each of them drew his gun. Clark turned the knob, paused, listened, then swung the door open. He stood still on the threshold for twenty seconds and examined the doorjamb, listening for the telltale beeping of an alarm panel. The house was quiet. The kitchen and nook were to the right; to the left, through an arch, a living room.

Clark stepped through and to the right, followed by Jack, then Dominic and Chavez, then moved left up to the arch. At

662

Clark's nod they started moving through the house. On the other side of the kitchen was an open doorway, and beyond that a hall. Clark peeked around the corner. Ten feet to his left, Ding's head appeared around another corner. The hall stretched to Clark's right. Three doors, one on each side and one at the end of the hall. Clark gestured for Ding and Dominic to take the left-hand door. As they came up, Clark and Jack slid up to the right-hand door. Both teams went in at the same time and came out ten seconds later. Both were guest bedrooms, and both were empty.

They stacked up at the door at the end: Clark, Jack, Chavez, and Caruso. Clark gestured: *Two by two, right and left.* Everyone nodded. Clark tried the knob, then turned and nodded. They pushed through the door, stepping right and left, guns tracking. Clark held up his fist—*hold*—then pointed at the lump under the covers on the bed. He then pointed at Chavez, then the closet. Ding checked it, shook his head.

Clark padded up to the bed. Jack and Dominic took the end, and Ding the other side. All four trained their guns on the figure under the covers. Clark holstered his gun, then clicked on his LED penlight, grabbed the edge of the sheet, and jerked it back.

"Shit," he said.

85

Kersen Kaseke left his house at four a.m., drove two blocks to an all-night gas station, and bought a large cup of coffee. On whether coffee was in fact *haraam*—forbidden to Muslims—Kaseke had yet to find a definitive answer; until that time, he would allow himself the indulgence. It was his only, after all. He neither smoked nor drank nor let his eyes linger too long on the relative nakedness of the women here.

He got back into his car and drove to Open Heart Congregational Church. The streets of the city, rarely crowded anyway, were especially quiet. It had been raining since mid-afternoon, and now the only people moving about were those who had no choice in the matter: early-morning workers, delivery drivers, police . . . Of the latter he saw no cars, a sign, he believed, that Allah was with him.

He circled the church once, then parked a couple of blocks north of the church in a video-store parking lot, then hefted his backpack over one shoulder and got out. Out of habit, he did not walk directly to the church but took a circuitous route. Finally satisfied he wasn't being followed, Kaseke cut across the church's front lawn to the hedges bordering the entrance steps, where he knelt down.

From his pack he withdrew the first mine. Officially known as the M18A1 and colloquially as a "Claymore," it was designed for use as an antipersonnel/area denial weapon. Shaped like a convex rectangle, the Claymore's guts were uncomplicated: a layer of C4 plastic explosive supporting a layer of seven hundred steel ball bearings, each the size of #4 buckshot, embedded in a layer of resin. Upon detonation, the C4 sprays the seven hundred fragments outward at four thousand feet per second. As instructed and as trained, Kaseke had the previous night removed the Claymore's outer casing and carefully sprinkled six ounces of rat-poison pellets amid the ball bearings. The poison's active ingredient, Difethialone, an anticoagulant, would with luck keep even the smallest of wounds from clotting. It was a tactic his Palestinian brothers had used to great effect in both the Gaza Strip and the West Bank. It hadn't taken Israeli first responders long to catch on, but during that all-too-short grace period, many dozens had died, bleeding to death from what would have otherwise been minor lacerations. Having never seen such attacks before, paramedics here would face the same horror and confusion.

Once satisfied the pellets were evenly distributed, Kaseke sealed the poison in place with a thin layer of candle wax, let it harden, then reassembled the Claymore's outer shell. The manual had recommended tissue paper coated in a sheer layer of spray-on fabric adhesive, but the wax would work just as well, he knew. Next he checked each screw in turn, then the gapping, to ensure the shells were properly fitted. The manual had been explicit about that, too: If the outer casings were misaligned, the explosive force may be diverted. This instruction he followed to the letter.

Now Kaseke extended the mine's scissor legs. He then made sure the label—*front toward enemy*—was pointing toward the entrance of that church that would in a few hours be bustling with activity, then jammed the legs into the soft earth inside the hedges. He got down on his belly, crawled through the hedges, then turned around and peered through the open sight affixed to the top of the mine.

Good. He'd chosen the perfect location. The blast would encompass not only the entrance and the steps but part of the sidewalk as well.

He checked the mine's clock against his own watch. They were synchronized. He set the countdown timer, pressed start, and watched a few seconds tick off before getting up and walking away.

As was their custom on weekends, Hank Alvey woke up early on Sunday morning and quietly got their three kids out of bed, fed them oatmeal and blueberry waffles, then got them settled in front of the TV—the volume turned way down—for cartoons. The previous night's rain clouds had moved on, leaving behind bright blue skies. Sunlight streamed through the living room windows and across the hardwood floors on which the kids now sat, entranced by the TV.

Shortly before seven, he made Katie her sourdough toast and coffee, and woke her up with breakfast in bed. The tire shop he managed was closed on Sunday, so this was the only day he could relieve his wife of what would otherwise be a seven-day-a-week job. Taking care of the kids so she could sleep in an hour was, she frequently assured him, so romantic, and so sexy—and on most Sunday nights after the kids went to bed, she showed him exactly how much she appreciated the gesture.

But that was for later, Hank reminded himself, pouring the coffee, which went on the tray next to the freshly buttered bread. Most mornings he was able to *almost* reach their bed before Katie rolled over and gave him a sleepy smile. This she did now.

"What's for breakfast?" she asked, smiling.

"Take a guess."

"Ah, my favorite." She sat up and shoved pillows behind her back. "What'd you do with the kids, lock them in the closet?"

"They're watching *Yo Gabba Gabba!* I think Jeremy's got a crush on Foofa."

Katie took a bite of toast. "Which one's that?"

"The pink flower bubble thing."

"Right. Are we going to church?"

"We'd better. We missed the last two Sundays. We can hit the nine o'clock, then take the kids to the park afterward."

"Okay, I'll make myself pretty."

"Done," Hank said, and headed for the door. "I'm going to let them out of the closet now."

Katie was down the stairs, dressed, her hair and makeup done, even before Hank was ready for shoes. Their oldest, Josh, could tie his own, but not so with Amanda and Jeremy, so Hank took one and Katie took the other, and then they were up and moving, looking for their coats and car keys, making sure the back door was locked. . . .

"We're going to be late," Katie called.

Hank checked his watch. "Not quite a quarter till. We'll be there in five minutes. Okay, kids, let's get a move on. . . ."

Then they were out the door.

Half a block north and west of the church, Kaseke was sitting on a bus bench, sipping his third cup of coffee of the day. From this angle he had a perfect vantage point of the front steps. *There.* The front doors opened, and people began emerging. Kaseke checked his watch: 8:48. Now from the path leading around the church to the rear parking lot came a line of nine a.m. worshippers. Leading the group was a young couple with three children, two boys and a girl, all three holding hands as they skipped ahead of their parents. Kaseke squeezed his eyes shut and asked Allah for strength. This was necessary. And the children, small as they were, would be killed instantly, so quickly that the pain wouldn't have time to register in their minds.

The incoming group reached the end of the path, where it joined the common area around the steps.

Kaseke checked his watch. Less than a minute now.

A hundred yards from where he'd planted the mine, he could not see that his plan was unraveling, and it would only be later, after he was captured, that the police would explain how he'd failed.

For the past five hours, as the Claymore sat first in the rain and then in the early morning sun, the candle wax Kaseke had used to cement the rat-poison pellets to the ball bearings and their resin base began to crack. This alone wouldn't have interfered with the mine's function, but what Kaseke didn't know was that this particular Claymore mine and eight others were more than two decades old and had spent the last eight years improperly stored either in a wooden box in a damp cave or buried in the sun-baked soil of Afghanistan's Nangarhar province.

As the candle wax cracked inside the casing, the resin, far past its effective lifespan and as brittle as a fortune cookie, also cracked, but only a few millimeters. It was enough, however, to loosen the sockets in which fourteen of the ball bearings rested. With overlapping metallic *tinks* that no one on the church steps would hear over the babble of voices, the fourteen ball bearings broke free and dropped against the shell's lower casing. If not for ten hours of rain that had fallen since the previous afternoon, this, too, wouldn't have hindered the mine's detonation, but the legs holding it upright in the soil, now softened to a mudlike consistency, succumbed to the weight of the fallen ball bearings. At 8:49:36, twenty-four seconds before detonation, Kaseke's carefully aimed Claymore tipped forward and came to a rest at a forty-five-degree angle, half its face pointing at the dirt, the other half pointing at the concrete.

When she would awake later that day in the hospital, Katie Alvey's first thoughts would be, *My husband's dead* and *I think my children are alive,* followed by the realization that dumb luck probably played a big part in both those outcomes.

As Kaseke's mine was tipping forward, the Alvey family mounted the front steps along with dozens of other late arrivals and started upward. Hank walked closest to the hedges bordering the steps, with Josh and Amanda to his left, then Katie and Jeremy, who was holding his mom's hand.

Witnesses would later describe the explosion as a whoosh

followed by the hailstorm from hell. Katie neither saw nor heard these things but had for some reason turned her head to look at Hank when the Claymore went off. Of the seven hundred bearings inside the mine, four hundred or so struck the dirt, cratering the bed and taking a yard-wide chunk out of the concrete. The remainder of the bearings either skittered along the concrete, punching through feet and calves, shattering bones and ripping away whole chunks of flesh, or bounced off the concrete and tore across the steps at various angles and trajectories. Those unlucky enough to be struck by these were either killed instantly or suffered horrific limb injuries. Hank Alvey, his body protecting his oldest boy and his daughter, caught a ball bearing beneath the left jaw, effectively cleaving his head into three portions. Katie saw this but had no time to react, no time to grab any of the children or to shield Jeremy with her body. As it turned out, none of it had been necessary.

Katie stood blinking, her ears ringing and her brain failing to immediately register the carnage around her. On either side of her, Josh, Jeremy, and Amanda were similarly stunned, but that passed quickly, and then the tears started to flow. The steps were awash in blood and littered with arms and legs and unidentifiable chunks of . . . who? She recognized no one. Dozens of people lay strewn across the concrete. Some weren't moving, while others writhed in pain or tried to crawl away or toward loved ones, their mouths moving but no sound coming out.

Then Katie's ears cleared and she heard the screaming. And sirens.

86

After making sure all the drapes were closed, they turned on lights around the house, then Jack called Pasternak and had him pull the van into the garage. The doctor walked through the kitchen door and stopped short. "Is that him?"

Jack said, "No, this is Tariq, the Emir's bodyguard."

In fact, it had taken ten minutes of talking to simply get Tariq to admit his own name. Beyond that, he'd said nothing. Chavez and Domingo were tossing the rest of the house, but so far it had all the individuality of a builder's model home. There were no personal touches.

"It appears we just missed the man himself," Jack said. "Go have a seat in the living room, Doc. We'll call you." He joined Clark at the table across from Tariq. They'd bound his hands and ankles with duct tape, then taped his feet to the kitchen-table leg.

"What happened to your hands?" Clark asked.

Tariq took them off the table and put them in his lap. "A fire."

"I assumed that. How specifically?"

"You invade my home, drag me from my bed. You are not the police. Who are you; what do you want?"

"You know why we're here," Jack said. "When did he leave?"

"Who? I live here alone."

"Shasif Hadi tells us a different story," Clark said.

At the mention of Hadi's name, Tariq's eyes narrowed ever so slightly, then went back to normal.

"Aren't you interested in how we found Hadi?" Jack asked. "We picked him up in Rio de Janeiro. After the attack on the Paulinia refinery, he was ordered by the Emir to break contact with Ibrahim, Fa'ad, and Ahmed. The Emir had told him the others had betrayed him."

"That's not—" Tariq stopped in mid-sentence.

Clark said, "Not true? You're right. The truth is we broke your crypto. All those onetime pads embedded in the website banners . . . We broke it, then uploaded a message to Hadi's storage site of the day, and sent him on the run—right into our laps." Clark looked at Jack. "It took, what, ten minutes for him to break?"

"Not even. Here's another piece of news, Tariq: The cargo ship *Losan*—we put a stop to that, too. The Salim kids are dead, and the Newport News Fire Department is offloading the propane tanks as we speak."

This time, Tariq couldn't help himself. "You're lying!"

"About what part?" Clark asked. "Hadi or *Losan*?"

"Both."

"So you admit who you are and that you know the Emir."

Tariq clasped his hands on the table before him and stared straight ahead.

From the hallway, Ding called, "John, you're gonna want to see this."

Clark and Jack found Ding and Dominic in the master bedroom. Sitting atop a chest of drawers was a laptop. Ding said, "We found it in the nightstand." He hit the return key.

After a few moments, the Emir's face appeared on the screen. The backdrop was the living room couch and wall. "My name is Saif Rahman Yasin. I am also known as the Emir, and I am the commander of the Umayyad Revolutionary Council. I speak to you today as a devout Muslim and a humble servant and soldier of Allah. By now the world has already witnessed the vengeance of Allah visited upon the infidel nation of America. . . ."

Clark tapped the return button, stopping the video. "That's the sonofabitch's last testament."

Jack asked, "What's the date on this?"

"Yesterday," Dominic answered.

"Christ."

They followed Clark down the hall and back to the dining nook. Clark sat down at the table while everyone else hung back.

"Tariq."

"What?"

"I want you to tell me where Saif is and what he's doing. Before you answer, you need to understand the ground rule: You get one chance to answer, and then—"

Tariq stared ahead. "You're going to kill me? Go ahead; I do not fear death. I'll be welcomed into paradise as a—"

"We're not going to kill you, Tariq, but before another hour passes, you're going to wish you were."

Tariq turned and looked at Clark. "I'm not afraid."

Clark regarded him solemnly for a few moments, and then, without taking his eyes off Tariq, said over his shoulder to Ding, "Go fill up the bathtub."

Clark had never quite understood the debate over whether or not waterboarding was torture. Anyone who'd either been through it or seen it firsthand knew that it was torture. It got results, the validity of which could be ascertained only by a particularly astute interrogator or subsequent intelligence gathering. Clark was blessed with the former attribute but lacked the time and resources for the latter.

Eight minutes, a saturated towel, and exactly thirty-two ounces of water was all it took. Satisfied, Clark rose from his crouched position over the barely conscious and sputtering Tariq and turned to Ding, who stood, arms folded, as he leaned against the bathroom wall.

"Pull the plug," Clark ordered. "Get him cleaned up and locked down."

"You buy it, John?"

"Yeah." Clark checked his watch. "Either way, we're outta time."

87

Clark strode back into the kitchen. "Jack, grab the phone book. We need the closest airfield. Commercial helicopter tours will be our best bet."

"On it."

"Dom, you'll drive. Doctor, are you comfortable staying here with him?" Ding was coming down the hall, dragging Tariq behind him. "We'll be back for you."

"Sure."

Jack called, "Paragon Air Helicopter Tours on Highway Two-fifteen. Three miles from here."

They were out the door in thirty seconds and on the highway in two minutes. Clark used the sat phone to dial The Campus. Rick Bell answered, and Clark said, "I need you, Gerry, and Sam on conference call right now."

"Hold on."

Thirty seconds passed. Hendley came on the line. "What've you got, John?"

"I've got Jack on the line, too. Our guy is gone, left yesterday. A bodyguard was still at the house. They've got a bomb, Gerry, probably something below ten kilotons but big enough for what they've got planned."

"Wait, back up? Is this credible?"

"I believe it is. We have to assume it is."

"Where'd they get it?"

"No idea. Our guy didn't have that info."

"Okay, what else?"

"The Emir's meeting with six other men about a hundred miles north of here. The bodyguard didn't have the nuts-and-bolts details, but their target is Yucca Mountain."

"As in the nuclear waste repository?"

"Yep."

"It's not even open yet. There's nothing there."

"There's groundwater," Jack replied.

"Come again?"

"Think of it as an underground nuclear test. Detonate a nuke under five thousand feet of rock and the shock wave goes straight down. The engineers there have already dug storage tunnels down to a thousand feet. The water table is five hundred feet below that. It's a geological sieve," Jack explained. "All the radiation from a nuke goes straight down into the aquifers, then to the rest of the southwest. Maybe all the way to the West Coast. We're talking about thousands of square miles poisoned for the next ten thousand years."

There was silence on The Campus end. Then Granger said, "Where the hell did they get this?"

Clark answered. "It's homemade—probably a simple gun-barrel setup: shoot one chunk of uranium called a 'slug' into a second, larger chunk called a 'pit' and you've got critical mass."

"And the material? Where'd they get that?"

"Not sure. The bodyguard said one of the Emir's captains was in Russia up until a couple weeks ago."

Hendley said, "You're the man on the ground, John. What do you wanna do?"

"We're handicapped, Gerry. Anybody we call isn't going to just send in the cavalry. There'll be a hundred questions before anybody moves: Who are we, where'd we get the info, what's our proof. . . . You know how it'll go."

"Yeah."

"We're about two minutes away from an airstrip. We're gonna see if we can borrow a helo. Depending on what we get, we could be over Yucca in thirty minutes. If we get there first, we'll hold the fort until you can get somebody to listen."

"And if you get there second?"

"Not even gonna think about it. I'll call you when we're airborne."

Ninety miles north of Las Vegas, on Death Valley's Highway 95, the Emir slowed his car and crossed over the median onto the shoulder. The dirt tract was barely perceptible through a berm of cactus scrub, but he picked his way down into a shallow spot and soon found himself in a pair of tire ruts. Through his windshield, a half-mile away, the Skeleton Hills rose from the barren terrain like mountains of the moon.

The tract kept descending, then swung north and began running parallel to a shallow canyon. A quarter-mile away, he saw a car parked. As he drew nearer, he saw it was a Subaru. Musa was standing beside the driver's door. The Emir slowed beside him, and he climbed in. They embraced. "Good to see you, brother," Musa said.

"And you, old friend. Are they here?"

"Yes, just up ahead."

"And the device?"

"Already loaded aboard."

The Emir followed Musa's directions another half-mile down the tract to where it curved around a low hill. Frank Weaver's flatbed was parked, nose facing the road. The GA-4 cask glinted in the sun. Three men were standing around near the driver's door.

The Emir and Musa got out and walked over. "My team from Russia," Musa said. "Numair, Fawwaz, and Idris."

The Emir nodded to each man in turn. "You've all done

675

well. Allah will smile on you all." The Emir checked his watch. "We leave in fifteen minutes."

The fit was tight, but they all managed to squeeze into the truck cab. Fawwaz, who bore the closest resemblance to Frank Weaver, drove. Five minutes later, they were back on the highway and heading north.

A sign on the shoulder said, HIGHWAY 373—6 MILES.

Chavez pulled into the parking lot of Paragon Air. Through the fence they could see two helicopters—both Eurocopter EC-130s—sitting on the tarmac. Chavez pulled up to the office, and Clark climbed out with Jack. "Ding, circle around to the maintenance gate. We'll let you in."

Clark and Jack walked into the office. A mid-sixties woman with a red beehive hairdo was sitting behind the counter. To the right through a half-glass door was the maintenance area.

"Morning," Clark said.

"Morning yourself. How can I help you?"

"Wondering if you've got a pilot around I could talk to."

"Maybe something I can help you with. Are you interested in a tour?"

"No, actually, I've got a technical question about the EC-130's rotational bearing manifold. My son here is studying avionics, and it'd be a big help if he could see one up close."

"Just a second, I'll see if Marty's got a minute."

She picked up the phone, spoke for minute, then said, "He'll be right up."

Clark and Jack wandered closer to the door. A man in gray coveralls walked up and opened the door. Clark stuck out his hand. "Hey Marty! Steve Barnes. This is my son, Jimmy. . . ." As Clark spoke, he stepped through the door, backing Marty along. "Gotta question about the EC-130."

Only two other people were visible in the hangar, both at the far end, near a Cessna.

"Sure," Marty replied. "But we should probably step back inside. . . ."

Clark lifted his shirttail and showed Marty the butt of his Glock.

". . . Oh, shit, hey . . ."

"Relax," Clark said. "We just want to borrow a helicopter."

"Huh?"

"And we want you to fly it."

"Is this a joke?"

"Nope. You're gonna help us or I'm going to shoot you in the leg and take your helicopter anyway. Go along, take us where we need to go, and you'll be back here in an hour. Say yes."

"Yes."

"Which bird is prepped?"

"Well, none—"

"Don't lie to me, Marty. It's a weekend. Prime time for tours and lessons."

"Okay. That one." Marty pointed.

"Go tell your receptionist you're going for a quick spin. Get hinky and I'll shoot you in the ass."

Marty opened the door, poked his head through, and did as he was asked.

Jack whispered to Clark, "What's a rotational bearing manifold?"

"No idea."

Marty turned back from the door and Jack asked, "Where're the controls for the side gate?"

"On the outside wall, opposite end of the hangar."

Jack started walking that way. Clark smiled at Marty. "Let's go."

"What's this all about?" Marty asked as they headed for the EC-130. "What're we doing?"

"You're saving the day, Marty."

As they neared the helo, Jack, Chavez, and Dominic came around the corner of the hangar and walked up. They got in the back while Clark took the front passenger seat. Marty climbed in, buckled up, and began preflighting.

"Where're we going?" he asked.

Jack said, "Northwest. When you reach Highway Ninety-five and Three seventy-three, head northeast." He gave Marty the latitude and longitude.

"That's restricted airspace, man," Marty said. "That's Nellis Range and the Nevada Test Site. We can't—"

"Sure we can."

They were airborne eight minutes later. Clark called Hendley and said, "We're up."

"Rick Bell's on the line, too. More shoes are dropping. CNN, MSNBC, Fox are all over it. An explosion of some kind at a church in Waterloo, Iowa; they're talking about fifty or sixty dead, maybe twice that many wounded. Something in Springfield, Missouri, too. A local news station was there, covering a statue unveiling; it looked like goddamned Omaha Beach. Some town in Nebraska . . . Brady . . . Someone walked into a high school swim meet and rolled grenades beneath the bleachers. Christ almighty."

"They're doing what they do," Clark said. "Terror. The *Losan,* the Paulinia fire, these attacks. The URC is sending a message: Nobody's safe anywhere."

"Well, there're gonna be a lot of believers after this."

"It's worse than that," Bell said. "Remember the dive the economy took after Nine-Eleven. Multiply that by a thousand, and that's what we're looking at. The Emir and the URC's trying to finish the job: to get our economy to devour the country from the inside out. They hit our new oil import source, they tried to hit a major port, they killed God knows how many in the heartland, and now they're trying to go nuke. People *are* the economy. Paralyze one, you paralyze the other. Add to that Kealty, who was already screwing the pooch, and we've got a big goddamned problem."

"It makes sense," Clark replied. "Nothing this guy does is one-dimensional."

Hendley asked, "What's your ETA?"

Clark asked Marty, "How long?"

"Twenty-two minutes."

88

Fifteen miles from the 373 junction, Highway 95 appeared below the EC-130, a straight gray line cutting through the brown desert. "How close is the Nellis Range?" Clark asked Marty.

"Reach out your window and you're almost touching it. That's what I'm telling you: As soon as we cut northwest, we're gonna light up radar screens. These folks don't fuck around."

"We need to get to Yucca."

"Shit. Please tell me you're not terrorists."

"We're the good guys."

"What kind of good guys?"

"Hard to explain. Can you get us there before they chase us down?"

"Which entrance, north or south?"

"South."

"If I'm balls to the wall I can get a hundred ninety miles an hour out of her, and if I put it on the deck . . . Figure four minutes after we turn off the highway. Do me a favor, huh?"

"What's that?"

"Threaten me again. When they slap the cuffs on me, I want some kind of defense."

Five minutes later, they saw through the windshield another gray line intersect 95 from the south. "Three seventy-three," Marty announced. As they swept over the junction, he banked to the northwest and began descending until they were thirty feet off the desert.

A ridge up before them. "Busted Butte," Marty announced, pulling up, then leveling out. "Three miles. Sixty seconds." He banked again, first left, then right, and dropped into a shallow valley.

A two-acre-square gravel lot appeared through the windshield. On the lot's far left side a keyhole shape had been cut into the hillside; at its center, an enormous tunnel entrance.

"Company," Jack called.

On the north side of the lot, a road extended into the desert. A flatbed truck carrying what looked like a giant stainless-steel dumbbell was pulling into the lot.

"What the hell is that?" Dominic shouted.

"GA-4 cask," Jack replied. "For transporting spent fuel rods."

"Thought this place wasn't open."

"It isn't." Jack scanned the binoculars north up the road to the white phone booth–sized guard shack. He could see two figures lying on the pavement. "Men down at the checkpoint," he called.

Clark asked Marty, "Can you put down in—"

"Not with that truck in there. I'll clip a rotor. Down the road about fifty yards I can."

"Do it."

"Coming around."

Marty banked sharply, spiraling back the way they'd come before stopping in a hover over the road. In the lot, the truck had stopped. Men were piling out of the cab.

"I count five," Dominic called.

As they watched, two of them sprinted down the length of the flatbed toward the EC-130. Still running, the men raised AK-47s and started firing.

"Shit!" Marty shouted. "What the fuck is going on?"

"Those are the bad guys," Clark told him.

Marty slid the helo to the right, away from the road and behind the hill.

"This'll do," Clark said.

Marty brought the EC-130 down in a one-bump landing. Clark and the others climbed out. Clark leaned back through the door and shouted, "Find cover and set down. Stay off the radio, and be here when we get back."

"Ah, come on—"

Clark pointed his gun in Marty's general direction. "That help?"

"Yeah!"

Clark slammed the door, then sprinted to where the others had clustered thirty feet away. Sand peppered them as Marty lifted off, then banked left and headed down the road, where he turned again behind a low hill. After twenty seconds, the chop of the rotors faded.

"Listen," Jack said.

Over the hill, the flatbed truck was moving.

With Chavez in the lead, they charged up the slope. They were ten feet from the ridgeline when they heard the chatter of automatic weapons. Controlled three-round bursts. Voices shouted, echoing off the canyon walls. Chavez dropped to his belly and crawled forward. After a moment, he signaled the others forward. Below, the flatbed was pulling into the notch in the hillside. As they watched, a man in a yellow hard hat sprinted across the lot, heading for the road. There were three overlapping pops, and the man pitched forward and went still.

"I count four others," Dominic said. "Don't see any of them moving. You guys?"

No one answered.

They sprinted down the slope to the concrete lip at the edge of the lot, then followed it up the opposite slope toward the edge of the entrance notch. They crept up to the edge, peeked over, and were met by the sounds of wrenching steel. The cab of the truck was disappearing into the mouth of the tunnel. The cask slipped into the entrance, scraping along the upper rim. The truck ground to a stop, lurched forward a few feet, then stopped again. The engine died.

A man appeared around the rear of the flatbed, his AK at his shoulder. Bullets thunked into the dirt at their feet. They backpedaled and dropped down. Chavez wiggled forward, peeked up, then rose to one knee, snapped off three shots, and dropped down again. "One down," he said.

"Do we know how big this thing is?" Jack asked.

"No bigger than a footlocker, I'd imagine," Clark replied. "Two men could carry it. Come on, let's move." They picked their way back along the concrete rim, then rolled over the edge one by one and dropped to the ground. Ahead, along the concrete wall, were stacks of crates, coils of wire, rolling tool chests, acetylene cutting rigs, and arc welding units. Beyond them, the corner leading to the notch.

They moved toward it in pairs, leapfrogging one another until Clark could see around the corner. He turned back, pointed to Jack, gestured him forward, then Dominic, then Chavez. At the entrance, nothing was moving. The flatbed was wedged tightly, both sides pressing against the walls and the cask against the roof.

From the tunnel came the humming of an engine. It faded.

"Sounds like a golf cart," Dominic said.

"Cushman utility vehicle. Sorta the same thing, but faster."

"What do you know about the layout?" Clark asked.

"Seen a few sketches on the Internet, but since it's not even done yet, I don't know—"

"Best guess."

"This main tunnel probably runs all the way to the north entrance. At intervals down the tunnel, there'll be ramps that angle downward."

"Straight shot or curved?"

"Straight."

"How deep?"

"Almost a thousand feet. At the bottom, the ramp will level out into a landing—how big I don't know. Branching off the landing will be storage tunnels for the casks. The good news is they're gonna want to plant that thing as deep as possible, which means a ramp. From the main tunnel to the bottom, it'll probably take them ten minutes."

At Clark's signal, Jack and Chavez sprinted to the rear of the flatbed, climbed up, and began moving forward past the cask. When they were almost to the cab, he and Dominic came around the corner, split around the truck, and sprinted to the walls on either side of the entrance. Clark slid along the wall, knelt down, and peeked under the truck chassis. He straightened up and signaled to Jack: *Two men inside.* Jack nodded and relayed it to Ding, who passed it on to Dominic on the other side.

Slowly, carefully, Jack slid open the cab's rear window, then accepted a boost from Chavez and squirmed through into the sleeper compartment. He slid down on the floorboard, crawled ahead to the dashboard. Out the side windows, the rock walls came to within a foot of the cab.

He poked his head up over the dash until he could see through the windshield. The tunnel was more massive than he'd originally imagined. Like the skeleton of a submarine, the walls and ceiling were braced by massive hoop girders.

Halogen lights affixed to the ceiling stretched into the distance.

Over the hood, Jack saw the top of a man's head move from right to left and disappear from view. Twenty feet down the tunnel, he saw another man crouching beside a yellow Cushman. Careful to keep his head out of sight, Jack wriggled into the driver's seat. From the sleeper compartment, he heard a single tap. One . . . Another tap. Two . . .

On three, Jack pressed his palm against the horn.

Gunfire erupted on either side of the cab. The man beside the Cushman stood up and fired a burst from his AK. There was a single pop, then another. The man stumbled backward, bounced off the Cushman, and slid to the ground.

"Come on out, Jack," Clark called.

In pairs, they wriggled beneath the truck and into the tunnel. The first man Jack had seen lay still a few feet away. Dominic trotted down to the Cushman and checked the other man. He turned back, drew his thumb across his throat.

They collected the two AKs and then, with Chavez at the wheel, climbed into the Cushman and started down the tunnel. "How stable is this thing they've got?" Jack asked Clark.

"Pretty stable. The slug has to be rammed into the pit with a lot of force. Takes a good-sized charge, and it has to be set. Why?"

"Working on an idea."

Fifty feet ahead, the string of halogen ceiling lights converged into a circle. "First ramp," Jack said.

"Easy, Dom," Clark ordered.

They pulled to within twenty feet, then stopped, got up, and walked up to the ramp's entrance. Lit from above by yet more halogen lights, the ramp angled down at twenty-five degrees.

"Should be able to hear their Cushman," Jack whispered.

They went silent and listened. Nothing.

They climbed back into the Cushman and kept going. The tunnel curved to the right. Dominic stopped short, and Jack got out and peeked around the bend. He came back. "Clear."

They kept going. They reached the second ramp and stopped to listen but heard nothing. Same with the third and fourth. As they approached the fifth, they heard a voice echo up the ramp. They got up and walked forward and looked down.

In the distance they could see the yellow speck of a Cushman appear under a halogen light, then move into shadow, then into light again.

"Three-quarters of the way down," Jack said.

"If you've got an idea, now's the time," Clark said.

"Depends on how sure you are about that thing's stability."

"Ninety percent."

Jack nodded. "Ding, need your help."

They climbed into the Cushman, did a Y-turn, and headed back down the tunnel. They returned thirty seconds later. From the rear of the Cushman, Jack and Ding each lifted out an acetylene cylinder. "Torpedo," Jack said.

"Are they full?"

"Mostly empty."

"Timing's going to be a bitch."

"I'll leave that up to you. You're the boss."

"Go ahead."

Jack and Chavez carried the cylinders to the ramp's entrance, laid them flat, then gave them a shove. At once they began to spin, gonging off the walls on their way down. Jack and Chavez ran back to the Cushman and got in. Dominic pulled up to the ramp and stopped.

Clark waited for a ten-count, then said, "Go."

*

Almost immediately it became apparent that the Cushman's brakes were inadequate. After fifty yards, the speedometer needle quivered past thirty mph. The overhead lights zipped by. Dominic braked, slowing them slightly, but smoke began gushing from the drums. Two hundred yards below them, the cylinders were spinning and tumbling like a pair of footballs. The Emir's Cushman was almost at the bottom.

"Gonna be close," Chavez said.

Clark said, "Slow us down, Dom."

Dominic tapped the brakes with no result. He stomped on the pedal. Nothing happened. "Keep your hands inside," he yelled, then veered right. The Cushman's front quarter panel scraped the tunnel wall, sending up a shower of sparks. They slowed slightly. He eased away from the wall, then back again.

A hundred yards down the ramp, the cylinders caught up with the Emir's Cushman. One cylinder took a bad bounce and tumbled past, but the second one crashed into the rear bumper. The Cushman skidded, turning broadside, then tipped onto its side and skidded onto the landing.

"Get us stopped," Clark ordered.

Dominic spun the wheel hard over, putting the whole left side into the wall. The Cushman slowly ground to a stop. They got out and started down the ramp. On the landing, the Emir's Cushman lay upside down. A few feet away, a body lay sprawled on the concrete. They paused at the entrance to the landing. To their left, the tunnel continued on another fifty feet before turning sharply left. There was no one in the tunnel. Chavez walked over to the body and knelt down. "Not him," he said.

They jogged down the tunnel. Around the corner, they found themselves in a thirty-foot-wide alley. Overhead, vaulted girders spanned the ceiling. They could see the circular entrances to the storage drifts, spaced at twenty-foot intervals along each side of the alley.

"I count twelve per side," Dominic said.

"Split up," Clark ordered. "Me and Jack will take the right, you two the left."

Clark and Jack sprinted across the alley to the opposite wall. Jack mouthed, *I'll take the last six.* Clark nodded. Jack took off in a sprint, glancing into each drift as he went. On the other side of the alley, Dominic was doing the same.

Jack dashed past the fifth drift, saw nothing, then continued past the seventh and eighth. He skidded to a stop, backed up, and looked again. He saw a flicker of light two hundred yards down the drift. He could just make out two figures crouched beside what looked like an industrial bait box. Jack looked around. Clark was working his way forward but too far away. Same with Dominic and Chavez.

"Hell with it."

He sprinted into the drift.

He'd covered half the distance to the figures when one of their heads snapped up. A muzzle flashed orange. Jack kept running. Raised his gun, snapped off two shots. From the alley, Clark yelled, "Over here!"

The man stepped forward, firing from the hip. Jack hunched over and pressed against the wall, trying to make himself small. He adjusted his aim, laid the sites on the man's center mass, squeezed off two rounds. The man spun and went down. The other figure ignored his fallen comrade and kept working, his hands moving in the box. He looked up, saw Jack, kept working. Thirty feet away. Jack raised his gun and kept firing until the slide locked open, the magazine now empty. Twenty feet. A head peeked around the box, disappeared again. Jack covered the last ten feet in two strides, then dropped his shoulder and slammed into the box. He heard something pop in his shoulder, felt the pain rush up his neck. The box skidded backward. Jack's feet went out from under him, and he slammed face-first into the concrete. Blood gushing from his shattered nose, he pushed himself to his knees. His eyesight sparkled. He looked around. The first man's body lay sprawled against the curved wall, his AK a few feet away. Jack crawled over to it, snagged the sling with his right hand, and dragged it toward him. He got to his feet and stumbled around the box.

Already on his feet, the Emir was stepping toward the box. He saw Jack and stopped. His eyes flicked to the box, then back to Jack's face.

"Don't!" Jack barked. "You're done. It's over."

Down the tunnel behind Jack came the pounding of footsteps.

"No, it's not," the Emir said, and knelt down before the box.

Jack fired.

89

Later, when asked by Hendley and Granger, Jack Ryan Jr. would remain cagey about whether he'd intended to simply wound the Emir or, in the heat of battle, he'd missed his center-mass target. The truth was, Jack wasn't sure himself. At the critical moment, the flood of adrenaline in his veins and the pounding of his heart had combined to seemingly both stretch and compress time in his brain. Contradictory thoughts fought for control of his fine motor skills: shoot to kill, stop the Emir; shoot to wound, gain an intel gold mine but risk the man getting a chance to push the button.

On seeing Jack standing before him in the darkened drift tunnel, the Emir had hesitated only seconds before returning his attention to the bomb—his eyes wide and feverish, fingers working inside the device's open panel. It took only a split second more for Jack to realize he wasn't facing a man who cared whether he lived or died—by gunfire or by nuclear detonation, the Emir had come here to finish his holy task.

Jack's weapon had bucked in his hand, and the tunnel had flashed with orange, and when the sound faded and the darkness returned, he saw the Emir lying on his back, arms splayed, the flashlight illuminating his face. Jack could see the AK's 7.62-millimeter bullet had entered the Emir's right thigh on an angle, traveled upward, and punched out his buttock. Jack took two quick steps forward, weapon raised, ready to fire again, when he heard footsteps pounding up behind him. Then Clark and Chavez and Dominic were there, pulling him away. . . .

Though they wouldn't discover the reason until a day later via a Homeland Security intercept, Clark and company had emerged from the main tunnel's entrance with their now bound-and-gagged quarry not to the sound of helicopter rotors and sirens but rather dead silence. As Clark had suspected, their helicopter's course north along Highway 95 and their subsequent intrusion of the airspace above the Yucca Mountain hadn't gone unnoticed on the radar net that blanketed the Nellis Air Force Range and the Nevada Nuclear Test Site. However, the alert that would have normally brought helicopters and security forces from Creech Air Force Base's 3rd Special Operations Squadron had been short-circuited by the DOE's test shipment from Callaway Nuclear Power Plant. Somewhere in the inevitable and often unfathomable bureaucratic process, the DOE had neglected to tell the Air Force they'd decided to forgo the helicopter escort for the shipment. As far as Creech was concerned, the stolen EC-130 on which Clark's team rode was air cover for the shipment.

Whether from fear or a suspicion that his passengers were indeed the good guys, Marty had taken Clark's "stick around" order to heart and had sat in the idling EC-130 until Clark and the others appeared jogging down the service road. Twenty-five minutes later they were back at Paragon Air, where they discovered Marty had also stayed off the radio.

"Hope I don't regret this," he'd said, as everyone climbed out.

"You'll probably never know it, but you did a good thing, my friend," Clark told him, then wiped down his Glock and laid it on the passenger-side floorboard. "Give us an hour, then call the police. Show them that gun and give them my description."

"What?"

"Just do it. It'll keep you out of jail."

And besides, I'm not exactly what you'd call "findable," Clark thought but didn't say.

Twenty minutes after leaving Paragon Air, they were back at the Emir's house, where they pulled into the garage and closed the door behind them. Chavez and Jack went inside to collect Tariq, while Pasternak and Dominic pulled the Emir from the rear of the vehicle and laid him out on the garage floor, where Pasternak knelt down and gave him a once-over.

"He live?" Clark asked.

Pasternak peeled back the hasty field bandage they'd applied before leaving Yucca, palpated the flesh around the puckered entrance wound, then slid his hands under the Emir's buttock.

"Through and through," Pasternak proclaimed. "No arteries, no bones, I don't think. Blood's clotting. What kind of round?"

"Jacketed seven-six-two."

"Good. No fragments. Barring infection, he'll make it."

Clark nodded. "Dom, you're with me."

The two of them returned inside to give the house a walk-through. Though they'd all worn gloves the entire time they'd been there, sooner or later the FBI would descend on the house, and the FBI was damned good at finding trace evidence where none should exist.

Satisfied, Clark nodded for Dom to return to the vehicle, then dialed The Campus. Within seconds he had Hendley, Rounds, and Granger on conference call. Clark brought them up to speed, then said, "We've got two choices, anonymously dump them on the steps of the Hoover Building or finish this ourselves. Either way, the less time we stay here, the better."

There was silence on the line. This was Hendley's call.

"Stand by," the director of The Campus said. He was back two minutes later. "Get back to the Gulfstream. The pilot knows where you're going."

Forty minutes later, they arrived at the North Las Vegas Airport and pulled onto the tarmac beside the plane, where they were met by the copilot, who ushered them aboard. Once airborne, Clark again called Hendley, who'd already begun the complicated and delicate process of informing the U.S. government that the Yucca Mountain Nuclear Waste Repository had been penetrated by now-deceased URC terrorists, and that while the suitcase nuke they'd left behind had been rendered safe, it might be wise to secure the device as soon as possible.

"How can you be sure this ain't going to blow back on us?" Clark now asked.

"I can't, but we don't have much choice in the matter."

"True."

"How's our patient?"

"Doc cleaned out the holes, stitched 'em shut, and put him on antibiotics. He's stable but in one hell of a lot of pain. Jack's given him a permanent limp, probably."

"Least of his worries now," Hendley observed. "Is he talking?"

"Not a word. Where're we going?"

"Charlottesville-Albemarle Airport. You'll be met."

"And then where?" Clark pressed. They had in their possession the world's most wanted terrorist; the sooner they found a bolt-hole where they could regroup and plan their next move, the better.

"Someplace quiet. Someplace Dr. Pasternak can work."

At this, Clark smiled.

Four short hours after they departed Las Vegas, they touched down on CHO's single runway and taxied up to the executive terminal. True to his word, Hendley had a pair of Chevy Suburbans waiting; in formation, they approached the Gulfstream's retractable stairs, did simultaneous three-point turns, and backed up to the bottom step. From the passenger door of the first Suburban, Hendley leaned out and signaled to Clark and Jack, who climbed into the backseat, while Caruso and Chavez, trailed by Pasternak, escorted their charges to the trailing Suburban. Within minutes they were off the airport grounds and heading north on Highway 29.

Hendley brought them up to speed. From what little Gavin Biery was able to glean from the flood of coded electronic traffic, Creech Air Force Base's 3rd Special Operations Squadron had arrived at Yucca within forty minutes of Hendley's call. Two hours after that, in a sure sign the Department of Energy, Homeland Security, and the FBI had descended en masse upon Yucca Mountain, the electronic traffic dried up.

"Are they onto the Emir's house?" Jack asked.

"Not yet."

"Won't take them long to find Paragon Air." This from Clark. "So spill it, Gerry. Where're we going?"

"I've got a few acres of horse land and a country house outside Middleburg."

"What's a few?"

"Thirty. Should give us some breathing room." Hendley checked his watch. "Dr. Pasternak's equipment should be there by now."

90

After the nearly constant adrenaline rush Clark and his team had experienced since touching down in Las Vegas twenty-four hours earlier, what followed immediately upon arriving at Hendley's country house was anticlimactic. To his obvious disappointment, Pasternak announced that it would be another day, perhaps two, before his patient would be stable enough to undergo interrogation. That left everyone with plenty of time to waste and nothing to do but play cards and watch cable news. Unsurprisingly, there wasn't a whiff of what had occurred at Yucca Mountain, but there was wall-to-wall coverage of what the networks had universally dubbed "The Heartland Attacks." The Claymore mine blast at the Waterloo, Iowa, church had claimed thirty-two dead and fifty wounded; the mortar attack at the Springfield, Missouri, statue unveiling, twenty-two dead, fourteen wounded; the grenade incident at the Brady, Nebraska, swim meet, only six dead and four wounded, thanks to a quick-thinking, off-duty volunteer police officer who shot the perpetrator dead after he'd rolled only three grenades beneath the bleachers. The Waterloo and Brady perpetrators, both of whom had been tracked to their respective homes within hours of the events, had taken their own lives.

Added to the other attacks, the casualties were climbing into triple digits.

Under the guiding hand of the FBI and Homeland Security, the near-miss chlorine attack aboard the *Losan* in Newport News had been attributed to a galley fire.

By four p.m. of their first day at Hendley's country house, as the plastic-pretty female and lantern-jawed male anchors that dominated afternoon cable news collectively announced that President Edward Kealty would be addressing the American people at eight p.m. eastern, Clark got up and wandered off to find Pasternak. He found the doctor in Hendley's woodworking shop, a fully appointed pole barn behind the house. The maple-topped bench had been converted into a makeshift medical suite, complete with halogen work lights, a Drager ventilator, and an EKG machine/resuscitator by Marquette, including manual external defibrillator paddles to convert an irregularly beating heart to normal sinus rhythm. Both machines were brand-new, fresh from their manufacturer's shipping cartons, which now lay stacked a few feet away. Everything was ready and present, save the guest of honor, who was ensconced in one of the guest bedrooms under a rotating watch manned by Chavez, Jack, and Dominic.

"All set?" Clark asked.

Pasternak pressed a series of buttons on the EKG and got a series of apparently satisfying beeps in reply. He powered down the unit and looked at Clark. "Yeah."

"Got second thoughts?"

"What makes you say that?"

"You ain't exactly a poker player, Doc."

Pasternak smiled at this. "Never was good at it. Guess it's the whole Hippocratic oath—kind of a hard thing to shake. I've had over ten years to mull it over, though. After Nine-Eleven, I couldn't figure out if it was just about revenge or about something bigger—the greater good and all that."

"What'd you decide?"

"It's both, but more of the latter. If we get something from this guy that helps save some lives, then I'll figure out a way to deal with what I've done—what I'm going to do. Or God willing, when the time comes."

Clark considered this, then nodded. "Doc, to lesser or larger degrees, we're all in that boat. All you can do is decide what you think is right, go with that, and let the rest come as it may."

The anticipation had everyone up at dawn the next day. Dominic, the best cook of the group, made a bowl of oatmeal and wheat toast for their guest, who, now fully awake and clearly in pain, stubbornly declined the meal.

At seven, Dr. Pasternak came to examine him. It took only a few minutes. Pasternak looked to Hendley, who stood in the doorway, the rest of the group behind him.

"No fever, no signs of infection. He's good to go."

Hendley nodded. "Let's move him."

The Emir neither struggled nor helped as Chavez and Dominic carried him out the back door and through the pole barn's side entrance. It wasn't until he saw the halogen-lighted workbench and makeshift leather restraints bolted to its surface that his face changed. Jack saw the fleeting expression but couldn't quite put his finger on its nature: fear or relief? Fear of what was coming, or relief because he suspected martyrdom was at hand?

As practiced the night before, Chavez and Dominic laid the Emir on the workbench. His right arm was cinched into the leather restraint, while the right, the one on the same side as the equipment, was stretched across a folded towel and similarly secured. Finally, both legs were locked down. Chavez and Dominic stepped back from the bench.

Now Pasternak began powering up the equipment: first the

EKG, then the ventilator, followed by a self-diagnostic test of the manual external defibrillator. Pasternak then turned his attention to the wheeled cart beside the table, on which lay an array of syringes and bottles. All of this the Emir watched closely.

He had to be curious, Jack thought, and he must be inwardly terrified. Nobody could be that indifferent to what was going on around him, all the more so a man who was fully accustomed to being the ultimate and total boss of everything that happened around him, used to having his every order obeyed with alacrity. The world around him was no longer in his control. There was no way he could be comfortable with that, but he retained a sense of dignity that was, in its way, rather impressive. Okay, he was courageous, but courage was not an infinite quality. It had its limits, and those in the room with him would be exploring those limits.

Dr. Pasternak rolled up the Emir's shirtsleeve and unbuttoned his shirt, then stepped away from the table, reached to the cart, and retrieved a plastic syringe and a glass vial. He checked his watch and looked up.

"I'm going with seven milligrams of the succinylcholine," Pasternak said, measuring the amount carefully into the plastic syringe as he withdrew the plunger. "Somebody write that down, please." On the chart Pasternak had asked Chavez to maintain, Ding wrote the information down: 7mg @ 8:58. "Okay . . ." the physician said. He stabbed the syringe into the brachial vein just inside the elbow and pushed the plunger in.

There was no real pain for Saif Rahman Yasin, just the momentary prick of something piercing his skin inside the elbow, and the needle was soon withdrawn. Were they poisoning him? he wondered. Nothing overt seemed to be happening. He looked at the man who'd just stabbed him and saw a face that was waiting for something. That was vaguely

696

frightening to him, but it was too late for fear. He told himself to be strong, to be faithful to Allah, to be confident in his faith, because Allah could handle anything men could do, and he, the Emir, was strong in his faith. He inwardly repeated his profession of faith, learned as a small boy more than forty years before, from his own father at the family house in Riyadh. *There is no God but God, and Mohammed is his prophet. Allahu akbar. God is great,* he told himself, thinking his profession of faith as loudly as he could in the silence of his own mind.

Pasternak watched and waited. His brain was racing. Was he doing the right thing? he wondered. It was too late to worry about that, of course, but even so, his mind asked the question. The man's eyes looked into his now, and the doctor told himself not to flinch. He was the one in control. Completely in control of the fate of the man who'd killed his closest relative, his beloved brother, Mike, the man who'd ordered the man driving the airplane to crash into the World Trade Center, causing the fire that would weaken the structural steel, and dropping the entire Cantor Fitzgerald office a thousand feet to the streets of lower Manhattan, crushing to death more than three thousand people, more than had been killed at Pearl Harbor. This was the face of the fucking murderer. No, he would not show weakness now, not before this fucking barbarian. . . .

The man was waiting for something, the Emir thought—but what? There was no pain, no discomfort at all. He'd just injected something into his bloodstream. What was it? If it was a poison, well, then the Emir would soon see Allah's face, and could report to Him that he'd done the Lord God's will, as all men did, whether they knew it or not, because everything that happened in the world was Allah's bidding, because everything that ever happened in heaven or on earth was written by God's own hand. But he had freely chosen to do Allah's will.

But nothing was happening. He didn't know, he couldn't tell, that his mind was racing at light speed, outstripping everything, even the blood in his own arteries, spreading whatever it was that the doctor had shot into him. He wished it were poison, for then he would soon see Allah's face, and then he could report on his life, how he had done Allah's will as best he understood it . . . or had he? the Emir asked himself, as the final doubts came. It was a time for ultimate truth. He'd done the Lord God's bidding, hadn't he? Had he not studied the Holy Koran his entire life? Did he not have the Holy Book virtually memorized? Had he not discussed its inner meaning with the foremost Islamic scholars in the Kingdom of Saudi Arabia? Yes, he had disagreed with some of them, but the nature of his disagreement had been honorable and direct, founded on his personal view of scripture, on his interpretation of God's word as written and distributed by the Prophet Mohammed, Blessings and Peace be upon him. A great and good man, the Prophet had been, as well he might be to have been chosen by God Himself to be His Holy Messenger, the conveyor of God's will to the people of the earth.

Pasternak was watching the sweep-second hand of his watch. One minute gone . . . another thirty seconds or so, he figured. Seven milligrams ought to be plenty for this application, delivered as it was, directly into the bloodstream. It would be fully distributed by now, infusing itself in all the man's bodily tissues . . . and first would be . . .

. . . the flutter nerves. Yes, they'd be first. The widely distributed nerves, the ones that worked peripheral systems, such as the eyelids, right about . . . now.

Pasternak moved his hand to the man's face, striking at his eyelids, and they didn't blink.

Yes, it was starting.

The Emir saw the hand slap at his face but stop short. He involuntarily blinked his eyes . . . but they didn't blink . . . *Huh?* He tried to lift his head, and it moved a centimeter or so, then collapsed back down. . . . *What?* He commanded his right fist to close and pull against the handcuffs, and it started to but stopped, falling back down to a resting position on the wooden surface of the table, the fingers unflexing of their own accord. . . .

His body was no longer his own . . . ? What was this? What was this? He moved his legs, and they moved under the command of his brain, just a little, but they moved as they should, as they had since before his childhood memory had begun, following the commands of his brain, as the body always did. Command your arm, an infidel philosopher had written, and it moves—command your mind, and it resists. But his mind was working, and his body was not. What was this? He turned his head to look around the room. His head did not move, despite his commands—neither would his eyes. He could see the white drop-ceiling panels. He tried to focus his eyes more closely on them, but his eyes were not working as they should. His body was like the body of another man; he could feel it, but he could not command it. He told his legs to move, and they barely fluttered, then froze limply in place. Limp like a corpse.

What was this? *Am I dying? Is this death?* But it wasn't death. Somehow he knew that and—

For the first time the Emir felt the beginnings of fear. He didn't understand what was happening. He only knew it would be very bad.

*

To Clark it looked as though the man was going to sleep. His body had stopped moving. There had been a few jerks and some little spasms, like a man settling to go to sleep in bed, but they'd stopped with surprising rapidity. The face became vacant, not focused, not proclaiming strength and power and lack of fear. Now he had the face of a mannequin. The face of a corpse. He'd seen that often enough in his life. He'd never thought what it was like for the mind behind the face. When death happened, the problem with that body was over for all time, allowing him to move on to the next problem, leaving this one behind for all time to come. It had never been necessary for Clark to destroy the body. When it died, the body was finished, right? Part of Clark wanted to approach the doc and ask him what was happening, but he didn't, unwilling to disturb the man in charge of the current operation quite yet. . . .

He could feel all of his body. It was all a matter of crystal clarity to Saif. He couldn't move any of it, but he could feel it all. He could feel the blood pumping through his arteries. But he couldn't move his fingers. What was this? They'd stolen his body from him. It was no longer his. He could feel it but not command it. He was a prisoner in a cell, and the cell was . . . himself . . . ? What was this? Were they poisoning him? Was this the onset of death? If so, shouldn't he welcome it? Was the face of God just moments away? If so, he told his mind to smile. If his body couldn't move, then his soul could, and Allah could see his soul as clearly as a large stone in the midst of the sea. If this were death, then he would welcome it as the culmination of his life, as a gift he'd given to so many men and women, the opportunity to see Allah's face, as he would soon do . . . yes . . . He felt the air entering his lungs, giving him the last few seconds of life as these infidels stole his life from him. But the Lord Allah would make them pay for this. Of that he was sure. Completely sure.

Pasternak checked his watch again. Coming up on two minutes, coming up on the last part. He turned and looked at the resuscitator. The green pilot light was on. The same was true of the ventilator. He'd have them when and if he needed them. He could restore this bastard's life. He wondered what Mike would think of that, but that thought was far too distant for him to latch on to it right now. What happened after death was unknown to living men. Everyone found out eventually, but none could return and relate it to the living. The great mystery of life, the subject of philosophy and religion, believed, perhaps, but not known. Well, this Emir guy was getting a look, of sorts. What would he see? What would he learn?

"Just a moment now," Pasternak told those around him.

The Emir heard that and understood the words. Just a moment until he saw God's face. Just a moment before Paradise. Well, he'd not gone all the way he'd hoped to go. He'd not become the world leader of the Faithful. He'd tried. He'd tried his best, and his best was very, very good. Just not good enough. That was a pity—a great pity. So much he could have done. Someone else would have to do it now? Ahmed, perhaps? A good man, Ahmed, faithful and learned, good of heart and strong of faith. Perhaps he'd be good enough. . . . The Emir felt the air going in and out of his lungs. He felt it so clearly. It was a beautiful feeling, the very feeling of life itself. How was it that he'd never appreciated it, the beauty of it, the wonder of it?

Then something else happened—

His lungs were stopping. His diaphragm wasn't—wasn't moving. The air wasn't coming into his lungs now. He'd been breathing since the moment of his birth. That was the first sign of life, when a newborn screamed its life to the world—but his lungs weren't filling with air. There was no air in his lungs now. . . . This was death coming. Well, he'd faced death for the last thirty years. At the hands of the Russians, the hands of the Americans, the hands of Afghans who'd not accepted his vision of Islam and the world. He'd faced death many, many times—enough that it held no terrors for him. Paradise awaited. He tried to close his eyes to accept his destiny, but his eyes wouldn't close. He still saw the panels of the drop ceiling over his head, just off-white rectangles that looked down at him without eyes. This was death? Was this what men feared? How strange a thing, his mind observed, waiting, not with patience but confusion, for the final blackness to overcome him. His heart continued to beat. He could feel it, thumping away, pumping blood through his body, and thus bringing life, bringing consciousness, soon to end, of course, but still present. When would Paradise come to him? the Emir wondered. When would he see Allah's face?

"Respiration stopped at three minutes, sixteen seconds," Pasternak reported. Chavez wrote that down, too. The doctor reached for the ventilator mask, checking again to be sure the system was turned on. He hit the button on the mask and was rewarded by the mechanical sound of rushing air in the rubber mask. Then he took the paddles off the resuscitator and pressed them to the man's chest, turning his eye to the EKG readout on the small computer screen. Normal sinus rhythm, he saw.

That wouldn't last long.

The Emir heard odd sounds around him, and he felt strange things but was unable even to make his eyes go look for the source of the sounds, locked as they were on the white ceiling panels. His heart was beating. *So,* he thought rapidly, *this is what death is like.* Was it like this for Tariq, shot in the chest? He'd failed his master, probably not because he'd been sloppy, just because the enemy in this case had been overly skillful and clever. That could happen to any man, and doubtless Tariq had died shamed at his failure to fulfill his mission in life. But Tariq was now in Paradise, the Emir was sure, perhaps enjoying his virgins, if that was really what happened there. Probably not, the Emir knew. The Koran didn't say that, not really. Enjoying the favor of Allah. That was sure enough, as he, the Emir, was about to discover. That would be sufficient.

It started to hurt some, right there in the center of his chest. He didn't know that when his breathing had stopped, so had stopped the infusion of oxygen into his system. His heart, a powerful muscle, needed oxygen to function, and when the oxygen stopped, then the heart tissues went into distress . . . and would soon start to die; the heart was full of nerves, and they reported the lack of oxygen as pain to his still-functioning brain. Great pain, the greatest pain a man could know.

Not quite yet, but going that way . . .

His face showed nothing at all, of course. The peripheral motor nerves were all dead, or effectively so, Pasternak knew. But the feelings would be there. Maybe they could measure that on an electroencephalograph, but that would just show traces of black ink on white fan-fold paper, not the searing agony that the tracings represented.

"Okay," he said quietly. "It's starting now. We'll give him a minute, maybe a little more."

Trapped within his nonfunctioning body, Saif felt the onset of pain. It started distantly, but it increased steadily . . . and quickly. His heart was being wrenched from his chest, as though a man had reached inside with his hand and was pulling it out, ripping the blood vessels as he did so, tearing it loose like wet paper from a destroyed book. But it wasn't paper. It was his heart, the very center of his body, the organ that provided life to the rest of him. It seemed to be on fire now, burning like kindling wood on open ground surrounded by rocks, burning, burning, burning . . . inside his chest, burning. His heart was burning alive, burning as he felt it. Not beating, not sending blood to his body, but burning like dry wood, like gasoline, like paper, burning, burning, burning . . . burning while he lived. If this was death, then death was a terrible thing, his mind thought . . . the worst thing. He'd inflicted this on others. He'd shot Russian soldiers—infidels, all of them, but still he'd ended their lives, put them through this . . . and thought it amusing? Entertaining. Part of Allah's will? Did Allah find this amusing, too? The pain continued to grow, to become unendurable. But he had to endure it. It would not go away. Nor could he. He could not run from it, not pray aloud to Allah to stop it, not deny it. It was there. It became all of reality. It overwhelmed all of his consciousness. It became everything. It was a fire in the middle of his body, and it was burning him up from the inside out, and it was more terrible than he'd ever imagined it to be. Was not death quick in coming? Was not Allah merciful in all things? Why, then, was Allah permitting this to happen to him? He wanted to grit his teeth to fight against the pain—he wanted, he needed, to scream aloud to protect himself from the agony that lived inside his body.

But he couldn't command his body to do anything at all. All of reality was pain. Everything he could see and hear and feel was pain. Even the Lord Allah was pain. . . .

Allah was doing this to him. If everything in the world was God's will, then had God willed this on him? How was that possible? Was not God a god of infinite mercy? Where the hell was His mercy now? Had Allah deserted him? *Why?*

Why?

WHY?

Then his mind faded into unconsciousness, with a final epilogue of searing pain to see him on his way.

On the EKG readout, the first irregularities showed up. That got Pasternak's attention. Ordinarily in the OR, as anesthesiologist, it was his job to keep watch on the patient's vital signs. That included the EKG machine, and he was, in fact, rather a skillful diagnostic cardiologist himself. He had to pay very close attention now. They didn't want to kill this worthless fuck, and more was the pity. He could have just given him a death such as few men had ever experienced, a fitting punishment for his crimes, but he was a physician, not an executioner, Pasternak told himself, pulling himself back from the edge of a tall and deadly cliff. No, they had to bring this one back. So he reached for the ventilator mask. The "patient," as he thought of him, was unconscious by now. He pressed the mask onto his face and pressed the button, and the machine shot air into the flaccid, deflated lungs. Pasternak looked up.

"Okay, mark the time. We're breathing him now. Patient is doubtless unconscious now, and we're infusing air into his lungs. This ought to take three or four minutes, I think. Could one of you come over here?"

Chavez was closest, and came at once.

"Put those paddles on his chest and hold them there."

Ding did that, turning to look at the EKG readout. The electronic tracings had settled down and were repeating themselves regularly but not in sinus rhythm, something his wife might have recognized but to him were just like things he'd seen on TV. To his left, Dr. Pasternak was hitting the ventilator button at regular intervals of maybe eight or nine seconds. "What's the score, Doc?" Chavez asked.

"His heart is settled down now that it's getting oxygen. The succinylcholine will wear off in another couple of minutes. When you see his body moving, then it'll be mostly

705

over. I'll breathe him for another four minutes or so," the doc reported.

"What did he go through?"

"You never want to find that out. We gave him the equivalent of a massive heart attack. The pain would have been intense—I mean, really miserable. For him, maybe that's just too damned bad, but it would have been pretty fucking awful. We'll see how he responds to it in a couple of minutes, guys, but he's been through something that nobody will ever want to repeat. He probably thinks he's just seen the bottom floor of hell. I guess we'll see what that does—did to him—in a few minutes."

It took four minutes and thirty seconds before the legs moved. Dr. Pasternak looked at the EKG readout on the resuscitator and relaxed. The Emir was out of the influence of the succinylcholine, and his muscles were now under the control of his nerves, the way they were supposed to be.

"He'll be unconscious for a few minutes, until his brain is fully suffused with oxygenated blood," the anesthesiologist explained. "We'll let him awaken normally, and then we can talk with him."

"What's his mental state going to be?" This was Clark asking the question. He'd never seen anything even remotely like this before.

"That depends. I suppose it's possible that he might remain strong and resistive, but I would not expect that. He's been through a singular and very, very adverse experience. He will not want to repeat it. He's been through pain that makes childbirth seem like a picnic in Central Park. I can only speculate how dreadful it's been for him. I don't know anyone who's been through this—well, maybe some people who've been through massive coronaries, but they don't usually remember the intensity of the pain. The brain doesn't work that way. It erases great pain as a defense mechanism. Not this time. He will remember the experience of it, if not the pain itself. If that experience doesn't frighten him beyond anything he's ever experienced, well, then we're talking about John Wayne on amphetamines. People like that do not exist in the real world. There's the complication of his religious beliefs. Those can be pretty strong. How strong, well, we'll have to see, but if he resists us from this point on, I will be surprised."

"If he does, can we repeat the experience?" Clark asked.

Pasternak turned. "Yes, we can—almost indefinitely. I've heard around the shop at Columbia that the East German Stasi used this technique to interrogate political and espionage prisoners, and that it was uniformly successful. They stopped using it—I don't know why. Maybe it was too evil even for them. As I said yesterday, this is off the syllabus from the Josef Mengele School of Medicine. The guy who ran the Stasi was Jewish, as I recall—Marcus Wolf, I think his name was—and maybe it affected him on that basis."

"How are you feeling, Rich?" Hendley asked.

"I'm fine. But he isn't." The doc paused. "Will they still execute this guy?"

"Depends on who ends up getting him," Hendley replied. "If the FBI gets him, he'll go through the federal court system, and if he does, then eventually he goes night-night at Terre Haute, Indiana, after due process of law. That's not our concern, really."

Because what he's just been through was quite a lot worse than that, Pasternak didn't say. His conscience was under control, but it was making noise. This really was out of Josef Mengele's playbook, and that wasn't something calculated to make a New York Jew happy. But his brother's body had never been recovered, squashed to atoms by the collapsing WTC tower. He didn't even have a grave that he could visit with Mike's kids. And this bastard had made that happen, and so Rich Pasternak told his conscience to be quiet. He was doing if not God's work, then his family's work, and that was fine with him. His conscience would have to be quiet about it.

"What's this guy's name exactly?" Pasternak asked.

Clark handled the answer: "Saif Rahman Yasin. He's child number fifty-plus of his father, a man of commendable vigor, his dad was, also tight with the Saudi Royal Family."

"Oh? I didn't know that."

"He hates the Saudi Royals more than he hates Israel," Clark explained. "They tried to whack him about six years ago, but they blew the mission. He hates them because of corruption, so he says. I guess they have some—I mean, a huge amount of—money controlled by a relatively small number of people, and you're going to get some, but compared to Washington, it isn't all that bad. I've been there. I learned the language there back in the 1980s. The Saudis I've met are pretty good people. Their religion is different from mine, but hell, so are the Baptists. The Saudis want this mutt dead more than we do, believe it or not. They'd love to drive him to Chop-Chop Square in Riyadh and take his head off with a sword. To them, he's spit on their country, and their king, and their religion. Three for three, and that's pretty bad over there. Doc, the Saudis are not the same as we are, but neither are the Brits, okay? I've lived there, too."

"What do you think we ought to do with him?"

"Above my pay grade, sir. We can always kill him, but better to do that in public—hell, do it at halftime at the Super Bowl with instant replay and color commentary from the network TV crew. I could live with that. But it's really a bigger question than that. He's a political figure, and his removal will be a political act also. That always screws things up," Clark concluded. He had little in the way of political instincts, and didn't really want any. His world was a simpler one: If you did murder, then you died for it. It wasn't elegant or very "sensitive," but it had, actually, worked once. As the legal system had worked a lot better before his country had been overrun with lawyers. But there was no going back, and he could not make it so. Clark had no illusions about ruling the world. His brain just didn't stretch that far. "Doc, what you just put him through, was it really that bad?"

"Far worse than anything I've ever come close to experiencing myself, worse than anything I've ever seen in twenty-six years of medical practice, worse than anything you can inflict on a person without killing him all the way dead. My knowledge of this is, really, theoretical, but it's not something I'd want to go through myself for any reason."

Clark thought back to a guy named Billy, and his time in Clark's recompression chamber. He remembered how coldly he'd tortured that little rapist fuck, how it had not touched his conscience one little bit. But that had been personal, not business, and his conscience still didn't care much about it. He'd left him alive in a farm field in Virginia, later to be driven to a hospital and treated futilely for a week or so before the barotrauma had stolen his worthless rapist life. Part of Clark wondered occasionally if Billy liked it in hell. But not often.

So this was worse than that? *Damn.*

Pasternak looked down and saw the eyelids flutter. Okay, he was coming all the way back. *Good. Sort of.*

Clark walked over to Hendley. "Who's going to interview him?" John asked.

"Jerry Rounds, to start."

"Want me to backstop him?"

"Probably a good idea if we all stand in here. I mean, it would be best if we had a psychiatrist handy—best of all, an Islamic theologian—but we don't. We're always shank's mare here, aren't we?"

"Cheer up. Langley would never have had the balls to do what we just did, not without a whole law school handy to kibitz, and a reporter from the *Post* to take notes and build up his moral outrage. That's one thing I really like about this place: no leaks."

"Part of me wants to discuss this with Jack Ryan. He's not a shrink, but I like his instincts. But I can't do that. You know why."

Clark nodded; he did. Jack Ryan also had been known to experience conscience problems. Nobody was perfect.

Hendley walked to a phone and punched in a few digits. Just two minutes later, Jerry Rounds came in. "Well?" Rounds asked.

"Our guest has had a bad morning," Hendley explained. "Now we need to talk to him. That's your job, Jerry."

"Looks unconscious," Rounds observed.

"He'll be that way for a couple of minutes," Pasternak clarified. "But he'll be okay," the doctor promised.

"Jesus, do we have enough people in here?" Rounds observed next. More people than the regular board meetings. Then the TV camera came in, set up on a tripod by Dominic, and the tarpaulin curtains they'd duct-taped together the night before were erected around the workbench. At his nod, Dominic hit the camera's record button, and Hendley took over, announcing off camera the time and date. Gavin Biery would, of course, later digitally alter Hendley's voice. Dominic replayed the sequence and pronounced the recording clean.

"Head games?" Rounds asked, almost to himself, but Clark was standing right next to him.

"Why not?" Clark responded. "No rules on this, Jerry."

"Right." Clark had a way of cutting down to the bone of the issue, the intel chief noted.

Clark wondered if everyone should wear cowboy dress, jeans, gunbelts, and ten-gallon hats, to distort him all the way, really to play head games with Saif. But it was better, probably, to keep it simple. Thinking too much about anything usually obfuscated everything and ended up leading nowhere. Simple was usually better. Almost always.

Clark walked to the table and saw that Saif was moving now, moving and twisting in his sleep. About ready to wake up. Would he be surprised to be alive? Clark wondered. Would he think he was in hell? For damned sure it wasn't paradise. He looked closely at the face. Little muscles were moving now. He was about ready to rejoin the world. Clark decided to stay where he was.

"John?" It was Chavez.

"Yeah, Ding?"

"It's really been that bad, eh?"

"That's what the doc says. He's the expert."

"Jesus."

"Wrong deity, man," Clark observed. "He's probably expecting to see Allah—or maybe the devil." *I guess maybe I can stand in for him,* John thought on reflection. He looked around. Jerry Rounds looked uneasy. Hendley had sent him up to bat in the bottom of the ninth, bases loaded and a full count. Well, he'd be inhuman not to be a little tight, John thought.

He felt himself being drawn into this. It was coming his way, and he suddenly knew it.

Oh, shit, Clark thought. What was he supposed to say to this bastard? This was a job for a psychiatrist. Maybe a serious Islamic churchman, or theologian—what did they call them? Mufti? Something like that. Somebody who knew Islam a hell of a lot better than he did.

But was this guy really a Muslim? Or was he a would-be politician? Did he himself even know what he was? At what point did a man become what he proclaimed himself to be? Those were deep questions for Clark. Too damned deep. But the man's eyelids were fluttering. Then they opened, and Clark was looking into them.

"Feels good to breathe, doesn't it?" Clark asked. There was

no answer, but there was confusion on the man's face. "Hello, Saif. Welcome back."

"Who are you?" the man asked, somewhat drunkenly.

"I work for the United States government."

"What have you done to me? What happened?"

"We induced a heart attack, then brought you back. They tell me it's an agonizing procedure."

To this Clark got no response, but he could see the flicker of terror in the Emir's eyes.

"You should know this: What you just went through can be replicated—indefinitely and without long-term damage. Fail to cooperate and your days will consist of nothing more than one heart attack after another."

"You cannot do that. You have—"

"Laws? Not here we don't. It's just me, you, and a syringe, for as long as it takes. If you don't believe me, I can have the doctor back here in two minutes. Make your choice."

The Emir's decision took less than three seconds. "Ask your questions."

Clark and Rounds quickly discovered that their interaction of the man known as the Emir wasn't going to be an interrogation but rather a cordial debriefing. Yasin had clearly taken Clark's warning to heart.

The first session lasted two hours and covered the mundane to the significant, questions to which they already had the answers, and mysteries they'd yet to unravel: How long had he been in America? Where and when had he undergone plastic surgery? His route after leaving Pakistan. How was the house in Las Vegas purchased? How big was the URC's operational budget? The locations of bank accounts; the URC's organizational structure, cell headquarters, sleeper agents, strategic goals . . .

And so it went, into the early evening, until Hendley called a halt. The next morning the group gathered in the kitchen of the main house to do a postmortem and to plan the day's questioning. Their time was limited, Hendley explained. Whatever their personal inclinations, the Emir didn't belong to The Campus, and justice was not theirs to dispense. The man belonged to the American people; justice to be dispensed according to their laws. Besides, once Yasin was in the hands of the FBI, months and years could be spent wringing from him every last drop of information. In the meantime, The Campus would make hay with what the Emir had so far disclosed. They had plenty of leads to run down, and enough intel to keep them busy for eight months to a year.

"I'd say there's just one last thing we need to get out of him," Jack Ryan Jr. said.

"What's that?" Rounds replied.

"The why of it all. This guy's thinking is too layered. All the pieces and parts of Lotus—Yucca Mountain, the *Losan,* the attacks in the Midwest . . . Was the whole point terror, or something bigger? It has to be more than Nine-Eleven writ large, right?"

Clark cocked his head thoughtfully and looked to Hendley, who took a beat, then said, "Damned good question."

By mid-morning they had what they wanted; they turned their attention to the tricky matter of turning Yasin over to the FBI. As symbolically and visually appealing as the idea might be, trussing up the Emir like a Christmas goose and shoving him from a moving car onto the steps of the Hoover Building was a nonstarter. The Campus had for weeks been skirting the gray line between remaining in the shadows where it was designed to operate and attracting the attention of the U.S. government.

So the question became how to "regift" the world's most

wanted terrorist without having it blow back on them. In the end, Dominic Caruso, having learned the lesson from Brian, came up with the solution.

"KISS," he said. "Keep it simple, stupid."

"Explain." This from Hendley.

"We're overthinking it. We've already got the perfect cutout: Gus Werner. He tapped me for The Campus, and he's in tight with Dan Murray, Director of the FBI."

"This is a damned big gift horse, Dom," said Chavez. "Think he'll go for it? Better question: Think he can make it work?"

"How would it go down?" asked Jack.

"He'll be arrested immediately and locked up in a very secure location. You know, read him his rights, offer him an attorney, try to talk to him some. Get a U.S. Attorney involved. They'll tell the Attorney General, who'll tell the President. After that, the snowball starts getting big. The press gets involved, and we sit back and watch the show. Listen, Gus knows how we work, and he knows how the Bureau works. If anybody can sell it, he can."

Hendley considered this for a few moments, then nodded. "Call him."

In the Hoover Building, Gus Werner's phone rang. It was his private line, and few people had access to that. "Werner."

"Dominic Caruso here, Mr. Werner. You got a few minutes this afternoon? Say, twenty minutes."

"Uh, sure. When?"

"Now."

"Okay, come on down."

Dominic parked a block from the Hoover Building and went into the main lobby, showing his FBI ID to the desk guards. That allowed him to walk around the metal detectors. FBI agents were supposed to carry sidearms. In fact, Dominic wasn't at the moment. He'd forgotten and left it at his desk, rather to his surprise.

Augustus Werner's office was on the top floor, complete with a secretary that he rated as a full assistant director of the FBI, just a few doors away from Dan Murray's rather larger director's office. Dominic announced himself to the secretary, and she whisked him right in. He took a seat across from the AD's desk. It was exactly 3:30 by his watch.

"Okay, Dominic, what do you want?" Werner asked.

"I have an offer to make."

"What offer is that?"

"You want the Emir?" Dominic Caruso asked.

"Huh?"

Dominic repeated the question.

"Sure, okay." Werner's expression said, *What's the punch line?*

"Tonight, at Tysons Corner. Upper-level parking area, say at nine-fifteen. Come alone. I know you'll have people close by, but not close enough to see the transfer. I'll personally hand him over to you."

"You're serious. You have him?"

"Yep."

"How the hell did that happen?"

"Don't ask, don't tell. We've got him and you can have him. Just leave us out of it."

"That'd be tough."

"But not impossible." Dominic smiled.

"No, not impossible."

"Anonymous tip, unexpected break—whatever."

"Right, right . . . I have to talk this one over with the director."

"I understand that."

"Stay by your phone. I'll be in touch."

*

As everyone knew it would, the call came quickly—within ninety minutes, in fact—and the time and place of the meeting was confirmed. Eight-thirty came soon enough, and then it was time to get ready. Dominic and Clark walked out to the workshop to find Pasternak giving the Emir a once-over under the watchful eye and ready Glock of Domingo Chavez.

"He good to go, Doc?" Dominic Caruso asked.

"Yes. Careful with the leg, though."

"Anything you say."

Clark and Dominic stood Yasin up, and Dominic took the flex-cuffs from his back pocket and attached them to his wrists. Next, Dominic took out an Ace bandage, which he wrapped around Saif's head half a dozen times. It would make a good blindfold. With that done, Clark grabbed him by the arm and walked him to the door, then across the backyard and through the back door to the garage. Hendley, Rounds, Granger, and Jack were standing beside the Suburban. They remained silent as Dominic opened the Suburban's rear passenger door and helped Yasin inside. Clark went around to the other side and slid in beside him. Dominic got in front and started up. The drive would be down U.S. 29 to the D.C. Beltway, and then west into northern Virginia. Dominic stayed right on the posted speed limit, which was unusual for him. The addition of an FBI ID in his wallet usually absolved him of all speed limits in America, but this evening he'd play everything strictly by the rules. Across the American Legion Bridge into Virginia, which turned into a sweeping left uphill turn. Another twenty minutes and Dominic took the right-hand exit to Tysons Corner. Traffic picked up, but mostly away from the shopping center. It was 9:25 now. He took the ramp to the upper level on the south side of the shopping center.

There, Dominic thought. An obvious Bureau car, a new Ford Crown Victoria with an extra radio antenna. He pulled to within thirty feet of it and just sat still. The Ford's driver-side front door opened. It was Gus Werner, dressed in his usual go-to-work suit. Dominic got out to join him.

"Got him?" Werner asked.

"Yes, sir," Dominic answered. "He looks a little different now. Bleached his skin some. Using this"—Dom handed over the half-used tube of Benoquin that he'd taken from the Las Vegas house—"and he's had some work done on his face, in Switzerland, he told us. I'll get him."

Dominic walked back to the Suburban, opened the rear door, helped Yasin down, then slammed the door shut and walked him toward Werner.

"He'll need some medical attention. Bullet injury to his thigh. It's been looked at, but he might need a little more attention. Aside from that, he's a hundred percent healthy. Hasn't eaten very much. Might be hungry. Taking him to D.C. Field Division?"

"Yep."

"Well, sir, he's all yours now."

"Dominic, someday I want to hear all of this story."

"Maybe someday, sir, but not tonight."

"Understood."

"One thing: Ask him about the Heartland Attacks first. Ask him about his sleepers."

"Why?"

"He's trying a little sleight of hand. It'd be best if nobody runs with it."

"Okay." Then Werner's voiced turned formal. "Saif Yasin, you are under arrest. You have the right to remain silent. Anything you say will be taken down and can be used against you in a court of law. You have the right to have an attorney present. Do you understand what I just told you?" Werner asked, taking the man's arm.

The Emir didn't say a word.

Werner looked to Dominic. "He understand English?"

Dominic grinned. "Oh, yeah. Believe me, he knows exactly what's happening."

Epilogue

Arlington National Cemetery

Though Jack Ryan Sr.'s Secret Service detail obviated any worries about unauthorized photographs being taken, most of the members of The Campus—Gerry Hendley, Tom Davis, Jerry Rounds, Rick Bell, Pete Alexander, Sam Granger, and Gavin Biery—had arrived several minutes early in three separate cars. Chavez and Clark came in a fourth vehicle with the recently retired and newly hired Campus member Sam Driscoll, who'd been spending half his time at The Campus bringing himself up to speed and the other half hunting for town houses and rehabbing at Johns Hopkins. Though he'd never met the fallen Caruso brother, Driscoll was a soldier to the core, and blood relation or not, known or not, a comrade in arms was a brother.

"Here they come," Chavez murmured to the group and nodded down the tree-lined drive.

Per Marine Corps standards, Brian's immediate family, escorted by Dominic, arrived in the lead limousine and stopped behind the hearse, where an eight-man escort platoon of Marine Corps pallbearers stood at attention, eyes forward and faces expressionless. Moments later the second limousine, carrying the Ryan clan, appeared and glided to a stop. At a nod from Special Agent Andrea Price-O'Day, rear doors on both limousines were opened, and the attendees emerged.

At the grave, Gerry Hendley and John Clark stood beside each other and watched as the members of the escort platoon stoically and smoothly slid the flag-draped coffin from the hearse and then fell into position behind the chaplain for the march across the lush lawn.

"Starting to sink in," the head of The Campus murmured.

"Yeah," Clark agreed. Six days had passed since Yucca, four since Brian's body had returned home from Tripoli. Only now had any of them had time to absorb everything that had transpired. For the country, The Campus had scored a big win, but it had come at a big price.

The rain that had been falling most of the morning had cleared away an hour earlier; the rows of stark-white head-stones seemed almost luminous in the midday sun. Paralleling the pallbearers' course to the grave, a Marine band contingent marched in lockstep while playing a somber drum cadence.

The casket reached the foot of the grave, and the family members took their positions. The escort commander softly barked, "Order . . . *arms* . . ." then "Parade . . . *rest*."

Per Dominic's request, the chaplain kept the ceremony short.

"Escort . . . ten-*hut*. Escort . . . present *arms*."

Then came the Marine Hymn and the gun salute, the Firing Party going through its crisp, almost robotic movements until the last shot echoed through the grounds. As it faded away, a lone bugler played taps as Brian's flag was carefully folded and then presented to the Carusos. The Marine band played the Navy Hymn, "Eternal Father, Strong to Save."

And it was over.

The next morning, Monday, The Campus resumed business, but the mood was predictably subdued. In the days leading up to Brian's funeral, each of them had, of course, written and submitted his own after-action report, but this would be the first time the members of the now dismantled Kingfisher Group would meet for a postmortem. Faces were grim as everyone filed into the conference room. By unspoken agreement, a single chair at the table was left open for Brian.

The answer to Jack's big "Why?" question had taken all of them by surprise. The Emir did, in fact, have larger aspirations for Lotus. The Heartland Attacks and the aborted *Losan* incident had been designed as jabs, the Yucca Mountain detonation as the uppercut that would awaken the sleeping giant. With an inept and reactionary Edward Kealty at the country's helm, the FBI and CIA would in due course unravel the identities of those responsible for the attacks, only to find carefully constructed and fully backstopped legends that would eventually lead directly to the doorstep of Pakistan's Directorate for Inter-Services Intelligence and radicalized elements of the Pakistan Army General Staff, both long suspected to be less-than-enthusiastic supporters of the war on terror.

Where the United States rightly invaded Afghanistan following 9/11, she would again react swiftly and overtly, expanding military operations east across the Safed Koh and Hindu Kush mountains. The inevitable destabilization of Pakistan, already a near-failed state, would, according to the Emir, create a power vacuum into which the Umayyad Revolutionary Council would step and take control of Pakistan's substantial nuclear arsenal.

"It's plausible," Jerry Rounds said. "Worst case, the plan succeeds; best case, we have to go into the area big, maybe quadruple our current presence."

"And stay there for a couple decades," Clark added.

"If we thought Iraq was a recruiting poster for militants . . ." Chavez observed.

"A win-win for the Emir and the URC," Jack added.

"I told Werner to dig into the legends first. He'll figure it out," Dominic Caruso said. "The question is, was this the only trick the bastard had up his sleeve?"

As if on cue, the phone beside Hendley's elbow buzzed. He picked it up, listened, then said, "Send her up." He hung up and said to the group, "Maybe one less question that needs answering."

Mary Pat Foley appeared in the doorway sixty seconds later. After greetings were exchanged, she laid a manila folder on the table before Hendley, who opened it and began reading.

Mary Pat said to Sam Driscoll, "Collage finally spit out an answer on your sand table."

"No shit?"

"Let me guess," Chavez said. "Old news. Yucca Mountain."

"No," Hendley said. He slid the file down the table to Clark and Jack, who scanned it together. Jack looked up at Mary Pat. "You sure this is right?"

"Crunched it a dozen times. We got eighty-two perfect geographical data point matches."

Dominic said, "Spit it out."

"Kyrgyzstan," Clark replied, without looking up from the file.

"What the hell does the Emir want with Kyrgyzstan?" Chavez said.

Gerry Hendley replied, "The million-dollar question. Let's start looking for the answer."

The meeting continued for another hour before breaking up. At eleven, Jack took an early lunch and drove to Peregrine Cliff. As he stepped onto the porch, Andrea Price-O'Day opened the front door.

"That's what I call service," Jack said. "How's things?"

"As always. Sorry about your cousin."

Jack nodded. "Thanks. Dad?"

"In his office. Writing," she added pointedly.

"I'll knock carefully."

Which he did, and was surprised to hear his father say, cheerfully, "Come on in."

Jack sat down and waited a few seconds for his father to

finish off a sentence on the keyboard. Ryan Senior swiveled in his chair and smiled. "How ya doing?"

"Okay. You getting close?" Jack asked, nodding at the autobiography on the computer monitor.

"I can see light at the end of the tunnel. After this, I'll let it cool off a little, then start rewriting. You went to work this morning."

"Yeah. We did the postmortem."

"What's the latest?"

"The FBI's got him. That's all we know. That's all we may ever know."

"He'll break," Ryan Senior predicted. "Might take a couple weeks, but he'll go."

"How can you be sure?"

"In his heart, he's a coward, son. Most of them are. He'll put on a good show, but it won't hold up. We gotta talk about something. Kealty's already taken the gloves off."

"Digging for dirt?"

The former President nodded. "Arnie's nosing around, but it sounds like Kealty's people are talking illegal espionage. Might be a story breaking in the *Post* next week."

"'Illegal espionage,'" Jack repeated. "Sounds a lot like The Campus. Could they—"

"Too early to tell. Maybe. If so, they'll use it as an opening salvo—try to blow us out of the water before the race really gets going."

"What can we do?"

"There's no 'we,' son," Ryan said gently, then smiled. "I'll handle it."

"You don't look worried. That worries me."

"It's politics. Nothing more. It's going to get uglier, but Kealty's days are numbered. The only question is how long it'll take him to realize it. Hell, I'll tell you what I'm really worried about."

"What's that?"

"Telling your mom you've gone into the family business."

"Ah, shit."

"If The Campus comes out and she reads about it in the paper or gets shanghaied by a reporter, you and I are in the doghouse."

"So how do we do it?"

"Keep it vague. I'll handle the part about The Campus. You tell her what you do there."

"Not all of it, right? Not the field stuff."

"No."

"Better that you don't know, either, huh?"

Ryan nodded.

"And if she asks?" Jack said.

"She won't. She's too smart for that."

"I gotta tell you, Dad, I'm not looking forward to this. She isn't gonna be happy."

"That's an understatement. Better now than later. Trust me."

Jack Ryan Jr. considered this, then shrugged. "Okay."

Ryan stood up, then clapped his son on the shoulder. "Come on, we'll face the fire together."